PENGUIN CLASSICS  DELUXE EDITION

# SODOM AND GOMORRAH

MARCEL PROUST was born in Auteuil in 1871. In his twenties, following a year in the army, he became a conspicuous society figure, frequenting the most fashionable Paris salons of the day. After 1899, however, his chronic asthma, the death of his parents, and his growing disillusionment with humanity caused him to lead an increasingly retired life. From 1907 on, he rarely emerged from a cork-lined room in his apartment on boulevard Haussmann. There he insulated himself against the distractions of city life and the effects of trees and flowers–though he loved them, they brought on his attacks of asthma. He slept by day and worked by night, writing letters and devoting himself to the completion of *In Search of Lost Time*. He died in 1922.

JOHN STURROCK is a writer and critic who has previously translated Victor Hugo, Stendhal, and a volume of Proust's essays for Penguin Classics. He is a consulting editor of the *London Review of Books*.

# Marcel Proust

# *Sodom and Gomorrah*

Translated with an Introduction
and Notes by John Sturrock

GENERAL EDITOR:
CHRISTOPHER PRENDERGAST

PENGUIN BOOKS

PENGUIN BOOKS
Published by the Penguin Group
Penguin Group (USA) Inc., 375 Hudson Street, New York, New York 10014, U.S.A.
Penguin Group (Canada), 90 Eglinton Avenue East, Suite 700, Toronto, Ontario,
Canada M4P 2Y3 (a division of Pearson Penguin Canada Inc.)
Penguin Books Ltd, 80 Strand, London WC2R 0RL, England
Penguin Ireland, 25 St Stephen's Green, Dublin 2, Ireland
(a division of Penguin Books Ltd)
Penguin Group (Australia), 250 Camberwell Road, Camberwell, Victoria 3124,
Australia (a division of Pearson Australia Group Pty Ltd)
Penguin Books India Pvt Ltd, 11 Community Centre, Panchsheel Park,
New Delhi – 110 017, India
Penguin Group (NZ), 67 Apollo Drive, Rosedale, North Shore 0632, New Zealand
(a division of Pearson New Zealand Ltd)
Penguin Books (South Africa) (Pty) Ltd, 24 Sturdee Avenue,
Rosebank, Johannesburg 2196, South Africa

Penguin Books Ltd, Registered Offices: 80 Strand, London WC2R 0RL, England

First published in the United States of America by Viking Penguin,
a member of Penguin Group (USA) Inc. 2004
Published in Penguin Books 2005

5   7   9   10   8   6

Translation, introduction, and notes copyright © John Sturrock, 2002
All rights reserved

THE LIBRARY OF CONGRESS HAS CATALOGED THE HARDCOVER EDITION AS FOLLOWS:
Proust, Marcel, 1871–1922.
[Sodome et Gomorrhe. English]
Sodom and Gomorrah / Marcel Proust ; translated with an introduction and
notes by John Sturrock ; general editor, Christopher Prendergast.
p.   cm.
Includes bibliographical references.
ISBN 0-670-03348-0 (hc.)
ISBN 978-0-14-303931-0 (pbk.)
I. France–Social life and customs–Fiction.   I. Sturrock, John.
II. Prendergast, Christopher.   III. Title.
PQ2631.R63S6313 2004
843'.912–dc22        2003069464

Printed in the United States of America
Set in Berthold Garamond
Designed by Francesca Belanger

# Contents

# Introduction

This fourth volume in the sequence of *In Search of Lost Time* is remarkable for giving a new and radical inflection to the narrative course of Proust's great novel, a turn which it would take an unusually clairvoyant reader of the earlier volumes to have foreseen. The volume's outspoken title, *Sodom and Gomorrah*, is a fair indication that the novel is about to take on a darker and sexually more adventurous tone, the twinned Biblical cities of Sodom and Gomorrah having been destroyed by God in the book of Genesis as punishment for the depravity of their inhabitants. In Proust, the names stand for the worlds of male and female homosexuality, to whose characteristic attitudes and habits *Sodom and Gomorrah* provides a sustained, unflattering introduction. This in fact is the cardinal moment in the developing novel, when the homosexual theme finally becomes essential to the drama. It is a theme made serious by its eventual repercussions in the Narrator's own emotional life, but it begins in the broadest comedy, with the delightfully camp first encounter, spied on by him, between the aging Baron de Charlus and the waistcoat-maker Jupien.

We are told at the start of *Sodom and Gomorrah* that the account of this portentous meeting has previously been deferred, that the Narrator has made "a discovery, involving M. de Charlus in particular, but so significant in itself that up until now, when I am able to give it the position and dimensions it requires, I have put off reporting it." This explanation is patently disingenuous; Proust's is not a novel in which narrative opportunities are anywhere at a premium. The Narrator's arch remark is more likely to allude indirectly to the considerable anxieties felt by Proust regarding the overtly homosexual content of the later stages of *In Search of Lost Time*. Given how pervasive the theme of "in-version," to use the novelist's own preferred term for it, now becomes, it seems surprising that he should have waited so long and advanced so far in his book before allowing it to move to the fore. It's not as if he had himself been ambushed, as he worked, by an erotic concern that he had not anticipated might loom so large; he had known all along that the book he was writing would have a homosexual coloring and might therefore be found obscene by some of those who read it. As far back as 1908, before he began to work systematically on the novel, he had told one of his friends in a letter that among the many and varied literary projects he had in mind was that of an "essay on pederasty," which would, he added, be "difficult to get published." That projected essay eventually found its way into the pages of *Sodom and Gomorrah*, which contain, in a more or less dispersed and dramatized form, much wickedly observant, if often also satirical, analysis of the homosexual condition as Proust himself had both studied and lived it. He did not mean *Sodom and Gomorrah* to be easily read, on the other hand, as the work of an "invert" outing himself in a roundabout manner by transfer-ring his own homosexuality onto a whole gallery of figures, some of them familiar from earlier volumes of the novel, who are now revealed to be gay. The unforgiving or even contemptuous nature of the por-trayal of gayness is a part of the novelist's cover story. Proust is no hero to the gay community today, unlike his contemporary André Gide (who in 1921 accused Proust of having portrayed only "the grotesque and abject aspects of Sodom"); he chose to remain in the closet, even though he had moved for years in the upper reaches of Parisian society, where homosexuality was practiced fairly openly and would have been talked about without inhibitions.

Once he had begun to work systematically at *In Search of Lost Time*, Proust felt it necessary to warn potential publishers of the book that what he was writing would, once complete, have a disreputable side to it that might get them into trouble with the censorship and would cer-tainly attract hostility from many *bien-pensant* readers. In 1909, when he was already angling to have the first hundred pages serialized in *Le Fi-garo*, he described the novel as he then envisaged it to one publisher as "extremely indecent in certain places" and as having a homosexual for one of its principal characters—clearly the character we now know as the Baron de Charlus, though at that stage he was still to be called M. de Guercy and to go without the aristocratic rank that means so much to the monstrous Baron. Three years later, Proust was still using words of caution to other possible publishers, and in 1916, when he came to a final agreement with Gaston Gallimard and wrote a letter of introduction for *Sodom and Gomorrah* to that most sophisticated of publishers, he once again stressed its "audacity." Gallimard's was the house he most wanted to be published by, but he feared that its owner might default on the arrangement once he had read what Proust was offering him.

By then, *Sodom and Gomorrah* was well under way, this volume having been written during the war years, between 1914 and 1918. It was not, however, published until three years after the war ended, appearing in two sections, in 1921 and 1922, the year of Proust's death. The first section contained in fact only the first thirty or so pages of the present volume, which carry the heading Part I, the remainder of the 1921 volume being made up of the concluding pages of *The Guermantes Way*. The second section, containing the several hundred pages of what appears here as Part II of *Sodom and Gomorrah*, came out in April 1922 in three volumes.

This timing has a lot to do with the unprecedented freedom with which Proust here enters on the descriptions of homosexual behavior among both men and women. There had been only passing hints in the earlier volumes that anything approaching this degree of openness might one day be expected from him. In the first volume, *Swann's Way*—the only section of the novel to have been published before the war—the demimondaine Odette confesses, for example, to her husband, Swann, that she has had a lesbian experience, and she is believed by many at the same time to be the mistress of the Baron de Charlus. Her husband is unable to credit the rumors he has heard to this effect, but we are not told in so many words why this should be; only when Charlus is brought back on in his true sexual nature in *Sodom and Gomorrah* can we fully enjoy the reason for Swann's incredulity at the stories that are circulating. Similarly, one of the novel's truly crucial scenes, which also occurs in *Swann's Way*, involves the daughter of the composer Vinteuil's profaning her father's photograph and engaging in lesbian fun and games with her girlfriend. This shocking scene, which did indeed upset some of Proust's first readers, is witnessed secretly from outside the window by the Narrator, and makes a pair with that other scene just now referred to at the start of *Sodom and Gomorrah*, when the concealed Narrator witnesses the first homosexual encounter between Charlus and Jupien. It had been Proust's intention originally that Charlus's homosexuality should be revealed by his behavior at a concert of Wagner's music; the revelation in the form that we actually have it is more dramatic, and no less telling for being highly comical.

That *Sodom and Gomorrah* should have been written during the Great War helps to explain the sudden-seeming detonation of the homosexual theme. In France, as in Britain, the war had led to a notable loosening of social taboos, including that on homosexual behavior, given the brutal and prolonged separation of the sexes that war on such a scale imposes on the young; and the loosening extended to the taboo on public reference to the subject. In consequence of the war, the guarded privacy of prewar years quickly gave way to the more forthcoming sexuality of the 1920s, when reportage and serious literature could both make freer with subject matter that had previously circulated mainly by word of mouth, and even then only in restricted circles. Thus, in *Sodom and Gomorrah*, Proust, a onetime socialite and gossip turned serious novelist, is able to play the role of the newly emancipated postwar moralist uncovering some of the less edifying secrets of the upper-class society of which he had once been a habitué, but which was now generally deemed to have suffered a deathblow in 1914. Though we have long since grown used to an extreme seaminess in modern fiction, it requires only a little historical imagination to respond appreciatively to the unwonted candor that Proust displays in the later volumes of *In Search of Lost Time*, less in the depiction of events themselves than in his cruelly penetrating analysis of people's motives when behaving in the ways they do.

*Sodom and Gomorrah* is far from belonging exclusively to Charlus, however, even if his increasingly arrogant and excitable behavior makes him this volume's most dominant presence. Mme Verdurin, another of Proust's memorably disagreeable creations, is also given a greater prominence here than in her earlier appearances in the novel, as the hostess of La Raspelière, the country house she and her husband have rented near the Normandy coast. The extraordinary ascent through society of this pretentious bourgeoise, who will end *In Search of Lost Time* as nothing less than the Princesse de Guermantes, is now under way, as she ingratiates herself with the people who have influence and bullies the ones who do not, and lords it over the members of the "faithful" who constitute her salon. Like Charlus, Mme Verdurin can be enjoyed as a comic character, but the egotism with which she advances her social cause is also sinister, and the outrageous worldly success that she is granted is Proust's bitter warning to us that the old, more graceful aristocratic society of before the war is heading for the abyss.

A third character who achieves a quite new status in *Sodom and Gomorrah* is Albertine, the fresh and athletic young girl who has passed for a time into the background of Proust's novel, following her first appearance before the Narrator during his first visit to the seaside resort of Balbec. She now becomes, for good and ill, the focus of his sentimental life, introducing the theme of sexual jealousy which comes largely to dominate the novel from this point on. Indeed, the two volumes that follow this one, *The Prisoner* and *The Fugitive,* are sometimes jointly known as "The Story of Albertine." That story begins in *Sodom and Gomorrah,* with the growing closeness and ambivalence of her relationship with the Narrator, who refers to her throughout as *"mon amie,"* which might mean anything from "my friend" to "my sweetheart"; I have attempted to preserve what I believe to be the slight irony in the French term as Proust uses it here by translating it as "my loved one."

A final comment must concern the title Proust gave to the final part of Chapter 1 in *Sodom and Gomorrah* Part II: "The Intermittences of the Heart." This had at one time been the title he intended to give to *In Search of Lost Time* as a whole, and it might seem strange to find it thus demoted, and allotted so seemingly slight a role. That role is very far from slight, however. The "intermittences of the heart" are the time delays that we may any of us experience between cause and effect in our emotional lives, between some more than usually significant event and our inward response to it. The first example of such a delay in *Sodom and Gomorrah* involves the death after a stroke of the Narrator's beloved grandmother, which had been described at some length in Part II of *The*

*Guermantes Way.* He had not then suffered its full effects. Now he does, when finding himself staying in the same hotel in Balbec where they had once stayed together, and sleeping next to exactly the same sort of partition wall on which he had tapped in moments of distress, knowing that she would hear him on her side and come to comfort him. The memory is enough to cause him finally and intensely to mourn her. It is thus one of the series of memories around which *In Search of Lost Time* is structured, the series of so-called involuntary memories, the most celebrated of which has the Narrator dipping a madeleine in his tea and finding whole swaths of the past being vividly restored to him.

In the final stages of *Sodom and Gomorrah,* another delayed memory proves equally disturbing to him: of the scene I referred to earlier when he was spying on Mlle Vinteuil and her lesbian lover. Only now, when he believes that he is in love with Albertine, but that Albertine is not to be trusted, does the full effect of that distant scene work on him. These two "intermittences of the heart" thus represent severe emotional crises for the Narrator, and the one involving Albertine opens the way directly to the painful "Story of Albertine" that fills the next two volumes of the novel. They are vital to both the psychological and the narrative structure of *In Search of Lost Time.*

John Sturrock

# A Note on the Translation

The present translation came into being in the following way. A project was conceived by the Penguin UK Modern Classics series in which the whole of *In Search of Lost Time* would be translated freshly on the basis of the latest and most authoritative French text, *À la recherche du temps perdu*, edited by Jean-Yves Tadié (Paris: Pléiade, Gallimard, 1987–89). The translation would be done by a group of translators, each of whom would take on one of the seven volumes. The project was directed first by Paul Keegan, then by Simon Winder, and was overseen by general editor Christopher Prendergast. I was contacted early in the selection process, in the fall of 1995, and I chose to translate the first volume, *Swann's Way*. The other translators are James Grieve, for *In the Shadow of Young Girls in Flower;* Mark Treharne, for *The Guermantes Way;* John Sturrock, for *Sodom and Gomorrah;* Carol Clark, for *The Prisoner;* Peter Collier, for *The Fugitive;* and Ian Patterson, for *Finding Time Again.*

Between 1996 and the delivery of our manuscripts, the tardiest in mid-2001, we worked at different rates in our different parts of the world—one in Australia, one in the United States, the rest in various parts of England. After a single face-to-face meeting in early 1998, which most of the translators attended, we communicated with one another and with Christopher Prendergast by letter and e-mail. We agreed, often after lively debate, on certain practices that needed to be consistent from one volume to the next, such as retaining French titles like Duchesse de Guermantes, and leaving the quotations that occur within the text—from Racine, most notably—in the original French, with translations in the notes.

At the initial meeting of the Penguin Classics project, those present had acknowledged that a degree of heterogeneity across the volumes was inevitable and perhaps even desirable, and that philosophical differences would exist among the translators. As they proceeded, therefore, the translators worked fairly independently and decided for themselves how close their translations should be to the original—how many liberties, for instance, might be taken with the sanctity of Proust's long sentences. And Christopher Prendergast, as he reviewed all the translations, kept his editorial hand relatively light. The Penguin UK translation appeared in October 2002, in six hardcover volumes and as a boxed set.

Some changes may be noted in this American edition, besides the adoption of American spelling conventions. One is that the UK decision concerning quotations within the text has been reversed, and all the French has been translated into English, with the original quotations in the notes. We have also replaced the French punctuation of dialogue, which uses dashes and omits certain opening and closing quotation marks, with standard American dialogue punctuation, though we have respected Proust's paragraphing decisions—sometimes long exchanges take place within a single paragraph, while in other cases each speech begins a new paragraph.

Lydia Davis

# Suggestions for Further Reading

Beckett, Samuel. *Proust.* New York: Grove Press, 1931.

Carter, William C. *Marcel Proust: A Life.* New Haven and London: Yale University Press, 2000.

Milly, Jean. *La Phrase de Proust.* Paris: Éditions Champion, 1983.

Painter, George D. *Proust: The Later Years.* Boston: Atlantic–Little, Brown, 1965.

Proust, Marcel. *Remembrance of Things Past,* vol. 4: *Cities of the Plain,* tr. C. K. Scott Moncrieff. New York: Modern Library, 1934.

——. *À la recherche du temps perdu,* ed. Jean-Yves Tadié, vol. 3: *Sodome et Gomorrhe* and *La Prisonnière.* Paris: Pléiade, Gallimard, 1988.

——. *In Search of Lost Time,* vol. 4: *Sodom and Gomorrah,* tr. C. K. Scott Moncrieff and Terence Kilmartin, rev. D. J. Enright. New York: Random House, 1993.

Shattuck, Roger. *Proust's Binoculars: A Study of Memory, Time and Recognition in À la recherche du temps perdu.* New York: Random House, 1963.

——. *Proust's Way: A Field Guide to In Search of Lost Time.* New York: W. W. Norton & Co., 2000.

Tadié, Jean-Yves. *Marcel Proust: A Life,* tr. Euan Cameron. New York: Viking, 2000.

White, Edmund. *Marcel Proust.* New York: Viking, 1999.

# PART I

*First appearance of the men-women, descendants of
those inhabitants of Sodom who were spared
by the fire from heaven.*

Woman will have Gomorrah and man will have Sodom.[1]

—Alfred de Vigny

A S WE KNOW, well before going that day (the day when the Princesse de Guermantes's soirée was taking place) to pay the call on the Duc and Duchesse that I have just recounted, I had been watching out for their return and had, in the course of my vigil, made a discovery, involving M. de Charlus in particular, but so significant in itself that up until now, when I am able to give it the position and dimensions it requires, I have put off reporting it. I had, as I have said, abandoned the splendid vantage point, so comfortably installed at the top of the house, from where you can take in the uneven inclines by which ascent is made to the de Bréquigny *hôtel*, gaily ornamented in the Italian style by the pink campanile of the coach house belonging to the Marquis de Frécourt. I had found it more practical, once I thought that the Duc and Duchesse were on the point of returning, to station myself on the staircase. I a little regretted ending my sojourn on high. But at this hour of the day, which was that following lunch, I had less cause for regret, for I would not have seen, as in the morning, the footmen from the de Bréquigny and de Tresmes *hôtel*, reduced by the distance to tiny figures in a painting, making their slow ascent of the abrupt rise, feather duster in hand, between the large sheets of transparent mica that stood out so pleasingly against the red foothills.[2] Lacking the perspective of the geologist, I at least had that of the botanist, and gazed through the shutters on the stairs at the Duchesse's small shrub and the precious plant, exhibited in the courtyard with that insistence with which the marriageable young are thrust forward, and I wondered whether, by some providential chance, the improbable insect would come to visit the tendered and forlorn pistil. Curiosity gradually emboldening me, I descended as far as the ground-floor window, which was also open, and whose shutters were only half closed. I could distinctly hear Jupien getting ready to leave, who could not have detected me behind my blind, where I remained motionless up until the moment when I sprang hurriedly aside for fear of being seen by M. de Charlus, who, on his way to visit Mme de Villeparisis, was slowly crossing the courtyard, potbellied, aged by the full daylight, graying. It had taken an indisposition on Mme de Villeparisis's part (a consequence of the illness of the Marquis de Fierbois, with whom he personally was at daggers drawn) for M. de Charlus to pay a visit, for perhaps the first time in his life, at this hour of the day. For, with that singularity of the Guermantes, who, instead of conforming to the life of society, modified it in accordance with their own habits (unworldly, so they believed, and deserving in consequence that worldliness, that thing of no value, should be humbled before them—thus it was that Mme de Marsantes did not have her "day" but entertained her women friends every morning, from ten till twelve), the Baron, setting this time aside for reading, or for hunting for old curios and the like, only ever went visiting between four and six in the evening. At six he would go to the Jockey Club or for a drive in the Bois.[3] A moment later, I once again drew back, so as not to be seen by Jupien; it would soon be his time to leave for his office, from where he returned only for dinner, or even not at all for the past week, since his niece had gone off to the country with her apprentices to a customer's to finish a dress. Then, realizing that no one could see me, I resolved not to be disturbed again for fear of missing, were the miracle to occur, the arrival, almost impossible to hope for (across all the obstacles, the distance, the contrary chances, the dangers), of the insect sent from afar as an ambassador to the virgin whose wait had been so protracted. I knew that this wait was no more passive than with the male flower, whose stamens had spontaneously turned so that the insect might the more easily receive him; similarly, the flower-woman that was here would, should the insect come, arch her "styles" coquettishly and, in order to be penetrated more fully by him, would imperceptibly, like a hypocritical but ardent young damsel, come to meet him halfway. The laws of the vegetable world are themselves governed by ever-higher laws. If the visit of an insect, that is to say, the bringing of the seed from another flower, is necessary as a rule to fertilize a flower, this is because self-fertilization, the fertilization of the flower by itself, like repeated marriages within the same family, would lead to degeneration and sterility, whereas the crossbreeding effected by insects gives to succeeding generations of the same species a vigor unknown among their elders. This new lease on life may be excessive, however, and the species develop disproportionately; then, just as an antitoxin protects us against disease, or as the thyroid controls our waistline, or as defeat comes to punish pride, or fatigue pleasure, and as sleep in turn reposes us from fatigue, so an exceptional act of self-fertilization comes at the appointed time to give its own turn to the screw, to apply the brake, and bring the flower that had exaggeratedly departed from the norm back within it. My reflections had been following an incline that I shall describe in due course, and I had already drawn from the conspicuous stratagem of the flowers a consequence bearing on a whole unconscious element in the work of literature, when I saw M. de Charlus coming out again from the Marquise's. Only a few minutes had elapsed since he had gone in. Perhaps he had learned from his elderly relative herself, or merely through a servant, of the great improvement or, rather, the complete recovery from what in Mme de Villeparisis's case had been only a passing indisposition. At that moment, when he thought no one to be watching him, his eyelids lowered against the sunlight, M. de Charlus had relaxed the tension in his face and muffled the factitious vitality sustained in him by animated chitchat and by force of will. Pale as a marble statue, he had a large nose, but his fine features no longer received a different meaning from a willful gaze that might detract from the beauty of their modeling; nothing more now than a Guermantes, he seemed already sculpted, he, Palamède XV, in the chapel at Combray. Yet these features common to a whole family took on, in M. de Charlus's face, a more spiritualized, above all a gentler, delicacy. I regretted for his sake that he should habitually adulterate, by his many violences, his disagreeable idiosyncrasies, his scandal-mongering, his severity, his touchiness, and his arrogance, that he should conceal, beneath a spurious brutality, the amenity and kindness I could see displayed so artlessly on his face at the moment when he emerged from Mme de Villeparisis's. Blinking against the sunlight, he seemed almost to be smiling, and in his face, seen thus in repose and as it were in its natural state, I found something so affectionate, so defenseless, that I could not help reflecting how angry M. de Charlus would have been had he known he was being watched; for what he put me in mind of, this man who was so enamored of, who so prided himself on, his virility, who found everyone hatefully effeminate, what he suddenly put me in mind of, so unmistakably did he have, fleetingly, the features, the expression, the smile of one, was a woman!

I was once again about to move so that he should not catch sight of me; I had neither the time nor the need. For what did I see! Face-to-face, in this courtyard where they had certainly never encountered each other before (M. de Charlus coming to the Guermantes *hôtel* only in the afternoons, at times when Jupien was at his office), the Baron, his half-closed eyes all of a sudden opened wide, was gazing with an extraordinary intentness at the former waistcoat-maker on the doorstep of his shop, while the latter, standing suddenly transfixed in front of M. de Charlus, rooted like a plant, was contemplating with an air of wonderment the aging Baron's embonpoint. But, even more astonishing, M. de Charlus's attitude having changed, that of Jupien was at once made to harmonize with it, as if in accordance with the laws of some secret art. The Baron, who was seeking now to disguise the impression he had felt, and who, for all his feigned indifference, seemed to be moving away only with regret, came and went, stared off into space in the manner that he believed best brought out the beauty of his eyes, and had assumed a self-satisfied, casual, and ridiculous expression. Jupien, meanwhile, at once shedding the humble, kindly expression I had always seen him wear, had—in perfect symmetry with the Baron—drawn back his head, set his torso at an advantageous angle, placed his fist on his hip with a grotesque impertinence, and made his behind stick out, striking poses with the coquettishness that the orchid might have had for the providential advent of the bumblebee. I had not known he could look so unsympathetic. But neither had I known that he was capable of playing his part impromptu in this sort of scene between two deaf-mutes, which (although he found himself in the presence of M. de Charlus for the first time) seemed to have been long rehearsed; we arrive at such perfection spontaneously only when meeting with a compatriot abroad, with whom understanding then comes of its own accord, the interpreter being one and the same, without ever having set eyes on each other before.

This scene was not positively comical; however, it was imbued with a strangeness, or if you like a naturalness, the beauty of which continued to grow. For all that, M. de Charlus had tried to assume a detached air, distractedly lowering his eyelids; every now and again he would raise them again and give Julien an attentive glance. But (no doubt because he thought that a scene such as this could not be prolonged indefinitely in this place, either for reasons that will be understood in due course, or else out of that sense of the brevity of all things that means we want every blow to strike home, and makes of any love affair a most affecting spectacle) each time M. de Charlus looked at Jupien, he saw to it that the look was accompanied by a word or two, which made it infinitely unlike the looks normally directed at someone whom we know or do not know; he gazed at Jupien with the peculiar fixity of someone who is about to say to you, "Forgive my butting in, but you have a long white thread hanging down your back," or else, "I can't be mistaken, you must be from Zürich, too; indeed, I believe I've often met you at the antique dealer's." Thus, every two minutes, the same question seemed to be being posed to Jupien with intensity by M. de Charlus's oglings, like those interrogative phrases in Beethoven, repeated indefinitely at equal intervals, and intended—with an exaggerated luxury of preparation—to bring in a new theme, a change of key, a "re-entry." But the beauty of M. de Charlus's and Jupien's glances came, on the contrary, from the very fact that, provisionally at least, these glances did not seem to have as their aim to lead to anything. It was the first time I had seen the Baron and Jupien manifest this beauty. In the eyes of both, it was the sky, not of Zürich, but of some Oriental city whose name I had not as yet divined, that had just arisen. Whatever the point that was able to detain M. de Charlus and the waistcoat-maker, agreement seemed to have been reached between them, and these useless glances seemed to be no more than the ritual preliminaries, like the entertainments given before a marriage that has been agreed on. Closer still to nature—and the multiplicity of these comparisons is itself all the more natural in that, examined over the course of a few minutes, the same man seems successively to be a man, a man-bird, or a man-insect, and so on—it was like two birds, the male and the female, the male seeking to advance, the female—Jupien—making no sign in response to this maneuver, but looking at her new friend without surprise, with an inattentive fixity, adjudged more disturbing no doubt and alone of use, from the moment that the male had made the first moves, and contenting herself with preening her feathers. Finally, Jupien's indifference no longer seemed to be enough for him; from the certainty of having made a conquest to getting himself pursued and desired was but a short step, and, making up his mind to leave for his work, Jupien went out through the porte cochere. It was only after turning his head two or three times, however, that he made his escape into the street, into which the Baron, fearful of losing the scent (whistling with a devil-may-care expression, and not without a loud *"au revoir"* to the concierge, who, half drunk and entertaining guests in his back kitchen, did not even hear him), dashed hurriedly out in order to catch up with him. At the self-same instant that M. de Charlus passed through the gateway whistling like a fat bumblebee, another one, a real one this time, entered the courtyard. Who knows whether it was not the one so long awaited by the orchid, that had come to bring her the rare pollen without which she would remain a virgin? But I was distracted from following the insect's frolics, for, a minute or two later, Jupien, making a greater claim on my attention (perhaps in order to collect a package that he later took away with him, and which, in the emotion caused in him by the appearance of M. de Charlus, he had forgotten, perhaps quite simply for some more natural reason), Jupien returned, followed by the Baron. The latter, resolved to precipitate matters, asked the waistcoat-maker for a light, but immediately remarked, "I'm asking you for a light, but I see I've forgotten my cigars." The laws of hospitality prevailed over the rules of flirtation. "Come inside, you'll be given everything you want," said the waistcoat-maker, on whose face disdain gave way to joy. The door of the shop closed on them, and I could no longer hear anything. I had lost sight of the bumblebee, I did not know whether it was the insect that the orchid needed, but I no longer doubted the miraculous possibility of a very rare insect and a captive flower being conjoined, now that M. de Charlus (a simple comparison of the providential chances, whatever they might be, without the least scientific pretension to drawing a parallel between certain botanical laws and what is sometimes quite wrongly called homosexuality), who for years past had come into this house only at the times when Jupien was not there, had, through the accident of Mme de Villeparisis's indisposition, encountered the waistcoat-maker and, with him, the good fortune reserved for men of the Baron's kind by one of those fellow creatures who may even be, as we shall see, infinitely younger than Jupien and better-looking, the man predestined so that they may receive their share of sensual pleasure on this earth: the man who loves only elderly gentlemen.

What I have just said here is in any case what I was to understand only a few minutes later, however, so closely do these properties of being invisible adhere to reality until some circumstance removes them. At all events, for the time being I was most annoyed no longer to be able to hear the conversation between the former waistcoat-maker and the Baron. I then noticed that the shop that was for rent was divided from Jupien's only by an exceedingly thin partition. To get into it, all I need do was to return upstairs to our apartment, go to the kitchen, descend the servants' staircase as far as the cellars, follow these internally for the whole width of the courtyard, and, having reached the point in the basement where, only a few months before, the cabinetmaker had been storing his joinery, and where Jupien was anticipating putting his coal, climb the few steps that gave access to the interior of the shop. Thus my whole route would be under cover; I should be seen by no one. That was the most prudent course. It was not the one that I adopted, but, keeping along the walls, I circled the courtyard in the open, trying not to be seen. If I was not seen, I owe it more to chance, I fancy, than to my good sense. And, supposing there to be one, I can see three possible reasons for the fact that I came to so rash a decision, when the cellar route was so safe. My impatience first of all. Then, perhaps, an obscure recollection of the scene in Montjouvain, hidden in front of Mlle Vinteuil's window.[4] Indeed, the staging of the things of this sort that I witnessed was always of the rashest and least probable nature, as if such revelations had to be the reward only for an action full of risk, though partly clandestine. Lastly, piece of childishness that it was, I hardly dare confess to the third reason, which was, I do believe, unconsciously determining. Since, in order to follow—and to see contradicted—the military principles of Saint-Loup, I had been following the Boer War in great detail, I had been led to reread old accounts of travel and exploration. These accounts had excited me, and I had applied them in my everyday life in order to give myself more courage. When my attacks had forced me to remain for several days and several nights on end not merely without sleeping but without lying down, and without drinking or eating, at the moment when my exhaustion and suffering had become such that I thought I would never re-emerge from them, I would think of some traveler cast up on the shore, poisoned by unwholesome plants, shivering with fever in clothes drenched in seawater, yet who felt better after a day or two and resumed his journey at random, in search of some inhabitants or other, who would perhaps be cannibals. Their example braced me, and gave me back some hope, and I felt ashamed of having momentarily lost heart. Thinking of the Boers, who, with English armies facing them, were not afraid to expose themselves at the moment when, before regaining the bush, they needed to cross a stretch of open country, "A fine thing," I thought, "that I should be more pusillanimous when the theater of operations is merely our own courtyard, and when the only steel I, who have just fought several duels without any fear, on account of the Dreyfus Affair, have to fear is that of the neighbors' gaze, who have better things to do than stare into the courtyard."

But once I was in the shop, avoiding making even the faintest creak of the floorboards, realizing that the slightest sound from Jupien's shop could be heard from mine, I reflected how imprudent Jupien and M. de Charlus had been, and the extent to which luck had been with them.

I did not dare move. The Guermantes' groom, taking advantage of their absence, no doubt, had in fact transferred a ladder previously stored in the coach house into the shop where I now found myself. And had I climbed up on it I could have opened the transom and heard as if I had been in Jupien's shop itself. But I was afraid of making a noise. Moreover, there was no point. I did not even need to regret having taken several minutes to get into my shop. For, to judge by what I heard in the early stages from Jupien's, which was simply inarticulate sounds, I assume few words were uttered. It is true that these sounds were so violent that, had they not constantly been taken up an octave higher by a parallel moaning, I might have thought that one person was slitting another's throat close beside me, and that the murderer and his resuscitated victim were then taking a bath in order to erase the traces of the crime. From which I later concluded that if there is one thing as noisy as suffering it is pleasure, especially when there is added to it—failing the fear of having children, which could not be the case here, in spite of the far-from-convincing example in the *Golden Legend*5—an immediate concern with cleanliness. Finally, at the end of half an hour or so (during which time I had surreptitiously hoisted myself up on my ladder so as to see through the transom, which I did not open), a conversation was joined. Jupien was energetically refusing the money that M. de Charlus wanted to give him.

Then M. de Charlus took a step outside the shop. "Why do you have your chin shaved like that?" he said to the Baron affectionately. "It's so handsome, a good beard!" "Pah, it's disgusting!" replied the Baron. He still lingered in the doorway, however, and asked Jupien for information about the neighborhood. "You don't know anything about the chestnut-vendor on the corner—not on the left, he's a horror, but on the even-numbered side, a big, strapping fellow, very dark? And the pharmacist opposite, he's got a very nice cyclist who delivers his medicines." These questions no doubt ruffled Jupien, for, drawing himself up in pique, like a great coquette betrayed, he replied, "I can see you're fickle." Uttered in a sorrowful, icy, and affected tone, this reproach no doubt found a response in M. de Charlus, who, in order to erase the bad impression his inquisitiveness had created, addressed an entreaty to Jupien, too low for me to be able to make out the words, which would no doubt necessitate their prolonging their stay in the shop, and which sufficiently affected the waistcoat-maker to erase his suffering, for he stared at the Baron's face, fat and flushed beneath his gray hair, with the supremely happy look of someone whose *amour-propre* has just been profoundly flattered, and, making up his mind to grant M. de Charlus what the latter had just requested, Jupien, after one or two remarks lacking in refinement—such as "You've got a fat behind!"—said to the Baron, with an expression at once smiling, emotional, superior, and grateful, "All right, come on, you great baby, you!"

"If I revert to the question of the tram-driver,"[6] M. de Charlus went on tenaciously, "it's because, aside from anything else, it might provide a bit of interest for the journey home. Like the Caliph who used to roam Baghdad mistaken for a simple merchant,[7] I sometimes indeed condescend to follow some curious young person whose silhouette has amused me." Here I made the same observation as I had made concerning Bergotte. If ever he had to answer before a court of law, he would use, not the phrases apt for persuading the judges, but those Bergotte-like phrases that his peculiar literary temperament prompted in him naturally and from the employment of which he derived pleasure. Similarly, M. de Charlus used the same language with the waistcoat-maker as he would have done with members of society from his own coterie, exaggerating its tics even, whether because the shyness against which he was laboring to fight had impelled him to an excess of pride, or because, by preventing him from being in command of himself (for we are more ill-at-ease in front of someone who is not from our own circle), it forced him to unveil, to lay bare his true nature, which was indeed arrogant and a little mad, as Mme de Guermantes used to say. "In order not to lose the scent," he went on, "I jump like a little school-teacher, like a good-looking young doctor, into the same tram as the young person herself, whom we speak of in the feminine only so as to observe the rule—just as we say when speaking of a prince, 'Is Son Altesse in good health?'[8] If she changes trams, I take, along perhaps with the microbes of the plague, that unbelievable thing known as a 'transfer,' a number that, although it is being handed to *me,* isn't always Number One! In this way I change 'carriages' as many as three or four times. I am sometimes left stranded at eleven o'clock in the evening at the Gare d'Orléans, and have to come home! If only it wasn't just from the Gare d'Orléans! But one time, for instance, not having been able to get into conversation earlier, I went as far as Orléans itself, in one of those frightful carriages where for a view you have, between the triangles of crochetwork known as 'luggage racks,' the photographs of the network's chief architectural masterpieces. There was only one seat free, and I had facing me, for a historical monument, a 'view' of Orléans Cathedral, which is the ugliest in France, and as wearisome to gaze at like that, against my will, as if I'd been forced to concentrate on its towers in the glass knob on those optical penholders that give you ophthalmia.[9] I got off at Les Aubrais at the same time as my young person, where, alas (when I had been assuming every defect in her bar that of having a family), her family was waiting on the platform! For consolation, while waiting for the train that would take me back to Paris, I had only Diane de Poitiers's house.[10] It may well have charmed one of my royal ancestors; I'd have preferred a more living beauty. It's for that reason, as a remedy for the tedium of these solitary return journeys, that I'd rather like to get to know a sleeping-car attendant or the driver of an omnibus. Anyway, don't be shocked," the Baron concluded, "it's all a question of class. With young society men, for example, I don't desire any physical possession, but I can't rest until I've touched them—I don't mean bodily, but touched some chord in them. Once, instead of leaving my letters unanswered, a young man never ceases writing to me, is mine to dispose of morally, I am appeased, or I would be at least if I wasn't soon gripped by concern about another one. It's rather curious, isn't it? Speaking of young society men, of the ones who come here, you don't know any of them?" "No, baby boy. Oh yes, one, dark, very tall, with a monocle, who's always laughing and turning around." "I can't tell who you mean." Jupien completed the portrait, but M. de Charlus could not manage to discover whose portrait it was, for he was unaware that the former waistcoat-maker was one of those people, more numerous than we imagine, who cannot remember the hair color of people they know only slightly. For me, however, who knew of this infirmity in Jupien, and who replaced dark by fair, the portrait seemed an accurate reference to the Duc de Châtellerault. "To get back to the young men who are not from the lower orders," resumed the Baron, "at this moment my head has been turned by a strange little fellow from the petty bourgeoisie, intelligent, who displays a prodigious incivility toward me. He has absolutely no notion of what a prodigious personage I am, and of the microscopic vibrio that he represents. But, after all, what does it matter? The little donkey can bray all he likes before my august bishop's robe." "Bishop!" exclaimed Jupien, who had understood nothing of the last words that M. de Charlus had just uttered, but who was stunned by the word "bishop." "But that hardly goes with religion," he said. "I have three popes in my family,"[11] replied M. de Charlus, "and the right to wear red mourning by virtue of a cardinal's title, the niece of the Cardinal, my great-uncle, having brought my grandfather the title of duke that was substituted for it. I can see you have no ear for metaphors and are indifferent to the history of France. Moreover," he added, by way less perhaps of a conclusion than of a warning, "the attraction exerted on me by the young persons who avoid me, out of fear, naturally, for respect alone seals their lips from shouting aloud that they love me, requires that they have an eminent position in society. There again, their feigned indifference may produce, for all that, the directly contrary effect. Foolishly prolonged, it nauseates me. To take an example from a class you will be more familiar with: When my town house was being repaired, so as not to provoke jealousy among all the duchesses vying for the honor of being able to tell me they had given me lodging, I went to spend a few days at a 'hotel,' as they say. One of the room waiters was known to me; I pointed out to him an intriguing young '*chasseur,*' who closed carriage doors, and who remained unamenable to my propositions. Exasperated, finally, to prove to him that my intentions were pure, I got them to offer him a ridiculously large sum merely to come up and talk to me for five minutes in my room. I waited for him in vain. I then took such a dislike to him that I used to go out by the service entrance so I wouldn't see that wicked young rogue's pretty little face. I learned later that he'd never got any of my letters, which had been intercepted, the first by the room waiter, who was envious; the second by the day porter, who was virtuous; the third by the night porter, who was in love with the young *chasseur* and used to sleep with him at the hour when Diana was rising. But my dislike has persisted all the same, and, were they to serve me up the *chasseur* simply as game on a silver dish, I would reject him and be sick. But, there, what a shame, we've been speaking of serious matters, and now it's over between us where what I'd been hoping for is concerned. But you could be of great service to me, as a go-between; and then, no, that idea in itself puts a bit of spunk back into me, and I feel nothing's yet over."

From the very beginning of this scene, a revolution had been effected in M. de Charlus in my newly opened eyes, as complete and as immediate as if he had been touched by a magic wand. Until now, because I had not understood, I had not seen. Vice (I put it thus for the sake of linguistic convenience), each person's vice accompanies him in the same fashion as the genie who was invisible to men for as long as they were unaware of his presence. Kindness, double-dealing, reputation, our social relations do not let themselves be discovered; we carry them concealed. Ulysses himself did not at first recognize Athena.[12] But the gods are immediately perceptible to the gods, as like equally soon is to like, and as M. de Charlus had been to Jupien. Until now, I had found myself in the same position when confronted by M. de Charlus as an absentminded man who, faced by a pregnant woman whose bulging waistline he has not noticed, persists, while she smilingly repeats to him, "Yes, I'm a little tired at present," in asking her tactlessly, "What's the trouble, then?" But should someone say to him, "She's expecting," he suddenly notices the belly and thereafter sees nothing else. It is reason that opens our eyes; an error dispelled lends us an extra sense.

Those who do not like to go for examples of this law to the MM. de Charlus of their acquaintance, whom for a very long time they had not suspected, until that day when, on the smooth surface of an individual no different from the rest, there have appeared, traced in a hitherto invisible ink, the characters making up that word beloved of the ancient Greeks, need only, in order to convince themselves that the world around them appears at first bare, stripped of the innumerable adornments it offers to those better informed, remember how many times in their lives it has happened that they were on the point of committing a gaffe. Nothing, on this or on that man's face, devoid of character as it is, could have given them to imagine that he was none other than the brother, or the fiancé, or the lover of a woman of whom they were about to say, "What a cow!" But then, fortunately, a word whispered to them by a neighbor arrests the fatal expression on their lips. At once the words appear, like a Mene, Tekel, Upharsin:[13] he is the fiancé, or he is the brother, or he is the lover of the woman, whom it is not right to call a "cow" in front of him. And this new notion in itself will entail a whole regrouping, the withdrawal or promotion of some fraction of the notions, henceforth complete, we had held concerning the rest of the family. In M. de Charlus, for all that another creature had been coupled with him, which differentiated him from other men, like the horse with the centaur, and that this other creature had formed one with the Baron, I had never noticed it. Now that the abstraction had been materialized, this creature, understood at last, had at once lost its capacity to remain invisible, and the transmutation of M. de Charlus into a new person was so complete that not only the contrasts in his face and his voice but, in retrospect, even the ups and downs in his relationship with me, all that thus far had appeared incoherent to my mind, became intelligible, showed itself to be self-evident, just as a sentence that had presented no meaning for as long as it remained broken up into letters arranged at random, expresses, if the characters find themselves restored to their rightful order, a thought we will not again be able to forget.

Moreover, I understood now why, a moment ago, when I had seen him coming out from Mme de Villeparisis's, I had been able to think that M. de Charlus had the look of a woman: he was one! He belonged to that race of beings, less contradictory than they appear to be, whose ideal is virile precisely because their temperament is feminine, and who are in life like other men in appearance only; there where each of us carries, inscribed in the eyes through which we see everything in the universe, a silhouette intaglioed into the facet of the pupil, for them it is not that of a nymph but of an ephebe. A race on which a malediction weighs, and which must live in falsehood and in perjury, because it knows that its desire, which, for every created being, is life's sweetest pleasure, is held to be punishable and shameful, to be inadmissible; which must deny its God, since, even if Christian, when they stand arraigned at the bar of the court they must, before Christ and in his name, defend themselves, as if from a calumny, from what is their life itself; sons without a mother, to whom they are obliged to lie even in the hour when they close her eyes; friends without friendships, notwithstanding all those that their frequently acknowledged charm inspires, and which their often kindly hearts would respond to; but can we give the name of friendship to relationships that vegetate only by virtue of a lie, and from which the first impulse of trust and sincerity that they might be tempted to show would cause them to be rejected in disgust, unless their dealings are with an impartial, or even a sympathetic spirit, but who then, misled in their regard by a conventional psychology, will ascribe to the vice confessed the one affection that is the most alien to it, just as certain judges presume and excuse murder more readily among inverts and betrayal among Jews, for reasons deriving from original sin and the fatality of the race? Finally—at least according to the first theory I had then sketched out, which we shall see being modified in due course, in which this would have angered them more than anything else had the contradiction not been hidden from view by the very illusion that made them see and live—lovers to whom the possibility of that love, the hope of which gives them the strength to bear so many risks and so much loneliness, is all but closed, simply because they are much taken with a man having nothing of the woman about him, with a man who is not an invert and cannot, in consequence, love them; so that their desire would be forever unsatisfiable were money not to deliver up real men to them, and imagination not finally to lead them to mistake the inverts to whom they have prostituted themselves for real men. Their only honor is precarious, their only liberty provisional until the crime be discovered; their only position unstable, as for the poet who was yesterday being fêted in every drawing room and applauded in every theater in London, only to be driven on the morrow from every lodging house, unable to find a pillow on which to lay his head,[14] turning the millstone like Samson and saying, like him, "The two sexes will die each on its own side,"[15] excluded even, save at times of high misfortune, when the majority rally around the victim, like the Jews around Dreyfus, from the sympathy—sometimes from the company—of their own kind, who are disgusted to be made to see themselves as they are, depicted in a mirror that no longer flatters them but brings out all the blemishes that they had not wanted to remark in themselves and makes them understand that what they had been calling their love (to which, by playing on the word, they had annexed, out of a social sense, all that poetry, painting, music, chivalry, and asceticism have been able to add to love) stems not from an ideal of beauty that they have chosen, but from an incurable malady; like the Jews once again (save those few who wish to associate only with those of their own race, and who have the ritual words and hallowed jokes constantly on their lips), shunning one another, seeking out those who are the most opposed to themselves, who want nothing to do with them, forgiving when rebuffed, elated when indulged; yet also brought together with their own kind by the ostracism that afflicts them, the opprobrium into which they have fallen, having finally acquired, by a persecution similar to that of Israel, the physical and moral characteristics of a race, sometimes beautiful, often ghastly, finding (despite all the ridicule that he who mixes more with and is better assimilated to the opposing race, and is relatively, on the surface, less inverted, heaps on him who has remained more so) relief in the frequentation of their own kind, a support even in their existence, so that, while denying that they are a race (the name of which is the gravest insult), they willingly unmask those who succeed in concealing that they belong to it, less in order to hurt them, to which they have no objection, than to excuse themselves, and going in search—as a doctor does of appendicitis—of inversion, even in history, taking pleasure in reminding you that Socrates was one of them, just as the Israelites tell you that Jesus was a Jew, without reflecting that no one was abnormal when homosexuality was the norm, no one anti-Christian before Christ, that opprobrium alone makes the crime, for it has allowed to survive only those who were recalcitrant to all preaching, all example, all punishment, by virtue of an innate disposition so special that it repels other men more (even though it may be accompanied by lofty moral qualities) than certain vices that contradict it, such as theft, cruelty, or bad faith, which are better understood and thus more readily excused by the common run of men; forming a freemasonry far more extensive, more effective, and less suspected than that of the lodges, for it rests on an identity of tastes, of needs, of habits, of dangers, of apprenticeship, of knowledge, of commerce, and of vocabulary, in which even the members who do not wish to know one another at once recognize one another by natural or conventional signs, whether involuntary or deliberate, which indicate to the beggar one of his own kind in the great nobleman whose carriage door he is closing, to the father in his daughter's fiancé, to the man who had wanted to be cured, or to confess, or to be defended, in the doctor or the priest or the lawyer of whom he has gone in search; all of them obliged to protect their secret, yet having their share in a secret of others that the rest of humanity does not suspect, and which means that for them the most improbable cloak-and-dagger stories seem true; for in this fabulous, anachronistic life, the ambassador is friends with the convict; the prince, with a certain freedom of manner lent him by his aristocratic upbringing, which no fearful petty bourgeois could have, when he comes out from the duchess, goes off to confer with the ruffian; a reprobate portion of the human collectivity, but a significant portion, suspected in places where it is not, flaunted, insolent, unpunished in places where it goes undetected; numbering adherents everywhere, among the common people, in the army, in the temple, in prison, on the throne; living, finally, a great number of them at least, in a dangerous, caressing intimacy with the men of the other race, provoking them, playing with them by speaking of their vice as if it were not theirs, a game made easy by the blindness or falseness of the others, a game that may be prolonged for years, up until the day of the scandal when these animal-tamers are devoured; obliged until then to keep their lives hidden, to avert their gaze from where they would like to be fixing it, to fix their gaze on what they would like to avert it from, to change the gender of many of the adjectives in their vocabulary, a small social constraint compared with the inner constraint that their vice, or what is improperly so called, imposes on them, in respect no longer of others but of themselves, and in such a way that it does not appear to them to be a vice. But some, more practical, more impatient, who do not have time to go and do their own bargaining or to give up the simplification of their lives and the saving in time that can result from cooperation, have created two societies, the second of which is made up exclusively of people like themselves.

This is striking among those who are poor and have come from the provinces, without connections, with nothing but the ambition of one day becoming a doctor or a celebrated attorney, having a mind as yet empty of opinions, and a body devoid of graces, which they expect rapidly to adorn, just as, for their little room in the Latin Quarter, they would buy furniture according to what they have observed and copied among those who have already "arrived" in the serious and useful profession in which they hope to enroll and to become famous; with these,

their special proclivity, inherited without their knowing, like an aptitude for drawing, for music, or for blindness, is perhaps their one deep-
rooted, despotic originality—which on certain evenings forces them to
miss some meeting or other useful to their careers with people whose
manner of speaking, of thinking, of dressing, of doing their hair they
have, on the other hand, adopted. In their own neighborhood, where
they otherwise associate only with their fellow disciples, their mentors,
or some compatriot who has arrived and taken them under his wing,
they have soon come across other young men drawn to them by the
same peculiar proclivity, just as in a small town the fifth-form teacher
and the notary become friends, both loving chamber music or medieval
ivories; applying to the object of their hobby the same utilitarian instinct, and the same professional spirit that guides them in their careers,
they meet at occasions to which laymen are not admitted, any more
than to those that bring together connoisseurs of old snuffboxes, Japanese prints, or rare flowers, and at which, because of the pleasure of
learning something new, the usefulness of the exchanges, and the fear
of competition, there reigns, as at a stamp market, at once the close understanding of specialists and the fierce rivalry of collectors. No one,
moreover, in the café where they have their table knows what the meeting is, whether of a fishing club, of subeditors, or of sons of the Indre,[16]
so correct is their costume, so cold and reserved their expression, and so
guarded the only glances they dare to give the fashionable young men,
the young "lions," who, a few yards away, are sounding off about their
mistresses, and among whom those who admire them without daring
to look up will learn only twenty years later, when some will be on
the eve of entering an academy, and others old men in a club, that
the most seductive, now a fat and graying Charlus, was in actual fact
like themselves, but elsewhere, in another world, beneath other external symbols, with alien signs, the difference of which has led them into
error. But these groupings are more or less advanced; and just as the
Union des Gauches differs from the Fédération Socialiste,[17] and this or
that Mendelssohn Society from the Schola Cantorum,[18] so, on certain
evenings, at another table, there are extremists who allow a bracelet to
protrude from beneath their cuff, or sometimes a necklace in the opening of their collar, who, by their insistent glances, their giggling, their

laughter, and their mutual caresses, force a band of schoolboys to take to their heels, and who are served, with a politeness beneath which there broods indignation, by a waiter who, as on the evenings when he serves Dreyfusards, would delight in going off to fetch the police were it not to his advantage to pocket the tips.

It is to these professional organizations that the mind opposes the taste of the solitaries, and without too much artifice in one respect, since in so doing it is only imitating the solitaries themselves, who believe that nothing differs more from organized vice than what appears to them a misunderstood love, yet with some artifice nonetheless, for these different classes correspond, every bit as much as to diverse physiological types, to successive moments in a pathological or merely social evolution. Indeed, it is very rarely that the solitaries do not, sooner or later, merge into organizations such as these, sometimes out of simple fatigue, or out of convenience (just as those who have been the most opposed to it end up installing the telephone, by receiving the Iénas or by shopping at Potin's).[19] They are generally none too well received there, however, for, in their relatively pure lives, the lack of experience, the saturation by daydreams to which they are reduced, have brought out more strongly in them those signs peculiar to effeminacy that the professionals have sought to erase. And it has to be admitted that, with some of these newcomers, the woman is not merely one with the man inwardly, but hideously apparent, agitated as they are in some hysterical spasm by a shrill laugh that convulses their knees and their hands, and no more resembling the common run of men than those monkeys, with their melancholy, dark-ringed eyes and prehensile feet, that put on dinner jackets and wear a black tie; with the result that these new recruits are deemed, and by those less chaste moreover, to be compromising company, and hard of admission; they are accepted, however, and they benefit then from the facilities by which commerce, the great enterprises, have transformed the lives of individuals, have brought within reach commodities hitherto too costly to acquire or even hard to find, but which now submerge them in a plethora of what, on their own, they had been unable to discover in the largest crowds. Yet, even with these innumerable outlets, the social constraint still weighs too heavily on some, who are recruited chiefly from among those in whom no mental constraint has been exercised and who still hold their kind of love to be more uncommon than it is. Let us leave aside for the time being those who, led by the exceptional nature of their inclination to believe themselves superior to women, despise them, who make of homosexuality the privilege of great geniuses and of glorious epochs, and who, when they seek to share their taste with others, do so less with those who seem predisposed to it, as a morphinomaniac does with morphine, than with those who seem to them worthy of it, out of an apostolic zeal, just as others preach Zionism, conscientious objection, Saint-Simonism,[20] vegetarianism, or anarchy. Some, if you come upon them unawares in the morning, still in bed, display an admirable woman's head, so general is the expression and symbolic of the sex as a whole; the hair itself declares it; its inflection is so feminine when loosened, it falls so naturally on the cheek in tresses, that you marvel that the young woman, the girl, Galatea,[21] barely awake as yet in the unconscious of this man's body in which she is imprisoned, should have been able so ingeniously, of her own accord, without having been taught by anyone, to take advantage of the humblest escape route from her prison and find what was necessary to her life. The young man whose delectable head this is doubtless does not say, "I am a woman." Even if—for so many possible reasons—he lives with a woman, he may deny to her that he is one, may swear that he has never had relations with a man. Let her look at him as we have just shown him, lying in a bed, in pajamas, his arms bare, his neck bare beneath his black hair. The pajamas have become a woman's shift, the head that of a pretty Spanish woman. The mistress is appalled by the confidences entrusted to her gaze, truer than any words could be, or even actions, and which actions moreover, if they have not done so already, will not fail to confirm, for every human being pursues his own pleasure; and if this human being is not too vicious, he seeks it in a sex opposite to his own. But for the invert vice begins, not when he establishes a relationship (for too many reasons may govern that), but when he takes his pleasure with women. The young man whom we have just tried to depict was so obviously a woman that the women who looked longingly at him were doomed (for lack of a particular proclivity) to the same disappointment as those who, in Shakespeare's comedies, are taken in by a young girl in disguise who passes herself off as an adolescent boy. The deception is the same, the invert knows it even, he can guess at the disillusionment the woman will experience once the travesty is removed, and senses how rich a source of poetic fancy it is, this mistake over gender. Moreover, for all that he may not confess, even to his exigent mistress (unless she is a citizen of Gomorrah), "I am a woman," with what stratagems and what agility will the unconscious yet visible woman within not seek out the masculine organ, with the obstinacy of a climbing plant! You have only to look at those curly tresses against the white pillow to understand that, in the evenings, if this young man slips from his parents' fingers, in spite of them, in spite of himself, it will not be to go to meet with women. His mistress may castigate him, may turn the key on him; the next day, the man-woman will have found the means of attaching himself to a man, just as the convolvulus throws out its tendrils wherever a hoe or a rake is to be found. Why, admiring in this man's face a delicacy that touches us, a grace and a natural affability such as men do not have, should we be distressed to learn that this young man seeks out boxers? These are different aspects of the one reality. And the aspect that repels us is in fact the most touching, more touching than all the delicacy, for it represents an admirable unconscious effort on the part of nature: the recognition of the sex by itself, despite that sex's deceptions, appears as the unavowed attempt to break out toward what an initial error on society's part has set far away from it. Some, those whose childhoods were the most self-conscious no doubt, hardly concern themselves with what sort of physical pleasure they receive, provided they can relate it to a masculine face. Whereas others, whose senses are no doubt more violent, give imperious localization to their physical pleasures. The confessions of these last would perhaps shock the world at large. They live less exclusively beneath the satellite of Saturn perhaps,[22] because for them women are not altogether excluded as they are for the first kind, with regard to whom they would not exist were it not for conversation, flirtation, and love in the head. But the second kind seek out the women who love women, who can procure a young man for them and add to the pleasure they get from finding themselves with him; much more, they can, in the same way, find the same pleasure with them as with a man. Whence it is that, in the case of those who love the first kind, jealousy is excited only by the pleasure they might be finding with a man and which alone seems to them a betrayal, since they have no part in the love of women, have practiced it only out of habit and so as to preserve the possibility of marriage, so little picturing to themselves the pleasure it may afford that they cannot bear for the man they love to enjoy it; whereas the second kind often inspire jealousy by their love affairs with women. For in the relationships they have with them they play the role of another woman for the women who love women, and the woman offers them at the same time more or less what they find in a man, so that the jealous friend suffers from feeling that the man he loves is inseparable from the woman who is for him almost a man, at the same time that he feels him almost escaping from him, because, for these women, he is something he does not know, a sort of woman. Let us not speak either of those young madmen who, out of a sort of childishness, in order to tease their friends or shock their parents, display a sort of fury in choosing clothes that look like dresses, in reddening their lips and blacking their eyes; let us leave them aside, for it is they whom we shall meet with again, once they have too cruelly paid the penalty for their affectation, spending a whole lifetime trying vainly to make reparation, by their severe, protestant demeanor, for the wrong they did themselves when they were carried away by the same demon that drives young women in the Faubourg Saint-Germain to live in a scandalous fashion, to break with all custom, to flout their families, up until the day when they set out perseveringly but unavailingly to reascend the slope that they had found such amusement in, or rather had been unable to stop themselves from descending. Let us leave until later, finally, those who have concluded a pact with Gomorrah. We shall speak of them when M. de Charlus comes to know them. Let us leave all those, of one variety or another, who will appear in their turn, and, to bring this first exposé to an end, say a word only about those of whom we began to speak a little earlier, the solitaries. Holding their vice to be more of an exception than it is, they have gone off to live on their own on the day when they discovered it, having long borne it without recognizing it, longer merely than others. For no one knows right away that he is an invert, or a poet, or a snob, or a miscreant. The schoolboy who was learning love poetry or looking at obscene pictures, if he then pressed up against a classmate, merely imagined that he was communing with him in the same desire for a woman. How could he believe that he was not like everyone else, when he recognizes the substance of what he feels in reading Mme de La Fayette, Racine, Baudelaire, Walter Scott, at a time when he is as yet too little able to observe himself to appreciate what he is adding to it of his own making, and that if the sentiment is the same its object is different, that what he desires is Rob Roy and not Diana Vernon?[23] With many of them, out of a prudent defensive instinct that precedes the clearer view of the intelligence, the mirror and walls of their room vanish beneath cheap color prints of actresses; they write verses such as:

> Chloë is the one for whom I care,
> She is divine, a girl so fair,
> Such love for her my heart doth bear.

Must we on this account set at the beginning of these lives a taste not to be met with again in them subsequently, like the blond curls of the children who will later become the darkest? Who knows whether the photographs of women are not a beginning of hypocrisy, and a beginning also of horror for the other inverts? But the solitaries are the very ones for whom hypocrisy is painful. Perhaps even the example of the Jews, of a different colony, is not strong enough to explain how weak a hold upbringing has over them, and with what artistry they succeed in reverting, not perhaps to something as simply atrocious as suicide (to which, whatever precautions we may take, madmen revert, and, having been rescued from the river into which they had thrown themselves, take poison, procure a revolver, and so on), but to a life not only that the men of the other race cannot understand or imagine, loathing its necessary pleasures, but whose frequent danger and permanent shame would fill them with horror. In order to depict them, we need perhaps to think, if not of those animals that cannot be domesticated, then of lion cubs supposedly tamed yet which are lions still, or at least of blacks, who are driven to despair by the comfortable existence of whites and prefer the risks of the uncivilized life and its incomprehensible joys. The day having come when they discover themselves to be incapable at once of lying to others and of lying to themselves, they go off to live in the country, fleeing their own kind (whom they believe to be few in number) out of horror at the monstrosity or fear of temptation, and the rest of humanity out of shame. Having never achieved genuine maturity, and having lapsed into melancholy, from time to time, on a Sunday when there is no moon, they take a walk along a lane as far as a crossroads where, without a single word having passed between them, one of their childhood friends who lives in a nearby château has come to wait for them. And they take up the games of old once again, on the grass, in the darkness, without exchanging a word. During the week, they meet in each other's houses, chat about this or that, without referring to what has taken place, exactly as if they had not done anything and were never going to do anything again, except, in their dealings, for a hint of coldness, of irony, of irritability, of resentment, and sometimes of hatred. Then the neighbor leaves on an arduous journey on horseback or by mule, scaling mountain peaks and sleeping in the snow; his friend, who identifies his own vice with a weakness of temperament, with his timid, home-loving life, realizes that the vice will not be able to survive in his emancipated friend, at so many thousands of meters above sea level. And, indeed, the other gets married. The abandoned one is not cured, however (in spite of the cases in which we shall see that inversion is curable). He insists on taking in the fresh cream himself in the mornings, in his kitchen, from the hands of the dairy boy, and on those evenings when he is too troubled by desire, he forgets himself to the extent of setting a drunkard back on his right road or straightening the blind man's shirt. No doubt the life of some inverts seems sometimes to change, and their vice (as we say) no longer shows in their habits; but nothing has been lost: a hidden jewel is recovered; when the quantity of urine decreases in an invalid, it is good that he should perspire more, but the excretion must still take place. One day this homosexual loses a young cousin, and by his inconsolable grief you realize that it was into this love, chaste perhaps and which had more to do with preserving esteem than obtaining possession, his desires had passed by a transference, just as, in a budget, certain expenses can be carried over into another financial year without affecting the total. As with those invalids in whom an attack of urticaria causes their habitual ailments to disappear for a time, so, in the invert, a pure love felt for a young relative seems momentarily to have replaced, by metastasis, habits that will sooner or later once again take the place of the vicarious, now cured sickness.

Meanwhile, the solitary's married neighbor has returned; faced with the beauty of the young wife and the affection shown her by her husband, on the day when the friend is obliged to invite them to dinner he feels shame for the past. Already in an interesting condition, she has to go home early, leaving her husband behind; the latter, when the time comes to go home, asks to be taken some of the way by his friend, who is not at first touched by any suspicion, but who then, at the crossroads, finds himself being thrown down on the grass, without a word, by the mountaineer soon to be a father. And the encounters recommence, up until the day when one of the young wife's male cousins comes and settles not far away, with whom the husband is now always going off. And should the abandoned one call and try to get close to him, the latter pushes him furiously away, indignant that the other should not have had the tact to sense the dislike he will from now on inspire. One time, however, a stranger presents himself, sent by the unfaithful neighbor; but the abandoned one is too busy and cannot receive him, and realizes only afterward with what object the stranger had come.

Then the solitary languishes alone. He has no pleasure other than going to the nearby seaside resort to ask for information from a certain railwayman. But the latter has been given promotion and been posted to the other end of France; the solitary will no longer be able to go and ask him the times of the trains or the price of a first-class ticket, and before returning home to dream in his tower, like Griselda,[24] he lingers on the beach, like some strange Andromeda whom no Argonaut will come to deliver, like a sterile jellyfish that will perish on the sand, or else he remains idly on the platform, before the departure of the train, casting glances at the crowd of passengers that will seem indifferent, disdainful, or distracted to those of another race, but which, like the brilliant luminescence with which certain insects adorn themselves to attract those of the same species, or like the nectar that certain flowers offer to attract the insects that will fertilize them, would not deceive the adept, almost impossible to find, of a pleasure too singular, too difficult to place, that is being offered to him, the confrère with whom our specialist might speak the unusual tongue; at most, some scarecrow on the platform will feign interest, but solely for material gain, like those who, at the Collège de France, in the hall where the professor of Sanskrit is speaking without any hearers, will follow the lecture, but only in order to get warm. Jellyfish! Orchid! When I was following only my own instinct, the jellyfish repelled me at Balbec; but had I known how to look at it, like Michelet,[25] from the point of view of natural history and of aesthetics, I would have seen a delectable girandole of azure. Are they not, with the transparent velvet of their petals, like the mauve orchids of the sea? Like so many creatures of the animal and vegetable kingdoms, like the plant that would produce vanilla but which, because in it the male organ is divided by a septum from the female organ, remains sterile unless hummingbirds or certain small bees transport the pollen from one to the other, or unless man fertilizes them artificially, M. de Charlus (and here the word "fertilization" must be taken in its moral sense, since in the physical sense the union of male with male is sterile, but it matters that an individual should be able to meet with the one pleasure he is capable of enjoying, and that "here below every soul" can give someone "its music, its flame, or its fragrance"),[26] M. de Charlus was one of those men who may be called exceptional because, however numerous they may be, the satisfaction, so simple with others, of their sexual needs depends on the coincidence of too many conditions, too difficult to encounter. For men like M. de Charlus (allowance being made for the accommodations that will gradually appear, and of which a hint may already have been given, demanded by the need for pleasure that resigns itself to a half-consent), a mutual love adds to the very great, at times insurmountable, difficulties it encounters among the common run of individuals, ones of its own so particular that what is always very rare for anyone at all becomes in their case almost impossible, and, should a truly happy encounter transpire, or one that nature makes to seem so, their happiness, far more even than that of the normal lover, has something extraordinary, something selective, something profoundly necessary about it. The hatred of the Montagues and the Capulets[27] was as nothing compared with the impediments of every kind that have been overcome, the special eliminations to which nature must have subjected the already far-from-common chances that lead on to love, before a former maker of waistcoats, who had been anticipating setting off quietly for his office, should reel about, bedazzled, in front of a fifty-year-old man with a potbelly. This Romeo and this Juliet have good cause to believe that their love is not a momentary whim but truly predestined, prepared for by the harmonies of their temperament, and not only by their own temperament but by that of their forebears, of their most remote heredity, so that the fellow creature now conjoined to them belongs to them from before birth, has attracted them by a force comparable to that which governs the worlds in which we have spent our previous lives. M. de Charlus had distracted me from looking to see whether the bumblebee had brought the orchid the pollen it had been awaiting for so long, and that it had the good fortune to receive only thanks to a chance so improbable it might be called a sort of miracle. But it was a miracle also which I had just witnessed, of almost the same kind, and no less marvelous. As soon as I had considered the encounter from this point of view, everything about it seemed imbued with beauty. The most extraordinary stratagems that nature has invented to force insects to ensure the fertilization of flowers that could otherwise not be fertilized, for the male flower is too far removed from the female flower, or that which, if it is the wind that must ensure the transporting of the pollen, makes it much easier to detach from the male flower and much simpler for the female flower to trap it as it passes, by suppressing the secretion of the nectar, which is no longer of use since there are no insects to attract, and even the brilliance of the corollas that attract them, and the stratagem which, so that the flower may be reserved for the pollen it requires, which can fructify in it alone, causes it to secrete a liquid that immunizes it against other pollens—this seemed to me no more marvelous than the existence of the subvariety of inverts destined to ensure the pleasures of love to the invert who is growing old: of the men who are attracted, not by all men, but—through a phenomenon of correspondence and of harmony comparable to those that govern the fertilization of such heterostyled, trimorphic flowers as *Lythrum salicaria*—only by men much older than themselves. Jupien had just offered me an example of this subvariety, though one less striking than others that any human herborist, any moral botanist, will be able to observe, despite their rarity, and one that will present them with a frail young man awaiting the advances of a robust, potbellied fifty-year-old and remaining indifferent to the advances of other young men, just as the short-styled hermaphroditic flowers of *Primula veris* remain sterile for as long as they are being fertilized only by other, likewise short-styled *Primula veris,* whereas they welcome with delight the pollen from the long-styled *Primula veris.*[28] Where M. de Charlus was concerned, however, I came to realize subsequently that for him there were various kinds of conjunction, certain of which, by their multiplicity, their barely perceptible instantaneity, and especially the absence of contact between the two agents, were even more reminiscent of those flowers which in a garden are fertilized by the pollen from a neighboring flower that they will never touch. There were indeed certain individuals that he found it enough to have come to him, and to hold them for a few hours under the sway of his tongue, to appease the desire kindled in him by some encounter. Merely with words the conjunction was made, as easily as may happen among the Infusoria. On occasions, as had no doubt transpired in my own case on the evening when I had been summoned by him after the Guermantes dinner party, assuagement came about thanks to a violent dressing down cast by the Baron into his visitor's face, just as certain flowers, thanks to a spring mechanism, spray the unconsciously complicit, disconcerted insect from a distance. M. de Charlus had passed from being the dominated to the dominator, and, feeling himself calmed and purged of his anxiety, dismissed the visitor he had at once ceased to find desirable. Finally, inversion itself arising from the fact that the invert approximates too closely to a woman to be able to have useful relations with her, it is thereby linked to a higher law which means that so many hermaphroditic flowers remain infertile—that is, to the sterility of self-fertilization. It is true that inverts in search of a male are often content with an invert as effeminate as themselves. But it is enough that they should not belong to the female sex, of which they have inside them an embryo they are unable to make use of, as occurs with so many hermaphroditic flowers and even certain hermaphroditic animals, like the snail, which cannot be fertilized by themselves, but can be so by other hermaphrodites. Hence inverts, who readily link themselves to the ancient East or the golden age of Greece, might go further back still, to those experimental epochs when neither dioecious flowers nor unisexual animals existed, to that initial hermaphroditism of which a few rudimentary male organs in the female anatomy and female organs in the male anatomy appear to conserve the trace.[29] I found the mimicry of Jupien and M. de Charlus, incomprehensible to me at the outset, as curious as those gestures of enticement addressed to insects, according to Darwin, by the flowers known as composites, which raise the florets of their capitula so as to be seen from farther away, like a certain heterostyled flower that turns its stamens over and arches them in order to clear a path for insects, or which offers them an ablution, or, quite simply, like the fragrance of the nectar, the brilliance of its corollas, which were at that very moment attracting insects into the courtyard. From that day forward, M. de Charlus was to alter the time of his visits to Mme de Villeparisis, not that he would have been unable to meet Jupien elsewhere, and more conveniently, but, just as they were for me, the afternoon sunlight and the flowering shrub were no doubt linked to his memory. He did not content himself, moreover, with recommending the Jupiens to Mme de Villeparisis, to the Duchesse de Guermantes, and to a whole brilliant clientele who were all the more attentive to the young embroideress inasmuch as the few ladies who had resisted or merely taken their time were the object of terrible reprisals on the part of the Baron, either so that they might serve as an example, or because they had excited his fury and stood up against his efforts at domination. He made Jupien's position more and more lucrative until finally he took him on as a secretary and set him up in the conditions in which we shall meet him later on. "Oh, that Jupien's one very lucky man," said Françoise, who had a tendency to play down or to exaggerate kindnesses according to whether they were shown to her or to others. This time, however, she had no need to exaggerate, nor, moreover, did she feel any envy, being genuinely fond of Jupien. "Oh, the Baron's such a good man," she added, "so respectable, so devout, so correct! If I had a daughter to marry off, and came from the world of the rich, I'd give her to the Baron with my eyes shut." "But, Françoise," said my mother gently, "she'd have lots of husbands, that daughter. Remember, you already promised her to Jupien." "Oh heavens, so I did," answered Françoise. "The fact is, he's someone else who'd make a woman very happy. It's all very well there being rich and dirt poor, that doesn't make you what you are. The Baron and Jupien, they're two of a kind right enough."

Faced by this initial revelation, I had greatly exaggerated the elective nature of so selective a conjunction. True, each of the men of M. de Charlus's kind is an extraordinary creature, since, if he makes no concessions to life's possibilities, he searches essentially for the love of a man of the other race, that is of a man who loves women (and who in consequence will not be able to love him); contrary to what I believed in the courtyard, where I had just seen Jupien circling around M. de Charlus like the orchid making advances to the bumblebee, these exceptional beings for whom we feel pity are legion, as we shall see in the course of the present work, for a reason that will be disclosed only at the end, and they complain themselves of being too many rather than too few. For the two angels who were posted at the gates of Sodom to learn whether its inhabitants, says Genesis, had done every one of the things report of which had risen as far as the Eternal had been, and we can but rejoice at the fact, very ill chosen by the Lord God, who ought to have entrusted the task only to a Sodomist. He would not have been led benevolently to lower the flaming sword or temper the sanctions by the excuses, "Father of six children, I have two mistresses, etc." He would have answered: "Yes, and your wife suffers the torments of jealousy. But even if these women were not chosen by you in Gomorrah, you spend your nights with a keeper of flocks from Hebron." And he would immediately have made him retrace his steps toward the town about to be destroyed by the rain of fire and brimstone. On the contrary, all the shameful Sodomists were allowed to flee, even if, on catching sight of a young boy, they looked away, like Lot's wife, without thereby being turned as she was into pillars of salt.[30] With the result that they had a numerous posterity, among whom this gesture has remained habitual, like that of those debauched women who, while appearing to stare at a display of shoes in a shopwindow, look around at a student. These descendants of the Sodomists, so numerous that another verse of Genesis may be applied to them—"So that if a man be able to number the dust of the earth, so thy seed also shall be numbered"[31]— have established themselves over the whole earth; they have had access to all the professions and gain admission so readily to the most exclusive clubs that, when a sodomist is not admitted, the black balls are in the majority those of the sodomists, who take care to incriminate sodomy, having inherited the lie that enabled their ancestors to leave the accursed city. It is possible that they will return there one day. Certainly, they form in every country a colony at once Oriental, cultivated, musical, and slanderous, which has charming virtues and unbearable defects. A more thorough picture of them will emerge in the course of the ensuing pages, but I have wanted provisionally to forestall the fatal error that would consist, just as a Zionist movement has been encouraged, in creating a sodomist movement and in rebuilding Sodom. But, no sooner arrived there, and the sodomists would be leaving the town so as to appear not to belong to it, would take a wife, would keep mistresses in other cities, where they would find, moreover, all the appropriate amusements. They would go to Sodom only on days of supreme necessity, when their own town would be empty, at those times when hunger brings the wolf out from the woods; that is to say that everything would proceed in sum as in London, Berlin, Rome, Petrograd,[32] or Paris.

At all events, on that particular day, before my visit to the Duchesse, I was not thinking so far ahead and was distressed at having, by attending to the Jupien–Charlus conjunction, perhaps missed the fertilization of the flower by the bumblebee.

# PART II

CHAPTER I

*M. de Charlus in society—A doctor—Characteristic face of Mme de
Vaugoubert—Mme d'Arpajon, the Hubert Robert fountain, and the merriment
of Grand Duke Vladimir—Mme d'Amoncourt, Mme de Citri, Mme de
Saint-Euverte, etc.—Curious conversation between Swann and the Prince
de Guermantes—Albertine on the telephone—Visits while awaiting my
second and last stay in Balbec—Arrival in Balbec—Jealousy with
regard to Albertine—The intermittences of the heart.*

A S I WAS NOT IN ANY HURRY to arrive at the Guermantes soirée, to
which I was not certain of having been invited, I whiled away the
time outside; but the summer daylight seemed in no greater
haste to move than I was. Although it was after nine o'clock, it was still
the daylight that, on the Place de la Concorde, had given to the Luxor
obelisk an appearance of pink nougat. Then it modified the tint and
turned it into a metallic substance, with the result that the obelisk did
not merely become more precious, but seemed thinner and almost
flexible. You fancied that you might have been able to twist it, that this
jewel had already been bent slightly out of true perhaps. The moon was
in the sky now like a quarter of an orange, delicately peeled but with a
small bite out of it. Later it would be made of the most resistant gold.
Huddled all alone behind it, a poor little star was about to serve as the
solitary moon's one companion, while the latter, even as it shielded its
friend, but more daring and going on ahead, would brandish, like an irresistible weapon, like a symbol of the Orient, its marvelous, ample
golden cresent.

In front of the Princesse de Guermantes's *hôtel*, I met the Duc de Châtellerault; I no longer remembered that half an hour before I was still haunted by the fear—which was soon indeed to take hold of me again—of coming without having been invited. We feel uneasy, and it is sometimes long after the moment of danger, forgotten thanks to our distraction, that we remember our unease. I said good day to the young Duc and made my way into the house. But here I must first note a trifling circumstance which will enable a fact that will follow shortly to be understood.

On that, as on the preceding evenings, there was someone who had the Duc de Châtellerault very much on his mind, without, however, suspecting who he was: this was Mme de Guermantes's doorman (known in those days as the "barker"). M. de Châtellerault, very far from being an intimate—as he was of the cousins—of the Princesse, was being received in her drawing room for the first time. His parents, who had quarreled with her ten years ago, had made it up two weeks ago, and, obliged to be away from Paris on that evening, had asked their son to stand in for them. Now, a few days before, the Princesse's doorman had met a young man in the Champs-Élysées whom he had thought charming but whose identity he had been unable to establish. Not that the young man had not proved as amiable as he was generous. All the favors that the doorman had imagined having to grant so young a gentleman, he had, on the contrary, received. But M. de Châtellerault was as cowardly as he was imprudent; he was the more determined not to disclose his incognito inasmuch as he did not know whom he had to deal with; he would have felt an even greater fear—though ill founded— had he known. He had merely passed himself off as an Englishman, and to all the doorman's impassioned questions, who was eager to see someone to whom he was indebted for so much pleasure and largesse again, the Duc had merely answered in English, all the way along the Avenue Gabriel, "*I do not speak French.*"

Although, in spite of everything—because of his cousin's maternal origins—the Duc de Guermantes affected to find something a trifle Courvoisier-like[1] about the Princesse de Guermantes-Bavière's salon, the general verdict on that lady's spirit of initiative and intellectual superiority was based on an innovation not to be met with anywhere else in those circles. After dinner, and whatever the importance of the rout that was to follow, the seats at the Princesse de Guermantes's were arranged in such a manner that you formed small groups, which, if need be, had their backs to one another. The Princesse would then mark her social sense by going and sitting in one of these, as if from preference. She was not afraid, however, of selecting and calling on a member of another group. If, for example, she had remarked to M. Detaille,[2] who had naturally agreed, what a pretty neck Mme de Villemur had, whose position in another group showed her from behind, the Princesse did not hesitate to raise her voice: "Mme de Villemur, M. Detaille, great painter that he is, is busy admiring your neck." Mme de Villemur understood this as a direct invitation to join in the conversation; with an agility born of her hours in the saddle, she caused her chair slowly to pivot through an arc of three-quarters of a circle and, without the least disturbance to her neighbors, sat almost facing the Princesse. "You don't know M. Detaille?" asked her hostess, for whom her guest's skillful but modest about-face was not enough. "I don't know him, but I know his work," replied Mme de Villemur, with a winning and respectful expression, and an aptness that many envied, even as she was directing an imperceptible nod at the celebrated painter, her being summoned not having amounted to a formal introduction to him. "Come, M. Detaille," said the Princesse, "I'm going to introduce you to Mme de Villemur." The latter then showed as much ingenuity in making room for the author of *The Dream*[3] as a little earlier in turning toward him. And the Princesse brought a chair forward for herself; indeed, she had summoned Mme de Villemur only so as to have a pretext for leaving the first group, where she had spent the regulation ten minutes, and granting an equal duration of her presence to a second. Within three-quarters of an hour, all of the groups had received her visit, which seemed every time to result from a sudden inspiration or a predilection, but which had the object above all of throwing into relief how naturally "a great lady knows how to entertain." But now the guests at the soirée were starting to arrive, and the hostess had taken her seat not far from the entrance—erect and haughty, in her quasi-royal majesty, her eyes ablaze with their own incandescence—between two plain-looking Highnesses and the Spanish ambassadress.

I lined up behind several guests who had arrived ahead of me. Facing me I had the Princesse, whose beauty, among so many others, is no doubt not the only one to remind me of that particular party. But our hostess's face was so perfect, had been struck like some beautiful medal, that for me it has preserved a commemorative value. The Princesse was in the habit of saying to her guests, when she met them a few days before one of her soirées, "You will come, won't you?," as if she felt a strong desire to talk with them. But since, on the contrary, she had nothing to say to them, the moment they arrived in front of her she contented herself, without getting up, with breaking off for a moment from her vacuous conversation with the two Highnesses and the ambassadress to thank them, by saying, "It's kind of you to come," not because she thought that the guest had given proof of kindness by coming, but in order to enhance even further her own; then, at once throwing him back into the river, she would add, "You'll find M. de Guermantes at the door into the gardens," so that you went off visiting and left her in peace. To some even she said nothing, contenting herself with displaying her admirable onyx eyes, as if you had come merely to an exhibition of precious stones.

The first person to go in ahead of me was the Duc de Châtellerault.

Needing to respond to all the smiles, all the waved greetings that came to him from the drawing room, he had not noticed the doorman. But the doorman had recognized him from the very first moment. In a moment, he was going to know the identity he had so longed to learn. As he asked his "Englishman" of two days before what name he should announce, the doorman was not merely moved, he judged himself to be indiscreet, tactless. He seemed to be about to reveal to all the world (who would suspect nothing, however) a secret that he was guilty of having uncovered in this way and of broadcasting publicly. On hearing the guest's reply, "the Duc de Châtellerault," he felt so overcome by pride that he remained speechless for a moment. The Duc looked at him, recognized him, saw himself ruined, as the manservant, meanwhile, who had regained control of himself and knew his armorial well enough to complete for himself an overmodest designation, shouted out with a professional vigor, mellowed by an intimate tenderness, "His

Highness Monseigneur the Duc de Châtellerault!" But now it was my turn to be announced. Absorbed in contemplation of our hostess, who had not yet seen me, I had not reflected on the functions, terrible for me—though in another way than for M. de Châtellerault—of this door-man, clad in black like an executioner and surrounded by a troop of footmen in the most cheerful liveries, lusty fellows ready to lay hands on an intruder and show him the door. The doorman asked my name, and I gave it to him as mechanically as a condemned man allowing himself to be attached to the block. He at once raised his head majesti-cally and, before I had been able to beg him to keep his voice down when announcing me so as to spare my *amour-propre* if I had not been invited, and that of the Princesse de Guermantes if I had been, he shouted out the disquieting syllables with a force capable of causing the roof of the house to vibrate.

The illustrious Huxley (he whose nephew currently occupies a pre-ponderant place in the English literary world)[4] recounts how one of his patients no longer dared go into society because often, in the very chair that was being politely indicated to her, she could see an elderly gentle-man sitting. She was quite sure that either the gesture of invitation, or the presence of the elderly gentleman, was a hallucination, for they would not have been showing her to a chair that was already occupied. When Huxley, in order to cure her, forced her to return to a reception, she experienced a moment of painful hesitation, wondering whether the hospitable sign they made to her was the real thing, or whether, in order to obey a nonexistent vision, she was about to sit down in public on the knees of a flesh-and-blood gentleman. Her brief uncertainty was cruel. Less so perhaps than my own. From the moment I heard my own name being roared out, like the sound preceding a possible cataclysm, I had, so as at all events to plead my good faith and as if I were not tormented by any doubts, to advance toward the Princesse with a reso-lute air.

She caught sight of me when I was a few feet away and, what left me no longer in any doubt that I had been the victim of a conspiracy, in-stead of remaining seated as for the other guests, she got up and came toward me. A second later, I was able to heave the sigh of relief of

Huxley's patient when, having made up her mind to sit down on the chair, she found it was unoccupied and realized that it was the elderly gentleman who was a hallucination. The Princesse had just held out her hand to me with a smile. She stayed standing for a few moments, with the kind of graciousness peculiar to the stanza in Malherbe which ends, "And to do them honor the Angels stand."[5]

She apologized for the fact that the Duchesse had not yet arrived, as though without her I must be bored. In order thus to bid me welcome, she performed about me, holding me by the hand, a very graceful pirouette, in whose vortex I felt swept away. I was almost expecting her then to hand me, like the leader of a cotillion, an ivory-knobbed cane or a wristwatch. Truth to tell, she gave me nothing like that, but as if, rather than dancing the Boston, she had been listening to a sacrosanct Beethoven quartet, the sublime strains of which she was afraid of disturbing, she halted the conversation there, or, rather, did not begin it, and, still radiant from having seen me enter, merely informed me of where the Prince was to be found.

I moved away and did not dare approach her again, sensing that she had absolutely nothing to say to me and that, in her immense goodwill, this marvelously tall and beautiful woman, noble as so many great ladies were who mounted the scaffold with such pride, could only, not daring to offer me some melissa cordial, have repeated what she had already twice told me: "You'll find the Prince in the garden." But to go up to the Prince was to feel my doubts revive in a different form.

At all events, someone had to be found to present me. Dominating every conversation could be heard the inexhaustible prattle of M. de Charlus, who was talking with His Excellency the Duc de Sidonia, whose acquaintance he had just made. As profession recognizes profession, so, too, does vice. M. de Charlus and M. de Sidonia had each immediately nosed out that of the other, which was, for both, to be, when in company, monologuists, to the extent of being unable to bear any interruption. Having at once adjudged that the malady was without remedy, as a famous sonnet has it,[6] they had made a resolve, not to stay silent, but each to speak without concerning himself with what the other would say. This had created that jumble of sound which, in Molière's comedies, is produced by several people saying different things at one and the same time. The Baron, with his resonant voice, was certain in any case of having the better of it, of drowning out the feeble voice of M. de Sidonia, without discouraging the latter, however, for, whenever M. de Charlus drew breath for a moment, the interval was filled by the susurration of the Spanish grandee, who had imperturbably continued discoursing. I might well have asked M. de Charlus to present me to the Prince de Guermantes, but I was afraid (with only too good reason) that he might be angry with me. I had behaved toward him in the most ungrateful fashion in not taking him up on his offer for a second time, and in not showing him any sign of life since the evening when he had seen me home so affectionately. Yet I had certainly not had as an anticipated excuse the scene that I had just witnessed, that very afternoon, taking place between Jupien and him. I had suspected nothing of the sort. It is true that, a little time before, when my parents were reproaching me for my laziness and for not having yet taken the trouble of dropping M. de Charlus a line, I had reproached them furiously for wanting to make me accept dishonorable propositions. But anger alone, and the desire to find the words that would be most disagreeable to them, had dictated this untruthful reply. In actual fact, I had not imagined there to have been anything sensual, or even sentimental, in the Baron's offers. I had said that to my parents out of sheer foolishness. But the future sometimes dwells in us without our knowing it, and the words thought to be untruthful describe an imminent reality.

M. de Charlus would no doubt have forgiven me my lack of gratitude. But what made him furious was that my presence that evening at the Princesse de Guermantes's, as for some little time past at her cousin's, seemed to make a mockery of his solemn declaration, "The only entrée to those salons is through me." A grave fault, an inexpiable crime perhaps: I had not followed the hierarchical path. M. de Charlus well knew that the thunderbolts that he brandished at those who did not submit to his commands, or to whom he had taken a strong dislike, were beginning to pass, in the eyes of many, for thunderbolts of cardboard, and no longer had the strength to expel anyone from anywhere. But perhaps he thought that his power, although diminished, was still great and remained intact in the eyes of a novice such as myself. So I did not consider it the wisest course to ask a service of him at a party where my mere presence seemed like an ironic challenge to his pretensions.

At which moment I was stopped by a somewhat vulgar man, Professor E——. He had been surprised to see me at the Guermantes'. I was no less so to find him there, for never before, and never again subsequently, had a person of his sort been seen at the Princesse's. He had just cured the Prince, who had already received the last rites, of an infectious pneumonia, and the very particular gratitude that Mme de Guermantes felt toward him for this was the reason why they had broken with custom and invited him. Since he knew absolutely no one in these drawing rooms and could not prowl about there indefinitely on his own like a minister of death, having recognized me, he had felt that, for the first time in his life, he had infinitely many things to say to me, which enabled him to keep in countenance and was one of the reasons why he had come toward me. There was a second reason. He attached great importance to never being mistaken in a diagnosis. Now, so many letters did he receive that he could not always remember clearly, when he had only seen a patient once, whether the illness had indeed followed the course he had assigned to it. It has not been forgotten perhaps that, at the time of my grandmother's stroke, I had taken her round to him on the evening when he was having all those decorations sewn on. Some time having elapsed, he no longer remembered the announcement he had been sent at the time. "Madame your grandmother is indeed dead, is she not?" he said to me, in a voice in which near certainty had stilled a slight apprehensiveness. "Ah, indeed! Anyway, from the very first moment I saw her, my prognosis was altogether gloomy, I remember very well."

Thus it was that Professor E—— learned or relearned of my grandmother's death, and I have to say to his credit, which is that of the medical body as a whole, without manifesting, or perhaps feeling, any satisfaction. The mistakes of doctors are innumerable. They err as a rule out of optimism as to the treatment, and pessimism as to the outcome. "Wine? In moderation it can't do you any harm, it's a tonic when all's said and done. . . . Physical pleasure? It's a function, after all. I permit it, but not to be overdone, you understand. Excess of any kind is a mistake." What a temptation all of a sudden for the patient to give up those two resuscitators, water and chastity! If, on the other hand, you have a heart or an albumin problem, or something of the kind, then there is not long to go. Grave but functional troubles are readily ascribed to an imaginary cancer. There is no point in keeping on with visits that could never stay an ineluctable disease. Should the patient, left to his own devices, now impose an implacable regimen on himself, and then be cured or at the very least survive, the doctor, greeted by him on the Avenue de l'Opéra when he thought him long since in the Père-Lachaise, will see in this tipping of the hat a gesture of sarcastic insolence. An innocent walk taken under his very nose would arouse no greater fury in the Assize Court judge who, two years before, had pronounced sentence of death on the seemingly fearless stroller. Doctors (this does not apply to all of them, naturally, and I do not omit, mentally, some admirable exceptions) are in general more disgruntled, more irritated by the quashing of their verdict than joyful at its execution. Which explains why Professor E——, whatever intellectual satisfaction he will have felt no doubt at finding he had not been mistaken, was able to speak only with sadness of the misfortune that had struck us. He was not keen to cut short the conversation, which was keeping him in countenance and was a reason for staying. He spoke to me of the heat wave we had been having in recent days, but although he was literate and could have expressed himself in good French, he said, "This hyperthermia doesn't upset you?" The fact is that medicine has made some small progress in knowledge since Molière, but none in its vocabulary. My interlocutor added: "What you need to do is to avoid the sudations weather like this causes, especially in overheated drawing rooms. You can remedy them, when you return home and want something to drink, by heat"—which means, obviously, hot drinks.

Because of the manner of my grandmother's death, the subject interested me, and I had recently read in a book by a great scientist that perspiration harmed the kidneys by causing what should issue elsewhere to pass through the skin. I had deplored the canicular weather during which my grandmother died, and had come close to holding it responsible. I made no mention of this to Dr. E—, but he said without being prompted, "The advantage of this very hot weather, when perspiration is very abundant, is that the kidney is correspondingly relieved." Medicine is not an exact science.

Now that he had hold of me, Professor E— asked only not to leave me. But I had just caught sight, making deep bows to the Princesse de Guermantes to left and to right, having taken a step backward, of the Marquis de Vaugoubert. M. de Norpois had recently introduced me to him, and I hoped that in him I would find someone capable of presenting me to our host. The proportions of the present work do not allow me to explain here the incidents during his youth in consequence of which M. de Vaugoubert was one of the few men (perhaps the only man) in society who found himself in what is known in Sodom as "confidence" with M. de Charlus.[7] But if our minister to King Theodosius had some of the same faults as the Baron, they ranked as no more than the palest reflections of them. It was only in an infinitely milder, sentimental, and simpleminded form that he displayed those alternations between sympathy and loathing through which the desire to charm and then the fear—equally imaginary—of being, if not despised, then at least discovered, caused the Baron to pass. M. de Vaugoubert nonetheless displayed these alternations, but rendered absurd by a chastity, a "Platonism" (to which, highly ambitious as he was, he had, ever since the days of the Foreign Ministry examination, sacrificed all pleasure), above all by his intellectual nullity. But whereas, in M. de Charlus's case, immoderate praises were trumpeted in a veritable sunburst of eloquence, and salted with the subtlest, most mordant raillery, which marked a man forever, with M. de Vaugoubert, on the contrary, sympathy was expressed with the banality of an utter mediocrity, a man of the fashionable world, and a functionary, and his grievances (generally a complete invention, as with the Baron) by a malevolence that was untiring but mindless and all the more shocking in that it was usually in contradiction of remarks the minister had been making six months earlier and would perhaps be making again before very long: a regularity of change that lent an almost astronomical poetry to the various phases of M. de Vaugoubert's life, even though, this aside, no one could have put one less in mind of a heavenly body.

The "good evening" that he returned had nothing of that which M. de Charlus would have wished me. To this "good evening," M. de Vaugoubert lent, apart from the high ceremoniousness he thought to be that of society and of diplomacy, a jaunty, brisk, smiling tone, so as to seem, on the one hand, overjoyed by life—whereas inwardly he was brooding over the setbacks to a career lacking in promotion and in danger of ending in a forced retirement—and, on the other hand, young, virile, and charming, though he could see, and no longer dared even to go and inspect in his mirror, the wrinkles forming on the outlying parts of a face all of whose seductiveness he would have liked to have preserved. It was not that he would have wished for actual conquests, the mere thought of which frightened him on account of hearsay, of scandal, and of blackmail. Having gone from an almost infantile debauchery to absolute continence on the day his thoughts turned to the Quai d'Orsay[8] and the desire to make a great career, he wore the look of a caged beast, casting glances in all directions expressive of fear, craving, and stupidity. His own was such that he did not pause to consider that the street boys of his adolescence were no longer children and that, when a newspaper-vendor yelled *"La Presse!"*[9] into his face, he shuddered in terror more even than in desire, believing he had been recognized and tracked down.

But, failing the pleasures sacrificed to an ungrateful Quai d'Orsay, M. de Vaugoubert—and it was on this account that he would have liked still to be found attractive—had sudden impulses of the heart. God knows with how many letters he had pestered the ministry, what personal stratagems he had deployed, and how many times he had drawn on the credit of Mme de Vaugoubert (who, because of her corpulence, her high birth, her masculine look, and especially because of the mediocrity of her husband, was thought to be endowed with superior qualities and fulfilling the true functions of the minister) in order, for no valid reason, to get a young man entirely devoid of merit taken on to the staff of the legation. It is true that, a few months or a few years later, should this insignificant attaché have appeared to show, without the least hint of any evil intent, signs of coldness toward his chief, the latter, believing himself despised or betrayed, devoted the same hysterical ardor to punishing him as once to gratifying him. He moved heaven and earth to get him recalled, and the director of political affairs would receive a letter daily: "What is keeping you from getting rid of this fellow for me? Give him a bit of a talking to, for his own good. What he needs is to be given a really hard time of it." For which reason, the post of attaché to the court of King Theodosius was far from pleasant. But in every other respect, thanks to his perfect good sense as a man of the world, M. de Vaugoubert was one of the French government's best representatives abroad. When, later on, a supposedly superior man, a Jacobin,[10] well informed in every sphere, replaced him, war was not long in breaking out between France and the country ruled over by the King.

Like M. de Charlus, M. de Vaugoubert did not like to be first with a greeting. Both preferred to "respond," forever fearful of the rumors that the person to whom they would otherwise have held out their hand might have heard about them since they last saw him. In my own case, M. de Vaugoubert did not have to ask himself the question, for in fact I had gone to greet him first, if only because of the difference in age. He answered me with a wondering and delighted look, his two eyes continuing to jump about as if there were forbidden clover to be grazed on either side. I thought it proper to solicit from him my introduction to Mme de Vaugoubert before that to the Prince, about which I was counting on speaking to him only afterward. The idea of bringing me into contact with his wife appeared to fill him with joy for himself, as for her, and he led me with resolute steps toward the Marquise. Arriving in front of her, and indicating me with both his hand and his eyes, with every possible mark of consideration, he remained nonetheless without speaking, and after a few seconds withdrew, with a fidgety look, so as to leave me alone with his wife. The latter had at once held out her hand to me, but without knowing to whom this mark of affability was being addressed, for I realized that M. de Vaugoubert had forgotten what my name was, had perhaps not recognized me even, and, not wanting, out of politeness, to admit it, had made the introduction consist of pure pantomime. So I was no further advanced; how to get myself presented to our host by a woman who did not know my name? Moreover, I found myself forced to talk for a few moments with Mme de Vaugoubert. This annoyed me from two points of view. I had no wish to remain forever at this party, for I had arranged with Albertine (I had given her a box for *Phèdre*)[11] that she would come and see me a little before midnight. It is true that I was not in love with her; by getting her to come that evening, I was obeying a wholly sensual desire, even though we were in that torrid season of the year when a liberated sensuality is more ready to visit the organs of taste and seeks coolness above all. More than for the kiss of a girl, it thirsts for an orangeade or for a bath, or to gaze indeed on that peeled and juicy moon that was quenching the thirst of the sky. But I was counting on ridding myself at Albertine's side—who brought back for me, moreover, the coolness of the waves—of the regrets I could not fail to be left with by so many charming faces (for the soirée the Princesse was giving was for girls as well as ladies). There was nothing attractive, on the other hand, about the morose Bourbon face of the imposing Mme de Vaugoubert.

It was said at the ministry, without the least hint of malice, that in this ménage it was the husband who wore the skirts and the wife the breeches. Now, there was more truth in this than they thought. Mme de Vaugoubert was a man. Whether she had always been one, or had become what I now saw her to be, hardly matters, for in either case we are dealing with one of nature's most touching miracles, whereby, in the second case especially, the human kingdom is made to resemble the kingdom of flowers. On the first hypothesis—whether the future Mme de Vaugoubert had always been so heavily mannish—nature, by a stratagem both diabolical and beneficent, gives to the young girl the deceptive aspect of a man. And the adolescent male who does not like women and wishes to be cured lights with joy on this subterfuge, of discovering a fiancée who for him is the embodiment of a market porter. In the contrary case, if the woman does not to start with have masculine characteristics, she gradually acquires them in order to please her husband, unconsciously even, by that sort of mimeticism whereby certain flowers give themselves the appearance of the insects they seek to attract. The regret she feels at not being loved, at not being a man, virilizes her. Even aside from the case that concerns us, who has not observed how many of the most normal couples end up resembling one another, sometimes even by exchanging their good qualities? A former German chancellor, the Prince von Bülow, had married an Italian woman.[12] In due course, on the Pincio, it was remarked how much Italian delicacy the German husband had acquired, and how much German coarseness the Italian Princess. To move out to a point eccentric to the laws we are tracing, everyone knows of an eminent French diplomat whose origin was recalled only by his name, one of the most illustrious in the East.[13] As he matured, as he aged, the Oriental whom no one had ever suspected was revealed, and on seeing him you regretted the absence of the fez that would have been the crowning touch.

To come back to habits wholly unknown to the ambassador whose ancestrally padded silhouette we have just evoked, Mme de Vaugoubert embodied the type, acquired or predestined, the immortal image of which is the Princesse Palatine, forever in her riding habit, who, having taken more from her husband than his virility, and espousing the defects of the men who do not like women, denounces in her gossipy letters the mutual dealings of all the great noblemen at the court of Louis XIV.[14] One of the factors that further accentuate the masculine appearance of women such as Mme de Vaugoubert is that the neglect they are left in by their husbands, and the shame that they feel, casts a gradual blight on everything womanly in them. In the end, they acquire the virtues and defects that the husband does not have. As he grows more frivolous, more effeminate, and more indiscreet, they become the charmless effigy, as it were, of the virtues that the husband ought to be practicing.

Traces of opprobrium, annoyance, and indignation had clouded Mme de Vaugoubert's regular features. I felt, alas, that she looked on me with interest and curiosity as one of the young men who appealed to M. de Vaugoubert, and whom she would have so much liked to be, now that her aging husband preferred youth. She looked at me with the attentiveness of those provincial women who copy out of a fashion catalogue the tailored dress that looks so well on the pretty young person in the drawing (the same one on every page, in point of fact, but illusorily multiplied into different individuals thanks to the difference in the poses and the variety of outfits). The vegetal attraction that drove Mme de Vaugoubert toward me was so strong that she went so far as to seize hold of my arm so that I might take her to drink a glass of orangeade. But I freed myself on the pretext that, on the point of leaving as I was, I had not yet had myself presented to our host.

The distance separating me from the entrance to the gardens, where he stood talking to one or two people, was not very great. But it made me more afraid than if, in order to cross it, I had had to expose myself to a running fire.

Many women by whom I fancied I might be able to get myself presented were in the garden, where, even as they feigned an impassioned admiration, they hardly knew what to do with themselves. Parties of this kind are generally anticipated. They scarcely become real until the next day, when they occupy the attention of the people who were not invited. If, on reading the article of a critic who has always evinced the greatest admiration for him, a true writer, devoid of the foolish *amour-propre* of so many literary people, finds the names of second-rate authors listed but not his own, he does not have time to dwell on what might for him be cause for astonishment: his books reclaim him. But a society woman has nothing to do, and, on discovering in *Le Figaro,* "Yesterday the Prince and Princesse de Guermantes gave a grand soirée, etc.," she exclaims, "What! I talked, three days ago, for an hour with Marie-Gilbert, without her so much as mentioning it!," and she racks her brains wondering what she might have done to the Guermantes. It has to be said that, where the Princesse's parties were concerned, the surprise was sometimes as great among those who were invited as among those who were not. For they exploded at the very moment when they were least expected, and sent a summons to people whom Mme de Guermantes had been neglecting for years. And almost all society people are so insignificant that each of their peers judges them only according to their degree of friendliness, cherishes them if invited, detests them if excluded. In the case of these last, if, indeed, the Princesse, even though they were among her friends, did not invite them, this often arose from her fear of displeasing "Palamède," who had excommunicated them. So I could be certain that she had not spoken about me to M. de Charlus; otherwise, I would not have found myself there. He was now leaning, facing the garden, next to the German ambassador, on the balustrade of the great staircase that led back into the house, so that, in spite of the three or four female admirers who had congregated around the Baron and were almost screening him, the guests were obliged to come and wish him good evening. He answered by styling people by their names. You heard successively, "Good evening, M. du Hazay; good evening, Mme de la Tour du Pin-Vercluse; good evening, Mme de la Tour du Pin-Gouvernet; good evening, Philibert; good evening, my dear Ambassadress," and so on. This made for a continuous yapping, interspersed with well-meaning advice or questions (to the answers to which he paid no heed), which M. de Charlus addressed in a tone at once gentler, artificial, in order to attest to his indifference, and benign: "Mind the little one doesn't catch cold, gardens are always a bit damp. Good evening, Mme de Brantes. Good evening, Mme de Mecklembourg. Is your young daughter here? Has she put on that ravishing pink dress? Good evening, Saint-Géran." Certainly, there was arrogance in this attitude. M. de Charlus knew he was a Guermantes occupying a preponderant place at this entertainment. But there was not only arrogance, and the very word "entertainment" evoked, for a man of aesthetic gifts, the sense of luxury and of curiosity that it may have if the entertainment in question is being given not by society people but in a painting by Carpaccio or Veronese. It is even more likely that the German Prince that was M. de Charlus was picturing to himself, rather, the entertainment that unfolds in *Tannhäuser,* with himself as the Margrave, having a kindly, condescending word for each of the guests at the entrance to the Warburg, as they disperse into the castle or the park, saluted by the long phrase, a hundred times repeated, of the famous March.[15]

I had to come to a decision, however. I was well able to recognize under the trees women with whom I was more or less friendly, but they seemed transformed because they were at the Princesse's and not at her cousin's, and because I saw them sitting not in front of a Saxe plate but beneath the branches of a chestnut tree. The elegance of the setting played no part in it. Had it been infinitely less than at "Oriane's," the same unease would still have existed inside me. Should the electricity happen to go off in our drawing room and have to be replaced by oil lamps, everything seems altered. I was rescued from my uncertainty by Mme de Souvré. "Good evening," she said as she came up to me. "Is it long since you saw the Duchesse de Guermantes?" She excelled at lending words of this kind an intonation that proved she was not uttering them out of pure stupidity, like those people who, not knowing what to talk about, are forever accosting you and naming some common acquaintance, often very vague. She, on the contrary, had a fine conductor wire in her eyes, which signified: "Don't think I didn't recognize you. You're the young man I've seen at the Duchesse de Guermantes's. I remember very well." Unfortunately, the protection extended over me by these seemingly stupid yet delicately intentioned words was extremely fragile and vanished the moment I sought to make use of it. Mme de Souvré had the art, if it was a matter of backing up a request to someone of influence, of appearing both to be recommending it in the eyes of the petitioner, and not to be recommending this petitioner in the eyes of the exalted personage, in such a way that this double-edged gesture opened a credit balance of gratitude from the former without incurring any debt vis-à-vis the other. Encouraged by this lady's good grace to ask her to present me to M. de Guermantes, she seized on a moment when our host's eyes were not turned in our direction, took me maternally by the shoulders, and, smiling at the Prince's face, which was turned away so that he could not see her, she thrust me toward him with a movement purportedly protective yet deliberately ineffective, which left me stranded almost at my point of departure. Such is the cowardliness of society people.

That of a lady who came up to greet me by calling me by my name was greater still. I tried to recover her name even as I was speaking to her; I remembered very well having dined with her, I remembered things she had said to me. But my attention, straining toward that inner region where these memories of her were, was unable to discover the name. Yet it was there. My mind was engaged on a sort of game with it, in order to grasp its contours and the letter it began with, and finally to illuminate it in its entirety. It was so much wasted effort; I could more or less sense its mass, its weight, but as for its forms, comparing these with the mysterious captive huddled in the darkness within, I said to myself, "That's not it." My mind might certainly have been able to create the most difficult names. But, alas, it had not to create but to reproduce. Any action of the mind is easy when it is not subject to reality.

Here I was forced to submit. At last, suddenly, the name came in its entirety: "Mme d'Arpajon." I am wrong to say that it came, for I do not believe it appeared to me under its own propulsion. Nor do I think that my numerous faint memories relating to this lady, whose help I did not cease to solicit (by exhortations such as, "Come on, this is the woman who's a friend of Mme de Souvré, who has so simpleminded an admiration for Victor Hugo, along with so much terror and repugnance")—I do not believe that all these memories, fluttering about between me and her name, served in the very least to refloat it. In the great game of "hide-and-seek" played out in the memory when we are trying to recover a name, there is not a series of graduated approximations. We can see nothing; then, all of a sudden, the exact name appears, and quite different from what we thought we could divine. It is not it that has come to us. No, I believe, rather, that, as we go on through life, we spend our time distancing ourselves from the zone where a name is distinct, and that it was by the exercise of my will and my attention, which enhanced the acuity of my inward gaze, that I had suddenly penetrated the semidarkness and seen clearly. At all events, if there are transitions between forgetfulness and memory, those transitions are unconscious. For the intermediate names through which we pass, before finding the right name, are themselves false, and bring us no closer to it. They are not even names, properly speaking, but often mere consonants not to be found in the rediscovered name. The work of the mind as it passes from nothingness to reality is so mysterious, on the other hand, that it is possible after all that these false consonants are a pole held clumsily out to us in advance, to help us grapple the right name. "All of which," the reader will say, "teaches us nothing about this lady's disobligingness; but since you've been at a standstill for this long, let me, M. l'Auteur, make you waste one minute more to tell you how regrettable it is that, young as you were (or as your hero was, if he is not yourself), you should already have had so little memory as to be unable to recall the name of a lady whom you knew very well." It is very regrettable, you are right, M. le Lecteur. And sadder than you think, once it is sensed as heralding the day when names and words will vanish from the illuminated zone of the mind and we shall have to give up forever naming to ourselves those whom we have known best. It is regrettable, indeed, that, from our youth on, it should require such labor to recover names we know well. But were this infirmity to occur only with names barely known and quite naturally forgotten, and which we do not want to weary ourselves by recalling, then this infirmity would not be without its advantages. "And what are they, pray?" Well, monsieur, the fact is that this malady alone causes us to take notice of and to learn, and enables us to analyze, the mechanisms of which we would otherwise be ignorant. A man who drops into his bed each evening like a dead weight and lives again only at the moment of coming awake and getting up, will that man ever dream of making, if not great discoveries, then at least some minor observations, concerning sleep? He hardly knows whether he sleeps. A spot of insomnia is not without its uses for appreciating sleep, for projecting a certain light into that darkness. An unfailing memory is no very powerful stimulus for studying the phenomena of memory. "So Mme d'Arpajon finally introduced you to the Prince?" No, but be quiet and let me take up my story again.

Mme d'Arpajon was even more cowardly than Mme de Souvré, but her cowardice had greater excuse. She knew she had always had little influence in society. This influence had been further weakened by the liaison she had had with the Duc de Guermantes; the latter's rejection of her was the final straw. The ill-humor produced in her by my request to be introduced to the Prince resulted in a silence, which she was naïve enough to think was an appearance of not having heard what I said. She did not even realize that anger had caused her to frown. Or perhaps she did realize but was not troubled by the contradiction, using it for the lesson in tact she could give me without being too impolite—I mean, a lesson that was wordless but no less eloquent on that account.

Mme d'Arpajon was in any case much annoyed, the gaze of many having been raised toward a Renaissance balcony at the corner of which, in place of the monumental statues that were so often placed there in those days, there leaned, no less sculptural than they, the magnificent Duchesse de Surgis-le-Duc, she who had just succeeded Mme d'Arpajon in the affections of Basin de Guermantes. Beneath the flimsy white tulle that protected her against the cool night air could be seen

the supple body of a *Winged Victory*. My one remaining recourse was to
M. de Charlus, who had gone back into a room below, which gave access to the garden. I had ample leisure (since he was pretending to be
absorbed in a simulated game of whist, which enabled him not to appear to see people) in which to admire the willful and artistic simplicity
of his dress coat, which, thanks to tiny details that a couturier alone
might have discerned, looked like a *Harmony in Black and White* by
Whistler;[16] or, rather, black, white, and red, for M. de Charlus wore, suspended by a broad ribbon against the jabot of his evening attire, the
white, black, and red enamel cross of a knight of the religious Order of
Malta. At that moment, the Baron's game was interrupted by Mme de
Gallardon, who had her nephew in tow, the Vicomte de Courvoisier, a
young man with a pretty face and an impertinent air: "Cousin," said
Mme de Gallardon, "allow me to introduce to you my nephew Adalbert.
Adalbert, you know, the famous Uncle Palamède you're always hearing
about." "Good evening, Mme de Gallardon," replied M. de Charlus.
And he added, without even looking at the young man, "Good evening, monsieur," with a surly look, and in so violently discourteous a
tone that everyone was astounded. Perhaps, knowing that Mme de Gallardon had her suspicions as to his habits and had been unable to resist
for once the pleasure of alluding to them, M. de Charlus was anxious to
forestall whatever embroidery she might add to a friendly reception of
her nephew, at the same time making a resounding profession of his indifference with respect to young men; or perhaps he considered that
the aforesaid Adalbert had not replied to his aunt's words with a sufficiently respectful air; or perhaps, eager to press home his attack later on
so attractive a cousin, he wanted to give himself the advantages of a previous act of aggression, like those sovereigns who, before engaging in a
diplomatic démarche, support it with a military action.

It was not as difficult as I had thought for M. de Charlus to accede
to my request for an introduction. For one thing, in the course of the
last twenty years, this Don Quixote had tilted against so many windmills (frequently relatives who he claimed had behaved badly toward
him), and had forbidden people to be invited with such regularity "as
someone unfit to be received," by either male or female Guermantes,
that the latter were beginning to be afraid of quarreling with all the peo-

ple whom they liked, and of being deprived until the day they died of the company of certain newcomers about whom they were curious, in order to espouse the thunderous yet unexplained grudges of a brother-in-law or cousin who would have wanted them to abandon wife, brother, and children for his sake. Being more intelligent than the other Guermantes, M. de Charlus had noticed that only one in two of his vetoes was effective, and, looking ahead to the future and fearing that one day it might be him of whom they would deprive themselves, he had begun to cut his losses, to lower, as they say, his prices. Moreover, if he was capable of giving an identical life to some hated individual for months, or for years, on end—to whom he would not have tolerated extending an invitation, but would rather have fought, like a street porter, with a queen, the rank of whatever stood in his way no longer counting for him—his explosions of anger, on the other hand, were too frequent for them not to be somewhat fragmentary. "The imbecile, the miserable devil! We're going to return him to where he belongs, sweep him into the gutter, where, alas, he won't do much for the salubriousness of the town," he would shout, even when alone at home, on reading a letter he considered irreverent, or on recalling a remark that had been repeated to him. But a fresh outburst against a second imbecile would dispel the earlier one, and, provided the first imbecile proved deferential, the attack he had occasioned was forgotten, not having lasted long enough to create a foundation of hatred on which to build. So perhaps—in spite of his ill-humor against me—I would have succeeded with him when I asked him to introduce me to the Prince, had I not had the unhappy idea of adding, out of scrupulousness, and so that he should not suppose me tactless enough to have entered on the off chance, relying on him to enable me to stay, "You know that I know them very well, the Princesse has been very kind to me." "Well, if you know them, what need have you of me to introduce you?" he snapped at me and, turning his back, resumed his make-believe game of cards with the nuncio, the German ambassador, and a personage whom I did not know.

Then, from the depths of those gardens where once the Duc d'Aiguillon had bred rare animals, there reached me, through the wide-open doors, a sniffing sound, of someone breathing in all this elegance and wanting none of it to go to waste. The sound drew closer; I made in its direction on the off chance, with the result that the words "good evening" were murmured into my ear by M. de Bréauté, not like the jagged, metallic sound of a knife being ground on the wheel, let alone the cry of the young wild boar that lays waste the crops, but like the voice of a potential savior. Less influential than Mme de Souvré, but less fundamentally afflicted than her by disobligingness, far more at ease with the Prince than was Mme d'Arpajon, under an illusion perhaps concerning my own place in the Guermantes circle, or perhaps knowing it better than I did, I yet had, in those first seconds, some difficulty in securing his attention, for, with nostrils dilated and the papillae of his nose quivering, he was facing in all directions, his monocle eye wide with curiosity, as though he had found himself faced by five hundred masterpieces. But, having heard my request, he welcomed it with satisfaction, led me toward the Prince, and presented me to him wearing a hungry, ceremonious, and vulgar expression, as though he were passing him, along with a recommendation, a plate of petits fours. Just as the Duc de Guermantes's greeting was, when he wanted, friendly, imbued with camaraderie, cordial, and familiar, so I found that of the Prince stiff, solemn, and haughty. He barely smiled at me, and addressed me gravely as "monsieur." I had often heard the Duc make fun of his cousin's aloofness. But from the first words he spoke to me, which, in their coldness and seriousness, formed the most complete contrast with Basin's way of speaking, I realized at once that the fundamentally disdainful man was the Duc, who spoke to you from your first visit "as an equal," and that, of the two cousins, the truly simple one was the Prince. In his reserve I found a greater sense, I will not say of equality, for that would have been inconceivable for him, but at least of the consideration one may accord an inferior, as occurs in any strongly hierarchical setting, at the Palais de Justice, for example, or in a university faculty, where a public prosecutor or a "dean," conscious of his high office, perhaps hides more actual simplicity and, once you get to know him better, more kindness, true simplicity, and cordiality beneath a traditional hauteur than someone more up-to-date in his affectation of a bantering camaraderie. "Are you expecting to follow Monsieur your father's career?" he said to me with a distant yet interested expression.

I replied summarily to his question, realizing he had only asked it in order to be gracious, and moved away to let him welcome the new arrivals.

I caught sight of Swann, and wanted to speak to him, but at that moment I saw that the Prince de Guermantes, instead of receiving Odette's husband's greeting there, where he stood, had immediately, with the force of a suction pump, dragged him off to the end of the garden, but, so certain persons informed me, "in order to show him the door."

So distracted in society that I did not learn until two days later, from the newspapers, that a Czech orchestra had been playing throughout the evening and that there had been, minute by minute, a constant succession of Bengal fire, I recovered a certain capacity for attentiveness at the thought of going to see Hubert Robert's celebrated fountain.[17]

It could be seen from afar, set up to one side, in a clearing sequestered by beautiful trees, several of which were as old as it was, slender, immobile, solidified, allowing only the faintest spray, falling back from its pale and tremulous plume, to be disturbed by the breeze. The eighteenth century had purified the elegance of its lines, but, in determining the jet's style, seemed to have arrested its life; at this distance, you had an impression of art rather than the sensation of the water. The moist cloud that was perpetually gathering at its summit had itself preserved the character of the age, like those that congregate in the sky around the palaces of Versailles. But from close up, you became aware that, even as they respected, like the stones of an ancient palace, the design traced out for them beforehand, the waters were being constantly renewed as they sprang upward, seeking to obey the ancient orders of the architect, and executing them accurately only by appearing to violate them, their innumerable scattered surges able to give the impression of a single impulse only from a distance. This last was in actual fact as frequently interrupted as the scattering of its fall, whereas, from a distance, it had seemed to me dense, inflexible, of an unbroken continuity. From quite close up, you could see that this continuity, altogether linear in appearance, was ensured at every point in the jet's ascent, wherever it ought to have been broken, by the coming into play, the lateral reprise, of a parallel jet that rose higher than the first and was itself, at a greater, and by now exhausting, height, relieved by a third. From close to, spent drops were falling back from the column of water and meeting their ascending sisters along the way, and now and again, torn and seized by an eddy of the air disturbed by this tireless upsurge, they drifted before capsizing into the basin. By their vacillations, and by traveling in the contrary direction, they frustrated, and with their soft vapor they blurred, the verticality and tension of this shaft, which bore above it an oblong cloud formed of innumerable droplets, yet appearing to have been painted an immutable golden brown, which rose, infrangible, immobile, slender, and rapid, to add itself to the clouds in the sky. Unfortunately, a puff of wind was enough to send it obliquely across the ground; at times even, a single disobedient jet would diverge and, had it not remained at a respectful distance, would have soaked the incautious crowd of onlookers to the skin.

One of these minor accidents, which hardly ever occurred except at moments when the breeze got up, was somewhat disagreeable. Mme d'Arpajon had been led to believe that the Duc de Guermantes—in actual fact not yet arrived—was with Mme de Surgis in the galleries of pink marble, which were reached through the double colonnade, hollow inside, that rose from the rim of the basin. Now, just as Mme d'Arpajon was about to enter one of these colonnades, a strong gust from the warm breeze twisted the jet of water and inundated the good lady so thoroughly that, with the water trickling down inside her dress from her décolletage, she was as soaked as if she had been plunged into a bath. Then, not far away, a rhythmical rumbling sounded, loud enough to be audible by an entire army, yet prolonged in periods as if it were addressed not to the whole assembly but successively to each section of the troops; it was the Grand Duke Vladimir,[18] laughing for all he was worth at the sight of Mme d'Arpajon's immersion, one of the jolliest things, he liked to say afterward, he had ever witnessed in all his life. A few charitable souls pointing out to the Muscovite that a word of condolence from him was perhaps in order and would give pleasure to the lady, who, although she would never see forty again, and even as she was mopping herself with her scarf, without asking for anyone's help, had extricated herself, despite the water that had made the rim of the basin treacherously wet, the Grand Duke, a kindly man at heart, thought action was called for, and, the last drumrolls of laughter having hardly been stilled, a fresh rumbling could be heard, still more violent than the earlier one. "Bravo, old girl!" he cried, clapping his hands as if at the theater. Mme d'Arpajon did not appreciate having her dexterity praised at the expense of her youth. And when someone said to her, deafened by the sound of the water, which was dominated even so by the thunder of Monseigneur, "I believe His Imperial Highness said something to you." "No, it was to Mme de Souvré," she replied.

I crossed the gardens and reascended the steps, where the absence of the Prince, who had vanished off to one side with Swann, had swollen the crowd of guests around M. de Charlus, just as, when Louis XIV was not at Versailles, more people gathered at Monsieur his brother's. I was stopped as I passed by the Baron, while behind me two ladies and a young man were approaching to greet him.

"It's nice to see you here," he said, offering me his hand. "Good evening, Mme de La Trémoïlle; good evening, my dear Herminie." But no doubt the memory of what he had said to me concerning his role as head of the Guermantes *hôtel* had given him the desire to appear to be feeling, with regard to what displeased him but which he had been unable to prevent, a satisfaction to which his lordly impertinence and his hysterical amusement at once lent a form of excessive irony: "It's nice," he repeated, "but above all it's very comic." And he began to let out roars of laughter that seemed to testify both to his delight and to the incapacity of human speech to give it expression, as certain people meanwhile, knowing both how hard of access he was and how liable to insolent "outbursts," approached in curiosity and then, with an almost indecent haste, took to their heels. "Come, don't be angry," he said, touching me gently on the shoulder, "you know I'm very fond of you. Good evening, Antioche, good evening, Louis-René. Have you been to see the fountain?" he asked me in a tone of voice more affirmative than questioning. "It's very pretty, is it not? It's marvelous. It could be even better, of course, by doing away with certain things, then there'd be nothing to equal it in France. But even as it is, it's among the best things. Bréauté will tell you they were wrong to hang lanterns, to try and make people forget it was he who had that absurd idea. But when all's said and done, he succeeded in making it only a little bit uglier. It's much harder to disfigure a masterpiece than to create it. We already had a vague suspicion anyway that Bréauté was no Hubert Robert."

I rejoined the line of visitors who were entering the house. "Has it been long since you saw my delightful cousin Oriane?" the Princesse asked me; she had shortly before deserted her armchair by the entrance, and with her I now returned to the drawing rooms. "She's due to be here this evening, I saw her during the afternoon," added our hostess. "She promised me. I believe, in any case, that you are dining with the two of us at the Queen of Italy's,[19] in the embassy, on Thursday. Every possible Highness will be there, it'll be most intimidating." They could in no way have intimidated the Princesse de Guermantes, whose drawing rooms teemed with them, and who used to say "my little Coburgs" as she might have said "my little dogs." And so Mme de Guermantes said, "It'll be most intimidating," out of sheer silliness, which, among society people, even outweighs their vanity. With respect to her own genealogy, she knew less than an *agrégé*[20] in history. Where her connections were concerned, she was keen to show that she knew the nicknames they had been given. Having asked me whether I would be dining the following week at the Marquise de la Pommelière's, often known as "la Pomme," the Princesse, having obtained a negative reply, was silent for a few moments. Then, for no reason other than a deliberate display of involuntary erudition, banality, and conformity to the prevailing spirit, she added, "She's quite an agreeable woman, la Pomme!"

It was just as the Princesse was talking with me that the Duc and Duchesse de Guermantes made their entrance. But I was unable at first to go forward to them, for I was snapped up in passing by the Turkish ambassadress, who, pointing to our hostess, whom I had just left, exclaimed, seizing hold of me by the arm: "Oh, what a delightful woman the Princesse is! A being so superior to all others! I fancy that were I a man," she added, with a hint of Oriental obsequiousness and sensuality, "I would devote my life to that heavenly creature." I replied that I indeed found her charming, but that I knew her cousin the Duchesse better. "But there's no comparison," the ambassadress said to me. "Oriane is a charming woman of the world who gets her wit from Mémé and Babal, whereas Marie-Gilbert is *somebody*."

I never much like thus being told without possibility of reply what I am to think about people whom I know. And there was no reason why the Turkish ambassadress's judgment as to the merits of the Duchesse de Guermantes should be any more sure than my own. On the other hand, which also explained my irritation with the ambassadress, the fact is that the defects of a mere acquaintance, or even of a friend, are for us true poisons, against which we are fortunately "mithridatized." But, without making the least show of scientific comparisons and talking of anaphylaxis, let me say that, at the heart of our friendly or merely social dealings, there is a hostility, cured temporarily but recurring in fits. Normally, we suffer little from these poisons as long as people are "natural." By saying "Babal" and "Mémé," to refer to people whom she did not know, the Turkish ambassadress had suspended the effects of the "mithridatism" that normally made her bearable. She had irritated me, which was the more unjust inasmuch as she had not spoken in this way in order to make me think she was an intimate of "Mémé," but because an over-rapid education had led her to name these noble lords according to what she believed was the local custom. She had completed her schooling in a few months without seeing it through to the end. But, on reflection, I discovered another reason for my displeasure at remaining with the ambassadress. It was not long since, at "Oriane's," this same diplomatic personage had told me, wearing a serious, considered expression, that the Princesse de Guermantes was frankly antipathetic to her. I saw fit not to dwell on this about-face: the invitation to this evening's party had brought it about. The ambassadress was perfectly sincere in telling me that the Princesse de Guermantes was a sublime creature. She had always thought so. But, never having until now been invited to the Princesse's, she thought she must give to this kind of noninvitation the form of a voluntary abstention founded on principle. Now that she had been invited, and very likely would be from now on, her sympathy could express itself freely. There is no need, in order to explain three-quarters of the opinions held about people, to go so far as a love that has been spurned or an exclusion from political power. Our judgment remains unsure: an invitation refused or received determines it. Moreover, the Turkish ambassadress, in the words of the Duchesse de Guermantes, who was carrying out an inspection of the drawing rooms with me, "did well." She was above all very useful. The true stars of society are weary of appearing there. Anyone who is curious to set eyes on them has often to immigrate into another hemisphere, where they are more or less alone. But women of the Ottoman ambassadress's kind, newly entered into society, do not fail to shine there, everywhere at once, so to speak. They are useful to performances of the kind known as a soirée or a rout, to which they would have themselves dragged from their deathbeds rather than miss them. They are the extras on whom you can always count, zealous in never missing a party. Thus foolish young men, unaware that they are false stars, see them as the queens of fashion, whereas instruction would be needed to explain to them the reasons in virtue of which Mme Standish, not known to them and who paints cushions, far away from society, is at least as great a lady as the Duchesse de Doudeauville.[21]

In the ordinary course of things, the Duchesse de Guermantes's eyes were distracted and a little melancholy; she only made them shine with a flame of wit each time she had to greet some friend, absolutely as if the latter had been some witticism, some delightful shaft, some gourmet delicacy, the sampling of which has brought an expression of joy and refinement to the face of the connoisseur. But with these grand soirées, since she had too many people to acknowledge, she had decided it would be wearisome, after each one of them, to turn off the light each time. A literary gourmet, going to the theater to see a new play by one of the masters of the stage, attests to his certainty that he will not be spending a bad evening by having already, even as he hands his things to the usherette, adjusted his lips for a judicious smile, and brought a light of sly approval into his eyes; so it was that, from the moment she arrived, the Duchesse would turn on the lights for the whole evening. And as she was handing over her evening cloak, of a magnificent Tiepolo red, to reveal a yoke of real rubies that encircled her neck, after casting the couturière's last rapid, meticulous, and complete glance at her dress, which is that of the society woman, Oriane checked on the sparkle in her eyes no less than on her other jewels. In vain did a few "well-wishers" like M. de Joinville dash up to the Duc to stop him from entering: "Don't you know, then, that poor Mama is at the point of death? They've just given him the last rites."[22] "I know, I know," replied M. de Guermantes, pushing the intruder away in order to enter. "The viaticum has worked wonders," he added with a smile of pleasure at the thought of the costume ball he was determined not to miss after the Prince's soirée. "We didn't want it known that we had returned home," the Duchesse said to me. She did not suspect that the Princesse had invalidated these words for me in advance by recounting how she had seen her cousin briefly, who had promised to come. The Duc, after a long stare, with which he crushed his wife for five whole minutes: "I told Oriane of the doubts you had." Now that she could see that they were unfounded and that she need take no steps to try to dispel them, she declared them to be absurd, and teased me at length. "Imagine supposing you weren't invited! One is always invited! And, then, there was me. Do you think I wouldn't have been able to get you invited to my cousin's?" I have to say that often, subsequently, she did far more difficult things for me; nevertheless, I was careful not to take her words in the sense of my having shown too great a reserve. I was beginning to know the precise value of the spoken or silent language of aristocratic amiability, an amiability happy to pour balm on the sense of inferiority of those in respect of whom it is exercised, but not, however, to the extent of dispelling it, in which event it would no longer have any *raison d'être*. "But you are our equal, if not better," the Guermantes seemed, by all their actions, to be saying; and they said it in the nicest way imaginable, so as to be liked and admired, but not so as to be believed; to tease out the fictitious nature of this amiability was to have been what they called well brought up; to believe that amiability to be real was to lack breeding. I received, as it happens, a short time after this, a lesson that finally taught me, with the most perfect exactitude, the extent and limits of certain forms of aristocratic amiability. It was at a matinée given by the Duchesse de Montmorency[23] for the Queen of England; a sort of small cortège had formed to go to the buffet, at the head of which walked the sovereign with, on her arm, the Duc de Guermantes. This was the moment of my own arrival. With his free hand, the Duc made, from a good forty meters away, innumerable gestures of summons and of friendship, which seemed to be saying that I could approach without fear, that I would not be eaten alive in place of the sandwiches. But, I, who was beginning to become word perfect in the language of the courts, instead of moving even a single step closer, gave a deep bow from my forty meters of distance, but without smiling, as I would have done faced with someone I hardly knew, then continued on my way in the opposite direction. I might have written a masterpiece, and the Guermantes would have done me less honor than for this bow. It did not go unobserved by the eyes either of the Duc, even though he had to respond to more than five hundred people that day, or of the Duchesse, who, having met my mother, recounted it to her, and, while being careful not to say that I had been in the wrong, that I should have gone up, told her that her husband had marveled at my bow, that it would have been impossible to make it any more expressive. They did not cease to discover all the virtues in that bow, without, however, mentioning that which had seemed the most precious, to wit that it had been discreet, nor did they cease paying me compliments, which I realized were less a reward for the past than an indication for the future, on the lines of that tactfully supplied to his pupils by the head of an educational establishment: "Don't forget, my dear children, that these prizes are less for you than for your parents, so that they will send you back next year." Thus it was that Mme de Marsantes, when someone from a different world entered her circle, extolled before him those discreet people "whom one finds when one goes in search of them, and who keep themselves to themselves the rest of the time," just as, in a roundabout way, you advise a servant who smells that bathing does wonders for the health.

While, before even she had left the entrance hall, I was talking with Mme de Guermantes, I heard a voice of a kind that, in the future, I was to be able to distinguish beyond possibility of error. It was, in this particular instance, that of M. de Vaugoubert, talking with M. de Charlus. A clinician has no need even for the patient under observation to lift his shirt nor to listen to his breathing; the voice is sufficient. How many times, later on, was I not struck in a drawing room by the intonation or the laugh of some man who was imitating exactly the language of his profession or the manners of his circle, and affecting a severe refinement or a coarse familiarity, yet the falsity of whose voice acted like a tuning fork on my practiced ear and was enough to tell me, "He's a Charlus"! At that moment, the entire staff of an embassy went by, and bowed to M. de Charlus. Although my discovery of the kind of sickness in question dated only from that same day (when I had caught sight of M. de Charlus and Jupien), I would not have needed, in order to make a diagnosis, to ask any questions or listen to any chests. But M. de Vaugoubert, talking with M. de Charlus, seemed unsure. Yet he ought to have known how things stood after the doubts of his adolescence. The invert believes he is the only one of his kind in the entire universe; only later does he imagine—another exaggeration—that the sole exception is the normal man. But, ambitious yet timorous, M. de Vaugoubert had not yielded for a long time past to what for him would have been pleasure. The diplomatic career had had the same effect on his life as if he had taken holy orders. Coupled with his assiduity at the École des Sciences Politiques,[24] it had condemned him since his twenties to the chastity of a Christian. Thus, just as each sense loses some of its strength and acuity and atrophies once it is no longer exercised, M. de Vaugoubert, like the civilized man who would no longer be capable of the feats of strength or the keenness of hearing of the caveman, had lost that special perspicacity which was rarely found wanting in M. de Charlus; and at official dinner tables, whether in Paris or abroad, the minister plenipotentiary no longer managed even to recognize those who, under the disguise of their uniforms, were in fact of his own kind. A few names uttered by M. de Charlus, indignant should his own tastes be mentioned but always amused to let those of others be known, came as a delightful surprise to M. de Vaugoubert. Not that, after all these years, he dreamed of taking advantage of any such windfall. But these rapid revelations, similar to those that, in Racine's tragedies, inform Athalie and Abner that Joas is of the race of David, or that Esther, seated in the purple, has kinsfolk who are "Yids,"[25] by altering the aspect of the X legation or of this or that department of the Foreign Ministry, rendered these palaces retrospectively as mysterious as the Temple of Jerusalem or the throne room of Suze.[26] For the embassy, the young personnel of which came up as one to shake M. de Charlus's hand, M. de Vaugoubert adopted the wondering expression of Élise exclaiming in *Esther:*

> Great Heaven! What a numerous swarm of innocent beauties
> Offers itself to my gaze, a crowd emerging on every side!
> What a lovely modesty is portrayed on their faces![27]

Then, anxious to be "better informed," he smiled and cast a fatuously questioning and concupiscent glance at M. de Charlus: "Oh, come, but of course," said M. de Charlus, with the learned expression of a scholar talking to an ignoramus. Instantly M. de Vaugoubert (which greatly annoyed M. de Charlus) could no longer take his eyes off these young secretaries, whom the ambassador of X to France, a habitual offender, had not selected at random. M. de Vaugoubert fell silent; I could see only his eyes. But, accustomed since childhood to attribute the language of the classics, even to what is speechless, I made M. de Vaugoubert's eyes speak the lines in which Esther explains to Élise that, out of zeal for his religion, Mordecai has wanted only girls who belonged to it to attend on the Queen.

> Meanwhile his love for our nation
> Has peopled this palace with daughters of Zion,
> Young and tender flowers agitated by their fate,
> Transplanted like myself under a foreign clime.
> In a place set apart from profane witnesses,
> He (the excellent ambassador) devotes his attention and his
>     care to forming them.[28]

M. de Vaugoubert finally spoke other than by his glances. "Who knows," he said mournfully, "whether, in the country where I reside, the same thing does not exist?" "It's likely," replied M. de Charlus, "starting with King Theodosius, although I don't know anything positive about him." "Oh no, absolutely not!" "Then it's not permitted to look like one to that extent. And he has his fancy ways. He's one of the 'darling' kind, the kind I detest most. I wouldn't dare show myself with him in the street. Anyway, you must certainly know him for what he is— it's common knowledge." "You're totally mistaken about him. He's charming, as it happens. The day when the agreement with France was signed, the King embraced me. I have never been so moved." "That was the moment to tell him what you wanted." "Oh, good God, how horrible, supposing he'd even suspected! But I have no fears on that score."

Words that I overheard, for I was not far away, and which led me to recite in my head:

> To this day the King does not know who I am,
> And this secret still keeps my tongue in chains.[29]

This dialogue, half mute, half spoken, had lasted only a few moments, and I had not yet taken more than a few steps into the drawing rooms with the Duchesse de Guermantes when a small dark-haired woman, extremely pretty, stopped her: "I'd very much like to call on you. D'Annunzio[30] caught sight of you from a box and wrote a letter to the Princesse de T— in which he says he'd never seen anything so lovely. He'd give his whole life for ten minutes' conversation with you. At all events, even if you can't or won't, the letter is in my possession. You must fix a time for us to meet. There are certain secret things I can't say here. I can see you don't recognize me," she added, addressing herself to me; "I met you at the Princesse de Parme's"—where I had never been. "The Russian Emperor would like your father to be sent to Petersburg. If you were able to come on Tuesday, Isvolsky[31] will in fact be there, he could talk to you about it. I've a present to give you, darling," she added, turning to the Duchesse, "which I wouldn't give to anyone except you. The manuscripts of three of Ibsen's plays,[32] which he had his old nurse bring me. I shall keep one and give you the other two."

The Duc de Guermantes was not enchanted with these offers. Unsure whether Ibsen and D'Annunzio were dead or alive, he could already see writers and dramatists coming to call on his wife and putting her into their works. Society people readily picture books to themselves as a sort of cube, one face of which has been removed, so that the author need waste no time in "bringing in" the people he meets. This obviously is underhanded, and they are people of little worth. Admittedly, it would not be without interest to meet them "in passing," for, thanks to them, when you read a book or an article you get to know the "inside story," can "remove the masks." But for all that, the wisest course is to

stick to authors who are dead. The one author whom M. de Guermantes considered "perfectly proper" was the gentleman who wrote the
death notices in *Le Gaulois*.[33] He at least contented himself with citing
the name of M. de Guermantes at the head of those persons noticed
"among others" at the funerals where the Duc had signed the list. When
the latter preferred that his name should not appear, instead of signing
he sent a letter of condolence to the deceased person's family, assuring
them of the deep sadness that he felt. Should this family then have inserted in the newspaper, "Among the letters received, let us cite that
from the Duc de Guermantes," etc., this was not the fault of the gossip
writer but of the son, brother, or father of the person deceased, whom
the Duc described as *arrivistes*, and with whom he was determined to
have no further dealings (what he called, being unclear as to the meaning of these locutions, "having a bone to pick"). The fact is that the
names of Ibsen and D'Annunzio, and their uncertain survival, brought
a frown from the Duc, not as yet far enough away from us not to have
heard the sundry civilities of Mme Timoléon d'Amoncourt. She was a
charming woman, of a quickness of mind, like her beauty, so captivat-
ing that one of these alone would have been sufficient attraction. But,
born outside the circles in which she was now living and, after aspiring,
to start with, only to a literary salon, successively and exclusively the
friend—never the lover; her morals were of the purest—of each great
writer who gave her all his manuscripts and wrote books for her, chance
having introduced her into the Faubourg Saint-Germain, these literary
privileges were of service to her there. Her situation was such now that
she had no need to dispense any favors other than those bestowed by
her presence. But, having got used in the old days to doing services for
people, and to handling them tactfully, she had persevered, even
though it was no longer necessary. She always had a state secret to reveal to you, a potentate whom you must meet, a watercolor by a master
to offer you. There was an element of falsehood certainly in all these futile attractions, but they made of her life a comedy of scintillating com-
plexity, and it was a fact that she had secured the appointment of
prefects and generals.

As she walked beside me, the Duchesse de Guermantes allowed the azure light of her eyes to float in front of her, but undirected, so as to avoid the people with whom she was keen not to come into contact, but whom she could sometimes make out in the distance like a menacing reef. We were advancing between a double hedge of guests who, aware that they would never get to know "Oriane," wanted at least, as a curiosity, to point her out to their wives: "Ursule, quick, quick, come and see Mme de Guermantes, who's talking with that young man." And you felt it would not have taken much for them to climb up onto chairs so as to have a better view, as at the July 14 parade or the Grand Prix.[34] It was not that the Duchesse de Guermantes had a more aristocratic salon than her cousin. The first was frequented by people whom the second would never have wished to invite, above all because of her husband. She would never have received Mme Alphonse de Rothschild, who, a close friend of Mme de La Trémoïlle and of Mme de Sagan, as was Oriane herself, was often to be seen at the last named's. And the same went for Baron Hirsch,[35] whom the Prince of Wales had brought to her house but not to that of the Princesse, who would not have taken to him, as well as for a number of great Bonapartist or even Republican celebrities, who interested the Duchesse but whom the Prince, a convinced Royalist, would have refused to receive. His anti-Semitism, being also a principle with him, made no concessions to the fashionable, however highly accredited, and if he received Swann, whose friend he had been from a long way back, being moreover the only one of the Guermantes who addressed him as "Swann" and not as "Charles," it was because, knowing that Swann's grandmother, a Protestant married to a Jew, had been the mistress of the Duc de Berry,[36] he tried, from time to time, to believe in the legend that had it that Swann's father was an illegitimate son of the Prince. On this hypothesis, which was, however, false, Swann, the son of a Catholic, who had himself been the son of a Bourbon and a Catholic woman, was Christian through and through.

"What, you don't know these splendors?" the Duchesse said to me, referring to the house we were in. But, having sung the praises of her cousin's "palace," she hastened to add that she infinitely preferred her own "humble abode." "It's admirable for *visiting* here. But I'd die of sadness if I had to stay and sleep in rooms where so many historical events have taken place. It would have the effect on me of having remained behind after closing time, of having been forgotten, in the château of Blois or Fontainebleau, or even at the Louvre, and of having as my one recourse against unhappiness to tell myself that I'm in the room where Monaldeschi was murdered.[37] As chamomile tea, that wouldn't do. Hello, there's Mme de Saint-Euverte. We had dinner there just the other day. As it's tomorrow she gives her big annual shindig, I thought she'd have gone off to bed. But she can't miss a party. If this one had been taking place in the country, she'd have climbed into a delivery van rather than not have gone to it."

In point of fact, Mme de Saint-Euverte had come there that evening less for the pleasure of not missing someone else's party than to ensure the success of her own, to recruit the final adherents and, as it were, review *in extremis* the troops who would the next day be maneuvering brilliantly at her *"garden party."* Because, for quite some years now, the guests at the Saint-Euverte parties had ceased to be at all the same as in the old days. The female notabilities of the Guermantes circle, at that time very thin on the ground, had—overwhelmed with courtesies by their hostess—little by little brought their women friends. At the same time, by her progressive hard work in parallel, but in the opposite direction, Mme de Saint-Euverte had, year by year, reduced the numbers of people unknown to the fashionable world. First one, then another had ceased to be seen there. For a time a system of "batches" operated, which, thanks to parties over which a veil was cast, enabled the reprobates to be invited to come and be entertained among themselves, which excused her from inviting them together with the people of substance. What cause for complaint could they have? Did they not get (*panem et circenses*) petits fours and a fine program of music? And so, in some sort of symmetry with the two duchesses in exile who, in the old days, when the Saint-Euverte salon made its bow, were to be seen, like two caryatids, holding up its tottering ridgepiece, in recent years, only two heterogeneous figures were to be made out, mingling with the *beau monde:* old Mme de Cambremer and an architect's wife with a beautiful voice whom they were often obliged to ask to sing. But, no longer knowing anyone at Mme de Saint-Euverte's, in mourning for their lost companions, and feeling themselves to be in the way, they looked as though they were ready to die of cold, like two swallows that have not emigrated in time. And so, the following year, they were not asked; Mme de Franquetot tried to intercede on behalf of her cousin, who was so very fond of music. But since she was unable to obtain any response on her behalf more explicit than the words, "But it's always possible to come in and listen to the music if it amuses you, there's no crime in that!," Mme de Cambremer did not consider the invitation sufficiently pressing and stayed away.

Such a transmutation having been effected by Mme de Saint-Euverte, from a salon for lepers into a salon for great ladies (the latest form, ultra-chic to all appearances, that it had taken), it might seem surprising that the person who tomorrow would be giving the season's most brilliant party should have needed to come on the eve to address a supreme appeal to her troops. But the fact was that the pre-eminence of the Saint-Euverte salon existed only for those whose social life consists merely in reading the accounts of matinées and soirées in *Le Gaulois* or *Le Figaro*, without ever having been to any of them. For those socialites who encounter society only by way of the newspaper, the enumeration of the ambassadresses of England, Austria, etc., and the Duchesses d'Uzès,[38] de La Trémoïlle, etc., etc., was enough to make them readily imagine the Saint-Euverte salon to be the first in Paris, whereas it was one of the last. Not that these accounts were untruthful. The majority of the people named had indeed been present. But every one of them had come as a result of entreaties, politenesses, and favors, and with a sense of doing Mme de Saint-Euverte infinite honor. Such salons, less sought after than shunned, to which you go only in the line of duty as it were, take in only the female readers of the "Society" column. They slide over a party, a truly fashionable one, to which the hostess, who might have had all the duchesses who crave being "among the chosen," has asked only two or three, and has not put the names of her guests in the newspaper. And so these women, either misunderstanding or else scorning the influence that publicity has today acquired, are fashionable for the Queen of Spain, but unrecognized by the crowd, because the first knows and the second do not know who they are.

Mme de Saint-Euverte was not among these women, but had come, like a good honeybee, to gather all who had been invited for the following day. M. de Charlus was not invited; he had always refused to go to her house. But he had quarreled with so many people that Mme de Saint-Euverte was able to put this down to his character.

True, if Oriane alone had been there, Mme de Saint-Euverte need not have put herself out, since the invitation had been given in person, and accepted, moreover, with that charming and deceitful good grace, the triumphant practitioners of which are the Academicians, from whose house the candidate emerges much moved and never doubting that he may count on their vote.[39] But others were there besides. The Prince d'Agrigente, would he be coming? And Mme de Durfort?[40] And so, in order to keep a weather eye open for squalls, Mme de Saint-Euverte had thought it more expedient to transport herself there in person; insinuating with some, imperative with others, to all she gave notice in veiled terms of unimaginable amusements, the like of which would not be seen again, and to each she promised that at her house they would find the person that they longed, or the personage they needed, to meet. And the sort of function with which she was invested on this one occasion in the year—like certain magistracies in the ancient world—of someone who will tomorrow be giving the most notable *garden party* of the season, conferred on her a momentary authority. Her lists were made up and closed, so that, as she moved slowly through the Princesse's drawing rooms in order to pour successively into each ear, "You won't forget me tomorrow," she experienced the ephemeral triumph of turning away, while continuing to smile, when she caught sight of some ugly duckling who was to be avoided or a country bumpkin who had been admitted to "Gilbert's" on the strength of having been a school friend but whose presence would add nothing to the *garden party.* She preferred not to speak to him so as to be able to say afterward, "I gave out my invitations in person, and unfortunately I didn't bump into you." Thus did she, a mere Saint-Euverte, her eyes darting this way and that, "sort through" the component parts of the Princesse's soirée. And in so doing, she saw herself as a true Duchesse de Guermantes.

It has to be said that neither was the latter as liberal as one might have thought with her greetings and her smiles. On the one hand, when she refused them, it was no doubt deliberately: "But she gets on my nerves," she would say. "Am I going to be obliged to talk to her about her reception for a whole hour?"

A very swarthy duchesse was seen to go past, whose ugliness and stupidity, and certain irregularities of behavior, had exiled her, not from society but from certain inner circles of the fashionable. "Oh," murmured Mme de Guermantes, with the exact, disabused glance of the connoisseur being shown a piece of paste jewelry, "they entertain that here!" Merely at the sight of this semi-imbecile, whose face was encumbered by too many speckles of black hair, Mme de Guermantes estimated this to be a second-rate soirée. She had been brought up with, but had broken off all relations with this lady; she replied to her greeting with the curtest of nods. "I don't understand," she said to me, as if to excuse herself, "why Marie-Gilbert should invite us with all these dregs. You could say there are people here from every parish. It was far better organized at Mélanie Pourtalès's.[41] She could have the Holy Synod and the Oratorian temple[42] if the fancy took her, but at least she didn't make us go on those days." But, in many cases, it was out of timidity, of fear of having a scene with her husband, who refused to let her entertain artists and the like (many of whom were Marie-Gilbert's protégés, you had to be careful not to be accosted by some illustrious German soprano), out of a certain fear also in respect of nationalism, which, possessing as she did, like M. de Charlus, the Guermantes spirit, she despised from the social point of view (in order to glorify the general staff, a plebeian general was now accorded precedence ahead of certain dukes), but to which, knowing herself to be adjudged a *mal pensante,* she nevertheless made large concessions, to the point of dreading having to hold out her hand to Swann in this anti-Semitic circle. In this respect she was very soon reassured, having learned that the Prince had not allowed Swann to enter but had had "a sort of altercation" with him. There was no danger of her having to make conversation in public with "poor Charles," whom she preferred to cherish in private.

"And who, again, is that one?" exclaimed Mme de Guermantes, on seeing a rather strange-looking short lady, in a black dress so simple you might have supposed her to have fallen on hard times, make her, along

with her husband, a deep curtsy. She did not recognize her and, insolent as she was capable of being, drew herself up as if offended, and
looked at her without replying: "Who or what is that person, Basin?"
she asked, with a look of astonishment, while M. de Guermantes, in order to atone for Oriane's rudeness, bowed to the lady and shook her
husband's hand. "But it's Mme de Chaussepierre, you were very rude."
"I know nothing of any Chaussepierre." "The nephew of old Mother
Chanlivault." "I know nothing of any of them. Who is the woman, why
does she curtsy to me?" "But you know only too well, it's Mme de
Charleval's daughter, Henriette Montmorency." "Oh, but I knew her
mother very well, she was charming, very quick-witted. Why did she
marry all these people I don't know? You say her name's Mme de
Chaussepierre?" she said, spelling out this last word with a questioning
air, and as if she was afraid of getting it wrong. The Duc looked severely
at her. "It's not so ridiculous as you appear to think, being called
Chaussepierre! Old Chaussepierre was the brother of the aforenamed
Charleval,[43] of Mme de Sennecour, and of the Vicomtesse du Merlerault. They're out of the top drawer." "Oh, stop," exclaimed the
Duchesse, who, like an animal-tamer, never wanted to look as though
she were allowing herself to be intimidated by the savage beast's vora-
cious stare. "Basin, you delight me. I don't know where you've dug
those names up from, but I compliment you heartily. I may not have
known Chaussepierre, but I've read Balzac, you're not the only one,
and I've even read Labiche.[44] I appreciate Chanlivault, I don't dislike
Charleval, but I confess that du Merlerault is the masterpiece. Let's admit, moreover, that Chaussepierre isn't bad, either. You've collected all
of them, it's not possible. You, who want to write a book," she said to
me, "you ought to hang on to Charleval and du Merlerault. You won't
find any better." "He'll quite simply find himself in court and will go to
prison; you're giving him very bad advice, Oriane." "I hope for his sake
that he has younger people he can call on if he feels like asking for bad
advice, and above all following it. But if the worst thing he means to do
is to write a book!" Some little distance from us, a marvelous, proud
young woman stood out quietly in a white dress, all diamonds and
tulle. Mme de Guermantes looked at her, talking before a whole group
magnetized by her grace. "Your sister is the belle of the ball; she looks

charming this evening," she said, as she was taking a chair, to the Prince de Chimay, who was passing.[45] Colonel de Froberville (he had the general of the same name for an uncle) came and sat down next to us, as did M. de Bréauté, while M. de Vaugoubert (out of an excess of politeness that he maintained even on the tennis court, where, by dint of asking for permission from anyone of importance before hitting the ball, he inevitably caused his own side to lose the game) went waddling back to M. de Charlus (until now almost enveloped by the immense skirt of the Comtesse Molé, whom he professed to admire above all other women), and, by chance, at the very instant when several members of a diplomatic mission new to Paris were greeting the Baron. At the sight of a young, particularly intelligent-looking secretary, M. de Vaugoubert fixed M. de Charlus with an expansive smile that was patently asking a single question. M. de Charlus would gladly have compromised anyone else perhaps, but to feel compromised himself by this smile coming from another and which could have only one meaning, exasperated him. "I have absolutely no idea, I must ask you to keep your curiosity to yourself. It leaves me more than cold. Besides, in this particular instance, you are committing a blunder of the first magnitude. I believe that young man to be the exact opposite." Here M. de Charlus, annoyed at having been given away by a fool, was not speaking the truth. Had the Baron been speaking truthfully, the secretary would have been the exception in that embassy. It was made up, indeed, of very different personalities, several of them extremely second-rate, so that, had you been searching for what the motive might have been for the choice that had fallen on them, you could have discovered only inversion. By setting at the head of this small diplomatic Sodom an ambassador who, on the contrary, loved women with the comic exaggeration of a music-hall master of ceremonies putting his battalions of transvestites through their regulation paces, they seemed to have been obeying the law of opposites. Despite the evidence of his own eyes, he did not believe in inversion. He gave instant proof of this by marrying his sister off to a chargé d'affaires who he quite wrongly believed went after tarts. From then on, he became something of an embarrassment and was soon replaced by a new Excellency, who ensured the homogeneity of the whole. Other embassies sought to compete with this one, but could not dispute the prize (as at the *concours général*,[46] when a particular *lycée* always wins), and more than ten years would have to pass before, heterogeneous attachés having been introduced into this very perfect whole, another embassy was finally able to snatch the fateful palm and march at the head.

Reassured as to her fear of having to talk with Swann, Mme de Guermantes now felt only curiosity concerning the conversation he had had with his host. "Do you know what about?" the Duc asked M. de Bréauté. "I did hear," replied the latter, "that it was apropos of a playlet that the writer Bergotte put on at their house. It was a delight, anyway. But it seems the actor was made up to look like Gilbert, whom the good Sir Bergotte may actually have wanted to portray." "You know, I'd have been amused to see a takeoff on Gilbert," said the Duchesse, smiling wistfully. "It was about that little performance," M. de Bréauté went on, thrusting forward his rodent's jaw, "that Gilbert wanted to have it out with Swann, who merely replied, which everyone thought very witty, 'But not at all, it's nothing like you, you're much more ridiculous than that!' It seems, moreover," M. de Bréauté went on, "that the little play was a delight. Mme Molé was there, she was vastly amused." "What, Mme Molé goes there?" said the Duchesse in astonishment. "Oh, it's Mémé who'll have arranged that. It's what always ends up happening in such places. One fine day all the world starts going there, and I, who have deliberately excluded myself on principle, I find myself all alone, feeling bored in my little corner." By now, after the account M. de Bréauté had just given them, the Duchesse de Guermantes had, as can be seen, adopted a fresh point of view (if not on the Swann salon, then at least on the hypothesis of meeting Swann in a few minutes' time). "The explanation you're giving us," said Colonel de Froberville to M. de Bréauté, "is a complete fabrication. I've my own reasons for knowing so. The Prince quite simply gave Swann a good talking to, and gave him to understand, as our forefathers put it, that he needn't show himself at the house again, given the opinions that he flaunts. And so far as I'm concerned, my uncle Gilbert was right a thousand times over, not simply to tell him off like that, but he should have had done with a declared Dreyfusard more than six months ago."

Poor M. de Vaugoubert, having on this occasion gone from being a too sluggish player to being the inert tennis ball itself, which is launched without ceremony, found himself being projected toward the Duchesse de Guermantes, to whom he presented his respects. He was none too well received, Oriane residing in the conviction that all the diplomats—or politicians—in her world were halfwits.

M. de Froberville had inevitably benefited from the favorable position in society accorded of late to military men. Unfortunately, if the woman whom he had married was a very genuine relation of the Guermantes, she was also an extremely poor one, and as he himself had lost his money, they had scarcely any connections and were among the people who got left to one side, except on big occasions, when they had the good fortune to lose or to marry off a relation. Then they truly became part of the communion of high society, like those nominal Catholics who approach the Lord's Table only once a year. Their material situation would have been wretched even had Mme de Saint-Euverte, loyal to the affection she had had for the late Général de Froberville, not helped the household out in every way, providing the two young daughters with outfits and amusements. But the colonel, good fellow though he was held to be, was not the soul of gratitude. He was envious of the splendors of a benefactress who herself celebrated them tirelessly and unrestrainedly. For him, his wife, and his children, the annual *garden party* was a wonderful pleasure that they would not have wanted to miss for all the gold in the world, but a pleasure poisoned by the thought of the vainglorious delight Mme de Saint-Euverte derived from it. The announcement of this *garden party* in the newspapers, which then, after a detailed account, added in Machiavellian fashion, "We shall have more to say about this brilliant entertainment," the complementary details about the costumes, given over several successive days, all this so hurt the Frobervilles—who were somewhat starved of pleasures, but who knew they could rely on that of the matinée—that they got to the point each year of hoping that its success might be spoiled by bad weather, of consulting the barometer and anticipating with joy the first hints of a storm that might cause the party to be a failure.

"I won't discuss politics with you, Froberville," said M. de Guermantes, "but as far as Swann is concerned, I can say frankly that his behavior toward us has been unspeakable. He was taken up by society in the old days, by ourselves and by the Duc de Chartres,[47] and they tell me he's openly Dreyfusard. I'd never have believed it of him, him, a discerning gourmet, a positive mind, a collector, a lover of old books, a member of the Jockey Club, a man highly respected on all sides, a connoisseur of good addresses who used to send us the best port you can drink, a dilettante, a family man. Oh, I've been badly let down. I'm not speaking of myself, it's agreed I'm an old fool whose opinion doesn't count, some sort of down-and-out, but, if only for Oriane's sake, he shouldn't have done that, he should have openly disowned the Jews and the condemned man's supporters."

"Yes, after the friendship my wife has always displayed toward him," the Duc went on, who obviously considered that to sentence Dreyfus for high treason, whatever opinion you might hold in your heart of hearts as to his guilt, constituted a form of gratitude for the way one had been received in the Faubourg Saint-Germain, "he should have broken ranks. For, ask Oriane, she had genuine affection for him." The Duchesse, thinking that a calm, ingenuous tone would lend her words a more dramatic and sincere quality, said in the voice of a schoolgirl, as if simply allowing the truth to issue from her mouth, and giving her eyes alone a somewhat melancholy expression, "But that's true, I've no reason to hide that I felt a sincere affection for Charles." "There, you see, I'm not putting words into her mouth. And after that, he takes ingratitude to the point of being a Dreyfusard!"

"Speaking of Dreyfusards," I said, "it seems that Prince Von is one." "Ah, you do well to bring him up," exclaimed M. de Guermantes. "I was about to forget that he's asked me to go and dine on Monday. But whether he's a Dreyfusard or not is all one to me, since he's a foreigner. I don't care two hoots. With a Frenchman, it's another matter. It's true, Swann is a Jew. But until today—forgive me, Froberville—I had been weak-minded enough to believe that a Jew can be a Frenchman, an honorable Jew, I mean, a man of the world. Now, Swann was that in the full force of the word. Well, he's forcing me to acknowledge I was mistaken, since he's taking the side of this Dreyfus—who, guilty or not, is in no way part of his circle, and whom he can never have met—against a society that had adopted him, had treated him as one of its own. There's no getting away from it, we'd all have vouched for Swann, I'd have answered for his patriotism as for my own. And this is how he rewards us! I confess I would never have expected it, not from him. I thought better of him. He had a quick wit—in his own way, of course. I'm well aware he'd already committed the insanity of his shameful marriage. By the way, do you know someone who was greatly hurt by Swann's marriage? It was my wife. Oriane often has what I shall call an affectation of insensitivity. But deep down she feels with an extraordinary intensity." Mme de Guermantes, overjoyed at this analysis of her character, listened to it wearing a modest expression but did not say a word, not liking to acquiesce in the eulogy, but fearing above all to interrupt it. M. de Guermantes might have spoken for an hour on this subject and she would no more have moved than if they had been making music for her. "Well, I recall when she heard about Swann's marriage, she felt offended; she decided it was wrong of someone to whom we had displayed so much friendship. She was very fond of Swann; she was greatly upset. Weren't you, Oriane?" Mme de Guermantes thought she must reply to so direct a challenge, on a point of fact that would enable her, without appearing to, to confirm the praises that she sensed were at an end. In a simple, diffident tone, and with an expression all the more studied for seeking to appear "felt," she said demurely and softly, "It's true, Basin is not mistaken." "Yet it still wasn't the same thing. But what do you expect? Love is love, although in my view it should stay within certain bounds. I might excuse a young man who's still wet behind the ears, letting himself be carried away by utopias. But Swann, an intelligent man, of a proven refinement, a shrewd connoisseur of paintings, a close friend of the Duc de Chartres, of Gilbert himself!" The tone in which M. de Guermantes had said this was perfectly sympathetic, with no hint of the vulgarity he too often showed. He spoke with a faintly indignant sadness, but everything about him breathed that gentle gravity which constitutes the broad and unctuous charm of certain figures in Rembrandt, the burgomaster Six,[48] for example. You felt that the question of the immorality of Swann's conduct over the Affair did not even arise for the Duc, so beyond all doubt was it; he had experienced the affliction of a father seeing one of his children, for whose education he has made the greatest sacrifices, willfully throwing away the magnificent situation he has created for him and, by indiscretions that the family's principles or prejudices cannot allow, bringing dishonor on a respected name. It was true that M. de Guermantes had not manifested so profound and sorrowful an astonishment earlier on, when learning that Saint-Loup was a Dreyfusard. But, for one thing, he regarded his nephew as a young man who had taken the wrong path and could do nothing that would surprise him until he had mended his ways, whereas Swann was what M. de Guermantes called "a levelheaded man, a man holding a position of the first rank." Then again, and especially, quite some time had passed during which, if, from the historical point of view, events had seemed in part to justify the Dreyfusist case, the anti-Dreyfusard opposition had become twice as violent, and, from being purely political at the outset, had become social. It was now a question of militarism, of patriotism, and the waves of anger whipped up in society had had time to acquire the force they never have at the beginning of a storm. "You see," M. de Guermantes went on, "even from the point of view of his beloved Jews, since he insists absolutely on supporting them, Swann has made a blunder of incalculable import. He is proving that they are all secretly united and are somehow obliged to lend their support to someone of their own race, even if they don't know him. That is a public menace. We've obviously been too easygoing, and the gaffe Swann is committing will reverberate all the more inasmuch as he was held in high esteem, received even, and was just about the only Jew whom one knew. People will say to themselves, *'Ab uno disce omnes.'*"[49] (The satisfaction of having found in his memory, at the appointed moment, so opportune a quotation, alone caused a proud smile to illuminate the melancholy of the great nobleman betrayed.)

I had a strong desire to know what exactly had transpired between the Prince and Swann, and to see the latter, if he had not yet left the soirée. "I must tell you," the Duchesse replied, to whom I had mentioned this desire, "that I am not myself excessively anxious to see him, because it seems, judging by what I was told a short while ago at Mme de Saint-Euverte's, that he would like, before he dies, for me to make the acquaintance of his wife and daughter. Heavens, it grieves me infinitely that he should be ill, but I hope, first of all, that it's not as serious as all that. And, then, that's not after all a reason, because it would really be too simple. A writer devoid of talent would only have to say,

'Vote for me at the Academy because my wife is about to die and I want to give her this last pleasure.' There wouldn't be salons any more if one was obliged to make the acquaintance of all the dying. My coachman could use it on me: 'My daughter's very ill, get me an invitation to the Princesse de Parme's.'[50] I adore Charles, and it would upset me greatly to refuse him, which is why I prefer to avoid his asking me. I hope with all my heart that he's not dying, as he says he is, but, truly, were that to happen, it would not be the moment for me to make the acquaintance of those two creatures, who've deprived me of the most agreeable of my friends these past fifteen years, and whom he would leave on my hands at a time when I wouldn't even be able to take advantage of it to see him, since he'd be dead!"

But M. de Bréauté had not ceased to ponder the contradiction inflicted on him by Colonel de Froberville. "I don't doubt the accuracy of your account, my dear friend," he said, "but I had mine from a good source. It was the Prince de La Tour d'Auvergne who related it to me." "I'm astonished that a knowledgeable man like yourself should still say 'the Prince de La Tour d'Auvergne,' " the Duc de Guermantes broke in. "You know he's nothing of the kind. There's only one member of that family left. That's Oriane's uncle, the Duc de Bouillon."[51] "The brother of Mme de Villeparisis?" I asked, recalling that the latter had been a Mlle de Bouillon. "Exactly so. Oriane, Mme de Lambresac is wishing you good day."

Indeed, a weak smile could be seen from time to time forming and vanishing like a shooting star, intended by the Duchesse de Lambresac for some person whom she had recognized. But instead of taking on definition as an active affirmation, in a language mute but clear, this smile was almost immediately drowned in a sort of ideal ecstasy that could discern nothing, while the head was inclined in a vacuous gesture of benediction reminiscent of that inclined toward the crowd of communicants by a somewhat doddery prelate. Mme de Lambresac was in no way doddery. But I was already familiar with this particular kind of obsolete refinement. In Combray and in Paris, all my grandmother's women friends were in the habit, at social gatherings, of greeting one another wearing as seraphic an expression as if they had just caught sight of someone of their acquaintance in church, at the moment of the

Elevation or during a funeral, and were bidding them a limp good day that ended in a prayer. And some words of M. de Guermantes's were about to complete the comparison I was making. "But you've seen the Duc de Bouillon," M. de Guermantes said to me. "He was leaving my library a little while ago as you were going in, a gentleman short in stature, and white-haired." He it was whom I had taken for some petty bourgeois from Combray but in whom I could now discern, on reflection, the resemblance to Mme de Villeparisis. The similarity between the evanescent greetings of the Duchesse de Lambresac and those of my grandmother's friends had begun to interest me, by demonstrating that in narrow and enclosed social circles, whether among the petty bourgeoisie or the high nobility, the old ways persist, enabling us to rediscover, like an archaeologist, how people may have been brought up, and the element of soul that it reflects, in the days of the Vicomte d'Arlincourt and Loïsa Puget.[52] Better still, the perfect conformity in appearance between a petty bourgeois of Combray of the same age and the Duc de Bouillon now reminded me (as had already struck me so forcibly when I saw Saint-Loup's maternal grandfather, the Duc de La Rochefoucauld, on a daguerreotype where, in dress, expression, and manner, he was exactly like my great-uncle) that social or indeed individual differences merge over time into the uniformity of an epoch. The truth is that the similarity in dress, and the spirit of the age as it is echoed by the face, occupy so much more significant a place in someone than his caste, which occupies a large place only in the person in question's self-esteem and in the imagination of others, that, to be made aware that a great nobleman of Louis-Philippe's time differs less from a bourgeois of Louis-Philippe's time than from a great nobleman of the time of Louis XV, there is no need to walk the galleries of the Louvre.

At that moment, a long-haired Bavarian musician, a protégé of the Princesse de Guermantes, greeted Oriane. The latter replied by inclining her head, but the Duc, enraged at the sight of his wife saying good evening to someone he did not know, who had so very strange a look about him, and who, as far as M. de Guermantes thought he knew, had a very bad reputation, turned to his wife with a terrible and inquisitorial air, as if to say, "Who is this Ostrogoth?" Poor Mme de Guermantes's situation was already somewhat complicated, and, had the musician felt some pity for that martyred spouse, he would have taken himself off as quickly as possible. But, whether out of a desire not to tolerate the humiliation that had just been inflicted on him in public, in the midst of his oldest friends from the Duc's circle, whose presence may well have been in part the reason for his silent bow, and to show that it was by right, and not without knowing her, that he had greeted Mme de Guermantes, or whether in obedience to the obscure but irresistible inspiration of his gaffe, which—at a moment when he should rather have relied on his wits—urged him on to apply protocol to the letter, the musician approached Mme de Guermantes more closely still and said, "Mme la Duchesse, I would like to solicit the honor of being presented to the Duc." Mme de Guermantes was most unhappy. But in the end, for all that she was a deceived wife, she was still the Duchesse de Guermantes and could not appear to have been robbed of her right to introduce people whom she knew to her husband. "Basin," she said, "allow me to present M. d'Herweck." "I won't ask you whether you're going tomorrow to Mme de Saint-Euverte's," said Colonel de Froberville to Mme de Guermantes, in order to dispel the uncomfortable impression produced by M. d'Herweck's untimely request. "The whole of Paris will be there." Meanwhile, turning in a single movement and as if he had no joints toward the tactless musician, the Duc de Guermantes, square on to him, monumental, unspeaking, wrathful, like Jove the Thunderer, remained thus without moving for several seconds, his eyes blazing with anger and astonishment, his frizzy hair seeming to emerge from a crater. Then, as if in the heat of an impulse that had alone enabled him to achieve the civility demanded of him, and after having seemed by his defiant posture to attest to those present that he did not know the Bavarian musician, he crossed his two white-gloved hands behind his back, tipped himself forward, and dealt the musician a bow so profound, imbued with so much rage and stupefaction, so abrupt, so violent, that the trembling artist recoiled even as he leaned forward so as not to receive a formidable butt in the stomach. "But it's just that I won't be in Paris," replied the Duchesse to Colonel de Froberville. "I must tell you—which I shouldn't admit—that I have reached my present age without having seen the stained-glass windows at Montfort-l'Amaury.[53] It's shameful, but there you are. So, to make amends for this culpable neglect, I've promised myself to go and see them tomorrow." M. de Bréauté gave a knowing smile. He understood indeed that, if the Duchesse had been able to go on not knowing the stained-glass windows of Montfort-l'Amaury until her present age, this artistic visit had not all of a sudden taken on the urgent character of an "emergency" operation and might, without danger, having been deferred for more than twenty-five years, been put back by twenty-four hours. The plan the Duchesse had formed was simply to decree, in the Guermantes manner, that the Saint-Euverte salon was decidedly not a truly respectable house, but a house to which you were invited so that you could be paraded in the account given in *Le Gaulois,* a house that would confer a badge of supreme elegance on those women, or, in any event, on that woman if there was only one of them, who would not be seen there. The tactful amusement of M. de Bréauté, coupled with the poetic pleasure that society people felt when they saw Mme de Guermantes doing things that their own lesser situation did not allow them to imitate, but the mere spectacle of which produced in them the smile of the peasant tied to his glebe, who sees men freer and more fortunate than himself passing above his head, this refined pleasure bore no connection to the disguised but frenetic delight at once experienced by M. de Froberville.

The efforts M. de Froberville was making so that his laughter might not be heard had made him go as red as a rooster, in spite of which he interspersed his words with hiccups of joy as he exclaimed in a compassionate tone: "Oh, poor aunt Saint-Euverte, what a song and dance she's going to make! No, the unfortunate woman isn't going to get her Duchesse, what a blow! It's enough to make her turn up her toes!" he added, doubled up with laughter. And in his euphoria he could not prevent himself from drumming his heels and rubbing his hands. Smiling out of one eye and only one corner of her mouth at M. de Froberville, whose friendly intentions she appreciated without finding him any less mortally tedious, Mme de Guermantes finally decided to leave him.

"Listen, I'm going to *have* to wish you good evening," she said, getting to her feet with an air of melancholy resignation, as if this for her were a misfortune. Beneath the incantation of her blue eyes, her softly musical voice put one in mind of the poetic lament of a fairy. "Basin wants me to go and see Marie for a bit." In point of fact, she had had enough of listening to Froberville, who had not ceased envying her going to Montfort-l'Amaury, when she knew full well that this was the first he had heard of the stained glass and, what was more, that he would not have relinquished the Saint-Euverte matinée for anything in the world. "Goodbye, I've hardly spoken to you, that's how it is in society, we don't meet, we don't say the things we'd like to say to one another; anyway, it's the same everywhere in life. Let's hope it'll be better organized after we're dead. At least we won't always have to wear low-cut dresses. Yet who knows? Perhaps we shall show off our bones and our worms on big occasions. Why not? I mean, look at old Mother Rampillon, d'you see any great difference between that and a skeleton in an open dress? It's true she has every right, she's at least a hundred years old. She was already one of those sacred monsters I refused to curtsy to when I was starting out in society. I thought she'd died long since; which would, as it happens, be the one explanation for the spectacle she's offering us. It's impressive and liturgical. Pure 'Campo Santo'!"[54] The Duchesse had left Froberville; he came closer: "I'd like one last word with you." A little irritated: "What is it now?" she said haughtily. And he, having feared that she might change her mind about Montfort-l'Amaury at the last minute: "I didn't dare mention it on account of Mme de Saint-Euverte, so as not to cause her any distress, but since you're not anticipating going, I can tell you I'm glad for your sake, because they've got measles in the house!" "Oh, good Lord!" said Oriane, who was afraid of diseases. "But that doesn't worry me, I've already had it. You can't get it twice." "It's the doctors who say that; I know people who've had it up to four times. Anyway, you've been warned." As for him, he would need actually to have had this fictitious measles and to be confined to his bed with it to resign himself to missing the Saint-Euverte party, looked forward to these many months. He would have the pleasure of seeing so many of the fashionable there, the greater pleasure of confirming that certain things had gone wrong, and the pleasure above all of being able to boast for a long time to come of having rubbed shoulders with the first and, by either exaggerating or inventing them, of deploring the second.

I took advantage of the fact that the Duchesse had changed her position to stand up also, so as to make my way to the smoking room and inquire after Swann. "Don't believe a word of what Babal's been recounting," she said to me. "Never would the little Molé have gone poking her nose in there. They tell us that to lead us on. They receive no one and are invited nowhere. He himself admits it: 'The two of us remain on our own by the fire.' Because he always says 'we,' not like the King but on behalf of his wife, I don't insist. But I'm very well informed," the Duchesse added. She and I passed two young men whose great but dissimilar beauty had its origins in the same woman. These were the two sons of Mme de Surgis, the Duc de Guermantes's new mistress. They were resplendent with their mother's perfections, but each with a different perfection. Into one there had passed, sinuous now in a male body, Mme de Surgis's regal bearing, and the same ardent, reddish, sacred pallor had flowed into the marmoreal cheeks of both the mother and this son; but his brother had received the Greek brow, the perfect nose, the statuesque neck, the boundless gaze; formed thus from the diverse gifts allotted by the goddess, their twofold beauty afforded the abstract pleasure of reflecting that the cause of this beauty lay outside them; it was as if their mother's principal attributes had been incarnated in two different bodies; that one of these young men was his mother's stature and her complexion, the other her gaze, like those divine beings who were nothing more than the Strength and the Beauty of Jupiter or Minerva. Full of respect for M. de Guermantes, of whom they used to say, "He's a great friend of our parents," the older one nevertheless thought it prudent not to come and greet the Duchesse, who he knew, without perhaps understanding the reason, felt hostility toward his mother, and on seeing us he turned his head slightly away. The younger one, who always imitated his brother because, being stupid and shortsighted into the bargain, he did not dare have an opinion of his own, inclined his head at the same angle, and the two of them glided toward the card room, one behind the other, like two allegorical figures.

Just as I arrived in this room, I was stopped by the Marquise de Citri, beautiful still though practically foaming at the mouth. Quite noble by birth, she had sought and made a brilliant match by marrying M. de Citri, whose great-grandmother was an Aumale-Lorraine.[55] But this satisfaction no sooner experienced, her negative character had led her to develop a deep dislike of people in high society, which did not absolutely rule out a social life. Not only, at a soirée, would she pour scorn on everyone, but this mockery had something so violent about it that even her laugh was insufficiently acerbic and turned into a guttural hissing: "Oh!" she said to me, pointing to the Duchesse de Guermantes, who had just left me and was already some little way off. "What staggers me is that she can lead this sort of life." Were these the words of an infuriated saint, astonished that the Gentiles should not come to the truth of their own accord, or of an anarchist thirsting for bloodshed? At all events, such an apostrophe had no possible justification. In the first place, the "life" that Mme de Guermantes led differed very little (indignation apart) from Mme de Citri's own life. Mme de Citri was astounded to find the Duchesse capable of this mortal sacrifice: of attending one of Marie-Gilbert's soirées. It has to be said, in this particular instance, that Mme de Citri was very fond of the Princesse, who was indeed very good-natured, and that she knew she was giving her great pleasure by attending her soirée. Thus, in order to come to this party, she had canceled a ballerina who she thought had genius and who was due to initiate her into the mysteries of Russian choreography. Another reason that somewhat devalued the concentrated fury felt by Mme de Citri when she saw Oriane greeting one or another guest is that, although at a much less advanced stage, Mme de Guermantes displayed the symptoms of the disease that was ravaging Mme de Citri. We have seen in any case that she had been carrying the germs of it since birth. Being more intelligent than Mme de Citri, Mme de Guermantes would have had better title than she to this nihilism (which was not only social), but it is a fact that certain virtues help us to tolerate our neighbor's failings rather than contributing to the pain that these cause us; a man of great ability will ordinarily pay less attention to other people's foolishness than would a fool. We have described the Duchesse's kind of cleverness at sufficient length to persuade anyone that, if it had nothing in common with high intelligence, it was at least cleverness, a cleverness adroit at employing (like a translator) different forms of syntax. But nothing of the sort seemed to entitle Mme de Citri to despise qualities so similar to her own. She considered everyone to be an idiot, but in her conversation, or in her letters, she showed herself inferior rather to the people whom she treated with such disdain. She had, moreover, so great a need to destroy that, once she had more or less renounced society, the pleasures she then sought underwent, one after the other, her terrible powers of dissolution. Having abandoned soirées for musical evenings, she started saying: "Do you like listening to that, to music? Good Lord, it depends on the moment. But it can be so very tedious! I mean, Beethoven, *la barbe!*"[56] With Wagner, then with Franck, and Debussy, she did not even trouble to say *"la barbe"* but was content to pass her hand across her face, like a barber. Soon what was tedious was everything. "Beautiful things, they're so tedious! Paintings, they're enough to drive you mad. . . . How right you are, it's so tedious, writing letters!" In the end, it was life itself that she declared to us was a bore, without one's quite knowing from where she was taking her term of comparison.

I do not know whether it was on account of what the Duchesse de Guermantes, on the first evening when I had dined with her, had said about this room, but the card room or smoking room, with its illustrated paving, its tripods, its faces of gods and animals that stared at you, the sphinxes lying along the arms of the seats, and especially the immense marble or enameled mosaic table, covered with symbolic signs roughly copied from Egyptian or Etruscan art, had the effect on me of a veritable magician's cell. And on a seat drawn up to the sparkling augural table, M. de Charlus, touching none of the cards himself and oblivious to what was going on around him, incapable of noticing that I had just entered, seemed exactly like a magician applying the full force of his willpower and his reasoning to the casting of a horoscope. Not only were his eyes, like those of a pythoness on her tripod, starting from his head, but, so that nothing might come to distract him from labors that required the cessation of the simplest movements, he had (like a calculator who means to do nothing else until such time as he has resolved his problem) put down beside him the cigar that, a short while before, he had had in his mouth, but which he no longer had the necessary freedom of mind to smoke. On remarking the two crouched divinities borne on its arms by the chair set facing him, you might have thought that the Baron was seeking to solve the riddle of the Sphinx, had it not been rather that of a young and living Oedipus, sitting in that selfsame chair, where he had installed himself in order to play. Now, the figure to which M. de Charlus was applying, and with such intensity, all his mental powers, and which was not, truth to tell, among those customarily studied *more geometrico*,[57] was that proposed to him by the lineaments of the young Marquis de Surgis's face; it seemed to be, so profound was M. de Charlus's absorption before it, some heraldic motto, some conundrum, some problem in algebra, the riddle or formula of which he was seeking to penetrate or reveal. In front of him, the sybilline signs and figures inscribed on this Table of the Law seemed to be the grimoire that would enable the old wizard to learn the direction in which the young man's destinies were oriented. All of a sudden, he saw that I was looking at him, raised his head as if emerging from a dream, and smiled at me, blushing. At that moment, Mme de Surgis's other son came up to the one who was playing, to look at his cards. Once M. de Charlus had learned from me that they were brothers, his face could not disguise the admiration inspired in him by a family capable of creating such splendid yet such different masterpieces. And what would have added to the Baron's enthusiasm would have been to learn that the two sons of Mme Surgis-le-Duc had not only the same mother but the same father. The children of Jupiter are unalike, but that comes from the fact that he married first of all Metis, part of whose destiny it was to bring wise children into the world, then Themis, and next Eurynome, and Mnemosyne, and Leto, and Juno only last of all. But by the one father, Mme de Surgis had given birth to two sons who had each received beauties from her, yet different beauties.

At last I had the pleasure of Swann's entrance into the room, which was very large, so that he did not notice me right away. A pleasure mixed with sadness, a sadness that the other guests perhaps did not feel, but which with them consisted in the sort of fascination exerted by the singular and unexpected forms of an imminent death, a death that is already, as the common people would put it, written on the face. And it was with an almost disobliging stupefaction, into which there entered a tactless curiosity, cruelty, and an at once calm yet concerned moment of self-awareness (a mixture at once of *suave mari magno* and *memento quia pulvis*,[58] Robert would have said), that every gaze became fixed on that face, whose cheeks had been so eroded by disease, like a waning moon, that, except from a certain angle, no doubt the one from which Swann looked at himself, they stopped short, like an insubstantial stage set to which an optical illusion alone can lend an appearance of depth. Whether because of the absence of the cheeks that were no longer there to diminish it, or whether arteriosclerosis, which is also a form of intoxication, had reddened it just as drink would have done, or deformed it as morphine would have done, Swann's Punchinello nose, for so long reabsorbed into a pleasing face, now seemed enormous, tumid, crimson, more that of an old Hebrew than an inquisitive Valois.[59] Perhaps, in any case, in recent days the race had caused the physical type characteristic of it to reappear more pronouncedly in him, at the same time as a sense of moral solidarity with the other Jews, a solidarity that Swann seemed to have neglected throughout his life, but which the grafting, one on to the other, of a mortal illness, the Dreyfus Affair, and anti-Semitic propaganda had reawakened. There are certain Israelites, very shrewd and refined men of the world though they be, in whom a boor and a prophet remain in reserve, or in the wings, so as to make their entrance at a given moment in their lives, as in a play. Swann had arrived at the age of the prophet. Certainly, with this face from which, under the effect of his illness, whole segments had disappeared, as from a block of ice that is melting and from which entire slabs have fallen away, he was much changed. But I could not help but be struck by how much more he had changed in relation to myself. I could not manage to understand how I had once been able to inseminate this excellent, cultivated man, whom I was very far from being bored at meeting, with a mystery such that his appearance in the Champs-Élysées caused my heart to pound, to the point where I was ashamed to approach his silk-lined Inverness cape, and that, at the door of the apartment where such a being lived, I could not ring without being seized by endless agitation and alarm; all this had vanished, not only from his home but from his person, and the thought of talking with him might or might not have been agreeable to me, but it had no effect whatsoever on my nervous system.

How he had changed, moreover, since that same afternoon, when I had come across him—only a few hours before, after all—in the Duc de Guermantes's study! Had he really had an altercation with the Prince, which had shaken him up? The supposition was not necessary. The least effort that is demanded of someone who is very ill quickly becomes for him an excessive strain. Already tired, he need only be exposed to the heat of a soirée for his face to become distorted and to turn blue, as an overripe pear may in less than a day, or milk that is turning. Moreover, Swann's hair had thinned in places and, as Mme de Guermantes said, was in need of a furrier: it looked camphorated, and badly camphorated. I was about to cross the smoking room to talk to Swann when, unfortunately, a hand came down on my shoulder: "Hello, *mon petit,* I'm in Paris for forty-eight hours. I came around, I was told you were here, so it's to you my aunt owes the honor of my presence at her party." It was Saint-Loup. I told him how beautiful I found the house. "Yes, very much the historical monument. But I find it dreary myself. Let's not get too close to my uncle Palamède, otherwise we'll be snapped up. As Mme Molé—for it's she who rules the roost at present—has just left, he's all at sea. It seems it was a real spectacle, he never strayed from her side, and only left her once he'd had her put into her carriage. I don't hold it against my uncle, only I find it comic that my family council, which has always come down so hard on me, should be made up of those very family members who've lived it up the most, starting with the most dissipated of the lot, my uncle Charlus, who's my surrogate tutor, who's had as many women as Don Juan, and who even at his age doesn't let up. There was a question at one time of my being made a ward of the court. I imagine that, when all those old lechers got together to consider the matter and sent for me to preach me a sermon and tell me I was causing distress to my mother, they can't have been able to look one another in the eye without laughing. Inspect the makeup of the council, they seem to have deliberately picked the ones who've had their hands up the most skirts." Leaving aside M. de Charlus, on the subject of whom my friend's surprise no longer seemed to me justified, but for other reasons, and ones that were, as it happens, to be modified later on in my mind, Robert was quite wrong to find it extraordinary that lessons in good behavior should be given to a young man by family members who have led wild lives, or are still doing so.

Were atavism and family resemblances alone to be involved, it is inevitable that the uncle who issues the reprimand should have more or less the same failings as the nephew he has been charged with berating. This is not the uncle being hypocritical, however, deceived as he is by the capacity men possess for believing that each fresh set of circumstances means that "things are different," a capacity that enables them to adopt artistic, political, etc., errors without noticing that these are the very errors that they took to be truths ten years ago, apropos of another school of painting that they condemned, or another political affair that they thought merited their hatred, but which they have got over, and now espouse without recognizing them in their new disguise. Moreover, even if the uncle's faults are different from those of the nephew, heredity may still to a certain extent be the causal law, for the effect does not always resemble its cause, as a copy its original, and even if the uncle's faults are worse, he may perfectly well believe them to be less serious.

When M. de Charlus had just been remonstrating indignantly with Robert, who anyway knew nothing of his uncle's true tastes in those days, and even if it had still been in the days when the Baron was denouncing his own tastes, he may perfectly well have been sincere in considering, from the point of view of a man of the world, that Robert was infinitely more blameworthy than himself. Had Robert not got himself all but ostracized from his society at the time when his uncle had been charged with making him see reason? Had he not come close to being blackballed at the Jockey Club? Was he not an object of ridicule for the sums he was lavishing on a woman of the lowest kind, for his friendships with people, authors, actors, Jews, not one of whom was a member of society; for his opinions, which were no different from those of traitors; for the pain he was causing to his whole family? How could this scandalous existence stand comparison with that of M. de Charlus, who had been able, until now, not only to preserve but even to enhance his position as a Guermantes, being an absolutely privileged individual in society, sought after, adulated in the most select circles, and who, married to a Bourbon princess,[60] an eminent woman, had been able to make her happy, had devoted a cult to her memory that was more fervent and more exact than is customary in society, and had thus been as good a husband as he had been a son?

"But are you sure M. de Charlus has had so many mistresses?" I asked, certainly not with the diabolical intention of revealing to Robert the secret I had chanced upon, but irritated nonetheless by hearing him maintain an error with so much assurance and self-satisfaction. He merely shrugged in response to what he thought to be naïveté on my part. "In any case, I'm not blaming him for it, I consider he's absolutely right." And he began outlining a theory to me that would have horrified him at Balbec (where he had not been content merely to denounce seducers, death seeming to him the one punishment proportionate to the crime). But then he had been still in love, and jealous. He went so far as to sing the praises of houses of ill-repute. "It's only there you can find a shoe that fits, what in the regiment we call your own size." He no longer felt the disgust for places of this sort that had excited him in Balbec when I alluded to them, and, hearing him now, I told him that Bloch had introduced me to them, but Robert answered that the one to which Bloch went must have been "exceedingly run-down, the poor man's paradise." "It depends, after all: where was it?" I avoided giving any details, for I remembered that it was there, in fact, that the Rachel with whom Robert had been so much in love used to give herself for one louis.[61] "Anyway, I'll introduce you to far better ones, where some stunning women go." Hearing me express the desire that he should take me as soon as possible to the ones he knew of, which had indeed to be much superior to the establishment that Bloch had pointed out to me, he evinced genuine regret at not being able to do so on this occasion, as he was leaving again the following day. "The next time I come," he said. "You'll see, there are even young girls," he added with an air of mystery. "There's a young Mlle de . . . d'Orgeville, I believe, I'll tell you precisely, who's the daughter of people right out of the top drawer; the mother was born more or less a La Croix–l'Évêque, they're from the cream of society, some sort of relation, if I'm not mistaken, of my aunt Oriane's. Anyway, you've only to set eyes on the child to tell she's the daughter of people of substance." For a moment, I was aware of the shadow of the Guermantes genius spreading itself over Robert's voice, which passed like a cloud, but at a great height, and did not pause. "She looks to me like a marvelous prospect. The parents are always ill and can't look after her. The child is looking to amuse herself, believe me, and I rely on you to find distractions for her!" "Oh, when will you be back?" "I don't know; if you're not absolutely set on duchesses"—that title being the only one that for the aristocracy denotes a peculiarly brilliant rank, just as among the lower orders they would say the same about princesses—"in another line of country there's Mme Putbus's head lady's maid."

At that moment, Mme de Surgis entered the card room to look for her sons. On noticing her, M. de Charlus went up to her with an affability by which the Marquise was all the more agreeably surprised for having expected great coldness from the Baron, he having always posed as Oriane's protector and, alone of the family—all too often indulgent of the Duc's whims because of his inheritance and out of jealousy with regard to the Duchesse—been merciless in keeping his brother's mistresses at arm's length. Thus Mme de Surgis might have well understood the motives of the attitude she feared in the Baron, but was far from suspecting those of the quite contrary welcome that she received from him. He spoke to her admiringly of the portrait that Jacquet[62] had made of her in the old days. This admiration grew even into an excitement that, if it was partly self-interested, in order to prevent the Marquise from moving away, to "grapple" her, as Robert used to say of hostile armies whose fighting strength one wants to keep pinned down, may also have been sincere. For, if everyone was pleased to admire in her sons Mme de Surgis's own queenly bearing and her eyes, the Baron was able to experience an inverse but equally keen pleasure in discovering these attractions converging once again in the mother, as in a portrait that does not itself kindle desires in us but nourishes those that it awakens with the aesthetic admiration that it inspires. These desires came retrospectively to lend a voluptuous charm to Jacquet's portrait itself, and at that moment the Baron would gladly have acquired it in order to study there the physiological genealogy of the two young Surgis. "You can see I wasn't exaggerating," Robert said to me. "Just look how attentive my uncle's being to Mme de Surgis. Yet, even there, it surprises me. If Oriane knew, she'd be furious. Frankly, there are enough women without going and throwing yourself at that particular one," he added; like all people who are not in love, he imagined that we choose the person we love after endless deliberation and after taking account of various qualities and kinds of suitability. What was more, while being mistaken about his uncle, who he thought was addicted to women, Robert, in his resentment, spoke of M. de Charlus too lightly. One is not always someone's nephew with impunity. It is very often by their intermediation that a hereditary habit is sooner or later handed down. A whole portrait gallery might be formed in this way, under the title of the German comedy *Uncle and Nephew*,[63] in which the uncle would be seen watching to make sure, jealously if unwittingly, that his nephew ends up resembling him. I shall even add that this gallery would be incomplete if it were not made to include the uncles who are not bonafide relations, being only the uncles of the nephew's wife. The MM. de Charlus of this world are so convinced indeed of being the only good husbands, the only ones, what is more, of whom a wife is not jealous, that, generally speaking, out of affection for their niece, they make her, too, marry a Charlus. Which ravels the skein of family likenesses. And to affection for the niece is sometimes conjoined an affection for her fiancé, too. Such marriages are not uncommon, and are often what is called happy.

"What were we talking about? Oh, about that tall blonde, Mme Putbus's lady's maid. She likes women, too, but I imagine you don't mind that; I can tell you honestly, I've never seen so lovely a creature." "I see her as somewhat Giorgione-like?"[64] "Pure Giorgione! Oh, if only I had time to spend in Paris, what splendid things there are to do! And then you move on to the next. Because love, that's just a joke, you know, I'm well and truly over all that." I soon found, to my surprise, that he was no less over literature, too, whereas it was only with the *littérateurs* that he had seemed to be disenchanted at our last meeting ("They're nearly all of them thoroughly bad," he had told me), which could have been explained by his justified resentment against certain of Rachel's friends. They, indeed, had convinced her that she would never have any talent if she allowed Robert, "a man of another race," to acquire influence over her, and, along with her, they made fun of him, to his face, at the dinner parties he gave for them. But in actual fact Robert's love of Letters had not gone very deep, it did not emanate from his true nature, it was only a by-product of his love for Rachel, and had been erased along with it, at the same time as his abhorrence of voluptuaries and his religious respect for women's virtue.

"What a strange look those two young men have! See, Marquise, that curious passion for cards, Marquise," said M. de Charlus, pointing her two sons out to Mme de Surgis, as if he had absolutely no idea who they were. "They must be two Orientals, they have certain characteristic features, perhaps they're Turks," he added, at once to further establish his feigned innocence and to attest to a vague antipathy that, when next it gave way to affability, would prove that this last was addressed purely to their status as sons of Mme de Surgis, having begun only when the Baron had learned who they were. Perhaps also M. de Charlus, whose insolence was a gift of nature that he took delight in exercising, was taking advantage of the short time during which he was supposed not to know who these young men were to amuse himself at the expense of Mme de Surgis and to indulge in his customary raillery, just as Scapin turns his master's being in disguise to profit by hitting him vigorously with a stick.[65]

"They're my sons," said Mme de Surgis, going red, as she would not have done had she been subtler without being any more virtuous. She would then have understood that the expression of absolute indifference or raillery that M. de Charlus was exhibiting toward a young man wasn't sincere any more than the wholly superficial admiration that he evinced for a woman expressed the true depths of his nature. The woman to whom he might have gone on indefinitely making the most complimentary remarks might have been jealous of the look that, even as he talked to her, he was casting at a man whom he then pretended not to have remarked. For that particular look was a look different from those that M. de Charlus had for women; a particular look that rose from the depths, and which, even at a soirée, ingenuously, he could not prevent himself from casting at young men, like the glances of a couturier, which betray his profession by the way they have of at once fastening onto the clothes.

"Oh, how strange!" replied M. de Charlus, not without insolence, while seeming to make his thoughts travel a long way to bring them back to a reality very different from that which he had pretended to assume. "But I don't know them," he added, afraid of having gone a little too far in expressing antipathy and of having thereby paralyzed the Marquise's intention of making them acquainted to him. "Would you like to allow me to introduce them to you?" asked Mme de Surgis diffidently. "But, good Lord, whatever you think, I'm very willing, I'm not so very entertaining a personage perhaps for such young men," intoned M. de Charlus, with the air of hesitation and coldness of someone allowing a politeness to be wrested from him. "Arnulphe, Victurnien, come quickly," said Mme de Surgis. Victurnien stood up unhesitatingly. Arnulphe, without seeing farther than his brother, followed him submissively.

"It's the sons' turn now, then," Robert said to me. "What a scream. Right down to the household dog, he strives to please.[66] It's all the more comic in that my uncle detests gigolos. And see how earnestly he's listening to them. If it'd been me who wanted to introduce them to him, he'd have soon sent me packing. Listen, I'm going to have to go and say hello to Oriane. I've so little time to spend in Paris that I want to try to see everyone here that otherwise I'd have to leave cards with." "How well brought up they seem, and what pretty manners they have," M. de Charlus was in the midst of saying. "You think so?" replied Mme de Surgis, enraptured.

Swann, having caught sight of me, came up to Saint-Loup and me. With Swann, a Jewish cheerfulness was less discriminating than the pleasantries of the man of the world. "Good evening," he said to us. "Good Lord! All three of us together, they're going to think it's a meeting of the Syndicate. In a minute they'll be looking to see where the cashbox is!" He had not noticed that M. de Beaucerfeuil was behind him and could hear him. The general gave an involuntary frown. We could hear the voice of M. de Charlus close beside us: "What, your name's Victurnien, like in the *Cabinet des antiques?*"[67] said the Baron in order to prolong the conversation with the two young men. "By Balzac, yes," answered the elder of the Surgis, who had never read a single line of that novelist, but whose teacher had pointed out to him, a few days before, the similarity between his first name and that of d'Esgrignon.

Mme de Surgis was overjoyed to see her son excelling himself, and M. de Charlus in ecstasies at meeting with so much knowledge.

"It seems Loubet[68] is entirely for us, from an altogether reliable source," Swann said to Saint-Loup, but this time dropping his voice so as not to be overheard by the general, his wife's Republican connections having become more advantageous to him since the Dreyfus Affair had been at the center of his concerns. "I'm telling you this because I know you're with us all the way."

"No, not that far; you're completely mistaken," answered Robert. "The whole affair began badly, and I very much regret sticking my nose in. It had nothing to do with me. If I could start again, I'd keep well out of the way. I'm a soldier, and for the army above all. If you remain for a minute with M. Swann, I'll find you again in a little while, I'm going over to my aunt." But I could see that it was with Mlle d'Ambresac that he was going to talk, and I was chagrined to think that he had lied to me about their possible engagement. I felt easier in my mind when I learned that he had been introduced to her half an hour before by Mme de Marsantes, who wanted the marriage, the Ambresacs being very wealthy.

"At last," said M. de Charlus to Mme de Surgis, "I find a young man of education, who has read, who knows who Balzac is. And it gives me all the more pleasure to meet him here, where it's become such a rarity, in the house of one of my peers, one of us," he added, laying stress on these words. In vain did the Guermantes make a pretense of finding all men equal; on the great occasions when they found themselves with people who were "well born," and especially less "well born," whom they desired and were able to flatter, they did not hesitate to bring out old family memories. "In the old days," the Baron went on, "aristocrats meant the best, in intelligence and in feeling. Yet here's the first one among us that I find knows who Victurnien d'Esgrignon is. I'm wrong to say the first. There's also a Polignac and a Montesquiou,"[69] added M. de Charlus, knowing that this double assimilation could but go to the Marquise's head. "Your sons, moreover, have someone to take after, their maternal grandfather had a celebrated eighteenth-century collection. I will show you my own if you'll do me the pleasure of coming to have lunch one day," he said to the young Victurnien. "I'll show you a curious edition of the *Cabinet des antiques* with corrections in Balzac's own hand. I shall be charmed to bring the two Victurniens face-to-face."

I could not make up my mind to leave Swann. He had arrived at that degree of fatigue in which the body of a sick man is no more than a retort in which chemical reactions are to be observed. His face was marked with small specks of Prussian blue, which appeared not to belong to the world of the living, and gave off that kind of smell which, at school, after "experiments," makes it so unpleasant to remain in a "science" classroom. I asked him whether he had not had a long conversation with the Prince de Guermantes, and whether he did not want to recount to me what form it had taken. "Yes indeed," he said, "but first go for a moment with M. de Charlus and Mme de Surgis, I'll wait for you here."

In fact, M. de Charlus having suggested to Mme de Surgis that they leave this overheated room and go to sit for a minute in another, had not asked her two sons to go with their mother, but me. In this way, he made it seem, having baited his hook, that he did not care about the two young men. He was, moreover, paying me a cheap compliment, Mme de Surgis-le-Duc being somewhat disapproved of.

Unfortunately, scarcely were we seated in a bay without any exit before Mme de Saint-Euverte, the target of the Baron's jibes, chanced to come by. She, in order perhaps to dissemble, or to disregard openly the hostile feelings she inspired in M. de Charlus, but above all to show she was on intimate terms with a lady who was talking so familiarly with him, wished the celebrated beauty a disdainfully amicable good day, who replied to it, while glancing at M. de Charlus out of the corner of her eye, with a mocking smile. But so constricted was the bay that when Mme de Saint-Euverte wanted, behind us, to continue flushing out her next day's guests, she found herself trapped and unable easily to disengage herself, a precious moment that M. de Charlus, anxious to show off his insolent verve to the watching mother of the two young men, took good care not to waste. An inane question that I put to him, without malice, furnished him with the opportunity for a triumphal diatribe of which the wretched Saint-Euverte, almost immobilized behind us, could hardly have lost a single word. "Would you believe that this impertinent young man," he said, indicating me to Mme de Surgis, "has just asked me, with none of the care one ought to take to hide these sorts of needs, whether I was going to Mme de Saint-Euverte's, that is, I fancy, whether I had the colic.[70] I should attempt in any case to relieve myself in some more comfortable spot than at the house of someone who, if memory serves, was celebrating her centenary when I was making my entry into society, i.e., not *chez elle*. Yet who would be more interesting to listen to than her? So many historical memories, seen or lived through, from the days of the First Empire and the Restoration,[71] so many intimate stories, too, with nothing 'saintly' about them for sure, but that must have been very *'vertes',*[72] to judge by how she still frisks about on those venerable hams! What would stop me from interrogating her about those exciting times is the sensitivity of my olfactory apparatus. Mere proximity to the lady is enough. I suddenly say to myself, 'Oh, good God, someone's burst my cesspit,' but it's simply that the Marquise, with the aim of getting some invitation, has just opened her mouth. And you'll understand that, were I to have the misfortune to go to her, the cesspit would be multiplied into a fearsome barrelful of sewage. Yet she bears a mystical name that always makes me think jubilantly, though she has long since passed the date of her own jubilee, of that stupid line of so-called deliquescent poetry: 'Ah! Green, how green was my soul that day....'[73] But I need more wholesome greenery. I'm told that this indefatigable old streetwalker gives *'garden parties,'*—myself, I'd call them 'invitations to a stroll in the sewers.' Are you going to soil yourself there?" he asked Mme de Surgis, who this time found herself in difficulties. For, wishing to pretend to the Baron that she wasn't going, yet knowing that she would give days of her life rather than miss the Saint-Euverte matinée, she got out of it by a compromise, by uncertainty that is. This uncertainty took so stupidly dilettantish and so miserably wardrobe-minded a form that M. de Charlus, unafraid of giving offense to Mme de Surgis, whom he was, on the other hand, anxious to please, started to laugh to show her that "it didn't wash" with him.

"I always admire the people who make plans," she said; "I often cancel at the last minute. There's the question of a summer gown that may alter things. I shall act on the inspiration of the moment."

For my own part, I was indignant at the abominable short speech that M. de Charlus had just delivered. I would have liked to shower the giver of *garden parties* with good things. In society, alas, as in the world of politics, the victims are so cowardly that you cannot hold it against their executioners for long. Mme de Saint-Euverte, who had managed to extricate herself from the bay whose entrance we had been obstructing, brushed unintentionally against the Baron in passing and, in a reflex of snobbery that annihilated all the anger in her, perhaps even in hopes of an overture of a kind at which this cannot have been her first attempt, exclaimed, "Oh, forgive me, M. de Charlus, I hope I didn't hurt you," as if she were kneeling before her lord and master. The latter did not deign to reply other than by a bold, ironic laugh and granted her only a "good evening," which, as if he had only become aware of the Marquise's presence once she had been the first to greet him, was one insult the more. At last, with a supreme obsequiousness which made me bleed for her, Mme de Saint-Euverte came up to me and, after taking me aside, said into my ear: "But how have I offended M. de Charlus? They claim he doesn't consider me smart enough for him," she said, laughing uproariously. I remained serious. For one thing, I found it stupid that she should appear to think, or to want it thought, that no one was in actual fact as smart as she was. And for another thing, people who laugh so loudly at what they say when it is not funny thereby excuse us from joining in by taking all the hilarity on themselves.

"Others assure me that he's put out I don't invite him. But he doesn't give me much encouragement. He seems to be avoiding me." The expression struck me as feeble. "Try to find out, and come and tell me tomorrow. And if he feels remorse and wants to come with you, bring him. Mercy for all sinners. It would even quite please me, on account of Mme de Surgis, whom it'd annoy. I give you carte blanche. You've got the most discerning flair for all that sort of thing, and I don't want to seem to be angling for guests. At all events, on you I count absolutely."

I reflected that Swann must be getting tired of waiting for me. I did not want, moreover, to be too late returning home, because of Albertine, and, taking leave of Mme de Surgis and M. de Charlus, I went to find my invalid again in the card room. I asked him whether what he had said to the Prince during their conversation in the garden was indeed what M. de Bréauté (whom I did not name) had retailed to us, and which had to do with a playlet by Bergotte. He burst out laughing: "There's not a word of truth in it, not one, it's a complete invention and would have been totally stupid. Really, it's unbelievable, this spontaneous generation of error. I won't ask you who told you that, but it would be really intriguing, in a setting as confined as this, to go back step by step and find out how it took shape. Moreover, how can what the Prince said to me be of any interest to anyone? People are very inquisitive. I've never been inquisitive myself, except when I've been in love and when I was jealous. And for all that that taught me! Are you jealous?" I told Swann that I had never felt jealousy, that I did not even know what it was. "Well, I congratulate you! When you're a little bit jealous, it's not altogether unpleasant, from two points of view. For one thing, because it enables people who are not inquisitive to interest themselves in the lives of other people, or at least of one other person. And then because it gives you quite a good sense of the sweetness of possession, of getting into a carriage with a woman, of not letting her go off alone. But that's only in the very early stages of the disease, or when the cure is almost complete. In between, it's the most frightful of tortures. Moreover, I have to say that I've seldom experienced even the two forms of sweetness I'm referring to; the first by the fault of my nature, which is incapable of any very prolonged reflection; the second because of circumstances, by the fault of the woman, I mean of the women, of whom I've been jealous. But that doesn't matter. Even when you no longer care about things, it still means something that you did so once, because it was always for reasons that escaped other people. We feel that the memory of those feelings is only in us; it's into ourselves we must return in order to look at it. Don't make too much fun of the idealist jargon, but what I mean is that I've loved life and have loved the arts. Well, now that I'm a bit too tired to live with other people, these old feelings that I've had, so personal to myself, seem very precious to me, which is the obsession of every collector. I open up my heart to myself like a sort of showcase, and I look one by one at so many loves that other people won't have known. And about this collection, to which I'm now even more attached than to other people, I tell myself, a little like Mazarin with his books,[74] but without any anguish as it happens, that it will be very tiresome to leave it all behind. But let's get on to my conversation with the Prince, I'm only going to tell one person about it, and that person will be you." My hearing him was made harder by the conversation that, right beside us, M. de Charlus, who had returned to the card room, was prolonging indefinitely. "And do you read, too? What do you do?" he asked the Comte Arnulphe, who did not know even the name of Balzac. But his shortsightedness, because he saw everything very small, made him appear to be seeing from a long way off, so that, a rare touch of poetry in a statuesque Greek god, remote and mysterious stars were as if inscribed in his pupils.

"Suppose we take a short turn in the garden, monsieur," I said to Swann, while the Comte Arnulphe, in a lisping voice that seemed to indicate that his mental development at least was incomplete, answered M. de Charlus with an artless and obliging precision, "Oh, with me it's more golf, tennis, football, running, polo especially." Just so, having subdivided herself, did Minerva, in a certain city, cease from being the goddess of wisdom and incarnate one part of herself in a purely sporting, hippic divinity, Athena Hippia. He also went to Saint-Moritz to ski, for Pallas Tritogeneia frequents the high peaks and outruns horsemen.[75] "Ah!" replied M. de Charlus, with the transcendent smile of the intellectual who does not even take the trouble to hide that he is making fun, but who anyway feels so superior to other people, and so despises the intelligence of those who are the least stupid, that he hardly differentiates between them and those who are the most stupid, as soon as they can be agreeable to him in some other fashion. By the mere act of talking to Arnulphe, M. de Charlus considered that he was conferring on him a superiority that the whole world must envy and acknowledge. "No," Swann replied, "I'm too tired to walk, let's rather sit down in some corner, I can't stand any longer." This was true, yet starting to talk had already given him back a certain animation. The fact is that, even in the most genuine fatigue, especially among the nervous, there is an element that depends on our awareness and is preserved only by the memory. We are suddenly weary the moment that we fear being so, and to overcome our fatigue it is enough to forget it. True, Swann was not quite one of those exhausted indefatigables who, having arrived drained, wilting, ready to drop, revive in conversation like a flower in water and can, for hours on end, draw, from their own words, a strength that they cannot, alas, transmit to those who are listening to them, who appear more and more dejected the more wide awake the speaker feels. But Swann belonged to that strong Jewish race, in whose vital energy and resistance to death its individuals themselves seem to share. Struck down by their particular illness, as it itself has been by persecution, they each struggle indefinitely in a terrible death agony that may be prolonged beyond any probable term, when all that can now be seen is a prophet's beard crowned by an immense nose, dilated in order to draw the final breaths, before the time comes for the ritual prayers and the punctual file-past to begin, of distant relatives, moving mechanically forward, as on an Assyrian frieze.

We went to sit down, but before moving away from the group formed by M. de Charlus, the two young Surgis, and their mother, Swann could not help fixing the latter's corsage with the lengthy, dilated, lustful glances of a connoisseur. He put in his monocle so as to have a better view, and even as he was talking to me, he would now and again cast a glance in that lady's direction. "Here, word for word, is my conversation with the Prince," he said to me once we were seated, "and if you recall what I told you just now, you'll see why I have chosen you as a confidant. And then for another reason, too, as you'll find out one day. 'My dear Swann,' the Prince de Guermantes said to me, 'you'll forgive me if I've seemed to be avoiding you for some little time.' I'd noticed nothing of the kind, being ill and avoiding company myself. 'In the first place, I'd heard, and could indeed foresee, that you held, in this unfortunate affair that is dividing the country, opinions wholly opposed to my own. Now, it would have pained me exceedingly had you professed them in my presence. So great was my nervousness that, the Princesse having heard her brother-in-law the Grand Duke of Hesse[76] say two years ago that Dreyfus was innocent, she didn't simply pick up on the remark very promptly; she didn't repeat it, so as not to annoy me. At almost the same time, the Swedish Crown Prince[77] had come to Paris and, having probably heard that the Empress Eugénie was a Dreyfusist,[78] got her confused with the Princesse—an odd confusion, you'll admit, between a woman of my wife's rank and a Spaniard, far less well born than they say, and married to a mere Bonaparte—and said to her, "Princesse, I'm doubly glad to meet you, because I know you have the same ideas as I do about the Dreyfus Affair, which doesn't surprise me, since Your Highness is from Bavaria." Which earned the Prince this reply: "Monseigneur, I'm nothing more than a French princess, and I think as all my compatriots do." Now, my dear Swann, about a year and a half ago, a conversation I had with Général de Beaucerfeuil gave me to suspect that not an error but grave illegalities had been committed in the conduct of the trial.' "

We were interrupted (Swann was anxious that his account should not be overheard) by the voice of M. de Charlus, who (without concerning himself with us) was on his way past, escorting Mme de Surgis out, and stopped in order to try and detain her further, either on account of her sons, or from that desire which the Guermantes had not to see the present moment brought to an end, which plunged them into a sort of anxious inertia. In which connection, Swann told me something a little later that removed from the name "Surgis-le-Duc" all the poetry I had been finding in it. The Marquise de Surgis-le-Duc had a far higher place in society, and far better connections by marriage, than her cousin the Comte de Surgis, who was poor and lived on his estates. But the term that ended the title, "le-Duc," was far from having the origin I had been lending to it, which had led me to compare it, in my imagination, to Bourg l'Abbé, Bois-le-Roi, and the like.[79] Quite simply, during the Restoration, a Comte de Surgis had married the daughter of an extremely wealthy industrialist, M. Leduc or Le Duc, himself the son of a manufacturer of chemical products, the wealthiest man of his day, and a peer of France.[80] For the male issue of this marriage, King Charles X had created the marquisate of Surgis-le-Duc, the marquisate of Surgis existing already in the family. The addition of the bourgeois name had not prevented this branch, on account of its enormous fortune, from marrying into the first families of the realm. And the present Marquise de Surgis-le-Duc, with her high birth, might have had a position of the first rank. A demon of perversity had driven her, despising a ready-made position, to flee the conjugal home, and to live in the most scandalous fashion. Then the world she had despised as a twenty-year-old, when it was at her feet, failed her cruelly at thirty, when, for the last ten years, no one, bar a few faithful women friends, any longer acknowledged her, and she had undertaken painstakingly to reconquer, bit by bit, what she had possessed at her birth (a not uncommon return journey).

As for the great noblemen, her kinsfolk, disowned of old by her and who had disowned her in their turn, she excused herself for the delight she would take in getting them back by the childhood memories she would be able to evoke with them. In saying which, in order to disguise her snobbery, she was perhaps being less untruthful than she thought. "Basin, it's my whole youth!" she said on the day when he returned to her. And, indeed, there was some truth in this. But she had miscalculated in choosing him for a lover. For all the Duchesse de Guermantes's women friends would be taking her side, and Mme de Surgis would thus descend for a second time the slope she had had so much difficulty in reascending. "Well," M. de Charlus was in the midst of saying to her, anxious to keep the conversation going, "you must lay my tribute at the feet of the beautiful portrait. How is it? What's become of it?" "But, you know, I no longer have it," replied Mme de Surgis, "my husband wasn't happy with it." "Not happy! With one of the masterpieces of the age, the equal of Nattier's *Duchesse de Châteauroux*,[81] and which aspired, moreover, to capture a goddess no less murderous and majestic! Oh, that little blue collar! I mean, never did Vermeer paint a fabric with greater mastery, let's not say that too loudly, so Swann doesn't attack us with the intention of avenging his favorite painter, the master of Delft." The Marquise, turning around, addressed a smile and held out her hand to Swann, who had risen to greet her. But, almost without disguising it, the advancing years having perhaps deprived him either of the moral will, out of an indifference to public opinion, or else of the physical capability, out of a heightening of desire and a weakening of the mechanisms that help to conceal it, the moment Swann had, as he shook the Marquise's hand, seen her bosom from close up and from above, he plunged an attentive, serious, absorbed, almost anxious, gaze into the depths of her corsage, and his nostrils, intoxicated by the woman's perfume, quivered like a butterfly ready to go and settle on the half-glimpsed flower. Abruptly, he tore himself free from the vertigo that had gripped him, and so contagious at times is desire, Mme de Surgis herself, though embarrassed, suppressed a deep sigh. "The painter was put out," she said to M. de Charlus, "and took it back. People have said it's now at Diane de Saint-Euverte's." "I shall never believe," answered the Baron, "that a masterpiece could have such poor taste."

"He's talking to her about her portrait. *I* could talk to her about that portrait as well as Charlus," Swann said, affecting a drawling, louche tone and following the retreating couple with his eyes. "And it would surely give me more pleasure than Charlus," he added. I asked him whether what was said about M. de Charlus was true, in which I lied twice over, for, if I did not know whether anything had ever been said, I knew very well, on the other hand, from a little earlier, that what I had meant was true. Swann shrugged, as if I had proffered an absurdity. "That's to say he's a delightful friend. But do I need to add that it's purely Platonic. He's more sentimental than others, that's all; on the other hand, because he never goes very far with women, that's given a sort of credibility to the nonsensical rumors you want to talk about. Charlus is very fond of his friends, perhaps, but take my word for it, that has never happened anywhere except in his head and in his heart. Anyway, we're perhaps going to get a couple of seconds' peace and quiet. So, the Prince de Guermantes went on: 'I'll admit to you that this notion, of a possible illegality in the conduct of the trial, was extremely painful to me, because, as you know, of the reverence I have for the army; I raised it again with the general, and I no longer had any doubts on that score, alas! I shall tell you frankly that the idea that in all this an innocent man might have suffered the most ignominious of punishments had never even crossed my mind. But, tormented by this idea of illegality, I set to studying what I had refused to read, and that was when I became haunted by doubts, not just about the illegality this time but about his innocence. I didn't think I should mention it to the Princesse. God knows she's become as French as I am. After all, I'd made such a point, from the day I married her, of showing her our France in all her beauty, and what for me is the most splendid thing about her, her army, that it was too cruel for me to let her into my suspicions, which only affected, it's true, a few officers. But I'm from a family of soldiers, I refused to believe that officers could be wrong. I raised it yet again with Beaucerfeuil, he confessed to me that guilty machinations had been set afoot, that the bordereau wasn't perhaps by Dreyfus, but that there existed glaring proof of his guilt. This was the Henry document.[82] And a few days later, we learned it was a forgery. From then on, on the sly from the Princesse, I started reading *Le Siècle* and *L'Aurore*[83] every day; soon I was no longer in any doubt, I could no longer sleep. I unburdened myself of my moral sufferings to our friend the Abbé Poiré, who I was astonished to find had the same conviction, and I had masses said by him for Dreyfus, for his unfortunate wife, and his children. At which juncture, one morning when I went in to the Princesse, I saw her lady's maid hiding something she'd had in her hand. I laughed and asked her what it was, she went red and wouldn't tell me. I had the utmost confidence in my wife, but this incident greatly disturbed me—the Princesse, too, no doubt, her lady's maid must have told her about it—because my dear Marie hardly spoke to me during the lunch that followed. That was the day when I asked the Abbé Poiré if he could say my mass for Dreyfus the next day.' Oh no!" exclaimed Swann in a low voice, breaking off. I looked up and saw the Duc de Guermantes coming toward us. "Forgive my disturbing you, *mes enfants.* Young fellow," he said, addressing himself to me, "I am delegated to speak to you by Oriane. Marie and Gilbert have asked her to stay and have supper at their table with five or six people only: the Princesse de Hesse, Mme de Ligne, Mme de Tarente, Mme de Chevreuse, and the Duchesse d'Arenberg.[84] Unfortunately, we can't stay, because we're going to a small costume ball of sorts." I was listening, but whenever we have something to do at an appointed moment, we depute a certain personage inside us accustomed to this sort of task to keep an eye on the clock and give us due warning. This internal servant reminded me, as I had asked him to a few hours earlier, that Albertine, at that moment very far from my thoughts, was to come around straight after the theater. So I turned down the supper. It was not that I was not enjoying myself at the Princesse de Guermantes's. Men may thus have several sorts of pleasures. The true pleasure is that for which they give up another. But this last, if it is apparent, or is alone apparent even, may act as a decoy for the first one, may reassure the jealous or throw them off the scent, may lead the world astray. And yet a little

happiness or a little suffering is all it takes for us to sacrifice it to the
other pleasure. Sometimes a third order of pleasures, more serious but
more essential, does not yet exist for us; its virtuality betrays itself only
by arousing regrets or discouragement. It is to these pleasures, however,
that we shall give ourselves later on. To cite an altogether minor example, a soldier in time of peace will sacrifice his social life to love, but
once war is declared (and without there being any need even to introduce the notion of a patriotic duty), love to the passion, stronger than
love, for fighting. For all that Swann had said he was glad to be recounting his history to me, I felt strongly that, because of the lateness
of the hour, and because he was too unwell, his conversation with me
was one of those exertions for which those who know that they are
killing themselves by late nights, and by excess, feel an exasperated regret on returning home, like that felt by prodigals at the huge sums they
have once again spent, yet who will be unable to prevent themselves on
the morrow from tossing money out of the window. Once past a certain
degree of weakness, whether it be caused by age or by sickness, any pleasure indulged at the expense of sleep, outside our habits, any disrup-
tion, becomes a worry. The talker continues to talk out of politeness, or
excitement, but he knows that the hour when he might still have been
able to get to sleep has already passed, and knows, too, the reproaches
he will be directing at himself during the insomnia and tiredness that
will ensue. Already, moreover, even the momentary pleasure has come
to an end, mind and body are too drained of their energies to welcome
with pleasure what to your interlocutor seems like a distraction. They
resemble an apartment on a day of departure or moving, when the visits
we receive sitting on trunks, our eyes glued to the clock, are such
drudgery. "Alone at last," he said to me; "I no longer know where I'd
got to. I told you, didn't I, that the Prince had asked the Abbé Poiré if
he could have his mass said for Dreyfus. ' "No," was the abbé's reply to
me'—I say 'me,' " Swann said, "because it's the Prince talking to me, you
understand?—' "because I've got another mass I've been instructed to
say for him also this morning." "What," I said to him, "there's another
Catholic besides myself who's convinced of his innocence?" "So it
would seem." "But this other supporter's conviction must be more recent than my own." "But this supporter was already making me say

masses when you still thought Dreyfus to be guilty." "Oh, I can tell it's not someone from our circle." "On the contrary!" "Really, there are Dreyfusists among us? You intrigue me; I'd like to unburden myself to this *rara avis,* if I know them." "You do know them." "Their name?" "The Princesse de Guermantes." While I had been afraid of upsetting nationalist opinions, the French faith of my dear wife had been afraid, on the other hand, of alarming my religious opinions, my patriotic sentiments. But, on her side, she'd been thinking as I had, though for longer than me. And what her maid had been hiding on entering her room, what she went out to buy her every day, was *L'Aurore.* There and then, my dear Swann, I thought of the pleasure I'd give you by telling you how closely akin my ideas on the matter were to your own; forgive me for not having done so sooner. If you go back to the silence I had maintained vis-à-vis the Princesse, you won't be surprised that being of the same mind as you should then have kept me away from you even more than thinking differently from you. For I found the subject infinitely painful to broach. The more I believe that an error, that crimes even have been committed, the more I bleed in my love for the army. I'd have thought that opinions similar to mine were far from filling you with the same sadness, when I was told the other day that you had strongly condemned the insults to the army and that the Dreyfusists should have agreed to ally themselves with the insulters. That decided me, I'll admit I found it cruel to confess to you what I think of certain officers, few in number happily, but it's a relief for me not to have to keep my distance from you any longer, and especially that you should feel that, if my feelings may have been other, it was because I was in no doubt at all as to the soundness of the verdict. As soon as I felt any doubt, I could wish for only one thing, for the error to be put right.' I confess to you that these words of the Prince de Guermantes moved me profoundly. If you knew him as I do, if you knew from where he had had to return to get to this point, you would feel admiration for him, and he deserves it. Not that his opinion surprises me, he's so upright a character!" Swann was forgetting that, that same afternoon, he had said to me, on the contrary, that opinions in the Dreyfus Affair were governed by atavism. At most, he had made an exception for intelligence, since in Saint-Loup's case it had succeeded in getting the better of atavism and making him into a Dreyfusard. But he had just found that this victory was of short duration and that Saint-Loup had gone over to the enemy. So the role devolved a little earlier on to intelligence was now given to uprightness of heart. In point of fact, we always discover after the event that our adversaries had a reason for taking the side they do take, and one that does not depend on the degree to which that side is in the right, and that those who think as we do have been constrained to do so by, if their moral nature is too contemptible to be invoked, intelligence, and if they have no great acumen, uprightness.

Swann now found those who were of his opinion to be uniformly intelligent, his old friend the Prince de Guermantes and my schoolmate Bloch, whom he had hitherto kept at arm's length but whom he invited to lunch. Swann interested Bloch greatly by telling him that the Prince de Guermantes was a Dreyfusard. "We must ask him to sign our lists for Picquart;[85] with a name like his, that would have a tremendous effect." But Swann, tempering the burning conviction of the Israelite with the diplomatic moderation of the man about town, whose habits he had imbibed too deeply to be able this belatedly to shed them, refused to sanction Bloch's sending the Prince a round-robin to sign, even a seemingly spontaneous one. "He can't do that, one mustn't ask for the impossible," repeated Swann. "Here we have a charming man who has traveled thousands of miles to get to where we are. He can be very useful to us. Were he to sign your list, he would simply be compromising himself with his own people, would be castigated on our account, would perhaps repent of his confidences and not give us any more." What was more, Swann withheld his own name. He thought it too Hebraic not to produce the wrong effect. Besides, although he approved of everything where the review was concerned, he wanted no part in the antimilitarist campaign. He was wearing, which he had never done up until now, the decoration he had won as a very young militiaman in '70,[86] and had added a codicil to his will asking that, contrary to his previous dispositions, he should be granted the military honors due to his rank as a chevalier of the Légion d'Honneur.[87] This assembled around the church at Combray a whole squadron of those troopers for whose future Françoise used to weep when she contemplated the prospect of a war. In short, Swann refused to sign Bloch's round-robin, so that, though he passed in the eyes of many for a fanatical Dreyfusard, my schoolmate considered him lukewarm, infected with nationalism, and a jingo.

Swann left me without shaking me by the hand so as not to be obliged to make his farewells in a room where he had too many friends, but he said to me: "You ought to come and see your friend Gilberte. She has really grown up and changed, you wouldn't recognize her. She'd be so happy!" I no longer loved Gilberte. She was for me like a dead person whom one has long mourned, but then oblivion has set in, and, were she to be resurrected, she would no longer be able to insert herself into a life no longer made for her. I had no desire to see her any more, nor the desire even to show her that I was not keen to see her, which every day when I loved her I promised myself I would display once I no longer loved her.

And so, seeking now only to make it look, where Gilberte was concerned, as if I had wished with all my heart to see her again, but had been prevented from doing so by so-called circumstances outside my control, which in fact occur, in any coherent way at least, only once our will does not go against them, very far from giving a cautious welcome to Swann's invitation, I did not leave him until he had promised me to explain in detail to his daughter the untoward events that had deprived me, and would deprive me still, of going to visit her. "Anyway, I shall write to her in a minute when I get home," I added. "But do tell her it will be a letter of threats, for in a month or two I shall be completely free, and then let her tremble, for I shall be around as often as in the old days even."

Before leaving Swann, I had a word with him about his health. "No, it's not as bad as all that," he replied. "At all events, as I told you, I'm rather tired, and I'm resigned in advance to accepting what may happen. Only I confess it would be very irritating to die before the end of the Dreyfus Affair. Those scum have more than one trick up their sleeves. I don't doubt they'll be beaten in the end, but they're very influential, they've got support everywhere. Just when it's going best, everything gives way. I'd like to live long enough to see Dreyfus rehabilitated[88] and Picquart a colonel."

Once Swann had left, I returned to the large drawing room, where the Princesse de Guermantes was, with whom I did not then know I was one day to be such good friends. The passion that she felt for M. de Charlus did not at first reveal itself to me. I merely observed that the Baron, from a certain time on, and without breaking out into any of that hostility toward the Princesse de Guermantes that with him was never a surprise, while continuing to have as much, or perhaps even more affection for her, seemed irritated and displeased whenever anyone mentioned her to him. He no longer ever put her name down on the list of people with whom he wished to dine.

It is true that, before this, I had heard a very malicious member of society say that the Princesse was altogether changed, that she was in love with M. de Charlus, but this slander had seemed to me absurd and made me indignant. I had certainly been surprised to observe that, when I was recounting something concerning myself, should M. de Charlus be introduced into the middle of it, the Princesse's attention was at once drawn a notch tighter, to become that of an invalid who, listening to us talking about ourselves, and consequently in a casual and distracted fashion, suddenly recognizes a name to be that of the illness he is suffering from, which both interests and delights him. Thus, were I to say to her, "M. de Charlus was in fact telling me . . . ," the Princesse would gather up the slackened reins of her attention. On one occasion, having said in her presence that at that moment M. de Charlus was quite drawn to a certain person, I was astonished to see insert itself into the Princesse's eyes the different, momentary line that traces something like the wake of a fissure in the pupils, and which originates in a thought that our words have, without our knowing, stirred up in the person to whom we are speaking, a secret thought that will not betray itself by words but will rise up from the depths we have disturbed to the momentarily impaired surface of the eyes. But if my words had affected the Princesse, I did not suspect in what way.

A little time later, she began talking to me about M. de Charlus, and almost openly. If she made allusion to the rumors that a few people were circulating concerning the Baron, it was only as though to absurd and infamous inventions. On the other hand, she said, "I consider that any woman who lost her heart to a man of Palamède's immense worth should have a sufficiently high outlook, and sufficient devotion, to accept and understand him as a whole, just as he is, to respect his freedom, his fancies, to seek only to smooth out his difficulties and console him for his sorrows." By which remarks, vague though they were, the Princesse de Guermantes revealed what she was seeking to magnify, in just the same way as M. de Charlus himself sometimes did. Have I not heard the latter say on more than one occasion to people who until then had been unsure whether he was being traduced or not, "I, who have had many ups and many downs in my life, who have known all sorts of people, thieves as well as kings, and even, I have to say, with a slight preference for the thieves, who have pursued beauty in all its forms," etc., and by these words, which he thought clever, and by denying rumors that they did not suspect had been circulating (or, to make an allowance for the truth, out of an inclination, or a sense of proportion, or a concern for verisimilitude that he alone adjudged to be minimal), he removed the last doubts concerning him in some, and inspired the first doubts in those who had not as yet felt any. For the most dangerous of all forms of concealment is that of the fault itself in the mind of the guilty person. His own permanent awareness of it prevents him from imagining how general ignorance of it is, how readily a complete falsehood would be believed, and, in return, from appreciating at what degree of truthfulness confession begins for others, in words that he believes to be innocent. Moreover, he would in any case have been quite wrong to seek to suppress it, for there are no vices that in high society cannot find complaisant support, and the domestic arrangements of a château have been known to be turned upside down so that a sister may sleep next to her sister the moment it was known that she did not have a merely sisterly love for her. But what suddenly revealed the Princesse's love to me was a particular fact that I shall not dwell on here, for it forms part of the very different story in which M. de Charlus allowed a queen to die rather than miss the hairdresser who was to use the curling tongs on him to impress a bus conductor by whom he found himself prodigiously intimidated.[89] However, in order to have done with the Princesse's love, let me say what the trifle was that opened my eyes. On the day in question, I was alone with her in her carriage. Just as we were going past a mailbox, she had the carriage stop. She had not brought a footman with her. She half drew a letter out from her muff and made as if to descend in order to put it in the box. I tried to stop her, she put up a slight struggle, and we both of us now realized that our first movement had been, hers compromising for seeming to be protecting a secret, mine tactless for opposing itself to that protection. She was quicker regaining possession of herself. Suddenly going very red, she gave me the letter; I no longer dared not take it, but as I put it into the box I saw, without wanting to, that it was addressed to M. de Charlus.

To go back in time, and to that first soirée at the Princesse de Guermantes's, I went to take my leave of her, for her cousins were driving me home and were in a great hurry. M. de Guermantes wanted, however, to say goodbye to his brother. Mme de Surgis having had the time, in a doorway, to tell the Duc that M. de Charlus had been charming to both her and her sons, this great kindness on his brother's part, the first in this connection that the latter had shown, touched Basin deeply and reawoke in him family feelings that were never dormant for long. Just as we were taking our leave of the Princesse, he insisted, without declaring his gratitude to M. de Charlus in so many words, on expressing his fondness for him, whether because he in fact found it hard to contain, or else so that the Baron might remember that the kind of action he had performed that evening had not gone unobserved by the eyes of a brother, just as, with the object of creating salutary associations of memories for the future, we give a lump of sugar to a dog that has sat up and begged. "Well, well, young brother," said the Duc, stopping M. de Charlus and taking him affectionately under his arm, "so that's how we walk past our older brother without so much as a small hello. I never see you any more, Mémé, and you don't know how much I miss you. Looking for some old letters, I in fact found some from poor Mamma that were all so full of affection for you." "Thank you, Basin," replied M. de Charlus in a strained voice, for he could never speak of their mother without emotion. "You ought to make up your mind to let me fix up a cottage for you at Guermantes," the Duc went on. "It's nice to see the two brothers so affectionate with each other," said the Princesse to Oriane. "Oh, indeed, I don't think you can find many brothers like that. I shall invite you with him," she promised me.

"You're not in his bad books? . . . But what can they have to say to each other?" she added in an anxious tone, for she could hear their words only imperfectly. She had always felt a certain jealousy at the pleasure M. de Guermantes experienced in talking with his brother about a past which he rather kept from his wife. She sensed that, when they were glad to be in each other's company like this, and when she, no longer able to restrain her impatient curiosity, came to join them, her arrival did not please them. But this evening, a second jealousy was added to this habitual one. For, if Mme de Surgis had recounted to M. de Guermantes the kindnesses his brother had shown, so that he might thank him, devoted women friends of the Guermantes couple had at the same time thought they should warn the Duchesse that her husband's mistress had been seen deep in conversation with his brother. And Mme de Guermantes agonized over that. "Remember how happy we were in the old days at Guermantes," the Duc went on, addressing himself to M. de Charlus. "If you were sometimes to come there in the summer, we could resume our good life. Do you remember old father Courveau: 'Why is Pascal *troublant*? Because he is *trou . . . trou . . .*' " "*—blé*," pronounced M. de Charlus, as if he were still answering his teacher. " 'And why is Pascal *troublé*? Because he is *trou . . .* because he is *trou . . .*' *—blanc*.[90] 'Very good, you will pass, you will certainly get a distinction, and Mme la Duchesse will present you with a Chinese dictionary.' Because you remember, Basin, at that time, Basin, I had a thing about Chinese." "Do I not remember, my dear Mémé! And that old porcelain vase that Hervey de Saint-Denis[91] brought you back, I can see it now. You'd been threatening us you'd go and spend the whole of your life in China, so smitten were you by the country; you already loved going off on long jaunts. Oh, you were someone out of the ordinary, for it can be said that in nothing did you have the same tastes as everyone else. . . ." But hardly had he spoken these words before the Duc went red as a beet, as they say, for he knew, if not of his brother's habits, then at least of his reputation. As he never spoke about it to him, he was all the more embarrassed at having said something that might seem to refer to it, and even more so at having appeared embarrassed. After a second's silence: "Who knows," he said, in order to erase his last words, "perhaps you were in love with a Chinese girl before loving so many white ones and finding favor with them, if I'm to judge by a certain lady to whom you have certainly given pleasure this evening by talking to her. She found you enchanting." The Duc had promised himself not to talk about Mme de Surgis, but in the midst of the disarray into which the gaffe he had made had just thrown his thoughts, he had snatched at the nearest one, which was the very one that ought not to have appeared in the conversation, even if it had led to it. But M. de Charlus had noticed his brother go red in the face. And, like a guilty man not wishing to appear embarrassed by having the crime he is supposed not to have committed discussed in front of him, and who thinks that he should prolong a perilous conversation: "I'm charmed," he replied, "but I insist on returning to what you said before that, which strikes me as profoundly true. You said that I have never had the same ideas as other people, you didn't say 'ideas,' you said 'tastes.' How right that is! I've never had the same tastes as other people in anything, how right that is! You said I had particular tastes." "No, no," protested M. de Guermantes, who in fact had not used those words and perhaps did not believe in the reality they denoted in his brother's case. Did he think he had the right, moreover, to harass him on account of singularities that had in any case remained sufficiently doubtful or sufficiently secret as in no way to harm the Baron's immense position? What was more, sensing that this position of his brother's was going to be of service to his mistresses, the Duc told himself that this was well worth a few kindnesses in return; had he had knowledge at that time of any "special" liaison of his brother's, M. de Guermantes, in the hope of the support the latter would lend him, a hope allied to the pious memory of days gone by, would have overlooked it, closing his eyes to it, and if need be lending a hand. "Come, Basin; good evening, Palamède," said the Duchesse, who, gnawed at by rage and curiosity, could stand no more. "If you've decided to spend the night here, we'd do better to stay to supper. You've been keeping Marie and me standing here for the last half-hour." The Duc left his brother after a meaningful embrace, and we all three descended the immense staircase of the Princesse's *hôtel*.

On either side, on the topmost steps, couples were spread out waiting for their carriages to be brought up. Erect, isolated, having at her side her husband and myself, the Duchesse stood on the left of the staircase, already wrapped in her Tiepolo cloak, the collar fastened by the clasp of rubies, being devoured by the eyes of women and of men seeking to chance upon the secret of her elegance and her beauty. Waiting for her carriage on the same stair as Mme de Guermantes, but at the opposite end, Mme de Gallardon, who had long since lost all hope of receiving her cousin's visit, had turned her back so as not to appear to have seen her, and above all so as not to present proof that the latter had not acknowledged her. Mme de Gallardon was in a very spiteful mood, because some gentlemen who were with her had thought they should bring up the subject of Oriane: "I'm not in the least anxious to see her," she had replied. "I caught sight of her just now, anyway, and she's beginning to age; it seems she can't come to terms with it. Basin himself says so. And I can well understand that, because, since she's not intelligent, is a thoroughly nasty piece of work, and has an offhand way with her, she certainly feels that, once she's no longer beautiful, she'll have nothing left at all."

I had put on my overcoat, for which M. de Guermantes, who was afraid of catching a chill, reproved me as he went down with me, because of how warm it was. And the generation of noblemen who have more or less passed through the hands of Monseigneur Dupanloup[92] speak such bad French (the Castellanes[93] excepted) that the Duc expressed his thought thus: "It's better not to be covered up before going outside, at least *as a general thesis.*" I can still see that whole departure, still see, if I am not mistaken in placing him on that staircase, a portrait removed from its frame, the Prince de Sagan,[94] whose last society soirée this was to be, uncovering himself in order to pay his respects to the Duchesse, with so sweeping a revolution of his top hat in his white-gloved hand, which matched the gardenia in his buttonhole, that you were surprised it was not a felt hat with a feather from the Ancien Régime, several ancestral faces from which were reproduced exactly in that of the great nobleman. He remained beside her for only a short time, but his attitudes, however momentary, sufficed to compose a whole *tableau vivant,* a scene from history, as it were. Moreover, as he has since died, and as I hardly did more than catch sight of him in his lifetime, he has become for me so much a character out of history, of the history of society at least, that I sometimes feel astonishment when

I reflect that a woman and a man whom I know are his sister and his nephew.

As we were going down the stairs, there came up them, with an air of lassitude that suited her, a woman who looked to be about forty, though she was more than that. This was the Princesse d'Orvillers, a natural daughter, it was said, of the Duc de Parme, whose soft voice was marked by a vague Austrian accent. She advanced, tall, stooped, in a dress of flowered white silk, allowing her delectable bosom to beat, palpitating and exhausted, through a harness of diamonds and sapphires. Tossing her head like a royal mare encumbered by its halter of pearls, of inestimable value but an uncomfortable weight, she rested her gentle, charming gaze first here, then there, of a blue that, as it began to weaken, became more caressing still, and gave a friendly nod of the head to the majority of the departing guests. "A fine time to be arriving, Paulette!" said the Duchesse. "Oh, I'm so very sorry! But, truly, there wasn't the physical possibility," answered the Princesse d'Orvillers, who had got this sort of expression from the Duchesse de Guermantes, but who brought to it her natural gentleness and the air of sincerity lent by the vigor of a remotely Teutonic accent in so affectionate a voice. She seemed to be alluding to complications in her life too lengthy to be spoken of, and not to common or garden soirées, though she was at that moment returning from several. But it was not these that had forced her to arrive so late. Since the Prince de Guermantes had for long years prevented his wife from receiving Mme d'Orvillers, the latter, once the ban was lifted, contented herself with replying to the invitations, so as not to appear to be craving them, simply by leaving a card. After two or three years of this method, she came in person, but very late, as if after the theater. In this way, she made it seem as if she cared nothing about the soirée, or about being seen there, but was simply coming to pay a visit to the Prince and the Princesse, for their sake alone, out of sympathy, at the time when, three-quarters of the guests having left, she would "enjoy them more." "Oriane has really sunk as low as you can go," grumbled Mme de Gallardon. "I don't understand Basin letting her talk to Mme d'Orvillers. M. de Gallardon wasn't the man to have let me do that." For my part, I had recognized in Mme d'Orvillers the woman who, near the Guermantes *hôtel,* had cast long, languorous looks at me, turned around, and stopped in front of shopwindows. Mme de Guermantes introduced me; Mme d'Orvillers was charming, neither too friendly nor prickly. She looked at me as at everyone else, out of her gentle eyes. . . . But never again was I to receive from her, when I met her, a single one of those overtures in which she had seemed to be offering herself. There are particular looks that appear to recognize you, that a young man only ever receives from certain women—or certain men—until the day when they get to know you and learn that you are the friend of people with whom they, too, are connected.

They announced that the carriage had been brought around. Mme de Guermantes gathered up her red skirt as if to go downstairs and get into the carriage, but, seized perhaps by remorse, or by the desire to give pleasure, and above all to take advantage of the brevity that the physical impediment to prolonging it imposed on so tiresome an action, she looked at Mme de Gallardon; then, as if she had only just noticed her, taken with an inspiration, she retraversed the whole length of the stair, before descending, and, having reached her delighted cousin, held out her hand to her. "How long it has been!" the Duchesse said, and then, so as not to have to expand on all that this formula purported to contain by way of regrets and legitimate excuses, she turned with an expression of alarm toward the Duc, who had, in fact, gone down with me to the carriage, and was furious on finding that his wife had set off toward Mme de Gallardon and was holding up the movement of the other carriages. "Oriane is still very beautiful, all the same!" said Mme de Gallardon. "People amuse me when they say there's no love lost between us; we may, for reasons we have no need to divulge to others, go for years without seeing each other, but we have too many memories in common ever to be separated, and deep down she knows very well that she loves me more than so many of the people she sees every day and who are not of her blood." Mme de Gallardon indeed was like those spurned lovers who want at all costs to make you believe that they are better loved than those whom their fair one dotes on. And (by the praises with which, untroubled by any contradiction with what she had been saying just before, she was so lavish when speaking of the

Duchesse de Guermantes) she proved indirectly that the latter had a thorough command of the maxims that should guide a woman of high fashion in her career, who, at the very moment when the most wonderful of her outfits is exciting, as well as admiration, envy, knows how to cross a whole staircase in order to disarm it. "At least take care not to get your shoes wet" (there had been a brief downpour), said the Duc, who was still furious at having waited.

On the way back, so exiguous was the coupé, the red shoes necessarily found themselves in close proximity to my own, and Mme de Guermantes, afraid they might even have touched them, said to the Duc: "This young man is going to be obliged to say to me, like in some cartoon or other, 'Madame, tell me here and now that you love me, but don't tread on my feet like that.' "⁹⁵ My thoughts, as it happens, were at some remove from Mme de Guermantes. Ever since Saint-Loup had spoken to me of a highborn girl who went into a brothel and of the Baronne Putbus's lady's maid, it was in these two individuals that, formed into a single whole, were now subsumed the longings inspired in me daily by so many beauties of two classes, the vulgar and magnificent on the one hand, the majestic lady's maids from great houses, puffed up with pride, who say "we" when speaking of duchesses, and, on the other hand, the girls whose names it was enough at times that I should have read in the account of a ball, without even having seen them go past in a carriage or on foot, for me to fall in love with them, and, having searched painstakingly through the *Annuaire des châteaux*⁹⁶ for where they were spending the summer (allowing myself very often to be led astray by a similarity in the names), I would dream of going by turns to inhabit the plains of the west, the sand dunes of the north, or the pine woods of the Midi. But even though I had fused together all the most exquisite carnal substance so as to constitute, following the ideal traced out for me by Saint-Loup, the dissolute young girl and Mme Putbus's lady's maid, my two possessible beauties lacked what I could not know until I had once set eyes on them: an individual character. I was to tire myself out seeking vainly to imagine, during the months when my desire turned rather to young girls, what the one whom Saint-Loup had talked to me about was like in her person, or who she was, and during the months when I would have preferred a lady's maid, that of Mme Putbus. But how restful, after being perpetually troubled by my anxious longings for so many fugitive creatures whose names even I often did not know, who were in any case so hard to find, even more so to get to know, and impossible perhaps to conquer, to have selected, from out of all this scattered, fugitive, and anonymous beauty, two choice specimens complete with their descriptions, whom I was at least sure of procuring for myself when I wanted! I deferred the moment of starting on this twofold pleasure, as I did that of working, but the certainty of enjoying it whenever I wanted excused me almost from taking it, like the sleeping pills that it is enough to have within reach of our hand for us no longer to need them but to fall asleep. I now desired only two women in the world, whose faces, it is true, I could not manage to picture to myself, but whose names Saint-Loup had given me, and whose compliance he had guaranteed. So that, if by his words of a little earlier he had imposed an arduous task on my imagination, he had, in return, procured a considerable relaxation and a lasting respite for my will.

"Well," the Duchesse said to me, "apart from balls, can I not be of any use to you? Have you found a salon where you'd like me to introduce you?" I replied that I was afraid that the only one that tempted me might be too unfashionable for her. "Who is it?" she asked in a husky, threatening tone, almost without opening her mouth. "The Baronne Putbus." This time she feigned genuine anger. "Oh no, not her, I think you're teasing me. I don't even know by what mischance I know the name of that cow. She's the dregs of society. It's like asking me to introduce you to my haberdasher. Or, then again, no, because my haberdasher is charming. You're a little mad, my poor boy. In any case, I ask you as a favor to be polite to the people I've introduced you to, to leave cards with them, to go and call on them, and not to mention the Baronne Putbus, who is not known to them." I asked whether Mme d'Orvillers was not a little loose. "Oh, not at all, you're confusing her with someone else, she's prudish if anything. Isn't she, Basin?" "Yes, at any event I don't think she's ever given rise to any talk," said the Duc.

"You won't come with us to the costume ball?" he asked me. "I'd lend you a Venetian cloak, and I know someone it'd damn well give pleasure to, to Oriane for one, but that's not worth saying, no, the Princesse de Parme. She's forever singing your praises, she swears only by you. You're lucky—since she's on the mature side—that her morals are impeccable. Otherwise she'd have certainly taken you for her *sigisbée*, as they used to say in my youth, a sort of *cavaliere servente*."

It was not the costume ball I wanted, but my rendezvous with Albertine. Thus I refused. The carriage had stopped; the footman asked for the porte cochere; the horses pawed the ground until it had been opened to its full width and the carriage entered into the courtyard. "Toodle-oo," the Duc said to me. "I've sometimes regretted living so near Marie," the Duchesse said to me, "for I may be very fond of her, but I'm less fond of seeing her. But I've never regretted the proximity so much as this evening, because it means my remaining so short a time with you." "Come on, Oriane, no speeches." The Duchesse would have liked me to go in with them briefly. She gave a loud laugh, as did the Duc, when I said I could not because in fact a girl was due to come and call on me. "You receive your calls at a very strange hour," she said. "Come on, *mon petit,* let's get a move on," said M. de Guermantes to his wife. "It's a quarter to midnight, and time to get our costumes on. . . ." In front of his door, he came up against its stern guardians, the two ladies with sticks who had not been afraid to come down from their mountaintop by night in order to avert a scandal. "Basin, we were anxious to warn you, in case you were seen at that costume ball: poor Amanien has just died, an hour ago." The Duc felt a momentary alarm. He had been able to see the famous costume ball foundering for him from the moment when, via these accursed mountain-dwellers, he had been warned of M. d'Osmond's death. But he very soon recovered himself, and into the remark that he hurled at the two cousins he put, along with the determination not to renounce a pleasure, his inability to assimilate accurately the locutions of the French language: "He's died! No, no, they're exaggerating, they're exaggerating!"[97] And, paying no further attention to his two kinswomen, who, alpenstocks at the ready, were about to make their ascent into the night, he hurried off to learn the latest by questioning his valet: "Has my helmet come?" "Yes, M. le Duc." "Is there a little hole to breathe through? I don't want to be asphyxiated, damn it all!" "Yes, M. le Duc." "Oh, hell's teeth, I'm having a bad evening. Oriane, I forgot to ask Babal whether the poulaine slippers were for you!" "But the wardrobe master from the Opéra-Comique is here, he'll tell us, dearest. I don't myself think they can go with your spurs." "Let's go and find the wardrobe master," said the Duc. "Goodbye, my boy. I'd certainly say, come in with us while we're trying them on, you'd be amused. But we'd talk, it's coming up to midnight, and we mustn't arrive late if the party's to be complete."

I, too, was in a hurry to leave M. and Mme de Guermantes as soon as I could. *Phèdre* had finished around half past eleven. Having had time to come, Albertine must have arrived. I went straight to Françoise: "Is Mlle Albertine here?" "No one has come." Good God, did that mean that no one would be coming? I was in torment, Albertine's visit now seeming all the more desirable for being less certain. Françoise, too, was annoyed, but for quite another reason. She had just sat her daughter down at the table for a succulent meal. But, hearing me arrive, and finding there was no time to remove the dishes and set out needles and thread, as if it were a matter of needlework and not of supper, "She's just had a spoonful of soup," Françoise said to me, "and I forced her to suck on a bit of the carcass," so as thus to reduce her daughter's supper to nothing, as though it would have been wrong for it to be plentiful. Even at lunch or at dinner, if I made the mistake of going into the kitchen, Françoise would act as if they had finished and even apologize by saying, "I just wanted a *bite of something,*" or "a *mouthful.*" But you were soon reassured on seeing the multitude of dishes littering the table, which Françoise, taken by surprise by my sudden entry, like the malefactor that she was not, had not had time to make disappear. Then she added: "Come on, off to bed, you've done enough work as it is today"—for she wanted her daughter to appear not only not to be costing us anything, to live by going without, but also to be working herself to death on our behalf. "You're only cluttering up the kitchen and above all getting in Monsieur's way, who's expecting a visit. Come on, upstairs," she went on, as if she were obliged to exert her authority to send her daughter to bed, who, the moment her supper had misfired, was there purely for effect and who, had I remained five minutes longer, would have decamped of her own accord. And, turning to me, in that beautiful, uneducated, yet slightly individual French of hers: "Monsieur can't see she's got sleep written all over her face." I remained, overjoyed at not having to talk to Françoise's daughter.

She came, as I have said, from a small village that was right next door to that of her mother, yet different by the nature of the soil, the cultivation, the patois, and certain peculiarities of the inhabitants above all. Thus "the butcher's wife" and Françoise's niece got along very badly but had this much in common, that, when going off on an errand, they would linger for hours "at the sister's" or "at the cousin's," being incapable of ending a conversation of their own accord, a conversation in the course of which the reason that had led them to go out vanished, to the point where, if you said to them on their return, "Well, will M. le Marquis de Norpois be at home at a quarter to six?," they wouldn't even slap their foreheads and say, "Oh, I've forgotten," but "Oh, I didn't realize Monsieur had asked that, I thought I was only to wish him good day." But although they might "go haywire" in this way concerning something said one hour earlier, it was impossible in return to rid their heads of what they had once heard the sister or the cousin say. Thus, if the butcher's wife had heard it said that the English had made war on us in '70 at the same time as the Prussians (and it was no good my explaining that this was not the case), every three weeks the butcher's wife would repeat to me in the course of a conversation, "It's 'cause of that war the English made on us in '70, at the same time as the Prussians." "But I've told you a hundred times you're mistaken." She would reply, implying that her conviction was in no way shaken: "That's no reason to hold a grudge against them, in any case. A lot of water's flowed under the bridge since '70," and so on. On another occasion, advocating a war with England, of which I disapproved, she said: "Of course, no war's always better; but since we must, better to get on with it right away. As the sister explained just now, since that war the English made on us in '70, the trade agreements have been ruining us. After we've beaten them, they won't let a single Englishman enter France without paying three hundred francs for admission, like us now to go to England."

Such, apart from a great deal of honesty and, when they spoke, a stubborn determination not to let themselves be interrupted, to take up again twenty times over at the point where they had been interrupted, which ended by lending to their remarks the unshakable solidity of a Bach fugue, was the character of the inhabitants of this small locality, who numbered barely five hundred and which was bounded by its chestnut trees, its willows, and its fields of potatoes and beets.

Françoise's daughter, on the other hand, regarding herself as a modern woman who had abandoned the well-worn paths, spoke the argot of Paris and avoided none of the jokes that went with it. Françoise having told her that I had just come from a princess's: "Ah, a bargain-basement princess, no doubt." Seeing that I was expecting a visit, she pretended to believe that my name was Charles. I replied innocently that it was not, which enabled her to get in: "Oh, I thought it was! And I'd been saying to myself 'Charlatan' "—*Charles attend.* It was not in very good taste. But I was less indifferent when, as consolation for Albertine's lateness, she said to me: "I imagine you can wait for her till you're blue in the face. She won't come. Oh, our good-time girls today!"

Thus her way of talking differed from that of her mother; but what is more intriguing is that her mother's way of talking differed from that of her grandmother, a native of Bailleau-le-Pin,[98] which was so close to Françoise's village. Yet the patois differed slightly, like the two landscapes. Françoise's mother's village, on a slope and descending into a ravine, was crowded with willow trees. And a long way from there, on the other hand, there was in France a small region where they spoke almost exactly the same patois as in Méséglise. I made this discovery simultaneously with experiencing the nuisance of it. In fact, I once found Françoise deep in conversation with one of the housemaids, who came from that area and spoke its patois. They almost understood each other; I understood them not at all; they knew this but did not for that reason desist, being excused, so they thought, by the joy of being fellow countrywomen though born so far away from each other, to go on speaking this alien tongue in my presence, as when we do not want to be understood. These colorful studies in linguistic geography and its attendant camaraderie were pursued each week in the kitchen, without my deriving any pleasure from them.

As, each time the porte cochere was opened, the concierge pressed an electric button that lit the staircase, and as none of the tenants had not now returned, I at once left the kitchen and went back to sit in the anteroom, to keep watch, at the point where the curtain, slightly too narrow to cover completely the glazed door to our apartment, let through the dark vertical strip made by the semiblackness on the stairs. Should this strip suddenly turn pale gold, it would mean that Albertine had just come in down below and would be with me in a couple of minutes; no one else could any longer be arriving at that hour. And there I stayed, unable to take my eyes off the strip, which persisted in remaining dark; I leaned right over, so as to be sure of seeing properly; but my looking was in vain, the vertical black line, for all my passionate longing, did not yield me the intoxicating happiness I would have felt had I seen it change, by some sudden, meaningful magic, into a luminous bar of gold. All this anxiety for that same Albertine, to whom I had not given three minutes' thought during the Guermantes soirée! But, by reawakening the feelings of expectancy I had felt of old in connection with other girls, with Gilberte above all, when she was late in arriving, the possible deprivation of a simple physical pleasure caused me cruel moral suffering.

I had to go back into my room. Françoise came in after me. Since I had returned from my soirée, she considered it pointless that I should keep the rose I had in my buttonhole, and came over to remove it. By reminding me that Albertine might no longer be coming, and by obliging me also to admit that I wanted to look smart for her, her action produced an irritation in me that was renewed by the fact that, in tearing myself violently free, I crumpled the flower and that Françoise said to me, "It'd have been better to let me take it away rather than spoil it like that." Her every least word exasperated me, moreover. When we are waiting, so much do we suffer by the absence of what we desire that we cannot tolerate another presence.

Françoise having left the room, I reflected that, if now it had come down to my fussing over my appearance with regard to Albertine, it was very unfortunate that I had so many times appeared before her ill shaven, with several days' growth of beard, on the evenings when I had let her come to renew our caresses. I felt that, neglectful of me, she had been leaving me alone. To improve my room a little, were Albertine still to arrive, and because it was one of the prettiest things I possessed, I put back, for the first time in years, on the table that stood beside my bed, the turquoise-studded slipcase Gilberte had had made for me to hold Bergotte's little volume, and which I had for a long time wanted to keep with me while I slept, next to the agate marble. At any event, as much perhaps as Albertine, who had still not come, her presence at that moment in an "elsewhere" that she had evidently found more agreeable, and that I did not know, produced in me a painful feeling that, despite what I had said scarcely an hour before to Swann, as to my inability to feel jealousy, might perhaps, had I seen my loved one at less distant intervals, have turned into an anxious need to learn where, and with whom, she was spending her time. I did not dare send round to Albertine's, it was too late, but in the hope that, having supper perhaps with friends, in a café, she might take it into her head to telephone me, I turned the selector switch and, by restoring the connection to my room, cut it off between the exchange and the concierge's lodge, to which it was ordinarily linked at that hour. To have had a receiver in the narrow corridor onto which Françoise's room opened would have been simpler and less of a disturbance, but useless. The progress of civilization enables each one of us to manifest unsuspected virtues or new vices, which make us either dearer or more unbearable to our friends. Thus it was that Edison's discovery[99] had enabled Françoise to acquire one more defect, which was to refuse, whatever its utility, however urgent it might be, to make use of the telephone. Whenever you tried to teach her, she found a means of escape, as others do on the point of being vaccinated. And so the telephone had been placed in my room, and, so that it should not inconvenience my parents, the bell had been replaced by a simple rotary sound. For fear of not hearing it, I did not move. So unmoving was I indeed that, for the first time in months, I noticed the ticking of the clock. Françoise came in to put things away. She talked with me, but I detested the conversation, beneath the uniformly trite continuity of which my feelings were changing minute by minute, passing from fear to anxiety, and from anxiety to total disappointment. Unlike the vaguely contented words I felt obliged to address to her, I sensed that my face looked so unhappy that I pretended I was suffering from a rheumatism in order to account for the disparity between my feigned indifference and this pained expression; and then I was afraid that the words uttered by Françoise, albeit in a low voice (not on account of Albertine, for she considered the hour of her possible arrival to have long passed), risked preventing me from hearing the saving call that would not now be coming. Finally, Françoise went off to bed; I dismissed her roughly but quietly, so that the noise she made going off should not drown that of the telephone. And I began once again to listen, and to suffer; when we are waiting, the double trajectory, from the ear that gathers in the sounds to the mind that processes and analyzes them, and from the mind to the heart to which it transmits its results, is so rapid that we are unable even to perceive its duration, and we seem to be listening directly with our hearts.

I was tortured by the ceaseless recurrence of my longing, ever more anxious but never fulfilled, for the sound of a call; having arrived at the culminating point of a harrowing ascent within the spirals of my solitary anguish, from the depths of a populous, nocturnal Paris, brought suddenly close to me, next to my bookcase, I all of a sudden heard, mechanical and sublime, like the brandished scarf or the shepherd's pipe in *Tristan*,[100] the spinning-top sound of the telephone. I dashed to it; it was Albertine. "I'm not disturbing you ringing at this hour?" "No, no . . ." I said, containing my delight, for what she had said about the untoward hour was no doubt her apology for being on the point of arriving this late, not because she was not going to come. "Are you coming?" I asked, in an indifferent voice. "Well . . . no, if you don't absolutely need me."

One part of me, which the other part was seeking to rejoin, was in Albertine. She had to come, but I did not tell her so at first; since we had made contact, I told myself I could always force her, at the last minute, either to come to me or to let me hurry around to her. "Yes, I'm close to home," she said, "and quite a ways from where you are; I didn't read your note properly. I've just found it again, and I was afraid you might be expecting me." I sensed that she was lying, and it was now, in my fury, more from a need to inconvenience her than to see her that I wanted to force her to come. But first I was anxious to refuse what I would try to obtain in a minute or two. But where was she? Other sounds were mixed in with her words: a cyclist's horn, the voice of a woman singing, a brass band in the distance sounded as distinctly as the cherished voice, as if to prove that it was indeed Albertine in her present surroundings who was close to me at that moment, like a clod of earth with which you have carried off all the grasses around it. The same sounds that I could hear were striking her ear also and hindering her from attending: truthful details, unconnected with the subject, futile in themselves, but all the more necessary to reveal to us the evidence of the miracle; prosaic, charming features, descriptive of some Parisian street, yet cruel, sharp-pointed features also of an unknown evening that, on her leaving after *Phèdre,* had prevented Albertine from coming to see me. "I must start by warning you that it's not so that you'll come, because at this hour you'll inconvenience me greatly," I said to her, "I can't keep my eyes open. Besides, well, a whole host of complications. I have to tell you that there was no possible misunderstanding in my letter. You answered that it was agreed. So, then, if you didn't understand, what did you mean by that?" "I said it was agreed, only I couldn't really remember what was agreed. But I can tell you're cross, and that bothers me. I regret having gone to *Phèdre*. If I'd known it was going to lead to such a fuss . . ." she added, like all people who, in the wrong over one thing, make a pretense of believing it is for another that they are being criticized. "*Phèdre* has nothing to do with my displeasure, since it was I who asked you to go to it." "Then, you're annoyed with me, it's a nuisance it's so late this evening, otherwise I'd have come around, but I'll come tomorrow or the day after to make my excuses." "Oh no, Albertine, please, having made me waste an evening, at least leave me in peace on the days following. I won't be free for a fortnight or three weeks. Listen, if it bothers you that we should be left with an impression of anger, and perhaps basically you're right, then I'd much prefer, it can't make me any more tired, since I've waited until this hour for you and you're still out, if you came right away, I'll have some coffee to wake me up." "Wouldn't it be possible to put it off till tomorrow, because the difficulty . . . ?" Hearing these words of excuse, uttered as if she were not going to come, I felt that a very different element was attempting painfully to unite itself with the desire to set eyes once again on that velvet face, which already at Balbec had directed all my days toward the moment when, in front of the mauve September sea, I would be beside that pink flower. I had learned to recognize this terrible need for another human being in Combray, in connection with my mother, to the point of wanting to die if she got Françoise to tell me she could not come upstairs. This effort of the old feeling to combine and form but a single element with the other, more recent one, whose voluptuous object was nothing more than the colored surface, the carnation pink of a flower of the seashore, such an effort often eventuates solely in the formation (in the chemical sense) of a new body, which may endure for a few moments only. On that evening, at least, and for a long time to come, the two elements remained dissociated. But already, from the last words heard on the telephone, I had begun to realize that Albertine's life was located (not physically, of course) at so great a distance from me that it would still have required wearisome investigations to lay my hand on it, organized, furthermore, like battlefield fortifications and, for greater surety, of the kind we later acquired the habit of referring to as "camouflaged." Moreover, Albertine was, at a more elevated level of society, part of that class of persons to whom the concierge promises your messenger she will give the letter when she returns—until the day when you realize that it is none other than she, the person met with outside and to whom you have taken the liberty of writing, who is the concierge, so that she does indeed live—if only in the porter's lodge—at the house she had indicated (which is, on the other hand, a small brothel, of which the concierge is the madam), or else who gives as her address a building where she is known by accomplices who will not betray her secret, from which your letters will be forwarded to her, but where she does not live, where she has at most only left some of her belongings. Existences disposed across five or six lines of retreat, so that when you try to visit or find out about this woman you strike too far to the right, or too far to the left, or too far in front, or too far behind, and you may, for months or years on end, learn nothing. With Albertine, I felt that I would never learn anything, would never succeed in unraveling this tangled multiplicity of authentic details and untruthful facts. And that it would always be thus, unless I were to put her in prison (but people escape) up until the end. On the evening in question, this conviction caused no more than a misgiving to pass through me, though in it I could sense that there quivered something like an anticipation of drawn-out suffering.

"No, no," I replied, "I've already told you I wouldn't be free for three weeks, tomorrow any more than any other day." "All right, then . . . I'll run around. . . . It's a nuisance, because I'm at a girlfriend's who . . ." I sensed that she hadn't thought I would accept her suggestion that she should come, which was not genuine therefore, and I wanted to make things difficult for her. "Your friend's no concern of mine. Come or don't come, that's your affair, it's not I who am asking you to come, it was you who suggested it." "Don't get angry, I'll jump into a cab and be with you in ten minutes." And so, out of that Paris from whose nocturnal depths there had already emanated, all the way into my room, measuring the radius of action of a distant being, the invisible message, what was about suddenly to materialize and to appear, following this first annunciation, was the Albertine I had known of old beneath the skies of Balbec, when the waiters at the Grand-Hôtel, as they set the tables, were blinded by the light of the setting sun, when, the windows having been drawn all the way back, the imperceptible evening breezes were free to enter from the beach, where the last strollers still lingered, into the vast dining room, where the first diners were not yet seated, and when, in the mirror set behind the bar, the red reflection of the hull went past, and there long lingered the gray reflection of the smoke, of the last boat for Rivebelle. I no longer asked myself what might have caused Albertine to be late, and when Françoise entered my room to tell me, "Mlle Albertine is here," if I answered without even moving my head, this was only in order to dissemble: "What's Mlle Albertine doing coming this late?" But then, looking up at Françoise, as if out of curiosity to get her response, which would corroborate the apparent sincerity of my question, I saw, with admiration and with fury, that, capable of rivaling La Berma herself in the art of getting inanimate garments and the features of her face to speak, Françoise had been able to teach their lines to her blouse, to her hair, the whitest of which had been brought to the surface and put on display like a birth certificate, and to her neck, bowed by tiredness and by obedience. They pitied her for having been dragged from her sleep and the fug of her bed, in the middle of the night, at her age, and forced to get dressed at high speed, at the risk of catching pneumonia. And so, afraid of having appeared to be apologizing for Albertine's tardy arrival: "Anyway, I'm very glad she's come, it's all for the best," and I let my profound joy burst forth. It did not go long unalloyed, once I had heard Françoise's reply. She, without proffering any complaint, looking even as if she were doing her best to suppress an irresistible cough, and merely drawing her shawl about her as if she were cold, began by retailing all that she had said to Albertine, not having failed to ask her for news of her aunt. "That's just what I was saying, Monsieur must've been afraid Mademoiselle's no longer coming, because this is no hour to arrive, it'll soon be morning. But she must've been in places where she was having a good time, because she didn't even say she was upset at having kept Monsieur waiting, she answered me as if she didn't give a fig for anyone, 'Better late than never!'" Then Françoise added the words that cut me to the quick: "She gave herself away, talking like that. She might well have wanted to hide perhaps, but . . ."

I had no call to be greatly surprised. I have just said that, after errands she was sent on, Françoise rarely gave any account, if not of what she had said, on which she gladly expounded, then at least of the expected answer. But if, exceptionally, she did repeat what our friends had said, however short it might be, she usually contrived, thanks if need be to the expression or tone by which, she assured us, they had been accompanied, to make them seem somehow hurtful. At a pinch, she would accept having suffered a snub, probably imaginary as it happens, from a tradesman to whom we had sent her, provided that, having been addressed to her as our representative, she having spoken in our name, this snub hit us on the rebound. You needed only to reply that she had misunderstood, that she was suffering from a persecution mania, and that the tradespeople were not all in league against her. Their feelings mattered little to me in any case. The same did not go for those of Albertine. And by repeating those ironic words, "Better late than never!," Françoise at once evoked for me the friends in whose company Albertine had ended her evening, finding more pleasure there than in my own. "She's comical, she's got a little flat hat, with her big eyes, it gives her a funny look, especially with her coat that she'd have done well to send to the invisible amender's, because it's all mangy. She amuses me," added, as though making fun of Albertine, Françoise, who rarely shared my impressions but felt a need to let her own be known. I did not even want to appear as if I understood that this laugh denoted disdain and mockery, but, in order to return blow for blow, I answered Françoise, though I did not know the little hat she had been referring to, "What you call a 'little flat hat' is something quite simply ravishing. . . ." "Like nothing at all, you mean," said Françoise, expressing, openly this time, her genuine contempt. Then (in a quiet, more deliberate tone, so that my untruthful reply might seem to be expressing not my anger but the truth, but wasting no time, on the other hand, so as not to keep Albertine waiting), I addressed these cruel words to Françoise: "You're an excellent person," I said smarmily, "you're kind, you've a thousand good qualities, but you're no further on than the day you arrived in Paris, either in knowing about women's clothes or in how to pronounce words properly and not commit howlers." This was a particularly stupid criticism, because the French words we are so proud of pronouncing accurately are themselves only "howlers" made by Gallic mouths in mispronouncing Latin or Saxon, our language being simply the defective pronunciation of a few others. The genius of the language in its living state, and the future and past of French, that is what should have interested me in Françoise's mistakes. Was her "amender" for "mender" not equally as curious as those animals surviving from remote epochs, such as the whale or the giraffe, which demonstrate to us the stages through which animal life has passed? "And," I added, "seeing that in all these years you haven't managed to learn, you'll never learn. But you can take consolation, that doesn't stop you from being a good soul, or making a wonderful *boeuf à la gelée* and countless other things besides. The hat you think is simple was copied from one of the Princesse de Guermantes's hats, which cost five hundred francs. Moreover, I expect very soon to offer Mlle Albertine an even better one." I knew that what was best able to annoy Françoise was that I should spend money on people she did not like. She answered me by a few words rendered almost unintelligible by a sudden breathlessness. When I later learned that she had a heart condition, how remorseful I felt at never having denied myself the ferocious and barren pleasure of answering her back in this way! Françoise loathed Albertine, in any case, because Albertine, being poor, could not add anything to what Françoise saw as my advantages. She smiled benevolently each time I got an invitation from Mme de Villeparisis. She was indignant in return that Albertine did not practice reciprocity. I had reached the point of being forced to invent purported presents I had received from her, in whose existence Françoise placed not the faintest credence. This lack of reciprocity shocked her above all in the matter of food. That Albertine should accept dinners from Mamma, if we had not been invited to Mme Bontemps's (who was not, however, in Paris half the time, her husband accepting "posts," as in the old days, when he had had enough of the ministry), seemed to her indelicate on the part of my loved one, whom she condemned indirectly by reciting the saying current in Combray:

"Let's eat my bread."
"All right, come on."
"Let's eat yours instead."
"My hunger's gone."

I made a pretense of being busy writing. "Who were you writing to?" Albertine said on entering. "To a pretty friend of mine, to Gilberte Swann. Do you know her?" "No." I forbore to put any questions to Albertine about her evening; I felt I would be reproaching her and, given the hour, that we would no longer have time to be sufficiently reconciled to move on to kisses and fondlings. So it was with these that I wanted to begin, from the very first moment. Moreover, if I had calmed down somewhat, I did not feel happy. The loss of one's bearings, of all sense of direction, that characterizes waiting, persists even after the arrival of the person awaited, and, having taken the place in us of the calm by virtue of which we had been picturing that arrival to ourselves as so great a pleasure, prevents us from deriving any pleasure from it at all. Albertine was here: my ravaged nerves, their agitation continuing, were still waiting for her. "Can I have a nice one, Albertine?" "As many as you like," she said, all kindness. Never had I seen her looking so pretty. "Another one? You know what great, great pleasure it gives me." "And me ever so many times greater," she replied. "Oh, what a pretty slipcase you've got there." "Take it, I give it to you as a memento." "You're so kind. . . ." We should be forever cured of our romanticism were we willing, in order to think of the one we love, to try to be the person we shall be once we no longer love them. The slipcase, Gilberte's agate marble, all that had once derived its importance from a purely internal state, since now, for me, they were just any old slipcase, any old marble.

I asked Albertine whether she wanted a drink. "I think I see some oranges and some water over there," she said. "That would be just the thing." I was thus able to enjoy, along with her kisses, the coolness that had seemed to me superior to them at the Princesse de Guermantes's. And, squeezed now into the water, the orange seemed, as I drank, to yield up the secret life of its ripening, of its fortunate action against certain states of that human body which belongs to a very different kingdom, which it is powerless to make live, but which in return it was able to favor by its irrigatory effects, innumerable mysteries disclosed by the fruit to my senses, not at all to my intellect.

Albertine having left, I recalled that I had promised Swann to write to Gilberte, and I thought it kinder to do so right away. It was without emotion and as if adding the final line to some tedious piece of homework, that I traced on the envelope the name Gilberte Swann, with which in the old days I had covered my exercise books so as to give myself the illusion of corresponding with her. The fact is that, if once it had been I who wrote that name, the task had now been devolved by habit onto one of the numerous secretaries on whom it can call. The latter was able to write Gilberte's name all the more calmly because, having found a place with me recently by habit, having recently entered my employ, he had not known Gilberte and knew only, without putting any reality underneath the words, because he had heard me speak of her, that she was a girl with whom I had been in love.

I could not accuse her of being unfeeling. The person that I was now with regard to her was the "witness" best qualified to understand what she herself had been. The slipcase and the agate marble had simply become for me, with regard to Albertine, what they had been for Gilberte, what they would have been for anyone who had not allowed the glow from an inner flame to play on them. But now there was a new agitation inside me, which had impaired in its turn the true power of words and things. And as Albertine was saying, to thank me once again, "I do so love turquoises!," I replied, "Don't let these die," thus entrusting to them, as if to precious stones, the future of our friendship, which, how-

ever, was no more capable of inspiring a sentiment in Albertine than it
had been of preserving that which had once united me to Gilberte.

At this time there occurred a phenomenon that deserves mention
only because it is to be found in all significant periods of history. At the
very moment when I was writing to Gilberte, M. de Guermantes, only
just returned from the costume ball and still crowned by his helmet,
was reflecting that the following day he would certainly be obliged to
go into official mourning, and decided to bring forward by a week the
cure that he was due to take. When he returned from it three weeks later
(to anticipate, since I have only just finished my letter to Gilberte), the
Duc's friends, who had watched him, originally so indifferent, become
a fanatical anti-Dreyfusard, were left speechless with surprise when they
heard him reply (as if the cure had acted on more than just his bladder):
"Well, the proceedings will be reviewed and he'll be acquitted; you
can't condemn a man against whom there's nothing. Have you ever
seen anyone as gaga as Froberville? An officer preparing Frenchmen for
the slaughter—for war, that is! Strange times!" Now, in the interim, the
Duc de Guermantes had got to know three charming ladies at the spa
(an Italian princess and her two sisters-in-law). Upon hearing them
comment briefly on the books they were reading and on a play being
performed at the casino, the Duc had at once realized that he was dealing with women of superior intellect, and with whom, as he put it, he
could not keep up. He had been all the happier to be invited to play
bridge by the Princess. But, hard on his arrival there, as he was saying,
with all the fervor of his unqualified anti-Dreyfusism, "Well, there's no
more talk of the famous Dreyfus getting his review," great had been his
stupefaction to hear the Princess and her sister-in-law say: "We've never
been so close to it. You can't keep someone in the penal colony who
hasn't done anything." "Oh, ah, what?" the Duc had stammered to begin with, as if on discovering some bizarre nickname employed in this
household in order to make someone he had hitherto thought intelligent appear ridiculous. But after a few days, just as, out of cowardice
and a spirit of imitation, we cry "Hello there, Jojotte,"[101] without knowing why, to a great artist we have heard being called that, in this house,
as yet much embarrassed by the new custom, the Duc was nevertheless

saying, "Indeed, if there's nothing against him!" The three charming ladies considered he was not moving fast enough and were quite hard on him: "But, basically, no one of intelligence can have believed there was anything." Each time a "crushing" fact was produced against Dreyfus, and the Duc, believing that this was going to convert the three charming ladies, came to announce it, they laughed uproariously and had no difficulty in demonstrating to him, with great dialectical subtlety, that the argument was without value and altogether ridiculous. The Duc had returned to Paris a rabid Dreyfusard. And, indeed, we shall not pretend that the three charming ladies were not, in this instance, the harbingers of the truth. But it should be remarked that every ten years, when you have left a man filled with a real conviction, it happens that an intelligent couple, or simply one charming lady, enter his society, and that after a few months he has been led to hold opposite opinions. And in this regard, there are many countries that behave like the man of sincerity, many countries that have been left filled with hatred for a people and that, six months later, have changed their views and reversed their alliances.

I did not see Albertine again for some time, but continued, failing Mme de Guermantes, who no longer spoke to my imagination, to see other fairies and their dwellings, no more separable from them than the mother-of-pearl or enamel valve, or the crenellated turret of its shell, from the mollusk that manufactured it and finds shelter there. I would not have known how to classify these ladies, the difficulty of the problem being that, as well as lacking all significance, it was impossible not only to resolve but to pose. Before the lady herself, the fairy *hôtel* had to be approached. Now, one of them being "at home" always after lunch during the summer months, even before arriving there, you had to have had the hood of the cab lowered, so fiercely was the sun beating down, the memory of which, without my being aware of it, would form part of the total impression. I thought I was simply going to the Cours-la-Reine;[102] in reality, before arriving at the gathering, which a practical man would perhaps have made fun of, I had, as though on a journey across Italy, known both bedazzlement and extreme pleasure, from which the house would never again be separated in my memory. Moreover, because of the warmth of the season and of the time of day, the lady had hermetically closed the shutters in the vast rectangular drawing rooms on the ground floor in which she entertained. I had difficulty at first in recognizing my hostess and her visitors, even the Duchesse de Guermantes, who, in her husky voice, asked me to come and sit beside her, in a Beauvais armchair figuring the *Rape of Europa*.[103] Then I made out on the walls the vast eighteenth-century tapestries representing ships with flowering hollyhocks for masts, beneath which I found myself in a palace not of the Seine but of Neptune, beside the river Oceanus, where the Duchesse de Guermantes had become like a divinity of the waters. I would never finish were I to enumerate all the salons that differed from this one. This example will suffice to demonstrate that into my judgments of society I introduced poetic impressions, of which I never took any account when drawing up the total, with the result that, when I assessed a salon's merits, my addition was never correct.

Admittedly, these sources of error were far from being the only ones, but I no longer have time, before my departure for Balbec (where, to my misfortune, I am going to stay for a second, which will also be the last, time), to start on depictions of society that will find their place much further on. Let me simply say that to this first false reason (my relatively frivolous life, which gave people to assume that I was a lover of society) for my letter to Gilberte and the return to the Swanns that it seemed to indicate, Odette might have added, just as inaccurately, a second. Up until now, I have been imagining the different aspects that society may take for the same person only by assuming that society does not change: if the same lady who used not to know anyone is now received everywhere, and another, who had a dominant position, has been abandoned, we are tempted to see in this the purely personal ups and downs that now and again lead, in the one society, consequent on speculation on the Bourse, to a resounding bankruptcy or an unhoped-for enrichment. But they are not only that. To a certain extent, social manifestations (greatly inferior to artistic movements, to political crises, and to the evolution that carries public taste toward the theater of ideas, then toward Impressionist painting, then toward complicated German music, then toward simple Russian music, or toward social ideas, ideas of justice, religious reaction, an outburst of patriotism) are nevertheless the distant, broken, uncertain, cloudy, shifting reflection of them. So that even the salons cannot be portrayed in the static immobility that may have been suitable hitherto for the study of characters, which must also be, as it were, swept along in a quasi-historical movement. The taste for novelty which leads those men of the world more or less genuinely desirous of keeping abreast of intellectual developments to frequent the circles where they can follow them, will normally cause them to prefer some hostess, previously unheard of, who represents the still-fresh hopes of a superior quality of mind, so withered and faded among the women who have long held sway over society, whose strengths and weaknesses they know, and who no longer speak to their imagination. Thus each age finds itself personified in new women, in a new group of women, who, closely identified with the very latest objects of curiosity, seem, by their dress, to appear only now, at this moment, like an unknown species born of the last flood, the irresistible beauties of each new Consulate, each new Directory.[104] But very often the new hostesses are quite simply, like certain statesmen whose first ministry it is but who had been knocking at all the doors for the last forty years without seeing them open, women who were not known to society but who had nevertheless, for a long time past and *faute de mieux,* been receiving a "few close friends." Admittedly, this is not always the case, and when, with the prodigious efflorescence of the Ballets Russes, revealing of, one after the other, Bakst, Nijinsky, Benois, and the genius of Stravinsky, the Princess Yourbeletieff,[105] the young godmother to all these new great men, appeared wearing on her head an immense, quivering aigrette unfamiliar to the women of Paris and which they all sought to copy, one might have thought that this marvelous creature had been brought with them, in their innumerable baggage and as their most precious treasure, by the Russian dancers; but when, beside her, in her stage box, we shall see installed, at every performance of the Russes, like a veritable fairy, unknown before today to the aristocracy, Mme Verdurin, we will be able to answer to those members of society who easily suppose Mme Verdurin to be newly disembarked with Diaghilev's troupe, that this lady had already existed in different times, and passed through various avatars, from which this one differed only in being the first finally to bring her the success, henceforth assured and progressing ever more rapidly, for which the Patronne had waited for so long, and in vain. In the case of Mme Swann, it is true, the novelty that she represented did not have the same collective character. Her salon had crystallized around a man, a dying man, who had passed almost overnight, at a time when his talent was running dry, from obscurity to great fame. The infatuation with the works of Bergotte was immense. He spent the whole day, on display, at Mme Swann's, who would whisper to a man of influence, "I'll speak to him, he'll write you an article." He was indeed in a position to write one, and even a short playlet for Mme Swann. Closer now to death, his health was a little better than in the days when he came to ask after my grandmother. The fact was that severe physical pain had imposed a regimen on him. Illness is the best heeded of doctors: to kindness or to knowledge, we only make promises; suffering we obey.

Certainly, the Verdurins' little clan was currently an altogether livelier source of interest than the mildly nationalist, even more literary, and above all Bergottian salon of Mme Swann. The little clan was the active center indeed of a long political crisis that had reached its maximum intensity: Dreyfusism. But society people were for the most part so antirevisionist that a Dreyfusian salon seemed something as impossible as, in another age, a Communard salon.[106] The Princesse de Caprarola, who had made the acquaintance of Mme Verdurin in connection with a large exhibition she had been organizing, had indeed paid the latter a lengthy visit, in hopes of debauching a few interesting elements of the little clan and adding them to her own salon, a visit in the course of which the Princesse (playing a cut-price version of the Duchesse de Guermantes) had argued against received opinions and declared those in her own world to be idiots, which Mme Verdurin had thought showed great courage. But this courage was not to extend so far later on as to dare, with the gaze of nationalist ladies trained on her, to acknowledge Mme Verdurin at the Balbec races. In the case of Mme Swann, on the other hand, the anti-Dreyfusards were grateful to her for being a *"bien-pensante,"* which, married as she was to a Jew, was doubly meritorious. Nonetheless, those who had never been there imagined she entertained only a few obscure Israelites and pupils of Bergotte. So it is that women far better qualified than Mme Swann are ranked at the very bottom of the social scale, either on account of their origins or because they do not like dining out or the soirées at which they are never seen, which is wrongly supposed to be due to their not having been invited, or because they never talk about their friendships in society but only about literature or art, or because people keep quiet about having visited them, or they, so as not to show impoliteness to others, keep quiet about having entertained them, in short for a thousand reasons that end by making one or another of them, in the eyes of some, the woman one does not receive. So it was with Odette. Mme d'Épinoy, looking at the time for a contribution to the Patrie Française,[107] having had to go and call on her, as if she were going into her haberdasher's, convinced moreover she would find only faces not despised even but unknown, remained as if transfixed when the door opened, not on the drawing room she had imagined, but on a magic chamber in which, as if thanks to a change of lighting in a fairy play, she recognized in the dazzling female extras, half reclining on divans or sitting on armchairs, addressing their hostess by her first name, the Highnesses and duchesses that she, the Princesse d'Épinoy, had the greatest difficulty in luring to her own house, and to whom, at that moment, beneath the benevolent gaze of Odette, the Marquis du Lau, the Comte Louis de Turenne, the Prince Borghese, and the Duc d'Estrées[108] were acting as pantlers and as cupbearers, carrying the orangeade and the petits fours. Since, without her being aware of it, the Princesse d'Épinoy saw people's place in society as internal to them, she was obliged to disincarnate Mme Swann and reincarnate her in a fashionable woman. Ignorance of the life actually led by women who do not exhibit it in the newspapers thus casts a veil of mystery over the social standing of some (thereby helping to diversify the salons). In Odette's case, at the outset, a few men of the very best society, curious to meet Bergotte, had been to dine at her house privately. She had had the tact, recently acquired, not to advertise the fact; there they had found—a memory, perhaps, of the little nucleus whose traditions Odette had preserved since the schism—the table set, and so forth. Odette had taken them, together with Bergotte, the death of whom this in fact finally proved to be, to the interesting "opening nights." They spoke of her to a few women of their own world capable of taking an interest in all this novelty. They were convinced that Odette, an intimate of Bergotte's, had more or less collaborated in his works, and thought her a thousand times more intelligent than the most remarkable women of the Faubourg, for the same reason as they had placed all their political hopes in certain staunch Republicans such as M. Doumer and M. Deschanel,[109] whereas they would have seen France as headed for the abyss had it been entrusted to the monarchist personnel whom they entertained to dinner, to the Charettes, the Doudeauvilles, etc.[110] This change in Odette's standing had been achieved on her part with a discretion that made it surer and more rapid, but allowed no inkling of it to reach a public inclined to depend on the columns of *Le Gaulois* for the advance or decline of a salon, with the result that one day, at the dress rehearsal of a play by Bergotte, given in one of the most fashionable auditoriums in aid of charity, it was a veritable *coup de théâtre* when they saw, in the front box, which was that of the author, coming to sit next to Mme Swann, Mme de Marsantes and the woman who, thanks to the progressive effacement of the Duchesse de Guermantes (sated with honors, and annihilating herself by putting up no resistance), was on the way to becoming the "lioness," the queen of the hour, the Comtesse Molé. "We hadn't even suspected she'd started to climb," it was said of Odette just as the Comtesse Molé was seen entering her box, "and now she's reached the top rung." With the result that Mme Swann was able to believe I was making up with her daughter out of snobbery. Despite her brilliant women friends, Odette nevertheless listened to the play with an extreme attentiveness, as though she were there purely in order to hear it, just as in the old days she had crossed the Bois for her health's sake and to get some exercise. Men who in the old days had paid her less attention came to the balcony, disturbing all and sundry, so as to hang on her hand and come close to the imposing circle by whom she was surrounded. She, with a smile still more friendly than ironic, replied patiently to their questions, affecting a greater calm than one would have credited and which was perhaps genuine, this exhibition being only the belated exhibition of a habitual and discreetly concealed intimacy. Behind the three ladies attracting all the stares was Bergotte, surrounded by the Prince d'Agrigente, the Comte Louis de Turenne, and the Marquis de Bréauté. And it is easy to understand that, for men who were received everywhere and could no longer expect further elevation save by seeking out originality, this demonstration of their worth that they thought to be giving, by allowing themselves to be lured by a hostess known for her high intellectuality, in whose company they expected to meet all the playwrights and novelists who were in vogue, was livelier and more exciting than the soirées at the Princesse de Guermantes's, which, lacking any program or fresh attraction, had succeeded one another these many years past, more or less similar to that which we have described at such length. In this exalted world of the Guermantes, from which curiosity had somewhat turned away, the new intellectual fashions were not embodied in amusements in their own image, as in the skits written for Mme Swann by Bergotte, or those veritable meetings of the Committee of Public Safety[111] (had society been able to take an interest in the Dreyfus Affair) when there gathered at Mme Verdurin's Picquart, Clemenceau, Zola, Reinach, and Labori.[112]

Gilberte, too, was of service to her mother's position, for an uncle of Swann's had just left the girl nearly eighty million francs, which meant that the Faubourg Saint-Germain was beginning to take notice of her. The obverse of this medal was that Swann, who was anyway dying, held Dreyfusist views, but even that did his wife no harm and was even of service to her. It did her no harm, because they said, "He's senile, an idiot, no one pays him any attention, only his wife counts and she's charming." But even Swann's Dreyfusism was useful to Odette. Left to her own devices, she would perhaps have gone and made overtures to smart women, which would have destroyed her. Whereas, on the evenings when she dragged her husband out to dine in the Faubourg Saint-Germain, Swann, remaining unsociably in his corner, did not hesitate, should he see Odette getting herself introduced to some nationalist lady, to say in a loud voice: "Come, Odette, you're mad. Calm down, I beg you. It would be ignominious on your part to get yourself introduced to anti-Semites. I forbid it." The society people after whom everyone runs are unaccustomed either to so much pride or to such lack of breeding. For the first time, they had found someone who thought himself "more" than them. These grumbles of Swann's were retailed, and Odette was showered with turned-down visiting cards. When she called on Mme d'Arpajon, there was a keen and sympathetic stir of curiosity. "It didn't annoy you, my introducing her to you," said Mme d'Arpajon. "She's very nice. I got to know her through Marie de Marsantes." "No, no, on the contrary, it seems she's as intelligent as could be, she's charming. On the contrary, I longed to meet her; tell me where she lives." Mme d'Arpajon told Mme Swann that she had enjoyed herself greatly at her house two days before and had been delighted to give up Mme de Saint-Euverte for her sake. Which was true, for to prefer Mme Swann was to prove that you were intelligent, like going to the concert rather than a tea party. But when Mme de Saint-Euverte came to Mme d'Arpajon's at the same time as Odette, since Mme de Saint-Euverte was a great snob and Mme d'Arpajon, even though she rather looked down on her, was fond of her receptions, Mme d'Arpajon did not introduce Odette, so that Mme de Saint-Euverte should not know who it was. The Marquise imagined that it must be some princess or other who very seldom went out for her never to have seen her, and prolonged her visit, replying indirectly to what Odette said, but Mme d'Arpajon was unyielding. And when the defeated Mme de Saint-Euverte was leaving, "I didn't introduce you," her hostess said to Odette, "because people don't much like going to her and she invites on the grand scale; you wouldn't have been able to extricate yourself." "Oh, that doesn't matter," said Odette, with some regret. But she retained the idea that people did not like going to Mme de Saint-Euverte's, which was to a certain extent true, and concluded from that that her own standing was much superior to that of Mme de Saint-Euverte, even though the latter had a very grand standing and Odette as yet none at all.

She was unaware of this, and although all Mme de Guermantes's women friends were friendly also with Mme d'Arpajon, when the latter invited Mme Swann, Odette would say, with a scrupulous air, "I'm going to Mme d'Arpajon's, but you're going to think me very *vieux jeu,* it shocks me, on account of Mme de Guermantes"—whom she did not, as it happens, know. Men of distinction thought that the fact that Mme

Swann knew few people in high society was because she must be a superior woman, probably a great musician, and that to go there would be a sort of extra-social qualification, as for a duke to be a doctor of science. Women who were complete nobodies were drawn to Odette for a contrary reason; learning that she went to the Colonne concerts[113] and declared herself to be a Wagnerian, they concluded that she must be a "practical joker" and were much excited by the thought of getting to know her. But, being themselves none too secure socially, they were afraid of compromising themselves in public by seeming to be friendly with Odette, and should they catch sight of Mme Swann at a charity concert, they looked the other way, deeming it out of the question, under the gaze of Mme de Rochechouart, to acknowledge a woman who was quite capable of having been to Bayreuth—which meant of committing all manner of excess.

Everyone, when they visited someone else, became different. To say nothing of the miraculous metamorphoses achieved in this way among the fairies, in Mme Swann's drawing room, M. de Bréauté, lent a sudden prominence by the absence of the people who customarily surrounded him, by the air of satisfaction he wore at finding himself as much at ease there as if, instead of going to a party, he had donned his spectacles in order to shut himself away and read the *Revue des deux mondes,*[114] and by the mysterious ritual he appeared to be fulfilling by coming to see Odette, M. de Bréauté himself seemed like a new man. I would have given a lot to see how much the Duchesse de Montmorency-Luxembourg might have changed for the worse in this new setting. But she was one of those people to whom Odette could never be introduced. Mme de Montmorency, who was much more kindly disposed toward Oriane than the latter was toward her, had greatly astonished me by saying to me, apropos of Mme de Guermantes: "She knows clever people, everyone likes her, I think that if she'd stuck at it more, she'd have managed to create a salon. The truth is, she wasn't keen on it, she's quite right, she's happy as she is, sought after by all." If Mme de Guermantes did not have a "salon," what, then, was a "salon"?

The stupefaction into which these words threw me was no greater than that which I caused Mme de Guermantes by telling her I much liked going to Mme de Montmorency's. Oriane thought her an old cretin. "Me, yes," she said, "I'm forced to, she's my aunt; but you! She doesn't even know how to attract agreeable people." Mme de Guermantes did not realize that the agreeable people left me cold, that when she said "the Arpajon salon" I saw a yellow butterfly, and "the Swann salon" (Mme Swann was "at home" in the winter from six to seven) a black butterfly, its wings felted with snow. Although inaccessible to her, she adjudged this latter salon, which was not one, to be excusable in my own case, because of the "clever people." But Mme de Luxembourg! Had I already "produced" something that had been noticed, she would have concluded that talent may coexist with an element of snobbery. And, to crown her disappointment, I admitted to her that I did not go to Mme de Montmorency's (as she thought) to "take notes" or "make a study." Mme de Guermantes was no more mistaken, however, than those society novelists who analyze the actions of a snob, or a purported one, cruelly from the outside, but never place themselves inside him, at the time when a whole social springtime is coming into flower in his imagination. When I tried to find what the great pleasure was that I felt on going to Mme de Montmorency's, I was myself somewhat disappointed. She lived in an old place in the Faubourg Saint-Germain, filled with detached houses divided by small gardens. Under the archway, a statuette, said to be by Falconet,[115] represented a spring, from which, indeed, there welled a perpetual moisture. A little farther on, the concierge, her eyes permanently red, whether from grief, or neurasthenia, or a migraine, or a cold, never answered you, but gestured vaguely to indicate that the Duchesse was in and allowed a few drops to fall from her eyelids over a bowl filled with forget-me-nots. The pleasure I got from seeing the statuette, putting me in mind as it did of a small plaster gardener that had stood in a garden in Combray, was as nothing compared with that produced in me by the great, damp, resonant staircase, full of echoes, like that in certain bathing establishments of old, from the vases filled with cinerarias—blue against blue—in the anteroom, and above all from the tinkling of the bell, which exactly matched that in Eulalie's room. This tinkling raised my enthusiasm to new heights, but seemed too humble for me to be able to explain it to Mme de Montmorency, so that that lady always saw me in a state of euphoria whose source she never divined.

## THE INTERMITTENCES OF THE HEART[116]

My second arrival in Balbec was very different from the first. The manager had come in person to wait for me at Pont-à-Couleuvre, repeating how much he valued his titled clientele, which made me fear that he had ennobled me until I realized that, in the darkness of his grammatical memory, *titré*, or "titled," meant simply *attitré*, or "regular." For the rest, as he proceeded to learn new languages, he grew worse at the old ones. He announced that he had put me right at the top of the hotel. "I hope," he said, "that you won't see that as a lack of discourtesy, I was worried about giving you a room you're unworthy of, but I did it with regard to the noise, because that way you won't have anyone overhead assailing your eardrops"–for "eardrums." "Rest assured, I'll have the windows closed so they don't bang. I'm intolerable where that's concerned." These words expressed not his own thought, which was that he would always be found inexorable on that subject, but very possibly that of his *garçons d'étage*. The rooms were in any case those of my first stay. They were no lower down, but I had risen in the manager's esteem. I could have a fire lit if I liked (for, on doctors' orders, I had left right after Easter), but he was afraid there might be "crocks" (for "cracks") in the ceiling. "Above all, always wait when lighting a blaze until the one before's been consummated"–for "consumed." "For the important thing's to avoid not setting fire to the fireplace, all the more because, to brighten things up a bit, I've had a big old Chinese-porcelain postiche placed above it, which might get ruined."

He informed me with much sadness of the death of the *bâtonnier*[117] from Cherbourg: "He was a woolly one," he said (probably for "wily"), and gave me to understand that his end had been hastened by a life of "débâcles," which meant "debauchery." "I'd been noticing for some time how after dinner he used to have a sneeze"–no doubt for a "snooze"–"in the lounge. Just lately, he was so much altered that, if you hadn't known it was him, to look at he was barely recognizant"–for "recognizable," no doubt.

In happy compensation, the First President[118] from Caen had just received the "ensign" of a commander in the Légion d'Honneur. "He has abilities, that's for sure, but it seems he was given it above all on account of his great impotence." Much had been made of this award, moreover, in the previous day's *Écho de Paris*,[119] of which the manager had as yet read only the first "paraph" (for "paragraph"). M. Caillaux's[120] policies had been given a good going over there. "I think they're right, what's more," he said. "He's putting us too much under the thimble"–instead of the "thumb"[121]–"of Germany." Since this sort of topic as treated by a hotelier struck me as tedious, I stopped listening. I thought of the mental images that had decided me to return to Balbec. They were very different from those of the other time; the vision that I had come in search of was as brilliant as the earlier one had been hazy; they were to be no less of a disappointment. The images chosen by memory are as arbitrary, as confined, and as elusive as those that imagination had formed and that reality has destroyed. There is no reason why, outside of us, a real place should possess the pictures painted by memory rather than those of our dreams. Besides, a new reality will perhaps make us forget, or even detest, the desires on whose account we had come away.

Those that had made me come away to Balbec stemmed in part from the fact that the Verdurins (of whose invitations I had never taken advantage, and who would certainly be glad to entertain me, were I to go to the country to apologize for never having been able to visit them in Paris), knowing that several of the faithful would be spending their holidays along this coast, and having for that reason rented for the whole season one of M. de Cambremer's châteaux (La Raspelière), had invited Mme Putbus. On the evening when I had learned of this (in Paris), I sent, like a veritable madman, our young footman to inquire whether that lady would be taking her lady's maid to Balbec. It was eleven o'clock at night. The concierge was a long time opening up and by some miracle did not send my messenger packing or summon the police, but was content merely to give him a rough reception, while supplying him with the desired information. He said that the head lady's maid would indeed be accompanying her mistress, first of all to take the waters in Germany, then to Biarritz, and, lastly, to Mme Verdurin's. From that moment on, I had felt calm and glad to have this prospect in store. I had been able to dispense with those pursuits in the street, when I was not armed with the letter of introduction to the beauties I encountered that my having dined that same evening, at the Verdurins, with her mistress, would represent to the "Giorgione." Moreover, she would perhaps think even better of me on learning that I knew not only the bourgeois tenants of La Raspelière but its owners, and especially Saint-Loup, who, unable to recommend me to the lady's maid from a distance (she not knowing Robert's name), had written an enthusiastic letter to the Cambremers on my behalf. He thought that, aside from the great usefulness they might have for me, I would find Mme de Cambremer, the daughter-in-law, née Legrandin, interesting to talk to. "She's an intelligent woman," he had assured me. "Within limits, of course. She won't say anything definitive"—"definitive" things had taken the place of "sublime" ones with Robert, who, every five or six years, would modify some of his pet expressions, while preserving the main ones—"but she's got character, she has a personality, intuition, she comes out with just what needs saying. She can get on your nerves now and again, she throws out silly remarks so as to seem 'upper crust,' which is all the more ridiculous since no one could be less fashionable than the Cambremers, she isn't always 'up to the minute' but, all in all, she's still one of the people it's most bearable to associate with."

As soon as Robert's recommendation had reached them, the Cambremers, whether from snobbery, which led them to want to make themselves indirectly agreeable to Saint-Loup, or from gratitude for what he had done for one of their nephews in Doncières, or more probably mainly out of kindness and a tradition of hospitality, had written long letters demanding that I should stay with them, or, if I preferred to be more independent, offering to look for lodgings. When Saint-Loup had pointed out that I would be staying at the Grand-Hôtel in Balbec, they replied that they would at least expect a visit from me right after I arrived, and if it were too long delayed would not fail to come and badger me with invitations to their *garden parties.*

Nothing of course connected Mme Putbus's lady's maid in any essential way to the neighborhood of Balbec; she would not be there for me like the peasant girl whom, alone on the Méséglise way, I had so often summoned up in vain, with all the strength of my longing.

But I had long since ceased trying to extract from a woman the square root of her unknown, as it were, which did not often survive a simple introduction. At least in Balbec, where I had not been for a long time, I should have the advantage, for want of the necessary connection that did not exist between the neighborhood and the woman, that my sense of reality would not be suppressed for me by habit, as it was in Paris, where, whether in my own house or in some familiar bedroom, pleasure with a woman was unable to give me for a single moment the illusion, in the midst of everyday objects, that it was opening the way for me to a new life. (For, if habit is a second nature, it prevents us from knowing the first, of which it has neither the cruelties nor the enchantments.) But I would perhaps have this illusion in a new landscape, where, before a ray of sunlight, the sensibility is reborn, and where the lady's maid whom I desired would indeed finally inflame me; but we shall see circumstances so decree not only that this woman should not come to Balbec, but that I dreaded nothing so much as that she might come, with the result that this principal object of my journey was neither attained nor even pursued. True, Mme Putbus was not due to go to the Verdurins' so early in the season; but the pleasures that we have chosen can be a long way off if their advent is certain and if, while we await them, we can give ourselves over in the meantime to an idle seeking to attract and to an incapacity for love. For the rest, I was not going to Balbec in as impractical a spirit as the first time; there is always less egotism in the pure imagination than in the memory; and I knew that I was going to find myself, as it happens, in one of those places teeming with beautiful women whom I did not know; a seaside resort displays no fewer of them than a ball, and I thought in advance of those strolls in front of the hotel, along the esplanade, with the same sort of pleasure that Mme de Guermantes would have procured for me if, instead of getting me invited to brilliant dinner parties, she had more often given my name, for their lists of male partners, to the hostesses where there was dancing. To make female acquaintances in Balbec would be as easy as it had been awkward for me in the old days, for I now had as many connections and supports there as I had been devoid of them on my first trip.

I was aroused from my reverie by the voice of the manager, to whose political dissertation I had not been listening. Changing the subject, he told me of the delight of the First President on learning of my arrival, and that he would be coming to call on me in my room that very evening. The prospect of this visit so alarmed me, for I was starting to feel tired, that I begged him to obstruct it (which he promised to do) and, for added security, for this first evening, to get his staff to mount guard on my floor. He did not seem overfond of them. "I'm obliged all the time to run after them, because they lack too much inertia. If I wasn't there, they wouldn't budge. I'll put the lift boy on sentry duty at your door." I asked whether he was at last "head *chasseur.*" "He's not yet senior enough in the house," he replied. "He's got workmates older than him, there'd be an outcry. There need to be granulations in everything. I allow he has a good aptitude"–for "attitude"–"there in front of his lift. But he's still a bit young for such positions. It would show up against others, who are too old. He's a bit lacking in responsibility, which is the primitive quality"–no doubt the "primordial," the most important, quality. "He needs to have his brains"–my interlocutor meant "head"– "screwed on a bit more. Anyway, he need only trust me. I know the ropes. Before winning my stripes as manager of the Grand-Hôtel, I first saw action under M. Paillard."[122] This comparison impressed me, and I thanked the manager for having come himself all the way to Pont-à-Couleuvre. "Oh, don't mention it! It made me waste only an infinite"– for "infinitesimal"–"amount of time." We had in any event arrived.

A convulsion of my entire being. On the very first night, as I was suffering from an attack of cardiac fatigue, trying to overcome the pain, I bent down slowly and cautiously to remove my boots. But hardly had I touched the first button of my ankle boot when my chest swelled, filled with an unknown, divine presence, I was shaken by sobs, tears streamed from my eyes. The person who had come to my assistance, who was rescuing me from my aridity of soul, was the one who, several years before, at an identical moment of distress and loneliness, a moment when I no longer had anything of myself, had entered, and who had restored me to myself, for it was both me and more than me (the container which is more than the content, and had brought it to me). I had just glimpsed, in my memory, bent over my fatigue, the tender, concerned, disappointed face of my grandmother, such as she had been on that first evening of our arrival; the face of my grandmother, not that of the one whom I had been surprised and self-reproachful at having missed so little, who had nothing of her but her name, but of my true grandmother, the living reality of whom, for the first time since the Champs-Élysées, where she had suffered her stroke, I had rediscovered in a complete and involuntary memory. This reality does not exist for us until such time as it has been re-created in our minds (otherwise, the men who have been involved in some titanic battle would all be great epic poets); thus, in a wild desire to hurl myself into her arms, it was only at this instant—more than a year after her funeral, on account of the anachronism which so often prevents the calendar of facts from coinciding with that of our feelings—that I had just learned she was dead. I had spoken of her often since that time and thought of her also, but beneath the words and thoughts of an ungrateful, selfish, and cruel young man there had never been anything that might resemble my grandmother, for, in my frivolity, my love of pleasure, and accustomed as I was to seeing her as an invalid, I contained within me the memory of what she had been only in a virtual state. At whatever moment we may consider it, our total soul has an almost fictitious value only, for all its great wealth of assets, for now some, and now others of these are unavailable, whether the riches concerned be actual, or be those of the imagination, and in my own case, for example, fully as much the riches contained in the ancient name of Guermantes, as those, so very much more solemn, of the true memory of my grandmother. For to the disturbances of memory are linked the intermittences of the heart. It is no doubt the existence of our body, similar for us to a vase in which our spirituality is enclosed, that induces us to suppose that all our inner goods, our past joys, all our sorrows, are perpetually in our possession. Perhaps this is as inaccurate as to believe that they escape or return. At all events, if they do remain inside us, it is for most of the time in an unknown domain where they are of no service to us, and where even the most ordinary of them are repressed by memories of a different order, which exclude all simultaneity with them in our consciousness. But if the framework of sensations in which they are preserved be recaptured, they have in their turn the same capacity to expel all that is incompatible with them, to install in us, on its own, the self that experienced them. Now, since the self that I had suddenly rebecome had not existed since that far-off evening when my grandmother had undressed me on my arrival in Balbec, it was, quite naturally, not after the day we were living, of which that self knew nothing, but—as if there were, in time, different and parallel series—without any break in continuity, immediately after that first evening in the past, that I adhered to the moment when my grandmother had leaned toward me. The self that I was then and which had vanished all that time ago, was once again so close to me that I seemed to hear still the words that had come immediately before, yet which were no more than a dream, just as a man not properly awake thinks he can perceive close beside him the sounds of his receding dream. I was nothing more than the being who had sought refuge in his grandmother's arms, to erase the traces of her sorrows by giving her kisses, the being I would have had as great difficulty in imagining to myself, when I was one or another of those who had been succeeding one another inside me for some time past, as the efforts it would now have required, sterile in any case, to re-experience the desires and joys of one of those beings that, for a time at least, I no longer was. I recalled how, an hour before the moment when my grandmother had thus leaned over, in her dressing gown, toward my boots, wandering in the stiflingly hot street, in front of the *pâtissier,* I had thought I could never, such was the need I had to embrace her, wait for the hour I had still to spend without her. And now that this same need was reborn, I knew that I could wait for hour upon hour, that never again would she be beside me, I had made the discovery only now because I had just, on being aware of her for the first time, alive, real, swelling my heart to bursting, on meeting her again, that is, realized that I had lost her forever. Lost forever; I could not understand, and I applied myself to suffering the pain of this contradiction: on the one hand, an existence, a tenderness, surviving in me such as I had known them, that is to say created for me, a love in which everything so much found in me its complement, its object, its constant direction, that the genius of great men, all the geniuses who may have existed since the world began, would have counted for less with my grandmother than a single one of my faults; and, on the other hand, as soon as I had relived, as though present, that felicity, to feel it traversed by the certainty, springing up like a repeated physical pain, of a nothingness that had erased my image of that tenderness, which had destroyed that existence, abolished retrospectively our mutual predestination, made of my grandmother, at the moment when I had found her again as if in a mirror, a mere stranger whom chance had led to spend a few years with me, as it might have been with anyone at all, but for whom, before and after, I was nothing, would be nothing.

Instead of the pleasures I had been enjoying for some time past, the only pleasure it would have been possible for me to enjoy at this moment would have been, by retouching the past, to lessen the sorrows my grandmother had once experienced. I did not remember her only in that dressing gown, a garment appropriate, to the extent of becoming almost symbolic of them, to the pains, unhealthy no doubt yet comforting also, she took on my behalf; little by little, I now remembered all the opportunities I had seized, by letting her see my sufferings, by, if need be, exaggerating them, of causing her a grief that I then imagined being expunged by my kisses, as if my affection were as capable as was my happiness of making hers; and, what was worse, I, who could conceive of no other happiness now than of being able to find it once again extended in my memory across the planes of that face, molded and bowed by tenderness, I had once shown a senseless fury in trying to extirpate from it even the smallest pleasures, as on the day when Saint-Loup had taken my grandmother's photograph and, finding it hard to conceal from her the almost ridiculously childish coquettishness she was putting into posing, with her broad-brimmed hat, in a fetching half-light, I had allowed myself to murmur a few impatient and hurtful words, which, I had sensed from the way her face contracted, had struck home, had wounded her; it was I whom they were lacerating, now that the consolation of a thousand kisses was forever impossible.

But never again would I be able to erase that contraction from her face, or that suffering from her heart, or, rather, from my own; for, since the dead exist only in us, it is ourselves that we strike unrelentingly when we persist in remembering the blows we have dealt them. I clung to these sorrows, however cruel they might be, with all my strength, for I felt that they were the effect of my memory of my grandmother, the proof that this memory which I had was indeed present in me. I felt that I truly remembered her only through sorrow, and would have wished the nails to be driven yet more firmly home that had riveted her memory inside me. I had not sought to make the suffering any easier, to embellish it, to pretend that my grandmother was only absent and momentarily invisible, by addressing words and entreaties to her photograph (the one that Saint-Loup had taken and which I had with me), as though to a being separated from us but who, having remained an individual, knows us and remains joined to us by an indissoluble harmony. I never did this, for I was anxious not to suffer only, but to respect the originality of my suffering, such as I had suddenly endured it against my will, and I wanted to continue to endure it, in accordance with its own laws, each time this strange contradiction between survival and oblivion, intersecting within me, returned. I knew not, certainly, whether I might one day isolate some element of truth in this painful and at present incomprehensible impression, but that, if I were ever able to extract that element of truth, it could only be from this same impression, so particular, so spontaneous, which had been neither traced by my intellect nor inflected or attenuated by my pusillanimity, but which death itself, the abrupt revelation of death, had hollowed out in me, like a thunderbolt, in accordance with some inhuman, supernatural diagram, like a double and mysterious furrow. (As for the forgetfulness of my grandmother in which I had been living up until now, I could not even think of attaching myself to that so as to draw some truth from it; for in itself it was nothing more than a negation, an enfeeblement of the mind, incapable of re-creating an actual moment of life and obliged to substitute for it conventional and indifferent mental images.) Perhaps, however, now that the instinct for self-preservation, or the intellect's ingenuity in shielding us against sorrow, was beginning to build on the still-smoking ruins, to lay the first foundations of its useful but ill-starred building work, I had been finding too much comfort in recalling one or another of the beloved being's judgments, in recalling them as if she were still able to pass them, as if she existed, as if I continued to exist for her. But as soon as I came to fall asleep, at that more truthful hour when my eyes were closed to the things without, the world of sleep (on the threshold of which my intellect and my will, momentarily paralyzed, could no longer contend with the cruelty of my genuine impressions) reflected, refracted the painful synthesis of survival and nothingness, in the organic depths, now become translucent, of the mysteriously illuminated viscera. World of sleep, where our inner knowledge, held in subjection by the disturbances in our organs, quickens the rhythm of our heart or of our breathing, for the same dosage of alarm, of sadness, of remorse is a hundred times more potent when thus injected into our veins; as soon as, in order to travel along the arteries of the subterranean city, we have embarked on the dark waves of our own blood, as if on the sixfold meanders of some internal Lethe,[123] tall, solemn forms appear to us, accost us, and then go from us, leaving us in tears. I searched in vain for that of my grandmother the moment I touched land beneath the gloomy porticos; yet I knew she existed still, but with a diminished life, as pale as that of memory; the darkness was increasing, and the wind; my father did not come, who was to conduct me to her. Suddenly my breath failed, I felt my heart as if hardened, I had just remembered that for long weeks I had forgotten to write to my grandmother. What must she be thinking of me? "Dear God," I said to myself, "how unhappy she must be in that small room that they've rented for her, as small as for some former maidservant, where she's all alone with the nurse they've sent in to look after her, and where she can't stir, for she's still partly paralyzed and hasn't once wanted to get up! She must think I've forgotten her since she died, how alone and abandoned she must feel! Oh! I must run and see her this very minute, I can't wait for my father to come, but where is it? How can I have forgotten the address? If only she still recognizes me! How can I have forgotten her all these months?" It's dark, I won't find her, the wind is stopping me from advancing; but here is my father walking in front of me; I cry out to him: "Where's Grandmother? Tell me the address. Is she all right? Is it quite certain she's got all she needs?" "No, no," my father says to me, "you can rest assured. Her nurse is an orderly person. We send a very small sum from time to time so they can buy her the little she has need of. She sometimes asks what's become of you. She's even been told you were going to write a book. She seemed pleased.

She wiped away a tear." Then I thought I remembered that, shortly after she died, my grandmother had said to me, sobbing, with a humble expression, like an old servant who has been dismissed, like a stranger: "You'll allow me to see you sometimes all the same, don't let me go too many years without visiting me. Remember that you were my grandson and that grandmothers don't forget." And seeing once again the face, so submissive, so unhappy, so gentle, that she wore, I wanted to run immediately and say what I ought then to have replied to her: "But, Grandmother, you'll see me as much as you want, I have only you in the world, I shall never leave you again." How my silence must have made her sob during all these months when I haven't been to where she's in bed! What may she have said to herself? And it was sobbing that I, too, said to my father, "Quick, quick, her address, take me." But he: "The fact is . . . I don't know if you'll be able to see her. Besides, she's very weak, you know, very weak, she's not herself any more; I think you'd find it rather upsetting. And I don't recall the exact number on the avenue." "But tell me, you who know, it's not true that the dead are no longer alive. It just can't be true, despite what they say, since Grandmother still exists." My father gave a sad smile: "Oh, very little, you know, very little. I think you'd do better not to go. She lacks for nothing. They come and keep everything tidy." "But she's often alone?" "Yes, but that's better for her. It's better that she shouldn't think, that could only cause her pain. Thinking often causes people pain. Anyway, you know, she's very low. I'll leave you exact directions so that you can go there; I can't see what you'd be able to do, and I don't think the nurse would let you see her." "You know very well, though that I shall always live near her, stags, stags, Francis Jammes, fork."[124] But already I had recrossed the river with its gloomy meanders, I had come back to the surface, where the world of the living opens out; so, if I was still repeating "Francis Jammes, stags, stags," this sequence of words no longer held the limpid, logical meaning they had expressed so naturally for me only a moment before and which I could no longer recall. I could no longer understand even why the word Aias,[125] spoken to me just now by my father, had at once signified, "Take care not to catch cold," beyond any possible doubt. I had forgotten to close the shutters, and the broad daylight had no doubt woken me up. But I could not bear to look out on those waves that my grandmother had once been able to contemplate for hours on end; the new image of their indifferent beauty was at once completed by the idea that she could not see them; I would have liked to block my ears against their sound, for now the luminous plenitude of the beach was hollowing out a void in my heart; everything seemed to be saying to me, like the paths and the lawns in the public gardens where I had once lost her, when I was very young, "We haven't seen her," and beneath the roundness of the pale, heavenly sky I felt oppressed, as if beneath an immense blue bell jar, shutting off a horizon where my grandmother was not. So as no longer to see, I turned toward the wall, but, alas, against me was the partition that had served of old between us as a morning messenger, that partition which, docile as a violin in rendering all the nuances of a feeling, spoke so exactly to my grandmother of my fear both of waking her up, or, if she was already awake, of not being heard by her, and of her not daring to move, then at once, like a second instrument taking it up, announcing her coming and exhorting me to stay calm. I no more dared to approach that partition than a piano on which my grandmother had been playing and that was vibrating still from her touch. I knew that now I could knock, more loudly even, that nothing could again wake her, that I would not hear any response, that my grandmother would never again come. And I asked nothing more of God, if there is a paradise, than to be able to give there the three little taps on that partition that my grandmother would recognize anywhere, and to which she would respond with those other taps that meant, "Don't fret yourself, little mouse, I realize you're impatient, but I'm just coming," and that he should let me remain with her for all eternity, which would not be too long for the two of us.

The manager came to ask me whether I did not want to go down. Just in case, he had taken care of my "placement" in the dining room. Not having seen me, he had been afraid that I might have had a recurrence of my breathless attacks from the old days. He hoped that it would be only some minor "throat troubles" and assured me that he had heard they could be eased with the aid of what he called "calyptus."

He handed me a brief note from Albertine. She had not been due to come to Balbec this year but, having changed her plans, had been for the last three days, not in Balbec itself, but ten minutes away by tram, at a neighboring resort. Afraid that I might be tired from the journey, she had stayed away on the first evening, but was now sending to know when I might be able to see her. I inquired whether she had come in person, not so as to see her, but so as to arrange not to see her. "She did indeed," the manager replied. "But she'd like it to be as soon as possible, unless you have absolutely necessitous reasons. You can see," he concluded, "that, when all's done and said, everyone here wants you." I, however, did not want to see anyone.

Yet, the day before, when I arrived, I had felt captured once more by the indolent charm of life in a seaside resort. The same silent "lift," out of respect this time, not disdain, and flushed with pleasure, had set the lift in motion. And as I rose along the ascending column, I traversed once more what had once been for me the mystery of an unfamiliar hotel, where, when you arrive, a tourist without either protection or prestige, every habitué returning to his room, every young girl going down to dinner, every maid passing down the strangely configured corridors, and the girl come from America with her chaperone going down to dinner, give you a look in which you can read nothing of what you would have wished for. This time, on the contrary, I had experienced the too restful pleasure of making the ascent of a hotel known to me, where I felt at home, where I had once more accomplished that operation having always to be begun afresh, longer and more difficult than the turning inside-out of an eyelid, which consists in imposing on objects the soul that is familiar to us in place of their own soul, which had alarmed us. Would I now, I had said to myself, unsuspecting of the abrupt change that lay in wait for my soul, have to go into yet other hotels, where I would dine for the first time, where habit would not yet have slain, on each floor, before each door, the terrifying dragon that had seemed to stand watch over an enchanted existence, where I would have to go up to those unknown women that grand hotels, casinos, and beach resorts serve merely to bring together and cause to live in common, like so many vast polyparies?

I had derived pleasure even from the fact that the tiresome First President should have been in such a hurry to call on me; I had seen, the first day, waves, the azure mountain ranges of the sea, its glaciers and its waterfalls, its elevation and its careless majesty—merely by smelling, for the first time in so long, as I washed my hands, the distinctive odor of the too highly scented Grand-Hôtel soap—which, seeming to belong simultaneously to the present moment and to my past stay, floated between them like the real charm of a particular way of life in which you return home only to change your tie. The sheets on the bed, too fine, too light, too vast, impossible to tuck in, to hold in place, and which remained puffed up around the blankets in shifting scrolls, would once have saddened me. On the unwieldy, billowing roundness of their sails, they merely cradled the glorious, hope-filled sunshine of early morning. But the sun did not have time to appear. During that same night, the dreadful, divine presence had been resurrected. I begged the manager to go, to ask that no one come in. I told him I would be staying in bed and rejected his offer of sending to the pharmacist's for his excellent preparation. He was overjoyed by my refusal, for he was afraid that the guests might be incommoded by the smell of "calyptus." Which earned me this compliment, "You're in the swim"—he meant to say "in the right"—and this piece of advice: "Mind you don't dirty yourself on the door, for, relating to the locks, I've had it 'coasted' with oil; if one of the staff were to dare knock at your room, he'd get a 'threshing.' And that can be taken as read, for I don't like 'recitations'"—which evidently meant, "I don't like having to recite things twice." "Only, for a pick-me-up, wouldn't you like a drop of the old wine I've got a bust of downstairs?" No doubt for "butt." "I won't bring it to you on a silver dish like the head of Jonathan,[126] and I must warn you it's not Château-Lafite, but it's more or less equivocal"—for "equivalent." "And because it's light, they could fry you a small sole." I refused everything, but was surprised to hear the name of the fish (*sole*) pronounced like the word for a willow tree (*saule*), by a man who must have ordered so many of them in his lifetime.

Despite the manager's promises, a little later on I was brought the turned-down visiting card of the Marquise de Cambremer. Having come to see me, the old lady had sent to ask whether I was there, and when she learned that my arrival dated only from the previous day, and that I was indisposed, she had not insisted, but (doubtless not without stopping off at the pharmacist's or the haberdasher's, where the footman had jumped from his seat to go in and pay some account or lay in supplies) the Marquise had left again for Féterne, in her ancient eight-spring calash and pair. Quite often, indeed, its rumble was to be heard, and its pomp admired, in the streets of Balbec and of several other small localities along the coast, situated between Balbec and Féterne. Not that these stops at suppliers' were the object of these outings. This, on the contrary, would be a tea party, or *garden party,* at the house of some squireen or bourgeois quite unworthy of the Marquise. But the latter, although by her birth and fortune she lorded it over the minor nobility of the district, was so afraid, in her perfect kindness and simplicity, of letting someone down who had invited her that she went to the most insignificant social gatherings in the neighborhood. Admittedly, rather than travel such a long way to come and hear, in the heat of some stifling small drawing room, a soprano generally devoid of talent and to whom, in her capacity as great lady of the district and a musician of repute, she would then have to offer her exaggerated congratulations, Mme de Cambremer would have preferred to go for a drive or to remain in her wonderful gardens at Féterne, at the foot of which the drowsy waves of a small bay come to expire amid the flowers. But she knew that her probable coming had been announced by the host, whether he was a nobleman or a freeman of Maineville-la-Teinturière or Chattoncourt-l'Orgueilleux. Now, if Mme de Cambremer had left home that day without putting in an appearance at the festivity, one or another of the guests coming from one of the small resorts along the sea could have heard and seen the Marquise's calash, which would have robbed her of the excuse of having been unable to leave Féterne. On the other hand, for all that these hosts had often seen Mme de Cambremer going to concerts given in the houses of people where they considered it was not her place to be, the slight lowering that, as they saw it, this fact inflicted on the standing of the too good-natured Marquise vanished as soon as it was they who were entertaining, and it was feverishly that they asked themselves whether they would or would not be getting her at their small tea party. What relief, for anxieties felt for several days past, if, after the first piece sung by the hosts' daughter or by some amateur vacationing locally, a guest announced (an infallible sign that the Marquise would be coming to the matinée) that they had seen the horses of the famous calash halted in front of the watchmaker or the druggist! Then Mme de Cambremer (who indeed would not be long in making her entrance, followed by her daughter-in-law and by guests she currently had residing with her, and whom she had asked permission, granted with what delight, to bring with her) would recover all her luster in the eyes of the hosts, for whom the reward of her hoped-for coming had perhaps been the determining but unacknowledged reason for the decision they had made a month earlier to inflict on themselves the bother and expense of giving a matinée. Seeing the Marquise present at their tea party, they no longer remembered her willingness to attend those of ill-qualified neighbors, but the antiquity of her family, the luxury of her château, and the rudeness of her daughter-in-law, née Legrandin, who, by her arrogance, threw into relief the somewhat mawkish good nature of the mother-in-law. They already fancied they could read, on the society page of *Le Gaulois*, the paragraph that they would themselves concoct *en famille*, behind locked doors, about "the little corner of Brittany where they know how to enjoy themselves, the ultra-select matinée from which no one tore themselves away without having made their hosts promise to repeat it without delay." Each day they would await the newspaper, concerned at not yet having seen any mention of their matinée, and fearing that they had got Mme de Cambremer for their guests alone and not for the multitude of readers. At last the blessed day arrived: "The season is exceptionally brilliant this year in Balbec. The fashion is for small afternoon concerts," etc. Lord be praised, Mme de Cambremer's name had been spelled correctly and "cited at random," but in first place. All that remained was to appear annoyed by this indiscretion on the part of the newspapers, which might lead to a falling-out with the people one had been unable to invite, and to ask hypocritically, in front of Mme de Cambremer, who could have been so perfidious as to send in this item of gossip, of which the Marquise, ever the benevolent *grande dame*, said, "I can understand its annoying you, but for my own part I'm only too happy for it to be known that I came to see you."

On the card I was handed, Mme de Cambremer had scribbled that she was giving a matinée in two days' time. And certainly, only two days before, however tired of socializing I might have been, it would have been a real pleasure to sample it transplanted into those gardens where, thanks to Féterne's exposure, fig trees, palms, and rosebushes grew out in the open, all the way down to a sea often of a Mediterranean calm and blue, across which the owners' small yacht would go, before the party began, to fetch the more important guests from the resorts on the far side of the bay, and serve, its awnings spread against the sun, once everyone had arrived, as a dining room for the tea, and set off again in the evening to take back those whom it had brought. A charming luxury, but so costly that it was partly in order to offset the expense it entailed that Mme de Cambremer had sought to increase her income in various ways, notably by renting, for the first time, one of her properties, very different from Féterne: La Raspelière. Yes, two days ago, what a change such a matinée, populated by unfamiliar minor nobility, in a new setting, would have made from the "high life" of Paris! But now pleasures no longer had any meaning for me. I wrote therefore to Mme de Cambremer to make my excuses, just as an hour earlier I had sent Albertine away: sorrow had abolished the possibility of desire in me as completely as a high fever takes away the appetite. My mother was to arrive the following day. It seemed to me that I was less unworthy of living beside her, that I would understand her better, now that a whole alien and degrading existence had made way for the resurgence of heartrending memories that had garlanded and ennobled my soul, like hers, with their crown of thorns. Or so I believed; in reality, there is every difference between genuine grief like that of Mamma—which literally takes away your life for long periods, sometimes forever, the moment you have lost the person that you love—and that other grief, ephemeral in spite of everything, as mine was to be, which goes away quickly just as it is late in coming, which we experience only long after the event because in order to feel it we needed to "understand" that event; grief such as so many people experience and from which the grief that was now torturing me differed only in its modality, of involuntary memory.

As for a grief as deep as that of my mother, I was to know that one day, as will be seen in due course in this narrative, but it was not now or thus that I pictured it to myself. Nevertheless, just as a narrator, who ought to know his lines and have taken up his place long before, but has arrived only at the last second and, having read what he is to say only once, is able to disguise the fact skillfully enough when the time comes to respond to his cue, so that no one is made aware of his late arrival, my newfound grief enabled me, when my mother arrived, to talk to her as if it had always been the same. She merely thought that the sight of the places where I had been with my grandmother (though this was not in fact it) had reawoken it. Then, for the first time, and because I felt a sorrow that was nothing in comparison with her own, but which had opened my eyes, I realized with terror what she might be suffering. I understood for the first time that the fixed, tearless gaze (which meant that Françoise felt little pity for her) that she had had since my grandmother's death had been dwelling on this incomprehensible contradiction between memory and nothingness. Moreover, though she was still in her black veils, but more dressed up in this new setting, I was the more struck by the transformation that had taken place in her. It is not enough to say that she had lost all her gaiety; having melted and become congealed into a sort of imploring image, she seemed to be afraid, by too abrupt a movement, too loud a tone of voice, of giving offense to the sorrowful presence that never left her. But above all, the moment I saw her enter in her crêpe coat, I realized—what had eluded me in Paris—that it was no longer my mother I saw in front of me, but my grandmother. Just as, in royal or ducal families, when the head of the family dies the son takes his title, and, from having been the Duc d'Orléans, Prince de Tarente, or Prince des Laumes, becomes King of France, Duc de La Trémoïlle, or Duc de Guermantes,[127] so, frequently, by an accession of a different order, and of a more profound origin, the dead man seizes hold of the living one, who becomes his successor in his own likeness, the perpetuator of his interrupted life. Perhaps all that the great grief does which, in a daughter such as Mamma was, ensues on the death of her mother is to break open the chrysalis a little sooner, to hasten the metamorphosis and the appearance of a being that we bear within us, and which, but for this crisis, which misses out the intermediate stages and covers long periods at a single bound, would only have supervened more slowly. Perhaps, in the regret for the one who is no more, there is a sort of suggestion that in the end produces on our own features similarities that were already latent in us, and that above all arrests our more particularly individual activities (in my mother's case, her common sense, and the mocking high spirits she had got from her father), which, for as long as the person greatly loved was alive, we were not afraid to exercise, be it at their expense, and which counterbalanced the character that we had got exclusively from them. Once she is dead, we would feel qualms about being other; we now admire only what she was, what we already were, but mixed in with something else, and what henceforth we shall be alone. It is in this sense (and not in that very vague, very false sense in which it is generally understood) that we can say that death is not without its use, that the dead person continues to exercise an influence on us. They influence us more even than the living, because, the true reality being set free only by the mind, being the object of a mental process, we truly know only what we are obliged to re-create by thought, what everyday life keeps hidden from us. . . . Finally, in this cult of regret for our dead, we make idols of that which they loved. Not only could my mother not be parted from my grandmother's bag, more precious for her now than if it had been of sapphires and diamonds, from her muff, from all the garments that brought out still more strongly how alike the two of them were in appearance, but even from the volumes of Mme de Sévigné[128] that my grandmother was never without, copies that my mother would not have exchanged for the manuscript of the *Letters* itself. She had teased my grandmother in the old days, who never once wrote to her without quoting a sentence from Mme de Sévigné or Mme de Beausergent.[129] In each of the three letters I received from Mamma before her arrival in Balbec, she quoted Mme de Sévigné at me, as if these three letters had been, not addressed by her to me, but addressed by my grandmother to her. She wanted to go down onto the esplanade to see the beach that my grandmother spoke of every day when writing to her. Holding her mother's *en-tout-cas*[130] in her hand, I saw her from the window, advancing all in black, with timid, pious steps, across the sand that cherished feet had trodden before her, and she seemed to be going in search of a dead body that the waves were to bring back to her. So as not to let her dine alone, I had to go downstairs with her. The First President and the widow of the *bâtonnier* had themselves introduced to her. And she was so sensitive to everything connected with my grandmother that she was infinitely touched, and preserved ever afterward the memory and her gratitude for what the First President said to her, just as she felt hurt and indignant at the fact that, on the other hand, the *bâtonnier*'s wife spoke not one word in remembrance of the dead woman. In point of fact, the First President felt no more concern for her than did the *bâtonnier*'s wife. The emotional words of the one and the silence of the other were only, although my mother set so great a distance between them, different ways of expressing the indifference that the dead inspire in us. But I believe that my mother took comfort above all from the words into which, against my will, I allowed a little of my pain to pass. It could but make Mamma happy (despite all the affection she had for me), like everything that ensured my grandmother's survival in our hearts. On each of the days following, my mother went down to sit on the beach, to do exactly as her mother had done, and read her two favorite books, the *Memoirs* of Mme de Beausergent and the *Letters* of Mme de Sévigné. She, or any of us, could not bear the last-named being referred to as the "witty Marquise," any more than La Fontaine as "*le Bonhomme*" or "good old La Fontaine."[131] But when in the letters she read the words "my daughter," she thought she heard her mother speaking to her.

She had the ill-luck on one of these pilgrimages when she did not want to be disturbed, to meet on the beach a lady from Combray, followed by her daughters. I believe her name was Mme Poussin. But among ourselves we only ever used to call her "We'll see how you like that," for it was by this phrase, constantly repeated, that she warned her daughters of the evils they were storing up for themselves, saying to the one who was rubbing her eyes, for example, "Once you've got a nice ophthalmia, we'll see how you like that." She addressed long, tearful greetings to my mother from a distance, not as a sign of condolence, but because such had been her upbringing. Even had we not lost my grandmother and had reason only to be happy, she would have done the same. Living a somewhat withdrawn life in Combray, in an immense garden, she considered that nothing was ever soft enough, and subjected the words and even the names of the French language to a softening process. She considered it too harsh to call the item of silver-ware that poured out her syrups a *cuiller* and would say in consequence, *cueiller;*[132] she would have been afraid of giving offense to the gentle songster of *Télémaque* by calling him, crudely, Fénélon[133]—as I did my-self, with good reason, having for my dearest friend the best, most intel-ligent, and bravest of human beings, unforgettable for all who knew him, Bertrand de Fénelon—and only ever said "Fénélon," considering that the acute accent added a certain mellowness. The not-so-soft son-in-law of this Mme Poussin, whose name I have forgotten, when he was a notary in Combray, ran off with the cashbox and caused my uncle, notably, to lose quite a considerable sum. But most of the people of Combray were so well disposed toward the other members of the family that no coldness resulted, and all they did was to feel sorry for Mme Poussin. She did not entertain, but every time you passed in front of her railings you stopped to admire the admirable shade under the trees, without being able to make out anything more. She hardly trou-bled us in Balbec, where I met her only once, at a moment when she was saying to her daughter, busy gnawing at her fingernails, "When you've got a nice whitlow, we'll see how you like that."

While Mamma was reading on the beach, I remained in my room on my own. I recalled the last days of my grandmother's life and every-thing connected with them, the staircase door that had been kept open when we went out for her last walk. In contrast to all of this, the rest of the world seemed scarcely real, and my suffering poisoned it in its en-tirety. Finally, my mother demanded that I go out. But at each step, some forgotten aspect of the casino, of the street along which, as I waited for her that first evening, I had gone as far as the statue of Duguay-Trouin,[134] prevented me, like a wind against which you cannot battle, from going any farther; I looked down so as not to see. And, having recovered some of my strength, I went back toward the hotel, toward the hotel where I knew it was henceforth impossible that, how-ever long I might wait, I would find my grandmother again, my grand-mother, whom I had once found, on the first evening of our arrival. Since this was the first time I had gone out, many of the servants that I had not yet seen looked at me curiously. On the actual doorstep of the hotel, a young *chasseur* took off his cap to salute me and promptly put it back on again. I imagined that Aimé had, to use his own expression, "passed on the order" that I was to be shown respect. But I saw in that same instant that, for someone else who was coming back in, he removed it again. The truth was that all this young man knew in life was how to take off and replace his cap, and this he did to perfection. Having realized that he was incapable of anything else but excelled at this, he performed it the greatest number of times he could each day, which earned for him a discreet but general sympathy on the part of the clientele, great sympathy, too, on the part of the porter, to whom fell the task of engaging the *chasseurs,* and who, until this *rara avis,* had been unable to find one who did not get himself dismissed within the week, to the great astonishment of Aimé, who used to say, "Yet in that trade little more's asked of them than to be polite, that shouldn't be so hard." The manager insisted also that they should look "present," as he put it, meaning that they should remain there, or, rather, having failed to retain the word "presentable." The appearance of the lawn that stretched behind the hotel had been modified by the creation of a few flower beds and the removal, not only of an exotic shrub, but of the *chasseur* who, the first year, had adorned the entrance externally with the supple stem of his body and the curious color of his hair. He had followed a Polish countess who had taken him on as a secretary, imitating in this his two elder brothers and his typist sister, snatched from the hotel by personalities of various countries and gender who had been smitten by their charms. The youngest alone remained, whom no one wanted because he had a squint. He was very happy when the Polish countess and the patrons of the other two came to spend some time at the hotel in Balbec. For, although he envied his brothers, he loved them and was thus able for a few weeks to cultivate family feelings. Was the abbess of Fontevrault not in the habit, for which she used to abandon her nuns, of going to share in the hospitality offered by Louis XIV to the other Mortemart, his mistress, Mme de Montespan?[135] As for him, this was the first year he had been in Balbec; he did not yet know me, but, having heard his longer-serving fellows follow the word "Monsieur" when they were speaking to me with my name, he imitated them from the very first occasion with an air of satisfaction, either at displaying his training in relation to a personality he adjudged to be well known, or

else at conforming to a usage of which he had been unaware five minutes previously but from which it seemed to him indispensable not to
depart. I understood very well the attraction this grand hotel might
have for certain people. It was arranged like a theater, and a numerous
cast of extras gave life to it all the way up into the flies. Although the
guest was only a sort of spectator, he was constantly involved in the
spectacle, not even as in those theaters where the actors perform one
scene in the auditorium, but as if the spectator's own life were unfold-
ing amid the sumptuousness of a stage set. The tennis player might re-
enter in a white flannel jacket, but the porter would have put on a blue
dress-coat with silver braid to hand him his letters. If this tennis player
did not want to walk up, he was no less involved with the actors for
having at his side, to take the lift up, the equally richly costumed "lift."
The upstairs corridors secreted an escape of chambermaids and guests'
maids, as lovely against the sea as the frieze of the Panathenaea,[136] all
the way to the little bedrooms to which the connoisseurs of ancillary female beauty would come by knowing detours. Downstairs, it was the
masculine element that dominated and turned this hotel, thanks to the
extreme and indolent youthfulness of its servants, into a sort of Judeo-
Christian tragedy that had become flesh and was in continuous performance. Thus I could not help repeating to myself, on seeing them, not,
for sure, the lines of Racine that had come into my head at the
Princesse de Guermantes's as M. de Vaugoubert was watching the young
secretaries from the embassy greeting M. de Charlus, but some other
lines from Racine, no longer from *Esther* this time, but from *Athalie*: for,
starting in the hallway, what in the seventeenth century was known as
the portico, there stood *"un peuple florissant"*[137] of young *chasseurs*, especially at teatime, like the young Israelites of Racine's choruses. But I do
not believe a single one of them would have been able to supply even
the vague answer that Joas finds for Athalie when the latter asks the
child prince, "What, then, is your occupation?,"[138] for they had none.
At the very most, had any one of their number been asked, like the old
queen, "But this whole people enclosed within this place / With what
does it occupy itself?,"[139] he might have been able to say, " 'I see the
stately order of these ceremonies,'[140] and have my part in them." From
time to time, one of these young extras would move toward some more

important character; then the young beauty would rejoin the chorus, and, unless it was a moment of contemplative respite, all would interweave in their futile, respectful, decorative, everyday maneuvers. For, except on their day off, "raised far from the world,"[141] and never going beyond the parvis, they led the same ecclesiastical existence as the Levites in *Athalie,* and, faced by this "young and faithful troupe,"[142] playing at the foot of stairs covered in magnificent carpets, I was able to wonder whether I was making my way into the Grand-Hôtel in Balbec or the Temple of Solomon.

I went directly up to my room. My thoughts had become habitually fixed on the last days of my grandmother's illness, on the sufferings that I was reliving, while increasing them by the element, even harder to endure than the actual suffering of others, added to them by the cruelty of our compassion; when we believe we are merely re-creating the pain of a beloved being, our compassion exaggerates it; yet perhaps it is the compassion that is right, rather than the awareness that those who are suffering have of their pain, from whom the sadness of their life is hidden, whereas compassion sees it and despairs. Even so, my compassion would have gained fresh impetus and exceeded my grandmother's sufferings had I known then what I was long unaware of: that, on the eve of her death, in a conscious moment, and after making sure that I was not there, she had taken Mamma's hand and, after pressing her fevered lips to it, had said to her, "Goodbye, daughter; goodbye forever." And it was perhaps this memory also that my mother never again ceased to gaze at so fixedly. Then the sweet memories came back to me. She was my grandmother and I was her grandson. The expressions of her face seemed written in a language that was for me alone; she was everything in my life; others existed only in relation to her, to the judgment she would pass on them; but, no, our relations were too fleeting not to have been accidental. She no longer knows me, I shall never see her again. We had not been created solely for each other, she was a stranger. I was busy looking at Saint-Loup's photograph of that stranger. Mamma, who had met Albertine, had insisted that I see her because of the kind things she had said to her about Grandmother and about myself. I had arranged to meet her therefore. I warned the manager, so that he would make her wait in the lounge. He told me he had known her from a long

way back, she and her friends, well before they had attained "the age of
purity," but that he resented things they had said about the hotel.
"They can't be so very 'illustrated' to talk like that. Unless they've been
slandered." I understood easily enough that he had said "purity" for
"puberty." While waiting for it to be time to go and find Albertine, I
kept my eyes fixed, as if on a drawing that in the end you are unable to
see by dint of having stared at it, on the photograph Saint-Loup had
taken, when all of a sudden I again thought, "It's Grandmother, I am
her grandson," just as an amnesiac rediscovers his name, or as an invalid changes personality. Françoise entered, to tell me that Albertine
was there, and, on seeing the photograph: "Poor Madame, it's her all
over, right down to the beauty spot on her cheek; the day the Marquis
photographed her, she'd been very ill, she'd had two bad turns. 'Above
all, Françoise,' she says to me, 'my grandson mustn't know.' And she
hid it so well, she was always cheerful in company. Alone, mark you, I
thought she seemed at times as if her spirits were a bit monotonous.
But it soon passed. And then she'd say to me right out: 'If anything
were ever to happen to me, he'd need to have a portrait of me. I've
never had a single one done.' Then she sent me to say to M. le Marquis,
advising him not to tell Monsieur it was her who'd asked him, whether
he couldn't take her photograph. But when I came back to tell her yes,
she wouldn't any more, because she thought she looked so ill. 'It'd be
even worse,' she says to me, 'than no photograph at all.' But as she
wasn't stupid, she finally arranged things very well by putting on a big
turned-down hat, so it no longer showed when she wasn't in the full
daylight. She was very pleased with her photograph, because at that moment she didn't think she'd be returning from Balbec. It was no good
my saying, 'You mustn't talk that way, madame, I don't like hearing
Madame talking that way,' she'd got it into her head. And, good Lord,
there were several days when she wasn't able to eat. That's why she
urged Monsieur to go and dine a long way off with M. le Marquis.
Then, instead of going to the table, she pretended to read, and as soon
as the Marquis's carriage had gone, she went up to bed. Some days she
wanted to warn Madame to come so she'd see her again. And then she
was afraid it would surprise her, as she hadn't said anything to her. 'It's
better she stays with her husband, you know, Françoise.'" Françoise,

her eyes on me, asked all of a sudden if I felt "indisposed." I told her
no; and she: "And then you keep me tied up here talking to you. Perhaps your visit's arrived already. I must go down. She's not a person for
here. And, always on the move as she is, she may have left again. She
doesn't like to wait. Oh, now, Mlle Albertine, she's quite a one."
"You're wrong, Françoise, she's quite respectable, too respectable for
here. But go and warn her I won't be able to see her today."

What pitying declamations I should have aroused in Françoise had
she seen me crying! I carefully hid it from her. Otherwise I would have
had her sympathy. But I gave her mine. We do not put ourselves sufficiently often into the hearts of these poor servants who cannot see us
cry, as if crying were harmful to us; or perhaps harmful to them,
Françoise having said to me when I was small, "Don't cry like that, I
don't like seeing you cry like that." We do not like high-flown phrases
or attestations, and we are wrong, we thereby close our hearts to the
pathos of the countryside, to the legend that the poor serving-woman,
having been dismissed, perhaps unjustly, for stealing, white-faced, become suddenly humbler as if to be accused were a crime, unfolds in in-
voking her father's honesty, her mother's principles, her grandmother's
good advice. Admittedly, these same servants who cannot endure our
tears will not hesitate to make us catch pneumonia because the housemaid downstairs likes drafts and it would not be polite to prevent them.
For the very ones who are right, like Françoise, have also to be wrong,
so that Justice becomes an impossibility. Even the humble pleasures of
women servants provoke either a refusal or the mockery of their employers. For it is always some trifle, foolishly sentimental and unhygienic. Thus they may say, "What, it's the one thing I ask for all year,
and I'm not granted it." Yet the employers would grant far more were
it not stupid or dangerous for them—or for themselves. True, there is
no withstanding the humility of the poor housemaid, trembling, ready
to confess to what she has not committed, saying, "I'll go this evening
if I have to." But we must be able also not to remain insensitive, for
all the solemn, threatening banality of the things she says, to her maternal heritage and the dignity of the "close," faced by an old cook
draped in an honorable life and ancestry, clutching her broom like a
scepter, playing her role for tragedy, interspersing it with tears, drawing

herself majestically up. On the day in question, I recalled or imagined such scenes, and I linked them to our old servant, after which, despite all the harm she was able to do Albertine, I loved Françoise with an affection–intermittent, it is true, but of the strongest kind–founded on compassion.

Certainly, I suffered all that day by remaining in front of my grandmother's photograph. It tormented me. Less, however, than did the manager's evening visit. As I was talking to him of my grandmother and he was renewing his condolences, I heard him say (for he loved using the words he mispronounced): "It's like the day when Madame your grandmother had that suncopy, I wanted to warn you, because on account of the clientele, you know? It might have been bad for the establishment. It would've been better for her to leave that same evening. But she begged me not to say anything and promised me she wouldn't have any more suncopies or that she'd leave at the first one. The *chef de l'étage* reported to me, however, that she'd had another one. But, good Lord, you were old patrons we were trying to please, and given that no one had complained . . ." So my grandmother had had syncopes and had kept them from me. Perhaps at the very time when I was being least nice to her, and when she was obliged, unwell though she was, to be careful to remain good-humored so as not to annoy me, and to appear to be healthy so as not to be shown the door of the hotel. "Suncopy" is a word that, so pronounced, I would never have imagined, which would perhaps, applied to others, have struck me as absurd, but which, by the strange novelty of its sound, similar to that of an original dissonance, long remained the thing that was capable of evoking the most painful sensations in me.

The next day, I went at Mamma's request to stretch out on the sand for a while, or, rather, in the dunes, at a point where you are hidden by their folds, and where I knew that Albertine and her friends would not be able to find me. My lowered eyelids let through only one, pink, light, that of the internal walls of my eyes. Then they closed altogether. And now my grandmother appeared to me, sitting in an armchair. She was so weak she seemed less alive than other people. Yet I could hear her breathing; now and again, a sign showed that she had understood what we were saying, my father and I. But it was in vain that I embraced her; I could not succeed in arousing a look of affection in her eyes or a spot of color in her cheeks. Absent from herself, she appeared not to love me, not to know me, perhaps not to see me. I could not guess the secret of her indifference, her dejection, her silent displeasure. I drew my father aside. "You can tell all the same," I said, "there's no denying it, she's taken everything in perfectly. It's a complete illusion of life. If only we could get your cousin to come who claims that the dead aren't alive! It's more than a year now since she died, yet all in all she's still alive. But why won't she embrace me?" "Look, her poor head is falling back." "But she'd like to go to the Champs-Élysées in a little while." "That's madness!" "Really, you think it could do her any harm, that she could die any more? It's not possible she no longer loves me. It'll be no good my embracing her; will she never smile at me again?" "What do you expect, the dead are the dead."

A few days later, I found comfort in looking at the photograph Saint-Loup had taken; it did not reawaken the memory of what Françoise had told me, because that had not left me again and I had become used to it. But in contrast to the idea I had formed of how serious and painful her condition was that day, the photograph, profiting still from the stratagems my grandmother had employed, which succeeded in deceiving me even now that they had been uncovered, showed her looking so elegant, so carefree beneath the hat that partly hid her face that I saw her as less unhappy and in better health than I had imagined. And yet, her cheeks having, without her knowing it, an expression of their own, something leaden and haggard, like the look of an animal that feels itself already chosen and marked down, my grandmother wore the air of someone under a death sentence, an involuntarily somber, unconsciously tragic air that had eluded me but which stopped Mamma from ever looking at this photograph, a photograph that seemed to her a photograph not so much of her mother as of the latter's illness, of an insult delivered by that illness to Grandmother's brutally abused face.

Then, one day, I made up my mind to let Albertine know that I would receive her shortly. The fact was that, one morning of great and premature heat, the innumerable shouts of the children playing, of the bathers as they joked, of the newspaper-vendors, had described to me, in lines of fire, in a latticework of sparks, the scorching-hot beach, which the ripples were coming one by one to sprinkle with their coolness; then the symphony concert had begun, mixed in with the lapping of the water, in which the violins vibrated like a swarm of bees strayed over the sea. I had at once longed to hear Albertine's laugh once more, to see her friends again, the young girls, outlined against the waves, who had remained in my memory as the inseparable charm, the characteristic flora of Balbec; and I had resolved to send word to Albertine by Françoise, for the following week, as, gently rising, at each unfurling of a wave, the crystalline flux of the sea completely drowned the melody, whose phrases seemed separated one from the next, like those angels with their lutes who, on the roof ridge of the Italian cathedral, rise up between the crests of blue porphyry and foaming jasper. But on the day when Albertine came, the weather had deteriorated again and grown cooler, and I had no opportunity in any case of hearing her laugh; she was in a very bad mood. "Balbec's a bore this year," she said. "I shall try not to stay long. You know I've been here since Easter; that's more than a month. There's no one. If you think that's a lot of fun." Despite the recent rain and the sky that was changing from minute to minute, after going with Albertine as far as Epreville, since Albertine, to use her own term, was "ferrying" between the small resort where Mme Bontemps's villa was and Incarville, where she had been taken in *"en pension"* by Rosemonde's parents, I left to take a walk on my own toward the main road that Mme de Villeparisis's carriage had taken when we went out with my grandmother; puddles of water that the bright sunshine had not dried out had turned the ground into a real quagmire, and I thought of my grandmother, who in the old days could not go two steps without getting mud on her. But the moment I reached the road, what bedazzlement. There, where in August, with my grandmother, I had seen only the leaves and as it were the emplacement of the apple trees, they were in full flower for as far as the eye could see, unimaginably luxuriant, their feet in the mud but wearing their ballgowns, not taking any precautions so as not to spoil the most marvelous pink satin that you ever set eyes on, made to shine by the sunlight; the far-off horizon of the sea provided the apple trees with what was in effect a background from a Japanese print; if I raised my head to look at the sky between the flowers, which made its blue appear the more cloudless, almost violent, they seemed to draw aside so as to display the depth of that paradise. Beneath this azure, a slight but fresh breeze was causing the reddening bouquets to shiver slightly. Blue tits were coming to settle on the branches and were leaping about among the indulgent flowers, as if it were some lover of exoticism and of colors who had artificially created this living beauty. But it moved one almost to tears, because, however excessive these effects of a refined artifice, you felt that it was natural, that these apple trees were there, in the heart of the countryside, like peasants, on one of the highways of France. Then to the rays of sunlight there suddenly succeeded those of the rain; they striped the entire horizon, drawing their gray mesh tight around the line of apple trees. But these continued to raise aloft their pink, flowering beauty, in a wind now become icy beneath the shower of rain that was falling: it was a day in spring.

CHAPTER 2

*The mysteries of Albertine—The girls she sees in the mirror—*
*The unknown lady—The lift boy—Mme de Cambremer—The pleasures*
*of M. Nissim Bernard—First outline of Morel's strange character—*
*M. de Charlus dines at the Verdurins'.*

IN MY FEAR that the pleasure found in this solitary walk might
weaken the memory of my grandmother in me, I sought to revive it
by thinking of some great moral suffering that she had experienced;
at my summons, this suffering tried to erect itself in my heart, throwing
up its immense pillars there; but my heart was doubtless too small for
it, I did not have the strength to bear so great a sorrow, my attention
slipped away just as it was re-forming into a whole, and its arches crum-
bled before they had come together, just as waves break before they
have completed their vault.

Meanwhile, if only from my dreams when I was asleep, I might have
learned that my grief at my grandmother's death was diminishing, for
she appeared there less oppressed by the idea I had been forming of her
nonexistence. I saw her as an invalid still, but on the way to recovering;
I thought she looked better. And if she alluded to what she had suffered, I stopped her mouth with my kisses and assured her that now
she was cured forever. I would have liked to make the skeptics acknowledge that death is in truth an illness from which we recover. Only I did
not find in my grandmother the rich spontaneity of old. Her words
were only an enfeebled, docile response, a mere echo almost, of my

own words; she was no longer anything more than the reflection of my own thoughts.

Incapable though I was as yet of again experiencing physical desire, Albertine was beginning, meanwhile, to fill me with something like a desire for happiness. Certain dreams of a shared tenderness, forever floating inside us, readily unite themselves by a sort of affinity to the memory (provided this has already become a little shadowy) of a woman with whom we have experienced pleasure. This feeling recalled for me aspects of Albertine's face, softer, less cheerful, rather different from those that physical desire would have evoked in me; and since it was also less pressing than this last, I would willingly have adjourned its realization to the following winter, without seeking to see Albertine again in Balbec before her departure. Yet, even in the midst of a still-keen grief, physical desire revives. From my bed, where I was made to stay resting for long periods each day, I wished that Albertine might come back and resume our old games. Are married couples not soon to be found once again intertwined, in the very bedroom where they have lost a child, in order to give the dead little one a brother? I tried to find distraction from this desire by going to the window to look at that day's sea. As in that first year, the seas were rarely the same from one day to the next. But they scarcely resembled those of that first year, on the other hand, either because now it was spring, with its storms, or because, even if I had come on the same date as the first occasion, the different, more changeable weather might not have recommended this coast to certain indolent, vaporous, and fragile seas that I had seen on days of burning heat, sleeping on the beach, lifting their blue bosom imperceptibly with a soft palpitation, or above all because my eyes, educated by Elstir to retain precisely those elements that I had once willfully discarded, dwelt at length on what that first year they had not known how to see. The opposition that had so struck me then, between the rustic excursions I took with Mme de Villeparisis and this fluid, inaccessible, mythological vicinity of the everlasting Ocean, no longer existed for me. On certain days, the sea itself now seemed to me, on the contrary, almost rural. On the quite rare days of truly fine weather, the heat had traced on the water, as if across the countryside, a white and dusty road, behind which there protruded, like a village steeple, the delicate tip of a fishing boat. A tugboat, of which only the funnel was visible, would be smoking in the distance like a secluded factory, while, alone on the horizon, a bellying white square, painted no doubt by a sail but which appeared compact and as if made of chalk, put you in mind of the sunlit corner of some isolated building, a hospital or a school. And the clouds and the wind, on the days when they were added to the sunshine, completed, if not the error of judgment, at least the illusion of a first glance, the suggestion it awakens in the imagination. For, on stormy days, the alternation between sharply defined areas of color, like those resulting in the countryside from the contiguity of different crops, the harsh, yellow, as if muddy irregularities of the sea's surface, the embankments and slopes that hid from view a boat on which a crew of agile sailors seemed to be harvesting, all this made of the ocean something as varied, as consistent, as uneven, as populous, as civilized, as the land that was navigable, where I would before long be driving again. On one occasion, unable any longer to withstand my desire, instead of going back to bed, I got dressed and went off to find Albertine in Incarville. I would ask her to go with me as far as Douville, where I would pay Mme de Cambremer a visit at Féterne, and, at La Raspelière, a visit to Mme Verdurin. During which time, Albertine would be waiting for me on the beach, and we would come back together in the dark. I went to catch the little branch-line train, all of whose local nicknames I had once learned from Albertine and her friends, it being known variously as the *Slow Coach,* on account of its innumerable detours, the *Rattletrap,* because of its slow progress, the *Ocean Liner,* on account of a fearsome siren it possessed to make passersby get out of the way, the *Decauville,*[1] and the *Funi,* even though it was nothing like a funicular, but because it climbed up the cliff, nor even, properly speaking, a Decauville, but because it had a sixty-centimeter track, the BAG because it went from Balbec to Grattevast via Angerville, the *tram* and the TSN because it formed part of the line of the Tramways du Sud de la Normandie. I installed myself in a carriage where I was alone; it was gloriously sunny, and stifling; I lowered the blue blind, which let only a strip of sunlight through. But I at once saw my grandmother, as she had been when sitting in the train on our departure from Paris for Balbec, and when, pained at seeing me drinking beer, she had preferred not to look, to close her eyes and pretend to be asleep. I, who had been unable to endure her sufferings in the old days when my grandfather took cognac, I had inflicted this pain on her, not simply even of seeing me take, at someone else's invitation, a drink she believed disastrous for me, but I had forced her to leave me free to swill it down as I pleased; worse still, by my rages and my breathless attacks, I had forced her to help me, to recommend it, in a supreme act of resignation whose wordless, despairing image I had before my memory, her eyes closed so as not to see. Such a memory, like a wave from a magic wand, had once again given back to me the soul I had been in the act of losing for some time past; what could I have done with Rosemonde[2] when across the whole of my lips there was passing only a desperate desire to kiss a dead woman? What could I have said to the Cambremers and the Verdurins when my heart was pounding because the sorrow that my grandmother had endured was constantly re-forming there? I could not remain in that carriage. As soon as the train stopped in Maineville-la-Teinturière, abandoning my plans, I got out. Maineville had for some time past been acquiring a considerable importance and a particular reputation, because a director of numerous casinos, a purveyor of well-being, had had built, not far from there, with an opulence of bad taste capable of competing with that of a grand hotel, an establishment to which we shall be returning, and which was, to make no bones about it, the first brothel for the smart set that anyone had thought to build on the coasts of France. It was the only one. Every port has its brothel, of course, but good only for sailors and for lovers of local color, who get amusement from seeing, right next door to the immemorial church, the madam, herself almost as old, venerable and moss-covered, standing in front of her door of ill-repute waiting for the fishing boats to return.

Avoiding the dazzling house of "pleasure," insolently erected there despite the family protests addressed in vain to the mayor, I rejoined the cliff and followed its winding paths in the direction of Balbec. I heard the summons of the hawthorns, without responding. As their less affluent neighbors, they found the apple blossom very heavy, while acknowledging the fresh complexions worn by the daughters, with their pink petals, of the great cider-makers. They knew that, though less richly dowried, they were yet more sought after, and that a rumpled whiteness was all they required by way of attraction.

When I got back, the hotel porter handed me a letter announcing a bereavement on the part of the Marquis and Marquise de Gonneville, the Vicomte and Vicomtesse d'Amfreville, the Comte and Comtesse de Berneville, the Marquis and Marquise de Graincourt, the Comte d'Amenoncourt, the Comtesse de Maineville, the Comte and Comtesse de Franquetot, the Comtesse de Chaverny, née d'Aigleville, and which I finally understood why it had been sent to me when I recognized the names of the Marquise de Cambremer, née du Mesnil La Guichard, and of the Marquis and Marquise de Cambremer, and when I saw that the dead woman, a cousin of the Cambremers, had been called Éléonore-Euphrasie-Humbertine de Cambremer, Comtesse de Criquetot. Nowhere in this extensive provincial family, the enumeration of which filled lines of fine, close-set writing, was there a single bourgeois, or a single familiar title, for that matter, but the whole *ban* and *arrière-ban* of the regional nobility, whose names—those of all the interesting places in the region—they made to sing with their joyful endings in *-ville*, or *-court*, or sometimes more dully (in *-tot*). Clad in the tiles of their château or the roughcast of their church, their nodding heads barely protruding above the vaulting or the *corps de logis*, and then only in order to be crowned by the Norman lantern or the half-timbering of the pepper-pot roof, they seemed to have sounded the rallying cry for all the pretty villages arranged in echelon or scattered for fifty leagues roundabout, and to have set them out in close formation, without one gap, or one intruder, on the compact, rectangular chessboard of this aristocratic, black-edged letter.

My mother had gone back up to her room, meditating on this sentence from Mme de Sévigné—"I see none of those who seek to distract me; in veiled words, the fact is they want to stop me from thinking of you, and that offends me"—because the First President had told her she would find some amusement. To me he whispered, "It's the Princesse de Parme." My fear was dispelled on seeing that the woman the magistrate was pointing to had no connection with Her Royal Highness. But since she had reserved a room in order to spend the night on returning from Mme de Luxembourg's, the news had the effect on many of making them assume that every newly arrived lady was the Princesse de Parme—and, on me, of making me go up and shut myself away in my garret. I would not have wanted to remain there alone. It was barely four o'clock. I asked Françoise to go and find Albertine, so that she might come and spend the end of the afternoon with me.

I think I would be lying if I said that the painful and perpetual mistrust that Albertine was to inspire in me had already begun, let alone the particular, above all Gomorran, character which that mistrust was to assume. True, from that day forward—though it was not the first—my expectations were a little fraught. Françoise, once gone, stayed away so long that I began to lose hope. I had not lit any lamps. It was barely daylight any longer. The wind was making the flag on the casino flap. And more sickly still, in the silence of the shore, where the sea was coming in—and like a voice, as it were, translating and enhancing the enervating uncertainty of that false, anxious hour of the day—a small barrel organ had stopped in front of the hotel and was playing Viennese waltzes. At last Françoise arrived, but alone. "I've been as quick as I could, but she wouldn't come, because she didn't think her hair was good enough. If she didn't stay a whole hour by the clock pomading herself, she didn't stay five minutes. It'll be a real perfume shop here. She's coming, she stayed behind to fix herself up in front of the mirror. I thought I'd find her here." It was still a long time before Albertine arrived. But her cheerfulness and kindness on this occasion dispelled my unhappiness. She announced (contrary to what she had said the other day) that she would be staying for the whole season and asked whether we could not, as the first year, see each other every day. I told her that at the moment I was too unhappy, and that instead I would send for her from time to time, at the last minute, as in Paris. "If ever you feel sad or if your heart tells you to, don't hesitate," she said, "send for me, I'll come running, and if you're not afraid it might cause a scandal in the hotel, I'll stay as long as you like." On bringing her back, Françoise had worn a happy expression, as on every occasion when she had put herself out on my behalf and succeeded in pleasing me. But Albertine herself counted for nothing in this delight, and the very next day Françoise was to speak these profound words to me: "Monsieur shouldn't see that young lady. I can easily tell the sort of character she has; she'll cause you unhappiness." Showing Albertine out, I caught sight through the lighted dining room of the Princesse de Parme. I merely looked at her while contriving not to be seen. But I will admit that I found a certain grandeur in the regal courtesy that had caused me to smile at the Guermantes'. It is a principle that sovereign princes are at home anywhere, and protocol translates this into dead and worthless customs such as that which has it that the host should keep his hat in his hand, in his own house, in order to show that he is no longer at home but at the Prince's. Now, the Princesse de Parme had not perhaps formulated this idea to herself, but so imbued with it was she that all her actions, invented on the spur of the moment to meet the circumstances, betrayed it. When she got up from the table, she handed Aimé a large tip, as if he had been there solely on her account, or as if, on leaving a château, she were rewarding a *maître d'hôtel* who had been detailed to attend on her. She did not content herself with the tip, moreover, but, with a gracious smile, addressed a few friendly and flattering words to him, with which her mother had supplied her. A minute more and she would be telling him that, just as the hotel was so very well maintained, so Normandy was prospering, and that of all the countries in the world she preferred France. Another coin slipped out of the Princesse's hand, for the sommelier, whom she had sent for, and to whom she insisted on expressing her satisfaction, like a general who has just reviewed his troops. The "lift" had come up at that same moment to give her a reply; he, too, received a word, a smile, and a tip, all combined with some humble and encouraging words intended to prove that she was nothing more than one of them. Since Aimé, the sommelier, the "lift," and the others thought it would be impolite not to wear the broadest of smiles for someone who was smiling at them, she was soon surrounded by a group of servants with whom she chatted benevolently; such manners being unusual in grand hotels, the people going past along the beach, not knowing her name, thought they were seeing a habituée of Balbec who, on account of her unimpressive origins or out of professional self-interest (she was perhaps the wife of a champagne sales representative), was less different from the domestic staff than the genuinely smart patrons. For my part, I thought of the palace in Parma, and of the advice, part religious and part political, given to the Princesse, who behaved toward the populace as though she must win them over in order to reign one day—or, rather, as though she were reigning already.

I went back up into my room, but I was not alone there. I could hear the mellow sound of someone playing Schumann. People, even those that we love the most, may, it is true, become saturated by the sadness or irritation that emanates from us. There is one thing, however, capable of a power of exasperation to which no human being will ever attain: a piano.

Albertine had made me take note of the dates on which she was due to be away, to go to her girlfriends' for a few days, and had made me write down their addresses also in case I had need of her on one of these evenings, since none of them lived too far away. This meant that, in order to find her, a chain of flowers, linking one girl to another, formed quite naturally around her. I dare to confess that many of her friends—I did not yet love her—afforded me moments of pleasure on one beach or another. These benevolent young companions did not seem many in number. But lately my mind has gone back to them, and their names have returned. I reckoned that, in that one season, twelve granted me their fragile favors. One name came back to me later, which made thirteen. I then felt a childish fear of remaining on that number. I reflected, alas, that I had overlooked the first of them, Albertine, who was no more, and who made the fourteenth.

To take up the thread of my story again, I had written down the names and addresses of the girls at whose houses I would find her on such-and-such a day when she would not be in Incarville, but I thought I would take advantage of those days rather to go to Mme Verdurin's. Our desires for different women are in any case not all equally strong. On a particular evening we cannot do without the woman who, afterward, will hardly trouble us for the next month or two. And, besides, apart from the reasons for alternating, for the study of which this is not the place, after the great exertions of the flesh, the woman whose image haunts our momentary senility is a woman whom we would hardly even kiss on the brow. As for Albertine, I saw her rarely, and only on those widely spaced-out evenings when I could not be without her. Should such a desire take hold of me when she was too far from Balbec for Françoise to be able to go there, I would send the "lift" to Epreville, La Sogne, or Saint-Frichoux, by asking him to stop work a little early. He would come into my room but leave the door open, for, although he did his "job" most conscientiously, which was arduous, consisting in much cleaning, starting at five o'clock in the morning, he could never find the strength to close a door, and if you pointed out to him that it was open, he would go back and, by succeeding in making a supreme effort, give it a gentle push. With the democratic vanity characteristic of him, but to which, in their careers, members of the fairly numerous professions, lawyers, doctors, men of letters, never attain, referring to another lawyer, man of letters, or doctor simply as "my colleague," he, making use, quite rightly, of a term reserved for exclusive bodies such as academies, for example, would say to me, when speaking of a *chasseur* who worked the lift one day in two, "I'm going to see my *associate* takes my place." This vanity did not prevent him, with the aim of improving what he called his "salary," from accepting remuneration for his errands, which had led Françoise to develop a strong dislike of him: "Yes, the first time you see him, he looks as if butter wouldn't melt in his mouth, but there are days when he's about as polite as a prison gate. They're all just money-grubbers." A category in which she had so often placed Eulalie, and in which, alas, for all the misfortunes to which it was one day to lead me, she had already classed Albertine, because she often saw me asking Mamma, on behalf of my far-from-wealthy loved one, for small objects, trinkets, which Françoise thought inexcusable, because Mme Bontemps had only the one maid of all work. Very soon, the "lift," having taken off what I would have called his uniform and what he termed his tunic, would appear in a straw hat, with a cane, attentive to his gait, and holding himself erect, for his mother had advised him never to adopt the style of a "workman" or *"chasseur."* Just as, thanks to books, knowledge is knowledge to a workman who is no longer a workman once his labors are over, so, thanks to the boater and to the pair of gloves, elegance had been brought within reach of the "lift," who, having stopped taking guests up for the evening, believed, like a young surgeon who has removed his gown, or Sergeant Saint-Loup his uniform, he had turned into a perfect man of the world. He did not in any case lack ambition, any more than a talent for handling his cage and not causing you to stop between floors. But his language was defective. I believed in his ambition because, in speaking of the hall porter, whose dependent he was, he would say "my hall porter," in the same tone of voice as a man who, owning in Paris what the *chasseur* would have called "a private mansion," would have spoken of his doorman. As for the lift boy's language, it is odd that someone who heard the guests calling out *"ascenseur"* fifty times a day should himself only ever have said *"accenseur."*[3] Certain things about this lift boy were extremely irritating: whatever I might have said to him, he would break in with a phrase, "I'll say!" or "Imagine!," that seemed either to signify that my remark was so self-evident that anyone at all might have thought of it, or else to transfer its merits onto himself, as if it were he who had drawn my attention to it. "I'll say!" and "Imagine!," exclaimed with the utmost vigor, came to his lips every two minutes, for things that would never have entered his head, which so irritated me that I at once began saying the opposite, to show him he understood not the first thing. But to my second assertion, incompatible though it was with the first, he would still answer, "I'll say!" or "Imagine!," as if these words were inevitable. I found it hard to forgive him also for employing certain terms of his trade, which would for that reason have been perfectly suitable if used literally, only in a figurative sense, which lent them a somewhat puerile pretension to wit, the verb "to pedal," for example. He never used it when he had run an errand by bicycle. But if, on foot, he had had to hurry so as to be on time, to signify that he had walked quickly he would say, "You can imagine how I pedaled!" The lift boy was on the small side, of poor physique, and somewhat ugly. Which did not stop him, whenever you mentioned a young man who was tall, slim, and fine-featured, from saying, "Oh yes, I know, one who's just my height." One day, when I was waiting for an answer from him as someone had been coming up the stairs, at the sound of footsteps I had in my impatience opened the door of my room, to see a *chasseur* as handsome as Endymion, with features of an unbelievable perfection, who had come for a lady whom I did not know. Once the lift boy had returned, in telling him with what impatience I had been awaiting his answer I told how I had thought it was he coming upstairs but that it was a *chasseur* from the Hôtel de Normandie. "Oh yes, I know the one," he said, "there's only one, a boy my own size. To look at, too, he's so like me we could be mistaken for one another, you'd say he was my twin." Finally, he liked appearing to have understood everything right from the start, which meant that as soon as you were advising him of something he would say, "Yes, yes, yes, yes, yes, I understand perfectly," with a decisiveness and an air of intelligence that took me in for a time; but as we get to know them, people are like a metal plunged into some corrosive mixture, and can be seen gradually losing their good qualities (as sometimes their defects). Before giving him my instructions, I saw that he had left the door open; I pointed this out, I was afraid we might be overheard; he condescended to my wishes and returned, having reduced the opening. "That's so as to please you. But there's no one on this floor any more but the two of us." I immediately heard one, then two, then three people go past. This annoyed me because of the possible indiscretion, but above all because I could see that it in no way surprised him but was simply the normal traffic. "Yes, it's the chambermaid from next door going to fetch her things. Yes, it's not of any importance, it's the sommelier bringing up his keys. No, no, it's nothing, you can speak, it's my associate who's going on duty." And since the reasons that all these people had for going past did not lessen my annoyance that they might overhear me, at my formal order he went, not to close the door, which was beyond the capacities of this cyclist who longed for a "motorbike," but to push it closed a little farther. "There, now we'll be nice and quiet." We were so much so that an American woman entered and withdrew, apologizing for having mistaken the room. "You're to bring the girl back here to me," I said to him, after myself slamming the door with all my strength (which brought another *chasseur* to make sure no windows were open). "I'm sure you can remember: Mlle Albertine Simonet. It's on the envelope, in any case. All you need do is tell her it's from me. She'll come very willingly," I added, to encourage him not to humiliate me too much. "I'll say!" "No, on the contrary, it's by no means a matter of course that she'll come willingly. It's very inconvenient to come here from Berneville." "I understand!" "You'll tell her to come with you." "Yes, yes, yes, yes, I understand perfectly," he replied in that precise, quick tone of voice that had long since ceased to create a "good impression" on me, because I knew it was more or less automatic and concealed beneath its seeming decisiveness much vagueness and stupidity. "What time will you be back?" "It'll not take me very long," said the "lift," who, taking to an extreme the rule, laid down by Bélise, of avoiding the recidivism of adding a *pas* to a *ne*, always contented himself with a single negative.[4] "I can very easily go there. In fact, time off was canceled this afternoon, because there was a private party of twenty for lunch. And it was my turn to be off this afternoon. It's only fair if I'm out for a bit this evening. I'll take my bike with me. That way I'll be quick." And an hour later he arrived, saying: "Monsieur's had to wait, indeed, but the young lady's come with me. She's downstairs." "Ah, thank you; the hall porter won't be angry with me?" "M. Paul? Doesn't know where I been, even. Even the door head had nothing to say." But once, when I had said to him, "You absolutely must bring her back here," he said to me with a smile: "You know I couldn't find her. She's not there. And I couldn't stay longer; I was afraid of being like my associate who was moved from the hotel"—for the "lift," who talked of rejoining a profession when one is joining it for the first time ("I'd be very happy to rejoin the post office"), by way of compensation, either so as to soften the blow if it was he who was involved, or else to insinuate it in a more mealy-mouthed and perfidious way if it involved someone else, suppressed the "re-" and said, "I know he was moved." It was not out of malice that he smiled, but on account of his shyness. He thought he could lessen the significance of his lapse by treating it as a joke. Similarly, when he had said, "*You know* I couldn't find her," it was not because he in fact believed I knew that already. On the contrary, he was in no doubt that I did not know and was above all alarmed. Thus he said "you know" so as to spare himself the agonies he would go through in uttering the words intended to inform me of it. We should never lose our tempers with those who, when we catch them out, start sniggering. They do so not because they are making fun, but are fearful that we may be displeased. Let us evince great compassion, show great gentleness to those who laugh. Like a veritable stroke, the "lift's" agitation had produced not only an apoplectic redness but a deterioration in his vocabulary, become suddenly familiar. He ended by explaining that Albertine was not in Epreville, that she would be back only at nine o'clock, and that if sometimes, which meant by any chance, she were to return sooner, she would be given the message, and she would at all events be with me before 1 a.m.

It was not even on that evening, however, that my cruel mistrust began to take shape. No, to have out with it and although the episode took place only several weeks later, it was born of a remark of Cottard's. Albertine and her friends had wanted, on that particular day, to drag me along to the casino in Incarville, and, as luck would have it, I would not have joined them there (wishing to go and pay a call on Mme Verdurin, who had invited me a number of times) had I not been held up in Incarville itself by the tram's breaking down, which was going to take some time to put right. Walking up and down while waiting for them to finish, I suddenly found myself face to face with Dr. Cottard, who had come to Incarville for a consultation. I almost hesitated to wish him good day, as he had not replied to any of my letters. But friendliness does not manifest itself in the same fashion in everyone. Not having been constrained by his upbringing to the same fixed rules of savoir-vivre as members of society, Cottard was full of good intentions of which we were unaware, which we denied, up until the day when he had the opportunity to display them. He apologized, had indeed received my letters, had signaled my presence to the Verdurins, who had a strong desire to see me and to whom he advised me to go. He even wanted to take me there that same evening, since he would be catching the little branch-line train again to go and dine there. As I was wavering, and as he still had a little time before his train, the breakdown projected to be quite prolonged, I made him enter the little casino, one of those that I had found so sad on the evening of my first arrival, full now of the tumult of young girls who, for want of male partners, were dancing together. Andrée came glissading up to me; I was anticipating leaving again in a moment with Cottard to go to the Verdurins', when I refused his offer once and for all, overcome by too keen a desire to remain with Albertine. For the fact was I had just heard her laughing. And that laugh at once summoned up the pink carnations, the perfumed walls against which it seemed to have just brushed, and from which, pungent, sensual, and revealing as the scent of geraniums, it seemed to be transporting with it a few almost ponderable, irritant, and secret particles.

One of the girls whom I did not know sat down at the piano, and Andrée asked Albertine to waltz with her. Happy, in this little casino, to reflect that I was going to remain with these girls, I pointed out to Cottard how well they danced. But he, from the specialized perspective of a doctor, and with his faulty upbringing, which took no account of the fact that I knew these girls, whom he must, however, have seen me greeting, replied: "Yes, but the parents are very unwise who let their daughters pick up such habits. I certainly wouldn't allow my own to come here. Are they pretty anyway? I can't make out their features. There, look," he added, pointing to Albertine and Andrée, who were waltzing slowly, pressed one against the other, "I've forgotten my eyeglass and I can't see properly, but they're certainly at the height of arousal. It's not sufficiently well known that it's chiefly through the breasts that women experience it. And look, theirs are touching, completely." Indeed, those of Andrée and of Albertine had not ceased to be in contact. I do not know whether they heard or guessed at Cottard's observation, but they drew slightly apart while continuing to waltz. At that moment, Andrée said something to Albertine and the latter laughed, with that same deep, penetrating laugh I had heard just before. But the disturbance it brought me this time was more than simply cruel; Albertine seemed to be demonstrating, to be making Andrée acknowledge, some secret and voluptuous tremor. It had the ring of the first or last chords of some unknown celebration. I left again with Cottard, my thoughts elsewhere as I talked with him, reflecting only at intervals on the scene I had just witnessed. Not that Cottard's conversation was interesting. At that particular moment it had turned sour even because we had just caught sight of Dr. du Boulbon, who did not see us. He had come to spend time on the far side of the Bay of Balbec, where he was in great demand. Now, although Cottard was in the habit of declaring that he did not practice medicine when on vacation, he had hoped to create for himself a select practice along this coast, to which du Boulbon found himself forming an obstacle. True, the Balbec doctor could not trouble Cottard. He was simply a very conscientious doctor who knew everything and to whom you could not mention the least itch without his immediately prescribing, in some complex formula, the appropriate pomade, liniment, or lotion. As Marie Gineste put it in her pretty way of talking, he knew how to "charm away" injuries and sores. But he lacked distinction. He had in fact caused Cottard some small annoyance. The latter, since he had been seeking to exchange his professorial chair for one in therapeutics, had made a special study of toxicants. Toxicants, a perilous innovation in medicine, serving to rewrite the labels of the pharmacists, all of whose products are declared to be, unlike similar drugs, absolutely nontoxic, or detoxicant even. This is the fashionable claim; the guarantee that the product has been carefully antisepticized survives, if only just, at the bottom, in illegible letters, like the faint vestige of a previous fashion. Toxicants serve also to reassure the patient, who learns to his delight that his paralysis is only some passing toxic malaise. Now, a grand duke, having come to spend a few days in Balbec and having a badly swollen eye, had sent for Cottard, who, in exchange for a few hundred-franc notes (the professor would not put himself out for less), had ascribed the inflammation to a toxic condition and prescribed a detoxifying treatment. The swelling did not go down, and the Grand Duke fell back on the usual Balbec doctor, who within five minutes had extracted a speck of dust. The next day, all sign of it had gone. A more dangerous rival, however, was a celebrated specialist in nervous diseases. He was a red-faced, jovial man, both because his close acquaintance with nervous collapse did not stop him from enjoying the rudest of health and also in order to reassure his patients by the loud laugh of his "good morning" and his "goodbye," even if his athlete's arms might later help to slip the straitjacket on them. All the same, the moment you spoke with him in company, whether about politics or about literature, he would listen to you with a benign attentiveness, as if to say, "What's the problem?," without pronouncing right away, as though this were a consultation. But he, after all, whatever his gifts, was a specialist. And so the whole of Cottard's fury had been transferred onto du Boulbon. For the rest, I soon left the professor, the friend of the Verdurins, in order to return home, promising him I would go and visit them.

The hurt that his remarks concerning Albertine and Andrée had caused me was profound, but the worst of the pain was not felt by me right away, as happens in those cases of poisoning that take effect only after a certain interval of time.

On the evening when the "lift" had gone to fetch her, Albertine did not come, despite his assurances. It is true that a person's attractions are a less frequent cause of love than some such phrase as, "No, this evening I won't be free." We pay little heed to those words if we are with friends; we remain cheerful throughout the evening, we are not preoccupied by a certain mental picture; during such time it is immersed in the requisite mixture; on coming home, we find the photograph, developed and perfectly clear. We realize that life is no longer the life we would have given up for a trifle the day before, for, though we may continue not to fear death, we no longer dare to contemplate separation.

At all events, after not one o' clock in the morning (the hour the lift boy had fixed) but three o' clock, I no longer suffered, as in the old days, from feeling the chances of her appearing to be diminishing. The certainty that she would not now be coming produced a complete calm in me, a freshness; the night was quite simply a night like so many others on which I had not seen her, that was the idea from which I began. And from that moment on, the thought that I would see her the next day or on other days, standing out against the nothingness that I had accepted, became sweet to me. Sometimes, on these evenings of waiting, our anguish is due to some medicament that we have taken. His feeling wrongly construed by whoever is suffering, he believes he is anxious on account of she who does not come. Love is born in such a case, like certain nervous diseases, from the inaccurate explanation of a painful malaise. An explanation that there is no point in rectifying, at least where love is concerned, a sentiment that (whatever its cause) is always erroneous.

The next day, when Albertine wrote that she had only just got back to Epreville, so had not received my note in time, and would come, with my permission, to see me that evening, behind the words of her letter, as behind those she had spoken to me once on the telephone, I thought I sensed the presence of pleasures, of persons, whom she had preferred to me. Once again, my whole being was agitated by a painful curiosity to know what she might have been doing, by the latent love we bear always within us; I was able to believe, for a moment, that it was about to attach me to Albertine, but all that it did was to quiver, there where it was, and its last murmurs died away without its having started moving.

During my first stay in Balbec, I misunderstood—and perhaps, indeed, Andrée had done as I had—Albertine's character. I had believed that it was innocent frivolity on her part if all our entreaties did not succeed in detaining her and causing her to miss a *garden party*, a donkey ride, or a picnic. During my second stay in Balbec, I suspected that that frivolity was only an appearance, and the *garden party* only a screen, if not an invention. Under various forms, the following episode occurred (I mean the episode as observed by me, from my side of the glass, which was by no means transparent, and without my being able to tell what truth there might be on the other side). Albertine would make me the most passionate protestations of her affection. She would look at the time because she was due to go and call on a lady who was "at home," it seemed, every day at five o'clock in Infreville. Tortured by a suspicion and feeling anyway unwell, I asked Albertine, I begged her, to stay. It was impossible (in fact, she could only stay for another five minutes), because it would annoy the lady in question, who was touchy and not very welcoming and, said Albertine, a bore. "But one can easily miss a visit." "No, my aunt has taught me politeness has to come first." "But I've seen you be impolite often enough." "That's not the same thing, this lady would hold it against me and make trouble for me with my aunt. I'm already rather in her bad books. She insists I should have been to see her once at least." "But since she's 'at home' every day . . ." Here Albertine, feeling she had been "cut off," modified the reason. "Of course she's 'at home' every day. But today I've arranged to meet some friends at her house. That way, we won't be so bored." "In that case, Albertine, you're preferring this lady and your friends to me, since, in order not to risk paying a tedious visit, you prefer to leave me on my own, ill and most unhappy?" "I wouldn't in the least mind the visit being tedious. But it's out of devotion to them. I shall bring them back in my trap. Otherwise, they'd no longer have any means of transport." I pointed out to Albertine that there were trains until ten o'clock in the evening from Infreville. "That's true, but, you know, it's possible we shall be asked to stay to dinner. She's very hospitable." "Well, you could refuse." "I'd be annoying my aunt again." "Anyway, you can have dinner and catch the ten o'clock train." "That's cutting it close." "Then I can never go out to dinner and come back by train. But listen, Albertine, we're going to do something very simple: I feel that the fresh air will do me good; since you can't give this lady up, I'm going to go with you as far as Infreville. Never fear, I won't go as far as the Tour Élisabeth"–the lady's villa–"I won't see the lady, or your friends." Albertine looked as if she had received a terrible blow. She broke off from speaking. She said that sea bathing had not benefited her. "If my going with you annoys you?" "But how can you say that? You know my greatest pleasure is going out with you." There had been an abrupt change of tack. "Since we're going to go somewhere together," she said, "why shouldn't we go to the other side of Balbec? We could have dinner together. It would be so nice. Basically, the coastline there's much prettier. I'm beginning to get fed up with Infreville and all these little places the color of spinach." "But your aunt's friend will be angry if you don't go and see her." "Well, she'll get unangry again." "No, we shouldn't make people angry." "But she won't even notice, she's 'at home' every day; whether I go there tomorrow, or the day after, in a week's time, a fortnight's time, that'll meet the bill." "And your friends?" "Oh, they've left me in the lurch enough times. It's certainly my turn." "But in the direction you're proposing, there's no train after nine o'clock." "Well, what of it? Nine is ideal. Besides, we should never let the problem of getting back stand in our way. We can always find a cart, or a bike, failing which we've got our legs." " 'Always find,' Albertine, you're getting carried away! The Infreville direction, where the little wooden stations are so close to one another, yes. But the opposite direction, it's not the same." "Even that way. I promise I'll get you back safe and sound." I sensed that Albertine was giving up on my account something she had arranged that she did not want to tell me about, and that there was someone who would be as unhappy as I had been. Finding that what she had wanted was not possible, since I wanted to go with her, she gave it up unhesitatingly. She knew it was not irremediable. For, like all women who have several things in their lives, she could rely for support on what never weakens: doubt and jealousy. Admittedly, she was not trying to excite them, on the contrary. But those in love are so suspicious that they instantly sniff out a falsehood. So that Albertine, being no better than anyone else, knew from experience (without guessing in the very least that she owed it to jealousy) that she would always be sure to see again the people she had left in the lurch one evening. The person unknown whom she had given up for my sake would suffer, would love her the more (Albertine did not know this was the reason), and, so as not to go on suffering, would return to her of his own accord, as I would have done. But I wanted neither to cause pain, nor to tire myself out, nor to enter onto the terrible path of inquiry, of a multiform, innumerable surveillance. "No, Albertine, I don't want to spoil your pleasure; go to your lady in Infreville, or at any rate to the person she's a pseudonym for, it's all the same to me. The real reason why I'm not going with you is that you don't want it, that the excursion you'd be making with me isn't the one you wanted to make, the proof of which is that you've contradicted yourself more than five times without noticing." Poor Albertine was afraid that her contradictions, which she had not noticed, might have been more serious, not knowing exactly what lies she had told: "It's very possible I contradicted myself. The sea air takes away all my powers of reason. I'm forever saying one name instead of another." And (which proved to me that she would not now have needed many sweet affirmations for me to believe her) I experienced the pain of a wound on hearing this admission of what I had only feebly assumed. "All right, it's agreed, I'm going," she said in a tragic voice, not without looking at the time, so as to see whether she was late or not for the other person, now that I had furnished her with the pretext for not spending the evening with me. "You're so unkind. I change everything so as to spend a nice evening with you, and it's you who don't want it, and you accuse me of lying. I've never seen you so cruel before. The sea will be my grave. I shall never see you again." My heart beat faster at these words, although I was certain she would be back the next day, which is what happened. "I shall drown myself, I shall throw myself into the water." "Like Sappho."⁵ "Yet another insult; you don't only have doubts about what I say but about what I do." "But, little one, I had no such intention, I swear, you know that Sappho hurled herself into the sea." "Yes, you did, you don't have any confidence in me." She saw from the clock that it was twenty of; she was afraid of missing what it was she had to do, and, selecting the briefest of farewells (which she apologized for, as it happens, by coming to see me the following day; on that particular following day, the other person probably was not free), she made her escape at a run, crying, "Farewell forever," wearing a heartbroken expression. And perhaps she was heartbroken. For, knowing what she was doing at that moment better than I did, at once more severe and more indulgent toward herself than I was to her, perhaps all the same she felt a doubt that I might not make her welcome after the way she had left me. I think that she cared for me, to the point where the other person was more jealous than I.

A few days later, in Balbec, when we were in the ballroom of the casino, Bloch's sister and cousin came in, both of whom were by now very pretty, but whom I no longer acknowledged because of my friends, for the younger of the two, the cousin, was living quite openly with the actress whose acquaintance she had made during my first stay. Andrée, allusion having been made to this under her breath, said to me, "Oh, I'm like Albertine about that, there's nothing the two of us find more disgusting." As for Albertine, starting to talk with me on the sofa where we were sitting, she had turned her back on the two disreputable girls. Yet I had observed that, prior to this movement, just as Mlle Bloch and her cousin had made their appearance, there had come into my loved one's eyes that sudden and profound attentiveness that sometimes lent this mischievous girl's face a serious, even solemn expression, and left her looking sad afterward. But Albertine had at once turned her gaze, still oddly immobile and thoughtful, back onto me. Mlle Bloch and her cousin having finally gone off, after giving a very loud laugh and uttering unseemly shouts, I asked Albertine whether the small, fair-haired one (she who was the girlfriend of the actress) was not the same girl who had the day before won the prize in the floral carriage race. "Oh, I don't know," said Albertine, "has one of them got fair hair? I have to tell you, they don't greatly interest me, I've never looked at them. Has one of them got fair hair?" she asked her three friends, with a detached, questioning look. Applied as it was to people whom Albertine met every day on the esplanade, this ignorance struck me as too extreme not to have been put on. "They don't appear to be looking at us much, either," I said to Albertine, perhaps on the hypothesis, though I did not as yet consciously entertain it, that Albertine liked women, so as to remove any regret on her part by demonstrating to her that she had not attracted the attention of these women, and that, generally speaking, even the most depraved of them do not usually concern themselves with young girls whom they do not know. "They didn't look at us?" replied Albertine unthinkingly. "They did nothing else the whole time." "But you can't know that," I said, "you had your back to them." "Well, what about that?" she replied, indicating, set into the wall facing us, a large mirror that I had failed to notice, and on which I now realized that, even while she was speaking to me, my loved one had not ceased to fix her beautiful, much-preoccupied eyes.

From the day when Cottard had gone with me into the little Incarville casino, without sharing the opinion he had given voice to, I no longer saw Albertine in the same light; the sight of her produced anger in me. I had myself changed so much that she seemed other. I had ceased to look kindly on her; in her presence, or out of her presence if it might get repeated to her, I spoke of her in the most wounding fashion. There were truces, however. One day I learned that Albertine and Andrée had both of them accepted an invitation to Elstir's. Not doubting that this was with a view to being able to amuse themselves on the way back like schoolgirls, by imitating girls of the disreputable sort, and derive in doing so an unconfessed, virginal pleasure that would wring my heart, without any announcement, in order to inconvenience them and to deprive Albertine of the pleasure on which she was counting, I arrived at Elstir's unexpectedly. But I found only Andrée there. Albertine had chosen another day, when her aunt was due to go there. So I told myself that Cottard must have been mistaken; the favorable impression produced in me by Andrée's being present without her friend did not go away, and fostered in me a gentler disposition in regard to Albertine. But this lasted no longer than the fragile good health of those delicate individuals liable to temporary improvements, but in whom the merest nothing suffices to bring about a relapse. Albertine had incited Andrée to games that, without going very far, were not perhaps altogether innocent; finding this suspicion painful, in the end I discarded it. Hardly was I cured before it was reborn in another form. I had just seen Andrée, in one of those graceful movements that were peculiar to her, lay her head coaxingly on Albertine's shoulder and kiss her on the neck, half closing her eyes; or else they had exchanged a quick glance; a comment had escaped someone who had seen them alone together on the way to bathe, trivial incidents such as habitually float in the ambient atmosphere, where the majority of people absorb them all day long without their health suffering or their mood changing for the worse, but which are morbid and generative of fresh pain for someone so predisposed. Sometimes, even, without my having seen Albertine again, and without anyone's having spoken of her to me, I rediscovered in my memory an attitude of Albertine's in the company of Gisèle that I had thought innocent at the time; it was enough now to destroy the state of calm I had been able to recover; I no longer needed to go out of doors to breathe in dangerous germs; I had, as Cottard would have said, intoxicated myself. I thought then about all that I had learned of Swann's love for Odette, and of the way in which Swann had been made a fool of all his life. Fundamentally, if I try to think about it, the hypothesis that led me little by little to construct Albertine's whole character, and to interpret painfully each moment of a life I was unable to control in its entirety, was the memory, the *idée fixe*, of the character of Mme Swann, such as I had been told that it was like. These accounts helped to ensure that in future my imagination played the game of supposing that, instead of being a good girl, Albertine might have the same immorality, the same capacity for deception, as a former whore, and I thought of all the suffering that would have awaited me in that event had I ever had to love her.

One day, in front of the Grand-Hôtel, where we had gathered on the esplanade, I had just directed the harshest and most humiliating words at Albertine, and Rosemonde said, "Oh, how you've changed toward her, at one time she was all that mattered, it was she who called the tune, now she's only good to be fed to the dogs." In order to make my attitude toward Albertine even more conspicuous, I was in the midst of saying all manner of friendly things to Andrée, who, though she might be afflicted with the same vice, seemed more excusable because she was unwell and neurasthenic, when we saw emerge, at a gentle trot, into the street perpendicular to the esplanade on the corner of which we were standing, Mme de Cambremer's calash and pair. The First President, who was at that moment advancing toward us, leaped out of the way when he recognized the carriage, so as not to be seen in our company; then, when he thought that the Marquise's glances might be about to meet his own, he bowed and gave an immense sweep of his hat. But the carriage, instead of continuing, as had seemed likely, along the rue de la Mer, vanished behind the entrance to the hotel. It was a good ten minutes after this that the "lift" arrived, all out of breath, to warn me: "It's the Marquise de Camembert who's come just to see Monsieur. I went up to the room, I looked in the reading room, I couldn't find Monsieur. Luckily, I had the idea of looking on the beach." Hardly had he concluded his narration when, followed by her daughter-in-law and by a very ceremonious gentleman, the Marquise advanced toward me, coming probably from a matinée or tea party in the vicinity, and bowed down under the weight, not so much of the years as of the host of luxurious articles in which she thought it more friendly and more befitting to her rank to be covered, so as to appear as "dressed up" as possible to those she had come to see. It was, in short, at the hotel, that "disembarkation" of the Cambremers that my grandmother had once so much dreaded when she wanted Legrandin not to be aware that we would perhaps be going to Balbec. Then Mamma would laugh at the fears inspired by an event she considered impossible. And yet now, at last, it had come about, but by another route and without Legrandin's having had any part in it. "Can I stay if I don't disturb you?" Albertine asked me—in whose eyes there remained, put there by the cruel things I had just been saying to her, a few tears that I observed without appearing to see them, and not without rejoicing—"I might have something to say to you." A hat with feathers, itself surmounted by a sapphire pin, had been set down anyhow on Mme de Cambremer's wig, like an insignia the display of which is necessary but sufficient, its placing of no importance, its elegance conventional, its immobility useless. Despite the heat, the good lady had put on a jet-black mantelet resembling a dalmatic, on top of which there hung an ermine stole, the wearing of which seemed to relate not to the temperature or the season, but to the nature of the ceremony. And on Mme de

Cambremer's bosom there hung a baron's coronet linked to a short chain, in the manner of a pectoral cross. The gentleman was a celebrated lawyer from Paris, of a nobiliary family, who had come to spend three days with the Cambremers. He was one of those men of a professional experience so complete as to cause them somewhat to look down on their profession, and who say, for example, "I know I argue well in court, so I no longer get any amusement from arguing," or "Operating no longer interests me; I know I operate well." As intelligent men, and as *artists,* they see, resplendent about a maturity handsomely endowed by success, the "intelligence" and the "artistic" nature that their colleagues acknowledge, and which confers on them a rough approximation to taste and discernment. They develop a passion for the paintings not of a great artist, but of an artist of great distinction nonetheless, to purchasing whose works they devote the large income that their career procures for them. Le Sidaner[6] was the artist selected by the friend of the Cambremers, who was in fact very agreeable. He talked well about books, the books not of the true masters, however, but of those who have mastered themselves. The one troublesome defect that this *amateur* displayed was that he consistently employed certain ready-made expressions, such as "for the most part," which lent something both important and incomplete to what he wished to talk about. Mme de Cambremer had taken advantage, she told me, of a matinée that some friends of hers had been giving that day near Balbec to come and see me, as she had promised Robert de Saint-Loup. "You know he's due shortly to come and spend a few days locally. His uncle Charlus is staying in the country at his sister-in-law's, the Duchesse de Luxembourg, and M. de Saint-Loup will take the opportunity both to go and greet his aunt and to revisit his old regiment, where he is greatly loved, greatly esteemed. We often entertain officers who all praise him to the skies. It would be so nice if you were to do us the pleasure of coming both of you to Féterne." I introduced Albertine and her friends to her. Mme de Cambremer named us to her daughter-in-law. The latter, so glacial toward the petty nobility with whom the neighborhood of Féterne forced her to associate, so full of reserve for fear of being compromised, held out her hand to me, on the contrary, with a radiant smile, in a place of safety, and delighted as she was to be faced by a friend of Robert de Saint-Loup's, and one whom the latter, preserving a greater social finesse than he liked people to see, had told her was a close friend of the Guermantes. Thus, in contrast to her mother-in-law, Mme de Cambremer had two infinitely different forms of politeness. It was at the very most the first form, distant and intolerable, that she would have accorded me had I met her through her brother Legrandin. But for a friend of the Guermantes she was all smiles. The most comfortable room in the hotel in which to receive people was the reading room, in the old days a very terrible place into which I now entered ten times a day, re-emerging freely, as my own master, like those lunatics, little affected, and so long resident in the asylum that the doctor has entrusted them with the key. Thus I offered to take Mme de Cambremer there. And because this hall no longer filled me with shyness or held any attraction for me, since the faces of things change for us just as those of people do, it was without feeling flustered that I made the suggestion. But she refused, preferring to remain out of doors, and we sat down in the open air, on the hotel terrace. There I found and rescued a volume of Mme de Sévigné that Mamma had not had time to take with her in her precipitate flight, when she heard that I had visitors. She dreaded these invasions by strangers as much as my grandmother had, and for fear of no longer being able to escape if she let herself be hemmed in, she made her escape with a rapidity that always led my father and me to make fun of her. In her hand, Mme de Cambremer held, together with the handle of a sunshade, several embroidered bags, a tidy, a gold purse from which hung ropes of garnets, and a lace handkerchief. It struck me that it would have been more convenient for her to put them down on a chair; but I sensed it would be improper and pointless to ask her to abandon the regalia of her pastoral rounds and her worldly ministry. We gazed at the calm sea, where stray gulls floated like white petals. Because of the level of simple "medium" to which worldly conversation reduces us, and also our desire to please with the help not of qualities of which we are ourselves unaware, but of what we believe must be prized by those we are with, I began instinctively to talk to Mme de Cambremer, née Legrandin, in the manner in which her brother might have done. "They have," I said, referring to the gulls, "the whiteness and stillness of water lilies." And, indeed, they appeared to be offering an inert target to the little waves that were rocking them, to the point where these, by contrast, seemed, in their pursuit, animated by some purpose, to have taken on life. The dowager Marquise did not weary of hymning the superb view of the sea that we got in Balbec, and envied me it, she who, at La Raspelière (where it so happens she was not living that year), could see the waves only from a long way off. She had two peculiar habits that derived at once from her exalted love of the arts (of music above all) and from her dental inadequacy. Whenever she talked aesthetics, her salivary glands, like those of certain animals in the rutting season, entered on a phase of hypersecretion such that the old lady's toothless mouth allowed a few droplets whose rightful place this was not, to come from the corners of her faintly mustachioed lips. She would at once swallow them down again with a deep sigh, like someone recovering their breath. And then, were the beauty of the music too much for her, in her enthusiasm she would raise her arms and proffer a few summary judgments, energetically masticated, and coming, if need be, from the nose. Now, it had never occurred to me that the commonplace beach of Balbec might indeed offer a "sea view," and Mme de Cambremer's simple words changed my ideas where that was concerned. In return, as I now told her, I had always heard people extolling the unique panorama from La Raspelière, situated at the top of the hill, and where, in a large drawing room with two fireplaces, one whole row of windows looks out, at the foot of the gardens, between the foliage, onto the sea as far as Balbec and beyond, and the other row onto the valley. "How kind of you, and how well you put it: the sea between the foliage. It's ravishing, it's like . . . a fan." And I sensed, from a deep breath intended to catch the saliva and dry the mustache, that the compliment was genuine. But the Marquise, née Legrandin, remained unmoved in order to show her disdain not for my words but for those of her mother-in-law. She did not merely despise the latter's intelligence, moreover, she deplored her affability, forever afraid that people might not have a sufficiently high regard for the Cambremers. "And what a pretty name," I said. "One would love to know the origin of all these names." "In the case of that one, I can tell you," the old lady answered quietly. "It's a family home, of my grandmother Arrachepel, it's not an illustrious family, but a very good and very ancient provincial family." "What, not illustrious?" her daughter-in-law broke in curtly. "A whole stained-glass window in Bayeux Cathedral is filled with its arms, and the principal church of Avranches contains their funerary monuments. If these old names amuse you, you've come one year too late. We had appointed to the benefice at Criquetot, despite all the difficulties there are in changing dioceses, the dean of a place where I myself have estates, a long way from here, in Combray, where the good priest felt he was becoming neurasthenic. Unfortunately, the sea air didn't succeed at his great age; his neurasthenia increased, and he went back to Combray. But while he was our neighbor, he amused himself by going to consult all the old charters, and he wrote a rather intriguing little booklet on the local place-names. That gave him a taste for it, moreover, for it seems he's occupying his closing years writing a large book on Combray and its surroundings. I shall send you his booklet on the region around Féterne. It's a labor of love. You'll read the most interesting things in it about our old Raspelière, about which my mother-in-law speaks much too modestly." "At all events, this year," replied the dowager Mme de Cambremer, "La Raspelière is no longer ours and doesn't belong to me. But I sense you're a painter at heart; you ought to draw, and I would so like to show you Féterne, which is much better than La Raspelière." For, now that the Cambremers had rented this last-named house to the Verdurins, its commanding position had abruptly ceased to appear as it had been for them during all these years, that is to say as offering the advantage, unique in the region, of having a view both out to sea and over the valley, and had suddenly—and after the event—presented them in return with the inconvenience that you had always to climb and descend in order to get there and then come away again. In short, you might have thought that if Mme de Cambremer had rented it out this was less in order to increase her revenues than to rest her horses. And she declared herself overjoyed at finally being able all the time to possess the sea from so close up, at Féterne, she who, for so long, ignoring the two months she used to spend there, had only seen it from high up and as if in a panorama. "I am discovering it at my age," she said, "and how I enjoy it! It does me a world of good! I'd rent La Raspelière for nothing so as to be constrained to live at Féterne."

"To get back onto more interesting matters," resumed Legrandin's sister, who addressed the old Marquise as "Mother" but had adopted an insolent manner toward her over the years, "you were talking of water lilies: I imagine you know those that Claude Monet has painted. What genius! It interests me all the more because, close to Combray, the place where I told you I owned land . . ." But she preferred not to speak too much about Combray. "Oh, that's surely the series we heard about from Elstir, the greatest of contemporary painters," exclaimed Albertine, who had said nothing hitherto. "Oh, one can tell Mademoiselle loves the arts," exclaimed Mme de Cambremer, sucking back a jet of saliva as she drew a deep breath. "You will permit me to prefer Le Sidaner, mademoiselle," said the lawyer, smiling with the air of a connoisseur. And, as he had once appreciated, or seen appreciated, certain of Elstir's "audacities," he added, "Elstir was gifted, he was almost part of the avant-garde even, but for some reason or other he didn't keep up, he has wasted his life." Mme de Cambremer came down in favor of the lawyer as far as Elstir was concerned, but, much to her guest's chagrin, ranked Monet with Le Sidaner. It cannot be said that she was stupid; she overflowed with an intelligence that I sensed was of not the slightest use to me. The sun just then getting lower, the seagulls were now yellow, like the water lilies in another canvas of that same series by Monet. I said that I knew it and (continuing to imitate the language of the brother whose name I had not as yet dared to cite) I added that it was a pity that she had not thought rather of coming the day before, for, at that same hour, she would have been able to admire a light out of Poussin. Confronted by some Normandy squireen not known to the Guermantes telling her that she should have come the day before, Mme de Cambremer-Legrandin would no doubt have stiffened with offense. But I could well have been more familiar still and she would have been all fond, melting sweetness; in the warmth of that lovely late afternoon, I could gather honey as I liked in the great honeycomb that Mme de Cambremer so seldom was, and which took the place of the petits fours I had not thought to hand around. But the name of Poussin, without taking away from the amenableness of the society woman, aroused the protests of the dilettante. On hearing that name, Mme de Cambremer gave vent six times, with scarcely any interval in between, to that brief clicking of the tongue against the lips which serves to signify to a child who is in the midst of doing something silly that he is both at fault for having started and forbidden to continue. "In heaven's name, after a painter like Monet, who's quite simply a genius, don't go and name an untalented old hack like Poussin. I tell you straight out that I consider him the most crashing of bores. There you are, but I can't call that painting. Monet, Degas, Manet, yes, they're painters! It's very odd," she added, fixing a rapt and searching gaze on some vague point in space where she could perceive her own thought, "it's very odd, at one time I preferred Manet. Nowadays, I still admire Manet, naturally, but I think I perhaps prefer Monet even more. Oh, the cathedrals!" She put as much scrupulousness as self-satisfaction into informing me of the direction in which her taste had evolved. And you had the sense that the phases through which that taste had passed were no less important, as she saw it, than the different manners of Monet himself. I had, moreover, no cause to feel flattered that she should have been confiding her admirations to me, for, even when faced by the most narrow-minded of provincial ladies, she could not go five minutes without feeling the need to confess them. When a noble lady from Avranches, who would have been incapable of telling Mozart from Wagner, said in front of Mme de Cambremer, "There was nothing new on of any interest during our stay in Paris, we did go once to the Opéra-Comique, they were doing *Pelléas et Mélisande,* it's ghastly," Mme de Cambremer not only seethed with anger but felt the need to exclaim, "On the contrary, it's a small masterpiece," and to "argue the matter." This perhaps was a habit from Combray, picked up from the sisters of my grandmother, who called it "fighting the good fight," and who loved dinner parties where they knew, week after week, that they would have to defend their gods against the Philistines. Thus Mme de Cambremer liked to "get the blood coursing" by "squabbling" about art, as others about politics. She took the side of Debussy as she would have done that of one of her women friends whose conduct had come under fire. Yet she must certainly have realized that when she said, "Not at all, it's a small masterpiece," she could never improvise, in whoever she was putting in their place, that whole progression in artistic culture at whose conclusion they might have reached agreement without any need to argue. "I shall have to ask Le Sidaner what he thinks of Poussin," the lawyer said to me. "He's a quiet one, keeps himself to himself, but I shall know how to draw him out."

"Anyway," Mme de Cambremer went on, "I have a horror of sunsets, so very romantic, so very operatic. That's the reason why I detest my mother-in-law's house, with its plants from the Midi. You'll see, it looks like a park in Monte Carlo. That's the reason why I like your shore better. It's sadder, more genuine; there's a little lane from where you can't see the sea. On rainy days, there's nothing but mud, it's a world of its own. It's like in Venice, I detest the Grand Canal and I know of nothing more affecting than the little alleyways. It's a question of ambience anyway." "But," I said to her, sensing that the one way of rehabilitating Poussin in Mme de Cambremer's eyes was to let her know that he was back in fashion, "M. Degas assures us that he knows of nothing more beautiful than the Poussins at Chantilly."[7] "Oh yes? I don't know the ones at Chantilly," said Mme de Cambremer, who did not want to be of a different opinion from Degas, "but I can talk about those in the Louvre, which are horrors." "Those, too, he admires enormously." "I shall have to look at them again. It's all a bit old in my head," she replied after a moment's silence, and as if the favorable judgment she would certainly soon be delivering on Poussin must depend, not on the news I had just conveyed to her, but on the supplementary and this time definitive examination to which she was relying on subjecting the Poussins in the Louvre so as to facilitate the reversing of her verdict. Contenting myself with what was the beginning of a retraction, since, if she did not yet admire the Poussins, she had adjourned for further deliberation, and so as not to leave her any longer on the rack, I told her mother-in-law what a lot I had heard about the admirable flowers at Féterne. Modestly, she spoke of the small mixed garden she had at the back, into which, by pushing open a door, she went in the mornings in her dressing gown to feed her peacocks, to look for new-laid eggs, and to pick zinnias or roses, which, by providing an edging of flowers along her table runner for the *oeufs à la crème* or the fried fish, reminded her of her garden paths. "It's true we have lots of roses," she said. "Our rose garden is almost too close to our living quarters, there are days when it gives me a headache. It's more agreeable from the terrace at La Raspelière, where the wind brings you the smell of the roses, but not so heady." I turned to the daughter-in-law: "It's straight out of *Pelléas*," I said, to satisfy her liking for modernism, "the smell of the roses coming all the way up to the terraces. It's so strong in the score that, because I get both hay fever and rose fever, it made me sneeze each time I heard that scene." "What a masterpiece *Pelléas* is!" exclaimed Mme de Cambremer. "I simply adore it." And, drawing closer, with the gestures of a female savage seeking to have her way with me, and making use of her fingers to pick out imaginary notes, she began humming something that I supposed for her represented Pelléas's farewell, keeping on with a vehement insistence, as though it were of importance that Mme de Cambremer should remind me of that scene at this moment, or, rather, perhaps demonstrate that she remembered it. "I think it's even more beautiful than *Parsifal*," she added, "because in *Parsifal* the most beautiful things have had a certain halo of melodic phrases added to them, obsolete therefore because melodic." "I know you are a great musician, madame," I said to the dowager. "I'd very much like to hear you." Mme de Cambremer-Legrandin looked at the sea in order not to take part in the conversation. Considering that what her mother-in-law liked was not music, she considered the gift she was recognized as possessing, purported according to her, but most remarkable in point of fact, as a virtuosity of no interest. It is true that Chopin's one surviving pupil had declared, rightly, that the Master's way of playing, his "feeling," had been handed down, through her, only to Mme de Cambremer, but to play like Chopin was far from being a commendation for the sister of Legrandin, who despised nobody so much as the Polish musician. "Oh, they're flying away!" exclaimed Albertine, pointing to the seagulls that, ridding themselves for a moment of their floral incognito, were rising as one toward the sun. " 'Their giant's wings hinder them from walking,' "[8] said Mme de Cambremer, confusing the seagulls with albatrosses. "I'm very fond of them, I saw some in Amsterdam," said Albertine. "They can smell the sea, they come and sniff it even through the paving in the streets." "Oh, you've been in Holland, do you know the Vermeers?" Mme de Cambremer asked imperiously, in the tone of voice in which she might have said, "Do you know the Guermantes?," for snobbery does not change its accent in changing its object. Albertine answered no; she thought they were living people. But it did not show. "I'd be very happy to play something for you," Mme de Cambremer said to me. "But, you know, I only play things that no longer interest your generation. I was brought up to worship Chopin," she said in a low voice, for she was fearful of her daughter-in-law and knew that the latter regarded Chopin as not being music, so that "to play him well" or "to play him badly" were expressions devoid of sense. She acknowledged that her mother-in-law had good technique and performed the virtuoso passages to perfection. "They'll never get me to say she's a musician," ended Mme de Cambremer-Legrandin. Because she saw herself as "advanced" and (in art only) "never far enough to the left," as she put it, she imagined that music not only progresses, but does so along a single line, and that Debussy was some sort of super-Wagner, a little more advanced even than Wagner. She had not realized that, if Debussy was not as independent of Wagner as she herself was to believe in a few years' time, for we use the weapons won in battle after all finally to liberate ourselves from him whom we have momentarily vanquished, he was nevertheless seeking, people beginning to have had their fill of works that were too complete, in which everything is expressed, to satisfy a contrary need. This reaction had been bolstered momentarily, of course, by theories similar to those that, in politics, come to the support of laws against the Congrégations, or wars in the East (teaching against nature, Yellow Peril, etc.).[9] An age of haste called, it was said, for rapidity in art, absolutely as they might have said that a future war could not last more than a fortnight, or that the out-of-the-way spots beloved of the stagecoaches would be forsaken by the railways but restored to honor by the motorcar. It was recommended not to tire the listener's attention, as though we did not have at our command different degrees of attention, the highest of which it is in fact up to the artist to awaken. For those who yawn with fatigue after ten lines of some second-rate article have been making the journey to Bayreuth year after year to hear the *Tetralogy*.[10] The day was coming, moreover, when, for a time, Debussy would be declared to be as fragile as Massenet,[11] and the joltings of *Mélisande* demoted to the rank of those of *Manon*. For theories and schools, like microbes and globules, devour one another and, by their struggles, ensure life's continuance. But that time had not yet come.

As, on the Bourse, when an upward movement occurs and a whole section of the market profits by it, a certain number of disdained authors had benefited from the reaction, either because they had not deserved such disdain, or simply—which enabled one to break new ground by extolling them—because they had brought it on themselves. And people even went looking, in an isolated past, for an independent talent whose reputation the current movement should not, seemingly, have affected, but whose name one of the new masters was thought to have cited favorably. Often it was because a master, whoever he might be, and however exclusive his school may be, is original in his judgments and does justice to talent wherever it is to be found, and to less than talent even, to a pleasing inspiration he has enjoyed in the past, linked to some cherished moment of his adolescence. At other times, because certain artists of another epoch have, in a single piece, achieved something that resembles what the master has gradually realized he has been seeking to do himself. He then sees this elder as something like a precursor; he likes in him, in another form, an effort that is momentarily, and in part, fraternal. There are bits of Turner in the work of Poussin, a phrase of Flaubert's in Montesquieu. But sometimes, too, the rumor of a master's predilection had resulted from an error, born who knows where and hawked about among his school. But the name cited then benefited from the imprint under whose protection it had come just in time, for if there is a certain freedom, genuine taste, in the choice of the master, schools for their part take their lead only from the theory. Thus it was that, following its customary course, which advances by digressions, veering off one time in this direction and the next in the contrary direction, the spirit of the age had brought back into the spotlight a certain number of works to which the need for justice, or for renewal, or the taste of Debussy, or some caprice of his, or some remark he had not perhaps made, had added those of Chopin. Extolled by judges in whom people had every confidence, and benefiting from the admiration aroused by *Pelléas,* they had rediscovered a new *éclat,* and even those who had not heard them again were so anxious to like them that they did so despite themselves, though with an illusion of freedom. But Mme de Cambremer-Legrandin remained for part of the year in the provinces. Even in Paris, as an invalid, she lived largely in her bedroom. It is true that this handicap managed to draw attention to itself mainly in the choice of expressions that Mme de Cambremer thought were fashionable, which would have been better suited to the written language, a nuance she had not discerned, for she derived them more from reading than from conversation. This last is necessary for an accurate knowledge less of people's opinions than of the new expressions. However, the rejuvenation of the Nocturnes had yet to be announced by the critics. News of it had been passed on only in casual conversation by "the young." It remained unknown to Mme de Cambremer-Legrandin. I took pleasure in informing her, though by addressing her mother-in-law for this purpose, as when, in billiards, you play off the cushion in order to strike a ball, that, very far from being old-fashioned, Chopin was Debussy's favorite musician. "Well, I never; how amusing," the daughter-in-law said with a smile, as though this were merely a paradox tossed off by the author of *Pelléas*. Nevertheless, it was quite certain now that she would only ever listen to Chopin with respect or even with pleasure. And so my words, which had just sounded the hour of her deliverance for the dowager, brought an expression of gratitude to me, and above all of joy, to her face. Her eyes shone like those of Latude in the play entitled *Latude or 35 years of Captivity*;[12] and her breast inhaled the sea air with that dilatation that Beethoven has emphasized so well in *Fidelio*, when his prisoners finally breathe in "the air that gives life."[13] I thought she was going to put her mustached lips to my cheek. "What, you like Chopin? He likes Chopin, he likes Chopin," she exclaimed with an impassioned nasal twang, as she might have said, "What, you know Mme de Franquetot, too?," with the difference that my connection with Mme de Franquetot would have been a matter of profound indifference to her, whereas my knowledge of Chopin threw her into a sort of artistic delirium. Salivary hypersecretion was no longer enough. Without even having tried to understand Debussy's role in the reinvention of Chopin, she simply felt that my verdict was favorable. She was seized by musical enthusiasm. "Élodie! Élodie! He likes Chopin." Her bosom swelled and she beat the air with her arms. "Ah, I'd sensed indeed you were a musician," she exclaimed. "I can understand, aaartist that you are, that you should like it. It's so beautiful!" And her voice was as flinty as if, in order to express her ardor for Chopin, she had, in imitation of Demosthenes, filled her mouth with all the pebbles from the beach. Finally, there came the reflux, reaching as far as her veil, which she had not had time to remove to safety and was drenched, and finally the Marquise took her embroidered handkerchief to the dribble of foam with which the memory of Chopin had just soaked her mustaches.

"Heavens," Mme de Cambremer-Legrandin said to me, "I think my mother-in-law's overstaying her welcome rather, she's forgetting we've got my uncle de Ch'nouville coming to dinner. And, besides, Cancan doesn't like to wait." Cancan remained beyond me; I thought perhaps it referred to a dog. But where the de Ch'nouville cousins were concerned, it was as follows. With age, the pleasure the young Marquise had taken in pronouncing their name in this fashion had died down. And yet, in the old days, it had been in order to enjoy it that she resolved on her marriage. In other social groups, when the name "de Chenouville" came up (every time, at least, that the *particule*[14] was preceded by a noun ending in a vowel, for in the contrary case one was indeed obliged to lay stress on the *de*, the tongue refusing to pronounce "Madam' d'Ch'nonceaux"), it was customary for the mute "e" of the *particule* to be sacrificed. They said "M. d'Chenouville." Among the Cambremers, the tradition was the reverse, but equally imperious. In every case, it was the mute "e" in "Chenouville" that was suppressed. Whether the name was preceded by *"mon cousin"* or *"ma cousine,"* it was always "de Ch'nouville" and never "Chenouville." (Where the father of these Chenouvilles was concerned, they said *"notre oncle,"* for they were not upper-crust enough at Féterne to pronounce it *"notre onk,"* as the Guermantes would have done, whose required jargon, suppressing consonants and nationalizing foreign names, was as hard to understand as old French or the modern patois.) Every person entering the Cambremer family at once received a warning, in this matter of the Ch'nouvilles, of which Mlle Legrandin had had no need. Visiting one day, and hearing a girl say *"ma tante d'Uzai,"* *"mon onk de Rouan,"* she had not recognized right away the illustrious names she was in the habit of pronouncing "Uzès" or "Rohan"; hers had been the surprise, the embarrassment, and the shame of someone who finds a newly invented utensil before them on the dinner table of whose use they are ignorant and with which they do not dare to start eating. But the night following and the next day, she had repeated, enraptured, *"ma tante d'Uzai,"* with that suppression of the final "s," a suppression that had astounded her the day before but which she now found it so vulgar not to be aware of that, one of her women friends having referred to a bust of the Duchesse d'Uzès, Mlle Legrandin had answered her ill-humoredly and in a haughty tone, "You might at least pronounce it correctly: *'Mame d'Uzai.'"* From that moment on, she had realized that, by virtue of the transmutation of solid matter into ever-more-subtle elements, the considerable and very honorably acquired fortune that she owed to her father, the thorough education that she had received, her assiduity at the Sorbonne, at Caro's lectures[15] along with those of Brunetière, and at the Lamoureux concerts,[16] all this was to be volatilized, to find its final sublimation in the pleasure of one day saying *"ma tante d'Uzai."* This did not exclude from her mind that she would continue to associate, at least in the early days following her marriage, not with certain women friends whom she liked but was resigned to giving up, but with certain others whom she did not like but to whom she wished to be able to say (since this was her reason for marrying), "I shall introduce you to my aunt d'Uzai," or, when she saw that this alliance was too difficult, "I shall introduce you to my aunt de Ch'nouville" or "I'll have you to dinner with the Uzais." Her marriage to M. de Cambremer had provided Mme de Cambremer with the opportunity of saying the first of these sentences but not the second, the society in which her parents-in-law moved not being that which she had imagined and of which she continued to dream. And so, after having said to me about Saint-Loup (adopting for the purpose an expression of Robert's own, for, if, in order to talk to her, I had spoken like Legrandin, she, by an opposite suggestion, had answered me in Robert's dialect, borrowed unbeknown to her from Rachel), bringing her thumb and forefinger together and half closing her eyes, as though she were gazing at something infinitely delicate that she had succeeded in capturing, "He has a pretty quality of mind," so wholehearted was she in her praise of him that you might have thought she was in love with him (it was claimed, as it happens, that in the old days, when he was at Doncières, Robert had been her lover), but in reality it was merely so that I might repeat it to him, and to lead up to: "You're very friendly with the Duchesse de Guermantes.

I'm ailing, I hardly get out, and I know she remains confined within a circle of select friends, which I fully approve of, so I know her only slightly, but I do know she's an absolutely superior woman." Knowing that Mme de Cambremer scarcely knew her, and to make myself as small as she was, I slid over this topic and said, in answer to the Marquise, that I had above all known her brother, M. Legrandin. At this name, she adopted the same evasive expression as I had worn in the case of Mme de Guermantes, but combining with it a look of displeasure, for she thought I had said this in order to humble not myself but her. Was she eaten away with despair at having been born Legrandin? That at least was what her husband's sisters and sisters-in-law claimed, provincial noblewomen who knew nobody and nothing, and were jealous of Mme de Cambremer's intelligence, her education, her wealth, and the physical attractions she had possessed before she fell ill. "She thinks of nothing else, it's that that's killing her," these spiteful women would say the moment they were talking about Mme de Cambremer to anyone at all, but preferably to a commoner, either, if he was conceited and stupid, so as to enhance the value, by this assertion of the shame attaching to the commoner's condition, of the affability they were showing him, or else, if he was shy and discerning and had applied the remark to himself, so as to have the pleasure, even as they received him courteously, of indirectly behaving insolently toward him. But if these ladies believed they spoke true where their sister-in-law was concerned, they were mistaken. The latter suffered all the less from having been born Legrandin for having lost all memory of the fact. She was annoyed that I should have reminded her of it and fell silent as if she had not understood, not regarding it as necessary to supply any details, or even to confirm mine.

"Our relations are not the main reason for cutting short our visit," the dowager Mme de Cambremer said to me, who was probably more blasé than her daughter-in-law where the pleasure to be had from saying "Ch'nouville" was concerned. "But, so as not to tire you out with too many people, Monsieur," she said, indicating the lawyer, "did not dare bring his wife and son all the way here. They're walking on the beach while they wait for us and must be starting to get bored." I had them carefully pointed out to me and hurried off to find them. The wife had a round face, like certain flowers of the Ranunculus family, and quite a large plantlike mark at the corner of her eye. And since the generations of men preserve their features like a family of plants, just as on the faded face of the mother, so the same mark, which might have helped to classify a variety, swelled beneath the eye of the son. The lawyer was touched by my attentiveness toward his wife and son. He showed interest in the subject of my stay in Balbec. "You must feel a bit out of place, for they're foreigners here for the most part." And he looked at me as he spoke, for, not liking foreigners, though many were his clients, he wanted to be sure that I was not hostile to his xenophobia, in which case he would have beaten a retreat by saying, "Of course, Mme X may be a charming woman. It's a question of principle." Since at that time I had no opinion concerning foreigners, I evinced no disapproval, and he felt himself on safe ground. He went so far as to ask me to call on him one day in Paris, to see his collection of Le Sidaners, and to bring the Cambremers along, with whom he obviously thought I was intimate. "I shall invite you with Le Sidaner," he said, convinced I would be living only in anticipation of that blessed day. "You'll see what a delightful man he is. And his pictures will enchant you. Of course, I can't compete with the big collectors, but I believe it's I who own the greatest number of his favorite canvases. It'll interest you all the more, coming from Balbec, because they're seascapes, in the majority at least." The wife and son, of a vegetable disposition, listened composedly. You sensed that their house in Paris was a sort of temple to Le Sidaner. These sorts of temple are not without their uses. When the god has doubts about himself, he can easily stop up the fissures in his own opinion with the irrefutable testimony of individuals who have devoted their lives to his work.

At a signal from her daughter-in-law, Mme de Cambremer started to stand up and said to me, "Since you don't want to install yourself at Féterne, won't you at least come and have lunch, one weekday, tomorrow for example?" And in her benevolence, in order to decide me, she added, "You'll find the Comte de Crisenoy there," whom I certainly had not lost, for the good reason that I did not know him. She was starting to hold out still other shining temptations to me, but stopped short. The First President, who, on returning, had learned that she was in the hotel, had been searching everywhere for her on the sly, had then waited for her, and, pretending to be meeting her by chance, came up to present his respects. I realized that Mme de Cambremer was not eager to extend to him the luncheon invitation she had just addressed to me. He, however, had known her for much longer than I had, having for years past been one of those regulars at the Féterne matinées whom I had so much envied during my first stay in Balbec. But seniority cannot do everything among society people. They reserve their lunches more readily for those new connections who can still prick their curiosity, especially when their arrival is preceded by a cordial and prestigious recommendation such as that of Saint-Loup. Mme de Cambremer calculated that the First President had not heard what she said to me, but in order to still the remorse that she felt, she addressed him in the most friendly manner. In the sunlight in which, on the horizon, the golden shoreline of Rivebelle, normally invisible, was bathed, we could make out, barely separate from the luminous azure, emerging from the water, pink, silvery, imperceptible, the little bells of the Angelus ringing out in the vicinity of Féterne. "Again, it's rather like *Pelléas*," I remarked to Mme de Cambremer-Legrandin. "You know the scene I mean." "I think I do, yes." But "I've no idea" was what her voice and her face proclaimed, uninformed by any memory, and her unsupported smile off into the air. The dowager could not get over the fact that the bells had carried all this way, and stood up, thinking of the time. "In fact," I said, "from Balbec you can't normally see that shoreline, or hear it, either. The weather must have changed and made the horizon twice as wide. Unless they've come to fetch you, for I can see they're making you leave; for you they are the dinner bell." The First President, none too responsive to the bells, was gazing furtively at the esplanade, which he was distressed to see so depopulated this evening. "You're a true poet," Mme de Cambremer said to me. "I can tell how vibrant you are, how artistic; come, and I will play you some Chopin," she added, raising her arms with an ecstatic air and pronouncing the words in a hoarse voice that seemed as if it were shifting pebbles. Then came the deglutition of the saliva, and the old lady instinctively wiped her "American" toothbrush mustache with her handkerchief. The First President rendered me a very great service in spite of himself by seizing the Marquise by the arm in order to conduct her to her carriage, a certain admixture of vulgarity, boldness, and a liking for ostentation having dictated a course of behavior that others would hesitate before adopting, but which is found far from displeasing in society. It had, in any case, been much more of a habit with him these many years past than with me. I may have blessed him, but I did not dare to imitate him, and walked beside Mme de Cambremer-Legrandin, who wanted to see the book I had in my hand. The name of Mme de Sévigné caused her to screw up her face; and, employing a word she had read in certain newspapers, but which, when spoken and put into the feminine, and applied to a writer of the seventeenth century, created a bizarre effect, she asked me, "Do you find her genuinely *talentueuse*?"[17] The Marquise gave the footman the address of a pâtisserie she needed to go to before taking again to the road, pink from the dust of evening, in which the stepped rumps of the cliffs had turned blue. She asked her old coachman whether one of her horses that felt the cold had been warm enough, whether another's shoe might not be hurting. "I shall write to you about what we have to arrange," she said to me in a low voice. "I saw you were talking literature with my daughter-in-law, she's adorable," she added, although she did not believe this but had got into the habit—maintained out of goodness of heart—of saying so, so that her son should not seem to have married for money. "Besides," she added, in a last enthusiastic mumble, "she's so aaartisssstic!" Then she climbed into her carriage, swaying her head and raising the handle of her sunshade, and went off again through the streets of Balbec, weighed down by the vestments of her ministry, like an old bishop on his confirmation rounds.

"She has invited you to lunch," the First President said to me sternly, once the carriage had moved off and I came back with the girls. "We're not on good terms. She thinks I neglect her. But, there, I'm easy enough to get on with. Should anyone have need of me, I'm always there to answer, 'Present.' But they tried to throw the grappling irons over me. Ah well, that!" he added, with a canny expression, and raising his finger like someone splitting hairs: "That I don't allow. That's an attack on my liberty when on vacation. I was obliged to say, 'Stop there!'

You seem to be very well in with her. When you get to be my age, you'll find that society is nothing, really, and you'll regret having attached so much importance to these trifles. Right, I'm going to take a turn before dinner. *Adieu les enfants,*" he cried to the world at large, as if he were already fifty meters away.

Once I had said goodbye to Rosemonde and Gisèle, they saw with astonishment that Albertine had stopped, without following them. "Albertine, what are you doing, you know the time?" "You go home," she replied authoritatively. "I have to talk with him," she added, indicating me with a submissive expression. Rosemonde and Gisèle looked at me, imbued, as far as I was concerned, with a new respect. I enjoyed feeling that, for the moment at least, and in the eyes even of Rosemonde and Gisèle, I counted for more with Albertine than the time of her return home, or than her friends, and might even share solemn secrets with her into which it was impossible that they be admitted. "Won't we be seeing you this evening?" "I don't know, that'll depend on him here." "Till tomorrow, anyway." "Let's go up to my room," I said to her, once her friends had gone. We took the lift; she held her tongue in front of the "lift." The habit of being obliged to rely on personal observation and on deduction in order to know the petty concerns of their masters, those strange people who talk among themselves but do not speak to them, develops a greater power of divination among "employees" (as the "lift" called the servants) than among the "employers." Our organs atrophy or become stronger or more subtle according as the need for them increases or diminishes. Since the existence of railways, the necessity of not missing the train has taught us to reckon the minutes, whereas among the ancient Romans, whose astronomy was not only more perfunctory but whose lives were less hurried, the notion, not of minutes, but even of fixed hours of the day, scarcely existed. So the "lift" had understood, and was counting on retailing to his fellows, that we were preoccupied, Albertine and I. But he talked to us without stopping, because he was without tact. I could see depicted on his face, however, substituted for the usual impression of friendship and delight at taking me up in his lift, a look of extraordinary dejection and anxiety. Since I was ignorant of its cause, in an attempt to distract him, and although more preoccupied with Albertine, I told him that the name of the lady who had just left was the Marquise de Cambremer and not de Camembert. On the floor that we were just then passing I caught sight of, carrying a bolster, a frightful-looking chambermaid who curtsied to me respectfully, hoping for a tip on my departure. I would like to have known whether it was the one I had so much desired on the evening of my first arrival in Balbec, but I was never able to be certain. The "lift" swore to me, with the sincerity of most false witnesses, though without abandoning his despairing expression, that it was certainly under the name of "Camembert" that the Marquise had asked him to announce her. And, truth to tell, it was quite natural that he should have heard a name he knew already. Besides, having, where the nobility and the nature of the names out of which titles are made are concerned, the very vague notions that are those of many people who are not lift boys, the name of Camembert had struck him as all the more probable in that, this cheese being universally known, there was no call to be surprised that a marquisate of such glorious renown should have been derived from it, unless it were that of the marquisate which had lent its celebrity to the cheese. All the same, as he could see that I did not wish to appear to have made a mistake, for he knew that the masters like to see their most futile whims being obeyed and their most blatant falsehoods accepted, he promised me, like a good servant, to say "Cambremer" from then on. It is true that no shopkeeper in the town or countryman from roundabout, where the name and the persons of the Cambremers were thoroughly familiar, would ever have been able to make the "lift's" mistake. But the staff at the Grand-Hôtel de Balbec were not in any sense locals. They had come in a straight line, with all their equipment, from Biarritz, Nice, and Monte Carlo, one part having been directed to Deauville, another to Dinard, and the third been kept for Balbec.

But the "lift's" sorrowful anxiety only grew. For him thus to have neglected to evince his devotion to me by his customary smiles, some misfortune had to have befallen him. Perhaps he had been "moved." I promised myself in that event to try to get him kept on, the manager having promised he would ratify whatever I might decide where his staff were concerned. "You can always do what you want, I rectify it in advance." Suddenly, just after leaving the lift, I fathomed the "lift's" distress, his downcast expression. Because of the presence of Albertine, I had not given him the hundred sous I was in the habit of handing him as we ascended. And instead of realizing that I did not want to make a show of tipping in front of a third party, the imbecile had begun to tremble, assuming that it was over once and for all, that never again would I give him anything. He had been imagining that I had "come a cropper" (as the Duc de Guermantes would have said), and that supposition had filled him, not with any compassion for me, but with a terrible, selfish disappointment. I told myself I was less unreasonable than my mother had thought one day when I had not dared not to give the exaggerated but feverishly anticipated sum that I had given the day before. But also the significance I had hitherto been lending, without the slightest doubt, to the customary expression of delight, which I had not hesitated to see as a sign of attachment, appeared less certain in meaning. Seeing the lift boy ready, in his despair, to throw himself down five stories, I wondered whether, had our respective positions in society been reversed, as the result of a revolution for example, instead of operating the lift for me so politely, the "lift," now a bourgeois, might not have thrown me from it, and whether there is not, among certain classes of the people, more duplicity than in society, where, no doubt, the disobliging remarks are reserved for when we are absent, but where the attitude toward us would not be insulting were we to fall on hard times.

It cannot be said, however, that at the Balbec hotel the "lift" was the most self-interested. As far as that went, the staff could be divided into two categories: On the one hand, those who made a distinction between the guests, being more responsive to the reasonable gratuity from an old nobleman (in a position, of course, to get him excused his twenty-eight days[18] by putting in a word with Général de Beautreillis) than to the reckless largesse of some foreign moneybags, who thereby betrayed a lack of breeding that was referred to as generosity only to his face. And, on the other hand, those for whom nobility, intelligence, celebrity, position, manners were nonexistent, being masked by a figure. For these there was only one hierarchy, the money that you have, or, rather, that you give. Aimé himself, although he aspired, on account of the large number of hotels in which he had served, to a wide knowledge of the world, perhaps belonged to this category. At most, he would give a social twist, as knowing the families, to this kind of appreciation, by saying of the Princess of Luxembourg, for example, "There's plenty of money there?"—the question mark being in order to gain information, or to check one last time on information already acquired, before procuring for a guest a "chef" for Paris, or guaranteeing him a table on the left as you go in, with a view of the sea, at Balbec. Despite which, without being devoid of self-interest, he would not have exhibited it with the same foolish despair as the "lift." However, the latter's artlessness perhaps simplified matters. The convenience of a grand hotel, or an establishment such as Rachel's once was, is that, without intermediaries, the sight of a hundred-franc note, and even more of a thousand-franc note, even when being given on this occasion to someone else, causes the hitherto frozen face of an employee or of a woman to smile and show willingness. In politics, on the other hand, or the relationship of a lover and a mistress, too many things are interposed between the money and the docility. So many things that even those in whom money finally kindles a smile are often incapable of following the inner process that links the two, and believe themselves to be, indeed are, more delicate. Besides, this refines polite conversation of all that "I know what there remains for me to do; tomorrow they'll find me in the morgue." Thus one meets in polite society with few novelists, or poets, or all those sublime creatures who talk about the very things that should not be said.

As soon as we were alone and had started down the corridor, Albertine said to me, "What have you got against me?" Had my severity toward her not been more painful to myself? Was it only an unconscious stratagem on my part, with a view to inducing in my loved one, vis-à-vis myself, that attitude of fear and entreaty that would enable me to question her and learn perhaps which of the two hypotheses I had long since formed about her was the right one? The fact is that, when I heard her question, I felt suddenly happy, like someone close to attaining a long-desired objective. Before answering her, I led her all the way to my door. As it opened, the latter caused the pink light that was filling the room to flow back and turned the white muslin of the curtains hanging against the evening into saffron lampas. I went as far as the window; the gulls had settled again on the waves, but now they were pink. I remarked on this to Albertine. "Don't change the subject," she

said, "be open like me." I lied. I declared that she would have to listen
to a preliminary confession, of a great passion that I had been feeling
for some time past for Andrée, and I made it to her with a simplicity
and candor worthy of the stage, but which we hardly ever have in life
save in the case of a love that we do not feel. Repeating the falsehood I
had used with Gilberte before my first stay in Balbec, but varying it, I
went so far, the better to make her believe me when I now told her that
I did not love her, as to let slip that in the old days I had been on the
point of falling in love with her, but that too much time had elapsed,
that she was no more to me than a good companion, and that, even
had I wanted, it would no longer have been possible for me again to
have more ardent feelings toward her. Moreover, by thus dwelling in Albertine's presence on the protestations of my indifference toward her,
all that I was doing—because of a particular circumstance and with a
particular end in view—was to make more apparent, to mark with
greater force, the binary rhythm that love assumes in all who are too
unsure of themselves to believe that a woman can ever love them, and
also that they can truly love her. They have sufficient self-knowledge to
know that, with the most dissimilar women, they have felt the same
hopes and the same anxieties, have invented the same fictions and uttered the same words, to have thus been made aware that their sentiments and their actions bear no close or necessary relation to the
beloved, but pass to one side of her, splashing her, circumventing her
like the tide that dashes itself along the rocks, and the sense of their
own instability even increases their mistrust as to whether this woman,
by whom they would like so much to be loved, loves them. Why would
chance so order it, when she is nothing more than a simple accident set
down before the outpouring of our desires, that we should be the object
of those that she feels? And so, even while needing to pour out all these
feelings toward her, so very different from the merely human feelings
inspired in us by our neighbors, the very special feelings that are those
of love, having taken a step forward, confessing to the one we love our
affection for her and our hopes, instantly fearful of displeasing her, embarrassed, too, at sensing that the language we have used was not created expressly for her, that it has served, will serve us, for others, that if
she does not love us she cannot understand us, that we have spoken

with the lack of good taste, the immodesty of the pedant addressing subtle phrases not designed for them to dunces, this fear, this shame, lead to a counterrhythm, a reflux, a need, be it by first of all drawing back, quickly to retract our previously confessed sympathy, to resume the offensive and recover our esteem, our dominance; this double rhythm is to be perceived in the various stages of a single love affair, in all the corresponding periods of similar love affairs, and in all those individuals who are better at analyzing than at valuing themselves. If, however, it was accentuated rather more forcefully than is customary in the speech I was in the midst of making to Albertine, this was simply to enable me to move more rapidly and energetically into the contrary rhythm, punctuated by my affection.

As though Albertine must be having difficulty believing what I had told her of the impossibility of my loving her again, because of the too long interval, I backed up what I had called a quirk of my character with examples taken from people with whom I had, either by their fault or my own, allowed the moment of loving them to pass, without being able, however much I might desire it, to rediscover it afterward. I thus appeared to be both apologizing to her, as if for an impoliteness, for this inability to start loving her again, and to be trying to make her understand the psychological reasons as if they had been peculiar to myself. But in explaining myself in this fashion, in elaborating on the case of Gilberte, in respect of whom what had become so untrue when applied to Albertine had been strictly true, I was simply making my assertions as plausible as I had pretended to believe that they were implausible. Sensing that Albertine had appreciated what she believed was my "frank talk," and had recognized in my deductions the clarity of the self-evident, I apologized for the former, telling her that I knew quite well that one always gave offense by speaking the truth, and that she must anyway have found it incomprehensible. She thanked me, on the contrary, for my sincerity, and added into the bargain that she understood perfectly a state of mind so common and so natural.

So as to appear wholly sincere and not to be exaggerating, I assured Albertine in passing, as if making a point of being polite, that this confession of an imaginary feeling for Andrée, and of indifference toward herself, was not to be taken too literally, and I was finally able, without fearing that Albertine might suspect love in it, to speak to her with a gentleness that I had for so long denied myself, and which I found delectable. I was almost caressing my confidante; as I spoke to her of her friend whom I loved, tears came into my eyes. But, coming to the point, I finally told her that she knew what love was like, its susceptibilities and its sufferings, and that perhaps, as a friend already of long standing, she would have her heart set on putting an end to the great unhappiness she had been causing me, not directly, since it was not her that I loved, if I might venture to repeat that without offending her, but indirectly, by injuring me in my love for Andrée. I broke off to look and to indicate to Albertine a large solitary, hurrying bird that, far ahead of us, was lashing the air with the regular beat of its wings and, traveling at great speed above the beach, stained here and there by reflections like small pieces of torn red paper, covered its entire length, without slackening its speed, without its attention being diverted, without deviating from its course, like an emissary carrying far off some urgent, critical message. "It at least goes straight to the mark!" said Albertine with a reproachful look. "You say that because you don't know what I'd have liked to say to you. But it's so difficult that I'd rather give up; I'm certain I'd make you angry; and then all it would lead to is this: I'd be in no way happier with the one I've given my heart to, but I'd have lost a good companion." "But since I swear I shan't be angry . . ." She looked so sweet, so sadly docile, to be waiting for her happiness to come from me, that I had difficulty restraining myself and not kissing—kissing with the kind of pleasure almost that I would have got from kissing my mother—that new face, which no longer had the alert, blushing appearance of a perverse and mischievous kitten, with its little pink, upturned nose, but seemed, in the fullness of its overwhelming sadness, to have melted, in broad, flattened, descending rivulets, into kindness. Leaving my love out of account, as though it were a chronic foolishness unconnected with her, and putting myself in her place, I felt pity faced by this good girl, accustomed to being treated fairly and kindly, yet against whom the good companion she may have thought I was for her had been conducting for weeks past a persecution that had finally reached a climax. It was because I had taken up a simply human vantage point, external to the two of us, from where my jealous love had vanished, that I felt this profound pity for Albertine, which would have been less so if I had not loved her. Moreover, in this rhythmic oscillation, which goes from the declaration to the quarrel (the surest, most dangerously effective means of forming, by contrary and successive movements, a knot that will not come untied, but which attaches us firmly to a person), and at the heart of the movement of withdrawal which constitutes one of the two elements in this rhythm, what use is it still to distinguish these refluxes of human pity, which, opposed to love yet perhaps having unconsciously the same cause, lead in any case to the same effects? When, afterward, we recall the sum total of all that we have done for a woman, we are often made aware that the actions inspired by the desire to demonstrate that we love her, to make ourselves loved, to win favors, occupy little more space than those attributable to the human need to set right the wrongs we have done to the one we love, out of a simple moral duty, as though we did not love them. "So, then, what have I managed to do?" Albertine asked me. There was a knock; it was the "lift"; Albertine's aunt, who had been passing the hotel in her carriage, had stopped on the off chance to see whether she might not be there and to take her back. Albertine sent answer that she could not come down, that they should eat without waiting for her, that she did not know what time she would be home. "But your aunt will be angry?" "Don't you believe it! She'll understand perfectly." And so—at this moment at least, such as would not perhaps recur—a conversation with me was, as Albertine saw it, the circumstances being what they were, a matter so self-evidently important that it must come before everything else, to which, referring herself no doubt instinctively to a familial jurisprudence, and enumerating the situations in which, when M. Bontemps's career had been at stake, a journey was not a consideration, my loved one was in no doubt that her aunt would think it perfectly natural to find the dinner hour being sacrificed. Having slid this remote hour that she spent without me, at her family's, all the way to me, Albertine gave it to me; I could use it as I saw fit. In the end, I ventured to tell her what had been reported to me as to her mode of life, and that, despite the profound disgust aroused in me by women afflicted with that same vice, I had not felt any concern until they named her accomplice to me, and that she could well understand, loving Andrée to the extent that I did, the grief that I had experienced. It would have been cleverer perhaps to say that other women, too, had been named, but ones who meant nothing to me. But Cottard's abrupt and terrible revelation had entered into me and lacerated me just as it was, in its entirety, with nothing to be added. And just as, before, I could never on my own have imagined that Albertine loved Andrée, or might at least play caressing games with her, had Cottard not drawn my attention to their attitude as they waltzed, so I had been unable to move on from that idea to the, for me, so very different one that Albertine might have relationships with women other than Andrée, which not even affection could excuse. Even before swearing to me that it was not true, Albertine, like anyone who has just been told they have been talked about in this way, displayed anger, unhappiness, and, where the unknown slanderer was concerned, a raging curiosity to learn who it was and a desire to come face-to-face with them, so as to be able to confound them. But she assured me that at least she did not hold it against me. "If it'd been true, I'd have confessed it. But Andrée and I are both as horrified as each other by that sort of thing. We haven't reached the age we are without seeing women with short hair, who have mannish ways and are of the kind you say, and nothing revolts us as much." Albertine merely gave me her word, a peremptory word, and unsupported by any proof. But that was the very thing best able to set my mind at rest, jealousy belonging to that family of unhealthy doubts far more easily removed by the vigor of an affirmation than by its plausibility. A peculiarity of love, moreover, is that it makes us at once more mistrustful and more credulous, makes us quicker to suspect the one we love than we would have another woman, and to be readier to lend credence to her denials. We must be in love to feel concern that there are not only honest women, or, in other words, to be made aware of it, and in love, also, if we are to hope, that is to say to be sure, that there are some. It is human to seek out sorrow and at once to be delivered from it. The propositions capable of succeeding in this easily strike us as true; we do not quibble for long over a sedative that works. And, besides, however multiple the person that we love may be, they may in any case present two essential personalities to us, according to whether they appear as ours or as turning their desires elsewhere than toward us. The first of these personalities possesses the peculiar power that prevents us from believing in the reality of the second, the specific secret for allaying the suffering that the latter has caused. The loved one is by turns the sickness and the remedy that suspends and aggravates the sickness. No doubt I had long been prepared, by virtue of the sway exercised over my imagination and my ability to be moved by the example of Swann, to believe that what I feared was true, instead of what I would have wished for. Thus the comfort brought by Albertine's affirmations was all but compromised for a moment because I recalled the story of Odette. But I told myself that, if it was right to make allowances for the worst not only when, in order to understand Swann's sufferings, I had tried to put myself in his place, but now that it involved myself, by seeking the truth as though it involved someone else, it must not, however, out of cruelty toward myself, a soldier choosing the post, not where he may be of the greatest use but where he is the most exposed, eventuate in the error of holding one supposition to be truer than the others solely because it was the most painful. Was there not an abyss between Albertine, a girl from quite a good bourgeois family, and Odette, a cocotte sold by her mother from an early age? The word of the one was not to be set alongside that of the other. Moreover, Albertine had none of the same interest in lying to me as Odette had to Swann. Besides, Odette had confessed to the latter what Albertine had just denied. I should therefore have committed an error of reasoning as serious—though opposite—as that which would have inclined me toward a hypothesis on the grounds that it would have caused me less suffering than the others, by not taking into account these real differences between their situations and reconstructing the actual life of my loved one solely in terms of what I had learned of Odette's. I had before me a new Albertine, already glimpsed on several occasions, it was true, toward the end of my first stay in Balbec, open, good-natured, an Albertine who, out of affection for me, had just forgiven me my suspicions and attempted to dispel them. She made me sit down beside her on my bed. I thanked her for what she had said, I assured her that our reconciliation was complete and that never again would I be hard on her. I told Albertine that she should, all the same, go back home for dinner. She asked me whether I was not comfortable as we were. And, drawing down my head for a caress she had never as yet given me, and which I owed perhaps to the ending of our quarrel, she passed her tongue lightly over my lips, and tried to part them. To start with, I kept them tightly shut. "You're being such a naughty boy!" she said.

I should have left that evening without ever seeing her again. I had a presentiment from then on that in a love that is not shared—or, in other words, in love, for there are people for whom there is no shared love—all we can taste of happiness is that simulacrum which had been granted me at one of those unique moments when a woman's kindness, or her caprice, or chance applies to our desires, in a perfect coincidence, the same words and the same actions as if we had truly been loved. The wise thing would have been to contemplate with curiosity, to possess with delight this small particle of happiness, lacking which I would have died without having suspected what it can be like for hearts less difficult or more favored; to suppose that it formed part of a vast and enduring happiness that had appeared to me at this point alone; and, so that the following day might not give the lie to this pretense, not to try to demand a further favor following that which had been due only to the artifice of an exceptional moment. I should have left Balbec, have shut myself away in solitude, have remained there in harmony with the dying vibrations of the voice I had been able to turn for a moment into that of love, and of which I would have demanded nothing more than never to address me further; for fear that by some fresh utterance, which from now on could only be different, it might wound by a dissonance the silence of the senses in which, as though thanks to some pedal, the tonality of happiness might have long survived within me.

Calmed by my discussion with Albertine, I began to live more in the company of my mother once again. She liked talking quietly to me about the days when my grandmother had been younger. Afraid that I might be reproaching myself for the sadnesses with which I may have darkened the end of that life, she went gladly back to the years when my early studies had given my grandmother satisfactions that hitherto had always been concealed from me. We spoke again of Combray. My mother told me that there at least I used to read, and that in Balbec I should certainly be doing the same, if I was not working. I replied that, in order indeed to surround myself with memories of Combray and the pretty painted plates, I would like to reread the *Arabian Nights*. As in the old days at Combray, when she gave me books for my name day, so as to make it a surprise, my mother sent secretly for both Galland's *Arabian Nights* and Mardrus's *Arabian Nights*.[19] But, having cast an eye over the two translations, my mother would certainly have wanted me to stick to that by Galland, while being afraid to influence me, on account of the respect she had for intellectual freedom, of a fear of intervening clumsily in the life of my mind, and of the feeling that, as a woman, on the one hand she lacked, as she thought, the necessary literary competence, and on the other should not be judging a young man's reading matter according to what she found shocking. Lighting upon certain of the tales, she had been revolted by the immorality of the subject matter and the coarseness of the expression. But above all, having conserved as precious relics, not only the brooch, the *en-tout-cas,* the cloak, and the volume of Mme de Sévigné, but also her mother's habits of thought and of language, and, searching at every opportunity for the opinion the latter might have expressed, my mother was in no doubt that my grandmother would have pronounced sentence on Mardrus's book. She recalled that at Combray, when, before setting off on the Méséglise walk, I had been reading Augustin Thierry,[20] my grandmother, happy with my reading and with my walks, was indignant all the same to find the man whose name had remained attached to the hemistich "Then Mérovée reigned" being referred to as Merowig, and refused to say "Carolingians" for the "Carlovingians," to whom she had remained faithful. In the end I had told her what my grandmother had thought about the Greek names that Bloch, following Leconte de Lisle,[21] had given to the Homeric gods, even going so far, in the case of the simplest things, to take it as a religious duty, in which he thought literary talent consisted, to adopt the Greek spelling. Having to say, for example, in a letter that the wine they drank at home was true nectar, he wrote "true nektar," with a "k," which enabled him to snigger at the name Lamartine.[22] Now, if an *Odyssey* from which the names of Ulysses and Minerva were missing was for her no longer the *Odyssey,* what would she have said on seeing the title of her *Arabian Nights* deformed on the cover itself, and on no longer finding, exactly transcribed as she had always been accustomed to saying them, the immortally familiar names of Scheherezade or Dinarzarde, or where the charming Caliph and the influential Djinns were barely recognizable, having been debaptized, if I dare apply that term in the case of Muslim tales, as, in the one instance, the "Kalifat," and, in the other, the "Gennis"? Meanwhile, my mother handed me the two books, and I told her I would read them on those days when I was too tired to go out for a walk.

Those days were not very frequent, as it happens. We went to have tea as a "gang," as in the old days, Albertine, her girlfriends, and I, on the cliffs or at the Marie-Antoinette farm. But there were times when Albertine gave me this great pleasure. She would say, "Today I want to be alone with you for a bit, it would be nicer if just the two of us met." Then she would say she had things to do, that in any case she did not have to account to anyone, and, so that the others, if they went off for a walk and for tea without us, would not be able to find us, we used to go off like two lovers all on our own, to Bagatelle or La Croix d'Heulan, while the gang, who would never have thought of looking for us there and never went there, remained indefinitely, in the hope of seeing us arrive, at Marie-Antoinette. I remember the warm weather we were then having, when a drop of sweat would fall vertically, regularly, intermittently, from the brow of the farm boys working in the sun, like the drip from a cistern, alternating with the fall of the ripe fruit coming away from the tree in the neighboring "close"; they have remained, still today, together with this mystery of a woman concealed, the most constant element in any love that is offered to me. I will break all my week's engagements to get to know a woman I have been told about but to whom I would not give a moment's thought, if it is a week when the weather is of this kind, and if I am to meet her at some isolated farmhouse. For all my knowing that weather and an assignation of this sort are not from her, they are the bait, familiar to me though it is, that I allow myself to take and which is enough to hook me. I know that in cold weather, in a town, I might have desired this woman, but without the accompaniment of any romantic feelings, without falling in love; the love is no less strong once, the circumstances being what they are, it has enslaved me; it is simply more melancholy, as our feelings for people become in life the more we perceive the increasingly small part they are playing and that the new love, which we would wish to be so enduring, and to be cut short at the same time as our life itself, will be the last.

There were few people in Balbec as yet, few girls. Sometimes I would see one or another of them stopped on the beach, without attractions yet who many coincidences seemed to certify was the same one as I had been in despair at not being able to go up to just as she was coming out with her friends from the riding school or the gymnastics class. If it was the same one (and I was careful not to mention her to Albertine), the girl I had thought intoxicating did not exist. But I was unable to attain any certainty, for the faces of these girls did not occupy a fixed magnitude on the beach, did not present any permanent form, contracted, dilated, transformed as they were by my own expectations, by my anxious longing, or a feeling of well-being that was sufficient unto itself, by the different outfits that they wore, by the pace they were walking at, or by their immobility. From close up, however, I found two or three of them adorable. Each time I saw one of these, I longed to take her down the Avenue des Tamaris, or into the dunes, or, better still, along the cliffs. But although into desire, as opposed to indifference, there already enters the boldness that is after all a first step, if a unilateral one, toward realization, between my desire and the action that would be my asking to kiss her, there lay the whole indefinite "blank" of hesitation and timidity. So then I would go to the *pâtissier-limonadier* and drink seven or eight glasses of port, one after the other. Instantly, in place of that unbridgeable gap between my desire and the action, the effect of the alcohol drew a line that conjoined both. No further room for hesitation or fear. I fancied that the girl would come flying to me. I went up to her, and these words came from my lips of their own accord: "I would like to go for a walk with you. Wouldn't you like to go along the cliffs, you're not disturbed by anyone behind the little wood which shields the portable house that's currently unlived in from the wind?" All life's difficulties had been smoothed away, there was no longer anything to impede the intertwining of our two bodies. No more impediments where I was concerned, at least. For they had not evaporated for the girl, who had not been drinking port. Had she done so, and had the universe lost a certain reality in her eyes, the long-cherished dream that might then have suddenly appeared realizable to her would by no means perhaps have been that of falling into my arms.

Not only were the girls few in number, but at that time of year, which was not yet the "season," they stayed only briefly. I remember one with the russet complexion of a coleus flower, with green eyes and two russet cheeks, whose thin, reversible face resembled the winged seeds of certain trees. I do not know what breeze brought her to Balbec, or what other breeze bore her away again. So abrupt was it that for several days I felt an unhappiness which I ventured to confess to Albertine, once I realized that she had gone forever.

It has to be said that several of them were either girls I did not know at all, or ones whom I had not seen in years. Often, before meeting them, I would write to them. What joy if their reply led me to believe in a possible love affair! At the outset of a friendship with a woman, even if it is not subsequently to be realized, we cannot be parted from the first letters we have received. We want to have them always beside us, like so many beautiful flowers we have been sent, still fresh, and which we break off from gazing at only in order to breathe them in from closer up. The phrase that we know by heart is pleasant to reread, and with those that we have learned less literally, we want to verify the degree of affection in a certain expression. Did she write "your dear letter"? A small disappointment in the sweetness we are breathing in, to be attributed either to our having read too fast or to our correspondent's illegible handwriting; she has not put "and your dear letter," but "on seeing your letter." But the rest is so affectionate. May more such flowers come tomorrow! Then that is no longer enough; her looks, her voice must be set next to the written words. We arrange a rendezvous, and—without her having changed, perhaps—where we had thought, from the given description or our own personal memory, we would be meeting the fairy Viviane, we find Puss in Boots.[23] We fix a rendezvous for the next day nevertheless, for it is after all *her*, and what we desired was her. But these desires for a woman of whom we have dreamed do not make the beauty of any precise feature absolutely necessary. These desires are simply the desire for some being or other; vague as fragrances,[24] as styrax was the desire of Prothyraia, saffron the ethereal desire, spices the desire of Hera, myrrh the fragrance of the clouds, manna the desire of Nike, incense the fragrance of the sea. But the fragrances of which the Orphic Hymns sing are far fewer in number than the divinities that they cherish. Myrrh is the fragrance of the clouds but also of Protogonos, of Neptune, of Nereus, and of Leto; incense is the fragrance of the sea, but also of the beautiful Dike, of Themis, of Circe, of the Nine Muses, of Eos, of Mnemosyne, of the Day, of Dikaiosyne. As for styrax, manna, and spices, there could be no telling all the divinities whom they inspire, so numerous are they. Amphietes has all the fragrances save incense, and Gaia rejects solely beans and spices. So also with the desires I felt for girls. Fewer in number than they were, they turned into disappointments and unhappinesses, one of which was much like another. Myrrh I have never wanted. I reserved that for Jupien and for the Princesse de Guermantes, since it is the desire of Protogonos "of the two sexes, having the bellow of the bull, of the countless, memorable, indescribable orgies, descending, joyfully, to the sacrifices of the Orgiophants."

But soon the season was in full swing; every day saw new arrivals, and for the suddenly increasing frequency of my walks, replacing the delightful reading of the *Arabian Nights,* there was a reason devoid of pleasure, which poisoned every one of them. The beach was now populated by girls, and the idea put into my head by Cottard having not furnished me with fresh suspicions but made me sensitive and vulnerable on that score, and careful not to allow any to form within me, as soon as a young woman arrived in Balbec, I felt uneasy and proposed the most distant excursions to Albertine, so that she might not make the acquaintance of, or even, if it were possible, set eyes on, the new arrival. I was naturally more fearful still of those whose dubious ways had been observed, or whose bad reputation was known; I attempted to persuade my loved one that this bad reputation was without foundation, was a slander, perhaps, without admitting it to myself, out of an as yet unconscious fear that she might try to strike up a friendship with the depraved woman in question, or regret not being able to seek her out on my account, or think, given the number of examples, that so widespread a vice was not to be condemned. By denying it in each instance of guilt, I came close to claiming that sapphism does not exist. Albertine adopted my own incredulity in respect of this or that woman's vice: "No, I think it's just a manner she's trying to put on, it's to give herself style." But then I would almost regret having pleaded their innocence, for it displeased me that Albertine, formerly so severe, might think that this "manner" was something sufficiently flattering, and sufficiently advantageous, for a woman exempt from such tastes to have sought to make it appear that she had them. I would have wished for no more women to come to Balbec; I trembled at the thought that, since this was more or less the time when Mme Putbus was due to arrive at the Verdurins', her lady's maid, whose preferences Saint-Loup had not concealed from me, might make an excursion as far as the beach and, if it was on a day when I was not at Albertine's side, might try to corrupt her. I found myself wondering, since Cottard had made no secret of the fact that the Verdurins were very attached to me and, while not wishing, as he put it, to appear to be pursuing me, would have given much to receive a visit, whether I might not, by dint of promising to bring to them in Paris every known Guermantes, persuade Mme Verdurin, on some pretext or other, to warn Mme Putbus that it was impossible that they should keep her in the house and make her leave again as quickly as possible.

In spite of these thoughts, and since it was above all the presence of Andrée that had been worrying me, the assuagement procured by Albertine's words persisted for some little while longer. I knew, moreover, that soon I would have less need of it, Andrée being due to leave with Rosemonde and Gisèle at almost the same time as everyone would be arriving, having only a few weeks more in the company of Albertine. During these weeks, moreover, Albertine seemed to plan everything she did and everything she said with a view to destroying my suspicions, should any remain, or stopping them from reviving. She saw to it that she was never left alone with Andrée and insisted, when we returned home, that I should go with her all the way to her door, so that I might come and fetch her from there when we were due to go out. Andrée, meanwhile, for her part, took equal pains and seemed to avoid seeing Albertine. And this apparent pact between them was not the only indication that Albertine must have informed her friend of our conversation and asked her to be good enough to lay my absurd suspicions to rest.

Around this time, there occurred a scandal at the Grand-Hôtel de Balbec that was not calculated to alter the course of my torments. Bloch's sister had for some little time had a secret relationship with a former actress that soon was no longer enough for them. To be seen seemed to them to add perversity to their pleasure, and they wanted to expose their perilous frolickings to the public gaze. It began with caresses that might after all be put down to an intimate friendship, in the card room, around the baccarat table. Then they grew bolder. Finally, one evening, in a not even unlit corner of the great ballroom, on a sofa, they no more stood on ceremony than if they had been in their bed. Two officers who were nearby with their wives complained to the manager. It was thought for a moment or two that their protest might have some effect. But against them was the fact that, having come to Balbec for the evening from Netteholme, where they were staying, they could be of no possible usefulness to the manager. Whereas, without her even knowing it, and whatever observations the manager may have made to her, there hovered over Mlle Bloch the protection of M. Nissim Bernard. I need to say why. M. Nissim Bernard practiced the family virtues in the very highest degree. Each year, he rented in Balbec a magnificent villa for his nephew, and no invitation could have deflected him from going back to dine at his, which was in reality their, house. He never ate lunch at home, however. Each day, at noon, he was at the Grand-Hôtel. For the fact was that, just as other men keep a young dancer, he kept a *"commis,"* rather like the *chasseurs* mentioned earlier, who put one in mind of the young Israelites in *Esther* and *Athalie*. Truth to tell, the forty years that separated M. Nissim Bernard from the young *commis* ought to have preserved the latter from a disagreeable contact. But as Racine puts it so very sagaciously in those same choruses:[25]

> Great heaven, with what uncertain steps
> Does a nascent virtue walk amid so many perils!
> May a soul that seeks you and would wish to remain innocent
> Find its designs obstructed![26]

For all that the young *commis* had been "raised far from the world," in the Temple Palace of Balbec, he had not followed the advice of Joas:

> Put not your trust in riches or in gold.[27]

He had resigned himself perhaps by saying, "The sinners cover the earth." Whatever the truth of the matter, and although M. Nissim Bernard could not have been hoping for so brief a delay, from the very first day,

> And whether from fear still or in order to caress him,
> By his innocent arms he felt himself pressed.[28]

From the second day, M. Nissim Bernard was taking the *commis* out, and "the contagion of this contact had marred his innocence." From then on, the young boy's life had changed. For all that he carried the bread and the salt, as ordered by his *chef de rang,* his whole face sang out:

> From flowers to flowers, from pleasures to pleasures
> Let us parade our desires.
> The number of our fleeting years is unsure.
> Let us make haste today to enjoy life!
> Honor and employment
> Are the price of a blind and sweet obedience,
> For the unhappy innocence
> That would come to raise its voice.[29]

From that day forward, M. Nissim Bernard had never failed to come and occupy his seat at lunch (as someone who is keeping a ballet dancer would have done his seat in the stalls, a ballet dancer in this case of a strongly characterized kind that still awaits its Degas).[30] It was M. Nissim Bernard's pleasure to follow, in the dining room and off into the distant vistas where the cashier sat enthroned beneath her palm tree, the maneuverings of this adolescent, assiduous in his attendance on one and all, though less so with M. Nissim Bernard since the latter had been keeping him, either because the young choirboy did not think it necessary to evince the same friendliness toward someone by whom he thought himself sufficiently loved, or because this love irritated him, or because he was afraid that, once discovered, it might make him

miss other opportunities. But this coldness in fact pleased M. Nissim
Bernard by all that it concealed. Whether out of an atavistic Hebraism,
or a profanation of Christian sentiment, he took a singular pleasure in
the Racinian ceremonial, whether Jewish or Catholic. Had it been a real
performance of *Esther* or *Athalie,* M. Bernard would have regretted that
the difference of centuries would not have allowed him to get to know
the author, Jean Racine, in order to obtain a more prominent role for
his protégé. But the ceremony of lunch not emanating from any writer,
he contented himself with being on good terms with the manager and
with Aimé, so that the "young Israelite" might be promoted to the
hoped-for role of either second-in-command or even *chef de rang.* He
had been offered that of sommelier. But M. Bernard forced him to
refuse, for he would no longer have been able to come every day and
see him running around the green dining room and be served by him
like a stranger. And so strong was this pleasure that M. Bernard came
back to Balbec year after year and ate his lunch away from home, habits
in which M. Bloch saw, in the first, a poetic liking for the beautiful
light, the sunsets along this coast that he preferred to any other; and, in
the second, the inveterate idiosyncrasy of an old bachelor.

Truth to tell, this error on the part of M. Nissim Bernard's relations,
who did not suspect the real reason for his annual return to Balbec, and
for what the pedantic Mme Bloch called his "culinary nights away," this
error was a deeper truth, to the second degree. For M. Nissim Bernard
was himself unaware of the extent to which his love of the beach at Balbec, and of the view you got over the sea from the restaurant, and his
obsessive habits entered into his liking for keeping, like a ballet dancer
of another sort as yet lacking its Degas, one of the male servants who
were still as yet girls. And so M. Nissim Bernard maintained excellent
relations with the manager of the theater that was the Balbec hotel, and
with Aimé, its director and stage manager—whose role in this whole affair was not of the most pellucid. One day they would scheme to obtain
a leading role, a position as *maître d'hôtel* perhaps. Meanwhile, M. Nissim Bernard's pleasure, however poetical and calmly contemplative it
might be, had something of the character of those ladies' men—Swann
in the old days, for example—who always know that by going into society they will meet with their mistress. Hardly would M. Nissim Bernard

be seated before he saw the object of his desires advancing onto the stage, bearing in his hand fruit or cigars on a tray. And so, each morning, having kissed his niece, fretted over my friend Bloch's labors, and fed lumps of sugar to his horses from his outstretched palm, he made feverish haste to arrive at the Grand-Hôtel in time for lunch. Had the house caught fire, or had his niece had a stroke, he would no doubt have left just the same. Thus he feared like the plague a cold that might keep him in bed—for he was a hypochondriac—and necessitate having Aimé asked to send his young friend around to him before teatime.

Moreover, he loved that whole labyrinth of corridors, secret offices, halls, cloakrooms, larders, and galleries that was the Balbec hotel. He had the atavistic love of an Oriental for harems, and when he left in the evenings, he was to be seen furtively exploring its byways.

Whereas, venturing all the way down into the basements, and trying in spite of everything not to be seen and to avoid scandal, M. Nissim Bernard put you in mind, in his quest for young Levites, of these lines from *La Juive*:[31]

> O God of our fathers,
> Descend among us,
> Conceal our mysteries
> From the eyes of the wicked![32]

I, on the contrary, was going up to the room of two sisters who had accompanied an old foreign lady to Balbec, as lady's maids. They were two what in hotel parlance are known as *courrières*, or guests' servants and, in that of Françoise, who imagined that a *courrier* or *courrière* is there to run *courses* or errands, two *coursières* or "coursers." Hotels, for their part, have remained, more nobly, in the days when they used to sing, "He's a ministerial messenger."[33]

In spite of the difficulty there was for a guest to go into the *courrières'* rooms, and vice versa, I had very soon struck up a very lively though very pure friendship with these two young people, Mlle Marie Gineste and Mme Céleste Albaret.[34] Born at the foot of the high mountains in the center of France, on the banks of streams and torrents (the water even passed underneath their family home, where a mill wheel turned, and which had several times been devastated by flooding), they seemed to have preserved their character. Marie Gineste was more uniformly quick and staccato, Céleste Albaret softer and more languid, slack like the waters of a lake, but with recurring fits of a terrible turbulence when her fury recalled the dangers of those spates and whirlpools that carry everything away and lay everywhere waste. They often used to come and visit me in the mornings, when I was still in bed. I have never known people so willfully ignorant, who had learned absolutely nothing at school, yet whose language had something so literary about it that, had it not been for the almost primitive nature of their accent, you would have thought their words affected. With a familiarity on which I am not embroidering, and despite the praises (which are here in order to celebrate not myself but the strange genius of Céleste) and the criticisms, both equally false, but perfectly sincere, which such remarks appear to imply in my regard, as I was dipping croissants in my milk, Céleste would say to me: "Oh, little black devil with hair like a jay, oh, what deep mischief! I don't know what your mother was thinking of when she made you, because you're just like a bird. Look, Marie, wouldn't you say he's smoothing down his feathers, and turning his neck so supply? He looks so light, you'd think he was busy learning to fly. Oh, you're lucky that the ones who created you had you born into the ranks of the rich; what'd have become of you, wasteful as you are? Look, he's throwing away his croissant because it touched the bed. Oh no, look how he's spilling his milk; wait till I put a napkin on you, because you wouldn't know how to go about it; I've never seen anyone so silly and so clumsy as you." And then you heard the more regular torrent sound of Marie Gineste, who was furious and took her sister to task: "Come, Céleste, will you be quiet? Are you crazy, talking to Monsieur in that way?" All Céleste did was to smile; and since I hated having a napkin tied on: "No, I'm not, Marie, look at him, whoosh!—he's sitting straight up now, like a snake. A real snake, I tell you." She did not stint, indeed, on these zoological comparisons, for, according to her, one never knew when I was asleep, I fluttered about all night long like a moth, and during the day I was as quick as the squirrels—"you know, Marie, like you see at home, so agile you can't follow them even with your eyes." "But, Céleste, you know he doesn't like having a napkin on when he's eating." "It's not that he doesn't like it, it's to tell you there's no changing what he's made up his mind to. He's a lord and master and wants to show he's a lord and master. You can change the sheets ten times a day if you have to, but he won't have given in. Yesterday's lasted the course, but today they've only just been put on and already they'll have to be changed. Oh, I was right to say he wasn't made to be born among the poor. Look, his hair's standing up, it's puffing up with anger like the feathers on a bird. Poor little dickybird!" At this Marie was not alone in protesting; I did so, too, for I did not at all feel myself to be a lord and master. But Céleste never believed that my modesty was genuine and, cutting me short: "Oh, bag of tricks, oh, sweet, yes, and treacherous, of all the cunning, lowdown . . . ! Oh, Molière!" (This was the only writer's name that she knew, but she applied it to me, meaning by it someone who would be capable simultaneously of composing plays and performing in them.) "Céleste!" cried Marie imperiously who, not knowing the name of Molière, was afraid it might be some further insult. Céleste went back to smiling: "Haven't you seen the photograph in his drawer, then, of when he was a child? He wanted to make us believe they always dressed him very simply. And there, with his little cane, he's nothing but fur and lace, like no prince ever had. But that's nothing compared with his immense majesty and his even more profound goodness." "So now you're rummaging in his drawers," scolded Marie the mountain torrent. To allay Marie's fears, I asked her what she thought about what M. Nissim Bernard had been doing. "Oh, monsieur, those are things I couldn't have believed they existed; I needed to come here." And, for once outdoing Céleste with a more profound observation, "But there you are, monsieur, you can never know what there may be in a life." To change the subject, I talked to her about my father's life, who used to work day and night. "Oh, monsieur, those are lives where people keep nothing for themselves, not a single minute, not a single pleasure; everything, everything entirely, is a sacrifice for others; those are *given* lives. . . . Look, Céleste, just to put his hand on the coverlet to pick up his croissant, such refinement! He can do the most insignificant things; you'd think the whole nobility of France, all the way to the Pyrenees, was changing its position in every one of his movements."

Crushed by this far-from-truthful portrait, I was silent; Céleste saw this as one more stratagem: "Oh, brow that looks so pure yet hides so many things, cool and friendly cheeks like the inside of an almond, little satin hands all plush, nails like claws, and so on. Say, Marie, look at him drinking his milk, so composedly it makes me want to say my prayers. How serious he looks! Now's when they should do his portrait, really. He's the complete child. Is it drinking milk like them that's kept you their clear complexion? Oh, youth, oh, what pretty skin! You'll never grow old. You're lucky, you'll never have to raise your hand against anyone, because you've got eyes that know how to impose their will. And look there, now he's angry. He's standing up, straight as what there's no denying."

Françoise did not at all like the women she called the two wheedlers coming to engage me in conversation like this. The manager, whose staff he made keep watch on everything that was going on, even pointed solemnly out to me that it was undignified for a guest to talk to the *courrières*. But I, who found the "wheedlers" superior to all the female guests in the hotel, merely laughed in his face, convinced that he would not understand my explanations. And the two sisters returned. "Look, Marie, at those delicate features. Oh, perfect miniature, finer than the most precious miniature you'd see in a glass case, for he's got the movements, and words to make you listen to him for days and nights on end."

It was a wonder that a foreign lady had been able to bring them, for, without knowing any history or geography, they confidently detested the English, the Germans, the Russians, the Italians, those foreign "vermin," and liked, with some exceptions, only the French. Their faces had preserved the moisture of the malleable clay of their rivers to such an extent that, as soon as mention was made of a foreigner staying in the hotel, in order to repeat what he had said, Céleste and Marie applied his face to their faces, their mouths became his mouth, their eyes his eyes, and you would have wanted to preserve these admirable stage masks. Céleste even, while pretending merely to be repeating what the manager had said, or one or another of my friends, would, without appearing to, insert fictitious remarks into her brief narrative, in which were mischievously depicted all the defects of Bloch, or the First President, and the like. In the form of an account of a simple errand that she had obligingly carried out, you got an inimitable portrait. They never read anything, not even a newspaper. One day, however, they found a book on my bed. It was some admirable but obscure poems by Saint-Léger Léger.[35] Céleste read a few pages and said to me, "But are you quite sure they're poetry? Aren't they more like riddles?" Obviously, for someone who had learned only one poem in her childhood, "Here below, all the lilacs are dying,"[36] there was a lack of transition. I think that their obstinate refusal to learn had something to do with their unhealthy native region. Yet they were as well endowed as a poet, with more modesty than these generally possess. For, if Céleste had said something remarkable and, unable to remember it properly, I asked her to remind me of it, she assured me she had forgotten. They will never read books, but neither will they ever write any.

Françoise was quite impressed on learning that the two brothers of these very simple women had married, one of them the niece of the Archbishop of Tours, the other a relation of the Bishop of Rodez. To the manager, this would have conveyed nothing. Céleste sometimes reproached her husband for not understanding her, and I was astonished, for my part, that he was able to put up with her. For there were certain moments when, quivering, furious, all-destroying, she was hateful. They claim that the saline liquid which is our blood is only what survives within us of our original element, the sea. In the same way, I believe that Céleste, not only in her rages but also in her moments of depression, had preserved the rhythm of her native streams. When she was exhausted, it was after their fashion; she had truly run dry. Nothing then could have brought her back to life. Then, all of a sudden, the circulation would resume in her tall, slender, magnificent body. The water flowed in the opaline transparency of her bluish skin. It smiled in the sunlight and became bluer still. At such moments she was truly celestial.

For all that Bloch's family had never suspected the reason why his uncle never lunched at home, but had accepted it from the outset as an old bachelor's idiosyncrasy, required of him perhaps by a liaison with some actress, everything that concerned M. Nissim Bernard was "taboo" for the manager of the Balbec hotel. And this was why, without even having referred the matter to the uncle, he had not dared in the end to find fault with the niece, while advising her to a certain circumspection. So the girl and her friend, who for several days had imagined that they would be banned from the casino and the Grand-Hôtel, finding that everything had been arranged, were happy to demonstrate to the patresfamilias who had shunned them that they could do whatever they liked with impunity. Not that they went so far, of course, as to repeat the public exhibition that had revolted everyone. But, gradually and imperceptibly, they resumed their old ways. And one evening, as I was leaving the casino more dead than alive, with Albertine and Bloch, whom we had met, they came past, intertwined, kissing without stopping, and, having drawn level with us, gave vent to giggles, laughter, and indecent shouts. Bloch looked down, so as to appear not to have recognized his sister, while I was in torments at the thought that this private and atrocious language was perhaps directed at Albertine.

Another incident fixed my preoccupations even more firmly in the direction of Gomorrah. On the beach I had seen a beautiful young woman, slender and pale, whose eyes disposed, around their centers, rays so geometrically luminous that, faced by her gaze, you thought of a constellation. I reflected on how much more beautiful this girl was than Albertine, and how it would be more sensible to give the other up. At the very most, this beautiful young woman's face had been subjected to an invisible planing by a life of great degradation, of the constant acceptance of coarse expedients, so that her eyes, though nobler than the rest of her face, had to radiate only appetite and lust. But the next day, this young woman being seated some distance from us in the casino, I could see that she never stopped letting the alternating and revolving light from her glances rest on Albertine. You would have said she was signaling to her, as if with the aid of a lighthouse. I was suffering lest my loved one see that she was the object of so much attention, and afraid that these endlessly kindled glances might carry the conventional meaning of a lovers' assignation for the following day. Who knows? That assignation might not perhaps be the first. The young woman with the

radiant eyes might have come to Balbec another year. It was perhaps because Albertine had already yielded to her desires or to those of a friend
that the latter felt free to address these dazzling signals to her. They
were doing more then than demand something for the present; their
authority for that had come from good times in the past.

In that case, the assignation would not be the first but a continuation of games played together in other years. And, indeed, the glances
were not saying, "Will you?" The moment the young woman had
caught sight of Albertine, she had turned her head all the way round
and shone glances at her laden with memories, as though she were
afraid and astounded that my loved one should not remember. Albertine, who could see her very clearly, remained phlegmatically without
moving, with the result that the other, with the same sort of tact as a
man who sees his former mistress with another lover, stopped looking
at her or taking any more notice of her than if she had not existed.

But a few days later, I received proof of this young woman's proclivities, and also of the probability that she had known Albertine in the
old days. Often, when, in the hall of the casino, two girls felt desire for
each other, there was produced something like a phenomenon of light,
a sort of trail of phosphorescence leading from one to the other. Let me
say in passing that it is with the aid of such materializations, imponder-
able though they be, by these astral signs setting fire to a whole portion
of the atmosphere, that, in every town and every village, that Gomorrah, having been scattered, tends to reunite its separated members, to
reconstitute the Biblical city, while everywhere the same efforts are being pursued, if only with a view to an intermittent rebuilding, by the
nostalgic, the hypocritical, and sometimes by the courageous exiles
from Sodom.

On one occasion I saw the unknown woman whom Albertine had
appeared not to recognize, just as Bloch's cousin was passing. Stars
came into the young woman's eyes, but it was easy to tell that she did
not know the young Israelite damsel. She was seeing her for the first
time, had felt desire, little doubt about that, but not at all the same certainty as in respect of Albertine—Albertine on whose camaraderie she
must have so much been counting that, faced by her indifference, she

had experienced the surprise of a stranger familiar with Paris but who does not live there and who, having returned to spend a few weeks, finds that a bank has gone up on the site of the little theater where he had been in the habit of spending happy evenings.

Bloch's cousin went and sat at a table, where she looked at a magazine. Soon the young woman came and sat down beside her, wearing an absent air. But beneath the table you would soon have been able to see their feet becoming agitated, and then their legs and hands, which were merged. Words followed, a conversation got under way, and the young woman's innocent husband, who had been looking for her everywhere, was astonished to find her making plans for that same evening with a girl he did not know. His wife introduced Bloch's cousin to him as a childhood friend, under some unintelligible name, for she had forgotten to ask her what her name was. But the presence of the husband advanced their intimacy by a step, for they addressed each other as *tu*, having met at the convent, an incident at which they laughed heartily later on, as well as at the deluded husband, with a merriment that was an opportunity for further intimacies.

As for Albertine, I cannot say that anywhere, in the casino or on the beach, her manner toward another girl was too free. I found it in fact excessively distant and insignificant, seeming more like a stratagem intended to deflect suspicion than the effect of a good upbringing. She had a quick, icy, proper way of answering this girl or that in a very loud voice—"Yes, I'll be going to play tennis around five. I shall have my bathe tomorrow morning around eight"—and at once leaving the person to whom she had just said this, which looked horribly like an attempt to mislead, and either to be arranging a rendezvous or, rather, having arranged one sotto voce, to be saying these, in effect insignificant, words loudly so as not to "draw attention to herself." And when next I saw her fetch her bicycle and ride off at top speed, I could not help thinking that she was on her way to join the girl to whom she had barely spoken.

At most, whenever some beautiful young woman got out of a motorcar at the corner of the beach, Albertine could not help looking round. And she would immediately justify herself: "I was looking at the new flag they've put up in front of the baths. They might have spent a bit more. The other one was pretty moth-eaten. But I really think this one's even shabbier."

On one occasion, Albertine was not content to remain indifferent, and I was all the more unhappy. She knew it bothered me that she might sometimes meet a friend of her aunt's, who "had a certain reputation" and sometimes came to spend two or three days with Mme Bontemps. Albertine had been kind enough to tell me she would not acknowledge her. And when this woman came to Incarville, Albertine said, "By the way, you know she's here. Did anyone tell you?," as if to demonstrate she was not seeing her on the sly. One day as she was saying this, she added, "Yes, I met her on the beach, and on purpose, out of rudeness, I practically brushed against her as I passed, I jostled her." As Albertine said this, there came back into my head some words of Mme Bontemps to which I had never given a second thought, when she had said to Mme Swann in my presence how impudent her niece Albertine was, as if this were a virtue, and how she had told some functionary or other's wife that the latter's father had been a kitchen boy. But a remark made by the woman we love does not preserve its purity for long; it spoils, it goes bad. One or two evenings later, Albertine's words came back to me, and what they seemed to signify was no longer the bad upbringing that was a source of pride to her—and which could but make me smile—but something else, and that Albertine, perhaps even without any precise object, in order to excite the woman's senses or to remind her mischievously of earlier propositions, accepted perhaps in the old days, had brushed quickly against her, had thought that I had perhaps found out about it, since it had been done in public, and had wanted to forestall an unfavorable interpretation.

But the jealousy caused in me by the women whom Albertine had perhaps loved was in any case about abruptly to cease.

We were, Albertine and I, in front of the Balbec station of the little local railway. We had had ourselves driven there by the hotel omnibus, on account of the weather. Not far away from us was M. Nissim Bernard, who had a black eye. He had recently been unfaithful to the choirboy from *Athalie,* with a boy from quite a thriving farm in the vicinity, Aux

Cerisiers. This red-faced boy, with his blunt features, seemed absolutely to have a tomato for a head. An exactly similar tomato served his twin brother for a head. For the disinterested onlooker, what is rather beautiful about these perfect resemblances between two twins is that nature, as if it had been momentarily industrialized, seems to be turning out similar products. M. Nissim Bernard, alas, saw things from a different point of view, and the resemblance was purely external. Tomato No. 2 found frenetic enjoyment in giving delight exclusively to the ladies; Tomato No. 1 was not at all loath to condescend to the tastes of certain gentlemen. Now, each time M. Bernard, shaken, as if by a reflex, by the memory of good times spent with Tomato No. 1, presented himself at Aux Cerisiers, the shortsighted (and shortsightedness was not essential in order to get them confused) old Israelite, unwittingly playing the role of Amphitryon,[37] would address the twin brother and say to him, "Will you meet me this evening?" He at once received a good "hiding." This might even be repeated in the course of the same meal, when he pursued with the one topics started on with the other. Eventually, by an association of ideas, he grew so to dislike tomatoes, even the edible kind, that every time he heard a traveler ordering them next to him at the Grand-Hôtel he would whisper: "Forgive me for addressing you without having been introduced, monsieur. But I heard you ordering tomatoes. They're not good today. I tell you this for your own good, as it's all one to me, I never eat them." The stranger would thank this disinterested and philanthropic neighbor effusively, call the waiter back, and pretend to be changing his mind: "No, definitely, no tomatoes." Aimé, for whom this was a familiar scene, would laugh to himself and think, "He's a sly old fox, M. Bernard, he's found a way of getting the order changed again." M. Bernard, as he waited for the tram, which was late, was not eager to greet Albertine and me, on account of his black eye. We were even less keen to speak to him. It would have been almost inevitable, however, if, at that moment, a bicycle had not borne down on us at high speed; from it jumped the "lift," out of breath. Mme Verdurin had telephoned shortly after our departure to get me to go to dinner in two days' time; it will soon be seen why. Then, having given me the details of this telephone call, the "lift" left us and, like those democratic "employees" who affect independence vis-à-vis the bourgeoisie and re-establish the principle of authority among themselves, meaning that the hall porter and the coachman might be displeased were he to be late, he added, "I'm off on account of my chiefs."

Albertine's friends had gone away for some time. I wanted to amuse her. Even supposing that she might have derived some happiness from spending the afternoons alone with me in Balbec, I knew that it never allows itself to be possessed totally and that Albertine, still at that age (which some never pass beyond) when we have yet to discover that this imperfection depends on the one who is experiencing the happiness, not on the one who is giving it, might have been tempted to trace the cause of her disappointment back to me. I preferred that she should impute it to circumstances that, having been arranged by me, would leave no opportunity for our being alone together, while preventing her from remaining in the casino or on the esplanade without me. And so, on the day in question, I had asked her to go with me to Doncières, where I would be going to visit Saint-Loup. In this same intention of keeping her occupied, I advised painting, which she had learned in the old days. While working, she would not be asking herself whether she was happy or unhappy. I would gladly also have taken her to dine now and again at the Verdurins' or the Cambremers', who would certainly, both of them, have gladly entertained a friend introduced by me, but I first had to be sure that Mme Putbus was not yet at La Raspelière. It was really only on the spot that I could find out, and I knew in advance that in two days' time Albertine would be obliged to go on an excursion with her aunt, so I had taken advantage of this to send a telegram to Mme Verdurin asking whether she could receive me on Wednesday. If Mme Putbus was there, I would contrive to meet her lady's maid, ascertain whether there was a risk of her coming to Balbec, and in that case find out when, so as to take Albertine well away on the day in question. The little local railway, making a loop that had not existed when I took it with my grandmother, now went through Doncières-la-Goupil, a large station from which important trains left, notably the express by which I had come to visit Saint-Loup from Paris and had then returned by. Because of the bad weather, the omnibus from the Grand-Hôtel took us, Albertine and me, to the station for the little tram, Balbec-Plage.

The little train was not yet there, but you could see the slow, lazy plume of smoke that it had left behind along the way, and which now, reduced to its own resources as a not very mobile cloud, was slowly climbing the green slopes of the Criquetot cliffs. At last, the little tram, which it had preceded only to then take a vertical direction, arrived in its turn, slowly. The passengers who would be catching it stood aside to give it room, but unhurriedly, knowing that they had to deal with a debonair, almost human stroller which, guided, like the bicycle of a learner, by the indulgent signals of the stationmaster, and under the powerful tutelage of the engine-driver, was in no danger of running any-one down and would have stopped wherever you wanted.

My telegram explained the Verdurins' telephone call, and it was all the more timely in that Wednesday (the day after next happened to be a Wednesday) was the day on which Mme Verdurin, at La Raspelière as in Paris, gave a big dinner party, which I had not known. Mme Verdurin did not give "dinners," but she had "Wednesdays." Her Wednesdays were a work of art. While knowing that there was nothing to equal them elsewhere, Mme Verdurin introduced fine distinctions between them. "This last Wednesday wasn't up to the one before," she would say. "But I think the next'll be one of the most successful I've ever given." She sometimes went so far as to confess: "This Wednesday wasn't worthy of the others. In return, I've got a big surprise for you for the one after that." In the final weeks of the season in Paris, before leaving for the country, the Patronne would announce that the Wednesdays were end-ing. It was an opportunity to spur on the faithful: "There are only three Wednesdays left, there are only two more," she would say, in the same tone of voice as if the world were about to end. "You're not going to let me down next Wednesday for the closure." But this closure was a sham, for she would warn them: "Now, officially, there are no more Wednes-days. That was the last for this year. But I shall be here all the same on Wednesdays. We'll have Wednesday among ourselves. Who knows? These little intimate Wednesdays will perhaps be the pleasantest." At La Raspelière, the Wednesdays were necessarily restricted, and since, ac-cording as some friend had been met with when passing through and had been invited for one evening or another, almost every day was a Wednesday. "I don't recall exactly the names of the guests, but I know Mme the Marquise de Camembert is one of them," the "lift" had said to me; the memory of our discussions relating to the Cambremers had not succeeded in finally supplanting the memory of the old word, whose familiar syllables, so full of meaning, had come to the aid of the young employee when he was having trouble with this difficult name, and had been instantly preferred and readopted by him, not out of laziness or as an old, ineradicable usage, but because of the need for logic and clarity that they satisfied.

We made haste to find an empty carriage where I would be able to kiss Albertine all through the journey. Not having found one, we got into a compartment where was already installed a lady with an enormous, ugly old face, and a mannish expression, very overdressed, who was reading the *Revue des deux mondes*. For all her vulgarity, she was pretentious in her gestures, and I amused myself by wondering to which social category she might belong; I at once concluded that she must be the manageress of some large brothel, a madam on her travels. Her face and mannerisms proclaimed it. I had simply been unaware until now that such ladies might read the *Revue des deux mondes*. Albertine drew my attention to her, not without winking as she smiled at me. The lady wore an extremely dignified air; and as, on my side, I carried within me the knowledge that I had been invited for the next day, at the terminus of the little railway, to the celebrated Mme Verdurin's, that at an intermediate station Robert de Saint-Loup was waiting for me, and that a little farther on I would have given Mme de Cambremer great pleasure by going to stay at Féterne, my eyes sparkled with irony as I contemplated this self-important lady, who seemed to think that, what with her studied attire, the feathers in her hat, and her *Revue des deux mondes*, she was a more considerable personage than myself. I was hoping that this lady would not remain much longer than had M. Nissim Bernard, and that she would at least be getting out at Toutainville, but no. The train stopped at Epreville; she remained sitting. Similarly at Montmartin-sur-Mer, at Parville-la-Bingard, at Incarville, so that, in despair once the train had left Saint-Frichoux, which was the last station before Doncières, I began to twine myself around Albertine without concerning myself with this lady. At Doncières, Saint-Loup had come to wait for me at the station, with the greatest difficulty, he told me, for, living as he was at his aunt's, my telegram had only just now reached him and, not having been able to organize his time in advance, he could only devote an hour to me. That hour appeared much too long for me, alas, for no sooner had she alighted from the carriage than Albertine's attention was all for Saint-Loup. She would not talk with me, scarcely answered if I addressed her, pushed me away when I approached. With Robert, on the other hand, she laughed her temptress's laugh, talked volubly, played with the dog he had brought, and, in teasing the animal, brushed deliberately against its master. I recalled that, on the day when Albertine had let herself be kissed by me for the first time, I had had a smile of gratitude for the unknown seducer who had produced so profound a modification in her and so greatly simplified my task. I thought of him now with horror. Robert must have realized that I was not indifferent to Albertine, for he did not respond to her flirting, which put her in a bad mood with me; then he spoke to me as if I were alone, which, once she had noticed it, made me rise again in her esteem. Robert asked me whether I would not like to try and find, among the friends with whom he had made me dine each evening in Doncières when I was staying there, those who were still there. And since he was inclined himself to the kind of irritating pretentiousness that he disapproved of— "What was the point of 'turning on the charm' for them so persistently if you don't want to meet them again?"—I turned down his proposal, because I did not want to risk being parted from Albertine, but also because I was now detached from them. From them, that is to say, from myself. We desire passionately that there should be another life in which we would be similar to what we are here below. But we do not reflect that, even without waiting for that other life, but in this one, after a few years we are unfaithful to what we have been, to what we had wanted to remain immortally. Even without supposing that death might modify us more than the changes that occur in the course of a lifetime, if in that other life we were to meet the self that we have been, we would turn away from ourselves as from those people to whom we have been close but whom we have not seen for a long time—those friends of Saint-Loup's, for example, that I was so pleased to find again every evening at the Faisan Doré, but whose conversation I would now find simply out of place and an embarrassment. In this respect, and because I preferred not to go and rediscover what had pleased me there, a walk through Doncières might have seemed to me to prefigure my arrival in paradise. We dream a great deal of paradise, or, rather, of numerous successive paradises, but they are all, long before we die, paradises lost, in which we would feel lost.

He left us at the station. "But you may have nearly an hour to wait," he said. "If you spend it here, you'll no doubt meet my uncle Charlus, who's taking the train to Paris again this afternoon, ten minutes before yours. I've already said my goodbyes to him, because I'm obliged to be back before the time of his train. I wasn't able to talk to him about you because I hadn't yet had your telegram." To the reproaches I directed at Albertine once Saint-Loup had left us, she replied that she had wanted, by her coldness toward me, to erase any ideas he might have chanced to get if, just as the train was stopping, he had seen me leaning against her with my arm around her waist. He had indeed remarked this position (I had not noticed him, otherwise I would have been sitting more correctly at Albertine's side) and had had time to say into my ear, "So, are these the very stuck-up girls you talked about, who wouldn't associate with Mlle de Stermaria because they didn't like the look of her?" I had indeed told Robert, and in all sincerity, when I went from Paris to visit him in Doncières, and as we were talking again about Balbec, that there was nothing doing with Albertine, that she was virtue itself. And now that I had long since learned for myself that this was not so, I wanted even more for Robert to believe it was true. It would have been enough for me to tell Robert that I loved Albertine. He was one of those people who are able to deny themselves a pleasure in order to spare their friend sufferings they would experience as if they were their own. "Yes, she's very childish. But you don't know anything about her?" I added anxiously. "Nothing, except that I saw you sat there like two lovers."

"Your attitude erased nothing at all," I said to Albertine once Saint-Loup had left us. "It's true," she said, "I was clumsy, I've made you suffer, I'm much more unhappy about that than you. You'll see, I'll never be like that again; forgive me," she said, holding out her hand to me with a sad expression. At that moment, from the back of the waiting room in which we were sitting, I saw, followed a little way behind by a porter carrying his bags, M. de Charlus go slowly past.

In Paris, where I encountered him only at soirées, motionless, tightly buttoned into his evening clothes, maintained in the vertical position by a haughty straightening of his back, the impulse to attract, and the rocket flight of his conversation, I had not realized to what extent he had aged. Now, in a light-colored traveling suit that made him look fatter, waddling as he walked, swinging a belly that was becoming a paunch and an almost symbolic behind, the cruelty of the broad daylight had broken down, into rouge on his lips, into rice powder fixed by cold cream on the tip of his nose, into black on the dyed mustache whose ebony color contrasted with his graying hair, everything that in an artificial light would have seemed to be enlivening the complexion of someone still young.

Even as I talked with him, only briefly, because of his train, I was looking at Albertine's carriage so as to signal to her that I was coming. When I turned back toward M. de Charlus, he asked me to be good enough to call over a soldier, a relation of his, who was on the other side of the tracks, exactly as if he were going to get into our train but in the opposite direction, that leading away from Balbec. "He's in the regimental band," M. de Charlus said. "Since you have the good fortune to be young enough, and I the nuisance of being old enough, for you to be able to spare me crossing all the way over there . . ." I made it my duty to go toward the soldier indicated and could see, indeed, from the lyres sewn onto his collar, that he was a bandsman. But how great was my surprise, and I may say my pleasure, when, just as I was about to discharge my commission, I recognized Morel, the son of my uncle's valet, who brought back so many memories! I forgot to carry out M. de Charlus's commission. "What, are you in Doncières?" "Yes, and I've been incorporated in the band, in the percussion." But he answered me in a curt, haughty tone. He had become a real "poseur," and the sight of me, reminding him as it did of his father's profession, was obviously disagreeable to him. I suddenly saw M. de Charlus bearing down on us. The delay had evidently made him impatient. "I'd like to hear a bit of music this evening," he said to Morel, without any preamble. "I'll give five hundred francs for the evening, that might be of some interest to one of your friends, if you have any in the band." For all that I was familiar with M. de Charlus's insolence, I was amazed that he should not even have greeted his young friend. The Baron left me no time for reflection, in any case. Holding out his hand affectionately, "*Au revoir,* dear boy," he said, to signify that all that remained was to go. I had in any case left my dear Albertine on her own for quite long enough. "You know," I said to her as we got back into the carriage, "the life of a resort and the life of travel make me realize that the theater of the world has fewer sets at its disposal than actors, and fewer actors than 'situations.'" "For what reason do you say that?" "Because M. de Charlus has just asked me to send one of his friends to him who, at this very instant, on the platform of the station here, I've just recognized as a friend of mine, too." But even as I said this, I was trying to think how the Baron might have met Morel. The social disproportion, which I had not at first considered, was too vast. My first idea was that it had been through Jupien, whose daughter, it will be remembered, had seemed very taken with the violinist. What had amazed me, however, was that, having to leave for Paris in five minutes, the Baron should have asked to hear some music in Doncières. But, seeing Jupien's daughter again in my memory, I was beginning to think that "recognitions," a lame expedient in works of artifice, might on the contrary express an important element in real life, were we able to attain to the true romance of it, when I had a sudden flash of inspiration and realized I had been very naïve. M. de Charlus had never in his life met Morel, nor Morel M. de Charlus, who, dazzled but also intimidated by a soldier, even by one wearing only lyres, had, in his agitation, commandeered me to bring him someone he had not suspected that I knew. At all events, the offer of five hundred francs must have made up in Morel's case for the absence of any previous connection, for I could see them continuing to talk without reflecting that they were next to our tram. And, recalling the manner in which M. de Charlus had come toward Morel and me, I seized on the resemblance to certain of his kinsmen when they picked up women in the street. The intended target had simply changed sex. After a certain age, and even if our inner development varies, the more we become ourselves, the more family characteristics are accentuated. For, while maintaining the harmonious design of its tapestry, Nature breaks up the monotony of the composition by the variety in the faces that it inserts. Moreover, the hauteur with which M. de Charlus had looked the violinist up and down is relative, according to the vantage point we adopt. It would have been recognized by three out of four society people, who bowed to him, but not by the chief of police, who, a few years later, was to put him under surveillance.

"The Paris train is signaled, monsieur," said the porter who was carrying the bags. "But I'm not catching the train, put all that in the cloakroom, confound it!" said M. de Charlus, giving the porter twenty francs, who was stupefied by this volte-face but enchanted by the tip. Such generosity at once attracted a flower-vendor. "Buy my carnations, see, this beautiful rose, *mon bon monsieur*, it'll bring you good luck." M. de Charlus, growing impatient, handed her forty sous, in exchange for which the woman offered him her blessing and once again her flowers. "God, if only she'd leave us alone," said M. de Charlus, addressing himself in an ironic, complaining tone, like a man all on edge, to Morel, in appealing to whom for support he found a certain comfort. "What we have to say is rather complicated as it is." Perhaps, the railwayman not yet being too far away, M. de Charlus was not eager to have a large audience, or perhaps these parenthetical words allowed his haughty timidity not to broach the request for a rendezvous too directly. The musician, turning with a frank, imperative, and resolute air toward the flower-vendor, raised a palm toward her, which thrust her away and signified that they did not want any of her flowers and that she should remove herself forthwith. M. de Charlus was in ecstasies at the sight of this virile, authoritative gesture, executed by the graceful hand for which it should as yet have been too heavy, too massively brutal, with a precocious firmness and suppleness that lent this as yet beardless adolescent the air of a young David capable of engaging Goliath in combat. Mixed involuntarily in with the Baron's admiration was the smile that we experience on seeing an expression on the face of a child that is too solemn for its years. "Here's someone I'd like to be accompanied by on my travels and helped by in my business affairs. How he would simplify my life!" M. de Charlus said to himself.

The Paris train (which the Baron did not take) left. Then Albertine and I got into ours, without my knowing what had become of M. de Charlus and Morel. "We mustn't ever be angry any more, I ask you to forgive me once again," Albertine repeated, referring to the Saint-Loup incident. "We must always both be kind," she said fondly. "As for your friend Saint-Loup, if you think he interests me in the very slightest, you're quite wrong. The one thing that attracts me about him is that he seems to be so fond of you." "He's a very good fellow," I said, carefully avoiding lending Robert any imaginary superior qualities, as I should not have failed to do out of friendship for him, had I been with anyone other than Albertine. "He's an excellent person, open, devoted, loyal, whom you can rely on for everything." In saying this, restrained by my jealousy, I was confining myself to speaking the truth about Saint-Loup, but it was certainly the truth that I spoke. But it had been expressed in exactly the same terms as Mme de Villeparisis had employed in talking to me of him, when I did not as yet know him, imagined him to be very different, very haughty, and used to tell myself, "People think him kind because he's a great nobleman." Similarly, when she had said to me, "He'd be so pleased," I imagined, having caught sight of him in front of the hotel, ready to drive off, that his aunt's words were a mere social commonplace, intended to flatter me. But I had then realized that she had spoken sincerely, thinking of what interested me, of my reading, and because she knew that that was what Saint-Loup liked, just as I was to have occasion to say sincerely to someone who was writing a history of his ancestor, La Rochefoucauld, the author of the *Maxims*,[38] and who would have liked to approach Robert for his advice, "He'll be so pleased." The fact was that I had learned to know him. But on meeting him that first time, I had not believed that an intelligence akin to my own could be swathed in so much outward elegance of dress and attitude. From his plumage, I had adjudged him to be from another species. It was Albertine now who, partly perhaps because Saint-Loup, out of kindness for me, had been so distant with her, said what I had once thought: "Oh, he's as devoted as that! I notice people always discover all the virtues in the people who come from the Faubourg Saint-Germain." Now, that Saint-Loup was from the Faubourg Saint-Germain was something that had not once crossed my mind during those years when, divesting himself of his prestige, he had displayed his virtues to me. A change of perspective from which to regard people, already more striking in friendship than in any mere social connection, but how much more so still in love, when desire sets the first signs of indifference on so vast a scale, magnifies them to such proportions, that it had taken a lot less than that shown at the outset by Saint-Loup to make me believe myself scorned at first by Albertine, to imagine her girlfriends to be wonderfully inhuman creatures, and to put Elstir's verdict down, when he said of the little gang, altogether in the same spirit as Mme de Villeparisis of Saint-Loup, "They're good girls," simply to the indulgence we feel toward beauty and a certain elegance. And was this not the verdict I would gladly have delivered when I heard Albertine say, "Anyway, devoted or not, I hope very much not to meet him again, because he led to us quarreling. We mustn't ever be angry again, the two of us. It's not nice"? Because she had seemed to feel desire for Saint-Loup, I felt more or less cured for some time of the idea that she loved women, which I imagined to be incompatible. And, confronted by Albertine's rubber raincoat, in which she seemed to have become another person, the indefatigable wanderer of rainy days, and which, close-fitting, malleable, and gray at that moment, seemed less to be to protect her clothes against the water than to have been soaked by her and to have been attached to my loved one's body in order to take an impression of her forms for a sculptor, I snatched at this tunic that was jealously molding a longed-for bosom and, drawing Albertine to me:

> "But you, indolent traveler, will you not
> Lay your brow on my shoulder, and dream?"[39]

I said, taking her head in my hands and pointing to the great silent, flooded meadows, stretching all the way in the gathering dusk to a horizon closed off by the parallel ranges of distant, blue-colored foothills.

Two days later, on the famous Wednesday, on the same little railway I had just taken in Balbec, to go and dine at La Raspelière, I was very anxious not to miss Cottard in Graincourt-Saint-Vast, where a fresh telephone call from Mme Verdurin had told me I would find him. He was to get on to my train and indicate where we needed to get off in order to find the carriages that were sent from La Raspelière to the station. And so, the little train stopping only for a moment at Graincourt, the first station after Doncières, I had stationed myself at the door ahead of time, so afraid was I of not seeing Cottard or of not being seen by him. Fears that proved quite baseless! I had not appreciated the extent to which, the little clan having shaped all the "regulars" to the same pattern, they, wearing full evening dress for good measure, were instantly recognizable as they waited on the platform, by a certain air of self-assurance, elegance, and familiarity, and by glances that passed, as though over an empty space where there is nothing to stay the attention, over the serried ranks of the common herd, watching for the arrival of some regular who had caught the train at a preceding station, and were already bubbling with the conversation to come. This sign of election, with which the habit of dining together had stamped the members of the little group, did not mark them out only when numbers of them were massed there in force, forming a more brilliant patch of color in the midst of the flock of travelers—what Brichot called the *pecus*[40]—on whose lackluster faces there could not be read any notion relating to the Verdurins, any hope of ever dining at La Raspelière. Moreover, these common travelers would have been less interested than I was had—despite the notoriety some had acquired—they heard spoken the names of those faithful whom I was surprised to find continuing to dine out, when several had already been doing so, according to the accounts I had heard, before I was born, in an epoch both sufficiently distant and sufficiently vague for me to be tempted to exaggerate its remoteness. The contrast between their continuing, not merely to exist but to be in the fullness of their vigor, and the annihilation of so many friends whom I had already seen depart at one time or another, produced in me the same feeling that we experience when, in the "Late News" column of the newspapers, we read the very report we had least expected, that of a premature death, for example, which seems fortuitous because the causes of which it is the outcome were not known to us. The sense we get is that death does not come to all men uniformly, but that a more advanced wave from its tragic tide, as it rises, carries off an existence situated at the same level as others that will yet long be spared by the waves that follow. We shall see, moreover, later on, the diversity of the deaths that circulate invisibly to be the source of that particular unexpectedness represented, in newspapers, by the obituaries.

Then I saw that, with time, not only do real gifts, which may coexist with the worst vulgarities in conversation, reveal and impose themselves, but also that second-rate individuals attain to those high positions that belong in our childhood imaginings to a few celebrated old men, without reflecting that, a certain number of years later, their disciples would be celebrated also, having become masters, and inspire the same respect and fear which they had felt in the old days. But if the names of the faithful were not known to them, their appearance attracted the stares of the *"pecus."* Even in the train (once the accident of what one or another of them had had to do during the day had brought them all together there), having only one more isolated member to pick up at the next station, the carriage in which they found themselves gathered, indicated by the elbow of Ski, the sculptor, and bedecked with Cottard's copy of *Le Temps*, blossomed in the distance like a deluxe carriage, and, at the station appointed, rallied their laggard comrade. The only one whom these promissory signs may have eluded, half blind as he was, was Brichot. But one of the regulars had gladly taken on the duties of lookout on behalf of the blind man, and the moment they caught sight of his straw hat, his green umbrella, and his blue spectacles, they steered him gently but hurriedly toward the compartment of election. So that it was unheard of for one of the faithful, short of exciting the gravest suspicions of being on the razzle or even of not having come by the train, not to meet up with the others along the way. On occasion, the opposite occurred: one of the faithful had had to go some distance during the afternoon and had in consequence to effect part of the journey on his own before being joined by the group; but even in isolation like this, alone of his kind, he did not fail most often to produce an effect. The Future for which he was heading singled him out to the person sitting on the seat opposite, who said to himself, "He must be somebody," and, with the obscure perspicacity of the travelers to Emmaus,[41] could discern, whether around Cottard's soft hat or Ski the sculptor, a vague halo, and was only half surprised when, at the next station, a fashionable crowd, if it was their final stop, welcomed this member of the faithful at the carriage door and went off with him toward one of the carriages that were waiting, all bowed very low to by the Douville porter, or else, if it were an intermediate station, invaded the compartment. Which is what, precipitately, for several had arrived late, just as the train, already in the station, was about to leave again, the troop did that Cottard led on the double toward the carriage at whose window he had seen my signals. Brichot, who was among the faithful in question, had become more so in the course of the same years that had seen the assiduity of others diminish. His progressively failing eyesight had obliged him, even in Paris, to do less and less work in the evenings. Moreover, he had little sympathy with the new Sorbonne, where German-style notions of scientific accuracy were beginning to prevail over humanism.[42] He confined himself exclusively now to his lectures and to examination juries; thus he had far more time to give to his social life, that is, to soirées at the Verdurins', or those given now and again for the Verdurins by one or another of the faithful, quaking with emotion. It is true that on two occasions love had nearly achieved what his work could not: detaching Brichot from the little clan. But Mme Verdurin, who "kept a weather eye open for squalls" and, what was more, having acquired the habit for the sake of her salon, had finally come to find a disinterested pleasure in these kinds of drama and executions, had turned him irremediably against the dangerous person, knowing, as she put it, how to "keep everything shipshape" and to "apply the cauterizing iron to the wound." This had been all the simpler for her in the case of one of these dangerous persons as it was only Brichot's washerwoman, and Mme Verdurin, who had free access to the professor's fifth-floor rooms, he blushing scarlet with pride whenever she deigned to undertake the climb, had merely had to show this worthless woman the door. "What," the Patronne had said to Brichot, "a woman like me does you the honor of coming up here, and you entertain a creature like that?" Brichot had never forgotten the service Mme Verdurin had rendered him by preventing his old age from sinking into the mire, and had become increasingly attached to her, whereas, in contrast to this renewal of affection and perhaps on account of it, the Patronne had begun to feel dislike for one of the faithful, who was far too docile, and of whose obedience she could be certain in advance. But from his intimacy with the Verdurins Brichot derived a prestige that marked him out among all his colleagues at the Sorbonne. They were dazzled by the accounts he gave them of dinner parties to which they

would never be invited, by the mention made of him in reviews, or by
the portrait exhibited at the Salon, by one or another renowned writer
or painter whose talents were held in high esteem by the holders of the
other chairs in the Faculty of Letters, but whose attention they had no
chance of attracting, and, finally, by the very elegance of dress of the
worldly philosopher, an elegance that they had mistaken at first for ca-
sualness until such time as their colleague kindly explained to them that
the top hat gladly allows itself to be put down on the floor in the course
of a visit, and is not worn for dinners in the country, however smart,
where it must be replaced by a soft hat, which looks very well with a
dinner jacket. During the first moments of the little group's being en-
gulfed by the carriage, I was not even able to speak to Cottard, for he
was choking, less from having run so as not to miss the train as from
amazement at having cut it so fine. More than joy at a triumph, he was
experiencing the hilarity almost of a merry prank. "Oh, that was a good
one!" he said, once he had recovered himself. "Another few seconds,
upon my word, that's what they call arriving on the dot!" he added with
a wink, not in order to ask whether the expression was correct, for these
days he oozed self-assurance, but out of self-satisfaction. Finally, he was
able to name me to the other members of the little clan. I was annoyed
to see that they were almost all of them dressed in what in Paris is called
a *smoking*. I had forgotten that the Verdurins had begun timidly to
evolve in the direction of society, an evolution slowed by the Dreyfus
Affair but accelerated by the "new" music, if one which they themselves
denied, and would continue to deny until it had come to fruition, like
the military objectives that a general announces only once he has attained them, in such a way as not to appear to have suffered a defeat
if he fails. For its part, moreover, the world was quite prepared to
move toward them. As yet, it looked on them as people to whom no
one from society went, but who did not thereby feel any regret. The
Verdurin salon passed for a temple of music. It was there, you were assured, that Vinteuil had found inspiration and encouragement. Now,
if Vinteuil's sonata remained wholly misunderstood and more or less
unknown, his name, spoken as that of the greatest of contemporary musicians, exerted an extraordinary prestige. Indeed, certain young men
from the Faubourg having made up their minds to be as well informed

as the bourgeoisie, three of their number had learned music, and among these Vinteuil's sonata enjoyed a huge reputation. Having returned home, they spoke of it to the intelligent mothers who had urged them on to cultivate themselves. And having taken an interest in their sons' studies, at concerts the mothers would gaze with a certain respect at Mme Verdurin, who was following the score from her front box. Until now, this latent society-mindedness on the Verdurins' part had betrayed itself by two actions only. On the one hand, Mme Verdurin had said of the Princesse de Caprarola:[43] "Ah, she's intelligent, that one, she's an agreeable woman. What I can't stand are the imbeciles, the people who bore me, they drive me crazy." Which would have given anyone in the least discerning to think that the Princesse de Caprarola, a woman of the very highest society, had paid a call on Mme Verdurin. She had even uttered her name in the course of a visit of condolences she had made to Mme Swann after the death of the latter's husband, and had asked her whether she knew them. "How did you say?" Odette had replied, suddenly looking sad. "Verdurin." "Oh, then I know!" she went on, desolately. "I don't know them, or, rather, I know of them without having met them, they're people I saw once at some friends' a long time ago, they're agreeable." The Princesse de Caprarola having left, Odette would very much have liked simply to have told the truth. But her instant falsehood was not the product of calculation, but the revelation of her fears and of her desires. She had denied not what it would have been astute to deny, but what she would have wished was not the case, even if her interlocutor was to learn within the hour that it was indeed the case. Not long afterward, she had regained her self-confidence and had even pre-empted questions by saying, so as not to appear to fear them, "Mme Verdurin, why, I knew her terrifically well," with an affectation of humility, like a great lady recounting how she has taken the tram. "The Verdurins have been much spoken of just lately," said Mme de Souvré. Odette, with the disdainful smile of a duchess, replied, "Oh yes, indeed, I imagine they're much spoken of. From time to time you get new people like that who arrive in society," without reflecting that she herself was one of the newest. "The Princesse de Caprarola has dined there," Mme de Souvré went on. "Ah!" replied

Odette, accentuating her smile. "That doesn't surprise me. It's always through the Princesse de Caprarola that these things start, then another one comes along, the Comtesse Molé, for example." In saying this, Odette appeared to have a profound disdain for the two great ladies, who were in the habit of being the earliest occupants of the newly opened salons. You sensed by her tone that this meant that they would never manage to get her, Odette, like Mme de Souvré, aboard any such ship of fools as that.

Following Mme Verdurin's admission as to the Princesse de Caprarola's intelligence, the second sign that the Verdurins were conscious of their future destiny was that they hoped very much that (without having requested it formally, of course) people would now wear evening dress when coming to dinner; M. Verdurin might now have been greeted without shame by his nephew, the one who was "in Queer Street."

Among those who got into my carriage at Graincourt was Saniette, who had been driven out from the Verdurins' in the old days by his cousin Forcheville but had returned. His defects, where his social life was concerned, had once been–for all his superior qualities–somewhat of the same kind as those of Cottard, shyness, a desire to please, and fruitless attempts to manage to do so. But if life had led Cottard to wear, if not at the Verdurins', where he had, thanks to the influence that past times exert over us when we find ourselves in an accustomed setting, remained much the same, then at least among his patients, when on duty at the hospital or at the Academy of Medicine, an exterior of coldness, disdain, and solemnity that was accentuated while he was coming out with his puns in front of his indulgent pupils, and had dug a veritable chasm between the present Cottard and the old one, the same defects had, on the contrary, become exaggerated in Saniette, even as he sought to correct them. Sensing that he was often boring, that he was not listened to, instead of then slowing down, as Cottard would have done, and compelling their attention by an air of authority, not only did he attempt, by a playful tone, to apologize for the too serious turn of his conversation, but he hurried his delivery, ignored all but the gist, used abbreviations so as to seem less long-winded and more familiar with the things he was talking about, and, by rendering these unintelligible, merely succeeded in seeming interminable. His self-assurance was not like that of Cottard, which caused his patients to freeze, who, to the people who acclaimed his amenableness in company, would answer, "He's not the same man any more when he receives you in his consulting room, you in the light, he with his back to it, with those piercing eyes." It did not impose itself; you felt it was masking too much self-consciousness, that the least thing would be enough to put it to flight. Saniette, whose friends had always told him he had too little belief in himself, and who indeed saw people whom he rightly regarded as very inferior obtaining with ease the successes that were denied to him, could no longer start on a story without smiling at its drollery, for fear that a serious expression might sell his wares short. At times, lending credence to the humor he himself appeared to find in what he was about to say, they granted him the favor of a general silence. But the story would fall flat. A kindhearted guest would sometimes slip Saniette the private, almost secret encouragement of a smile of approval, conveying it to him furtively, without attracting attention, as someone slips you a note. But no one went so far as to assume the responsibility, to risk the public adhesion, of laughing out loud. Long after the story had finished, and fallen flat, the dejected Saniette alone remained smiling to himself, as if enjoying, alone, the delectation in it that he pretended to find sufficient, and which the others had not felt. As for the sculptor Ski, so called because of the difficulty they found in pronouncing his Polish name, and because he himself, since he had been living in a certain society, had affected not to wish to be confused with relations who were very well placed but somewhat boring and very numerous, he, aged forty-five and extremely ugly, had a sort of impishness, of dreamy whimsicality, that he had preserved from having been, until the age of ten, the most ravishing child prodigy in the world, the apple of every lady's eye. Mme Verdurin claimed he was more artistic than Elstir. Any resemblance he bore to the latter was purely external, however. It was sufficient for Elstir, who had met Ski on one occasion, to feel for him that profound repulsion that is inspired in us, even more than by those people who are our complete opposites, by those who resemble us only on our worst side, in whom are displayed what is least good about us, the faults which we have cured, unfortunate reminders to us of how we may have appeared to some before we became what we are. But Mme Verdurin believed that Ski had more temperament than Elstir, because there was no art for which he did not have an aptitude, and she was convinced that he might have developed that aptitude into a talent had he had less laziness. This last even seemed to the Patronne to be one more gift, being the opposite of hard work, which she thought was the lot of those without genius. Ski would paint anything you wished, on cuff links or over doors. He sang with the voice of a composer, and played from memory, giving an imitation of an orchestra at the piano, less by his virtuosity than by the false bass notes that signified his fingers' inability to indicate that at this point there was a cornet, which he imitated in any case with his mouth. Searching for words as he spoke, to make people believe in an interesting impression, in the same way he would hold back a chord and then strike it, saying "ping," to make the brass section sound, he passed for being wonderfully intelligent, but in point of fact his ideas amounted to two or three very limited ones. Annoyed by his reputation as a fantasist, he had taken it into his head to demonstrate that he was a practical, positive person, whence a triumphant affectation in him of false precision and false good sense, made worse by the fact that he had no memory and that his information was always inaccurate. The movements of his head, his neck, and his legs might have been graceful had he still been nine years old, with blond curls, a big lace collar, and little red leather boots. Having arrived ahead of time with Cottard and Brichot at the station in Graincourt, they had left Brichot in the waiting room and gone to take a stroll. When Cottard had wanted to go back, Ski had replied: "But there's no rush. It's not the local train today, but the departmental train." Overjoyed at observing the effect that this pedantic nuance produced in Cottard, he added, speaking of himself: "Yes, because Ski loves the arts, because he models in clay, people think he isn't practical. Nobody knows this line better than I." Nevertheless, they were on their way back to the station when, suddenly, catching sight of the smoke of the little train as it arrived, Cottard let out a cry and shouted, "We'll have to run like the very devil." They had in fact arrived just in time, the distinction between the local and the departmental trains having ever existed only in Ski's head. "But isn't the Princesse on the train?" asked Brichot in a quavering voice, whose enormous spectacles, resplendent like the reflectors that laryngologists attach to their foreheads to shine down their patients' throats, seemed to have borrowed their vitality from the professor's eyes and, perhaps because of the effort he was making to adjust his vision to them, seemed, even at the most insignificant moments, to be themselves gazing with a sustained attention and an extraordinary fixity. Moreover, by gradually depriving Brichot of his sight, his illness had revealed to him the beauties of this sense, just as we often need to have decided to part with an object, by making a present of it for example, to look at it, to miss it, and to admire it. "No, no, the Princesse has gone to take some of Mme Verdurin's guests back to Maineville, who were catching the Paris train. It's not impossible even that Mme Verdurin, who had things to do in Saint-Mars, went with her! In that case she'd be traveling with us, and we'd all be doing the journey together, it'd be delightful. The thing is to keep an eye open at Maineville, and the right one! Ah well, never mind, we very nearly missed the boat, and no mistake. When I saw the train, I was thunderstruck. That's what they call arriving at the psychological moment. If we'd missed the train, you know, if Mme Verdurin saw the carriages coming back without us, picture the scene!" added the doctor, who was not yet recovered from his agitation. "That was no ordinary escapade. I say, Brichot, what d'you think of our little adventure?" asked the doctor with a certain pride. "My word," replied Brichot, "yes indeed, if you hadn't found the train still there, as the late Villemain[44] would have said, that would have put the lid on things!" But I, distracted from the very start by these people whom I did not know, I recalled all of a sudden what Cottard had said to me in the ballroom of the little casino, and, as if an invisible chain had managed to connect an organ to the pictures in my memory, that of Albertine leaning her breasts against those of Andrée gave me a terrible pain in my heart. The pain did not last; the idea of Albertine's possible relations with women no longer seemed possible, since two days earlier, when the advances my friend had made to Saint-Loup had excited a new jealousy in me, which had caused me to forget the earlier one. I had the innocence of those people who believe that one taste necessarily excludes another. At Arembouville, as the tram was crowded, a farmer in a blue smock, who had only a third-class ticket, got into our compartment. The doctor, adjudging that the Princesse could not be allowed to travel with him, summoned a porter, displayed his card as doctor to one of the great railway companies, and forced the stationmaster to make the farmer get out. This scene so pained the kind heart and alarmed the timidity of Saniette that, the moment he saw it start, fearful already, because of the number of country people there were on the platform, that it might take on the dimensions of a peasants' revolt, he feigned a stomachache and, in order not to be accused of having some share in the doctor's violence, he slipped into the corridor on the pretense of looking for what Cottard called the "WC." Not finding one, he gazed at the countryside from the other end of the "slow coach." "If this is your first time at Mme Verdurin's, monsieur," Brichot said to me, anxious to show off his talents to a "newcomer," "you'll find there's no circle where you get a stronger sense of *'douceur de vivre,'* in the words of the inventors of dilettantism, of couldn't-care-less-ism, of a lot of words in '-ism' fashionable among our jumped-up shopgirls—I refer to M. le Prince de Talleyrand."[45] For, when he spoke of these great noblemen from the past, he thought it was witty and lent "period color" to put "Monsieur" in front of their title, and would say "M. le Duc de La Rochefoucauld," or "M. le Cardinal de Retz," whom he also called from time to time "that *'struggle-for-lifer'* de Gondi, that *'boulangiste'* de Marcillac."[46] And he never failed to call Montesquieu, with a smile, "M. le Président Secondat de Montesquieu." A clever man of the world would have been irritated by this pedantry, which smelled of the schools. But there is pedantry, too, in the perfect manners of the man of the world, revealing of another caste, that in which, when speaking of a prince, they put "the Emperor" in front of the name of William,[47] and talk to a Royal Highness in the third person. "Ah, to him we must take off our hats," Brichot went on, alluding to "M. le Prince de Talleyrand." "He's an ancestor." "It's a delightful circle," Cottard said to me. "You'll find a bit of everything, for Mme Verdurin is not exclusive: illustrious scholars like Brichot, the high nobility like, for example, the Princesse Sherbatoff, a great Russian lady, a friend of the Grande Duchesse Eudoxie, who even visits her alone, at the times when no one is admitted." The Grande Duchesse Eudoxie indeed, not caring that the Princesse Sherbatoff, who had not been received by anyone for a long time past, should come to her when she might have people there, only let her come very early in the day, when Her Highness had none of the friends with her for whom it would have been as disagreeable to encounter the Princesse as it would have been embarrassing for the latter. As, for the last three years, immediately after leaving, like a manicurist, the Grande Duchesse, Mme Sherbatoff had gone off to Mme Verdurin's, who had only just woken up, and did not leave her again, it could be said that the Princesse's loyalty infinitely exceeded that of Brichot even, assiduous though he was at the Wednesdays, where he had the pleasure of believing himself, in Paris, to be a sort of Chateaubriand at the Abbaye-aux-Bois,[48] and where, in the country, he got the impression of having become the equivalent of what the man whom he always called (with the mischievous satisfaction of the literary man) "M. de Voltaire" may have been for Mme de Châtelet.[49]

The absence of connections had enabled the Princesse Sherbatoff to display a fidelity to the Verdurins in recent years that made her more than an ordinary member of the "faithful," but the very type, the ideal, that Mme Verdurin had long believed was inaccessible, and which, having reached the change of life, she had at last found made flesh in this new female recruit. However much the Patronne might be racked by jealousy, it was unprecedented for even the most assiduous of the faithful not to have "defaulted" once. The most stay-at-home had let themselves be tempted by a journey; the most continent had had an amorous adventure; the most robust may have caught the flu, the idlest been trapped by their twenty-eight days, the most indifferent gone to close the eyes of their dying mother. And it was in vain that Mme Verdurin would then say to them, like the Roman Empress,[50] that she was the one general whom her legion must obey, like Christ or the Kaiser,[51] that whoever loved his father and mother as much as her but was not prepared to leave them in order to follow her, was unworthy of her, that, instead of growing weak in bed or letting themselves be made a fool of by a whore, they would do better to remain close to her, she, their one remedy and their one delight. But destiny, which is sometimes pleased to embellish the conclusion of lives that are long-drawn-out, had caused Mme Verdurin to meet the Princesse Sherbatoff. Having quarreled with her family, an exile from her homeland, no longer knowing anyone except the Baronne Putbus and the Grande Duchesse Eudoxie, to whom, because she had no wish to meet the women friends of the first, and because the second had no wish for her women friends to meet the Princesse, she went only at those morning hours when Mme Verdurin was still asleep, not recalling having kept to her room on a single occasion since the age of twelve, when she had had measles, and having replied on December 31 to Mme Verdurin, who, concerned at being on her own, had asked her without warning whether she could not stay overnight, despite New Year's Day, "But what would be able to stop me, no matter what day it is? Moreover, that's a day when we remain *en famille,* and you are my family," living in a *pension* and swapping whenever the Verdurins moved, following them on their holidays in the country, the Princesse was, for Mme Verdurin, so much the embodiment of Vigny's line,

You alone appeared to me that which we are always seeking.[52]

that the lady president of the little club, desirous of securing one of the "faithful" even unto death, had asked her that whichever of them was the last to die should have herself buried next to the other. Before strangers—among whom must always be counted that stranger to whom we lie the most because it is by them that it would be most painful to be despised: ourselves—the Princesse Sherbatoff took care to represent her only three friendships—with the Grande Duchesse, with the Verdurins, and with Mme Putbus—as the only ones not that cataclysms independent of her will had allowed to emerge amid the destruction of all the rest, but which a free choice had caused her to elect in preference to any other, and to which a certain liking for solitude and simplicity had led her to confine herself. "I see *no one* else," she would say, stressing the inflexible character of what had the appearance more of a self-imposed rule than of a necessity to be endured. She would add, "I frequent only three houses," like those authors who, afraid of being unable to stretch to a fourth, announce that their play will have only three performances.

Whether or not M. and Mme Verdurin lent credence to this figment, they had helped the Princesse to instill it into the minds of the faithful. And the latter were persuaded both that the Princesse, out of the thousands of connections available to her, had chosen the Verdurins alone, and that the Verdurins, solicited in vain by the whole of the upper aristocracy, had consented to make only one exception, in favor of the Princesse.

As they saw it, the Princesse, too superior to her original milieu not to be bored there, and out of all the people with whom she might have associated, had found the Verdurins alone to be agreeable, and the latter, in return, deaf to the overtures of the whole aristocracy that had been offering itself to them, had consented to make only one exception, in favor of a great lady more intelligent than her peers, the Princesse Sherbatoff.

The Princesse was very rich; at every opening night she had a large ground-floor box, to which, authorized by Mme Verdurin, she took the faithful and never anyone else. People would point out this pale, enigmatic figure who had aged without turning white but, rather, had gone red, like certain long-lasting, shriveled fruit in the hedgerows. They admired both her influence and her humility, for, though always having with her an Academician, Brichot, a celebrated scholar, Cottard, the leading pianist of the day, and later on M. de Charlus, she still did her best to book the gloomiest *baignoire* and remained at the back, paying no attention to the auditorium but living exclusively for the little group, who, a little before the end of the performance, would withdraw in the train of this strange sovereign who was not without possessing a shy, fascinating, worn-out beauty. But if Mme Sherbatoff did not look at the auditorium, and remained in the shadows, it was in order to try to forget that there existed a living world that she desired passionately but was unable to get to know; the "coterie" in a *baignoire* was for her what their almost corpselike stillness is for certain animals in the presence of danger. Nonetheless, the taste for novelty and for curiosity which exercises society people meant that they perhaps lent greater attention to this mysterious stranger than to the celebrities in the front boxes on whom everyone came calling. They imagined her to be other than the people whom they knew, that a wonderful intelligence, wedded to a clairvoyant goodness, had retained this small circle of the eminent around her. Were someone's name to be mentioned, or someone introduced to her, the Princesse was forced to feign a great indifference so as to keep up the fiction of her horror of society. Nonetheless, with the support of Cottard or of Mme Verdurin, a few newcomers succeeded in meeting her, and her euphoria at meeting one of them was such that she forgot the fable of her voluntary isolation and lavished attention on this new arrival. If he was a nonentity, everyone was astonished. "What a peculiar thing, that the Princesse, who refuses to meet anybody, should go and make an exception for someone so inappropriate!" But these fertilizing acquaintances were rare, and the Princesse lived strictly confined in the midst of the faithful.

Cottard was far more inclined to say, "I'll see him on Wednesday at the Verdurins'" than "I'll see him on Tuesday at the Academy." He spoke also of the Wednesdays as of an occupation just as important, and just as ineluctable. Cottard, moreover, was one of these little-sought-after people who make it an imperious duty to accept an invitation as though it constituted an order, like a military or judicial summons. He needed to be called out on a truly important visit for him to "default" from the Verdurins' on a Wednesday, its importance having more to do, moreover, with the status of the sick person than the seriousness of their condition. For Cottard, kindly man though he was, would renounce the comforts of a Wednesday not for a workman who had had a stroke but for the headcold of a minister. Even in this last instance he would say to his wife: "Make my sincere apologies to Mme Verdurin. Warn her I'll be late getting there. His Excellency might well have picked another day to catch cold." One Wednesday, their elderly cook having cut the vein in her arm, Cottard, already in a dinner jacket in order to go to the Verdurins', had given a shrug when his wife timidly asked him whether he could not dress the wound. "But I can't, Léontine," he had exclaimed with a groan, "you can see I've got my white waistcoat on." So as not to provoke her husband, Mme Cottard had sent posthaste for the *chef de clinique*. The latter, in order to save time, had taken a cab, with the result that, his carriage entering the courtyard at the same moment as that of Cottard was about to leave to take him to the Verdurins', they had wasted five minutes advancing and retreating. Mme Cottard was embarrassed that the *chef de clinique* should have seen her lord and master in his evening clothes. Cottard had cursed at the delay, perhaps out of remorse, and left in an execrable temper that it required all the pleasures of a Wednesday finally to dispel.

Were a patient to ask Cottard, "Do you sometimes come across the Guermantes?," it was in the best of good faith that the professor would reply: "Perhaps not the Guermantes exactly, I don't know. But I meet all those sorts of people at some friends of mine. You've certainly heard speak of the Verdurins. They know everybody. And they at least aren't smart folk who've gone down in the world. There's money there all right. Mme Verdurin's generally reckoned to have thirty-five million. I mean, that's a tidy sum, thirty-five million. So she doesn't do things by halves. You mentioned the Duchesse de Guermantes. I'm going to tell you the difference. Mme Verdurin is a great lady, the Duchesse de Guermantes is probably on her uppers. You get the distinction, don't you? In any event, whether the Guermantes go to Mme Verdurin's or not, she entertains, which is better, the d'Sherbatoffs, the d'Forchevilles, *e tutti quanti*, people out of the very top drawer, all the nobility of France and Navarre, who you'd see me talking to as equals. What's more, those sorts of individuals are happy to seek out the princes of science," he added, with a beatifically self-regarding smile, produced on his lips by the presumptuous satisfaction, not so much that an expression once reserved for such as Potain and Charcot[53] should now be applied to him, but that he was finally able to make suitable use of all those expressions authorized by custom of which, after much burning of the midnight oil, he now had a thorough command. And so, after citing the Princesse Sherbatoff to me among the people received by Mme Verdurin, Cottard added, with a wink, "You can tell the type of establishment it is, you understand what I mean?" He meant the most chic imaginable. Now, to entertain a Russian lady who knew only the Grande Duchesse Eudoxie meant little. But the Princesse Sherbatoff might even not have known her without lessening the opinion Cottard held as to the supreme elegance of the Verdurin salon or his delight at being received there. The splendor in which the people with whom we associate appear clothed is no more intrinsic than that of those characters on the stage, to dress whom it is quite pointless for a director to spend hundreds of thousands of francs on authentic costumes and real jewelry that will have no effect, when a great designer will create an impression of luxury a thousand times more sumptuous by directing a beam of artificial light at a doublet of coarse cloth strewn with glass bottletops, and a cloak made of paper. A man may have spent his life amid the great ones of the earth, who to him were either tedious relatives or tiresome acquaintances, because in his eyes a habit contracted from the cradle had stripped them of all glamour. But in return, this same glamour needed only, by some accident, to be added to the most obscure individuals for Cottards without number to live bedazzled by titled women whose salons they imagined to be the center of aristocratic elegance, and who were not even what Mme de Villeparisis and her friends were (great ladies fallen from favor with whom the aristocracy that had been brought up with them no longer associated); no, were the many people who took pride in their friendship with such ladies to publish their memoirs, citing their names and those of the women whom they received, no one, Mme de Cambremer any more than Mme de Guermantes, would be able to identify them. But what matter! In this way, a Cottard has his Baronne or his Marquise, who for him is "the Baronne" or "the Marquise," just as in Marivaux, where the Baronne's name is never spoken and we have no idea even that she ever had one.[54] Cottard believes all the more strongly that he has here found the very essence of the aristocracy—which has no knowledge of this lady— because, the more doubtful the titles, the more space the coronets occupy on the glasses, the silver, the notepaper, and the luggage. Numerous Cottards, who thought they were spending their lives in the heart of the Faubourg Saint-Germain, have had their imaginations more bewitched perhaps by feudal dreams than those who have lived among princes in actuality, just as, for the small shopkeeper who on Sundays goes now and again to visit "olde-world" buildings, it is sometimes from those buildings all of whose stones are of our own world, and whose ceilings have been painted blue and strewn with gold stars by pupils of Viollet-le-Duc,[55] that they get the strongest sense of the Middle Ages. "The Princesse will be at Maineville. She will travel with us. But I won't introduce you right away. It'd be better were Mme Verdurin to do that. Unless I find some neat way in. You can rely on me then, I shall jump at it." "What were you talking about?" said Saniette, who acted as if he had been out getting a breath of air. "I was quoting to Monsieur," said Brichot, "a remark you know well, of the man who in my opinion is first among all the *'fins de siècle'*—of the eighteenth *siècle*, be it understood—first name Charles-Maurice, abbé of Périgord.[56] He had begun by promising to be a very good journalist. But he went to the bad, I mean he became a minister! These falls from grace happen in life. A none-too-scrupulous politician, what's more, with all the disdain of a thoroughbred nobleman, but who found no difficulty in working in his time for nothing, let's not hide the fact, and died an incorrigible member of the center-left."

At Saint-Pierre-des-Ifs there got on a splendid girl who, alas, was not part of the little group. I could not take my eyes off her magnolia flesh, her black eyes, the high and admirable construction of her breasts. After a moment, she wanted to open a window, because it was rather hot in the compartment, and, not wanting to ask everyone for permission, since I alone had no overcoat, she said to me, in a quick, fresh, laughing tone, "You don't find it disagreeable, monsieur, the fresh air?" I would have liked to say to her, "Come with us to the Verdurins'," or "Tell me your name and address." I replied, "No, the fresh air doesn't worry me, mademoiselle." And afterward, without moving from her seat, "The smoke won't worry your friends?," and she lit a cigarette. At the third station, she jumped out. The next day, I asked Albertine who it could have been. For, foolishly, believing that we can love only one thing, and jealous of Albertine's attitude in respect of Robert, I felt reassured where women were concerned. Albertine told me, perfectly sincerely I believe, that she did not know. "I'd so much like to meet her again!" I exclaimed. "Don't worry, we always do meet again," answered Albertine. In this particular instance, she was wrong; I have never again met, nor identified, the beautiful girl with the cigarette. We shall see, moreover, why for a long time I had to leave off searching for her. But I have not forgotten her. It often happens that when I am thinking of her I am seized by a wild longing. But these recurrences of desire force us to reflect that, if we wanted to meet these girls again with the same pleasure, we should have also to go back to the year in question, which has since been followed by ten others, in the course of which the girl has faded. We can sometimes find a person again, but not abolish time. All this up until that unforeseen day, sad as a winter's night, when we are no longer seeking that particular girl, or any other, and when to find one would alarm us even. For we no longer feel we have sufficient attractions to please, or the strength to love. Not, of course, that we are, in the true sense of the word, impotent. So far as love is concerned, we would love more than ever. But we feel that it is too great an undertaking for the little strength that we preserve. Our eternal rest has already introduced intervals, in which we cannot go out, cannot speak. To place a foot on the step that is needed is a triumph, like not missing a somersault. To be seen in this state by a girl whom we love, even if we have kept the face and the fair hair we had as a young man! We can no longer assume the fatigue of falling into step with youth. So much the worse if the desires of the flesh are redoubled instead of being deadened! On their account, we send for a woman whom we shall make no effort to please, who will share our couch for one evening only, and whom we shall never see again.

"We must still be without news of the violinist," said Cottard. The event of the day among the little clan had indeed been the defection of Mme Verdurin's favored violinist. He, who was doing his military service near Doncières, came three times a week to dine at La Raspelière, since he had leave up until midnight. But two days before, for the first time, the faithful had not managed to discover him on the tram. It was assumed he had missed it. But although Mme Verdurin had sent to the tram following, and finally to the last one, the carriage had come back empty. "He's been confined to barracks for sure, there's no other explanation for his flight. In the soldiering trade, you know, with those strapping young fellows, it only takes a grumpy NCO." "It'll be all the more mortifying for Mme Verdurin," said Brichot, "if he lets her down again this evening, because our charming hostess is entertaining to dinner for the very first time the neighbors who have leased La Raspelière to her, the Marquis and Marquise de Cambremer." "This evening, the Marquis and Marquise de Cambremer!" exclaimed Cottard. "But I had absolutely no idea. Of course, I knew, as you all did, that they were due to come one day, but I didn't know it'd be so soon. *Sapristi!*" he said, turning to me. "What did I tell you? The Princesse Sherbatoff, the Marquis and Marquise de Cambremer." And, having repeated these names, savoring their melodiousness, "You can see that we do well for ourselves," he said. "Never mind, for your first time, you've scored a bull's-eye. It's going to be an exceptionally brilliant roomful." And, turning to Brichot, he added: "The Patronne must be furious. It was high time we arrived to lend her a hand." Since Mme Verdurin had been at La Raspelière, she had indeed affected in front of the faithful to be under an obligation and in despair at having to invite the owners. In this way she would get better terms for the following year, she said, and was doing it only out of self-interest. But she claimed to feel such terror, to fuss so about nothing more than a dinner with people not from the little group, that she was always putting it off. It did frighten her a little, as it happens, for the reasons that she proclaimed, even though she exaggerated them, if from another point of view it charmed her, for snobbish reasons about which she preferred to remain silent. She was thus half sincere; she thought the little clan something so unique in the world, one of those bodies such that it would take centuries to constitute its like, that she trembled at the thought of seeing introduced into it these provincials, unfamiliar with the *Tetralogy* and the *Meistersinger,* who would not know how to sustain their part in the concert of the general conversation and were capable, by coming to Mme Verdurin's, of ruining one of the famous Wednesdays, those fragile and incomparable masterpieces, like the Venetian glass that one false note is enough to shatter. "What's more, they're bound to be as *anti* as can be, and all top brass," M. Verdurin had said. "Oh, *that,* that's all one to me, that particular story's been being talked about for quite some time," Mme Verdurin had replied, who was genuinely pro-Dreyfus but would still have liked to earn some worldly reward from the preponderant Dreyfusism of her salon. But Dreyfusism had triumphed politically, not socially. For society people, Labori, Reinach, Picquart, and Zola remained traitors of a kind that could only alienate them from the little nucleus. And so, after this incursion into politics, Mme Verdurin was anxious to get back into art. Were d'Indy and Debussy not anyway "in the wrong" over the Affair?[57] "So far as the Affair is concerned, we'd only need to sit them next to Brichot," she said (the university man being the only one of the faithful who had taken the side of the General Staff, which had lowered him greatly in Mme Verdurin's esteem). "We're not obliged to go on everlastingly about the Dreyfus Affair. No, the truth is that the Cambremers get on my nerves." As for the faithful, as much excited by the unconfessed desire they felt to meet the Cambremers as taken in by the annoyance Mme Verdurin affected to feel at entertaining them, they daily took up again, when talking with her, the unworthy arguments she had herself used in favor of the invitation and attempted to make them irresistible. "Make up your mind to it once and for all," repeated Cottard, "and they'll knock something off the rent, they'll pay the gardener, you'll have the use of the field. All that's well worth an evening of boredom. I mention it only for your sake," he added, although his heart had beaten faster one time when, in Mme Verdurin's carriage, he had met that of the old Mme de Cambremer along the road, and above all had been made to feel small in front of the porters when, at the station, he found himself next to the Marquis. For their part, the Cambremers, who lived much too far outside the social swim to be able even to suspect that certain fashionable women might speak of Mme Verdurin with a certain consideration, imagined the latter to be someone who could know only bohemians, was not even lawfully married perhaps, and, as far as people "of birth" were concerned, would only ever meet themselves. They had resigned themselves to dining there only in order to stay on good terms with a tenant who they hoped would return for many more seasons, especially since they had learned, the previous month, that she had just inherited all those millions. It was in silence and without any tasteless jokes that they prepared themselves for the fateful day. The faithful no longer expected it ever to arrive, so many times had Mme Verdurin fixed in their presence a date that was forever shifting. These false resolutions had as their aim not only to make a display of the nuisance this dinner party was causing her, but to keep in suspense those members of the little group who lived in the vicinity and were inclined at times to default. Not that the Patronne had guessed that the "great day" was as agreeable for them as for her, but because, having persuaded them that for her this dinner party was the most terrible drudgery, she could appeal to their devotion. "You're not going to leave me on my own, hobnobbing with that lot! On the contrary, we need to be there in numbers to put up with the boredom. Of course, we won't be able to talk about anything that interests us. As a Wednesday it'll be a failure, but there you are!"

"In fact," replied Brichot, addressing himself to me, "I don't believe Mme Verdurin, who is highly intelligent and very fastidious in working out her Wednesdays, was very keen to entertain these squireens of high pedigree but no brains. She couldn't bring herself to invite the dowager Marquise but has resigned herself to the son and daughter-in-law." "Ah, we shall be seeing the Marquise de Cambremer?" said Cottard, with a smile that he thought he should make both suggestive and bantering, although he did not know whether Mme de Cambremer was pretty or not. But the title of marquise had evoked dashing and glamorous images in him. "Oh, I know her," said Ski, who had met her once when out driving with Mme Verdurin. "You don't know her in the Biblical sense?" said the doctor, one of whose favorite jokes this was, sliding a louche glance from beneath his eyeglass. "She's intelligent," Ski said to me. "Of course," he went on, noticing that I had said nothing and smilingly laying weight on every word, "she's intelligent yet she isn't, she lacks education, she's frivolous, but she has an instinct for pretty things. She'll fall silent, but she'll never say anything stupid. Besides, her coloring is pretty. Hers is a portrait it'd be amusing to paint," he added, half closing his eyes, as if he were gazing at her posing in front of him. Since I thought the complete opposite of what Ski had expressed with so many qualifications, I contented myself with saying that she was the sister of a very distinguished engineer, M. Legrandin. "Well, you see, you'll be introduced to a pretty woman," Brichot said to me, "and one never knows what that may lead to. Cleopatra wasn't even a great lady, she was the little woman, the thoughtless and terrible little woman of our Meilhac,[58] and think of the consequences, not only for that simpleton of an Antony but for the ancient world." "I've already been introduced to Mme de Cambremer," I answered. "Ah, so you're going to find yourself in familiar country." "I'll be all the more glad to see her," I replied, "because she promised me a book by the former *curé* of Combray about the local place-names, and I'll be able to remind her of her promise. I'm interested in the priest and in etymologies also." "Don't put too much trust in those he gives," replied Brichot. "The book, which is at La Raspelière and which I've amused myself by looking through, tells me nothing of any value; it's littered with errors. I'll give you an example. The word *bricq* enters into the formation of a number of place-names hereabouts. The good cleric has had the somewhat cranky notion that it comes from *briga*, a height or fortified place. He finds it already in the Celtic tribes, Latobriges, Nemetobriges, and so on, and traces it even in names like Briand, Brion, etc. To come back to the region we have the pleasure of traversing with you at this moment, Bricquebosc would signify the wood of the height; Bricqueville the habitation of the height; Bricquebec, where we shall be stopping in a moment before getting to Maineville, the height near the stream. Yet that's not it at all, for the good reason that *bricq* is the old Norse word signifying quite simply a bridge. Just as *fleur*, which Mme de Cambremer's protégé takes infinite pains to link at one point to the Scandinavian words *floi* and *flo*, and at others to the Irish words *ae* and *aer*, is, on the contrary, and beyond any doubt, the *fiord* of the Danes, and signifies a harbor. Similarly, the excellent priest thinks that the station of Saint-Martin-le-Vêtu, which is next door to La Raspelière, signifies Saint-Martin-le-Vieux (*vetus*). It's a fact that the word *vieux* has played a major role in the toponymy of the region. *Vieux* generally comes from *vadum* and signifies a ford, as in the place known as Les Vieux, or as in the English 'Oxford' and 'Hereford.' But in this particular instance, *vieux* comes not from *vetus* but from *vastatus*, a bare, de-vastated place. Near here you have Sottevast, the vast of Setold, Brillevast, the vast of Berold. I'm all the more certain that the *curé* is in error because Saint-Martin-le-Vieux was at one time called Saint-Martin-du-Gast, or even Saint-Martin-de-Terregate. Now, the 'v' and the 'g' in those words are the same letter. We say *dévaster* but also *gâcher*. *Jachères* and *gâtines*[59]– from the High German *wastinna*–have the same sense. 'Terregate,' therefore, is *terra vasta*. As for Saint-Mars, in the old days (*honni soit qui mal y pense!*) Saint-Merd,[60] that is Saint-Medardus, which is sometimes Saint-Médard, Saint-Mard, Saint-Marc, Cinq-Mars, all the way to Dammas. It mustn't be forgotten, moreover, that, very near here, places bearing this same name of Mars are evidence merely of a pagan origin (the god Mars) that's still very much alive in the region, but which the man of

God refuses to acknowledge. The heights dedicated to the gods in particular are very numerous, like the mountain of Jupiter (Jeumont). Your *curé* is having none of it, but, on the other hand, wherever Christianity has left traces, they elude him. He extended his travels as far as Loctudy, a barbarian name, he says, whereas it's *Locus sancti Tudeni;* nor, in 'Sammarcoles,' has he divined *Sanctus Martialis.* Your *curé,*" Brichot went on, noticing that he was interesting me, "makes the words *hon, home,* and *holm* come from the word *holl (hullus),* a hill, whereas it comes from the Norse *holm,* an island, which you're certainly familiar with in 'Stockholm,' and which is so widespread throughout the region: La Houlme, Engohomme, Tahoume, Robehomme, Néhomme, Quettehou, and so on." These names brought to mind the day when Albertine had wanted to go to Amfreville-la-Bigot (from the name of two of its successive lords, Brichot told me), and when she had then suggested we should eat together in Robehomme. As for Montmartin, we would be passing it in a minute. "Is Néhomme," I asked, "not near Carquethuit and Clitourps?" "Exactly, Néhomme is the *holm,* the island or peninsula, of the famous Vicomte Nigel, whose name has survived also in Néville. For Mme de Cambremer's protégé, Carquethuit and Clitourps, which you spoke of, are an opportunity for other errors. He can see easily enough, of course, that *carque* is a church, the Germans' *Kirche.* You're familiar with Querqueville and Carquebut, not to mention Dunkerque. For we'd do better then to pause at this famous word *dun,* which for the Celts signified an elevation. That you'll find throughout France. Your abbé has been hypnotized faced by Duneville. But in the Eure-et-Loir he'd have found Châteaudun; Dun-le-Roi in the Cher; Duneau in the Sarthe; Dun in the Ariège; Dune-les-Places in the Nièvre; and so on and so forth. This *dun* leads him to commit a curious error in connection with Douville, where we shall be getting out, and where the comfortable carriages of Mme Verdurin await us. Douville: in Latin *donvilla,* so he says. Indeed, Douville is at the foot of the big heights. Your *curé,* who knows everything, senses all the same he has blundered. He has in fact read *Domvilla* in an old *terrier.* Then he retracts; Douville, according to him, is a fief of the abbé, *domino abbati,* of Mont-Saint-Michel. That delights him, which is rather bizarre when one reflects on the scandalous life that, since the capitulary of Saint-Clair-sur-Epte, they led at

Mont-Saint-Michel, and which would be no more extraordinary than finding the King of Denmark as suzerain of this whole coast, where he celebrated the worship of Odin far more than that of Christ. On the other hand, the supposition that the 'n' got changed into a 'u' doesn't shock me and requires less of a deformation than the very correct 'Lyon,' which also comes from *dun* (*Lugdunum*). But the abbé has in fact got it wrong. Douville was never Donville, but Doville, *Eudonis Villa,* the village of Eudes. Douville was once called Escalecliff, where you scaled the rise. Around 1233, Eudes the Cupbearer, lord of Escalecliff, left for the Holy Land; at the moment of departure, he handed over the church to the Abbey of Blanchelande. An exchange of courtesies: the village took his name, whence present-day Douville. But I will add that toponymy, where I'm anyway quite ignorant, is not an exact science; did we not have this historical evidence, Douville might very well come from d'Ouville, i.e., les Eaux, the waters. Forms in 'ai' (Aigues-Mortes), from *aqua,* very often turn into 'eu,' or 'ou.' And there were renowned waters very close to Douville. As you can imagine, the *curé* was only too happy to find some Christian vestige there, even if the region seems to have been hard enough to evangelize, since it took successive attempts by Saint Ursal, Saint Gofroi, Saint Barsanore, and Saint Laurent de Brèvedent, who finally made way for the monks of Beaubec. But where *tuit* is concerned, the author is mistaken; he sees it as a form of *toft,* a hovel, as in Criquetot, Ectot, Yvetot, whereas it's the *thveit,* or assart, land freshly cleared, as in Braquetuit, Le Thuit, Regnetuit, and so on. Similarly, if in 'Clitourps' he recognizes the Norman *thorp,* which means 'village,' he wants the first part of the name to derive from *clivus,* an incline, whereas it comes from *cliff,* a rockface. But his grossest blunders stem less from ignorance than from his prejudices. However good a Frenchman you may be, do you have to deny what is self-evident and take Saint-Laurent-en-Bray to be the well-known Roman priest, whereas the saint in question is Saint Lawrence O'Toole, Archbishop of Dublin? But more than his patriotic sentiments, it's your friend's religious *parti pris* that leads him to commit crude errors. Thus, not far from the house of our hosts at La Raspelière, you have two Montmartins, Montmartin-sur-Mer and Montmartin-en-Graignes. With Graignes, the worthy *curé* has not made any mistake, he's seen clearly that Graignes, *grania* in

Latin, *krene* in Greek, signifies ponds, marshland; how many Cresmays, Croens, Grennevilles, Lengronnes could one not cite? But with Montmartin your purported linguist insists it's a question of parishes dedicated to Saint Martin. His authority for this is the fact that that saint is their patron, but he's unaware that he was only adopted as such after the event; or, rather he's blinded by his hatred of paganism; he won't see that people would have said Mont-Saint-Martin as they say Mont-Saint-Michel, had it been a question of Saint Martin, whereas the name Montmartin applies in a far more pagan fashion to temples consecrated to the god Mars, temples of which, it's true, we possess no other vestiges, but which would be made extremely likely by the undeniable presence in the vicinity of vast Roman camps, even without the name Montmartin, which settles any doubts. So you can see, the little book that you'll find at La Raspelière is not so very well done." I protested that in Combray the *curé* had often taught us interesting etymologies. "He was probably better on his home ground, the journey to Normandy will have disoriented him." "And not cured him," I added, "because he arrived with neurasthenia and left with the rheumatics." "Ah, that's the fault of the neurasthenia. He fell from neurasthenia into philology, as my good master Poquelin[61] would have said. I say, Cottard, does it seem to you that neurasthenia can have a harmful influence on philology, and philology a calming influence on neurasthenia, and that the cure for neurasthenia can lead to rheumatism?" "Absolutely, rheumatism and neurasthenia are two vicarious forms of neuroarthritis. You can pass from one to the other by metastasis." "The eminent professor," said Brichot, "expresses himself, may God forgive me, in a French mixed in with as much Latin and Greek as M. Purgon himself might have done, of Molièrish memory! Help, Uncle, I mean Sarcey,[62] our national . . ." But he was unable to finish his sentence. The professor had just given a start and let out a shout: "Damn it all, what the . . . ," he cried, finally moving on to articulated speech. "We've passed Maineville—hey, there!—and even Renneville." He had just noticed that the train had stopped at Saint-Mars-le-Vieux, where almost all the passengers alighted. "They can't have gone through it without stopping, though. We can't have been paying attention, talking about the Cambremers." "Listen, Ski, wait, I'm going to tell you 'a good thing,' " said Cottard, who had developed a fondness for this expression, common in certain medical circles. "The Princesse must be on the train; she won't have seen us but has got into another compartment. Let's go and look for her. Just as long as all this isn't going to create ructions!" And he led all of us off in search of the Princesse Sherbatoff. He found her in the corner of an empty carriage, busy reading the *Revue des deux mondes.* Over long years, she had, from a fear of rejection, got into the habit of staying put, of remaining in her corner, and of waiting until someone wished her good day before giving her hand. She continued to read when the faithful entered her carriage. I recognized her instantly; this woman, who might have come down in the world but was nevertheless of noble birth, who was in any case the pearl of a salon like that of the Verdurins, was the lady who, in this same train, two days earlier, I had thought might be the madam of a brothel. Her very uncertain social personality became clear to me the moment I learned her name, as when, having toiled over a riddle, we finally learn the solution, which makes clear everything that had remained obscure, and which in the case of people is their name. To learn two days later who the person was next to whom one had traveled on the train without managing to decide on their social standing is a far more amusing surprise than reading in the latest issue of a review the solution to the conundrum posed in the previous issue. Great restaurants, casinos, "slow coaches," these are the family museums of such social conundrums. "Princesse, we must have missed you in Maineville! Will you allow us to come and sit in your compartment?" "Why, of course," said the Princesse, who raised her eyes from her review only when she heard Cottard address her, eyes that, like those of M. de Charlus, although gentler, saw very clearly the people whose presence she had pretended not to have noticed. Cottard, reflecting on the fact that being invited with the Cambremers was for me a sufficient recommendation, took, after a moment, the decision to introduce me to the Princesse, who bowed with great courtesy but gave the impression of hearing my name for the first time. "Damnit," exclaimed the doctor, "my wife's forgotten to change the buttons on my white waistcoat. Oh, women, they never think. Don't ever get married, d'you hear," he said to me. And as this was one of the pleasantries he thought appropriate when there was nothing to be said, he glanced out of the corner of his eye at the Princesse and at the other faithful, who, because he was a professor and an Academician, smiled in admiration of his good humor and lack of presumption. The Princesse informed us that the young violinist had been found. He had kept to his bed the previous day on account of a migraine, but would be coming this evening and bringing an old friend of his father's whom he had met again in Doncières. She had learned this through Mme Verdurin, with whom she "had had lunch that morning," she told us quickly, in a voice in which the rolled "r"s of her Russian accent were quietly mumbled at the back of her throat, as if they were not "r"s but "l"s. "Ah, you had lunch with her this morning," said Cottard to the Princesse—but looking at me, for the words were intended to demonstrate to me how intimate the Princesse was with the Patronne. "You're truly one of the faithful!" "Yes, I like the little gloup, intelligent, agleeable, without malice, velly simple, not snobbish, and where they've blains all the way down to their fingertips." "Damnation, I must have lost my ticket, I can't find it," exclaimed Cottard, without being unduly concerned, however. He knew that at Douville, where two landaus would be awaiting us, the porter would allow him through without a ticket and would simply doff his cap all the lower in order, by this salute, to give the explanation of his indulgence, to wit, that he had indeed recognized Cottard to be a Verdurin regular. "They won't be putting me in the police room for that," the doctor concluded. "You were saying, monsieur," I asked Brichot, "that there were some renowned waters near here; how do you know?" "The name of the next station confirms it, together with much other evidence. It's called Fervaches." "I don't complehend what he means," grumbled the Princesse, in the tone of voice in which she might have said to me, out of kindness, "He's getting on our nerves, isn't he?" "But, Princesse, Fervaches means 'warm waters,' *fervidae aquae.* . . . But . . . apropos of the young violinist," Brichot went on, 'I was forgetting, Cottard, to speak to you about the big news. Did you know that our poor friend Dechambre, formerly Mme Verdurin's favorite pianist, has just died? It's frightening." "He was still young," replied Cottard, "but he must have got something amiss with his liver, he must have had something nasty there, he'd looked rotten for some time." "But he wasn't that young," said Brichot. "In the days when El-stir and Swann used to come to Mme Verdurin's, Dechambre already had a reputation in Paris, and, what is admirable, without having received his baptism of success abroad. *He* was no adept of the Gospel according to Saint Barnum."[63] "You're getting him confused, he couldn't have been going to Mme Verdurin's at that time, he was still in swaddling clothes." "But unless my old memory's playing me false, I fancy Dechambre was playing the Vinteuil sonata for Swann when that club-man, who'd broken with the aristocracy, hardly suspected he would one day become the *embourgeoisé* prince consort of our national Odette." "That's impossible, Vinteuil's sonata was played at Mme Verdurin's long after Swann was no longer going there," said the doctor, who, like those people who work a great deal and think they should retain many things that they imagine may be useful, forget many others, which enables them to go into ecstasies at the memory of people who have nothing to do. "You're doing your knowledge an injustice; your mind isn't going, however," smiled the doctor. Brichot conceded his mistake. The train stopped. It was La Sogne. The name intrigued me. "I'd love to know what all these names mean," I said to Cottard. "But ask M. Brichot, he'll know perhaps." "But La Sogne is La Cicogne, *Siconia*, the stork," replied Brichot, whom I was longing to question about many other names.

Forgetting how keen she was on her "corner," Mme Sherbatoff kindly offered to change places with me so that I would be better able to talk with Brichot, whom I wanted to ask about other etymologies that interested me, and she assured me that it was a matter of indifference to her whether she traveled forward, backward, standing up, or any other way. She remained on the defensive for as long as she did not know the intentions of the new arrivals, but once she had recognized that these were friendly, she tried in every way possible to please each one of them. Finally, the train stopped at the station of Douville-Féterne, which, being more or less equidistant from the village of Féterne and that of Douville, bore on account of this peculiarity both their names. "Zounds," exclaimed Dr. Cottard, once we were in front of the barrier where the tickets were collected, and pretending only now to have noticed, "I can't find my ticket, I must have lost it." But the porter, removing his cap, assured him it was of no account and smiled respectfully. The Princesse (giving an explanation to the coachman, as a sort of lady-in-waiting to Mme Verdurin might have done, who, on account of the Cambremers, had not been able to come to the station, which she did only rarely in any case) took me, together with Brichot, with her in one of the carriages. Into the other there got the doctor, Saniette, and Ski.

The coachman, though very young, was the Verdurins' head coachman, the only one actually to bear the title; during the day, he took them on all their outings, for he knew all the roads, and in the evenings went to fetch and later take back the faithful. He was accompanied by auxiliaries (chosen by him) in case of need. He was an excellent lad, sober and skillful, but with one of those melancholy faces whose too fixed gaze signifies someone who is soon worked up, or even gets dark thoughts, over nothing at all. But at that moment he was very happy, for he had managed to get his brother, another excellent sort, taken on by the Verdurins. We went first through Douville. Here grassy hillocks ran right down to the sea, in ample grazing made lush, velvety, and exceptionally vivid in color from its saturation by the damp and the salt. The islets and indentations of Rivebelle, much closer together here than in Balbec, lent this part of the sea the appearance, new to me, of a relief map. We passed small chalets, almost all of them rented by painters; we took a track on which some loose cows, just as alarmed as our horses, barred our way for ten minutes, then we entered on the road along the corniche. "But, by the immortal gods," asked Brichot all of a sudden, "to revert to poor Dechambre; do you think Mme Verdurin *knows*? Has she been *told*?" Like almost all society people, Mme Verdurin, precisely because she had need of the company of others, never gave them another thought after the day they died and were no longer able to come to her Wednesdays, or her Saturdays, or eat in a dressing gown. And it could not have been said of the little clan, the image in this of all the salons, that it was made up more of the dead than the living, seeing that the moment you were dead it was as if you had never existed. But in order to avoid the nuisance of having to speak of the deceased, or even to suspend the dinners, something quite out of the question for the Patronne, as a sign of mourning, M. Verdurin would pretend that the death of the faithful so affected his wife that, in the interests of her health, it was not to be mentioned. Moreover, and perhaps indeed just because the death of others struck him as so common and final an accident, the thought of his own death filled him with horror, and he avoided any reflection that might bear on it. As for Brichot, since he was a very decent man and completely taken in by what M. Verdurin had said about his wife, he dreaded on his friend's account the emotions of such an upset. "Yes, she's *known everything* since this morning," said the Princesse. "We couldn't *keep it from her.*" "Oh, great thundering Zeus," exclaimed Brichot. "Oh, that must have been a terrible blow, a friend of twenty-five years' standing! And who was one of us!" "How right, how right, but there you are," said Cottard. "These are always painful circumstances; but Mme Verdurin is a strong woman, she's a cerebral even more than an emotive." "I'm not altogether of the doctor's opinion," said the Princesse, whose rapid way of speaking and muttered accent gave her an expression decidedly at once sullen and mischievous. "Beneath a cold exterior, Mme Verdurin conceals treasures of sensitivity. M. Verdurin told me he had great difficulty stopping her from going to Paris for the ceremony; he was obliged to give her to believe it would all take place in the country." "Ah, good heavens, she wanted to go to Paris. But I know very well she's a woman of heart, too much heart perhaps. Poor Dechambre! As Mme Verdurin was saying not two months since, 'Compared with him, Planté, Paderewski, Risler even,[64] none of them count.' Ah, he had better reason than that showoff Nero, who has found a way of hoodwinking German learning itself, to say *Qualis artifex pereo!*[65] But Dechambre at least must have died in the fulfillment of his ministry, in the odor of Beethovenian devotion; and bravely, I don't doubt; by rights, that officiant of German music would have deserved to pass away while celebrating the Mass in D.[66] For all that, he was a man to welcome the Grim Reaper with a trill, for that performer of genius sometimes rediscovered in his ancestry, Parisianized man of Champagne that he was, the swank and elegance of a *garde-française.*"[67]

From the height at which we already were, the sea no longer looked, as it did from Balbec, like the undulations of upraised mountains, but, on the contrary, the way a blue-colored glacier or a dazzling plain situated at a lower altitude appears from a peak, or from a road that hugs the mountainside. The jagged swirls seemed to have become immobilized, and to have traced their concentric circles once and for all; the very enamel of the sea, which changed color imperceptibly, took on, toward the end of the bay, where an estuary had been scooped out, the bluish whiteness of milk, in which small black ferryboats seemed trapped like flies, unable to advance. I fancied that from nowhere else could you have discovered so vast a tableau. But at each bend in the road, a new portion was added to it, and when we reached the tollhouse of Douville, the spur of cliff that had hitherto hidden one half of the bay from us drew back, and I suddenly saw to my left a gulf as deep as that which hitherto I had had in front of me, but whose proportions it altered while doubling its beauty. In this very elevated spot, the air had become of a keenness and purity that intoxicated me. I loved the Verdurins; that they should have sent a carriage for us seemed so kind as to be touching. I would have liked to kiss the Princesse. I told her I had never seen anything so beautiful. She, too, professed to love this country more than any other. But I had a strong sense that for her, as for the Verdurins, the important thing was not to gaze on it like tourists, but to eat well there, to entertain company that they enjoyed, to write letters, to read, in short to live in it, allowing its beauty to wash passively over them rather than making it the object of their concerns.

From the tollhouse, the carriage having stopped for a moment at such a height above the sea that, as from a mountaintop, the view of the blue gulf almost gave you vertigo, I opened the window; the softness and clarity of the sound of each wave as it broke, distinct to the ear, had something sublime about it. Was it not like an index of measurement that, overturning our customary impressions, proves that vertical distances can be assimilated to horizontal distances, contrary to the representation our minds usually make of them; and that, bringing the sky closer to us as they do, they are not great; that they are less great even for a sound that covers them, as that of the little waves was doing, because the medium that it has to traverse is purer? Indeed, if you drew no more than two meters back from the tollhouse, you could no longer make out the sound of the waves, which two hundred meters of cliff

had not robbed of its delicate, meticulous, gentle precision. I told myself that my grandmother would have felt for it the admiration inspired
in her by all those manifestations of nature or of art into whose simplicity grandeur may be read. My exaltation was at its height, and raised
up all that surrounded me. I was touched that the Verdurins should
have sent to fetch us from the station. I said as much to the Princesse,
who seemed to think I was making far too much of a quite simple courtesy. I know that she later confessed to Cottard that she found me very
enthusiastic; he replied that I was too emotional, that I would have
needed sedatives and to take up knitting. I remarked to the Princesse
upon each tree, each little house crumbling beneath its roses; I made
her admire everything; I would like to have pressed her to my heart.
She told me she could see I had a gift for painting, that I should draw,
that she was surprised I had not been told that before. And she admitted that the country here was indeed picturesque. We went through,
perched on its height, the little village of Englesqueville (*Engleberti Villa*,
Brichot told us). "But are you quite sure that this evening's dinner is
taking place, despite Dechambre's death, Princesse?" he added, without
reflecting that the fact that the carriages in which we were had come to
the station was in itself an answer. "Yes," said the Princesse, "M. Vel-
dulin was insistent it shouldn't be put off, plecisely in order to stop his
wife from 'thinking.' Besides, after all these years when she has never
failed to entertain on a Wednesday, the change in her habits might have
left its mark on her. She is tellibly nervous these days. M. Verdurin was
especially pleased you were coming to dinner this evening, because he
knew it would be a great distraction for Mme Verdurin," said the
Princesse, forgetting her pretense of not having heard of me. "I think
you'd do well not to say *anything* in front of Mme Verdurin," added the
Princesse. "Ah, you do well to tell me," replied Brichot artlessly. "I'll
pass that recommendation on to Cottard." The carriage stopped for a
moment. It started off again, but the noise the wheels had been making
in the village ceased. We had entered the grand driveway of La
Raspelière, where M. Verdurin was waiting for us on the steps. "I did
right putting on a dinner jacket," he said, ascertaining with pleasure that
the faithful were in theirs, "since I have such smart men." And as I
apologized for my own jacket: "Oh, come, that's ideal. Here we dine

among friends. I'd gladly offer to lend you one of my dinner jackets, but it wouldn't fit you." The very feeling handshake that, as he entered the hallway of La Raspelière, and by way of condolences for the death of the pianist, Brichot gave the Patron, provoked no comment from the latter. I told him of my admiration for the region. "Ah, so much the better, yet you've seen nothing, we'll show it to you. Why don't you come and stay here for a few weeks? The air is excellent." Brichot feared that his handshake might not have been understood. "Well, well, poor Dechambre!" he said, but in a low voice, for fear that Mme Verdurin might not be far away. "It's frightful," replied M. Verdurin cheerfully. "So young," Brichot went on. Annoyed at being detained by these futilities, M. Verdurin replied hurriedly and with a shrill groan, not of grief but of irritated impatience, "Well, yes, but there you are, there's nothing we can do about it, our words aren't going to bring him back to life, are they?" And, gentleness returning along with his joviality: "Come on, my good Brichot, put your things down quickly. We've got a bouillabaisse that won't wait. Above all, in the name of goodness, don't go mentioning Dechambre to Mme Verdurin! You know she hides a lot of what she feels, but she's so sensitive it's like a genuine sickness. I swear to you, when she heard that Dechambre was dead, she almost wept," said M. Verdurin in a profoundly ironic tone. Hearing him, you would have said that it required a sort of dementia to mourn for a friend of thirty years' standing, while gathering, on the other hand, that the perpetual union of M. Verdurin and his wife did not preclude the former from constantly passing judgment on her and the latter from frequently irritating him. "If you mention it to her, she'll go and get ill again. It's lamentable, three weeks after her bronchitis. And in these cases, it's me who's the sick-nurse. You can understand, I've only just been through it. Grieve all you want for the fate of Dechambre in your heart. Think about it, but don't speak of it. I loved Dechambre dearly, but you can't begrudge me loving my wife even more dearly. Here, there's Cottard, you'll be able to ask him." And, indeed, he knew that there are many small services a family doctor is able to render, such, for example, as prescribing that we must not feel grief.

Cottard had said, docilely, to the Patronne, "Upset yourself like that and tomorrow you'll be giving *me* a temperature of thirty-nine degrees," as he might have said to the cook, "Tomorrow you can give me a *ris de veau*." For want of curing us, medicine busies itself altering the meanings of verbs and pronouns.

M. Verdurin was happy to confirm that, despite the rebuffs he had suffered two days earlier, Saniette had not deserted the little nucleus. In their idleness, Mme Verdurin and her husband had in fact developed cruel instincts, for which the great occasions were too infrequent any longer to suffice. They had been able indeed to turn Odette against Swann, and Brichot against his mistress. And they would repeat it with others, that was understood. But the opportunity did not present itself every day. Whereas, thanks to his quivering sensitivity, and his fearful, quickly panic-stricken shyness, Saniette offered them an everyday whipping boy. And so, for fear of his defaulting, they took care to invite him with friendly and persuasive words such as those who have been held back a year at the *lycée*, or old sweats in the army, use to a tyro whom they want to butter up so as to be able to grab hold of him, with the one aim of then tickling or bullying him once he can no longer escape. "Above all," Cottard, who had not heard M. Verdurin, reminded Brichot, "not a word in front of Mme Verdurin." "Fear not, O Cottard, you see before you a sage, as Theocritus has it.[68] Besides, M. Verdurin is right, what use are our lamentations?" he added, for, capable of assimilating forms of words and the ideas to which they gave rise in him, but being without finesse, he found M. Verdurin's words admirable for their very courageous stoicism. "All the same, it's a great talent who has left us." "What, are you still talking about Dechambre?" said M. Verdurin, who had gone ahead of us but, noticing that we were not following, had turned back. "Listen," he said to Brichot, "there's never any need to exaggerate. Because he's dead isn't a reason to make him into the genius he wasn't. He played well, agreed, above all he had the right setting here; transplanted, he no longer existed. My wife became besotted with him and made his reputation. You know how she is. I shall say, moreover, that, for that same reputation's sake, he died at just the right moment, *à point*, just as the *demoiselles de Caen* are about to be, I hope, grilled in accordance with the incomparable recipes of Pampille[69]— unless you're going to keep on forever with your jeremiads here in this Casbah open to all the winds. You surely can't want to kill all of us off just because Dechambre is dead, when for the last year he'd been obliged to play scales before giving a concert, so as to get his suppleness back temporarily, very temporarily. In any case, this evening you're going to hear, or at least encounter, for after dinner the young monkey too often abandons art for cards, someone who's far more of an artist than Dechambre, a youngster my wife discovered, just as she discovered Dechambre, and Paderewski and the others: Morel. The confounded fellow hasn't arrived yet. I'm going to be obliged to send a carriage to the last train. He's coming with an old friend of his family's who he's met again and who bores him to death, but who otherwise, so as not to have his father complaining, he'd have been obliged to remain with in Doncières, to keep him company: the Baron de Charlus." The faithful went in. M. Verdurin, who had stayed behind with me while I took off my things, took me jokingly by the arm, like a host at a dinner party who has no lady guest to give you to take in. "Did you have a good journey?" "Yes, M. Brichot taught me things that interested me greatly," I said, thinking of the etymologies, and because I had heard that the Verdurins greatly admired Brichot. "I'd have been surprised if he hadn't taught you something," said M. Verdurin. "He's such a self-effacing man, who talks so seldom about the things he knows." This compliment did not strike me as very accurate. "He has a charming way with him," I said. "Exquisite, delightful, not at all pedantic, whimsical, light-hearted, my wife adores him, I do, too!" replied M. Verdurin, in a tone of exaggeration and as if reciting a lesson. Only then did I realize that what he had said about Brichot was ironic. And I wondered whether M. Verdurin, since those distant days of which I had heard speak, had not shaken off his wife's tutelage.

The sculptor was much surprised to learn that the Verdurins had consented to receive M. de Charlus. Whereas in the Faubourg Saint-Germain, where M. de Charlus was so well known, his habits were never referred to (not known to the great majority, an object of uncertainty for others, whose idea was more of intense but Platonic friendships and indiscretions, and carefully concealed by those alone in the know, who would shrug their shoulders when some ill-natured Gallardon ventured an insinuation), these same habits, scarcely known about save to a few intimates, were on the contrary denounced daily far away from the circle in which he lived, like the gunfire that is heard only after the interference of a zone of silence. Moreover, in those bourgeois and artistic circles where he was looked on as the very embodiment of inversion, his high standing in society and his exalted origins were wholly unknown, through a phenomenon analogous to that whereby, among the people of Romania, the name of Ronsard is known for that of a great nobleman, whereas his poetic oeuvre is unknown there.[70] On top of which, Ronsard's nobility rests on an error in Romania. Similarly, if in the world of painters and actors M. de Charlus had such a bad reputation, this stemmed from the fact that he had been confused with a certain Comte Leblois de Charlus, who was not even faintly, or only very distantly related to him, and who had been arrested, perhaps in error, during a police raid that was still talked about. In short, all the stories recounted of M. de Charlus applied to the false one. Many professionals swore that they had had dealings with M. de Charlus, and in good faith, believing the false Charlus to be the true one, and the false one perhaps encouraging, half as parading his noble birth, half as concealing his vice, a confusion that was for a long time prejudicial to the real Charlus (the Baron whom we have met), but which then, once he was on the slippery slope, became a convenience, since it enabled him also to say, "It wasn't me." At present, indeed, the talk was not of him. What added to the falsehood of the comments about a true fact (the Baron's tastes) was that he had been the close and perfectly innocent friend of an author who, in the world of the theater, had, no one knew why, the same reputation without in any way deserving it. When they were seen together at an opening night, people said, "You know," just as it was believed that the Duchesse de Guermantes had an immoral relationship with the Princesse de Parme; an indestructible legend, for it would have evaporated only at a proximity to these two great ladies to which the people who retailed it would most likely never attain, save when turning their lorgnettes on to them at the theater and slandering them to the occupant of the next stall. The sculptor was all the less hesitant about concluding from M. de Charlus's habits that the Baron's standing in society also must be bad because he possessed no information of any kind about the family to which M. de Charlus belonged, neither his title nor his name. Just as Cottard thought that everyone knows that the title of doctor of medicine means nothing, and that of house surgeon something, so society people are mistaken in imagining that everyone holds the same ideas as themselves and those of their circle concerning the social significance of their names.

The Prince d'Agrigente passed for a foreign vulgarian in the eyes of a club *chasseur* to whom he owed twenty-five louis, and resumed his importance only in the Faubourg Saint-Germain, where he had three sisters who were duchesses, for the great nobleman has some effect, not on people of modest means, in the eyes of whom he counts for little, but on the brilliant ones, well informed as to his status. For the rest, M. de Charlus was to be able to realize that same evening that the Patron had only very superficial notions concerning the most illustrious ducal families. Convinced that it would be a faux pas on the Verdurins' part to allow a tainted individual to be introduced into their very "select" salon, the sculptor thought he should take the Patronne aside. "You're entirely mistaken, anyway I never believe that sort of thing, and besides, even if it were true, I can tell you it wouldn't exactly be compromising me!" replied Mme Verdurin, furious, for, Morel being the principal ingredient of her Wednesdays, she was anxious before all else not to upset him. As for Cottard, he could not give an opinion, for he had asked to go upstairs for a moment "on a brief errand" in the *buen retiro*,[71] and then to write a very urgent letter on behalf of a patient in M. Verdurin's bedroom.

An important publisher from Paris, there on a visit and who had thought he would be asked to stay, went abruptly off, without delay, understanding that he was not fashionable enough for the little clan. He was a tall, powerful man, very dark, studious, with something sharp-edged about him. He looked like an ebony paper knife.[72]

Mme Verdurin, who, in order to receive us in her immense drawing room, where trophies of ornamental grasses, poppies, and wildflowers, picked that same day, alternated with the same motif painted in camaïeu, two centuries earlier, by an artist of exquisite taste, had got up for a moment from a game of cards she was having with an old friend, and asked for two minutes' grace in order to finish it while going on talking to us. What I told her of my impressions was only half agreeable to her, however. For one thing, I was shocked to find that she and her husband came back in every day long before it was time for the sunsets that were held to be so beautiful seen from these cliffs, and even more so from the terrace at La Raspelière, for the sake of which I would have traveled great distances. "Yes, they're incomparable," said Mme Verdurin offhandedly, with a glance at the immense casements that formed a French window. "For all that we see them all the time, we never grow tired of them," and her eyes went back to the cards. But my very enthusiasm had made me demanding. I complained of not being able to see from the drawing room the rocks at Darnetal that Elstir had told me were adorable at this hour of the day, when they refracted so many colors. "Oh, you can't see them from here, you'd need to go to the end of the garden, to the 'Bayview.' From the seat there, you can take in the whole panorama. But you can't go there on your own, you'd get lost. I'll take you there, if you like," she added, lamely. "No you don't, come on, weren't the pains you had the other day enough, d'you want to get more of them? He can come back, he'll see the view of the bay another time." I did not insist, and I realized that for the Verdurins it was enough to know that the setting sun was here in their drawing room or their dining room, like a magnificent painting, or a precious Japanese enamel, justifying the high price at which they were renting La Raspelière fully furnished, but to which they seldom raised their eyes; their main business here was to live agreeably, to go on excursions, to eat well, to talk, to entertain agreeable friends whom they made play amusing games of billiards, have good meals and cheerful tea parties. I found later on, however, how intelligently they had learned to know the locality, taking their guests on excursions as "original" as the music to which they made them listen. The part that the flowers at La Raspelière, the roads along by the sea, the old houses, and the unknown churches played in M. Verdurin's life was so great that those who saw him only in Paris, and who had themselves replaced the life of the seaside and the country with the luxuries of the city, could scarcely comprehend the idea he had formed of his own life, and the importance that his pleasures lent it in his own eyes. This importance had been further increased by the fact that the Verdurins were convinced that La Raspelière, which they were counting on buying, was a property unique in the world. As they saw it, the superiority that their *amour-propre* had led them to ascribe to La Raspelière justified my enthusiasm, which would otherwise have somewhat irritated them, including as it did the disappointments (like those I had once suffered on first hearing La Berma) of which I had made sincere confession to them.

"I hear the carriage returning. Let's hope it found them," the Patronne suddenly murmured. Let it be said in a word that Mme Verdurin, aside even from the changes made inevitable by age, no longer resembled what she had been in the days when Swann and Odette were listening to the little phrase in her house. Even when it was being played, she was no longer obliged to wear that look of exhausted admiration she had adopted in the old days, for it had become her face. Under the impact of countless attacks of neuralgia, brought on by the music of Bach, Wagner, Vinteuil, and Debussy, Mme Verdurin's forehead had assumed vast proportions, like limbs finally deformed by rheumatism. Her temples, like two beautiful burning spheres, pain-filled and milky white, in which Harmony rolls undyingly around, had pushed back her silvery tresses on either side and proclaimed, on the Patronne's behalf, without the latter's having any need to speak, "I know what awaits me this evening." Her features no longer took the trouble to formulate the succession of too strong aesthetic impressions, for they were themselves their permanent expression, as it were, in a face both ravaged and majestic. This attitude of resignation to the ever-imminent sufferings inflicted on her by the Beautiful, and of the courage that it took to put on a gown when one was scarcely recovered from the last sonata, meant that, even when listening to the cruelest music, Mme Verdurin kept a disdainfully impassive face, and even hid herself in order to swallow her two spoonfuls of aspirin.

"Ah yes, here they are!" exclaimed a relieved M. Verdurin, seeing the door open on Morel, followed by M. de Charlus. The latter, for whom to dine *chez* Verdurin was certainly not to go into society but into some place of ill-repute, was as self-conscious as a schoolboy entering for the first time into a brothel and overdoing his respects to the madam. Thus M. de Charlus's customary wish to appear virile and unmoved was overcome (when he appeared in the open doorway) by those notions of a traditional politeness that reawaken the moment self-consciousness destroys an artificial attitude and summons up the resources of the unconscious. When this sense of an instinctive, atavistic politeness toward strangers takes effect in a Charlus, whether he be a nobleman or a bourgeois for that matter, it is always the soul of a relative of the female sex, auxiliary like a goddess or incarnate like a double, who undertakes to introduce him into a new drawing room and to shape his attitude until such time as he arrives in front of his hostess. Thus will a young painter, brought up by a saintly Protestant cousin, enter, his head to one side and tremulous, looking up at the sky, his hands clutching an invisible muff, the evoked shape of which, together with the real tutelary presence, will assist the self-conscious artist to cross, without any agoraphobia, the chasm-filled space leading from the anteroom into the small drawing room. Thus it was that the pious relative, the memory of whom is guiding him today, had entered many years ago, with so mournful an expression that they wondered what misfortune she had come to announce, when, from her opening words, they realized, as now with the painter, that she had come to pay a digestive call. By virtue of the same law which holds that, in the interests of an action as yet unperformed, life should exploit, utilize, denature, by a perpetual prostitution, the most respectable, at times the most sacred, and sometimes only the most innocent legacies from the past, and although it might then engender a different aspect, the one of Mme Cottard's nephews who had caused distress to his family, by his effeminate ways and the company that he kept, always made his entry joyfully, as if he had come to give you a surprise or announce an inheritance, radiating a happiness of which it would have been pointless to inquire the cause, but which derived from his unconscious heredity and his misplaced sex. He would walk on tiptoe, was himself astonished, no doubt, not to be holding in his hand a book of visiting cards, held out his hand while opening his mouth into a heart shape, as he had seen his aunt doing, and his one worried glance was at the mirror, where he seemed to want to make sure, bare-headed though he was, whether, as Mme Cottard had asked Swann one day, his hat was not on crooked. As for M. de Charlus, whom the society in which he had lived had provided, at this critical juncture, with different examples, other arabesques of affability, and the maxim that we must be able, in certain cases, even for members of the petty bourgeoisie, to show off and exploit our rarest charms, normally held in reserve, it was fluttering affectedly, and with the same ampleness to his waddlings as though they were hobbled and made broader by his being in a skirt, that he made for Mme Verdurin, wearing so flattered and honored an expression that you might have thought that to be introduced to her was for him a supreme favor. His half-bowed face, on which self-satisfaction did battle with propriety, was creased by small lines of affability. You might have thought you saw Mme de Marsantes coming forward, so conspicuous at that moment was the woman that nature's error had introduced into M. de Charlus's body. It is true that the Baron had labored hard to conceal that error, and to acquire a masculine appearance. But hardly had he succeeded before, having during this same time preserved the same tastes, the habit of feeling, as a woman lent him a new feminine appearance, engendered this time not by his heredity but by his individual way of life. And since he had gradually come to think, even about social matters, in the feminine, and this without even noticing, for it is not only by dint of lying to others, but also of lying to ourselves, that we cease to notice that we are lying, although he had demanded of his body that it manifest (at the moment of entering the Verdurins' house) all the courtesy of a great nobleman, that body, which had clearly grasped what M. de Charlus had ceased to understand, deployed all the seductiveness of a *grande dame,* to the point where the Baron might have merited the epithet of "ladylike." Can we in any case entirely separate M. de Charlus's appearance from the fact that, sons not always taking after their fathers, even if they are not inverts and go in pursuit of women, they may consummate the profanation of their mothers in their faces? But let us here leave what would merit a chapter on its own: the profanation of mothers.

Although other reasons may have presided over this transformation in M. de Charlus, and purely physical ferments have caused matter to "work" in him and his body gradually to pass over into the category of women's bodies, the change we are here registering was spiritual in origin. By dint of believing ourselves to be ill, we become so, we lose weight, we no longer have the strength to get up, we suffer from nervous enteritis. By dint of having tender thoughts about men, we become a woman, and a false skirt impedes our steps. In such cases, the *idée fixe* can modify (as in other cases our health) our gender. Morel, who was behind him, came to greet me. From that moment on, because of a twofold change that had occurred in him, he created (I was unable to take account of it soon enough, alas!) a bad impression on me. Here is why. I have said that Morel, having escaped from servitude under his father, generally indulged in a very disdainful familiarity. On the day when he had brought me the photographs, he had spoken without even once calling me "monsieur," treating me condescendingly. How surprised I was, then, at Mme Verdurin's, to find him bowing very low to me, and to me alone, and to hear, even before any other utterance, words of respect, most respectful—the words I had thought it impossible to bring beneath his pen or onto his lips—being addressed to me! I at once got the impression he had something to ask of me. Leading me aside a minute or two later: "Monsieur would be doing me a very great service," he said, going so far this time as to address me in the third person, "by concealing altogether from Mme Verdurin and her guests the kind of profession that my father exercised at his uncle's. It would be better to say that, in your family, he was the steward of estates so vast that it made him the equal practically of your parents." Morel's request annoyed me very greatly, because it forced me to exaggerate not his father's situation, which was all one to me, but my own father's at least apparent wealth, which I thought ridiculous. But so unhappy and so urgent was his expression that I did not refuse. "No, before dinner," he said in a tone of entreaty, "Monsieur has countless pretexts for taking Mme Verdurin aside." Which was what in fact I did, attempting as best I could to enhance the distinction of Morel's father, without exaggerating overmuch the "standard of living" or the "worldly wealth" of my family. This was accepted without a murmur, despite the astonishment of Mme Verdurin, who had known my grandfather slightly. But as she lacked tact, and detested families (that solvent of the little nucleus), after telling me that she had once caught sight of my great-grandfather, and speaking of him as of some semi-imbecile who would not have understood the first thing about the little group, and who, as she put it, "was not one of us," she said, "Families are such a nuisance in any case, one aspires only to escape from them"; and she at once recounted one of my grandfather's traits of which I was unaware, although at home I had had suspicions (I never knew him, but he was much talked about) as to his uncommon avariciousness (as opposed to the rather too ostentatious generosity of my great-uncle, the friend of the lady in pink and Morel's father's employer): "The very fact that your grandparents had such a smart steward proves that there are people of every stripe in a family. Your grandfather's father was so miserly that, almost gaga by the end of his life—between ourselves, he was never very bright, you make up for all of them—he couldn't bring himself to spend three sous on an omnibus. So that they were obliged to have someone go after him, to pay the conductor separately, and give the old skinflint to believe that his friend M. de Persigny,[73] a minister of state, had arranged for him to travel on the buses gratis. Anyway, I'm very glad that *our* Morel's father should have been so respectable. I'd understood he taught at a *lycée,* but never mind, I'd misunderstood. But it hardly matters, for I must tell you that here we appreciate only people's inner worth, the personal contribution, what I call participation. Provided you are of the guild, provided in short you are of the brotherhood, the rest matters little." Morel's way of being of it—as far as I could make out—was to be sufficiently fond of both men and women to give pleasure to either sex with the help of the experiments he had conducted on the other, as will be seen in due course. But what it is essential to say here is that, the moment I had given him my word to approach Mme Verdurin, the moment I had done so, above all, when there was no going back, Morel's "respect" for me took wing as if by magic, the respectful formulas vanished, and for a time he avoided me even, contriving to make it look as though he despised me, so that if Mme Verdurin wanted me to say something to him, to ask him for a particular piece of music, he went on talking to one of the faithful, then moved on to another, and changed his position if I went up to him. They were obliged to tell him up to three or four times that I had addressed him, after which he would answer me, briefly, with an air of constraint, unless we were alone. In which case, he was expansive and amicable, for he had charming sides to his character. I concluded nonetheless from that first evening that he must be base by nature, that he would not shrink when need be from any obsequiousness and knew nothing of gratitude. In which he resembled the common run of mankind. But as I had something of my grandmother in me, and took pleasure in men's diversity without expecting anything from them or holding anything against them, I overlooked his servility, took pleasure in his gaiety when it showed itself, and even in what I took to have been genuine friendship on his part when, having reviewed the full range of his false knowledge of human nature, he realized (in fits and starts, for he had strange regressions to his blind and primitive savagery) that my kindness toward him was disinterested, that my indulgence stemmed not from a lack of clearsightedness but from what he called goodness of heart, and above all I was enchanted by his artistry, which was hardly anything more than an admirable virtuosity, but which caused me (without his being in the intellectual sense of the word a true musician) to hear again, or to get to know, so much beautiful music. Moreover, a manager, M. de Charlus, of whose talents in this direction I had been unaware (although Mme de Guermantes, who had known a very different Charlus in their young days, claimed that he had written her a sonata, had painted a fan for her, and so on), modest where his own superior abilities, first-rate though they were, were concerned, had been able to harness this virtuosity to a manifold artistic sense, which magnified it tenfold. You are to imagine some merely skillful performer from the Ballets Russes, trained, taught, and brought on in every sense by M. de Diaghilev.

I had just passed on to Mme Verdurin the message I had been entrusted with by Morel, and was talking to M. de Charlus about Saint-Loup, when Cottard entered the drawing room to announce, as if there were a fire, that the Cambremers were arriving. So as not to appear, in front of newcomers like M. de Charlus (whom Cottard had not seen) and myself, to attach too great an importance to the arrival of the Cambremers, Mme Verdurin did not stir, made no response to the announcement of this news, but contented herself with saying to the doctor, fanning herself gracefully and in the same artificial tone of voice as a marquise at the Théâtre-Français, "The Baron was just saying . . ." This was too much for Cottard! Less animatedly than would once have been the case, for his practice and his high positions had slowed down his delivery, but with the emotion all the same that he recovered at the Verdurins': "A baron! Where, where's a baron? Where's a baron?" he exclaimed, looking around for him with an astonishment bordering on incredulity. Mme Verdurin, with the affected indifference of a hostess one of whose servants has just smashed a precious glass in front of her guests, and with the artificial, over-shrill intonation of a first-prize–winner at the Conservatoire playing in Dumas *fils,*[74] replied, indicating Morel's patron with her fan, "But the Baron de Charlus, to whom I am about to introduce you . . . M. le Professeur Cottard." Mme Verdurin was not displeased, as it happens, to have an opportunity to play the lady. M. de Charlus held out two fingers, which the professor shook with the benevolent smile of a "prince of science." But he stopped dead on seeing the Cambremers enter, while M. de Charlus drew me into a corner to say a word to me, not without feeling my muscles, which is a German custom. M. de Cambremer bore little resemblance to the old Marquise. He was, as she used affectionately to put it, "altogether on his father's side." For anyone who had only heard speak of him, or even of letters from him, of a lively and apt turn of phrase, his physical appearance was a surprise. No doubt you would grow accustomed to it. But his nose, in order to come and take up its crooked position above his mouth, had chosen perhaps the one oblique line, out of so many, that you would never have thought of tracing on that face, one that denoted a common stupidity, made even worse by the proximity of an apple-red Norman complexion. It is possible that M. de Cambremer's eyes had preserved in their lids something of that Le Cotentin sky, so soft on those beautiful sunny days when the stroller is amused to see, halted beside the road, and to count in their hundreds, the shadows of the poplar trees, but those heavy, rheumy, badly drooping eyelids would have prevented intelligence itself from passing through. And so, disconcerted by the thinness of that blue gaze, you turned back to the big, crooked nose. By a transposition of the senses, M. de Cambremer looked at you with his nose. This nose of M. de Cambremer's was not ugly but, rather, a little too beautiful, too strong, too vain of its own importance. Hooked, polished, shiny, spanking new, it was quite prepared to make up for the spiritual insufficiency of his gaze; unfortunately, if the eyes are sometimes the organ in which intelligence is revealed, the nose (whatever their intimate solidarity and the unsuspected repercussions of one feature on the others), the nose is generally the organ in which stupidity exhibits itself the most readily.

Although the decorousness of the somber clothing that M. de Cambremer always wore, even in the mornings, reassured those dazzled and exasperated by the insolent brilliance of the beach costumes of the people whom they did not know, you could not understand why the wife of the First President should declare, with an air of expertise and of authority, as someone having had greater experience of Alençon's high society than yourself, that with M. de Cambremer you at once felt yourself, even before knowing who he was, in the presence of a man of great refinement, a man of perfect breeding, who made a change after the Balbec kind, a man, in short, in whose company you could breathe freely. On her, asphyxiated as she was by so many Balbec tourists, who knew nothing of her world, he had the effect of a flask of smelling salts. He struck me, on the contrary, as one of those people whom my grandmother would have at once found to be "quite unpresentable," and since she did not understand snobbery, she would no doubt have been amazed that he had managed to be married to Mlle Legrandin, who must have been very hard to satisfy when it came to refinement, she whose brother was so very "presentable." At best, it might have been said of M. de Cambremer's common ugliness that it rather belonged to the locality, possessing something of its ancient past; faced by his defective features, which one would have liked to rectify, you thought of the names of those small Normandy towns about whose etymology my *curé* had been mistaken, because the country people, articulating badly or having understood amiss the Norman or Latin word that designated them, had finally perpetuated a misconception and a corrupt pronunciation in a barbarism that was already to be found in the cartularies, as Brichot would have said. Life in these small old towns can anyway be spent agreeably, and M. de Cambremer must have had his good qualities, for, if it was only natural that, as a mother, the old Marquise should have preferred her son to her daughter-in-law, she often declared in return, she who had several children, two or three of whom were not without talents, that the Marquis was in her opinion the best one of the family. During the short time he had spent in the army, his comrades, finding "Cambremer" too much of a mouthful, had given him the nickname of Cancan,[75] which he had, as it happens, in no way deserved. He knew how to adorn a dinner party to which he had been invited by saying, on the arrival of the fish course (even were the fish to be high) or

the entrée: "Really, though, what a fine beast we seem to have here."
And his wife, having, on entering the family, adopted all that she
thought formed part of this society's style of living, put herself on the
same level as her husband's friends, and sought perhaps to please him
like a mistress, as if in the old days she had been involved in his life as a
bachelor, by saying with a detached air when talking about him to officers: "You'll be seeing Cancan. Cancan has gone to Balbec, but he'll be
back this evening." She was furious to be jeopardizing her reputation
this evening at the Verdurins' and had done so only at the entreaties of
her mother-in-law and husband, for the sake of the tenancy. But, being
less well brought up than they, she made no secret of the motive, and
for the past fortnight had been having a good laugh with her women
friends about this dinner. "You know, we're having dinner with our tenants. That'll be well worth an increase. Basically, I'm rather curious to
find out what they may have done to our poor old La Raspelière"—as
though she had been born there, and found it full of mementos of her
family. "Our old keeper told me only yesterday the whole place has become unrecognizable. I don't dare to think about all that must be going
on in there. I think we'd do well to have it all fumigated before we
move back in." She arrived haughty and morose, with the air of a great
lady whose château, on account of a war, has been occupied by the
enemy, but who feels at home nonetheless and is keen to show the vic-
tors that they are intruders. Mme de Cambremer could not see me to
start with, for I was in a bay to one side with M. de Charlus, who was
telling me he had learned from Morel that his father had been a "steward" in my family, and that he, Charlus, was relying sufficiently on my
intelligence and my magnanimity (a term common to both him and
Swann) to deny myself the mean and unworthy pleasure that common
young imbeciles (I had been warned) would not fail to take in my position by revealing to our hosts details that the latter might think demeaning. "The mere fact that I take an interest in him and extend my
protection over him has something supereminent about it and abol-
ishes the past," concluded the Baron. Even as I was listening to him,
and pledging him the silence which I would have kept even without the
hope of being thought in exchange intelligent and magnanimous, I was

looking at Mme de Cambremer. And I had difficulty recognizing the melting, toothsome article whose company I had enjoyed the other day at teatime, on the terrace in Balbec, in the Normandy *galette* I saw now, hard as a pebble, into which the faithful would have tried to sink their teeth in vain. Irritated in advance by the easygoing side that her husband had got from his mother, and which meant that he would assume an honored expression when the faithful were being introduced to him, but anxious all the same to fulfill her functions as a woman of the world, once Brichot had been presented to her she wanted him to make the acquaintance of her husband, as she had seen the more elegant of her women friends doing; but, fury or pride prevailing over the flaunting of her savoir-vivre, she said, not, as she should have done, "Allow me to introduce my husband," but "Meet my husband," thus keeping the flag of the Cambremers flying high, in spite of themselves, for the Marquis bowed as low in front of Brichot as she had anticipated. But Mme de Cambremer's whole mood changed suddenly when she noticed M. de Charlus, whom she knew by sight. Never had she succeeded in getting herself introduced to him, even in the days of the liaison she had had with Swann. For M. de Charlus, who always took the woman's side, of his sister-in-law against M. de Guermantes's mistresses, of Odette, at that time not yet married, but an old liaison of Swann's, against the new ones, was a stern defender of morality and a loyal protector of married couples, and had given Odette—and kept—his word that he would not allow himself to be presented to Mme de Cambremer. The latter had certainly never suspected that it was at the Verdurins' that she would finally meet this unapproachable man. M. de Cambremer knew that it was so great a delight to her that he was himself affected, and he looked at his wife with an expression that signified, "You're glad you decided to come, aren't you?" He spoke, as it happens, very little, knowing that he had married a superior woman. "Me, unworthy," he was forever saying, readily quoting a fable of La Fontaine's and another by Florian[76] that he saw as applying to his own ignorance, and as enabling him, on the other hand, under the guise of a disdainful flattery, to demonstrate to the men of learning who were not members of the Jockey Club that one could both be a sportsman and have read fables. The unfortunate thing was that he only really knew two. Thus these recurred frequently. Mme de Cambremer was not stupid, but she had various very irritating habits. In her case, the deformation of people's names had absolutely nothing of aristocratic disdain about it. She would not have said, unlike the Duchesse de Guermantes (whose birth should have shielded her, more so than Mme de Cambremer, against such an absurdity), so as to appear not to know the far-from-fashionable name (whereas it is now that of one of the least approachable of women) of Julien de Monchâteau: "a little Mme . . . Pico della Mirandola."[77] No, when Mme de Cambremer got a name wrong it was out of kindness, so as to appear not to know something, and when, out of sincerity, she all the same admitted it, she thought she could hide it by removing the name tag. If she was defending a woman, for example, she would seek to disguise the fact, while wanting not to lie to someone who was begging her to tell the truth, that Mme Such-and-Such was currently the mistress of M. Sylvain Lévy, and would say, "No . . . I know nothing whatsoever about her, I believe she's been criticized for having kindled a passion in some gentleman whose name I don't know, something like Cahn, Kohn, Kuhn; anyway, I believe that this gentleman has long since died and that there was never anything between them." The procedure is similar—though the reverse of theirs—to that of those liars who, by editing their activities when recounting them to a mistress or simply to a friend, imagine that neither one nor the other will at once see that the sentence spoken (as in the case of Cahn, Kohn, Kuhn) is an interpolation, is of another species from those making up the conversation, that it has a false bottom.

Mme Verdurin asked in her husband's ear: "Do I give my arm to the Baron de Charlus? Since you'll have Mme de Cambremer on your right, we could have swapped courtesies." "No," said M. Verdurin, "as the other is higher in rank"—meaning that M. de Cambremer was a marquis—"M. de Charlus is in fact his inferior." "Very well, I'll put him next to the Princesse." And Mme Verdurin introduced Mme Sherbatoff to M. de Charlus; the pair of them bowed silently, as much as to say they knew all about each other but promised to keep a mutual secret. M. Verdurin introduced me to M. de Cambremer. Even before he had spoken, in his loud voice with its slight stammer, his tall stature and high color had displayed in their oscillation the martial hesitation of a superior officer who tries to put you at your ease and says, "They've had a word with me, we'll sort things out; I'll get your punishment lifted; we're not man-eaters; it'll all be all right." Then, shaking my hand, "I believe you know my mother," he said. The verb "believe" he thought appropriate to the wariness of a first introduction but in no way to express doubt, for he went on, "Anyway, I have a letter from her for you." M. de Cambremer was artlessly happy to revisit the place where he had lived for so long. "I am rediscovering myself," he said to Mme Verdurin, as his wondering gaze recognized the painted flowers on the trumeaux above the doors, and the marble busts on their tall pedestals. He may, however, have felt disoriented, for Mme Verdurin had brought in any amount of fine old things that she owned. From this point of view, Mme Verdurin, though regarded by the Cambremers as having turned everything upside down, was not a revolutionary but intelligently conservative, in a sense which they could not understand. Thus they accused her, wrongly, of hating the old house and of dishonoring it with simple fabrics in place of their own opulent plush, like an ignorant *curé* criticizing the diocesan architect for reinstating the old wooden carvings that had been stored away, for which the cleric had seen fit to substitute ornaments bought on the Place Saint-Sulpice.[78] What was more, in front of the château, a small mixed garden had started to replace the flower beds that had been the pride and joy not only of the Cambremers but of their gardener. The latter, who looked on the Cambremers as his sole masters, and groaned beneath the yoke of the Verdurins, as if the land had been temporarily occupied by an invader and a troop of marauding soldiery, went off secretly bearing his grievances to the dispossessed owner, waxed indignant at the contempt in which his araucarias, his begonias, his sempervivums, and his double dahlias were held, and that anyone should dare, in so opulent a residence, to grow such commonplace flowers as anthemis or maidenhair fern. Mme Verdurin had sensed this stubborn resistance and had decided, should she take a long lease or even buy La Raspelière, to set as a condition the dismissal of the gardener, to whom the old owner was, on the contrary, exceedingly attached. He had served her for nothing in times of hardship, and adored her; but, thanks to the bizarre compartmentalization of opinion among the common people, where the profoundest moral contempt may be enclosed within the most heartfelt esteem, which in its turn overlaps with old, unended grudges, he often used to say about Mme de Cambremer, who, in '70, in a château she owned in the east, surprised by the invasion, had had, for a whole month, to endure the contact of the Germans: "What Mme la Marquise's been much criticized for is, during the war, to have taken the Prussian side and even put them up in her house. At any other time, I'd have understood; but in time of war, she shouldn't have done it. It's not right." So that he was undyingly loyal to her, revered her for her kindness, yet credited that she had been guilty of treason. Mme Verdurin was piqued that M. de Cambremer should claim to recognize La Raspelière so easily. "You must find a few changes all the same," she replied. "First of all, there were those terrible great Barbedienne bronzes[79] and some nasty little plush chairs that I wasted no time packing off to the attic, which is still too good for them." After which acerbic rejoinder directed at M. de Cambremer, she offered him her arm to go to the table. He hesitated for a moment, saying to himself, "All the same, I can't go in ahead of M. de Charlus." But, imagining that the latter was an old friend of the household, seeing that he did not have the place of honor, he decided to take the arm he was being offered and told Mme Verdurin how proud he was to have been admitted into the *cénacle* (which is how he referred to the little nucleus, not without a short laugh of satisfaction at knowing the term). Cottard, who was sitting next to M. de Charlus, looked at him underneath his monocle so as to make his acquaintance and break the ice, with winks that were far more insistent than they would once have been, and not diluted by any shyness. His winning glances, magnified by their smile, were no longer contained by the eyepiece but overflowed it on every side. The Baron, who was quick to find men of his own kind wherever he was, did not doubt that Cottard was one such, and was giving him the eye. He at once displayed to the professor the severity of the invert, as contemptuous of those who feel attracted by him as he is all ardor and attentiveness toward those for whom he feels an attraction. Although everyone talks, untruthfully, of the comforts, forever denied to us by fate, of being loved, it is no doubt a general law, whose writ is very far from running to the Charluses alone, that we should find the person whom we do not love but who loves us unbearable. To such a person, to the woman of whom we will say not that she loves us but that she has her hooks into us, we prefer the company of any other woman at all, who has neither her charm, nor her attractions, nor her brains. She will only get these back, as far as we are concerned, once she has ceased loving us. In which sense, we might see, in the irritation produced in an invert by a man he finds unattractive but who seeks him out, simply the transposition, in a comical form, of this universal rule. With him, however, it is far more powerful. Thus, whereas the common run of men try to conceal it even as they experience it, the invert is implacable in letting the man who has provoked it know, as he would certainly not let a woman know, M. de Charlus, for example, with the Princesse de Guermantes, whose passion annoyed yet flattered him. But when they find another man displaying a particular proclivity toward them, then, whether it be incomprehension that it should be the same as their own, or an unfortunate reminder that this proclivity, found beautiful by them for as long as it is they who are experiencing it, is looked on as a vice, or a desire to rehabilitate themselves by an outburst in circumstances where it will not cost them anything, or out of a fear of detection which they suddenly rediscover when desire is no longer leading them on, blindfold, from one rash act to the next, or in fury at suffering, by virtue of someone else's equivocal attitude, the injury they would not have shrunk from causing that other person by their own attitude had they found him attractive, the men who are not embarrassed to follow a young man for miles on end, or never to take their eyes off him at the theater even if he is with friends, thereby risking causing a rift between them, they can be heard to say, the minute someone for whom they feel no attraction looks at them, "Who do you take me for, monsieur?"—simply because they are being taken for what they are—"I don't understand you, no, no good insisting, you're making a mistake," going as far as a slap in the face if necessary, and, in front of someone who knows the rash individual in question, becoming indignant: "What, you know this horror? The way it has of looking at one! Such manners!"

M. de Charlus did not go as far as this, but he assumed the frosty, of-fended expression that women who are not loose have when people ap-pear to think that they are, and even more the women who are so. Moreover, the invert brought face-to-face with an invert sees not simply a displeasing image of himself which, purely inanimate, could injure only his self-esteem, but another himself, alive, active in the same direc-tion, and capable therefore of injuring him in his amours. Thus he is following his instinct for self-preservation when he puts this potential rival down, either to the people who are capable of doing the latter harm (without Invert No. 1's concerning himself about being taken for a liar when thus condemning Invert No. 2 in the eyes of people who may be well informed about his own case), or to the young man whom he has "started," who is going perhaps to be taken away from him, and who needs to be convinced that the same things that he would find every advantage in doing with him would be the greatest of misfortunes were he to allow himself to do them with the other. For M. de Charlus, mindful perhaps of the (quite imaginary) dangers that the presence of this Cottard, whose smile he had misinterpreted, would incur for Morel, an invert who did not attract him was not merely a caricature of himself, he was also a rival designate. If, when setting foot in the provincial town where he has come to settle permanently, a tradesman in an unusual line of business sees directly facing him, in the same square, the same business being carried on by a competitor, he is not any more discomfited than a Charlus who, having gone off to conduct his love life privately in some tranquil spot, catches sight, on the day of his arrival, of the local squire, or the barber, whose appearance and mannerisms leave him in no doubt. The tradesman will often develop a hatred for his competitor; this hatred sometimes degenerates into mel-ancholy, and if his heredity be even slightly tainted, the tradesman in small towns has been known to show the first signs of insanity, which can be cured only by persuading him to sell his "goodwill" and expatri-ate himself. The fury of the invert is more obsessional still. He has real-ized from the very first instant that the squire and the barber have desired his young companion. It is no good his repeating to the latter a hundred times a day that the barber and the squire are ruffians any con-tact with whom would dishonor him; he is obliged, like Harpagon,[80] to watch over his treasure and gets up during the night to see whether it is being stolen from him. Which is what no doubt, more even than desire or the convenience of a common habit, and almost as much as that experience of ourselves which is alone true, makes one invert able to sniff out another with an almost infallible rapidity and certainty. He may be momentarily mistaken, but is quickly able to redivine the truth. Thus M. de Charlus's error was short-lived. A godlike discernment showed him a moment later that Cottard was not of his own kind and that he had no need to fear his advances, either for himself, which would merely have exasperated him, or for Morel, which would have seemed to him more serious. He recovered his composure, and since he was still under the influence of the transit of Venus Androgyne, he smiled feebly now and again at the Verdurins without taking the trouble to open his mouth, but simply uncreasing one corner of his lips, and for a second allowed his eyes to light up affectionately, he who was so besotted with virility, just as his sister-in-law the Duchesse de Guermantes would have done. "Do you do much hunting, monsieur?" Mme Verdurin said contemptuously to M. de Cambremer. "Has Ski told you about our great adventure?" Cottard asked the Patronne. "I hunt mainly in the forest of Chantepie," answered M. de Cambremer. "No, I haven't told her anything," said Ski. "Does it deserve its name?"[81] Brichot asked M. de Cambremer, having glanced at me out of the corner of his eye, for he had promised to talk etymologies, while asking me to keep from the Cambremers the contempt with which those of the *curé* had filled him. "It's no doubt because I'm incapable of understanding, but I don't follow your question," said M. de Cambremer. "I mean, do many magpies sing there?" answered Brichot. Cottard, meanwhile, was suffering from the fact that Mme Verdurin was not aware that they had all but missed the train. "Come on, now," said Mme Cottard to her husband, in order to encourage him, "recount your odyssey." "Yes indeed, it's quite out of the ordinary," said the doctor, who recommended his narrative. "When I saw that the train was in the station I was thunderstruck. And all by the fault of Ski. You're somewhat quaint with your information, *mon cher*! And with Brichot waiting for us at the station." "I thought," said the university man, casting what remained of his gaze around him and smiling with his thin lips, "that if you had been delayed at Graincourt it was because you had encountered some lady of the peripatetic school." "Hold your tongue, will you? Supposing my wife were to hear you!" said the professor. "The little woman, he jealous." "Oh, that Brichot," exclaimed Ski, whose traditional gaiety had been aroused by Brichot's risqué joke, "ever the same," although he did not know, truth to tell, whether the university man had ever been dirty-minded. And in order to add the ritual gesture to these hallowed words, he acted as if he were unable to resist the urge to pinch his leg. "Quite a lad, he never changes," Ski went on, and, not reflecting on how sad and how comic the academic's semiblindness made the words seem, he added, "Ever one eye on the ladies." "There, you see," said M. de Cambremer, "that's what it's like when you encounter a scholar. I've been hunting in the forest of Chantepie these past fifteen years, and not once did I ask myself what the name might mean." Mme de Cambremer cast a stern glance at her husband; she would not have wanted him to humble himself like this in front of Brichot. She was even more displeased when, each time Cancan employed a "ready-made" expression, Cottard, who knew both their strengths and their weaknesses, having learned them so laboriously, demonstrated to the Marquis, who had admitted to being stupid, that they did not mean anything: "Why 'dull as ditchwater'? Do you think ditchwater is duller than anything else? You say 'forty winks.' Why forty particularly? Why 'sleep like a log'? Why 'go west'? Why 'paint the town red'?" But then Brichot undertook to defend M. de Cambremer, by explaining the origins of each expression. But Mme de Cambremer was chiefly occupied in examining the changes the Verdurins had brought about at La Raspelière, so as to be able to criticize some of these and to import others, or the same ones perhaps, into Féterne. "I ask myself what that chandelier is that's all askew. I have difficulty recognizing my old Raspelière," she added, with a familiarly aristocratic air, as though she had been speaking of a retainer, and claiming less to be denoting his age than saying that he had seen her born. And as she was somewhat bookish in her language, "All the same," she added in an undertone, "I fancy that, were I to live in someone else's house, I'd be rather ashamed to alter everything like this." "It's unfortunate you didn't come with them," said Mme Verdurin to M. de Charlus and Morel, hoping that M. de Charlus would "be back" and would yield to the rule of all arriving by the same train. "You're sure 'Chantepie' means the magpie that sings, Chochotte?" she added, to demonstrate that, great hostess that she was, she took part in all the conversations at once. "Tell me a little bit about this violinist," Mme de Cambremer said to me. "He interests me; I adore music, and I fancy I've heard speak of him; you must educate me." She had found out that Morel had come with M. de Charlus, and wanted, by getting the first to come, to try and make a friend of the second. She added, however, so that I might not guess this reason, "M. Brichot, too, interests me." For, though she was highly cultivated, just as certain people predisposed to obesity eat hardly anything and walk all day long without ceasing visibly to put on weight, so, for all that Mme de Cambremer had delved more deeply, at Féterne especially, into an increasingly esoteric philosophy and an increasingly learned kind of music, she emerged from these studies only to contrive schemes that might enable her to drop the bourgeois friendships of her young days and form relationships that she had thought at first were part of her in-laws' society but which she had then realized were situated much higher up and much further off. A philosopher who was not sufficiently modern for her, Leibniz, has said that the journey from the intellect to the heart is a long one. Mme de Cambremer had proved no more up to making it than her brother. Ceasing to read Stuart Mill only to start reading Lachelier,[82] the less she came to believe in the reality of the external world, the greater the zeal with which she tried to create a position for herself in it before she died. Besotted as she was with realism in art, no object seemed to her humble enough to serve as the painter's or the writer's model. A society picture or novel she would have found nauseating; Tolstoy's muzhiks, or Millet's peasants,[83] were the absolute limit, socially speaking, which she would not allow the artist to go beyond. Yet to overstep that which limited her own social dealings, to ascend to associating with duchesses, was the aim of all her endeavors, so ineffective was the spiritual discipline to which she subjected herself through the study of masterpieces against the morbid and congenital snobbery that had grown up in her. This last had in the end cured certain tendencies toward avarice and adultery to which she had been liable when young, in which it resembled those singular and permanent pathological states that appear to immunize those afflicted by them against other diseases. Listening to her, I could not for the rest help but acknowledge, without deriving any pleasure from it, the refinement of her expressions. They were those common, in any given period, to everyone of the same intellectual caliber, so that the refined expression at once supplies an arc of the circle, as it were, the means of describing and limiting the whole circumference. Thus these expressions mean that the people who employ them at once annoy me, as being already familiar, yet also pass for being superior, and were often held out to me as delightful and unappreciated neighbors. "You are not unaware, madame, that many forest regions derive their names from the animals that populate them. Next to the forest of Chantepie, you have the woods of Chantereine." "I don't know who the queen in question is,[84] but you're not being very gallant to her," said M. de Cambremer. "Take that, Chochotte!" said Mme Verdurin. "Apart from which, did you have a good journey?" "We encountered only vague specimens of humanity, who filled the train. But I must answer M. de Cambremer's question; the *reine* here isn't a queen, the wife of a king, but a frog. It's the name it kept for a long time in these parts, witness the station of Renneville, which ought to be written as 'Reineville.' " "You seem to have a fine beast there," said M. de Cambremer to Mme Verdurin, pointing to a fish. This was one of the compliments with the help of which he thought he could pay his way at a dinner party, and already return the courtesy. ("There's no point in inviting them," he would often say to his wife, referring to one or another group of friends. "They were delighted to have us. It was they who thanked me.") "Anyway, I have to tell you that I've been going just about every day to Renneville for many years, and I've not seen any more frogs there than elsewhere. Mme de Cambremer brought the *curé* of a parish where she owns a lot of property here, who's of the same way of thinking as yourself, I imagine. He's written a book." "He has indeed, I read it with the utmost interest," answered Brichot, hypocritically. The satisfaction that his vanity received indirectly from this answer brought a long laugh from M. de Cambremer. "Ah well, the author of, how shall I put it, this geography, this glossary, holds forth at length on the name of a small locality of which we were once, if I may say so, the lords, by the name of Pont-à-Couleuvre. Now, I'm obviously just a common ignoramus compared with that fount of learning, but I've been to Pont-à-Couleuvre scores of times to his once, and I'll be damned if I've ever seen even one of those nasty serpents,[85] I say 'nasty,' despite the praise the good La Fontaine bestows on them." ("The Man and the Snake" was one of his two fables.) "You've not seen any, and it's you who has seen aright," replied Brichot. "True, the writer you speak of knows his subject backward, he's written a remarkable book." "Indeed!" burst out Mme Verdurin. "That book, it's fair to say, is a true labor of love." "No doubt he consulted a few *terriers*"—meaning by that the lists of benefices and *curés* for each parish—"which may have supplied him with the names of the lay patrons and ecclesiastical collators. But there are other sources. One of my most learned friends has drawn on them. He found that the same place was given the name of Pont-à-Quileuvre. This bizarre name inspired him to go further back still, to a Latin text in which the bridge that your friend believes to be infested with snakes is given as *pons cui aperit*. A closed bridge opened only on payment of a fair toll." "You talk of frogs. Finding myself in the midst of such learned people, I have the impression of being the frog before the Areopagus"—this was the second fable[86]—said Cancan, who made this joke frequently, laughing loudly, thinking by means of it, in his humility and very aptly, at once to profess his ignorance and make a display of his learning. As for Cottard, blocked by the silence of M. de Charlus and searching for air in other directions, he turned to me and put one of those questions that impressed his patients if he had guessed right and thus shown that he was, so to speak, inside their bodies; and if on the contrary, he had guessed wrong, enabled him to rectify certain theories and broaden his former points of view. "When you come to these relatively elevated situations, such as that where we find ourselves in at this moment, have you noticed whether it increases your tendency to breathless attacks?" he asked me, certain either of making me admire him, or else of completing his education. M. de Cambremer heard the question and smiled. "I can't tell you how much it amuses me to hear you have breathless attacks," he threw at me across the table. By which he did not mean that it cheered him up, although that was in fact the case. For this excellent man could not hear speak of another's misfortune without a sense of well-being and a spasm of hilarity that quickly made way for the compassion of a kind heart. But his words had another meaning, made clear by those that followed: "It amuses me," he said, "because in fact my sister does, too." In short, it amused him as if he had heard me naming as one of my friends someone who had been a frequent visitor to their house. "What a small world," was the reflection that he formulated to himself, and which I saw written on his smiling face when Cottard mentioned my breathless attacks. And, starting with that dinner party, these became like a sort of common link, for news of which M. de Cambremer never failed to ask me, if only in order to pass it on to his sister.

Even as I replied to the questions his wife put to me concerning Morel, I was thinking about a conversation I had had with my mother during the afternoon. As, while not advising me against going to the Verdurins' if it might amuse me, she was reminding me that it was a milieu that would not have appealed to my grandfather but would have made him shout, "Turn out the guard!," my mother had added: "Listen, President Toureuil and his wife told me they had had lunch with Mme Bontemps. I wasn't asked anything. But I thought I gathered that a marriage between you and Albertine would be her aunt's dearest wish. I think the real reason is they all find you very sympathetic. At the same time, I fancy the luxury they think you would be able to give her, the connections they more or less know we have, all that's not unconnected with it, I fancy, though secondary. I wouldn't have mentioned it to you, because I'm not keen on it, but as I imagine people will bring it up, I preferred to forestall them." "But you, what do you think of her?" I had asked my mother. "Me? *I* won't be marrying her. You could certainly do a thousand times better where marriage is concerned. But I don't think your grandmother would have liked you to be influenced. At present, I can't tell you what I think of Albertine, I don't think of her. I shall say to you, like Mme de Sévigné, 'She has good qualities, or so I believe. But at the start, I am able to praise her only with negatives. She is not this, she does not have a Rennes accent. In time I shall perhaps say, she is that.'[87] And I shall always think well of her if she makes you happy." But by these same words, which put the decision concerning my happiness back into my own hands, my mother had plunged me into that state of doubt in which I had been already when, my father having given me permission to go to *Phèdre*, and above all to become a man of letters, I had suddenly felt too heavy a responsibility, the fear of upsetting him, and the melancholy that comes when we cease to obey orders that, day by day, hide the future from us, and realize that we have at last begun to live life in earnest, as a grown-up person, to live the one life of which each of us is free to dispose.

It would be best perhaps to wait a little, to begin by seeing Albertine as in the past, so as to try and find out whether I truly loved her. I could amuse her by bringing her to the Verdurins', and that reminded me that I had come there myself this evening only in order to discover whether Mme Putbus was staying there, or would be coming. She was not dining, at all events. "Apropos of your friend Saint-Loup," Mme de Cambremer said to me, thus making use of an expression that indicated a greater logic in her thoughts than her words might have given one to suppose, for, though she had been talking to me about music, her mind had been on the Guermantes, "you know everyone's talking about his marriage with the Princesse de Guermantes's niece. I must tell you that for my own part, I don't give a *fig* for all this social tittle-tattle." I was seized by a fear of having spoken unsympathetically in front of Robert about a girl whose originality was false and whose mind was as second-rate as her character was violent. There is almost no piece of news we learn that does not cause us to regret some remark of ours. I replied to Mme de Cambremer, what was in any case the truth, that I knew nothing about it, and that anyway his fiancée had struck me as still very young. "That's perhaps the reason why it's not yet official; it's on everyone's lips, anyway." "I prefer to warn you," said Mme Verdurin curtly to Mme de Cambremer, having heard that the latter had been talking to me about Morel and thought, when she dropped her voice to talk about Saint-Loup's engagement, that she was still talking about him. "What we make here isn't light music. It's frightening how progressive they are, you know, in matters of art, my Wednesday faithful, my children, as I call them," she added, with a look of vainglorious terror. "I sometimes say to them, 'My dear good people, you're marching faster than your Patronne, not that audacity was ever thought to frighten her.' Every year, they go a bit further; I can see the day coming when they'll no longer march for Wagner or for d'Indy." "But it's very good being progressive, we're never progressive enough," said Mme de Cambremer, while inspecting every corner of the dining room, seeking to identify the things her mother-in-law had left behind and those that Mme Verdurin had brought in, and to catch the latter red-handed in her lack of good taste. Meanwhile, she was trying to talk to me on the subject that interested her most, M. de Charlus. She found it touching that he should have a violinist for a protégé. "He looks to be intelligent." "Extremely full of life even, for a man who's already getting on," I said. "Getting on? But he doesn't look as though he's getting on, see, his hair's still yellow." (For the last three or four years, the normal word for "hair," *les cheveux,* had been used in the singular, *le cheveu,* by one of those unknown launchers of literary fashions, and everyone on the same radius as Mme de Cambremer said *le cheveu,* not without an affected smile. At the present moment, people are still saying *le cheveu,* but out of a surfeit of the singular, the plural will be reborn.) "What mainly interests me in M. de Charlus," she added, "is that you can sense the gift in him. I must tell you that I set little store by knowledge. What is learned doesn't interest me." These words are not at variance with the particular virtue of Mme de Cambremer, which was indeed imitative, and acquired. But one of the things that you needed to know at that particular moment was that knowledge is nothing, is not worth a straw compared with originality. Mme de Cambremer had learned, like everyone else, that one must never learn anything. "That's the reason why Brichot," she said to me, "who has his intriguing side, for I don't turn up my nose at a certain appetizing erudition, interests me much less." But Brichot, at that moment, had only one preoccupation: hearing that they were talking music, he was fearful lest the subject remind Mme Verdurin of the death of Dechambre. He wanted to say something that would dismiss that fateful memory. M. de Cambremer gave him the opportunity with this question: "Wooded places are always named after animals, then?" "Not so," replied Brichot, happy to deploy his knowledge in front of so many newcomers, among whom, as I had told him, he was sure to interest at least one. "You only need to see how, in the names of people themselves, a tree is preserved, like a fern in a lump of coal. One of our conscript fathers[88] is called M. de Saulces de Freycinet, which, if I'm not mistaken, signifies a place planted with willows and ash, *salix et fraxinetum;* his nephew, M. de Selves, unites even more trees, since his name is 'de Selves,' *sylva.*"[89] Saniette was delighted to find the conversation taking so animated a turn. He was able, since Brichot was talking the whole time, to observe a silence that would keep him from becoming the target of M. and Mme Verdurin's gibes. And, having become more susceptible still in his joy at being rescued, he had been touched to hear M. Verdurin, for all the solemnity of such a dinner party, telling the *maître d'hôtel* to set a jug of water beside M. Saniette, who drank nothing else. (The generals who get the most soldiers killed insist that they be well fed.) And then, at one moment, Mme Verdurin had smiled at Saniette. No question about it, they were good people. He would never again be tortured. At that moment, the meal was interrupted by a guest whom I have forgotten to mention, an illustrious Norwegian philosopher who spoke French very well but very slowly, for the twofold reason, first, that, having only recently learned it and wishing not to make mistakes (he made a few all the same), he referred for each word to a sort of internal dictionary; and then because, as a metaphysician, he was always thinking about what he meant as he was saying it, which, even in a Frenchman, is a cause of slowness. He was for the rest a delightful creature, though similar in appearance to many others, except in one respect. This man who was so slow of speech (there was a silence after each word) became vertiginously quick to make his escape the moment he had said his farewells. His precipitateness gave you to suppose, the first time, that he had a stomachache or some even more pressing need.

"My dear ... associate," he said to Brichot, having deliberated to himself whether "associate" was the appropriate term, "I have a sort of ... desire to know whether there are other trees in the ... nomenclature of your beautiful ... French ... Latin ... Norman ... language. Madame"–he meant Mme Verdurin, although he did not dare look at her–"has told me that you know everything. Is this not the precise moment?" "No, it's the moment to eat," broke in Mme Verdurin, who could see the dinner's never being over. "Ah, very well!' replied the Scandinavian, lowering his head to his plate, with a sad smile of resignation. "But I must point out to Madame that if I ventured on this questionnaire ... I'm sorry, this questation ... it's because tomorrow I must return to Paris to dine at the Tour d'Argent or at the Hôtel Meurice.[90] My French ... colleague ... M. Boutroux[91] is to talk to us there about the spiritualist séances ... I'm sorry, the spirituous evocations ... that he has supervised." "It's not as good as they make out, the Tour d'Argent," said Mme Verdurin in irritation. "I've even had some detestable dinners there." "But am I mistaken, or is the food that one eats at Madame's not the very finest French cuisine?" "Good heavens, it's not positively bad," said Mme Verdurin, mollified. "And if you come next Wednesday, it'll be better." "But I leave on Monday for Algiers, and from there I am going to the Cape. And once I'm at the Cape of Good Hope, I won't be able to meet my illustrious associate any more. . . . Forgive me, I won't be able to meet my colleague any more." And, having supplied these retrospective excuses, he began obediently to eat at breakneck speed. But Brichot was only too happy to be able to provide further vegetable etymologies, and he replied, so interesting the Norwegian that the latter stopped eating once again, but indicating that they could take away his full plate and move on to the next course. "One of the Forty,"[92] said Brichot, "has the name Houssaye, or a place planted with *houx*, or holly; in the name of a subtle diplomatist, d'Ormesson, you find *orme*, or elm, the *ulmus* beloved of Virgil, and which gave its name to the town of Ulm; in that of his colleagues, M. de la Boulaye, the *bouleau*, or birch; M. d'Aunay, the *aulne* or alder; M. de Bussière, the *buis* or box; M. Albaret, the *albier* or alburnum"— I promised myself I would tell Céleste that—"M. de Cholet, the *chou*, or cabbage; and the *pommier* or apple tree in the name of M. de la Pommeraye, whom we heard lecture, Saniette, d'you remember, in the days when the good Porel had been sent off to the other end of the earth, as proconsul in Odéonia?"[93] Hearing Brichot pronounce the name of Saniette, M. Verdurin cast an ironic glance at his wife and at Cottard, which unnerved that self-conscious man. "You were saying that Cholet comes from *chou*," I said to Brichot. "Does a station that I went through before getting to Doncières, 'Saint-Frichoux,' also come from *chou*?" "No, Saint-Frichoux is *Sanctus Fructuosus*, just as *Sanctus Ferreolus* gave Saint-Fargeau, but it's not Norman at all." "He knows evelything there is to be known, he's borling us," gurgled the Princesse quietly. "There are so many other names that interest me, but I can't ask you everything at once." And, turning to Cottard, "Is Mme Putbus here?" I asked him. "No, thank God," replied Mme Verdurin, who had overheard my question. "I tried hard to divert her holidays to Venice, we're rid of her for this year." "I shall myself have a right to two trees," said M. de Charlus, "for I've more or less taken a small house between Saint-Martin-du-Chêne and Saint-Pierre-des-Ifs."[94] "But that's very near here, I hope you'll come over often, together with Charlie Morel. You'll only need to make arrangements concerning the trains with our little group, you're no distance from Doncières," said Mme Verdurin, who hated people's not coming by the same train and at the times when she had sent carriages. She knew how severe the climb was up to La Raspelière, even going round by the network of small roads behind Féterne, which delayed you by half an hour, and she was afraid that those looking to be independent might not find carriages to bring them, or might even, having in actual fact remained at home, seize on the pretext of not having found one at Douville-Féterne and not having felt up to making such an ascent on foot. In response to this invitation, M. de Charlus contented himself with a mute nod of the head. "He can't always be so accommodating, he looks so stiff," whispered the doctor to Ski, having remained very simple despite the superficial coating of vanity, and who did not try to hide the fact that Charlus had snubbed him. "He's no doubt unaware that in all the watering places and even in Paris in the clinics, the doctors, for whom I am of course 'number one,' make it a point of honor to introduce me to all the noblemen who are there and are afraid of hearing the worst. That even makes staying in a resort rather agreeable for me," he added offhandedly. "Even in Doncières, the major of the regiment, who is the doctor in attendance on the colonel, invited me to have lunch with him, telling me I was in a position to dine with the general. And this general is a M. de Something. I don't know whether his titles of nobility are more or less ancient than those of the Baron here." "Don't get all excited, it's not much of a coronet," replied Ski in an undertone, and he added something indistinct with a verb of which I could make out the final syllables, "*-arder*,"[95] preoccupied as I was with listening to what Brichot was saying to M. de

Charlus. "No, I regret to tell you, it's probable you have only one tree, for if Saint-Martin-du-Chêne is obviously *Sanctus Martinus juxta quercum*, the word *if*, conversely, may simply be the root *ave, eve*, which means 'damp,' as in Aveyron, Lodève, Yvette, and which you see surviving in our *éviers*, or kitchen sinks. It's the '*eau*,' the water, which in Breton is *Ster, Stermaria, Sterlaer, Sterbouest, Ster-en-Dreuchen*." I did not hear the conclusion, for, whatever pleasure I might have taken in hearing the name of *Stermaria* once again, I could not help hearing Cottard, near to whom I was sitting, saying in a low voice to Ski: "Ah, but I didn't know! He's a gentleman who knows how to manage things, then. What, he's one of the brotherhood! Yet he hasn't got those puffy eyelids. I shall need to watch out for my feet underneath the table, he'd only have to squeeze one, so far as I'm concerned. Anyway, it only half surprises me. I see several noblemen in the shower, in the altogether, they're degenerates more or less. I don't speak to them, because, after all, I'm a public servant and it might do me harm. But they know perfectly well who I am." Saniette, who had been alarmed by Brichot's interpellation, was beginning to breathe freely again, like someone who is afraid of storms but finds that the flash of lightning has not been followed by any sound of thunder, when he heard M. Verdurin question him while fixing him with a stare that did not let go of the poor wretch all the time he was speaking, in such a way as instantly to intimidate him and not allow him to gather his wits. "But you've always kept it from us, Saniette, that you used to frequent matinées at the Odéon?" Trembling like a recruit in front of a bullying sergeant, Saniette answered, making his words occupy the smallest possible space so as to have a better chance of avoiding the blows, "Once, to *La Chercheuse*."[96] "What's that he says?" shouted M. Verdurin, looking both disgusted and furious, and knitting his brows, as though his full attention would not be enough if he was to understand something unintelligible. "For a start, we don't understand what you're saying, what have you got in your mouth?" demanded M. Verdurin with increasing violence, and alluding to Saniette's faulty pronunciation. "Poor Saniette, I won't have you making him unhappy," said Mme Verdurin in a falsely pitying tone and so as to leave no one in any doubt as to her husband's insolent intentions. "I went to *La Che*—" "*Che, che, che,* do try to speak clearly," said M. Verdurin, "I can't

even hear you." Hardly one of the faithful could forbear from guffaw-
ing, and they looked like a band of cannibals whose taste for blood has
been reawakened by a wound inflicted on a white man. For the instinct
for imitation and lack of courage govern societies as they do crowds.
And everyone laughs at someone who is seen being made fun of, while
being quite prepared to venerate him ten years later in a circle where he
is admired. It is in this same fashion that the common people drive out
or acclaim a king. "Come, it's not his fault," said Mme Verdurin. "It's
not mine, either; you don't dine out if you can no longer articulate." "I
was at Favart's *La Chercheuse d'esprit.*" "What, it's *La Chercheuse d'esprit*
that you call *La Chercheuse?* Oh, that's magnificent, I could have gone
on searching for a hundred years and not found that," exclaimed
M. Verdurin, who would, however, have decided right away that someone was not well read or an artist, "was not one of us," if he had heard
him give certain works their full title. You had, for example, to say *Le
Malade, Le Bourgeois;* and anyone adding *"imaginaire"* or *"Gentilhomme"*
would have made it clear they were not "of the club," just as in a salon
someone proves that he is not a member of society by saying "M. de
Montesquiou-Fezensac" instead of "M. de Montesquiou." "But it's not
so extraordinary," said Saniette, breathless with emotion yet smiling,
though he may not have wanted to. Mme Verdurin burst out: "Oh yes
it is!" she sniggered. "You can be sure that no one in the world could
have guessed you meant *La Chercheuse d'esprit.*" M. Verdurin resumed
more quietly, and addressing both Brichot and Saniette, "It's a jolly
play as it happens, *La Chercheuse d'esprit.*" Uttered in a serious tone,
these simple words, in which no trace of malice was to be detected, did
Saniette as much good and evoked as much gratitude in him as a kindness. He was unable to proffer a single word but maintained a contented silence. Brichot was more talkative. "That's true," he replied to
M. Verdurin, "and were it to be passed off as the work of some Sarma-
tian or Scandinavian author, *La Chercheuse d'esprit* might be proposed as
a candidate for the situation vacant of masterpiece. But let it be said
without disrespect to the shade of the gentle Favart, his temperament
was not that of an Ibsen." He at once blushed up to the ears, remembering the Norwegian philosopher, who wore an unhappy look because
he had been trying in vain to identify what vegetable substance the *buis*

might be that Brichot had mentioned just now in connection with Bussière. "Anyway, Porel's satrapy now being occupied by a functionary who is a Tolstoyan of the strict observance, maybe we shall be seeing *Anna Karenina* or *Resurrection* beneath the Odéonian architrave."[97] "I know the portrait of Favart you mean," said M. de Charlus. "I saw a very good proof engraving of it at the Comtesse Molé's." The name of the Comtesse Molé had a powerful effect on Mme Verdurin. "Ah, so you go to Mme de Molé's," she exclaimed. She thought that you said "the Comtesse Molé" or "Mme Molé" simply as an abbreviation, as she had heard people say "the Rohans," or out of disdain, as she herself said "Mme La Tremoïlle." She was in no doubt that the Comtesse Molé, knowing as she did the Queen of Greece and the Princesse de Caprarola, had as good a right to the *particule* as anybody, and she had decided for once to grant it to this very brilliant person who had shown herself so well disposed toward her. And so, to make quite clear that she had spoken as she had deliberately, and did not begrudge the Comtesse the *de,* she went on, "But I had no idea you knew Mme de Molé!," as if it had been doubly extraordinary both that M. de Charlus should have known that lady and that Mme Verdurin should not have known that he knew her. Now, society, or at least what M. de Charlus called by that name, forms a relatively homogeneous and closed whole. Just as it is understandable that in the disparate vastness of the bourgeoisie a lawyer should say to someone who knows one of his school friends, "But how the devil did you come to meet So-and-So?," to be surprised on the other hand that a Frenchman should know the meaning of the word *temple* or *forêt* would be hardly any more extraordinary than to wonder by what accident M. de Charlus had been brought together with the Comtesse Molé. Moreover, even had such an acquaintance not followed naturally from the laws of society, if it had been fortuitous, how could it have been strange that Mme Verdurin should not know of it, when she was meeting M. de Charlus for the first time, and his connection with Mme Molé was far from the only thing she did not know in relation to a man of whom, in truth, she knew nothing? "Who was in that *Chercheuse d'esprit,* my dear Saniette?" asked M. Verdurin. Although feeling that the storm had passed, the former archivist hesitated before answering. "There, now," said Mme Verdurin, "you're intimidating him, you make fun of everything he says and then you want him to respond. Come on, say who was in it, and we'll give you some galantine to take home," said Mme Verdurin, making an unkind allusion to the ruination Saniette had brought down on himself in trying to save a married couple with whom he was friends. "I only remember that it was Mme Samary who played La Zerbine," said Saniette. "La Zerbine? What on earth's that?" cried M. Verdurin, as though the house were on fire. "It's a stock role in the old repertoire, see *Le Capitaine Fracasse*,[98] as you might say the Braggart or the Pedant." "Ah, it's you who's the pedant. La Zerbine! No, but he's out of his mind," exclaimed M. Verdurin. Mme Verdurin looked at her guests and laughed, as if to excuse Saniette. "La Zerbine, he imagines everyone knows instantly what that means. You're like M. de Longepierre, the stupidest man I know, who said to us familiarly the other day 'the Banat.' Nobody knew what he was talking about. Finally we found out it was a province in Serbia." To put an end to Saniette's ordeal, which was causing me more pain than it was him, I asked Brichot if he knew what "Balbec" meant. " 'Balbec' is probably a corruption of 'Dalbec,' " he told me. "One would need to be able to consult the charters of the Kings of England, the suzerains of Normandy, because Balbec was a dependency of the barony of Dover, on which account it was often known as Balbec d'Outremer or Balbec-en-Terre. But the barony of Dover itself came under the bishopric of Bayeux, and, despite the rights held momentarily over the abbey by the Templars, starting with Louis d'Harcourt, the Patriarch of Jerusalem and Bishop of Bayeux, it was the bishops of that diocese who were collators of the benefice of Balbec. That's how the Dean of Doville explained it to me, a bald, eloquent, fanciful man and a gourmet, who lives in the obedience of Brillat-Savarin and expounded some dubious pedagogy to me in ever so slightly sybilline terms while making me eat some admirable *pommes frites*."[99] While Brichot was smiling, to show how witty it was to associate such disparate matters and to employ an ironically elevated language on down-to-earth matters, Saniette was looking to introduce some shaft of wit that might set him back on his feet after his collapse of a moment before. The shaft of wit was what used to be known as an *à-peu-près*,[100] or pun, but which had changed its form, because plays on words evolve as do literary genres, or epidemics, which vanish only to be replaced by others, and so on. In the old days, the form the *à-peu-près* took was that of "the last word." But this was out of date, no one any longer used it, it was only Cottard now who might sometimes say in the middle of a game of piquet: "Do you know the last word in absentmindedness? Believing that the Édit de Nantes was an Englishwoman."[101] Last words had been replaced by nicknames. Basically, it was still the old *à-peu-près*, but because the nickname was in vogue, people failed to notice. Unfortunately for Saniette, when these *à-peu-près* were not his own, and generally unfamiliar to the little nucleus, he came out with them so self-consciously that, despite the laugh by which he followed them in order to signal their humorous nature, no one understood them. But if, conversely, the *bon mot* was his own, since he had generally hit upon it when talking with one of the faithful, the latter had repeated it on taking possession of it and the witticism was then known, but not as coming from Saniette. Thus, when he slipped one of these in, it was recognized, but because he was its author, he was accused of plagiarism. "Now, then," Brichot went on, "*bec* in Norman is 'stream'; there is the Abbey of Bec; Mobec, the stream of the marshland (*mor* or *mer* meant 'marsh,' as in Morville, or in Bricquemar, Alvimare, Cambremer); Briquebec, the stream of the height, coming from *briga*, a fortified place, as in Bricqueville, Bricquebosc, Le Bric, Briand, or else from *brice*, a bridge, which is the same as *Bruck* in German (Innsbruck) and in English *bridge*, which ends so many place-names (Cambridge, etc.). You have a lot of other *becs* in Normandy: Caudebec, Bolbec, Le Robec, Le Bec–Hellouin, Becquerel. It's the Norman form of the Germanic *Bach*, Offenbach, Anspach. Varaguebec, from the old word *varaigne*, the equivalent of *garenne*, a private wood or pond. As for *dal*," Brichot went on, "that's a form of *Thal*, a valley: Darnetal, Rosendal, and even, near Louviers, Becdal. The river that lent its name to Balbec is charming, as it happens. Seen from a *falaise* or cliff (*Fels* in German; you even have, not far from here, on a height, the pretty town of Falaise), it adjoins the spires of the church, though in reality situated a long way off, and appears to be reflecting them." "I can believe that," I said. "It's an effect Elstir is very fond of. I've seen several sketches of it in his house." "Elstir! You know Tiche?" exclaimed

Mme Verdurin. "But you must know that he and I were once really close. Thank heaven, I no longer see him. No, but ask Cottard, or Brichot, he used to have his place set at my table, he came every day. And he's one of whom it can be said it did him no good leaving our little nucleus. In a moment I'll show you some flowers he painted for me; you'll see the difference from what he's doing nowadays, which I don't like at all, not at all! Why, I got him to paint Cottard's portrait, not counting everything that he did from me." "And he gave the professor mauve hair," said Mme Cottard, forgetting that at that stage her husband was not even an *agrégé.*[102] "I don't know whether you find that my husband has mauve hair, monsieur." "That's of no account," said Mme Verdurin, lifting her chin with an expression of disdain for Mme Cottard and admiration for the man of whom she had been speaking. "That was the work of a famous colorist and a fine painter. Whereas," she added, addressing herself once again to me, "I don't know whether you call that painting, all those terrible great compositions, those great contraptions he's been exhibiting since he's no longer been coming to me. I call them daubs, they're so trite, and then they lack any relief, any personality. There's a bit of everybody in them." "He is bringing back the grace of the eighteenth century but in a modern form," said Saniette precipitately, invigorated and restored to the saddle by my friendliness. "But I prefer Helleu."[103] "There's no connection with Helleu," said Mme Verdurin. "But there is, it's eighteenth-century febrile. He's a Watteau *à vapeur,*"[104] and he started to laugh. "Oh, heard it, heard it a hundred times, I've been having that served up to me for years," said M. Verdurin, who had indeed once been told it by Ski, though as his own creation. "You're out of luck when the one time you pronounce something intelligibly it isn't your own." "It pains me," Mme Verdurin went on, "for he was someone of ability, he's thrown away a fine artistic temperament. Oh, if only he'd stayed here! He'd have become the leading landscapist of the day. And it's a woman who's dragged him down so! Not that that surprises me, for he was an attractive man, if vulgar. Basically, a second-rater. I can tell you, I sensed that right away. All in all, he never interested me. I was very fond of him, that's all. For one thing, he was so dirty! Do you much care for that, people who never wash?" "What's this thing we're eating, of such a pretty shade?" asked Ski. "It's called a strawberry mousse," said Mme Verdurin. "But it's ra-vish-ing. We ought to be opening bottles of Château-Margaux, Château-Lafite, port." "I can't tell you how amusing I find him, he only drinks water," said Mme Verdurin, in order to disguise, beneath the charm she found in this flight of fancy, the alarm occasioned in her by such prodigality. "But not so as to drink them," Ski went on. "You will fill all our glasses with them, they'll bring in wonderful peaches, huge nectarines, there, facing the setting sun; it'll have the luxuriance of a beautiful Veronese." "And cost almost as much," muttered M. Verdurin. "But take away these cheeses of such a villainous shade," Ski said, trying to remove the Patron's plate, who defended his Gruyère with all his might. "You can understand why I don't miss Elstir," Mme Verdurin said to me; "this one has twice the talent. Elstir is hard work, the man who's incapable of letting go of his picture when he wants to. He's the good student, examination fodder. Ski, on the other hand, follows his fancy. You'll see him lighting his cigarette in the middle of dinner." "By the way, I don't know why you've refused to have his wife," said Cot-tard; "it would be like the old days then." "Watch what you're saying, will you! No prize tart enters my house, M. le Professeur," said Mme Verdurin, who had, on the contrary, done her very best to get Elstir to return, even with his wife, but before they got married she had tried to come between them, she had told Elstir that the woman he loved was stupid, dirty, immoral, and had stolen. For once, she had not succeeded in bringing about a split. Instead, Elstir had broken with the Verdurin salon; and he had congratulated himself on having done so, just as con-verts bless the illness or the setback that has impelled their withdrawal and set them on the road to salvation. "He's splendid, is the professor," she said. "Why not say that my drawing room is a house of assignation? Anyone'd think you don't know what Mme Elstir is like. I'd rather en-tertain the lowest of street girls! No, no, I'd rather starve. I tell you in any case, I'd have been all the more stupid to overlook the wife when the husband no longer interests me, it's out of date, it's not even drawn any more." "That's extraordinary for a man of such intelligence," said Cottard. "Oh no," replied Mme Verdurin, "even in the days when he had talent, for he had that, the wretch, and to spare, what was tiresome about him was that he wasn't the least bit intelligent." Mme Verdurin had not waited for their quarrel, and no longer to like his painting, to pass this verdict on Elstir. The fact was that, even in the days when he formed part of the little group, Elstir would sometimes spend entire days with some woman or other who Mme Verdurin thought, rightly or wrongly, was "bird-brained," which in her view was not the behavior of an intelligent man. "No," she said, with an air of being even-handed, "I think his wife and he are just right for each other. God knows, I know of no more boring creature anywhere on earth, and I'd go out of my mind if I had to pass two hours with her. But they say he finds her very intelligent. You simply have to admit the fact, our *Tiche* was above all *excessively stupid*! I've seen him bowled over by women you can't imagine, by honest-to-God idiots we'd never have wanted in our little clan. Well, he used to write to them, to argue with them! Him, Elstir! Not that that stops him having his charming side—oh, charming, charming and delightfully absurd, of course." For Mme Verdurin was convinced that truly remarkable men commit countless follies. A false idea, yet with some truth in it. Certainly, people's "follies" are unbearable. But a lack of balance that we discover only with time is a consequence of the entry into a human brain of susceptibilities to which it is not customarily suited. With the result that the oddities of people who are charming exasperate us, but there are few if any charming people who are not, in some way, odd. "Here, I'm going to be able to show you his flowers right away," she said to me, seeing her husband signaling to her that we could get up from the table. And she took M. de Cambremer's arm once again. As soon as he had left Mme de Cambremer, M. Verdurin sought to make his apologies to M. de Charlus, and give his reasons, mainly for the pleasure of discussing these social nuances with a man of title, and momentarily the inferior of those who had assigned him the place to which they adjudged he had a right. But first of all he was anxious to demonstrate to M. de Charlus that he held too high an opinion of him intellectually to suppose that he paid any heed to such bagatelles: "Forgive me for mentioning these trifles," he began, "for I can well imagine the scant importance you attach to them. Bourgeois minds may heed them, but the others, the artists, the ones truly of our own kind, don't give a damn. And I realized you were one of us from the very first words we exchanged!" M. de Charlus, who had placed a very different interpretation on this expression, gave a sudden start. Following the doctor's oglings, the Patron's insulting frankness made him choke. "Don't protest, *cher* monsieur, you are one of us, it's as clear as day," M. Verdurin went on. "Note that I do not know whether you practice some art or other, but that isn't necessary, nor is it always sufficient. Dechambre, who has just died, played perfectly, with the most robust technique, but he wasn't one, you sensed right away he wasn't. Brichot isn't one. Morel is, my wife is, I sense that you are." "What were you going to say to me?" M. de Charlus broke in, who was beginning to feel reassured as to M. Verdurin's meaning, but would rather he did not shout these ambiguous words from the rooftops. "We put you only on the left," M. Verdurin replied. M. de Charlus, with a good-natured, understanding, insolent smile, replied, "Oh, come! That's of no account at all *here!*" And he gave a little laugh that was peculiar to him, a laugh that had probably come down to him from some Bavarian or Lorraine grandmother, who had herself got the identical laugh from one of her forebears, so that it had been ringing out like this, unchanged, for a good few centuries in the lesser courts of old Europe, and its precious quality had been enjoyed, like that of certain old musical instruments now grown very uncommon. There are times when, in order to depict someone in their entirety, a phonetic imitation would need to be added to the description, and that of the character which M. de Charlus was playing risks incompleteness for want of this little laugh, so delicate and so light, just as certain of Bach's suites are never rendered accurately because the orchestras lack the "little trumpets," with their particular tone, for which the composer wrote one or another part. "But," explained M. Verdurin, wounded, "it was on purpose. I attach no importance at all to titles of nobility," he added with that disdainful smile that I have seen so many people I have known, unlike my grandmother and my mother, have for all the things they do not possess, in front of people who will then, so they believe, be unable to use these to establish their superiority over them. "But, then, since M. de Cambremer was in fact there and he's a marquis, and you're only a baron . . ." "Permit me," replied M. de Charlus with a haughty expression, to the astonished M. Verdurin, "I am also Duc de Brabant, Damoiseau de Montargis, and Prince d'Oléron, de Carency, de Viareggio, and des Dunes. It's of absolutely no importance, however. Do not torment yourself," he went on, resuming his delicate smile, which grew broader at these final words: "I could tell right away that you weren't in the habit of it."

Mme Verdurin came up to show me Elstir's flowers. If the act, long since become a matter of such indifference to me, of dining out had, on the contrary, in a form that had entirely revived it, that of a journey along the coast, followed by an ascent by carriage up to two hundred meters above sea level, produced a sort of intoxication, this last had not been dispelled at La Raspelière. "Here, just look at that," the Patronne said to me, pointing to some large and magnificent roses by Elstir, but whose unctuous scarlet and frothy whiteness had boiled over with rather too creamy a relief against the jardinière on which they had been placed. "D'you think he'd still have the touch to capture that? Is that not pretty good? Besides, the subject matter's so beautiful, it would be amusing to finger them. I can't tell you how amusing it was watching him painting them. You felt it interested him, searching for that effect." And the Patronne's gaze paused dreamily on this present from the artist, in which was encapsulated not only his great talent but their long friendship, which survived only in these mementos of it that he had left to her; behind the flowers once picked for her by him, she thought she could once again see the beautiful hand that had painted them, in a single morning, in their freshness, so that the ones on the table, and the other leaning against a chair in the dining room, had been able to represent, for the Patronne's lunch party, a tête-a-tête between the still-living roses and the semilikeness of their portrait. A semilikeness only, Elstir being able to see a flower only by first transplanting it into that interior garden in which we are obliged always to remain. In this watercolor he had shown the roses as they had first appeared to him, and in a way that, but for him, we should never have known; so that they could be said to be a new variety with which the painter, like an ingenious horticulturist, had enriched the rose family. "From the day he left the little nucleus, the man was finished. It seems that my dinner parties made him waste time, that I was harming the development of his *genius*," she said, in an ironic tone. "As if associating with a woman such as myself could be anything but salutary for an artist!" she exclaimed in an impulse of vanity. Right beside us, M. de Cambremer, who had already sat down, and seeing M. de Charlus standing, made as if to get up and offer him his chair. This offer corresponded in the Marquis's mind perhaps simply to a vague intention of being polite. M. de Charlus preferred to attach to it the significance of a duty that a mere gentleman knew he must render to a prince, and thought that there was no better way of establishing his right to such precedence than by declining it. And so he exclaimed, "What's this? I beg you! The idea!" There was already something very "Guermantes" about the astutely vehement tone of this protestation, which was more strongly marked still in the imperious, useless, and familiar gesture with which M. de Charlus pressed down with both hands, as if forcing him to be seated again, on the shoulders of M. de Cambremer, who had not got up. "Oh, come now, my dear fellow," the Baron insisted, "that'd be all we need! There's no reason! In our day we reserve that for princes of the blood." The Cambremers were no more moved than Mme Verdurin by my enthusiasm for their house. For I was unresponsive to the beauties they pointed out to me but excited by my confused reminiscences; now and again I even confessed to my disappointment on finding that something did not conform to what its name had given me to imagine. I made Mme Verdurin indignant by telling her that I had thought it would be more countrified. Conversely, I paused in ecstasy to sniff the fragrance of the air coming through the doorway. "I see you like drafts," they said. My praise of the piece of green luster stopping up a broken windowpane was no more successful: "But it's horrible!" exclaimed the Marquise. The last straw was when I said: "My greatest joy was when I arrived. When I heard my footsteps echoing along the gallery, I thought I'd entered the offices of some village *mairie* or other, where there's a map of the canton." This time, a determined Mme de Cambremer turned her back on me. "You didn't find it all too badly arranged?" her husband asked her, with the same pitying solicitude as if he were inquiring how well his wife had withstood some unhappy ceremony. "There are some good things." But since, when the fixed rules of a sure taste do not impose inevitable limits on it, malevolence finds fault with everything about the person or the house of the people who have supplanted you: "Yes, but they're not in the right place. Indeed, are they all that good?"

"You'll have noticed," said M. de Cambremer, with a sadness restrained by a certain firmness, "some of the Jouy cretonne is showing through, things worn completely out in this drawing room!" "And that piece of material with its big roses like a peasant woman's bedspread," said Mme de Cambremer, whose quite spurious culture applied exclusively to idealist philosophy, Impressionist painting, and the music of Debussy. And so as not to make her case solely in the name of luxury but also of good taste: "And they've put up draft curtains! What a lack of style! But what d'you expect, such people don't know, where could they have learned? They must be retired wholesalers. They've not done so badly, considering." "I thought the chandeliers were good," said the Marquis, without anyone's knowing why he should make an exception of the chandeliers, just as, inevitably, each time a church was mentioned, whether it was Chartres Cathedral, or Rheims, or Amiens, or the church in Balbec, what he always hastened to cite as admirable was "the organ case, the pulpit, and the workmanship on the misericords." "As for the garden, the less said the better," said Mme de Cambremer. "It's been massacred. The paths have gone all skewwhiff!"

I took advantage of the fact that Mme Verdurin was serving the coffee to go and take a look at the letter that M. de Cambremer had handed me, in which his mother had invited me to dinner. In these few lines of ink, the handwriting betrayed an individuality recognizable for me from now on among all others, without there being any need to resort to the hypothesis of special pens, any more than rare pigments of mysterious manufacture are necessary to the painter to express his original vision. Even a paralytic, suffering from agraphia after a stroke, and reduced to seeing the characters as a pattern without being able to read them, would have realized that Mme de Cambremer belonged to an old family in which the enthusiastic cultivation of literature and the arts had let some air into its aristocratic traditions. He would also have guessed around what age the Marquise had learned simultaneously to write and to play Chopin. It was the epoch when people of breeding observed the rule of being agreeable and the so-called rule of the three adjectives. Mme de Cambremer combined the two. One laudatory adjective was not enough for her; she would follow it (after a dash) by a second, then (after a second dash) by a third. But what was peculiar to her is that, contrary to the social and literary objective she had set herself, in Mme de Cambremer's letters the sequence of the three epithets wore the aspect, not of a progression, but of a diminuendo. Mme de Cambremer told me in this first letter that she had met Saint-Loup and had appreciated more than ever his "unique–rare–real" qualities, and that he was due to return with one of his friends (the one, indeed, who was in love with the daughter-in-law), and that, if I cared to come, with or without them, to dinner at Féterne, she would be "overjoyed–happy–pleased." Perhaps it was because the desire to be agreeable was not matched in her by any fertility of imagination or richness of vocabulary that, eager to utter three exclamations, this lady had the resources to provide in the second and third only an enfeebled echo of the first. There need only have been a fourth adjective for nothing to have remained of her initial affability. Finally, out of a certain refined simplicity that can but have created a considerable impression among her family and even the circle of their connections, Mme de Cambremer had acquired the habit of substituting for the word *sincère*, which might end by appearing untruthful, the word *vrai*, or true. And to make quite clear that something sincere was indeed involved, she broke the conventional alliance that would have put *vrai* in front of the substantive and set it bravely down behind. Her letters would end with: *"Croyez à mon amitié vraie." "Croyez à ma sympathie vraie."*[105] Unfortunately, so much had this become a formula that the affectation of candor gave a stronger impression of a mendacious politeness than those ancient formulas to whose meaning we no longer give a thought. My reading was not helped, in any case, by the confused sound of conversations, dominated by the raised voice of M. de Charlus, not having let the topic drop and saying to M. de Cambremer: "By wanting me to take your place, you reminded me of a gentleman who sent me a letter this morning addressed 'To His Highness the Baron de Charlus' and which began 'Monseigneur.' " "Indeed, your correspondent was exaggerating somewhat," replied M. de Cambremer, giving way to a discreet merriment. M. de Charlus had provoked it; he did not share in it. "But in actual fact, my dear fellow," he said, "you'll observe that, heraldically speaking, it's he who is in the right; I'm not turning it into a personal matter, as you can imagine. I speak of it as though it concerned someone else.

But what will you, history is history, there's nothing we can do about it, and it's not up to us to rewrite it. I won't cite the case of the Emperor William, who in Kiel has never stopped Monseigneuring me. I've heard it said that he called all French dukes that, which is improper, but is perhaps simply a thoughtful gesture aimed above our heads, at France." "Thoughtful and more or less sincere," said M. de Cambremer. "Oh, I'm not of your opinion. Personally speaking, you'll observe that a nobleman of the lowest rank such as this Hohenzollern, a Protestant what's more, and who dispossessed my cousin the King of Hanover,[106] is unlikely to appeal to me," added M. de Charlus, who seemed to take Hanover more closely to heart than Alsace-Lorraine. "But I believe that the inclination the Emperor bears toward us is deeply sincere. The imbeciles will tell you that he's a stage emperor. On the contrary, he's wonderfully intelligent. He knows nothing about painting, and he forced M. Tschudi[107] to withdraw the Elstirs from the national collections. But, then, Louis XIV didn't like the Dutch masters, also had a liking for ostentation, yet, when all's said and done, was a great sovereign. And then William II has armed his country from the military and naval points of view, as Louis XIV did not, and I trust that his reign will never experience the reverses that darkened the end of the reign of the man tritely referred to as the Sun King. The Republic committed a grave error, in my view, in spurning the Hohenzollern's civilities, or in returning them in driblets. He himself is very conscious of this and says, with that gift for expression that he has, 'What I am looking for is a handshake, not a sweep of the hat.' As a man, he is despicable; he has abandoned, betrayed, reneged on his best friends in circumstances in which his silence was as wretched as theirs was magnificent," continued M. de Charlus, who, borne off down the slope, was slithering toward the Eulenburg Affair,[108] and recalled the remark made to him by one of the highest placed of those inculpated: " 'What confidence the Emperor must have in our discretion to have dared to permit such a trial! But, then, he was not wrong to have put his trust in our discretion. We'd have kept our mouths shut even on the scaffold.' Anyway, all this has nothing to do with what I meant to say, namely that, in Germany, as mediatized princes we are *Durchlaucht*,[109] and that in France our rank of Highness was publicly recognized. Saint-Simon claims we acquired it improperly, in which he is completely mistaken. The reason he gives, namely that Louis XIV had us forbidden to call him the Most Christian King, and ordered us to call him the King and nothing more, merely proves that we were answerable to him, and not at all that we did not have the rank of prince. Otherwise, he would have had to deny it to the Duc de Lorraine and a great many others! As it happens, several of our titles come from the House of Lorraine, through Thérèse d'Espinoy, my great-grandmother, who was the daughter of the Damoiseau de Commercy." Having noticed that Morel was listening to him, M. de Charlus went into the reasons for his pretension more fully. "I have pointed out to my brother that the entry on our family ought to be found not in the third section of the *Gotha* but in the second, not to say in the first," he said, not realizing that Morel did not know what the *Gotha* was. "But that's his affair, he's my *chef d'armes*, and as long as he finds it right the way it is and lets the matter rest, I have only to close my eyes." "M. Brichot interested me greatly," I said to Mme Verdurin, who had come up to me as I was putting Mme de Cambremer's letter into my pocket. "A good man, and with a cultivated mind," she answered coldly. "He obviously lacks originality and taste, and has a terrible memory. It used to be said of the 'forefathers' of the people we have here this evening, the *émigrés*,[110] that they had forgotten nothing. But at least they had the excuse," she said, taking over a *bon mot* of Swann's, "of never having learned anything. Whereas Brichot knows everything and hurls piles of dictionaries at our heads during dinner. I imagine you now know everything there is to be known about what the name of this or that town or village means." As Mme Verdurin was speaking, I was thinking that I had promised myself to ask her something, but I could not remember what it was. "I'm sure you're talking about Brichot," said Ski. "Chantepie, Freycinet, really, he spared you nothing. I had my eye on you, *ma petite* Patronne." "I saw you indeed, I nearly exploded." I would not be able to say today how Mme Verdurin was dressed on that particular evening. I had no better idea at the time perhaps, for I am not observant by nature. But, sensing that her toilette was not without its pretensions, I said something friendly or even admiring to her. She was like almost all women, who imagine that the compliment they receive is a strict expression of the truth, that it is a judgment passed impartially, irresistibly, as though it applied to an art object unconnected with a particular individual. And so it was with a seriousness that made me blush at my own hypocrisy that she put the vain and artless question customary in such circumstances, "You like it?" "You're talking about Chantepie, I'm sure," said M. Verdurin, coming up to us. I had been alone, with my mind on my green luster and a smell of wood, in not noticing that, as he enumerated his etymologies, Brichot was being laughed at. And since the impressions that for me gave things their value were of the kind that other people either do not experience or else suppress unthinkingly as insignificant, so that in consequence, had I been able to communicate them, they would have remained misunderstood or would have been scorned, they were quite unserviceable and had the additional drawback of making me appear stupid in the eyes of Mme Verdurin, who could see that I had "swallowed" Brichot, as I had already seemed stupid to Mme de Guermantes because I had enjoyed myself at Mme d'Arpajon's. However, where Brichot was concerned, there was another reason. I was not one of the little clan. And in every clan, be it social, political, or literary, they develop a perverse capacity for discovering in a conversation, an official speech, an item of news, a sonnet, everything that the straightforward reader would never have dreamed of finding there. How many times has it not happened that, reading with a certain emotion a tale artfully spun by a wordy and somewhat antiquated Academician, I have been on the point of saying to Bloch, or to Mme de Guermantes, "It's very amusing!," when, before I had opened my mouth, they would exclaim, each in a different language: "If you want to have a moment's enjoyment, read a short story by So-and-So. Human stupidity has never gone so far." Bloch's contempt derived above all from the fact that certain, as it happens, agreeable effects of style were somewhat jejune; that of Mme de Guermantes from the fact that the story seemed to prove the exact reverse of what the author had intended, for factual reasons that she was ingenious enough to deduce, but of which I would never have thought. I was as surprised to find the irony that lay concealed behind the apparent amiability of the Verdurins toward Brichot as to hear, a few days later at

Féterne, the Cambremers say to me, faced by the enthusiastic praises I was bestowing on La Raspelière, "You can't possibly mean it, after what they've done there." It is true they admitted that the dinner service was good. I had not noticed it, any more than the scandalous draft curtains. "So now, when you go back to Balbec, you'll know what Balbec signifies," said M. Verdurin, ironically. It was indeed the things that Brichot had taught me that interested me. As for what they called his wit, it was exactly the same as that which had once been so much enjoyed among the little clan. He spoke with the same irritating facility, but his words no longer carried, had to overcome a hostile silence or disagreeable echoes; what had changed was not what he trotted out but the acoustics of the drawing room and the attitude of mind of the audience. "Careful!" said Mme Verdurin in an undertone, pointing to Brichot. The latter, having kept his hearing, more acute than his eyesight, cast at the Patronne a myopic philosopher's glance, soon averted. If his eyes were not so good, those of his mind took a correspondingly broader view of things. He had seen how little was to be expected from human affection, and had resigned himself to the fact. Admittedly, it pained him. It happens that even the man who, on the same evening, in a circle where he is accustomed to please, guesses that he has been found too frivolous, or too pedantic, or too clumsy, or too cavalier, and so on, returns home unhappy. Often it is over a matter of opinion, or a system, that he has appeared absurd to others or passé. Often he knows perfectly well that these others are his inferiors. He would have no difficulty dissecting the sophisms with the aid of which they have tacitly condemned him, he wants to go and visit someone, or to write a letter; wiser to do nothing, but wait for the following week's invitation. Sometimes, too, instead of ending in a single evening, these falls from favor last for months. They further increase the instability of social judgments to which they are attributable. For the man who knows that Mme X despises him, feeling himself to be appreciated at Mme Y's, declares her to be much superior and immigrates to her salon. This, however, is not the place to depict the men who are above the life of society but have not been able to realize themselves outside of it, glad to be received, embittered by being misunderstood, and discovering year by year the flaws in the hostess they had been idolizing, and the genius of the one whose true worth they had not appreciated, only to return to their first love once they have endured the disadvantages that the second love had also, and once those of the first have been somewhat forgotten. From these brief falls from favor you can judge of the unhappiness produced in Brichot by one that he knew was final. He was not unaware that Mme Verdurin sometimes made fun of him in public, of his infirmities even, and although knowing how little was to be expected of human affection, having accepted that, he still looked on the Patronne as his best friend. But from the flush that covered the university man's face, Mme Verdurin realized that he had heard her and promised herself she would be kind to him in the course of the evening. I could not help saying to her that she had not been at all so to Saniette. "What, not nice! But he adores us, you don't know how much we mean to him! My husband is a little irritated at times by his stupidity, and you have to admit, with good reason, but why at such times doesn't he bridle up more, instead of wearing that hangdog expression? It's not being open. I don't like that. That's not to say I don't always try to calm my husband down, because, if he went too far, Saniette would only not have to come back; and I wouldn't want that, because I can tell you he's penniless, he needs his dinners. But, then, after all, if he takes offense, if he doesn't come back, that's no concern of mine, when you have need of other people you try not to be so idiotic." "The dukedom of Aumale was in our family for a long time before entering the House of France," M. de Charlus was explaining to M. de Cambremer, in front of an openmouthed Morel, for whom this whole discourse was, if not addressed to him, intended. "We took precedence over all the foreign princes; I could cite you a hundred examples. When, at the burial of Monsieur,[111] the Princesse de Croy attempted to kneel after my great-great-grandmother, the latter pointed out to her in no uncertain terms that she had no right to the cushion, had it removed by the officer on duty, and took the matter to the King, who ordered Mme de Croy to go to Mme de Guermantes's and make her apologies. The Duc de Bourgogne having come to us with the ushers, with their rods of office raised, we obtained the King's consent to have them lowered. I know it's bad form to speak of

the virtues of one's own kinsfolk. But it's well known that ours were always to the fore in times of danger. Our battle cry, once we had given
up that of the Ducs de Brabant, was '*Passavant.*'[112] So that, all in all, it
was quite legitimate that the right everywhere to be first, to which we
had laid claim during all those centuries in war, we should then have
obtained at court. And it's always been recognized there, I can assure
you. For further proof, I shall cite the Princesse de Baden. She having so
far forgotten herself as to try to dispute her rank with that same
Duchesse de Guermantes of whom I spoke just now, and having sought
to go in ahead of her to the King by taking advantage of a momentary
hesitation on my kinswoman's part (although there was no need for
one), the King quickly called out, 'Enter, cousin, enter, Mme de Baden
knows all too well what is due to you.' And it was as Duchesse de Guermantes that she held that rank, even though she was well enough born
in her own right, since through her mother she was niece to the Queen
of Poland, the Queen of Hungary, the Elector Palatine, the Prince de
Savoie-Carignan, and the Prince of Hanover, later King of England."[113]
"*Maecenas atavis edite regibus!*"[114] said Brichot, addressing M. de Charlus, who responded to this compliment with a slight nod of the head.
"What were you saying?" Mme Verdurin asked Brichot, with whom she
would have liked to try to make amends for her words of a little earlier.
"I was referring, may God forgive me, to a dandy who was the orna-
ment of the upper crust"—Mme Verdurin gave a frown—"in, roughly
speaking, the century of Augustus"—Mme Verdurin, reassured by the remoteness of this "upper crust," adopted a more serene expression—"to a
friend of Virgil and Horace, who carried their toadying to the point of
acclaiming his more-than-aristocratic, his *royal* ascendancy to his face,
in short, I was referring to Maecenas, to a bookworm who was the
friend of Horace, of Virgil, and of Augustus. I'm sure M. de Charlus
knows very well, in every respect, who Maecenas was." Looking gra-
ciously at Mme Verdurin out of the corner of his eye, because he had
heard her arranging a rendezvous with Morel in two days' time, and was
afraid of not being invited, "I fancy," said M. de Charlus, "that Maecenas was something like the Verdurin of the ancient world." Mme Verdurin could only half suppress a smile of satisfaction. She went up to

Morel. "He's agreeable, your parents' friend," she said. "You can tell he's an educated man, well bred. He'll do well in our little nucleus. Where does he live in Paris?" Morel maintained a haughty silence and simply asked to play a game of cards. Mme Verdurin first demanded something on the violin. To general astonishment, M. de Charlus, who never spoke of the great gifts he possessed, accompanied, in the purest style, the last part (uneasy, tormented, Schumannesque, though in fact earlier than the Franck sonata) of Fauré's sonata for piano and violin."[115] I felt that he would give Morel, wonderfully gifted where tone and virtuosity were concerned, precisely what he lacked, culture and style. But I reflected with curiosity on what unites a physical taint and a spiritual gift within the same man. M. de Charlus was not very different from his brother, the Duc de Guermantes. He had even, a moment or two earlier (which was rare with him), spoken in equally bad French. Berating me (no doubt so that I might speak warmly about Morel to Mme Verdurin) for never going to see him, and I having pleaded discretion, he had replied, "But since it's I who am asking you, it's only I who *might've taken umbrage.*" It could have been the Duc de Guermantes speaking. M. de Charlus was in sum only a Guermantes. But it was enough that nature should have thrown his nervous system out of balance sufficiently for him to prefer, instead of a woman, as his brother the Duc would have done, one of Virgil's shepherds or Plato's pupils, and qualities foreign to the Duc de Guermantes but often linked with this imbalance had turned M. de Charlus into a delightful pianist, an amateur painter who did not lack taste, and an eloquent talker. Who could have divined that the quick, anxious, charming style in which M. de Charlus had played the Schumannesque passage from Fauré's sonata had its correlation in–I do not dare say, was caused by–the purely physical elements of M. de Charlus, in the defectiveness of his nerves? We shall explain the term "defectiveness of his nerves" later on, and the reasons why a Greek from the time of Socrates, and a Roman from the time of Augustus, could be what we know they were while remaining absolutely normal men, and not men-women such as we see today. In addition to a real aptitude for the arts, never brought to fruition, M. de Charlus had, far more than the Duc, loved their mother, and loved his wife, and even years later, when people spoke of them, tears would come, but superficial tears, like the perspiration of an overweight man, whose brow is beaded with sweat at the least exertion. With the difference that to the latter people say, "You're overheated!," whereas they pretend not to notice other people's tears. They, that is to say, society; for the common people are concerned by seeing someone cry, as if a sob were more serious than a hemorrhage. His sadness following the death of his wife did not, thanks to his habit of lying, debar M. de Charlus from a way of life that was out of keeping. Later on, he stooped so low as to let it be understood that, during the funeral ceremony, he had found a means of asking the altar boy for his name and address. And this may have been true.

The piece having finished, I took the liberty of demanding some Franck, which seemed to cause Mme de Cambremer so much pain that I did not insist. "You can't like that," she said. She asked instead for Debussy's *Fêtes*,[116] which brought cries of "Oh, it's sublime!" from the very first note. But Morel realized that he knew only the opening bars, and out of a sense of mischief, without any intention of mystifying, he began a march by Meyerbeer. Unfortunately, as he left few transitions and made no announcement, everyone thought it was still Debussy, and they went on calling out, "Sublime!" By revealing that the composer was that not of *Pelléas* but of *Robert le Diable*,[117] Morel cast a certain chill. Mme de Cambremer scarcely had time to experience it personally, as she had just come upon a book of Scarlatti[118] and had flung herself on it with the impulsiveness of a hysteric. "Oh, play this, look, this, it's divine," she cried. And yet what, in her fever of impatience, she had selected from that long-despised composer, recently promoted to the highest honors, was one of those accursed pieces that have so often stopped you from sleeping, and which a merciless learner begins over and over again on the floor adjoining yours. But Morel was done with music, and since he insisted on playing cards, M. de Charlus, in order to take part, wanted whist. "He told the Patron just now he was a prince," Ski said to Mme Verdurin, "but that's not true, his family's bourgeois merely, of minor architects." "I want to know what you were saying about Maecenas. It amuses me, so there!" Mme Verdurin repeated to Brichot, out of an amiability that went to the latter's head. To shine in the eyes of the Patronne, therefore, and perhaps in my own, "Well, truth to tell, madame, Maecenas interests me mainly because he was the first apostle of note of that Chinese god who numbers more sectaries today in France than Brahma, than Christ himself, the almighty god Je-Men-Fou."[119] Mme Verdurin was no longer content in such cases to sink her face into her hands. She descended with the abruptness of the insects known as mayflies on the Princesse Sher-batoff; if the latter was within range, the Patronne would clutch at the Princesse's armpit, digging in her nails, and hide her head there for a moment or two like a child playing hide-and-seek. Masked by this protective screen, she was presumed to be laughing until the tears came, but was as likely to be thinking of nothing at all as those people who, while reciting a somewhat lengthy prayer, take the sensible precaution of burying their faces in their hands. Mme Verdurin imitated them when listening to Beethoven quartets, at once to show that she regarded these as a prayer and not to let it be seen that she was asleep. "I speak in all seriousness, madame," said Brichot. "Too many in number I think are the people today who spend their time contemplating their navel as if it were the center of the universe. As sound doctrine, I raise no objection to some nirvana or other that tends to dissolve us into the Great All—which, like Munich and Oxford, is much closer to Paris than Asnières or Bois-Colombes[120]—but it is not the mark of a good Frenchman, or even of a good European, when the Japanese are perhaps at the gates of our Byzantium, that collectivized antimilitarists should be solemnly debating the cardinal virtues of free verse." Mme Verdurin thought she could now let go of the Princesse's bruised shoulder, and she allowed her face to reappear, not without pretending to wipe her eyes and to catch her breath two or three times. But Brichot wanted that I should share in the feast, and, having remembered, from the *soutenances de thèses*[121] over which he presided so incomparably, that there is no better way of flattering the young than by taking them to task, by granting them some importance and getting them to treat you as a reactionary, "I wouldn't want to blaspheme against the Gods of Youth," he said, casting at me one of those furtive glances that an orator accords on the sly to someone present in the audience whom he has mentioned by name. "I wouldn't want to be damned as a heretic or a backslider in the Mallarméan chapel, in which our new friend, like all those of his age, will have served at the esoteric mass, as an altar boy at least, and proved himself a deliquescent or a Rosicrucian.[122] But, really, we've seen too many of these intellectuals worshipping Art with a capital 'A,' and who, when taking to the bottle with Zola is no longer enough, inject Verlaine into their veins. Having become etheromanes in their devotion to Baudelaire, they'd no longer be capable of the manly effort their homeland may some day demand from them, anesthetized as they are by the great literary neurosis in the hot, enervating atmosphere, heavy with the unwholesome effluvia from an opium-den symbolism." Unable to feign even the faintest admiration for Brichot's motley and inept declamation, I turned away toward Ski and assured him that he was entirely mistaken as to the family to which M. de Charlus belonged; he replied that he was sure of his facts and added that I had even told him that his real name was Gandin, Le Gandin. "I told you," I replied, "that Mme de Cambremer was the sister of an engineer, M. Legrandin. I've never mentioned M. de Charlus. He and Mme de Cambremer are about as closely connected by birth as the Great Condé[123] and Racine." "Oh, I thought they were," said Ski offhandedly, no more apologizing for his mistake than a few hours earlier for that which had almost caused us to miss the train. "Are you planning to stay long on the coast?" Mme Verdurin asked M. de Charlus, whom she could foresee being one of the faithful and was fearful of seeing him return too soon to Paris. "Good Lord, one never knows," replied M. de Charlus in a nasal drawl. "I would like to stay until the end of September." "You're right," said Mme Verdurin, "that's when we get the good storms." "To be perfectly truthful, that's not what would decide me. For some time I've been too neglectful of the Archangel Saint Michael, my patron, and I would like to make amends by remaining until his feast day, September 29, at the Abbaye du Mont."[124] "Does that sort of thing much interest you?" asked Mme Verdurin, who might perhaps have managed to suppress the injury to her anticlericalism had she not been afraid that so lengthy an excursion might lead to the violinist and the Baron's "defaulting" for forty-eight hours. "You are perhaps afflicted by an intermittent deafness," replied M. de Charlus insolently. "I have told you that Saint Michael was one of my glorious patrons." Then, smiling in a benevolent ecstasy, his eyes fixed on the distance, and his voice swelling with an exaltation that seemed to me more than aesthetic, but religious, "It's so fine at the Offertory, when Michael stands beside the altar, in a white robe, swinging a gold censer, and with such a mass of perfumes that the fragrance of them rises all the way up to God!" "We might go as a group," suggested Mme Verdurin, for all her horror of the cassock. "At that moment, from the Offertory," M. de Charlus went on, who, for different reasons but in the same manner as the good orators in the Chamber, never responded to an interruption but pretended not to have heard it, "it would be gorgeous to see our young friend Palestrina-ing or even performing an aria by Bach. He would be wild with joy, the good abbé also, and it's the greatest homage, the greatest public homage at any rate, that I can render to my patron. So very edifying for the faithful! We will discuss it in a little while with the young musical Angelico, a soldier, like Saint Michael."

Called on to be dummy, Saniette declared that he did not know how to play whist. And Cottard, noticing that there was not now long to go before the time of the train, at once started on a game of *écarté* with Morel. M. Verdurin, furious, marched on Saniette wearing a terrible expression: "You don't know how to play anything, then!" he shouted, furious at having lost an opportunity for a game of whist, but overjoyed at finding one for insulting the former archivist. The latter, terror-stricken, adopted a humorous expression: "Yes I do, I know how to play the piano," he said. Cottard and Morel had sat down facing each other. "Your honor," said Cottard. "Suppose we move a bit closer to the table," M. de Charlus said to M. de Cambremer, worried at seeing the violinist with Cottard. "It's as interesting as those questions of etiquette that, in our own day, no longer much signify. The only kings left to us, in France, at any rate, are the ones in a pack of playing cards, and I fancy there are kings galore in our young virtuoso's hand," he soon added, out of an admiration for Morel that even extended to the way he played cards, to flatter him also, and, indeed, to justify the movement he was making, of leaning over the violinist's shoulder. "Me terrump you," said Cottard, putting on his vulgar, rich foreigner's voice, he whose children used to burst out laughing, as did his students and the *chef de clinique,* when, even at the bedside of a seriously ill patient, the Master, wearing the expressionless mask of an epileptic, came out with one of his customary jests. "I don't quite know what I ought to play," said Morel, consulting M. de Cambremer. "As you like, you'll be beaten either way, this one or that one, it matters not, *c'est égal.*" "Égal . . . Galli-Marié?"[125] said the doctor, sliding a kindly and insinuating glance in the direction of M. de Cambremer. "She was what we call a true diva, a dream, a Carmen such as we won't see again. The role was made for her. I liked hearing Ingalli-Marié[126] in it, too." The Marquis stood up with the contemptuous vulgarity of the well-born, who do not realize that they are insulting their host by appearing unsure whether their guests are to be associated with, and who take the English custom as their excuse for employing a disdainful expression: "Who is that gentleman playing cards? What's his occupation in life? What does he *sell*? I rather like to know who I find myself with, so as not to become intimate with just anyone at all. But I didn't catch his name when you did me the honor of introducing me to him." If M. Verdurin had, on the strength of these last words, indeed introduced him to his guests, M. de Cambremer would have thought it very wrong. But, knowing that it was the opposite that had taken place, he thought it gracious and to be running no risks to assume a modest, good-natured expression. The pride that M. Verdurin took in his intimacy with Cottard had only grown since the doctor had become an illustrious professor. But it no longer expressed itself in the naïve form of old. Then, when Cottard was scarcely known, should anyone speak to M. Verdurin of his wife's facial neuralgia, "There's nothing you can do," he would say, with the naïve smugness of people who suppose that those whom they know are famous and that everyone has heard the name of their daughter's singing teacher. "If her doctor were in the second rank, we might be looking for a different treatment, but when your doctor's name is Cottard"—a name he pronounced as though it had been Bouchard or Charcot[127]—"there's no point in looking elsewhere." Employing a contrary procedure, and knowing that M. de Cambremer had certainly heard speak of the famous Professor Cottard, M. Verdurin assumed a simple-minded expression. "He's our family doctor, a dear good soul whom we adore and who'd go through fire and water for us; he's not a doctor, he's a friend; I don't suppose you know him, or that his name means anything to you; at all events, for us it's the name of a thoroughly good man, of a very dear friend, Cottard." This name, murmured wearing a modest expression, deceived M. de Cambremer, who had thought someone else had been meant. "Cottard? You're not speaking of Professor Cottard?" At which exact moment the voice of the said professor was to be heard who, the play having gone against him, said as he held up his cards: "And then it was prepare to meet thy doom." "Oh yes, the very same, he's a professor," said M. Verdurin. "What, Professor Cottard! You're not mistaken! You're quite sure it's the same one, the one who lives on the rue du Bac!" "Yes, he lives on the rue du Bac, number 43. You know him?" "But everyone knows Professor Cottard. He's a top man! It's like asking me whether I know Bouffe de Saint-Blaise or Courtois-Suffit.[128] I could tell by listening to him right enough that he was no ordinary man, that's why I took the liberty of asking you." "Let's see, now, what do I need to put down, a trump?" asked Cottard. Then, abruptly, with a vulgarity that would have been irritating even in heroic circumstances, where a soldier tries to give a familiar expression to his contempt for death, but which became doubly foolish in the safe pastime of cards, Cottard, making up his mind to play a trump, assumed a grim, "fire-eater" air and, in an allusion to those who risk their skins, staked his card as though it were his life, exclaiming, "After all, I don't give a damn!" It was not what he should have played, but he found a consolation. In the middle of the drawing room, in a wide armchair, Mme Cottard, yielding to the after-effects, irresistible in her case, of dinner, had, after a losing struggle, succumbed to the vast if light sleep that had taken possession of her. Even though she straightened up now and again, to smile, either in self-mockery or else out of a fear of leaving some friendly word that might have been addressed to her unanswered, she would then fall helplessly back, in the grip of an implacable but delightful sickness. Rather than the noise, what had thus aroused her, for a second only, was the glance (which, in her fondness, she could see even with her eyes closed, could foresee, for the same scene took place every evening and haunted her sleep, like the hour when we shall have to get up), the glance by which the professor indicated his spouse's slumbers to those present. He was content at the start to look at her and smile, for, if as a doctor he was critical of this after-dinner sleep (he at any rate gave this scientific reason so as to become angry toward the end, but it is not certain that it was determinant, so various were the views he held on the matter), as an all-powerful husband and a tease he was delighted to make fun of his wife, to only half wake her at first, so that she might go back to sleep and he have the pleasure of waking her again.

Mme Cottard was now fast asleep. "Here, Léontine, you're napping!" the professor called out to her. "I'm listening to what Mme Swann is saying, *mon ami*," Mme Cottard replied, weakly, and sank back into her lethargy. "It's nonsensical," exclaimed Cottard, "in a minute she'll be declaring she hasn't been asleep. It's like the patients who come to an appointment and claim that they never sleep." "They imagine it, perhaps," laughed M. de Cambremer. But the doctor was as fond of contradicting as he was of teasing, and above all could not allow a layman to dare talk medicine to him. "We can't imagine that we don't sleep," he proclaimed in a dogmatic tone. "Ah," replied the Marquis, bowing respectfully, as Cottard would once have done. "One can easily tell," Cottard went on, "that you've haven't, as I have, administered up to two grams of trional without managing to induce somnolescence." "Indeed, indeed," laughed the Marquis with a superior air, "I've never taken trional, or any of the drugs that soon cease to have any effect but which do things to your stomach. When you've been shooting all night, as I have in the forest of Chantepie, I can assure you you don't need trional in order to get to sleep." "It's the ignoramuses who say that," replied the professor. "Trional can sometimes raise nerve tone in a remarkable way. You talk about trional, do you even know what it is?" "But ... I've heard that it's a medicine for sleeping." "You're not answering my question," replied the professor pompously, who three times a week, in the Faculty, acted as an "examiner." "I'm not asking you whether it makes one sleep or not, but what it is. Can you tell me what proportion it contains of amyl and ethyl?" "No," replied M. de Cambremer, in embarrassment. "I prefer a good glass of brandy, or even

345 port."[129] "Which are ten times more toxic," broke in the professor. "As for trional," ventured M. de Cambremer, "my wife subscribes to all that sort of thing, you'd do better to talk with her about it." "She must know just about as much as you do. Anyway, if your wife takes trional to make her sleep, you can see that my wife has no need of it. Come, Léontine, move yourself, you'll get stiff; do I go to sleep after dinner? What'll you be like when you're sixty if you drop off like an old woman now? You'll start to get stout, you're stopping the circulation. . . . She can't even hear me any more." "These little naps after dinner are bad for the health, are they not, Doctor?" said M. de Cambremer, in order to rehabilitate himself with Cottard. "After a good meal one should take some exercise." "An old wives' tale!" replied the doctor. "They've taken equal quantities of food from the stomach of a dog that hadn't moved, and from the stomach of a dog that had been running, and digestion was more advanced in the first." "So it's sleep that shortens digestion?" "That depends on whether we're talking about esophageal, stomachic, or intestinal digestion; no point in giving you explanations you wouldn't understand, since you've never studied medicine. Come on, Léontine, by the front . . . quick march! It's time we went." This was not true, for the doctor was merely about to go on with his game of cards, but he was hoping by this more abrupt means to interfere with the sleep of the speechless woman to whom he had been addressing the most scientific exhortations without receiving any further response. Either because the will to keep sleep at bay persisted in Mme Cottard, even in the somnolent state, or because the armchair lent it no support, her head was being jerked mechanically about in space, from left to right and up and down, like some lifeless object, and Mme Cottard, well balanced where her head was concerned, appeared now to be listening to music and now to have entered on the final phase of her death agony. But where the increasingly vehement remonstrations of her husband had failed, a sense of her own foolishness succeeded: "My bath is just the right temperature," she murmured, "but the feathers of the dictionary . . ." she exclaimed, coming upright. "Oh, good heavens, I'm so silly! What am I saying? I was thinking about my hat, I must have said something foolish, I was just about to doze off, it's that wretched fire." Everyone started to laugh, for there was no fire.

"You're making fun of me," said Mme Cottard, laughing herself, as she wiped the last traces of sleep from her brow with her hand, with the light touch of a mesmerist and the neatness of a woman rearranging her hair. "I would like to present my humble apologies to dear Mme Verdurin and to learn the truth from her." But her smile quickly turned unhappy, because the professor, who knew that his wife was seeking to please him and was fearful of not having succeeded, had just called out to her, "Look at yourself in the mirror, you're as red as if you'd come out in acne, you look like an old peasant woman." "He's charming, you know," said Mme Verdurin, "he's got a lovely bantering, good-natured side to him. Besides, he brought my husband back from the edge of the grave when the whole Faculty had given him up. He spent three nights beside him, without going to bed. So for me, you know," she added, in a solemn, almost menacing tone, raising her hand to the twin spheres of her musical temples with their white tresses, and as if we had wanted to lay hands on the doctor, "Cottard is sacred! He could ask for whatever he wanted. Moreover, I don't call him Dr. Cottard, I call him Dr. God! And even when I say that, I'm slandering him, for this God does everything in his power to put right some of the evils the other one is responsible for." "Play a trump," M. de Charlus told Morel, with a happy expression. "A trump, so as to see," said the violinist. "You should have declared your king first," said M. de Charlus. "You're distracted, but how well you play!" "I've got the king," said Morel. "He's a fine-looking man," replied the professor. "What's that affair up there with the pickets?" asked Mme Verdurin, indicating to M. de Cambremer a superb carved escutcheon above the fireplace. "Are they your *arms?*" she added, with ironic disdain. "No, they're not ours," replied M. de Cambremer. "We bear Or with three bars embattled, counter-embattled Gules of five pieces each charged with a trefoil of the field. No, those are the arms of the Arrachepels, who weren't of our stock, but from whom we inherited the house, and those of our line have never wanted to change it. The Arrachepels—Pelvilains in the old days, so it's said— bore Or with five piles couped Gules. When they intermarried with the Féternes, their coat of arms changed but remained cantoned with twenty crosses crosslet with pile pery fitchy Or with dexter a vol ermine." "So much for you," said Mme de Cambremer under her breath. "My great-grandmother was a d'Arrachepel or de Rachepel, as you wish, because both names are found in the old charters," M. de Cambremer went on, suddenly blushing, for only now did the thought occur to him that his wife had put him in dread of, and he was afraid that Mme Verdurin might have applied to herself words that were in no way aimed at her. "History has it that in the eleventh century the first Arrachepel, Macé, known as Pelvilain, showed himself particularly skilled during a siege at uprooting stakes. Whence the nickname of Arrachepel,[130] under which he was ennobled, and the stakes you see persisting through the centuries in their arms. The stakes in question are those that, to make the fortifications harder to approach, they planted, they bedded, if you'll allow the expression, in the ground in front of them, and then joined them together. It's they that you quite rightly called pickets and which had no connection with the floating sticks of our good La Fontaine.[131] For they were held to make a place impregnable. That brings a smile, obviously, what with modern artillery. But you must remember we're talking about the eleventh century." "It lacks topicality," said Mme Verdurin, "but the little campanile has character." "You have," said Cottard, "the luck of a . . . cuckoo clock," a word he happily repeated in order to avoid Molière's word.[132] "Do you know why the king of diamonds failed his army physical?" "I wish I'd been in his shoes," said Morel, who was bored with his military service. "Oh, he's no patriot," exclaimed M. de Charlus, who could not restrain himself from pinching the violinist's ear. "No, you don't know why the king of diamonds failed his physical?" Cottard went on, who insisted on his jokes, "it's because he's only got one eye." "You've got a hard game on your hands, Doctor," said M. de Cambremer, to show Cottard that he knew who he was. "This young man is astonishing," M. de Charlus broke in artlessly, pointing to Morel. "He plays like a god." This observation did not much appeal to the doctor, who replied: "Time will show. He may be too cunning for his own good." "Queen, ace," announced Morel triumphantly, the luck having been with him. The doctor bowed his head as if unable to deny this good fortune and admitted, fascinated, "That's good." "We're so glad to have dined with M. de

Charlus," said Mme de Cambremer to Mme Verdurin. "You didn't know him? He's quite agreeable, he's unusual, he's from *another era*"—she would have found it hard to say which—replied Mme Verdurin, with the self-satisfied smile of a dilettante, a judge, and a hostess. Mme de Cambremer asked me whether I would be coming to Féterne with Saint-Loup. I could not contain a cry of admiration on seeing the moon suspended like an orange-colored lantern from the vault of oak trees that led away from the château. "It's nothing as yet; in a minute, when the moon is higher and the valley is lit up, it'll be a thousand times more beautiful. That's something you don't have at Féterne!" she said scornfully to Mme de Cambremer, who did not know how to reply, not wishing to run her own property down, especially in front of her tenants. "Will you be staying some time yet in these parts, madame?" M. de Cambremer asked Mme Cottard, which might have passed for a vague intention to invite her but which excused him for the present from any more precise arrangement. "Oh, certainly, monsieur, I insist on this annual exodus for the children's sake. No matter what people say, they need the fresh air. I'm perhaps very primitive in these matters, but I find that there's no treatment for children like good air, even if the contrary were to be proved to me by A plus B. Their dear little faces are quite altered already. The Faculty wanted to send me to Vichy; but it's too airless, and I'll start worrying about my stomach once these great big boys have grown a bit more. Besides, the professor, with the examinations he puts them through, always has his nose to the grindstone, and the heat tires him out. I consider that you need frankly to relax when you've been hard at it like him all year long. We shall be here for a good month yet, whatever happens." "Ah, then we shall be seeing one another again." "I'm all the more obliged to remain, in any case, because my husband has to do a tour of Savoie, and it'll be another fortnight before he's stationed here permanently." "I like the valley side even more than the sea side," Mme Verdurin went on. "You're going to have splendid weather for your return." "We'll even have to see whether the carriages are harnessed up, in the event of your absolutely insisting on going back to Balbec this evening," M. Verdurin said to me, "because I don't see the necessity for it myself. We could have you driven back tomorrow morning by carriage. It'll certainly be fine. The roads are admirable." I said that it was out of the question. "It's not time, in any case," objected the Patronne. "Let them be, they've plenty of time. Much good it'll do them arriving at the station an hour ahead of time. They're better off here. And you, my young Mozart," she said to Morel, not daring to address herself directly to M. de Charlus, "will you not stay? We have some lovely bedrooms overlooking the sea." "But he can't," replied M. de Charlus, on behalf of the attentive card-player, who had not heard. "He has leave only up to midnight. He must go back there to sleep, like a very good, very obedient little boy," he added, in a voice at once self-satisfied, affected, and insistent, as though he were deriving a sadistic and voluptuous pleasure from employing this chaste comparison, as well as letting his voice dwell in passing on what concerned Morel, from touching him with, for want of a hand, words that seemed to be palpating him.

From the sermon that Brichot had directed at me, M. de Cambremer had concluded that I was a Dreyfusard. Since he was as anti-Dreyfusard as it was possible to be, out of courtesy toward an enemy he began to eulogize a Jewish colonel to me who had always treated a cousin of the Chevregnys with great fairness and had got him the promotion he deserved. "And my cousin's ideas were absolutely opposed to his," said M. de Cambremer, sliding over what these ideas were, but which I sensed to be as ancient and ill formed as his own face, ideas that a few families in certain small towns must have held for a long time past. "Well, you know, I find that very fine!" M. de Cambremer concluded. It is true that he was hardly using the word "fine" in the aesthetic sense, where, in the case of his mother or his wife, it might have described different works, but works of art. M. de Cambremer preferred to make use of this qualifier when, for example, congratulating someone delicate on having put on a little weight. "What, you've put back three kilos in two months? You know, that's fine!" Refreshments were being served from a table. Mme Verdurin invited the gentlemen to go themselves to choose the drink that suited them. M. de Charlus went and drank his glass and came quickly back, to sit beside the card table, and did not stir again. Mme Verdurin asked him, "Did you have some of my orangeade?" Then M. de Charlus, with a gracious smile and in a crystalline tone that was rare with him, and with endless pursings of the lips and wigglings of his torso, replied, "No, I preferred its neighbor, the *fraisette*[133] I fancy, it's delicious." It is strange that a certain category of secret actions should have as their external consequence a manner of speaking or of gesticulating that betrays them. If a gentleman believes, or not, in the Immaculate Conception, or in Dreyfus's innocence, or in the plurality of worlds, but wishes to keep it to himself, you will find nothing in his voice, or in his bearing, that enables you to see his thoughts. But on hearing M. de Charlus say, in that high-pitched voice, and with that smile and those movements of the arm, "No, I preferred its neighbor, the *fraisette*," you could have said, "Aha, he likes the strong sex," with the same certainty as that which enables a judge to condemn a criminal who has not confessed, or a doctor a general paralytic who perhaps does not know himself what is wrong with him but who has made certain mistakes in pronunciation from which it can be deduced that he will be dead within three years. Perhaps the people who infer from the way of saying, "No, I preferred its neighbor, the *fraisette*," a so-called antiphysical love, have no need of so much science. But that is because in this case there is a more direct relationship between the tell-tale sign and the secret. Without quite putting it into words, we sense that it is a gentle, smiling lady who is answering and who appears affected because she is passing herself off as a man and because we are not accustomed to seeing men put on so many airs and graces. And it is more gracious perhaps to imagine that for a long time now a certain number of angelic women have been included by mistake in the male sex, where, as exiles, even as they vainly beat their wings at the men whom they fill with a physical repulsion, they know how to arrange a drawing room or create an "interior." M. de Charlus was unconcerned that Mme Verdurin should be standing up, and remained installed in his armchair so as to be closer to Morel. "Do you not think it a crime," said Mme Verdurin to the Baron, "that that person there, who might be enthralling us with his violin, should be at the *écarté* table. When you can play the violin like he does!" "He plays cards well, he does everything well, he's so intelligent," said M. de Charlus, keeping an eye on the cards in order to advise Morel. This was not, as it happens, his only reason for not getting up from his chair for Mme Verdurin. With the peculiar amalgam that he had created out of his social conceptions, as at once a great nobleman and an *amateur* of the arts, instead of being polite in the same way as another man from his world would have been, he had created for himself *tableaux vivants* of a sort based on Saint-Simon; at this moment, he was amusing himself playing the Maréchal d'Huxelles, other aspects also of whom were of interest to him, whose vanity was such, so it was said, that he refused to rise from his seat, seemingly out of laziness, for the most distinguished members of the court. "Tell me, Charlus," said Mme Verdurin, who was beginning to grow familiar, "you wouldn't have in your Faubourg some broken-down old nobleman who might come and be my porter?" "But of course ... of course," replied M. de Charlus, smiling jovially, "but I don't advise it." "Why?" "I'd be afraid for your sake that fashionable visitors might not get any farther than the lodge." This was the first of the skirmishes between them. Mme Verdurin hardly heeded it. There were, alas, to be others, in Paris. M. de Charlus continued not to leave his chair. He could not, however, help smiling imperceptibly when he saw, in the submission so readily obtained from Mme Verdurin, confirmation of his favorite maxims as to the prestige of the aristocracy and the cravenness of the bourgeoisie. The Patronne appeared in no way surprised by the Baron's posture, and if she left him it was only because she had been concerned to see me being badgered by M. de Cambremer. Before that, however, she wanted to elucidate the question of M. de Charlus's relations with the Comtesse Molé. "You told me you knew Mme de Molé. Do you go there?" she asked, giving to the words "go there" the sense of being received by her, of having being authorized to call on her. M. de Charlus replied, with an inflection of disdain and an affectation of precision, and in a singsong tone, "But yes, now and again." This "now and again" sowed doubts in Mme Verdurin, who asked, "Have you met the Duc de Guermantes there?" "Well, I don't recall." "Ah, you don't know the Duc de Guermantes?" "But how could I not know him?" replied M. de Charlus, a smile causing his mouth to undulate. This smile was ironic; but as the Baron was afraid of allowing a gold tooth to show, he suppressed it beneath a reflux of his lips, so that the resulting sinuosity was that of a smile of benevolence. "Why do you say, 'How could I not know him?'" "But he's my brother," said M. de Charlus offhandedly, leaving Mme Verdurin plunged in stupefaction and uncertainty as to whether her guest was making fun of her, or was a natural child, or the son of another marriage. The idea that the Duc de Guermantes's brother might be called the Baron de Charlus never entered her head. She made her way over to me: "I heard M. de Cambremer inviting you to dinner just now. That's all right with me, you understand. But in your own best interest, I very much hope you won't go. For one thing, it's infested with bores. Oh, if you enjoy dining with provincial counts and marquises that no one knows, you'll have your fill of them." "I think I shall be obliged to go there once or twice. I'm not so free, as it happens, for I have a young cousin whom I can't leave on her own." I had found that this purported kinship simplified things where going out with Albertine was concerned. "But where the Cambremers are concerned, since I've already introduced her to them . . ." "You must do as you wish. I can tell you this: it's excessively unhealthy; and what good is it going to do you to pick up an inflammation of the chest, or a nice little family rheumatism?" "But is it not a very pretty spot?" "Mmmyesss . . . if you like. But I confess to you frankly that I like the view over the valley a hundred times better from here. For one thing, even if they'd paid us, I wouldn't have taken the other house, because the sea air is fatal for M. Verdurin. Your cousin only needs to be a bit high-strung. . . . But, then, you're high-strung, I imagine . . . you have breathless attacks. Well, you'll see! Go there once and you won't sleep for a week. No, it's not the place for you." And without thinking how contradictory her next words would be of the earlier ones: "If it'd amuse you to see the house, which isn't bad, 'pretty' would be overstating it, but amusing after all, with the old moat, the old drawbridge, as I shall have to go through with it and dine there one time, well, come here that day, I'll try to bring all my little circle, then it'll be nice. The day after tomorrow we're going to Arembouville by carriage. The road is magnificent, they have delicious cider. Come with us. You, Brichot, you must come, too. And you, too, Ski. It'll make an outing that my husband must have planned in advance in any case. I'm none too sure who he's invited. M. de Charlus, are you one of them?"

The Baron, who heard only these final words and did not know they had been talking about an excursion to Arembouville, gave a start. "Strange question," he murmured in a sardonic tone, by which Mme Verdurin felt piqued. "Anyway," she said to me, "while we wait for the Cambremer dinner party, why shouldn't you bring your cousin here? Does she like conversation, intelligent people? Is she agreeable? Yes, well then, very good! Come with her. The Cambremers aren't the only people in the world. I can understand their being glad to invite her, they can't manage to get anyone. Here she'll have good air, and always men who are intelligent. At all events, I'm counting on you not letting me down next Wednesday. I've heard you were having a tea party in Rivebelle with your cousin, M. de Charlus, and I don't know who else. You ought to plan to transport the whole lot here, it'd be nice, a small consignment en masse. Communications couldn't be simpler, the roads are ravishing; if need be, I'll have you fetched. I don't know, for that matter, what you can find attractive in Rivebelle, it's infested with mosquitoes. Perhaps you're thinking of the reputation of its *galettes*. The ones my cook makes are in a different class. I'll make you eat Normandy *galettes*, the real thing, and the local shortbread, I say no more. Oh, if you insist on the filth they serve in Rivebelle, I want none of it, I don't murder my guests, monsieur, and even if I wanted, my cook would refuse to make those unspeakable objects and would change establishments. You don't know what they're made from, the *galettes* from there. I know a poor girl who got peritonitis from them, which carried her off in three days. She was only seventeen. It's sad for her poor mother," added Mme Verdurin, with a melancholy expression beneath the spheres of her temples, weighed down by sorrow and experience. "But, there, go and have tea in Rivebelle if it amuses you to be fleeced and to throw money out of the window. Only, I beg you, I'm entrusting you with a confidential mission: on the stroke of six o'clock, bring all your people here, don't let them disband and all go off home one by one. You can bring whom you please. I wouldn't say that to everyone. But I'm sure your friends are nice, I can see here and now that we understand one another. Apart from the little nucleus, some very agreeable people are coming on Wednesday, in fact. You don't know little

Mme de Longpont? She's a delight, and so quick, not in the least bit snobbish, you'll see, you'll really take to her. She's also due to bring a whole group of friends," added Mme Verdurin, to show that this was quite the thing and to encourage me by example. "We'll see who has the most influence and brings the most people, Barbe de Longpont or you. Besides, I believe they're due to bring Bergotte, too," she added with a vague expression, the collaboration of that celebrity having been rendered all too improbable by a notice that had appeared in the papers that morning to the effect that the great writer's health was giving rise to the gravest anxiety. "Anyway, you'll see, it'll be one of my most successful Wednesdays, I don't want any women who are tiresome. Don't judge by this evening's, in any case, that was a total failure. Don't protest, you can't have been any more bored than I was, I found it tedious myself. It won't always be like this evening, you know! I'm not talking about the Cambremers, moreover, who are impossible, but I've known society people who passed for being agreeable, well, compared to my little nucleus, they didn't exist. I heard you say you thought Swann intelligent. My opinion, first of all, is that that was much exaggerated, but not even to speak of the man's character, which I always found fundamentally unsympathetic, sly, underhanded, I often had him to dinner on Wednesdays. Well, you can ask the others, even compared with Brichot, who's certainly no genius, but a good fifth-form teacher whom I got into the Institute just the same, Swann was nothing any more. He was so dreary!" And as I was emitting a contrary opinion: "That's the way it was. I don't want to say a word against him, since he was your friend; he was very fond of you, for that matter, he spoke about you in a delightful way, but ask these people whether he ever said anything interesting at our dinners. That's the acid test, after all. Well, I don't know why, but Swann when he came to me never produced, never gave us anything. And yet the little that he was worth, he acquired it here." I assured her that he was very intelligent. "No, you only thought that because you hadn't known him for as long as I had. Basically, you very soon got the measure of him. He bored *me*." Translation: he went to the La Trémoïlles and the Guermantes and knew that I didn't. "And I can stand anything except boredom. That, no, never!" Her horror of being bored was now the reason on which Mme Verdurin relied to explain the

makeup of her little circle. She had not yet entertained duchesses because she was unable to be bored, as she was to go on a cruise on account of seasickness. I told myself that what Mme Verdurin had been
saying was not wholly false, and whereas the Guermantes might have
declared Brichot to be the stupidest man they had ever met, I remained
unsure whether he was not at bottom superior, if not to Swann himself,
then at least to those people having the Guermantes sense of humor,
who would have had the good taste to avoid and the decency to blush
at his pedant's facetiousness, or so I asked myself, as if a measure of
light might be thrown on the nature of intelligence by the answer I
gave, with the seriousness of a Christian influenced by Port-Royal posing the problem of Grace to himself.[134] "You'll see," Mme Verdurin
continued, "when you have society people together with truly intelligent people, people from our circle, that's where you need to see them,
the cleverest man of the world in the kingdom of the blind is no more
than a one-eyed man here. He freezes the others, moreover, who no
longer feel any confidence. To the point where I ask myself whether, instead of trying out the combinations that ruin everything, I won't have
series for the bores alone, so as to enjoy my little nucleus properly. We
must stop: you will come with your cousin. That's agreed. Good. At
least here the two of you'll get to eat. At Féterne, it's hunger and thirst.
Oh, I mean, if you like rats, go there this instant, you'll be offered your
fill of them. And they'll keep you there as long as you like. I mean,
you'll die of hunger. Anyway, when I go, I shall dine before setting out.
And to make it more fun, you must come and fetch me. We'll have a
hearty tea and supper when we get back. Do you like *tarte aux pommes*?
Yes, well, our chef's better at them than anybody. You can see, I was
right to say you were meant to live here. So come and stay. You know
the house is far roomier than it looks. I don't tell people, so as not to attract bores. You could bring your cousin here permanently. She'd get
quite different air here from Balbec. With the air here, I claim I can
cure the incurable. Take my word for it, I've cured some, and not just
recently. Because I lived quite near here in the old days, something I'd
unearthed that I got for a crust of bread and which had far more character than their Raspelière. I'll show it to you if we take a drive. But I acknowledge that even here the air is really bracing. But, then, I don't

want to talk about it too much—all I need is for the Parisians to start liking my little hideaway. That's always been my luck. Anyway, tell your
cousin. We'll give you two pretty rooms overlooking the valley, you'll
see it in the mornings, the sun in the mist! And who's this Robert de
Saint-Loup you were talking about?" she said anxiously, for she had
heard that I was due to go and visit him in Doncières and was afraid he
might cause me to default. "You could bring him here instead, if he's
not a bore. I've heard about him through Morel, I fancy he's one of his
great friends," said Mme Verdurin, telling a complete lie, because Saint-
Loup and Morel did not even know of each other's existence. But, having heard that Saint-Loup knew M. de Charlus, she thought that this
was through the violinist and wanted to appear to be in the swim of
things. "He isn't studying medicine by any chance, or literature? You
know, if you need a word put in on the examinations, Cottard can do
anything, and I can do what I like with him. As for the Academy, for
later on, for I imagine he's not yet of an age, I can call on several votes.
Your friend'll be on familiar ground here, and it'd perhaps amuse him
to see the house. It's not much fun, Doncières. Anyway, you must do as
you like, whatever suits you best," she ended, without insisting, so as
not to appear to be trying to get an introduction to the nobility, and
because her claim was that the name of the regime under which she
made the faithful live, her tyranny, was liberty. "Hello, what's the matter?" she said, catching sight of M. Verdurin, who, gesturing impa-
tiently, had gone out onto the wooden veranda that stretched above the
valley on one side of the drawing room, like a man who is choking with
rage and has need of fresh air. "Is it Saniette again who's been annoying
you? But since you know he's an idiot, resign yourself to the fact, and
don't get into these states. . . . I don't like it," she said to me, "because
it's bad for him, he goes blue in the face. But I have to say, too, that
you sometimes need the patience of an angel to put up with Saniette,
and to remind yourself above all that it's an act of charity to take him
in. For my own part, I confess, such is the magnificence of his stupidity,
it delights me rather. I imagine you heard his *bon mot* after dinner: 'I
can't play whist, but I can play the piano!' Isn't that lovely! The greatest
thing you've ever heard, and a lie as it happens, because he can't play

one any more than the other. But my husband, underneath his rough exterior, is very sensitive, very kind, and that sort of selfishness in Saniette, forever taken up with the effect he's going to create, drives him wild. . . . Come, *mon petit,* calm yourself, you know very well Cottard told you it was bad for your liver. And it's I who'll have to bear the brunt," said Mme Verdurin. "Tomorrow Saniette's going to come with his little *crise de nerfs* and his tears. Poor man! He's very ill. But, then, that's no reason why he should kill others. Besides, even at the times when he's too unwell, when you'd like to feel sorry for him, his silliness stops pity dead. He's simply too stupid. You just need to tell him very gently that these scenes are making the two of you ill, that he mustn't come back; since that's what he most dreads, it'll have a calming effect on his nerves," whispered Mme Verdurin to her husband.

You could barely make out the sea through the right-hand windows. But those on the other side showed the valley, on which there had now fallen the snow of the moonlight. From time to time, the voice of Morel and that of Cottard could be heard. "Have you got a trump?" A *yes* in English. "Oh, you've got some good ones, *vous en avez de bonnes,*" said M. de Cambremer to Morel, in answer to his question, for he had seen that the doctor's hand was full of trumps. "Here's the wife of diamonds," said the doctor. "That's a trump, you know? Me play, me take . . . But there isn't a Sorbonne any more," said the doctor to M. de Cambremer, "there's only the University of Paris now." M. de Cambremer confessed himself ignorant of why the doctor had made this remark. "I thought you were talking about the Sorbonne," the doctor went on. "I heard you say, 'You're bringing out the right one, *tu nous la sors bonne,*' " he added with a wink, to show that this was a witticism. "Wait," he said, pointing to his adversary, "I'm getting ready to deliver the knockout blow." And the blow had to be an excellent one, so far as the doctor was concerned, for in his delight he began as he laughed to shake both shoulders voluptuously, which in the family, in the Cottard "genus," was an almost zoological mark of satisfaction. In the previous generation, the gesture of rubbing the hands together as if one were soaping them had accompanied this movement. Cottard himself had originally used this double mimicry simultaneously, but one fine day, without anyone's knowing to what conjugal, or perhaps magisterial, intervention it was to be attributed, the rubbing of the hands had disappeared. Even at dominoes, when he forced his partner to "draw" and take the double six, which was for him the keenest of pleasures, the doctor contented himself with the movement of the shoulders. And when—as rarely as possible—he went to his native village for a few days, and met his first cousin again, who for his part was still at the hand-rubbing stage, he would say on returning to Mme Cottard, "I thought poor René very common." "Have you got any of these little theengs?" he said, turning to Morel. "No? Then I shall play this old David."[135] "But you've got five then, you've won!" "A fine victory, Doctor," said the Marquis. "A victory à la Pyrrhus," said Cottard, turning to the Marquis and peering over his eyeglass to judge the effect of his *bon mot*. "If we've still got time," he said to Morel, "I'll give you your revenge. It's me to . . . Ah, no, here are the carriages, it'll be for Friday, and I'll show you a trick you don't see every day." M. and Mme Verdurin led us outside. The Patronne was especially ingratiating with Saniette, so as to be sure he would come back the next day. "But you don't look covered up to me, *mon petit*," M. Verdurin said to me, his advanced years sanctioning this fatherly form of address. "It's as though the weather had changed." These words filled me with joy, as if the profound life, the sudden appearance of different combinations that they implied in nature, must herald other changes, occurring this time in my own life and creating new possibilities there. Merely by opening the door onto the gardens before leaving, you felt that a different "weather" had just then occupied the scene; breaths of cool air, one of summer's delights for the senses, were stirring in the pine wood (where Mme de Cambremer had once dreamed of Chopin) and almost imperceptibly, in caressing meanders and capricious eddies, had begun their faint nocturnes. I refused the rug that I would accept on the subsequent evenings when Albertine would be there, more for the secrecy of our pleasures than against the risks of the cold. The Norwegian philosopher was searched for in vain. Had he been taken with a stomachache? Had he been afraid of missing the train? Had an airplane come to fetch him? Had he been carried up in an Assumption? The fact was that he had vanished without anyone's

having had the time to notice, like a god. "You're wrong," M. de Cambremer said to me, "it's as cold as charity." "Why charity?" asked the
doctor. "Watch out for breathless attacks," the Marquis went on. "My
sister never goes out in the evenings. But, then, she's none too good at
present. Don't stay bare-headed like that, anyway, get your headgear on
quickly." "They're not breathless attacks *a frigore*," said Cottard senten-
tiously. "Oh, in that case," said M. de Cambremer, bowing, "since
that's your opinion. . ." "Get a second opinion," said the doctor, sneak-
ing glances outside his eyeglass for a laugh. M. de Cambremer did
laugh but, convinced that he was right, he insisted. "Yet each time my
sister goes out in the evenings," he said, "she has an attack." "There's no
point in quibbling," answered the doctor, without being aware of his
own rudeness. I don't practice medicine at the seaside in any case, unless summoned to a consultation. I'm here on vacation." He was even
more so, as it happens, than he might have wished. M. de Cambremer
having said to him as they got into the carriage together, "We're fortunate in having another medical celebrity, Dr. du Boulbon, so close by,
not on your side of the bay, on the other, but it's so shut in at that
point," Cottard, who normally, on *deontological* grounds, abstained
from criticizing his colleagues, could not help exclaiming, as he had in
front of me on that fateful day when we had gone into the little casino:
"But he's not a doctor. He practices literary medicine, a therapeutics of
fantasy, quackery. We're on good terms even so. I'd take the boat to go
and visit him one time were I not obliged to absent myself." But from
the expression that Cottard assumed in order to discuss du Boulbon
with M. de Cambremer, I sensed that the boat on which he would have
gladly gone in search of him bore a close resemblance to the vessel that
the doctors of Salerno had fitted out to go and destroy the waters discovered by another literary doctor, Virgil (who had also taken away
their entire clientele), but which foundered with them during the crossing.[136] "Goodbye, *mon petit* Saniette, don't fail to come tomorrow, you
know that my husband is very fond of you. He likes your wit, your intelligence; yes, he does, you know that, he likes putting on a show of
brusqueness, but he can't do without seeing you. It's always the first
question he puts to me: 'Is Saniette coming? I so love seeing him!' "

"I've never said that," said M. Verdurin to Saniette, with a simulated candor that seemed perfectly to reconcile what the Patronne had been saying with his own treatment of Saniette. Then, looking at his watch, no doubt so as not to prolong the farewells in the evening damp, he advised the coachmen not to dawdle, but to be careful on the descent, and assured us that we would get there before the train. The latter would be setting down the faithful, one at one station, another at another, ending with myself, none of the others going as far as Balbec, and starting with the Cambremers. They, so as not to make their horses go all the way up to La Raspelière in the dark, took the train with us to Douville-Féterne. The nearest station to them was not in fact this one, which is some little way from the village and even farther from the château, but La Sogne. On arriving at the station of Douville-Féterne, M. de Cambremer insisted on "crossing the palm," as Françoise used to put it, of the Verdurins' coachman (the same gentle, sensitive coachman, with the melancholy ideas), for M. de Cambremer was generous, being "from his mamma's side" rather in this. But whether it was that "his papa's side" intervened at this juncture, even as he gave it, he felt qualms that a faux pas was being committed—either by himself, because, unable to see properly, he might for example be giving a sou instead of a franc, or by the recipient, who could not notice the size of the gift he was getting. He drew attention to it, therefore. "That *is* a franc I'm giving you, isn't it?" he said to the coachman, causing the coin to reflect the light, and so that the faithful might report it to Mme Verdurin. "Isn't it? It's twenty sous, as it's only a short ride." He and Mme de Cambremer left us at La Sogne. "I shall tell my sister that you have breathless attacks," he repeated to me. "It's sure to interest her." I realized he meant: to please her. As for his wife, in taking leave of me, she employed two of those abbreviations that, even when written, used in those days to shock me in a letter, although we have grown accustomed to them since, but which, when spoken, seem to me still, even today, to have about them, in their studied familiarity, something intolerably pedantic: "Glad to have spent the evening with you," she said to me; "regards to Saint-Loup if you see him." In saying these words, Mme de Cambremer pronounced it "Saint-Loupe." I have never found out who had pronounced it like that in her presence, or what had given her to believe that it was to be so pronounced. The fact remains that for several weeks she pronounced it "Saint-Loupe," and that a man who had great admiration for her and followed her in everything did likewise. If other people were to say "Saint-Lou," they insisted, emphasizing the "Saint-Loupe," either indirectly to put these other people right, or else to mark themselves off from them. But no doubt women more brilliant than Mme de Cambremer told her, or gave her indirectly to understand, that it should not be pronounced that way, and that what she had taken to be originality was an error which would have it thought that she was not *au fait* with the ways of society, for, shortly afterward, Mme de Cambremer was again saying "Saint-Lou," and her admirer likewise abandoned all resistance, either because she had lectured him, or because he had noticed she was no longer sounding the final consonant, and had told himself that if a woman of her worth, her energy, and her ambition had given in it had to be with good reason. The worst of her admirers was her husband. Mme de Cambremer loved teasing other people, often very impertinently. As soon as she set about someone in this way, whether myself or somebody else, M. de Cambremer began looking at the victim and laughing. As the Marquis had a squint—which can lend an intention of wit to the amusement even of an imbecile—the effect of this laugh was to bring a bit of the pupil back into the otherwise unbroken white of his eye. Thus does a bright interval produce a patch of blue in a sky fleecy with clouds. The monocle, moreover, protected this delicate operation like the glass over a valuable painting. As for the actual intention behind the laugh, one hardly knew whether it was friendly—"Ah, you rascal, you're to be envied, and no mistake. You've found favor with a woman with a strong sense of humor"—or catty—"Well, monsieur, I hope that's taught you a lesson, put that in your pipe and smoke it"—or obliging—"I'm here, you know, I can laugh because it's all in fun, but I won't let you be maltreated"—or cruelly complicit—"I don't have to add my own pennyworth, but you can see I find the insults she's heaping on you hilarious. I'm convulsed, so I approve, I, her husband. And so, if you take it into your head to return the compliment, you'll find you've got me to deal with, *mon petit monsieur.* First you'd receive two good sound slaps on the cheek, then we'd go and cross blades in the forest of Chantepie."

Whatever the truth of these various interpretations of the husband's mirth, the wife's passing whims soon came to an end. M. de Cambremer would then leave off laughing, the temporary pupil would vanish, and as you had, for the past few minutes, lost the habit of that completely white eye, it lent this red-faced Norman something at once bloodless and ecstatic, as though the Marquis had just been operated on, or were imploring heaven, beneath his monocle, for a martyr's crown.

## CHAPTER 3

*Sorrows of M. de Charlus—His fictitious duel—*
*The stations of the "Transatlantic"—*
*Weary of Albertine, I want to break with her.*

I COULD NOT keep awake. I was taken up as far as my floor in the lift, not by the lift boy, but by the cross-eyed *chasseur*, who struck up a conversation to relate to me that his sister was still with the very rich gentleman, and that one time, because she had wanted to return home rather than behave responsibly, her gentleman had sought out the mother of the cross-eyed *chasseur*, and of the other, more favored children, who had taken the nonsensical girl back to her friend as quickly as possible. "You know, monsieur, she's a great lady, my sister. She plays the piano and can speak Spanish. You might not believe it, of the sister of the mere employee who takes the lift up, but she denies herself nothing; Madame has her own maidservant, it wouldn't amaze me if one day she had her own carriage. She's very pretty, if you could see her, a bit too stuck up, but, Lord, that's understandable! She's quite a humorist. She never leaves a hotel without relieving herself in a wardrobe or a chest of drawers, so as to leave a small memento for the chambermaid who'll have to clean up. Sometimes she even does it in a cab, and after she's paid her fare, she hides in a corner, so's to have a good laugh watching the driver curse and swear when he's got to wash down his cab again. My father had a stroke of luck, too, finding that Indian Prince he'd met in the old days for my young brother. Of course, that's a different kind of arrangement. But it's a superb position. If it weren't for the traveling, what you dream of. There's only me up till now who's been left out. But you can never tell. Luck runs in my family; who knows whether I won't one day be president of the Republic? But I'm making you chatter on." I had not said a single word and was starting to fall asleep listening to his words. "Good night, monsieur. Oh, thank you, monsieur! If everyone was as kindhearted as yourself, there'd be no poor people any more. But as my sister says, there'll always need to be some so that now I'm rich, I can tell them to go to blazes. Pardon the expression. Good night, monsieur."

Every night perhaps, we accept the risk of experiencing, while we sleep, sufferings that we consider to be null and void because they will be endured only in the course of a sleep that we believe is without consciousness. In fact, on the evenings when I returned home late from La Raspelière, I was very sleepy. But as soon as the cold weather arrived, I was unable to get to sleep right away, because the fire was so bright it was as if a lamp had been lit. It had only flared up, however, and—as with a lamp, or the daylight when dusk falls—its too bright light was not long in dying down; and I entered into sleep, which is like a second apartment that we have, into which, abandoning our own, we go in order to sleep. It has its own system of alarms, and we are sometimes brought violently awake there by the sound of a bell, heard with perfect clarity, even though no one has rung. It has its servants, its particular visitors who come to take us out, so that, just when we are ready to get up, we are obliged to recognize, by our almost immediate transmigration into the other apartment, that of our waking hours, that the room is empty, that no one has come. The race that inhabits it, like that of the earliest humans, is androgynous. A man there will appear a moment later in the aspect of a woman. Objects have the ability to turn into men, and men into friends or enemies. The time that elapses for the sleeper, in sleep of this kind, is utterly different from the time in which a waking man's life transpires. Its passage may now be far more rapid, a quarter of an hour seeming like a whole day; or at other times much longer, we think we have just dozed off, and have slept right through the day. And then, on sleep's chariot, we descend into depths where the memory can no longer keep pace with it, and where the mind stops short and is forced to turn back. Sleep's horses, like those of the sun, move at so uniform a pace, in an atmosphere where no resistance can any longer arrest them, that some small alien aerolite is needed (hurled from the azure by Unknown Hand?) if this regular sleep is to be affected (which would otherwise have no reason to stop but would endure with a similar motion until the end of time) and made to return, wheeling suddenly about, toward reality, traversing without drawing breath the borderlands of life–the sounds of which, vague almost as yet, but already perceptible, though distorted, the sleeper will soon be hearing–and come abruptly to earth at our waking. From these deep sleeps we then awake in a dawn, not knowing who we are, being nobody, quite new, prepared for anything, our brain finding itself emptied of the past that had hitherto been our life. And perhaps it is better still when the return to earth of our waking is a brutal one and when our sleeping thoughts, concealed behind a vestment of oblivion, do not have time progressively to return before sleep has ended. Then, from the black storm through which we seem to have passed (but we do not even say "we"), we emerge lying prostrate, without any thoughts: a "we" it may be without content. What hammer blow has this person or thing that is here received, that it should be aware of nothing, be stupefied, until such time as the memory comes hurrying back, and restores its consciousness or personality? For these two kinds of reawakening, however, we must not go to sleep, not even deeply, under the law of habit. For habit keeps watch over all that it imprisons in its nets; we must elude it, find sleep at the moment when we thought we were doing something quite other than sleeping, find the sleep, in short, that does not dwell under the tutelage of foresight, in the company, even concealed, of reflection. At all events, in reawakenings such as I have just described, and which were mine most often after I had dined the evening before at La Raspelière, everything took place as if this were how it was, and I can testify, I, the strange human being who, while waiting for death to deliver him, lives behind closed shutters, knows nothing of the world, stays unmoving as an owl, and, like an owl, can see with any clarity only in the dark. Everything takes place as if this were how it was, but perhaps only a layer of cotton wool has prevented the sleeper from perceiving the inner dialogue between his memories and the incessant verbiage of sleep. For (and this can be explained just as readily, for that matter, in the first, vaster, more mysterious, more astral system), at the moment when waking occurs, the sleeper hears an inner voice that says to him, "Will you be coming to that dinner this evening, my dear friend? How pleasant that would be!," and thinks, "Yes, since it'll be pleasant, I shall go"; then, his wakefulness increasing, he suddenly remembers, "My grandmother has only a few weeks to live, so the doctor assures us." He rings the bell, weeps at the thought that, unlike in the past, it will not be his grandmother, his dying grandmother, who will come to answer it, but an indifferent *valet de chambre*. Moreover, when sleep carried him so far away from the world inhabited by memory and thought, through an ether in which he was alone, more than alone, without that companion even in whom we perceive ourselves, he was outside of time and its measurement. The *valet de chambre* is already entering, and he does not dare ask him the time, for he does not know whether he has been asleep, or how many hours he has slept (he wonders whether it is not how many *days,* having returned so broken in body, so rested in spirit, and so homesick in his heart, as if from a journey too distant not to have lasted for a long time). True, we can claim that there is only one time, for the futile reason that it is by looking at the clock that we have confirmed that what we thought was a whole day was only a quarter of an hour. But at the moment when we confirm it, we are of course a man awake, plunged into the time of waking men, we have deserted the other time. Perhaps even more than another time: another life. We do not include the pleasures we have during sleep when reckoning up those we have experienced in the course of our existence. To allude only to the most crudely sensual of them, which of us, on waking, has not felt some irritation at having experienced, while we slept, a pleasure that, unless we want to overtax ourselves, we cannot, once awake, repeat indefinitely on that particular day? It is as if a part of our substance has been wasted. We have felt pleasure in another life that is not ours. Were we to include the pains and pleasures of our dreams (which generally vanish very quickly on waking) in a budget, it would not be in that of our everyday life.

Two kinds of time, I have said; perhaps there is only one, not because that of the waking man holds good for the sleeper, but perhaps because the other life, that in which we sleep, is not—in its profound part–subject to the category of time. That is what I imagined when, in the aftermath of the dinners at La Raspelière, I fell so completely asleep. Here is why. I was beginning to feel desperate when, on waking, I found that, after I had rung ten times, the valet had not arrived. At the eleventh, he entered. It was only the first time. The other ten had been mere adumbrations in my still-continuing sleep of the summons that I wanted. My numbed hands had not even moved. On these mornings (which is what makes me say that sleep perhaps knows nothing of the law of time), my attempt to wake up consisted above all in an attempt to introduce the obscure, undefined block of sleep that I had just been living into the framework of time. This is no easy task; the sleep that does not know whether we have slept for two hours or for two days cannot provide us with a point of reference. And if we do not discover one outside of it, and do not succeed in re-entering time, we go back to sleep again, for five minutes that seem to us like three hours.

I have always said–and proved by experience–that sleep is the most potent of hypnotics. Having slept deeply for two hours, fought with any number of giants, and formed any number of undying friendships, it is far more difficult to come awake than after taking several grams of veronal. And so, reasoning from one to the other, I was surprised to learn through the Norwegian philosopher, who had had it from M. Boutroux, his eminent "associate–forgive me, colleague," what M. Bergson thought about the particular ill-effects on the memory produced by hypnotics. "Of course," M. Bergson will have said to M. Boutroux, if the Norwegian philosopher is to be believed, "hypnotics taken from time to time in moderate doses do not affect the solid memory of our everyday lives, so firmly fixed in us. But there are other kinds of memory, higher and more unstable ones. One of my colleagues is lecturing on ancient history. He has told me that if the night before, he had taken a pill to get to sleep, he had difficulty, during his lecture, in recovering the Greek quotations that he needed. The doctor who had recommended the pills to him assured him they did not affect the memory. 'Perhaps that's because you don't have to give Greek quotations,' the historian had replied, not without a mocking vanity."

I do not know whether this conversation between M. Bergson and M. Boutroux is accurate. The Norwegian philosopher, very profound and lucid though he was, and so passionately attentive, may have mis-understood. My personal experience has given me the opposite results. The moments of oblivion that ensue, the next day, after we have in-gested certain narcotics, bear only a partial, if troubling, resemblance to the oblivion that reigns in the course of a night of deep, natural sleep. Now, what I forget in either case is not some line of Baudelaire's that wearies me rather, "like a dulcimer,"[1] not some concept from one of the philosophers I have been citing, but the very reality of the common ob-jects that surround me—if I am asleep—my nonperception of which turns me into a madman; it is—if I am awake and emerging after an arti-ficial sleep—not the system of Porphyry or Plotinus, which I am as able to discuss as on any other day, but the answer I have promised to give to an invitation, the memory of which has been replaced by a complete blank. The elevated idea has remained in place; what the hypnotic has disabled is our capacity to act in minor matters, in everything that calls for action if we are to repossess it just in time, to seize hold of some memory of our everyday life. Despite all that may be said about sur-vival after the destruction of the brain, I observe that to every deterio-ration in the brain there corresponds a fragment of death. We possess all our memories, if not the faculty of recalling them, says, following M. Bergson, the great Norwegian philosopher, whose language I have not tried to imitate, so as not to slow things down any further. If not the faculty of recalling them. But what is a memory that we cannot re-call? Or let us go further. We do not recall our memories of the last thirty years, but we are totally steeped in them; why, then, stop at thirty years, why not continue this previous existence back beyond our birth? Given that I do not know a whole portion of the memories that are behind me, given that they are invisible to me, that I do not have the faculty of summoning them, who is to say that in this mass that is un-known to me there are not memories that date back long before my life as a man? If I can have, in me and around me, so many memories that I do not remember, this oblivion (a *de facto* oblivion at least, since I do not have the faculty of seeing anything) may apply to a life that I have lived in the body of another man, or even on another planet. The one oblivion erases everything. But what, then, would be signified by the immortality of the soul whose reality the Norwegian philosopher had asserted? The person that I shall be after death has no more reason to remember the man that I have been since my birth than this latter remembers what I was before it.

The *valet de chambre* had entered. I did not tell him that I had rung several times, for I realized that hitherto all I had done was to dream that I had rung. I was alarmed to think, however, that this dream had had the clarity of a cognition. Could cognition, by the same token, have the unreality of a dream?

I asked him, on the other hand, who had rung so many times during the night. He told me "no one," and could say that with certainty, because it would have shown up on the "board." Yet I had heard repeated, almost furious peals, which vibrated still in my ear and were to remain audible for several days. It is rare, however, for sleep thus to discharge into waking life memories that do not die with it. Such aerolites can be counted. If it is an idea that sleep has forged, this quickly disintegrates into tenuous, irretrievable fragments. But here sleep had fabricated sounds. Being more physical and simpler, they had lasted longer. I was astonished at the relatively early hour the *valet de chambre* told me it was. I felt rested nonetheless. It is light sleeps that are of long duration, because, being intermediate between waking and sleeping, and preserving a partly erased but permanent notion of the former, they require an infinitely longer time to refresh us than does a deep sleep, which may be short. I felt thoroughly at ease for another reason. If reminding ourselves that we are tired is enough to make us painfully aware of our tiredness, to say to ourselves, "I feel rested," is enough to create repose. Now, I had dreamed that M. de Charlus was 110 years old and had just twice slapped his mother, Mme Verdurin, in the face for spending five billion on a bunch of violets; I was assured, therefore, of having slept deeply, and of having dreamed the contrary of my notions of the day before and of all the possibilities of my current life; that was enough for me to feel fully rested.

I would have greatly astonished my mother, who could not understand M. de Charlus's assiduousness *chez* Verdurin, if I had told her (on the very day on which Albertine's toque had been ordered, without my saying a word to her, so that it might come as a surprise) with whom M. de Charlus had come to dine in a private room at the Grand-Hôtel in Balbec. His guest was none other than the footman of a cousin of the Cambremers. This footman was dressed with great elegance, and when he crossed the hall with the Baron, "played the man-of-the-world" in the eyes of the tourists, as Saint-Loup would have put it. Even the young *chasseurs,* the "Levites," a crowd of whom were descending the steps of the temple at that moment, which was that of their going off duty, paid no attention to the two new arrivals, one of whom, M. de Charlus, was anxious to show, by his lowered gaze, how very little he was according them. He seemed to be pushing his way through their midst. "Prosper, dear hope of a sacred nation,"[2] he said, recalling some lines from Racine, quoted in a very different sense. "I beg your pardon?" asked the footman, none too well versed in the classics. M. de Charlus did not answer, for he took a certain pride in discounting questions and in walking straight ahead, as if there were no other guests in the hotel and as if he alone, the Baron de Charlus, existed in the world. But, having continued with Josabeth's lines, "Come, come, my daughters,"[3] he felt distaste and did not add, as she does, "they must be summoned,"[4] for these children had not yet reached the age when sexuality is fully developed, and which appealed to M. de Charlus. Although, moreover, he had written to Mme de Chevregny's footman, because he did not doubt his docility, he had hoped he would be more virile. On seeing him, he found him more effeminate than he would have liked. He told him that he would have expected to be dealing with someone else, for he knew another of Mme de Chevregny's footmen by sight, having in fact noticed him on her carriage. This was a sort of country bumpkin, the complete opposite of the present one, who, adjudging his fancy ways to be so many marks of superiority, and not doubting that it was these man-of-the-world qualities that had seduced M. de Charlus, could not even understand whom the Baron meant. "But I've no colleagues except for one, and you can't have had your eye on him, he's a fright, he looks like a great fat peasant." And at the thought that it was perhaps this yokel whom the Baron had seen, he felt punctured in his self-esteem. The Baron guessed as much and, widening his inquiries: "But I haven't made a special vow to know only Mme de Chevregny's people," he said. "Couldn't you, whether here or in Paris, since you'll soon be going, introduce many of your colleagues to me, from one house or another?" "Oh no," replied the footman, "I don't associate with anyone from my own class. I only speak to them when on duty. But there's one highly respectable person I could introduce you to." "Who?" asked the Baron. "The Prince de Guermantes." M. de Charlus was greatly put out that he should be offered only a man that old, and with whom, what was more, he had no need of a recommendation from a footman. Thus he curtly declined the offer and, not allowing himself to be deterred by the flunky's social pretensions, he began again to explain to him what he would like, the style, the type, a jockey maybe, and so on. Afraid that the lawyer who was passing at that moment might have overheard him, he thought it canny to show that he had been talking about something quite other than what might have been supposed, and said with insistence, and to the company at large, but as if all he were doing was continuing the conversation: "Yes, despite my years, I have kept my taste for curio-hunting, my taste for pretty curios, I'll spend more than I can afford on an old bronze or an antique chandelier. I worship Beauty." But to get the footman to understand the change of subject that he had executed so rapidly, M. de Charlus laid so much stress on each word, and in addition, so that the lawyer should hear, shouted them all out so loudly, that this whole bit of playacting would have sufficed to reveal what it was concealing to ears more alert than those of the legal official. The latter no more suspected anything than any other of the hotel guests, all of whom saw an elegant foreigner in the very well-turned-out footman. On the other hand, if the men of the world were deceived and took him for an ultra-smart American, hardly had he appeared before the servants when they saw through him, just as one convict will recognize another convict, even quicker, nosed out from afar, as one animal is by certain others. The *chefs de rang* raised an eyebrow. Aimé cast a suspicious glance. The sommelier, shrugging his shoulders, said behind his hand, because he thought this was politeness, a disobliging phrase that everyone heard. And even our old Françoise, whose sight was failing and who was passing the bottom of the stairs at that moment, to go and eat with the guests' servants, looked up, recognized a domestic where the hotel guests had not suspected one—just as the old nurse Euryclea recognizes Ulysses long before the suitors at the banquets[5]—and, seeing M. de

Charlus walking with him in this familiar manner, appeared overcome, as if all of a sudden wicked things that she had heard spoken but had not believed had assumed in her eyes a distressing probability. She never mentioned this incident, to me or to anyone else, but it must have set her brain to working hard, for later on, whenever in Paris she had occasion to see "Julien," of whom she had hitherto been so fond, she always treated him with politeness, but now it had cooled and was always diluted by a strong admixture of reserve. This same incident led someone else to entrust me with a confidence, on the other hand; this was Aimé. When I passed M. de Charlus, the latter, who had not been expecting to come across me, had called out, raising his hand, "Good evening," with the indifference, apparent at least, of a great nobleman who believes he is a law unto himself and deems it more adroit not to appear to be hiding. But Aimé, who had just then been observing him with a distrustful eye and saw that I greeted the companion of the man in whom he was sure of having recognized a domestic, asked me that same evening who he was. For Aimé had for some time now liked to chat or, rather, as he put it, no doubt in order to mark the, as he saw it, philosophical nature of these chats, to "debate" with me. And as I had frequently told him it embarrassed me that he should remain standing beside me as I ate, when he could have sat down and shared my meal, he declared that he had never come across a guest having "such sound powers of argument." He was talking at that moment with two waiters. They had bowed to me, I did not know why; their faces were not known to me, although there sounded in their conversation a confused murmur that did not seem new. Aimé was upbraiding the two of them for having become engaged, of which he disapproved. He called me as a witness; I said I could not have an opinion, not knowing them. They reminded me of their names, and that they had often waited on me in Rivebelle. But one of them had let his mustache grow, the other had shaved his off and been shorn; as a result, although it was the old heads that were set on their shoulders (and not a different one, as in the faulty restorations at Notre-Dame),[6] they had remained as invisible for me as those objects that elude the most painstaking search yet are simply lying in full view, unnoticed by anyone, on a mantelpiece.[7] The moment I learned their names, I recognized exactly the uncertain music of their voices, for I could again see the old faces that had determined it. "They want to get married and they don't even know English!" Aimé said to me, without reflecting that I was not well up on the profession of hotelier and hardly understood that if you do not know foreign languages you cannot count on finding a position. I, who had expected him to find out soon enough that this new diner was M. de Charlus, and even imagined that he must remember him, having waited on him in the dining room when the Baron had come to see Mme de Villeparisis during my first stay in Balbec, told him his name. Not only did Aimé not remember the Baron de Charlus, but the name appeared to make a strong impression on him. He told me that the next day he would hunt among his belongings for a letter that I might be able to explain to him. I was all the more surprised in that M. de Charlus, when he had wanted to give me one of Bergotte's books in Balbec, that first year, had made a special point of asking for Aimé, whom he must have come across again subsequently in the restaurant in Paris where I had had lunch with Saint-Loup and his mistress, and where M. de Charlus had come to spy on us. It is true that Aimé had not been able to carry out these missions in person, having been in the one instance in bed and the second time busy serving. I had serious doubts, however, as to his sincerity when he claimed not to know M. de Charlus. For one thing, he must have suited the Baron. Like all the *chefs d'étage* at the Balbec hotel, and like several of the Prince de Guermantes's *valets de chambre*, Aimé belonged to a race more ancient than that of the Prince and hence more noble. When you asked for a private room, you thought at first you were alone. But soon, in the pantry, you observed a sculptural *maître d'hôtel*, of that red-haired Etruscan kind of which Aimé was the type, somewhat aged by an excess of champagne and seeing the moment for Contrexéville water unavoidably approaching. Not all the guests asked them only to wait on them. The *commis* waiters, who were young, scrupulous, and in a hurry, with a mistress waiting for them in the town, made their escape. And so Aimé would criticize them for their irresponsibility. He had the right. He *was* responsible. He had a wife and children, and was ambitious for them. Thus he did not repel the advances made to him by a stranger, male or female, even though he might have to remain all night. For work must come before anything else. He was so much the kind of person to appeal to M. de Charlus that I suspected him of a falsehood when he told me he did not know him. I was wrong. It was the simple truth when the *chasseur* told the Baron that Aimé (who had hauled him over the coals the next day) had gone to bed (or gone out), and on the other occasion was busy serving. But the imagination goes beyond the reality in supposition. And the *chasseur*'s embarrassment had probably sown doubts in M. de Charlus as to the genuineness of his excuses, doubts that had wounded feelings in him that Aimé had not suspected. We have seen also that Saint-Loup had prevented Aimé from going to the carriage, in which M. de Charlus, who had somehow or other obtained the *maître d'hôtel*'s new address, had suffered a fresh disappointment. Aimé, who had not noticed him, felt the astonishment one can imagine when, on the evening of the same day on which I had had lunch with Saint-Loup and his mistress, he received a letter sealed with the Guermantes arms, from which I shall quote a few passages as an example of unilateral madness in an intelligent man addressing an imbecile of good sense. "Monsieur, I have not succeeded, in spite of efforts that would surprise many people seeking uselessly to be received and acknowledged by me, in getting you to listen to the few explanations for which you did not ask me but which I thought it befitting both my dignity and your own to offer you. I shall therefore write here what it would have been simpler to say to you in person. I shall not hide from you that, the first time I set eyes on you in Balbec, I found your face frankly unsympathetic." There then followed reflections on the resemblance—remarked only on the second day—to a deceased friend for whom M. de Charlus had felt great affection. "I then had the idea for a moment that you might, without its at all hindering you in your profession, come and have with me the games of cards with which his gaiety was able to dispel my sadness, and give me the illusion that he was not dead. Whatever the nature of the more or less foolish suppositions that you have probably arrived at, and more within reach of a servant (who does not even deserve that name, since he has refused to serve) than the comprehension of so elevated a sentiment, you probably thought to make yourself seem important, not knowing who I was and what I was, by sending reply, when I made them ask you for a book, that you were in bed; but it is a mistake to believe that an incivility can ever add to one's charms, of which you are in any case totally devoid. I would have broken things off then had I not, by chance, been able to speak to you the following morning. Your resemblance to my poor friend became so marked, causing even the unbearable shape of your protuberant chin to vanish, that I realized that it was the deceased who, at that moment, was lending you something of his own very kindly expression so as to enable you to take hold of me again, and prevent you from wasting the unique good fortune that was being offered to you. Indeed, although I do not wish, since all this has no longer any object, and I shall have no further occasion to meet you in this life, to bring into all this brutal questions of self-interest, I would have been only too happy to obey my dead friend's prayer (for I believe in the communion of saints and their urge to intervene in the destiny of the living), to behave toward you as toward him, who had his own carriage and his servants, and to whom it was perfectly natural that I should devote the greater part of my resources since I loved him like a son. You have decided otherwise. To my request that you bring me a book, you sent reply that you had to go out. And this morning, when I sent to ask you to come to my carriage, you, if I can so put it without committing a sacrilege, denied me for a third time. You will forgive me for not enclosing in this envelope the elevated gratuities that I had counted on giving you in Balbec, and to which I would find it too painful to adhere with regard to someone with whom I had thought for a moment to share everything. You might at the very least spare me making a fourth futile approach to you, in your restaurant, to which my patience will not extend." And here M. de Charlus gave his address, an indication of the times when he could be found in, etc. "Farewell, monsieur. Since I believe that, resembling as you do the friend that I have lost, you cannot be entirely stupid, as otherwise physiognomy would be a false science, I am persuaded that if, one day, you think back on this incident, it will not be without experiencing a certain regret and a certain remorse. For my own part, believe me when I quite genuinely say that I harbor no bitterness. I would have preferred us to part on a less unhappy memory than this third futile overture. It will be quickly forgotten. We are like those vessels that you must have seen now and again from Balbec, which have crossed for a moment; it might have been to the advantage of either one to stop; but one of them has seen things differently; soon they will be out of sight of one another on the horizon, and the encounter is erased; but before this final separation, each salutes the other, as does here, monsieur, wishing you every good fortune, the Baron de Charlus."

Aimé had not even read this letter to the end, able to make neither head nor tail of it, but suspecting a hoax. Once I had explained to him who the Baron was, he appeared somewhat thoughtful and experienced that regret which M. de Charlus had predicted. I would not even swear that he did not then write to apologize to a man who gave carriages to his friends. But in the interim, M. de Charlus had made the acquaintance of Morel. At most, his relations with the latter being perhaps Platonic, M. de Charlus would now and again seek out company for an evening such as that in which I had just met him in the hall. But he could no longer turn away from Morel the violent sentiments that, free a few years earlier, had asked for nothing better than to attach themselves to Aimé and had dictated the letter that made me feel embarrassed for M. de Charlus's sake and which the *maître d'hôtel* had shown me. It was, because M. de Charlus's love was of an antisocial kind, a more striking example of the imperceptible yet mighty force of these currents of passion, in which the lover, like a swimmer being swept away unawares, very soon loses sight of land. Doubtless the love of a normal man also can, when, by the successive inventions of his desires, his regrets, his disappointments, and his projects, the lover constructs an entire novel around a woman whom he does not know, enable us to measure the notable divergence between the two legs of the compass. At the same time, this divergence was singularly widened by the nature of a passion that is not usually shared, and by the difference in status between M. de Charlus and Aimé.

I went out with Albertine every day. She had made up her mind to go back to painting and had chosen to work first at the church of Saint-Jean-de-la-Haise, which no one any longer visits and is known to very few, hard to get directions to, impossible to find without being guided, and takes a long time to reach in its isolation, more than half an hour from the station at Epreville, the last houses in the village of Quetteholme having been left well behind. Where the name Epreville was concerned, I found no agreement between the *curé*'s book and Brichot's indications. According to the one, Epreville was the ancient *Sprevilla;* the other gave *Aprivilla* as the etymology. The first time, we took the little railway in the opposite direction from Féterne, that is to say, toward Grattevast. But it was the dog days, and terrible enough in itself to be leaving straight after lunch. I would have preferred not to go out so soon; the burning, luminous air awoke thoughts of indolence and refreshment. It filled my and my mother's rooms, according to their exposure, with unequal temperatures, like rooms at a spa. Mamma's bathroom, festooned with sunlight, of a brilliant, Moorish whiteness, seemed plunged in the bottom of a well, on account of the four plaster walls on which it looked out, while up above, in the square left empty, the sky, whose fleecy, superimposed billows of cloud could be seen gliding past, one above the other, resembled (because of the longing you felt) a pool, situated on a terrace (or seen inverted in a mirror attached to the window) and filled with blue water, reserved for your ablutions. Despite the burning temperature, we had gone to catch the one o'clock train. But Albertine had felt very hot in the compartment, and hotter still during the long journey on foot, and I was afraid she might catch cold by then remaining motionless in that damp hollow to which the sun does not reach. On the other hand, having realized, ever since our first visits to Elstir, that she would appreciate not simply the luxury but even a certain measure of comfort of which her lack of money had deprived her, I had arranged with a livery stable in Balbec that a carriage should come to fetch us every day. To avoid the heat, we took the road through the forest of Chantepie. The invisibility of the innumerable birds, some of them half seabirds, that were calling to one another in the trees beside us, gave the same impression of repose as you get with your eyes shut. At Albertine's side, imprisoned by her arms in the back of the carriage, I listened to these Oceanides. And when I chanced to catch sight of one of these musicians, passing from one leaf underneath another, there was so little apparent connection between it and its songs that I could not believe I was seeing their source in that humble little body as it hopped, surprised and unseeing. The carriage could not take us right to the church. I made it stop on the way out of Quetteholme and said goodbye to Albertine. For she had alarmed me by saying about this church, as about other monuments and about certain paintings: "It'd be such a pleasure to see it with you!" That was a pleasure I did not feel capable of giving. I felt it in front of beautiful things only if I was alone, or pretended to be so, and was silent. But since she had thought she would be able to experience, thanks to me, artistic sensations that cannot be communicated in this way, I found it wiser to tell her that I was leaving her, would come to fetch her at the end of the day, but that meanwhile I needed to go back with the carriage to pay a call on Mme Verdurin or the Cambremers, or even to spend an hour with Mamma in Balbec, but never any farther. The first times, at least. For, Albertine having once said to me out of caprice, "It's a nuisance that nature has arranged things so badly and put Saint-Jean-de-la-Haise on one side and La Raspelière on the other, so that you're incarcerated for the whole day in the place that you've chosen," as soon as I had received the toque and the veil, I ordered, as my ill-fortune would have it, a motorcar in Saint-Fargeau (*Sanctus Ferreolus,* according to the *curé*'s book). Albertine, whom I had kept in ignorance, and who had come to fetch me, was surprised to hear the throb of the engine in front of the hotel and overjoyed when she learned that the car was for us. I made her come upstairs to my room for a moment. She was jumping for joy. "Are we going to pay a call on the Verdurins?" "Yes, but it would be better not to go there dressed like that, since you're going to have your car. Here, you'll look better in these." And I brought out the toque and veil, which I had hidden. "Are they for me? Oh, you're so sweet!" she exclaimed, jumping at my neck. Aimé encountered us on the stairs and, proud of Albertine's elegance and of our means of transport, for such vehicles were something of a rarity in Balbec, granted himself the pleasure of descending the stairs behind us. Albertine, wanting to be seen for a moment in her new outfit, asked me to have the top folded back, which we could lower later on so as to have greater freedom together. "Come on," said Aimé to the mechanic, whom he did not in fact know, and who had not stirred, "didn't you hear them say to fold the top back?" For Aimé, educated in the ways of the world by life in a hotel, where he had, moreover, achieved an eminent rank, was not so shy as the cabdriver, for whom Françoise was a "lady"; despite the lack of any earlier introduction, he addressed plebeians whom he had never met as *tu*, without your quite knowing whether this was aristocratic disdain on his part or fraternizing with the people. "I'm not free," replied the chauffeur, who did not know me. "I was ordered for Mlle Simonet. I can't drive Monsieur." Aimé gave a guffaw: "Come on, you great oaf," he replied to the mechanic, whom he at once convinced, "this is Mlle Simonet, in fact and Monsieur, who is ordering you to fold your top back, is in fact your employer." And since Aimé, although personally not feeling any sympathy for Albertine, was, on account of me, proud of the outfit she was wearing, he whispered to the chauffeur: "You'd be happy to drive a princess like her every day if you could, wouldn't you?" On this first occasion, I was not able to go to La Raspelière alone, as I did on other days while Albertine was painting; she wanted to go with me. She intended for us to stop here and there along the way, but thought it impossible to start by going to Saint-Jean-de-la-Haise, that is to say, in a different direction, and to make an excursion that seemed meant for another day. She learned, on the contrary, from the mechanic that nothing could be simpler than to go to Saint-Jean, where he would be in twenty minutes, and where we could remain, if we wanted, for several hours, or push on much farther, for from Quetteholme to La Raspelière he would not take more than thirty-five minutes. We realized this the moment the car leaped forward and in a single bound covered twenty paces of an excellent horse. Distances are simply the ratio of space to time and vary with it. We express the difficulty that we have in getting to a place in a system of leagues and kilometers, which becomes false the moment that difficulty decreases. The art of distance, too, is modified, since a village that had seemed to be in a different world from some other village becomes its neighbor in a landscape whose dimensions have altered. At all events, learning that there perhaps exists a universe in which two and two make five, and where a straight line is not the shortest distance between two points, would have surprised Albertine much less than hearing the mechanic tell her that it was easy to go in one afternoon to Saint-Jean and to La Raspelière. Douville and Quetteholme, Saint-Mars-le-Vieux and Saint-Mars-le-Vêtu, Gourville and Balbec-le-Vieux, Tourville and Féterne, prisoners hitherto as hermetically locked away in the cells of separate days as Méséglise and

Guermantes of old, and on which the same pair of eyes could not rest in a single afternoon, released now by the giant in the seven-league boots, came to congregate around our teatime their towers and their belfries, and their old gardens, which the nearby wood had been eager to disclose.

Having arrived at the foot of the corniche road, the car climbed it in a single movement, with a continuous sound, like a knife being ground, while the sea dropped away and broadened out beneath us. The ancient rustic houses of Montsurvent came rushing up, clutching their vines and rosebushes tightly to them; the pine trees of La Raspelière, more agitated than when the evening wind came up, ran off in all directions to avoid us, and a new manservant whom I had never seen before came to open the door to us on the front steps, while the gardener's son, betraying a precocious aptitude, gazed hungrily at the driver's seat. As it was not a Monday, we did not know whether we would find Mme Verdurin, for except on that day, when she was "at home," it was unwise to call on her without warning. No doubt she stayed in "in principle," but this expression, which Mme Swann had used in the days when she, too, was attempting to form her little clan and attract a clientele without having to stir, even though this often failed to pay its way, and which she translated mistakenly into "on principle," simply meant "as a general rule," that is to say, with numerous exceptions. For not only did Mme Verdurin like going out, but she carried her duties as a hostess to extremes, and when she had had company for lunch, immediately after the coffee, the liqueurs, and the cigarettes (despite the first torpor from the heat and from having to digest, when they would have preferred to watch the Jersey packet passing across the enamel sea through the foliage on the terrace), the program included a series of excursions, in the course of which the guests, forcibly installed in carriages, were taken willy-nilly to one or another of the lookout points that abound round Douville. This second part of the entertainment was not, however (the effort of getting up and climbing into the carriage having been achieved), found any less attractive by guests already prepared, by the succulent dishes, the fine wines, or the sparkling cider, to let themselves be easily intoxicated by the purity of the breeze and the magnificence of the beauty spots. Mme Verdurin showed these off to strangers a little as if they were (more or less distant) annexes of her own property, which you could not fail to go and see once you came to lunch with her, and which, conversely, you would not have known about had you not been entertained by the Patronne. This pretension, of arrogating to herself the sole rights to their excursions, as to Morel's and, in the old days, Dechambre's playing, and of constraining the landscape to form part of the little clan, was not, however, as absurd as it may at first seem. Mme Verdurin made fun of the lack of taste which, as she saw it, the Cambremers had shown in the furnishing of La Raspelière and the arrangement of the garden, as well as in the excursions they took, or made others take, in the neighborhood. Just as, according to her, La Raspelière had only begun to be what it should have been since it became the asylum of the little clan, so she declared that the Cambremers, forever retracing in their barouche, along the railway line, beside the sea, the one unpleasant road to be found in the vicinity, had always lived in the district but did not know it. There was some truth in this assertion. From routine, a lack of imagination, and a want of curiosity about a region that seemed trite for being so close by, the Cambremers only ever left home to visit the same places and by the same roads. To be sure, they laughed heartily at the Verdurins for presuming to teach them about their own neighborhood. But had they been cornered, they, and even their coachman, would have been incapable of taking us to the splendid, slightly secret places to which M. Verdurin conducted us, here lifting the gate into a private but abandoned property where others would not have felt free to venture, there getting down from the carriage in order to follow a lane that was not negotiable, but always with the certain reward of a marvelous landscape. Let me say for the rest that the garden at La Raspelière was in some sense a summation of all the excursions one could make for many kilometers around. First of all on account of its commanding situation, overlooking the valley on one side, and the sea on the other, and then because, even on the one side, that of the sea for example, clearings had been created amid the trees, so that from here you took in one horizon, from there a different one. At each of these lookout points, there was a garden seat; you went and sat by turns on the one from which you could make out Balbec, or Parville, or Douville. In one direction even, seats had been placed more or less above the sheer cliff, and a little way back from it. From these, you had a foreground of greenery and a horizon that already seemed the vastest possible, but which became infinitely larger if, by continuing along a small path, you went as far as the next seat, from which you took in the whole amphitheater of the sea. Here you could perceive the precise sound made by the waves, which did not, on the other hand, penetrate to the more sunken parts of the garden, from where the waves still allowed themselves to be seen, but no longer heard. For our hosts, these places of repose at La Raspelière bore the name of "views." And, indeed, they had gathered around the house the best "views" of the neighboring villages, beaches, and woodlands, glimpsed much reduced by the distance, like Hadrian assembling in his villa scale reproductions of the most celebrated monuments from various provinces. The name that accompanied the word "view" was not necessarily that of a place on the coast, but often on the opposite side of the bay, which you could make out, and which had preserved a certain relief despite the extensiveness of the panorama. Just as you might take down a volume from M. Verdurin's shelves to go and read for an hour at "the Balbec view," so, if the weather was clear, you went to have liqueurs at "the Rivebelle view," on condition, however, that there was not too much wind, for, despite the trees planted on either side, the air there was keen. To come back to the excursions by carriage that Mme Verdurin used to organize in the afternoons, if, on her return, the Patronne found the cards of some society person who was "passing along the coast," she pretended to be overjoyed, but was desolate at having missed their visit and (although they might have come only to see "the house" or to meet for a day with a woman whose artistic salon in Paris was celebrated but unfrequentable) quickly made M. Verdurin invite them to dinner for the following Wednesday. As, frequently, the tourist was obliged to leave before then, or was afraid of returning late at night, Mme Verdurin had agreed that on Saturdays she was always to be met with at teatime. There were not so very many of these tea parties, and I had known more brilliant ones in Paris at the Princesse de Guermantes's, Mme de Gallifet's, or Mme d'Arpajon's. But, then, this was no longer Paris, and for me the charm of the setting reacted not only on the attractions of the gathering but on the quality of the visitors. The encounter with some society person that, in Paris, afforded me no pleasure at all, but that, at La Raspelière, where he had come from some way off via Féterne or the forest of Chantepie, changed in character and significance, became an agreeable incident. Now and again it was someone I knew perfectly well and would not have taken a single step to meet again at the Swanns'. But his name had a different ring to it on these cliffs, like that of an actor whom you often hear in a theater appearing on the playbills in a different color for some unscheduled or gala performance, where his celebrity is suddenly magnified by the unexpectedness of the context. Since, in the country, there is no standing on ceremony, the society person would often take it upon himself to bring the friends with whom he was staying, emphasizing to Mme Verdurin in an undertone by way of an excuse that he could not leave them behind, living as he was in their house; to his hosts, in return, he made out that it was as a sort of courtesy that he was offering to introduce them to this distraction, amid the monotony of seaside life, of going into a center of the mind, of touring a magnificent house, and of eating an excellent tea. This at once made up a gathering of several half-worthy individuals; and if a small patch of garden with a few trees, which would look mean in the country, acquires an extraordinary charm on the Avenue Gabriel or the rue de Monceau, where multimillionaires alone can treat themselves to one, inversely, noblemen who take a back seat at a Paris soirée acquired their full value on Monday afternoons at La Raspelière. No sooner seated around the table, covered with a cloth embroidered in red, on which, beneath the trumeaux painted in camaïeu, they were served *galettes,* Normandy *feuilletés,* boat-shaped tarts filled with cherries like coral pearls, and "diplomats,"[8] than these guests at once underwent, from their closeness to the deep bowl of azure onto which the windows gave, and which one could not help seeing at the same time, an alteration, a profound transmutation which turned them into something more precious. What was more, even before having seen them, when you came to Mme Verdurin's on a Monday, the people who in Paris looked only with a weariness born of habit at the elegant turnouts drawn up in front of a sumptuous *hôtel,* felt their hearts beat faster at the sight of two or three wretched traps halted in front of La Raspelière, beneath the tall pine trees. No doubt it was because the rustic setting was different and,

thanks to this transposition, your social impressions had been re-
freshed. It was also because the miserable vehicle hired in order to go
and visit Mme Verdurin evoked a beautiful drive and a costly "arrangement" reached with a coachman who had demanded "so much" for the
whole day. But the faint stirrings of curiosity felt toward new arrivals, as
yet impossible to distinguish, derived also from the fact that everyone
asked themselves, "Who's it going to be?," a question that was hard to
answer, not knowing who might have arrived to spend a week at the
Cambremers' or elsewhere, but which we always like to put to ourselves
in these solitary, rural existences, in which the encounter with a human
being you have not seen for a long time, or the introduction to someone you do not know, ceases from being the tiresome affair it is living
in Paris, and makes a delightful interruption in the empty space of lives
that are too isolated, in which even the arrival of the postman becomes
a pleasure. And the day when we arrived by motorcar at La Raspelière,
since it was not a Monday, M. and Mme Verdurin must have fallen victim to that need to see company, which troubles both men and women,
and makes the invalid who has been shut away in isolation, far from his
family, to get cured, long to throw himself from the window. For the
new servant, who was more mobile, and familiarized already with such
expressions, having answered that "if Madame had not gone out she
must be at 'the Douville view' " and that he would go and find out, he
at once returned to say that she would receive us. We found her looking
a little disheveled, for she had come from the garden, the farmyard, and
the kitchen garden, where she had gone to feed her peacocks and her
chickens, to look for eggs, and to pick flowers and fruit for her "table
runner," a reminder, in miniature, of one of her garden walks; but on
the table it conferred the distinction of making it support only things
that were useful and good to eat; for around the other gifts from the
garden that were the pears and the whipped egg whites, there rose the
tall stems of viper's bugloss, pinks, roses, and coreopsis, between which
were to be seen, as if between flowering signposts, through the window-
panes, the boats going past out to sea. From the surprise that M. and
Mme Verdurin displayed, breaking off from arranging the flowers in order to receive the visitors who had been announced, on seeing that

these visitors were none other than Albertine and myself, I could tell that the new servant, full of zeal but not as yet familiar with my name, had repeated it wrongly and that Mme Verdurin, hearing the name of unknown guests, had nonetheless said for them to come in, feeling a need to see anyone at all. And the new servant was studying the spectacle from the doorway in order to understand what role we played in the household. Then he went off at a run, with long strides, for he had been taken on only the day before. Once Albertine had shown off her toque and her veil to the Verdurins, she gave me a look to remind me that we did not have too much time ahead of us for what we wished to do. Mme Verdurin wanted us to wait for tea, but we refused, when all of a sudden a plan was unveiled that would have reduced to nothing all the pleasures I had been promising myself from my outing with Albertine: the Patronne, unable to make up her mind to leave us, or perhaps to allow a new diversion to elude her, wanted to go back with us. Long accustomed to the fact that offers of this kind on her part did not give pleasure, and being uncertain probably whether this one would cause us any, she concealed the diffidence that she felt in making it beneath an excessive self-assurance, and, not even looking as though she supposed there to be any doubt as to our answer, she asked us no questions but said to her husband, referring to Albertine and me, as if she were doing us a favor, "*I'll* bring them back!" At the same time, there was applied to her lips a smile that did not belong to her personally, a smile I had already seen on certain people when they said to Bergotte, with a knowing air, "I've bought your book, it's tremendous," one of those collective, universal smiles that, when they have need of them—just as we make use of the railway and of moving vans—individuals borrow, except for a few ultra-refined ones, such as Swann or M. de Charlus, on whose lips I have never seen that particular smile settle. From that moment on, my visit was poisoned. I made a pretense of not having understood. After a moment, it became obvious that M. Verdurin would be of the party. "But M. Verdurin'll find it very long," I said. "No, no," replied Mme Verdurin with a cheerful, condescending expression, "he says it'll amuse him greatly to retrace with young people the road he traveled so often in the old days; if need be, he can get up next to the driver, that doesn't frighten him, and we'll come quietly back together by the train, like a good husband and wife. See, he looks delighted." She seemed to be talking about some great painter, old but full of bonhomie, who, younger than the young, finds delight in scrawling likenesses to get a laugh from his grandchildren. What added to my unhappiness was that Albertine seemed not to share it but to find it fun to drive all around the countryside like this with the Verdurins. For my own part, the pleasure I had promised myself I was going to take with her was so imperious that I refused to allow the Patronne to spoil it; I invented falsehoods that Mme Verdurin's irritating threats had made excusable, but which Albertine, alas, contradicted. "But we've a call to make," I said. "What call?" asked Albertine. "I'll explain, it's essential." "All right, we shall wait for you," said Mme Verdurin, resigned to anything. At the last minute, my anguish at feeling a long-desired happiness being snatched away from me lent me the courage to be impolite. I refused point-blank, alleging in Mme Verdurin's ear that, because of some trouble that Albertine had had, about which she wished to consult me, I had absolutely to be alone with her. The Patronne assumed a look of fury. "Right, we won't come," she said to me, in a voice quivering with anger. I sensed that she was so angry that, to seem to be giving way a little: "But we might have been able to . . ." "No," she went on, more furious still, "once I've said no, it's no." I thought I was in her bad books, but she called us back in the doorway to advise us not to "let her down" on Wednesday next, and not to come in that contraption, which was dangerous in the dark, but by the train with all the little group, and she got the car to stop when it was already going down the sloping driveway into the gardens because the new servant had forgotten to put in it the square of tart and the shortbreads she had had packed up for us. We set off again escorted for a moment by the little houses that had come hurrying up with their flowers. The face of the locality seemed quite altered, so far is the notion of space from playing the major role in the topographical image of each one that we create for ourselves. I have said that the notion of time divides them further. Nor is it alone. Certain scenes that we see always isolated seem to us to lack any common measure with the rest, almost outside the world, like the people whom we have known at special periods in our lives, in the army, during our childhood, whom we connect with nothing. The year of my first stay in Balbec, there was an eminence to which Mme de Villeparisis liked to take us because from it you could see nothing but the water and the woodland, and which was called Beaumont. As the road she made them take to go there, which she thought the prettiest because of its old trees, was all uphill, her carriage was obliged to go at a walk and took a very long time. The top once reached, we got down, we took a short walk, we got back into the carriage, and we returned by the same road, without having encountered a single village or a single house. I knew that Beaumont was something very curious, very distant, very high up, but I had no idea in which direction it lay, never having taken the road for Beaumont to go anywhere else; it took, in any case, a long time to get there by carriage. It obviously formed part of the same *département* (or the same province) as Balbec, but for me was situated on a different plane, and enjoyed a special privilege of extraterritoriality. But the motorcar is no respecter of mystery, and after passing Incarville, whose houses I could still see before me, and as we were descending the cross-gradient that leads to Parville (*Paterna villa*), catching sight of the sea from the piece of level ground on which we were, I asked what this place was called, and before the chauffeur had even answered, I recognized Beaumont, near to which I had thus passed without realizing it every time I took the little railway, for it was two minutes from Parville. Just like an officer in my regiment who might have struck me as someone special, too kindly and simple to be from a grand family, too remote and mysterious to be simply from a grand family, and who I learned was the brother-in-law or cousin of one or another lot of people with whom I had been to dinner, so Beaumont, linked all of a sudden to places from which I had thought it quite distinct, lost its mystery and took up its place in the region, leading me to reflect in terror that Mme Bovary and La Sanseverina[9] would perhaps have struck me as creatures like any other had I come across them anywhere except in the enclosed atmosphere of a novel. It might seem as though my love of fantastic journeys by train would have prevented me from sharing Albertine's wonderment at the motorcar, which takes us, even an invalid, where we will, and prevents us—as I had been doing up until now—from regarding their location as the individual sign, the irreplaceable essence of immovable beauties. And doubtless the motorcar did not make of this location, as the railway once had, when I had come from Paris to Balbec, an objective abstracted from the contingencies of normal life, ideal almost when you set off and which, remaining so on your arrival, the arrival in that great house where nobody lives but which simply bears the name of the town and the station, seems finally to promise its accessibility, just as it is its materialization. No, the motorcar did not carry us in this fantastic way into a town that we saw first of all as the whole encapsulated in its name, and with the illusions of a spectator in the theater. It made us go backstage, into the streets, stopping to ask directions of an inhabitant. But as compensation for this very familiar progression, you have the very hesitations of the chauffeur, unsure of his road and turning back, the *chassés-croisés* of the perspective, causing a château to play hide-and-seek with a hill, a church, and the sea, as you approach, huddle in vain though it may beneath its centuries-old foliage; these ever-tightening circles that the motorcar describes around a fascinated town that runs off in all directions in order to escape it and onto which it finally swoops down vertically, in the bottom of the valley, where the town lies prostrate; so that the motorcar, having seemed to strip the location, this unique point, of the mystery of the express train, gives us, on the contrary, the impression of discovering it, of ourselves determining it as if with a compass, of helping us to feel, with a more lovingly exploratory hand, with a more delicate precision, its true geometry, the beautiful "measure of the earth."

What I did not, alas, know at that time, and only learned more than two years later, was that one of the chauffeur's customers was M. de Charlus, and that Morel, responsible for paying him and keeping part of the money for himself (by getting the chauffeur to triple or quintuple the number of kilometers), had struck up a close friendship with him (while pretending he did not know him in front of company) and used his vehicle for distant errands. Had I known this at the time, and that the confidence which the Verdurins soon felt in this chauffeur had derived, unbeknown to them, therefrom, perhaps many of the sorrows of my life in Paris the following year, many of my misfortunes relative to

Albertine, might have been avoided; but I had not the least suspicion of it. In themselves, the drives that M. de Charlus took in the car with Morel were of no direct interest to me. They were in any case confined most often to lunch or dinner in a restaurant along the coast, where M. de Charlus passed for a penniless old domestic and Morel, whose business it was to settle the bill, for an overgenerous member of the gentry. I shall recount one of these meals, which may give an idea of the others. It was in an oblong-shaped restaurant in Saint-Mars-le-Vêtu. "Couldn't they remove this?" M. de Charlus asked Morel, as if to an intermediary, so as not to address the waiters directly. By "this" he denoted three wilted roses with which a well-intentioned *maître d'hôtel* had thought fit to decorate the table. "Yes . . . ," said Morel, embarrassed. "You don't like roses?" "I am proving, on the contrary, by the request in question that I do like them, since there are no roses here"—Morel seemed surprised—"though in point of fact I do not like them a lot. I am somewhat sensitive to names; and as soon as a rose is at all beautiful, one finds out that it is called the Baronne de Rothschild or the Maréchale Niel,[10] which puts one right off. Do you like names? Have you found some pretty titles for your little concert pieces?" "One of them's called *Poème triste*." "That's ghastly," snapped M. de Charlus in a high-pitched voice that was like a slap in the face. "Did I not ask for champagne?" he said to the *maître d'hôtel*, who supposed that he had brought some, setting two glasses filled with sparkling wine down beside the two customers. "But, monsieur . . ." "Remove this filth, which bears no relation to even the worst champagne. It's the vomitive known as 'cup' where they generally trail three rotting strawberries in a mixture of vinegar and seltzer water. . . . Yes," he went on, turning back to Morel, "you appear not to know what a title is. And even in the interpretation of what you play best, you seem not to notice the mediumistic aspects of the thing." "You're saying?" asked Morel, who, having understood not the first thing in what the Baron had said, was afraid of being deprived of some useful piece of information, such as, for example, an invitation to lunch. M. de Charlus having omitted to take "You're saying?" as a question, Morel, in consequence, having received no response, thought he should change the conversation and turn it in a sensual direction: "There, the little blonde who's selling the flowers you don't like; another one who's bound to have a young friend. And the old woman eating at the table down the end, too." "But how do you know all this?" asked M. de Charlus, amazed by Morel's pre-science. "Oh, I can see through them in an instant. If the two of us were walking in a crowd, you'd see I'm never wrong twice." And whoever had been observing Morel at that moment, with his girlish look in the midst of his masculine beauty, would have understood the obscure divination that marked him out to certain women no less than them to him. He was keen to supplant Jupien, vaguely desirous of adding to his "salary" the income that, so he believed, the waistcoat-maker was extracting from the Baron. "And I'm even more expert where gigolos are concerned, I'd help you avoid making any mistakes. It'll soon be the Balbec fair, we'd find lots of things. And then in Paris! You'd have fun, you'll see." But the hereditary wariness of a servant led him to give the sentence on which he had already begun a different twist. With the result that M. de Charlus thought it still had to do with girls. "You know," said Morel, anxious to excite the Baron's senses in a manner that he adjudged to be less compromising for himself (although it was in point of fact more immoral), "my dream would be to find a perfectly innocent young girl, make her fall in love with me, and take her virginity." M. de Charlus could not refrain from tenderly pinching Morel's ear, but added artlessly: "What good would that do you? If you took her maidenhead, you'd certainly be obliged to marry her." "Marry her?" exclaimed Morel, who felt the Baron must be drunk, or else was oblivious of the man, more scrupulous, all things considered, than he imagined, to whom he was speaking. "Marry her? Rubbish! I'd promise, but the minute the little operation had been brought to fruition, I'd ditch her the same evening." M. de Charlus was in the habit, when a fiction was able to produce in him a moment's sensual pleasure, of giving it his approval, while being prepared to withdraw this altogether a few moments later, once the pleasure had worn off. "Really, you'd do that?" he said to Morel, laughing and holding him all the tighter. "Would I not!" said Morel, seeing that he was not displeasing the Baron by continuing genuinely to explain what was indeed one of his desires. "It's dangerous," said M. de Charlus. "I'd pack my bags in advance and clear off without leaving an address." "And what about me?" asked M. de Charlus. "I'd take you with me, of course," Morel hastened to say, who had not thought about what might become of the Baron, who was the least of his concerns. "Listen, there's a little one who'd appeal to me greatly, as far as that goes, a young seamstress who has her shop in M. le Duc's house." "Jupien's daughter!"[11] exclaimed the Baron, as the sommelier entered. "Oh, never!" he added, whether because the presence of a third party had cast a chill, or because, even in these sorts of black mass during which he took pleasure in defiling the most sacred things, he could not bring himself to involve people for whom he felt friendship. "Jupien's a good fellow, the little one is charming, it would be dreadful to cause them any unhappiness." Morel sensed that he had gone too far and fell silent, but his gaze continued to fix itself, in the void, on the girl in front of whom one day he had wanted me to address him as *"cher grand artiste,"* and from whom he had ordered a waistcoat. The young girl was very hardworking and had not taken any vacation, but I have learned since that, while the violinist was in the neighborhood of Balbec, she could not stop thinking of his handsome face, ennobled by the fact that, having seen Morel with me, she had taken him for a "gentleman."

"I never heard Chopin play," said the Baron, "yet I could have, I took lessons with Stamati,[12] but he forbade me from going to hear the master of the Nocturnes at my aunt Chimay's." "What a silly thing to do!" exclaimed Morel. "On the contrary," replied M. de Charlus sharply, in a shrill voice. "It was proof of his intelligence. He'd realized I was a 'natural' and that I'd come under Chopin's influence. It doesn't matter, because I gave up music when I was quite young, like everything else, for that matter. Besides, one can use one's imagination," he added, in a protracted nasal drawl; "there are always people who did hear, who can give you an idea. But, anyway, Chopin was only a pretext for getting back to the mediumistic aspect that you're neglecting."

It will be observed that, after an interpolation in the vulgar tongue, that of M. de Charlus had abruptly become once more as precious and haughty as usual. The fact was that the idea that Morel would have no compunction in "ditching" a girl he had violated had suddenly caused him to experience total pleasure. From that moment on, his senses were appeased for a time, and the sadist (who truly was mediumistic) who had momentarily taken the place of M. de Charlus had fled and handed the floor back to the real M. de Charlus, full of artistic refinement, sensitivity, and kindness. "The other day, you played the transcription for piano of Quartet No. 15, which is absurd in itself, because nothing could be less pianistic. It's meant for people who get earache from the glorious Deaf One's overtaut strings. Yet it's that same almost sour mysticism which is divine. At all events, you played it very badly, altering all the tempi. You need to play it as if you were composing it: the young Morel, afflicted with a temporary deafness and a nonexistent genius, remains motionless for an instant; then, seized by the sacred frenzy, he plays, he composes the opening bars; then, exhausted by this attempt to cast a spell, he collapses, letting his pretty lock of hair fall to please Mme Verdurin, and takes the time, in addition, to re-create the prodigious quantity of gray matter that he called upon for the Pythic objectification; then, having recovered his strength, and, seized by a fresh, supereminent inspiration, he springs toward the sublime, inexhaustible phrase that the Berlin virtuoso"—we believe M. de Charlus was here referring to Mendelssohn—"was unwearyingly to imitate. It's in this, the one truly transcendent and enlivening manner, that I shall make you play in Paris." When M. de Charlus gave him advice of this nature, Morel was much more alarmed than on seeing the *maître d'hôtel* remove his spurned roses and "cup," for he asked himself anxiously what effect this might have on the "class." But he could not dwell on these reflections, for M. de Charlus was saying to him imperiously, "Ask the *maître d'hôtel* if he's got any *bons Chrétiens*." "*Bons Chrétiens?* I don't understand." "As you can see, we've got to the fruit, it's a pear. You can be sure Mme de Cambremer'll have some at her house, because the Comtesse d'Escarbagnas, which she is, used to have them. M. Thibaudier sends them to her and she says, 'Here's a really beautiful *bon Chrétien.*' "[13] "No, I didn't know." "I can see, for that matter, that you don't know anything. If you haven't even read Molière ... Oh well, since you can't know how to order any more than the rest, quite simply ask for a pear that's in fact picked near here, the *Louise-bonne d'Avranches.*" "The ... ?" "Wait, since you're so awkward, I'll ask myself for others that I prefer. *Maître d'hôtel*, do you have any *doyenné des comices?* Charlie, you must read the ravishing passage written about that pear by the Duchesse Émilie de Clermont-Tonnerre." "No, monsieur, I don't have any." "Do you have any *triomphe de Jodoignes?*" "No, monsieur." "Any *Virginie-dallet?* Any *passe-Colmar?* No? Oh well, since you don't have anything, we shall leave. The *Duchesse d'Angoulêmes* aren't yet ripe; come, Charlie, we're going." Unfortunately for M. de Charlus, his lack of common sense, and perhaps the chasteness of the relationship he probably enjoyed with Morel, made him rack his brains from that time on to overwhelm the violinist with strange acts of kindness that the latter could not understand, and to which his nature, wild in its way, yet also mean and ungrateful, could respond only with an ever-increasing indifference or violence, which plunged M. de Charlus—once so proud, now quite timid—into fits of genuine despair. We shall see how, in the smallest things, Morel, who saw himself as having become an infinitely more important M. de Charlus, had understood amiss, by taking them literally, the Baron's arrogant teachings concerning the aristocracy. For the present, let me simply say, while Albertine is waiting for me in Saint-Jean-de-la-Haise, that if there was one thing that Morel set above the nobility (and this was, as a principle, noble enough, especially in someone whose pleasure it was to go in search of young girls—"without anyone's being any the wiser"—with the chauffeur) it was his artistic reputation and what his violin class might think. It was ugly, no doubt, that, because he felt M. de Charlus belonged exclusively to him, he should have appeared to disown him, to make fun of him, just as, the moment I had promised to keep the secret of his father's duties at my great-uncle's, he treated me with lordly disdain. On the other hand, his name as an artist graduated from the Conservatoire, Morel, seemed to him superior to a "name." And when M. de Charlus, in his dreams of Platonic affection, tried to make him accept a title from his own family, Morel energetically refused.

When Albertine found it more sensible to stay in Saint-Jean-de-la-Haise to paint, I would take the car, and it was not just to Gourville and Féterne, but to Saint-Mars-le-Vieux and as far as Criquetot, that I was able to go before returning to collect her. While pretending to have other things than her on my mind, and to be obliged to desert her for other pleasures, I thought only about her. Very often, I went no farther than the broad plain that overlooks Gourville, and since it a little resembles that which begins above Combray, in the direction of Méséglise, even when quite some distance from Albertine I had the joy of reflecting that, though my gaze might not be able to go all the way to her, the powerful but mild sea breeze that was passing beside me would outreach it, would go hurrying down, with nothing that might arrest it, all the way to Quetteholme, and come to stir the branches of the trees that bury Saint-Jean-de-la-Haise beneath their foliage, caressing the face of my loved one, and thus throw up a double link between her and me in this indefinitely enlarged yet safe retreat, as in those games when two children find themselves momentarily out of sight and earshot of one another, yet, though separated, remain joined. I returned by the roads from which you can see the sea, and where once, before it appeared between the branches, I used to close my eyes to reflect that what I was about to see was indeed the plaintive ancestress of the earth, pursuing, as in the days when no human beings as yet existed, its crazed, immemorial agitation. Now they were nothing more for me than the means of going to rejoin Albertine; when I recognized them, quite unchanged, knowing how far they would run straight ahead, and where they would bend, I remembered that I had followed them thinking of Mlle de Stermaria, and that I had been in just the same hurry to find Albertine again in Paris, when going down the streets along which Mme de Guermantes had passed; they had taken on for me the profound monotony and the moral significance of a sort of line that my character was following. It was natural, but not thereby a matter of indifference; they reminded me that my fate was to pursue only phantoms, beings whose reality lay in large part in my imagination; there are human beings indeed—and this had been my own case since my early days—for whom whatever has a fixed value, recognizable by others, fortune, success, a high position, counts for nothing; what they must have is phantoms. To this they sacrifice all the rest, use every possible means, bend all their efforts, to encounter some phantom. But the latter is not long in vanishing; then they pursue some other phantom, while being ready to return later to the first one. This was not the first time that I had gone in search of Albertine, the girl glimpsed that first year in front of the sea. Other women, it was true, had been interposed between the Albertine loved on that first occasion and the one whom at present I hardly ever left; other women, notably the Duchesse de Guermantes. But, people will say, why agonize so over Gilberte, or go to so much trouble over Mme de Guermantes, if, having become the latter's friend, it was solely in order not to think about her any more, but only about Albertine? Swann, before his death, might have known the answer, he who had been a connoisseur of phantoms. These Balbec roads were full of them, of phantoms pursued, forgotten, sought after afresh, sometimes for a single interview and so as to touch an unreal life that had at once made its escape. Reflecting that their trees, pears, apples, and tamarisks would outlive me, I seemed to be receiving from them the advice finally to set to work while the hour of eternal rest had yet to sound.

I got out of the car in Quetteholme, ran down the steep, sunken lane, crossed the stream by a plank, and found Albertine painting in front of the church, which was all turrets, thorny and red, in blossom like a rosebush. The tympanum alone was smooth; and on the smiling surface of the stone there appeared angels, who continued, before our twentieth-century couple, to celebrate, taper in hand, the ceremonies of the thirteenth. It was they whose portrait Albertine was attempting to paint on her prepared canvas, and, in imitation of Elstir, she was making long strokes with the brush, attempting to obey the noble rhythm that, the great master had told her, made these angels so different from all those that he knew. Then she gathered up her things. Leaning against each other, we reascended the sunken lane, leaving the little church as quiet as if it had not seen us, to listen to the constant sound of the stream. Soon the car was speeding along, taking us a different road back from the one we had come by. We passed in front of Marcouville-l'Orgueilleuse. Over its church, half new, half restored, the declining sun had spread a patina as lovely as that of the centuries. Through it, the great bas-reliefs seemed to be seen only beneath a fluid coating, half liquid, half luminous; the Holy Virgin, Saint Elizabeth, Saint Joachim were still swimming in the impalpable eddies, almost in the dry, on the surface of the water or the sunlight. Looming suddenly into view in a warm dust, the numerous modern statues rose on their columns, halfway up the golden veils of the sunset. In front of the church, a tall cypress seemed to be in a sort of consecrated enclosure. We got out for a moment to look at it, and took a few steps. As much as of her limbs, Albertine was directly conscious of her Italian straw toque and her silk scarf (which for her were no lesser a seat of feelings of well-being), and received from them, as we walked around the church, another kind of impulsion, betrayed by a contentment that was inert yet which for me had charm; a scarf and toque that were only a recent, adventitious part of my loved one, but which was already dear to me and whose wake I followed with my eyes, along the cypress, in the evening air. She herself could not see it, but suspected that this elegance was having its effect, for she smiled at me, cocking her head in harmony with the headgear that completed it: "It doesn't appeal to me, it's been restored," she said, pointing to the church and remembering what Elstir had said to her about the precious, the inimitable beauty of the old stonework. Albertine knew at once how to recognize a restoration. You could not but be astonished at the sureness of taste that she already possessed in architecture, instead of the deplorable taste she had preserved in music. No more than had Elstir did I like this church; it was without affording me any pleasure that its sunlit façade had come and set itself down before my eyes, and I had got out to look at it only as a kindness to Albertine. Yet I found that the great Impressionist was in contradiction with himself; why make a fetish of the objective architectural value, without taking any account of the transfiguration of the church in the setting sun? "No, I definitely don't like it," Albertine said. "I like its name of Orgueilleuse. But what we must remember to ask Brichot is why Saint-Mars is called 'le Vêtu.' We'll go next time, won't we?" she said, looking at me out of her black eyes, over which her toque had been pulled down, like her little cap in the old days. Her veil was floating loose. I got back into the car with her, glad that the next day we were to go together to Saint-Mars, where, in this torrid weather, when your one thought was of bathing, the two ancient, salmon-pink belfries, with their diamond-shaped tiles, slightly out of true and as if palpitating, looked like old, pointed fish, imbricated with scales, moss-covered and ruddy, which, without appearing to move, were rising in a blue, transparent water. On leaving Marcouville, to take a short cut, we forked off at a crossroads where there is a farm. Sometimes Albertine made us stop there and asked me to go on my own and fetch, so that she could drink it in the car, some Calvados or cider, which we were assured was not fizzy yet which sprayed all over us. We sat pressed one against the other. The people from the farm could barely see Albertine in the closed car, and I gave them back the bottles; we left again, as if to carry on with our life, the two of us together, with the lovers' life which they may have supposed we led, in which this pause to drink would have been simply one insignificant moment; a supposition that might have seemed all the less improbable had they seen us after Albertine had drunk her bottle of cider; she then, indeed, seemed unable any longer to tolerate a gap between herself and me, which normally did not trouble her; under her linen skirt her legs were pressed against my legs, she brought close to mine cheeks that had become pallid, hot, and red over the cheekbones, with something burning and faded about them such as street girls have in the suburbs. At these times, she changed her voice almost as quickly as her personality, lost her own in order to assume another, hoarse, brazen, almost crapulous. Dusk was falling. What a pleasure to feel her against me, with her scarf and her toque, reminding me that it is always thus, side by side, that we encounter those who love one another! I perhaps felt love for Albertine, but did not dare to let her see it, so that if it existed in me it could only be as a truth without value until it had been able to be verified by experience; but it seemed to me unrealizable, and outside the plane of life. As for my jealousy, it led me to leave Albertine as seldom as possible, although I knew that it would be cured altogether only by parting from her forever. I was even capable of feeling it in her presence, but then contrived not to allow the circumstances to recur that had excited it. Thus it was that, on a day of fine weather, we went to have lunch in Rivebelle. The big glass doors of the dining room, and of the corridor-shaped hall that was used for teas, had been opened, level with the lawns, turned to gold by the sun, of which the huge, luminous restaurant seemed to form part. The waiter with the pink face, and the black hair twisted like a flame, dashed about in this vast expanse less rapidly than before, for he was no longer a *commis* but a *chef de rang;* nevertheless, because of his natural industry, now in the distance, in the dining

room, and now closer up, but outside, serving customers who had preferred to eat in the garden, you saw him first in one place, then in another, like the successive statues of a young god running, some in
the—well-lit—interior of a house that extended into the green lawn, others beneath the foliage, in the bright light of life in the open air. Momentarily, he was at our side. Albertine replied distractedly to what I
had been saying. She was gazing at him through widened eyes. For a
minute or two, I felt that you could be close to the person that you love
yet not have them with you. They appeared to be involved in a mysterious tête-à-tête, rendered wordless by my presence, and the continuation
perhaps of former assignations of which I knew nothing, or simply of a
look that he had given her—where I was the intrusive third party from
whom one hides. Even when, after a violent summons from his superior, he had gone off, Albertine, while continuing to eat her lunch, appeared to regard the restaurant and gardens as nothing more than an
illuminated running track, on which there appeared here and there,
against various backgrounds, the running god with the black hair. For a
moment I wondered whether, in order to follow him, she might not be
going to leave me on my own at the table. But from the days that followed I began to forget this painful impression once and for all, because I had decided never to return to Rivebelle, and had made
Albertine promise, who assured me that this was the first time she had
been there, that she would never go back. And I denied that the waiter
with the nimble feet had had eyes only for her, so that she might not
believe that my company had deprived her of a pleasure. It so happened that I did, on occasion, go back to Rivebelle, but alone, and
drank too much, as I had done there before. As I drained a last glass, I
looked at a rosette painted on the white wall, and transferred onto it the
pleasure that I felt. It alone in the world existed for me; I pursued it,
touched it, and lost it by turns with my shifting gaze, and I was indifferent to the future, content with my rosette, like a butterfly that circles
about a butterfly that has settled, with which it is about to end its life in
an act of supreme voluptuousness. But I thought it dangerous to allow
there to take up residence in me, in however mild a form, a sickness
that resembles those habitual pathological states to which we pay no
heed, but that, should the least accident, unforeseeable but inevitable,

befall it, suffice at once to lend it an extreme gravity. The moment was particularly well chosen perhaps to renounce a woman whom no very recent or very acute suffering obliged me to ask for that balm against a sickness that those who have caused it possess. I was calmed by these same excursions, which, although I looked on them at the time simply as an anticipation of a tomorrow that itself, in spite of the longing with which it filled me, would be no different from the day before, had the attraction of having been wrenched away from the places where Albertine had been until now but where I had not been with her, at her aunt's, or at her girlfriends'. The attraction not of a positive joy, but simply of the allaying of an anxiety, yet very powerful even so. For, within the space of a few days, when I thought back to the farm in front of which we had drunk our cider, or simply to the few steps we had taken in front of Saint-Mars-le-Vêtu, remembering that Albertine had walked beside me under her toque, the sense of her presence added such healing properties all of a sudden to the indifferent image of the new church that, at the moment when the sunlit façade came thus and set itself down of its own accord in my memory, it was like a great soothing compress that had been applied to my heart. I set Albertine down in Parville, but only so as to meet her again in the evening and go and stretch out beside her, in the darkness, on the shore. I did not see her every day, it is true, yet I was able to tell myself, "Were she to recount the timetable of her life, it's I still who would have pride of place"; and we passed long hours on end together, which introduced so sweet an intoxication into my days that, even when, in Parville, she jumped down from the car that I would be sending back for her in an hour's time, I no more felt alone in the car than if, before getting out, she had left flowers behind. I could have gone without seeing her every day; I would be happy when I left her, I sensed that the calming effect of this happiness might endure for several days. But then I would hear Albertine, as she left me, saying to her aunt or to a girlfriend: "Tomorrow at eight-thirty, then. We mustn't be late, they'll be ready by a quarter past eight." The conversation of a woman that you love is like the earth covering a dangerous, subterranean lake; you are constantly aware of the presence, behind the words, of the penetrating cold of an invisible sheet of water; here and there it is to be seen oozing perfidiously out, but the lake itself remains hidden. As soon as I heard Albertine's words, my calm was destroyed. I wanted to ask to see her the next morning, so as to prevent her going to this mysterious rendezvous at half past eight, which had been referred to in my presence only in veiled terms. She would no doubt have obeyed me the first times, while regretting having to give up her plans; then she would have discovered my permanent need to disrupt them; I would be the one from whom everything must be kept. It is of course likely that these entertainments from which I was excluded amounted to very little, and that it was perhaps out of a fear that I might find one or another female guest vulgar or tedious that I was not invited. Unfortunately, this life, so closely involved with that of Albertine, did not have its effect only on myself; to me it brought peace of mind; in my mother it caused anxieties the confession of which destroyed that peace of mind. As I returned home contented, determined to bring to an end from one day to the next an existence whose termination I believed depended on my own volition alone, my mother said to me, hearing me send to the chauffeur to go and fetch Albertine after dinner, "All the money you're spending!" (Françoise, in her simple and expressive language, put it more forcefully: "Money burns a hole in your pocket.") "Try," Mamma went on, "not to become like Charles de Sévigné, whose mother used to say, 'His hand is a crucible in which money melts.' Besides, I do think you've been out enough with Albertine. I assure you, you're overdoing it, that even she may find it ridiculous. I've been delighted that it takes your mind off things, I'm not asking you not to see her again, but just so that's it's not impossible to meet one of you without the other." My life with Albertine, a life devoid of great pleasures—as perceived by me, at least—this life that I was counting on changing from one day to the next, by choosing a moment of calm, suddenly became necessary to me once again for a time, when it found itself under threat from Mamma's words. I told my mother that her words had just put back by two months perhaps the decision that they were demanding, which, but for them, would have been taken by the end of the week. Mamma began to laugh (so as not to make me unhappy) at the effect that her advice had instantly produced, and promised not to mention it again so as not to prevent my good intentions from being revived. But since my grandmother's death, every time that Mamma allowed herself to laugh, the laughter was cut short almost before it began, and ended on an almost sobbing expression of suffering, either out of remorse at having been able for a moment to forget, or else out of the recrudescence whereby this short-lived forgetfulness had again revived her cruel preoccupation. But to that caused by the memory of my grandmother, lodged in my mother like an *idée fixe,* I sensed that this time another preoccupation had been added, having to do with myself, and with the fact that my mother dreaded the consequences of my intimacy with Albertine; an intimacy she did not dare stand in the way of, however, on account of what I had just told her. But she did not seem convinced that I was not deceiving myself. She could remember all those years during which she and my grandmother had no longer raised the question of my work or of a healthy form of life, on which, I used to say, only the agitation into which their exhortations cast me was preventing me from starting, but which, despite their obedient silence, I had not pursued.

After dinner the car brought Albertine back; there was still a little daylight left; the air was less hot, but after a burning-hot day we were both dreaming of unknown forms of coolness; then, to our fevered eyes, the moon appeared, all narrow at first (as on the evening when I had gone to the Princesse de Guermantes's and when Albertine had telephoned me), like the thin, fragile rind, then like the fresh quarter of a fruit that an invisible knife had begun to peel in the sky. On occasion, it was I who went to fetch my loved one, a little later in that case; she was to wait for me in front of the market arcade in Maineville. To start with, I could not make her out; I was already worried that she might not be coming, that she had misunderstood. Then I would find her, in her white blouse with the blue polka dots, jumping into the car beside me with the light spring more of a young animal than of a girl. And it was like a dog, again, that she at once began endlessly to fondle me. Once the darkness was complete and, as the manager of the hotel used to say, the sky was all skittered with stars, if we did not go for a drive in the forest with a bottle of champagne, unconcerned by the strollers still sauntering along the dimly lit esplanade, who would not have been able to see a thing two paces away on the black sand, we would stretch out below the dunes; and that same body, in whose suppleness there lived all the feminine, marine, and sportive grace of the girls I had seen that first time passing across the horizon of the waves, I now held it pressed tightly against my own, under the same rug, on the very edge of the motionless sea, divided by a trembling shaft of moonlight; and we listened to it without wearying and with the same pleasure, whether as it held its breath, long enough suspended for you to suppose its reflux had been halted, or as, finally, it exhaled the anticipated but delayed murmur at our feet. In the end, I would take Albertine back to Parville. Having arrived in front of the house, we had to interrupt our kisses for fear of being seen; having no desire to go to bed, she would come back with me as far as Balbec, from where I took her back for a last time to Parville; in those early days of the motorcar, chauffeurs were men who went to bed at all hours. In fact, I got home to Balbec only with the first dampness of early morning, alone this time, but still surrounded by the presence of my loved one, gorged with a supply of kisses that I would be long in exhausting. On my table I would find a telegram or a postcard. It was from Albertine again! She had written them at Quetteholme while I was off on my own in the car, to tell me that she was thinking of me. I reread them as I got into bed. Then, above the curtains, I would see the band of broad daylight and tell myself that we must be in love after all, to have spent the night kissing each other. When, the next morning, I saw Albertine on the esplanade, I was so afraid that she would answer that she was not free that day and could not agree to my request that we go out together that I delayed for as long as I could before making it. I was the more concerned in that she appeared distant and preoccupied; people of her acquaintance were passing; no doubt she had made plans for that afternoon from which I was excluded. I looked at her, I looked at that entrancing body, at those pink features of Albertine's, raising the enigma of their intentions in front of me, the unknown decision on which turned the happiness or unhappiness of my afternoon. It was a whole state of being, a whole future existence, which had assumed in front of me the fateful, allegorical form of a girl. And when at last I had come to a decision, when, with as indifferent an air as I could, I asked, "Shall we go off together this afternoon and this evening?," and she replied, "I'd love to," then the whole sudden replacement, in that pink face, of my prolonged anxiety by a delectable quietude made more precious to me still those contours to which I was perpetually indebted for my well-being, the assuagement we feel after a storm has broken. I repeated to myself, "She's so sweet, what an adorable creature!" in an exaltation less fertile than that owed to intoxication, hardly any more profound than that of friendship, but much superior to that of life in society. We canceled the car only on the days when there was a dinner party at the Verdurins', and on those when, Albertine not being free to go out with me, I took the opportunity to let the people who wished to visit me know that I would be remaining in Balbec. I authorized Saint-Loup to come on these days, but on these days alone. For once when he had arrived without warning, I had preferred to forgo seeing Albertine rather than risk his meeting her, jeopardizing the state of contented calm in which I had been for some time now, and reviving my jealousy. I felt easy in my mind only once Saint-Loup had left again. He therefore bound himself, regretfully but scrupulously, never to come to Balbec without a summons from me. In the old days, reflecting enviously on the hours that Mme de Guermantes spent with him, I had set such great store by seeing him! People never cease to change position in relation to ourselves. In the world's imperceptible but everlasting march, we think of them as motionless, in a moment of vision, too brief for us to perceive the motion that is bearing them along. But we need only choose from our memory two pictures of them taken at different times, yet sufficiently close together for them not to have changed in themselves, perceptibly at least, and the difference between the two pictures measures the displacement they have effected relative to ourselves. He worried me dreadfully by talking about the Verdurins; I was afraid he might ask me to have him received there, which would have been enough, because of the jealousy I would not have ceased to feel, to mar all the pleasure that I enjoyed there with Albertine. But happily, Robert admitted that, quite to the contrary, he wished above all not to meet them. "No," he said, "I find that type of clerical circle exasperating." I did not at first understand the adjective "clerical" as applied to the Verdurins, but Saint-Loup's concluding words enlightened me as to his thought, and to the concessions to linguistic fashion that one is often surprised to find adopted by intelligent men. "They're circles," he said, "where they play at being tribes, where they play at being congregations and chapels. You're not going to tell me it isn't a small sect; they're all sweetness and light to the people who belong, and couldn't be more contemptuous of the ones who don't. The question isn't, as for Hamlet, to be or not to be, but to be one of them or not to be one of them. You're one, my uncle Charlus is one. What d'you expect? I've never liked all that, it's not my fault."

Naturally, I enacted the rule I had imposed on Saint-Loup, not to come and visit me except when summoned, equally strictly in the case of the people, whoever they were, with whom I had gradually become friendly in La Raspelière, Féterne, Montsurvent, and elsewhere; and when from the hotel I saw the smoke of the three o'clock train, whose plume long remained stationary, clinging to the sides of the green slopes in the anfractuosities of the Parville cliffs, I felt no hesitation concerning the visitor who was coming to have tea with me but was as yet, in the manner of a god, concealed beneath that little cloud. I am obliged to confess that this visitor, previously authorized by me to come, was almost never Saniette, and I have often reproached myself for this. But Saniette's consciousness of being a bore (even more so when paying a visit, naturally, than when recounting a story) meant that, although he was better educated, more intelligent, and better than many others, it seemed impossible to experience in his company, not only any pleasure, but anything except an almost intolerable lowness of spirits which spoiled your afternoon. Probably, if Saniette had confessed openly to the boredom he was afraid of causing, you would not have dreaded his visits. Boredom is one of the less serious evils that we have to endure, and his existed perhaps only in the imagination of others, or had been inoculated in him thanks to a kind of suggestion through them, which had found a purchase on his likable modesty. But so anxious was he not to let it be seen that he was not sought after, that he did not dare offer himself. Admittedly, he was right not to behave as the people do who are so glad to take off their hats to you in a public place that, not having seen you in a long while but catching sight of you in a box together with a brilliant set whom they do not know, they cast you a furtive but resounding good evening, while apologizing for the pleasure, for the emotion, they felt on seeing you, on discovering that you were returning to old pleasures, that you were looking so well, and so forth. Saniette, on the contrary, was far too lacking in boldness. He could, at the Verdurins' or in the little tram, have told me that he would have great pleasure in coming to call on me in Balbec were he not afraid of putting me out. Such a proposal would not have alarmed me. On the contrary, he offered nothing, but with a tortured face and a gaze as indestructible as a fired enamel, but into the composition of which there entered, together with a breathless desire to see you—unless he found someone more amusing—the determination not to let that desire show, he said to me with a detached air: "You don't know what you're doing these days? Because I'll no doubt be coming near Balbec. But, no, it's of no account, I was only asking you on the off chance." There was no mistaking his expression, and the inverse signs with the help of which we express our feelings by their opposite are so transparent that you wonder how there can still be people who say, for example, "I've had so many invitations I don't know which way to turn," to hide the fact that they have not been invited. Moreover, this offhand air, because most likely of what had entered into its turbid composition, produced in you what the fear of boredom or a frank admission of the desire to call on you could never have produced, namely, that sort of unease, or repulsion, which, in the order of relations of simple social politeness, is the equivalent of the disguised offer made to a lady during a love affair by the lover whom she does not love, to see her the following day, while protesting that he does not insist, or not even this offer, but an attitude of false indifference. There at once emanated from Saniette's person some *je ne sais quoi* that meant that you answered him wearing the most affectionate of expressions, "No, unfortunately, this week, I'll explain . . ." And I allowed there to come instead people who were by no means his equal but who did not have his melancholy-filled eyes, or a mouth puckered by all the bitterness of all the visits that he longed, while not saying a word, to pay to one person or another. Unfortunately, only rarely did Saniette fail to meet on the "slow coach" the guest who had just been to see me, even supposing that the latter had not said to me, at the Verdurins', "Don't forget I'll be coming to see you on Thursday," the selfsame day on which I had told Saniette I would not be free. So that he ended up by imagining life as being filled with amusements arranged without him knowing, if not actually against him. On the other hand, since we are never all of a piece, this too discreet man was morbidly indiscreet. The one time when he chanced to call on me in my despite, a letter, from I forget whom, was lying on the table. After a moment, I saw that he was listening with only half an ear to what I was telling him. The letter, of whose provenance he was wholly ignorant, had fascinated him, and I thought that at any moment his enameled eyes were going to detach themselves from their sockets and join the letter, without importance yet which his curiosity had magnetized. He was like a bird that is about to hurl itself fatally at a snake. Finally, he could no longer restrain himself, and first of all changed its position as if he were tidying up my room. This being no longer enough for him, he picked it up, turned it over, turned it back again, as if mechanically. Another form of tactlessness was that, once riveted to you, he could not leave. As I was unwell on the day in question, I asked him to catch the next train and leave in half an hour. He did not doubt I was unwell, but replied, "I'll stay for an hour and a quarter, and after that I'll go." Since then, I have suffered for not having told him, whenever I could have done so, to come. Who knows? Perhaps I would have exorcised his ill-fate, others might have invited him, for whom he would at once have given me up, so that my invitations would have had the twofold advantage of restoring his happiness and ridding myself of him.

On the days that followed those on which I entertained, I was naturally not expecting any visits, and the car returned to fetch us, Albertine and me. And when we got back, Aimé, on the top step of the hotel, could not help watching, through impassioned, inquisitive, and greedy eyes, to see what tip I was giving the chauffeur. It was no use my closing my fist around my coin or note, Aimé's gaze would part my fingers. He would look away a moment later for he was discreet, well brought up, and himself content with relatively small perquisites. But the money someone else received aroused an incompressible curiosity in him and made his mouth water. For a few brief instants, he would wear the feverish, attentive expression of a child reading a Jules Verne novel, or of a diner sitting not far away from you in a restaurant who, seeing them carving for you a pheasant to which he cannot or will not treat himself, abandons his serious thoughts for an instant to fix on the poultry eyes made to smile by love and envy.

Thus did these excursions by motorcar follow one another daily. But one time, just as I was going back up in the lift, the lift boy said to me, "This gentleman came, he left me a message for you." The lift boy spoke these words in a terribly croaky voice, and coughing and spitting in my face. "I've got such a bad cold!" he added, as if I were incapable of noticing it for myself. "The doctor says it's whooping cough," and he began again to cough and spit over me. "Don't tire yourself by talking," I said with a kindly expression, which was put on. I was afraid of catching whooping cough, which, with my tendency to breathless attacks, would have been very distressing. But, like a virtuoso refusing to cry off sick, he prided himself on talking and spitting all the while. "No, it doesn't matter," he said (to you perhaps, I thought, but not to me). "Anyway, I'll soon be going back to Paris" (so much the better, provided he does not give it to me first). "It seems," he went on, "that Paris is very magnificent. It must be even more magnificent than here and than Monte Carlo, although *chasseurs,* guests even, and all the way up to *maîtres d'hôtel* who used to go to Monte Carlo for the season, have often told me that Paris was less magnificent than Monte Carlo. They got it wrong maybe, though to become a *maître d'hôtel* you mustn't be an imbecile; you need brains in your head to take all the orders and reserve the tables! I've been told it's even more terrifying than writing plays and books." We had almost reached my floor when the "lift" made me go all the way down again because he had found the button was not working properly, and in a trice he had fixed it. I told him I preferred to go back up on foot, the hidden meaning of which was that I preferred not to catch whooping cough. But with a cordial and contagious fit of coughing, the lift boy thrust me back into the lift. "There's no longer any risk, I've fixed the button." Seeing that he had not left off talking, and preferring to know the name of my visitor and the message he had left to the parallels between the beauties of Balbec, Paris, and Monte Carlo, I said to him (as to a tenor who is overtaxing you with Benjamin Godard,[14] "Sing me some Debussy instead"), "But who was it who came to see me?" "It was the gentleman you went out with yesterday. I'll go and fetch his card, it's with the porter." Since the day before I had dropped Saint-Loup off at the station in Doncières before going to fetch Albertine, I thought the "lift" meant Saint-Loup, but it was the chauffeur. And by referring to him as "the gentleman you went out with," he had taught me at the same time that a workman is just as much a gentleman as is a society man. A verbal lesson simply. Because, as for the thing itself, I had never made any distinction between the classes. And if, on hearing a chauffeur referred to as a gentleman, I had felt the same astonishment as the Comte X, who had been that only for the past week and whom, by saying "the Comtesse looks tired," I had caused to look behind him to see whom I was talking about, this was simply because I was unused to the vocabulary; I had never discriminated between workmen, bourgeois, and great noblemen, but would have accepted all of them as friends without distinction, with a certain preference for workmen, and after them the noblemen, not from taste, but knowing that you can demand greater courtesy from them toward workmen than you can obtain from the bourgeoisie, either because great noblemen do not despise workmen, as the bourgeoisie does, or else because they are ready to be courteous to anyone at all, like pretty women, happy to bestow a smile they know will be received with so much delight. I cannot say, on the other hand, that this way that I had of putting the common people on an equal footing with members of society, although the latter were very happy to accept it, always gave my mother entire satisfaction. Not that, humanly speaking, she made any distinction at all between people, and if ever Françoise was upset or unwell, she was always comforted and tended by Mamma with the same affection and the same devotion as her best friend. But my mother was too much my grandfather's daughter not, socially speaking, to be a respecter of caste. For all that the people of Combray showed themselves kindhearted and sensitive, and had taken on the noblest theories of human equality, my mother, when a *valet de chambre* got above himself, used *vous* one time and slipped imperceptibly into no longer addressing me in the third person, showed the same displeasure at these usurpations as bursts out in Saint-Simon's *Memoirs* each time a nobleman who has no right to it seizes on a pretext to assume the title of "Highness" in some legal instrument, or not to show a proper deference to dukes, with which he gradually dispenses. There was a "Combray spirit," so refractory that it will take centuries of kindness (my mother's was boundless), and of egalitarian theories, to succeed in dissolving it. I cannot say that, in my mother's case, certain particles of this spirit had not remained insoluble. She would have found it as hard to offer her hand to a manservant as it was easy to give him ten francs (which anyway afforded him far greater pleasure). For her, whether she admitted it or not, masters were masters, and servants the people who ate in the kitchen. When she saw a chauffeur eating with me in the dining room, she was not altogether pleased, and used to say to me, "It seems to me you could do better where friends are concerned than a mechanic," as she might have said, were it a question of marrying, "You could find a better match." The chauffeur (luckily, I had never thought of inviting this one) had come to tell me that the car company that had sent him to Balbec for the season was recalling him to Paris as of tomorrow. This excuse, all the more so because the chauffeur was charming and expressed himself so simply that you would always have said it was the Gospel truth, seemed to us to have to conform to the truth. It only half did so. There was indeed nothing to do any more in Balbec. And in any case, the company only half trusting in the veracity of the young evangelist, bent over his wheel of consecration, wished for him to return to Paris as soon as possible. And indeed, if the young apostle had achieved a miraculous multiplication of the kilometers when reckoning them up for M. de Charlus, in return, once it was a question of accounting to his company, he divided what he had earned by six. As a consequence of which, the company, believing either that no one was any longer taking excursions in Balbec, which the season made seem plausible, or that it was being robbed, considered that on either one of these hypotheses the best thing was to summon him back to Paris, where, as it happens, there was also little activity. The desire of the chauffeur was to avoid, if possible, the off season. I have said—what I did not then know, and knowledge of which would have spared me much unhappiness—that he was very friendly (without their ever seeming to be acquainted in front of other people) with Morel. As of the day on which he was recalled, without our yet knowing he had a means of not leaving, we had to make do for our excursions with hiring a carriage, or sometimes, in order to amuse Albertine and since she liked riding, saddle horses. The carriages were bad. "What an old rattletrap!" Albertine would say. I would anyway often have liked to be in them on my own. Without being willing to fix a date, I wanted an end to this life, which I reproached with making me renounce not so much work as pleasure. However, it could also happen that the habits which were holding me back were suddenly abolished, most often when some former self, full of the desire to live with cheerfulness, replaced my present self momentarily. I experienced this longing for escape most notably one day when, having left Albertine at her aunt's, I rode over on horseback to call on the Verdurins and had taken an unmarked route through the woods whose beauty they had extolled to me. Hugging the contours of the cliffs, by turns it climbed and then, hemmed in between dense clumps of trees, sank deep into wild gorges. For a moment, the bare rocks by which I was surrounded, and the sea, which could be glimpsed through the jagged gaps, floated before my eyes like fragments from some other universe: I had recognized the landscape of mountains and sea that Elstir has used as the setting for those two admirable watercolors, *Poet Meeting with a Muse* and *Young Man Meeting with a Centaur*, which I had seen at the Duchesse de Guermantes's. The memory of them relocated the place in which I found myself so far outside the present-day world that I would not have been surprised if, like the young man of ante-historic times painted by Elstir, I had in the course of my ride come upon some mythological personage. All of a sudden my horse reared; he had heard a strange noise; I had difficulty in controlling him and not being thrown to the ground; then I raised my tear-filled eyes to the spot from where the noise appeared to be coming, and I saw, fifty meters or so above me, in the sunlight, between two great wings of glittering steel that were bearing him away, a being whose indistinct face I fancied resembled that of a man. I was moved as might a Greek have been setting eyes for the first time on a demigod. I was weeping also, for I had been ready to weep from the moment when I recognized that the noise was coming from above my head—airplanes were still a rarity in those days—and at the thought that what I was about to see for the first time was an airplane. Then, as when you sense some moving words to be approaching in a newspaper, I waited only to have seen the airplane before bursting into tears. The aviator, meanwhile, seemed to be hesitating over his course; I felt there to lie open before him—before me, had habit not made me its prisoner—every course through space, or through life; he flew farther on, glided for a moment or two above the sea, then, abruptly making up his mind, seeming to yield to some inverse attraction to that of gravity, as if returning to his native land, with a slight movement of his golden wings, he headed straight up into the sky.

To come back to the mechanic, he asked of Morel not just that the Verdurins should replace their carriage with a car (which, given the Verdurins' generosity in respect of the faithful, was relatively easy), but also, something much more awkward, their head coachman, the sensitive young man given to gloomy thoughts, by him, the chauffeur. This was effected within a few days in the following manner. Morel had begun by getting them to steal from the coachman everything he needed to harness up. One day he could not find the bit, another day the curb chain. On other occasions it was his seat cushion that had vanished, or even his whip, his blanket, the martingale, the sponge, the chamois leather. But he always came to an arrangement with neighbors; only he would arrive late, which made M. Verdurin annoyed with him, and plunged him into a state of sadness and black thoughts. The chauffeur, in a hurry to be taken on, declared to Morel that he was returning to Paris. Some masterstroke was required. Morel persuaded M. Verdurin's menservants that the young coachman had declared that he was going to lead them all into an ambush and had boasted of getting the better of all six of them, and he told them that they could not allow this to happen. For his own part, he could not get involved, but he was warning them so that they might get their blow in first. It was agreed that, while M. and Mme Verdurin and their friends were out walking, they would all set on the young man in the stables. I must record that, although it was only the occasion for what was about to take place, but because the persons concerned interested me later on, on the day in question a friend of the Verdurins was vacationing with them, whom they wanted to take out on foot before his departure, fixed for that same evening.

What greatly surprised me when we left to go out was that, on that particular day, Morel, who was coming with us on our walk, where he was to play his violin under the trees, said to me, "Listen, I've got a bad arm; I don't want to tell Mme Verdurin, but ask her to bring one of her footmen, Howsler for example; he can carry my instruments." "I think one of the others'd be a better choice," I replied. "They need him for dinner." A look of anger passed across Morel's face. "No, no, I'm not entrusting my violin to just anybody." Afterward, I understood the reason for this preference. Howsler was the much-loved brother of the young coachman and, had he stayed at the house, could have gone to his assistance. During the walk, low enough for the elder Howsler to be unable to hear us: "He's a good fellow, that one," said Morel. "His brother is, too, for that matter. If it wasn't for that fatal habit of drinking . . ." "What, drinking?" said Mme Verdurin, turning pale at the thought of having a coachman who drank. "You wouldn't notice it. I'm forever telling myself it's a miracle he hasn't had an accident while he was driving you." "But does he drive other people, then?" "You only need to see how many times he's tipped over, his face today is covered in bruises. I don't know how he hasn't killed himself, he's broken his shafts." "I've not seen him today," said Mme Verdurin, trembling at the thought of what might have happened to her. "You distress me." She wanted to cut the walk short so as to get home, but Morel chose an air by Bach with countless variations so as to make it last. As soon as we got back, she went to the coach house, saw the brand-new shaft and Howsler all bloodied. She was about to tell him, without remarking on it, that she no longer had need of a coachman and to hand him some money, but he, of his own accord, not wishing to accuse his colleagues, to whose animosity he had retrospectively attributed the daily theft of all the saddles and the like, and finding that his forbearance led merely to his letting himself be left for dead on the floor, asked to leave, which settled the whole affair. The chauffeur came in the following day, and afterward, Mme Verdurin (who had been obliged to take on a second one) was so satisfied with him that she recommended him to me warmly as someone totally trustworthy. I, all unknowing, employed him by the day in Paris; but I am getting too far ahead of myself, all this will be met with again in the story of Albertine. At this moment, we are at La Raspelière, where I have come to dine for the first time with my loved one, and M. de Charlus with Morel, the purported son of a "steward" who earned a salary of thirty thousand francs a year, had a carriage, and a number of subordinate majordomos, gardeners, factors, and farmers at his beck and call. But since I have been running ahead, I do not want all the same to leave the reader under the impression that Morel might have been wicked through and through. Rather, he was full of contradictions, capable on certain days of genuine kindness.

I was naturally most surprised to learn that the coachman had been shown the door, and even more so to recognize his replacement as the chauffeur who had been taking Albertine and me out. But he reeled off some complicated story, according to which he was supposed to have returned to Paris, whence he had been sent for on behalf of the Verdurins, and I did not doubt him for a moment. The sacking of the coachman was a reason for Morel to talk briefly with me, so as to express his sadness at the good fellow's departure. For the rest, even aside from the times when I was alone, when he would literally bound toward me in an effusion of delight, Morel, finding that everyone welcomed me with open arms at La Raspelière, and feeling that he had been willfully excluding himself from familiarity with someone who did not represent any danger to him, since he had made me burn my bridges and removed any possibility of my behaving patronizingly toward him (which I had as it happens never had any thought of doing), ceased to keep his distance from me. I put his change of attitude down to the influence of M. de Charlus, which had indeed made him less limited and more artistic in some things, but in others, where he applied the eloquent, mendacious, and anyway ephemeral formulas of the master to the letter, had made him even more stupid. What M. de Charlus had been able to tell him was in fact the one thing that I had assumed. How at the time could I have guessed what I was told afterward (and of which I have never felt certain, Andrée's assertions concerning anything connected with Albertine, later on especially, having always struck me as needing to be taken with caution, for, as we saw earlier, she was not genuinely fond of my loved one but was jealous of her), what in any event, if it were true, had been remarkably well hidden from me by the two of them: that Albertine knew Morel well? The new attitude that, around the time of the coachman's dismissal, Morel adopted toward me allowed me to alter my opinion of him. I retained the low opinion of his character I had been led to form by the obsequiousness that this young man had displayed toward me when he had need of me, followed, immediately the service had been rendered, by a contempt taken to the point of seeming not to see me. To which had to be added the evidence of his venal relationship with M. de Charlus, as well as of the instinct for incoherent bestiality whose nongratification (when that occurred), or the complications that it entailed, was the source of his unhappiness; that character was not uniformly ugly, however, but was full of contradictions. It resembled an old book of the Middle Ages, full of errors, of absurd traditions, of obscenities, it was extraordinarily composite. I had thought at first that his art, in which he was truly a past master, had given him superior abilities that went beyond the virtuosity of the performer. Once, when I was telling him of my desire to get down to work: "Work, achieve renown," he said to me. "Who's that from?" I asked him. "From Fontanes, to Chateaubriand."[15] He also knew a collection of Napoleon's love letters.[16] Good, I thought, he's literate. But this phrase that he had read who knows where was most probably the only one he knew in the whole of literature, ancient or modern, for he repeated it to me every evening. Another one, which he repeated even more frequently, to stop me from telling anyone anything about him, was the following, which he thought equally literary, but which is scarcely French, or at least presents no sort of sense, except perhaps to a manservant obsessed with secrets: "Put no trust in the mistrustful." In fact, by going from this stupid maxim to Fontanes's words to Chateaubriand, you would have scanned one whole part, varied but less contradictory than it seems, of Morel's character. This boy who, provided there was money to be made by it, would have done no matter what, and without remorse—perhaps not without a bizarre contrariness, going as far as nervous overexcitement, but which was far from meriting the name of remorse—who would, if he thought it was in his own interest, have plunged whole families into grief or even into mourning, this boy who put money ahead of everything else, ahead of, let alone kindness, the most natural sentiments of a common humanity, this same boy yet put ahead of money his diploma as first-prize-winner at the Conservatoire and that no disobliging remarks should be made about him to his flute or counterpoint classes. Thus his greatest rages, his gloomiest and least justifiable outbursts of bad temper, stemmed from what he called (no doubt generalizing from a few particular instances when he had encountered men of ill-will) the universal duplicity. He flattered himself he avoided this by never discussing anyone, by keeping his cards hidden, by mistrusting everybody. (As misfortune would have it, given what was to result from it after my return to Paris, his mistrust had not "worked" in respect of the Balbec chauffeur, in whom he had no doubt recognized one of his own kind, that is to say, contrary to his maxim, a man mistrustful in the proper meaning of the word, who remains stubbornly silent when with decent people but at once sees eye to eye with a debauchee.) It seemed to him—and he was not altogether wrong—that this mistrust would always enable him to come off unscathed, to slip uncaught through the most perilous adventures, without their being able to hold, let alone prove, anything against him in the establishment on the rue Bergère.[17] He would work, would achieve renown, would one day perhaps, his respectability intact, be chairman of the violin jury at the prestigious Conservatoire.

But it is perhaps again to introduce too great a logic into Morel's head to make his contradictions follow one from the other. In actual fact, his nature was really like a sheet of paper in which so many folds have been made in every direction that it is impossible to know where you are. He seemed to have quite lofty principles, and in a magnificent handwriting, marred by the crudest spelling mistakes, spent hours writing to his brother that he had behaved badly toward his sisters, that he was the oldest and their support; to his sisters, that they were guilty of a breach of good manners vis-à-vis himself.

Soon now, with summer coming to an end, when you alighted from the train at Douville, the sun, muffled by the mist, was no more than a block of red in the uniformly mauve sky. To the great peace that descends in the evening on these lush, saline meadows, which had induced many Parisians, painters for the most part, to come and spend their vacations in Douville, there was added a dampness which made them return in good time inside their little chalets. In several of these, the lamp was already lit. A few cows alone remained outside, gazing at the sea and lowing, while others, more interested in humankind, turned their attention to our carriages. One painter alone, who had set up his easel on a narrow eminence, was working to try and render this great calm and the still light. The cows perhaps would be serving him as unwitting and benevolent models, for their contemplative air and their solitary presence, once the human beings had returned home, contributed in their way to the powerful impression of repose that the evening gives off. And a few weeks later, the transposition was no less agreeable when, with the autumn advancing, the days became decidedly short and the journey had to be made in the dark. If I had been taking a stroll during the afternoon, I needed to go home and get dressed by five at the latest, by which time the round, red sun had already descended halfway down the slanting mirror I had once detested, and, like Greek fire, had set light to the sea in the glass fronts of all my bookcases. Some incantatory gesture having excited, as I was putting on my dinner jacket, the alert and frivolous self that had been mine when I used to go with Saint-Loup to dine in Rivebelle, or on the evening when I thought I would be taking Mlle de Stermaria to dine on the island in the Bois, I was unconsciously humming the same tune as then; and it was only on becoming aware of this that, by the song, I recognized the intermittent singer, who indeed knew only that one song. The first time that I had sung it, I was beginning to be in love with Albertine, but I thought I would never get to know her. Later, in Paris, it was when I had ceased loving her and a few days after having possessed her for the first time. Now, it was on loving her again and at the moment of going to have dinner with her, to the great regret of the manager, who thought I would end up living at La Raspelière and abandoning his hotel, and who assured me he had heard that fevers were rife there, due to the marshes of Le Bec and their "pregnant" waters. I was pleased by this multiplicity, which I could see thus deployed in my life on three planes; besides, when we become for a moment a former self, different that is from the one that we have been for a long time, our sensibilities, no longer deadened by habit, receive from the least shock impressions so vivid as to make all that has gone before seem pallid, and on which, because of their intensity, we fasten with the fleeting exaltation of a drunkard. It was already dark when we got into the omnibus or the carriage that was to take us to the station to catch the little train. And in the foyer the First President would say to us: "Ah, you're going to La Raspelière! *Sapristi*, she's got a nerve, Mme Verdurin, making you spend an hour in the train in the dark, just to have dinner. And then start the journey all over again at ten o'clock at night, in the very devil of a wind. It's obvious you can't have anything to do," he added, rubbing his hands. He no doubt spoke thus out of displeasure at not having been invited, and also because of the satisfaction that "busy" men feel—be their work perfectly fatuous—at "not having the time" to do what you are doing.

It is legitimate, admittedly, for the man who drafts reports, lines up figures, answers business letters, or follows prices on the Bourse to feel, when you say to him sneeringly, "It's all right for you, who have nothing to do," an agreeable sense of his own superiority. But the latter would assert itself equally contemptuously, if not more so (for the busy man, too, dines out), were your recreation writing *Hamlet* or simply reading it. In which busy men are unthinking. For they ought to reflect that the disinterested culture which strikes them as a comic pastime for the idle when they come upon it at a moment when it is being practiced is the same as that culture which, in their own métier, singles out men who are not perhaps better magistrates or administrators than themselves, but before whose rapid promotion they bow their heads, saying, "It appears he's very well read, altogether someone of distinction." But above all the First President did not realize that what pleased me about these dinners at La Raspelière was that, as he rightly said, though in criticism, they "represented a real journey," a journey whose attraction seemed all the keener because it was not an end in itself, that one was not looking for any enjoyment from it, this last being assigned to the gathering for which one was bound, and which never failed to be greatly modified by the whole atmosphere surrounding it. It was already dark now when I exchanged the warmth of the hotel—of the hotel that had become my home—for the compartment into which we got with Albertine, where the reflection of the lamplight on the window told us, at certain of the wheezy little train's stops, that we had arrived in a station. So as not to risk Cottard's failing to notice us, and not having heard the station being shouted out, I would open the door, but what came dashing into the carriage was not the faithful but the wind, the rain, and the cold. In the darkness, I could make out the fields and I could hear the sea, we were in open country. Before we joined the little nucleus, Albertine would inspect herself in a little mirror taken from a gold vanity case that she carried. The first times, indeed, Mme Verdurin having made her go upstairs to her dressing room so that she could tidy herself before dinner, I had, in the midst of the profound calm in which I had been living for some time past, experienced a slight stirring of disquiet and jealousy at being obliged to leave Albertine at the foot of the stairs, and I had felt so anxious while I was alone in the drawing room in the midst of the little clan, and wondering what my loved one was doing upstairs, that the following day I had, by telegram, after asking M. de Charlus for advice as to what was most fashionable, ordered from Cartier's a vanity case that was the joy of Albertine and of myself. For me it was a token of my peace of mind as well as of my solicitude for my loved one. For she had certainly guessed that I did not like her remaining without me at Mme Verdurin's and had contrived to make all her toilet preparations before dinner, in the compartment.

To the number of Mme Verdurin's regulars, and the most faithful of all, there had for several months now been added M. de Charlus. Regularly, three times a week, the passengers parked in the waiting rooms or on the platform at Doncières-Ouest would see this fat man going past, with his gray hair, his black mustache, and red makeup on his lips that was less noticeable at the end of the season than in the summer, when the broad daylight had made it more garish and the heat half liquid. As he made his way toward the little train, he could not help (merely out of a connoisseur's habit, since he now had an attachment that had made him chaste, or at least, most of the time, faithful) casting, at the laborers, the soldiers, the young men in tennis clothes, a furtive glance, at once inquisitorial and timorous, after which he would at once lower his eyelids over eyes that were almost closed, with the unctuousness of an ecclesiastic busy telling his beads, and the reserve of a bride plighted to her one love, or of a well-brought-up young girl. The faithful were the more convinced that he had not seen them when he entered a compartment other than theirs (as the Princesse Sherbatoff also often did), like a man who has no idea whether people will be happy or not to be seen with him and who gives you the option of coming to look for him if you so desire. No such desire had been felt in the very early days by the doctor, who had wanted us to let him remain on his own in his compartment. Making a virtue of his hesitant nature now that he stood so high medically, it was with a smile, and leaning back, while looking at Ski from over the top of his eyeglass, that he said, either out of mischievousness or to learn his companions' opinion by a roundabout means: "You understand, if I was on my own, a bachelor . . . but because of my wife, I ask myself whether I can allow him to travel with us after what you've told me," whispered the doctor. "What's that you're saying?" asked Mme Cottard. "Nothing, it's none of your business, it's not for women," replied the doctor with a wink, and with a majestic self-satisfaction that came halfway between the poker-faced expression that he maintained in front of his pupils and his patients, and the anxiety that had accompanied his shafts of wit in the old days at the Verdurins', and he went on talking in an undertone. Mme Cottard made out only the words "of the brotherhood" and *"tapette,"*[18] and since in the doctor's idiom the first denoted the Jewish race and the second those who talked too much, Mme Cottard concluded that M. de Charlus must be a garrulous Israelite. She could not understand why the Baron should be ostracized on that account, and thought it her duty as the clan's doyenne to demand that he should not be left on his own, and we all made our way toward M. de Charlus's compartment, guided by a still-perplexed Cottard. From the corner where he was reading a volume of Balzac, M. de Charlus remarked this hesitation; he had not, however, looked up. But just as deaf-mutes can recognize, by a current of air imperceptible to others, that someone has come up behind them, he had, for alerting him to the coldness felt toward him, a veritable hyperacuity of the senses. This, as it customarily does in whatever domain, had given rise in M. de Charlus to imaginary sufferings. Like the neuropaths who, feeling a slight freshness, infer that a window must be open on the floor above, fly into a rage and start sneezing, M. de Charlus, if someone had displayed a preoccupied expression in his presence, concluded that a comment he had made about that person had been repeated to them. But there was no need even for anyone to be wearing a distracted, or a grim, or a laughing expression, he would invent them. In return, cordiality easily masked from him the backbiting of which he was unaware. Having detected Cottard's hesitation the first time, although, much to the surprise of the faithful, who did not think they had yet been noticed by this reader with the lowered eyes, he held out a hand to them when they were a suitable distance away, he contented himself with an inclination of his whole body, at once quickly straightened, for Cottard, without taking the hand that the doctor had held out in his own suede-gloved hand. "We absolutely insisted on doing the journey with you, monsieur, and not leaving you on your own like this in your little corner. It's a great pleasure for us," Mme Cottard said good-naturedly to the Baron. "I'm most honored," recited the Baron, bowing coldly. "I was very glad to learn that you had finally chosen this region to set up your tabern—" She was going to say "tabernacles," but the word struck her as Hebraic and disobliging for a Jew who might see some allusion in it. So she caught herself up to choose another of the expressions with which she was familiar, namely a solemn expression: "to set up, I meant to say, your 'penates.'" (It is true that these divinities do not belong to the Christian religion, either, but to one that has been dead for so long it no longer has any adepts to whom one might be afraid of giving offense.) "We, alas, what with the academic year starting, and the doctor's hospital duties, we can never elect domicile for very long in one place." And, pointing to a cardboard box, "You can see, what's more, how we women are less fortunate than the strong sex; to go only as far as to our friends the Verdurins', we're obliged to take with us a whole range of impedimenta." During this time, I was looking at the Baron's volume of Balzac. This was not a paperback copy, bought at random like the volume of Bergotte he had lent me the first year. It was a book from his library, and as such bearing the device *"Je suis au Baron de Charlus,"* or "I belong to the Baron de Charlus," for which was sometimes substituted, to display the studious tastes of the Guermantes, *"In proeliis non semper"* or still another one, *"Non sine labore."*[19] But we shall soon see these being replaced by others, in order to try and please Morel. After a moment, Mme Cottard took up a subject she considered was more personal to the Baron. "I don't know if you're of my opinion, monsieur," she said after a moment, "but I'm very broadminded, and as I see it, provided you practice them sincerely, all religions are good. I'm not like those people who start frothing at the mouth at the sight of a . . . Protestant." "I was taught that mine was the true one," replied M. de Charlus. "He's a fanatic," thought Mme Cottard; "Swann, except toward the end, was more tolerant; it's true he was a convert." But, quite to the contrary, the Baron was not simply a Christian, as we know, but pious in the fashion of the Middle Ages. For him, as for the sculptors of the thirteenth century, the Christian church was, in the living sense of the word, peopled by a crowd of beings he believed to be perfectly real: prophets, apostles, angels, sacred personages of every sort, surrounding the Word made flesh, his mother and her espoused, the Eternal Father, all the martyrs and doctors, the race of whom, in high relief, crowd the porch or fill the nave of the cathedrals. From among them all, M. de Charlus had chosen as his patron intercessors the Archangels Michael, Gabriel, and Raphael, with whom he held frequent conversations so that they might convey his prayers to the Eternal Father, before whose throne they stand. Thus Mme Cottard's error amused me greatly.

To get off the terrain of religion, let us say that the doctor, having come to Paris with the meager baggage of a peasant mother's advice, then been absorbed by the almost purely physical studies to which those who wish to carry their medical careers all the way through are obliged to devote themselves for a great many years, had never become cultured; he had acquired more authority, but not experience; he took the word "honored" literally, was at once gratified by it because he was vain and pained because he was a good-natured fellow. "That poor de Charlus," he said that evening to his wife, "he upset me when he told me he was honored to be traveling with us. You sense, poor devil, that he has no connections, that he's demeaning himself."

But soon, without having needed to be guided by the charitable Mme Cottard, the faithful had succeeded in overcoming the awkwardness they had all more or less felt at the start, on finding themselves next to M. de Charlus. No doubt, in his presence they kept always before them the memory of Ski's revelations and the idea of the sexual strangeness enclosed within their traveling companion. But this strangeness even held a sort of attraction for them. For them, it lent the

Baron's conversation, remarkable in any case but in parts that they were hardly able to appreciate, a savor that, by comparison, made the conversation of even the most interesting of the others, of Brichot himself, seem a little colorless. They had been pleased to acknowledge right from the start, moreover, that he was intelligent. "Genius may lie next to madness," announced the doctor, and if the Princesse, hungry for instruction, insisted, he would say no more, this axiom being all that he knew about genius, and seeming moreover less demonstrable than anything having to do with typhoid or arthritis. And since he had become arrogant and remained ill bred: "No questions, Princesse, don't interrogate me, I'm at the seaside for a rest. In any case, you wouldn't understand me, you don't know medicine." And the Princesse would apologize and fall silent, finding that Cottard was a charming man and gathering that celebrities are not always approachable. In this first period, they had in the end therefore found M. de Charlus to be intelligent in spite of his vice (or what is generally so termed). Now, it was, without their realizing it, because of that vice that they found him more intelligent than the others. The simplest maxims that, at the adroit provocation of the university man or the sculptor, M. de Charlus pronounced concerning love, jealousy, or beauty, because of the singular, secret, refined, and monstrous experience from which they had been drawn, assumed for the faithful that charm of the foreign which a psychology analogous to that offered to us from time immemorial by our own dramatic literature wears in a Russian or a Japanese play, as performed by artistes from those places. They still risked, when he was out of earshot, an unkind joke: "Oh!" the sculptor would whisper, catching sight of a young railwayman with the long eyelashes of a nautch-dancer whom M. de Charlus had been unable to stop himself from eyeing. "If the Baron's starting to make eyes at the ticket collector, it'll take us forever to get there, the train'll start going arsy-versy. Just look at the way he's looking at him, we're not on a train any more but in queer street." In fact, however, if M. de Charlus did not come, they felt disappointment almost at traveling only among people who were like everyone else and not to have next to them this bedizened, potbellied, and impenetrable personage, reminiscent of a box, of some suspect and exotic provenance, that gives off a curious smell of fruit, the mere thought of sampling which would turn the stomach. From this point of view, the faithful of the masculine sex derived a keener satisfaction, during the short section of the journey between Saint-Martin-du-Chêne, where M. de Charlus got in, and Doncières, the station where we were joined by Morel. For, as long as the violinist was not there (and provided the ladies and Albertine, keeping to themselves so as not to hamper the conversation, remained at a distance), M. de Charlus did not hold back, so as not to appear to be avoiding certain topics, from talking about "what it is agreed should be termed vice." Albertine could not embarrass him, for she was always with the ladies, out of the graciousness of a girl who does not want her presence to restrict the freedom of the conversation. But I was easily able to bear not having her beside me, always on condition that she remained in the same carriage. For I, who no longer felt jealousy or scarcely any love for her, and gave no thought to what she might be doing on the days when I did not see her, when, in return, I was there, a simple partition that might conceivably have been concealing a betrayal was unbearable to me, and if she went with the ladies into the next-door compartment, a moment later, no longer able to remain in my seat, and at the risk of offending whoever might be speaking, Brichot, Cottard, or Charlus, to whom I was unable to explain the reason for my flight, I would get up, leave them sitting there, and, in order to see whether something abnormal might not be going on, move next door. And all the way to Doncières, M. de Charlus, not being afraid to shock, would talk, often very crudely, of habits that he declared, for his own part, he considered neither good nor bad. He did so out of cleverness, to display his broad-mindedness, persuaded as he was that his own habits had aroused hardly any suspicions in the minds of the faithful. He believed, indeed, that there existed in the world a few people who had, following an expression that later became common with him, "got him straight." But he imagined that there were no more than three or four such persons, and that none of them were on the Normandy coast. This illusion may seem surprising on the part of someone so discerning and so anxious. Even in the case of those whom he thought more or less in the know, he flattered himself that it was only in the abstract, and, according to whether he said one thing or another, aspired to place the person in question outside the suppositions of an interlocutor who, from politeness, pretended to take him at his word. Even suspecting what I might know or suppose about him, he imagined that this opinion, which he thought was of longer standing on my part than in reality it was, was quite general, and that it was enough for him to deny some detail in order to be believed, whereas, on the contrary, even if knowledge of the whole always precedes that of the details, it makes the investigation of these infinitely simpler and, having destroyed the capacity for invisibility, no longer allows the dissembler to hide whatever he pleases. Certainly, when M. de Charlus, asked out to dinner by one or another of the faithful or some friend of the faithful, took the most complicated detours in order to introduce, in the midst of the names of ten people whom he was citing, the name of Morel, he hardly suspected that to the reasons he gave, always different, for the pleasure or convenience he might find in being invited with him on that particular evening, his hosts, while appearing to believe him implicitly, had substituted a single reason, always the same, which he thought was not known to them, namely that he was in love with him. Similarly, Mme Verdurin, seeming always to appear quite to have accepted the motives, part artistic, part humanitarian, that M. de Charlus gave her for the interest he took in Morel, never stopped thanking the Baron feelingly for the touching kindnesses, as she put it, that he showed the violinist. But how astonished would M. de Charlus have been if, on a day when he and Morel were late and had not come by the train, he had heard the Patronne say, "We won't wait for the young ladies any longer!" The Baron would have been all the more astounded in that, hardly ever stirring from La Raspelière, the figure he cut there was that of chaplain, of a stage abbé, sometimes (when Morel had a forty-eight-hour leave) sleeping there two nights in a row. Mme Verdurin would then give them two communicating rooms, and, to set them at their ease, say, "If you feel like making music, don't hesitate; the walls are like those of a fortress, you've no one on your floor, and my husband sleeps like the dead." On these days, M. de Charlus would relieve the Princesse and go to meet the new arrivals at the station, apologizing for Mme Verdurin's not having come on account of a state of health that he described so graphically that the guests entered wearing suitably concerned expressions and let out a cry of surprise on finding the Patronne up and about, in a demi-décolletage.

For M. de Charlus had become, momentarily, for Mme Verdurin the faithful of faithfuls, a second Princesse Sherbatoff. She was much less sure of his social standing than of the Princesse's, imagining that, if the latter wished to see only the little nucleus, this was out of contempt for others and a predilection for it. Since this selfsame pretense was peculiar to the Verdurins, who treated as bores all those with whom they could not associate, it is incredible that the Patronne should have believed the Princesse to be a soul of steel, detesting what was fashionable. But she stuck by her opinion and was convinced that in the case of the *grande dame*, too, it was in all sincerity and out of a taste for intellectuality that she did not associate with bores. The number of these had in any case gone down where the Verdurins were concerned. The life of a seaside resort removed from an introduction the consequences for the future that might have been dreaded in Paris. Brilliant men, having come to Balbec without their wives, which made things easier, put out feelers toward La Raspelière, and went from boring to delightful. This was the case with the Prince de Guermantes, whom the absence of the Princesse would not, on the other hand, have decided to go to the Verdurins' "as a bachelor," had the magnet of Dreyfusism not been so powerful as to cause him to ascend the rise leading to La Raspelière in a single go, on a day, alas, when the Patronne was out. Mme Verdurin was not certain in any case that he and M. de Charlus were from the same social world. The Baron had certainly said that the Duc de Guermantes was his brother, but that perhaps was the falsehood of an adventurer. However fashionable he had shown himself to be, however affable, and however faithful to the Verdurins, the Patronne yet hesitated almost to invite him with the Prince de Guermantes. She consulted Ski and Brichot: "The Baron and the Prince de Guermantes, do they go together?" "Good heavens, madame, where one of them's concerned, I think I can say . . ." "One of them, what good's that to me?" Mme Verdurin had gone on, in annoyance. "I'm asking you whether they go together." "Ah, madame, that sort of thing's very hard to find out." There was no malice in this on Mme Verdurin's part. She was certain as to the Baron's habits, but in expressing herself as she did it was not they that she had in mind, wanting only to know whether the Prince and M. de Charlus could be invited together, whether they would hit it off. There was no unkind intention in her use of these ready-made expressions, which are favored by the "little clans" of the artistic. To parade M. de Guermantes, she wanted to take him, on the afternoon following the lunch party, to a charity event when some sailors from the coast would be enacting a ship setting sail. But, not having the time to take care of everything, she delegated her functions to the faithful of faithfuls, to the Baron. "You understand, they're not to stay standing about, like mussels; they've got to be coming and going, be seen clearing the decks for action, or whatever you call all that. But you, who often go to the harbor in Balbec-Plage, you could certainly make them rehearse without tiring yourself. You must have a better idea than I do, M. de Charlus, of how to get young sailors going. But, then, we're giving ourselves a lot of trouble over M. de Guermantes. Perhaps he's one of those imbeciles from the Jockey Club. Oh, good heavens, I'm saying bad things about the Jockey Club, and I seem to remember you're one of them. What, Baron, you're not answering, are you one of them? Will you not come out with us? Look, here's a book I've received, I think it'll interest you. It's a Roujon. It's got a pretty title: *Parmi les hommes*."[20]

For my own part, I was all the happier that M. de Charlus should quite often have stood in for Princesse Sherbatoff, in that I was in ill odor with the latter, for a reason at once trivial and profound. One day when I was on the little train, showering attentions, as ever, on the Princesse Sherbatoff, I saw Mme de Villeparisis get in. She had in fact come to spend a few weeks with the Princess of Luxembourg, but, shackled to this daily need to see Albertine, I had never replied to the proliferating invitations from the Marquise and her royal hostess. I felt remorse at the sight of my grandmother's friend and, purely as a duty (without leaving the Princesse Sherbatoff), I talked with her for quite some time. I had absolutely no idea, however, that Mme de Villeparisis knew very well who my companion was but had no wish to meet her. At the next station, Mme de Villeparisis left the compartment, and I even reproached myself for not having helped her alight; I went to resume my seat next to the Princesse. But it was as though—a cataclysm common among people whose position is insecure and who fear that you may have heard ill reports of them, and despise them—a change of scenery had been effected. Ensconced in her *Revue des deux mondes*, Mme Sherbatoff did little more than move her lips in answer to my questions, and finally told me that I was giving her a migraine. I had no inkling of what my crime was. When I said goodbye to the Princesse, the usual smile did not light up her face, a curt nod depressed her chin, she did not even offer me her hand, and she has never spoken to me since. But she must have spoken—but what to say, I do not know—to the Verdurins, for, the moment I asked them whether I would not do well to make some polite gesture to the Princesse Sherbatoff, they came hastily out in chorus: "No, no, no! That least of all. She doesn't like courtesies!" This was not done so as to cause a rift between us, but she had managed to make them believe that she was indifferent to attentions, a soul impervious to the vanities of this world. One needs to have met the politician who passes for being the most plainspoken, the most intransigent, the most unapproachable once he has come to power; one needs to have seen him in his days out of favor, timidly soliciting, with the dazzling smile of a lover, the haughty salute of some journalist or other; one needs to have seen the straightened spine of Cottard (whom his new patients mistook for a ramrod), and to know from what unrequited passions, what snobbish rebuffs, the seeming haughtiness, the universally acknowledged antisnobbery of the Princesse Sherbatoff had been formed, to understand that the rule among humankind—which allows of exceptions, naturally—is that the hard are the weak whom no one has wanted, and that the strong alone, caring little whether they are wanted or not, have that gentleness that the crowd mistakes for weakness.

For the rest, I must not judge the Princesse Sherbatoff harshly. Hers is so very common a case! One day, at the funeral of a Guermantes, a distinguished man standing beside me pointed out a slim gentleman graced by a pretty face. "Of all the Guermantes," my neighbor said, "that's the most extraordinary, the oddest. It's the Duc's brother." I answered unwisely that he was mistaken, that the gentleman was no relation at all to the Guermantes but was named Fournier-Sarlovèze.[21] The distinguished man turned his back on me and has never acknowledged me since.

A great musician, a member of the Institute, a high official dignitary who knew Ski, stopped off in Arembouville, where he had a niece, and came to one of the Verdurins' Wednesdays. M. de Charlus was especially affable toward him (at Morel's request), above all so that, on his return to Paris, the Academician might enable him to attend various private performances, rehearsals, and the like, where the violinist would be playing. The Academician, flattered, and a charming man in any case, promised, and kept his promise. The Baron was deeply touched by all the kindnesses that this personage (who in fact, where he himself was concerned, loved only, and with passion, women) showed him, by all the facilities he procured for him so that he might meet Morel in those official places into which the layman cannot go, by all the opportunities offered the young virtuoso by the celebrated artist to put himself forward, to become known, by nominating him, in preference to others equally talented, for recitals that would be much talked about. But M. de Charlus did not suspect that he owed the maestro all the more gratitude in that the latter, doubly deserving, or, if you prefer, twice as culpable, was fully aware of the relationship between the violinist and his noble patron. He encouraged them, while admittedly having no sympathy with them, being unable to understand any love except that for a woman, which had inspired all his own music, but out of moral indifference, a professional wish to please and to be of service, a worldly amiability and snobbery. As for his doubts concerning the nature of that relationship, so few did he have that, at the very first dinner at La Raspelière, he had asked Ski, referring to M. de Charlus and Morel, as he might have done to a man and his mistress: "Have they been together long?" But, too much the man of the world to allow any of this to appear to those concerned, and prepared, had it given rise to tittle-tattle among Morel's fellow students, to suppress it and to reassure Morel by saying to him in a fatherly way, "They say that about everyone these days," he did not cease to shower the Baron with kindnesses, which the latter thought charming but natural, being incapable of suspecting the celebrated maestro of so much vice or so much virtue. For no one was so mean-spirited as to repeat to M. de Charlus the witticisms spoken in his absence, or the *à-peu-près* about Morel. Yet this simple situation suffices to demonstrate that even that universally decried thing, which would nowhere find anyone to defend it, "gossip," has, whether we are ourselves its object, so that it then becomes particularly disagreeable, or whether it teaches us something we did not know about a third person, its psychological value. It prevents the mind from falling asleep over the factitious view that it takes of what it believes things to be like, which is only their outward appearance. It turns this inside out with the magical dexterity of an idealist philosopher and quickly offers us an unsuspected corner of the reverse side of the fabric. Could M. de Charlus have imagined these words spoken by a certain fond female relative: "How can you expect Mémé to be in love with me? You're forgetting I'm a woman!" Yet she had a genuine, deep attachment to M. de Charlus. Why be surprised, then, that, in the case of the Verdurins, on whose affection and kindness he had no right to rely, the remarks that they made when far away from him (and it was not only remarks, as we shall see) should have been so unlike what he imagined them to be, that is to say the simple echo of those that he heard when he was there? These last alone decorated with fond inscriptions the little ideal pavilion into which M. de Charlus sometimes went in order to dream on his own, when he would introduce his imagination for a moment into the idea that the Verdurins had of him. The atmosphere there was so sympathetic, so cordial, the respite so comforting, that, when M. de Charlus, before going to sleep, had come there for a moment to relax from his cares, he never re-emerged without a smile. But for each of us a pavilion of this kind is double: facing what we think is the only one, there is the other, customarily invisible to us, the real one, symmetrical with the one that we know yet very different, whose decoration, where we would recognize nothing of what we were expecting to see, would alarm us as being formed of the odious symbols of an unsuspected hostility. How aghast M. de Charlus would have been had he found his way into one of these adverse pavilions, by virtue of some piece of gossip, as if by one of those servants' staircases where obscene graffiti have been chalked on the doors of the apartments by disgruntled tradesmen or dismissed domestics! But, just as we are devoid of that sense of direction with which certain birds are endowed, so we lack the sense of visibility as we lack that of distances, imagining as close the concerned attention of people who, on the contrary, never give us a thought, and not suspecting that during this same time we are the sole preoccupation of others. Thus M. de Charlus lived deluded, like the fish that believes that the water in which he is swimming extends beyond the glass of his tank, which offers him his reflection, whereas he does not see beside him, in the shadows, the amused passerby who is following his antics, or the all-powerful pisciculturalist who, at the unforeseen and fatal moment, deferred at this moment in the case of the Baron (for whom the pisciculturalist, in Paris, will be Mme Verdurin), will pull him ruthlessly out from the medium in which he had liked living, to toss him into another one. Whole nations, what is more, insofar as they are simply collections of individuals, can provide examples, vaster yet identical in each of their parts, of this profound, obstinate, and disconcerting blindness. Until now, though it may have been a reason why M. de Charlus passed remarks in the little clan of a pointless cleverness or a daring that gave rise to surreptitious smiles, it had not yet had for him, nor was it to have in Balbec, any serious disadvantages. A little albumen, or sugar, or cardiac arrhythmia does not stop life from continuing normally for someone who does not even notice them, while the doctor alone sees them as prophetic of catastrophes. At present, M. de Charlus's liking—whether Platonic or not—for Morel merely led the Baron readily to say in Morel's absence that he found him very good-looking, thinking this would be taken quite innocently, and thereby behaving like a shrewd man who, summoned to testify in court, will not be afraid to enter into details that seem on the face of it to be to his disadvantage, but which, on this very count, have more that is natural and less that is vulgar about them than the conventional protestations of a stage defendant. With the same freedom, always between Doncières-Ouest and Saint-Martin-du-Chêne—or, conversely, on the return journey—M. de Charlus gladly talked about people who have, it seems, very strange habits, and would even add, "I say 'strange' after all, I don't know why, for there's nothing so very strange about it," in order to prove to himself how thoroughly at ease he felt with his audience. And he was so, in fact, provided that the initiative in these proceedings lay with him and he knew that the gallery was mute and smiling, disarmed by credulity or by a good upbringing.

When M. de Charlus was not speaking of his admiration for Morel's beauty, as if it had no connection with a proclivity known as a vice, he would deal with this vice, but as if it were by no means his own. At times, indeed, he did not hesitate to call it by its name. When, after looking at the fine binding on his Balzac, I asked what he liked best in the *Comédie humaine,* he answered, steering his thought toward an *idée fixe:* "All one thing or all the other, the little miniatures like *Le Curé de Tours* or *La Femme abandonnée,* or the great frescos like the series of the *Illusions perdues.* What, you don't know *Les Illusions perdues*? It's so fine, the moment when Carlos Herrera asks the name of the château his barouche is passing: it's Rastignac, the home of the young man he had once been in love with. Whereupon the abbé falls into a reverie that Swann used to call, which was very witty, the 'Tristesse d'Olympio' of pederasty.[22] And the death of Lucien! I no longer recall what man of taste[23] it was whose reply, to whoever asked him what event had most distressed him in his life, was, 'The death of Lucien de Rubempré in *Splendeurs et misères.*'" "I know everyone's wearing Balzac this year, just as last year it was pessimism," Brichot broke in. "But at the risk of grieving those souls yearning for a Balzacian deference, and without aspiring, damn it all, to the role of literary gendarme and to institute charges of faults of grammar, I will admit that the copious improviser whose alarming lucubrations you appear strangely to overrate has always seemed to me an insufficiently meticulous wielder of the pen. I have read those *Illusions perdues* of which you speak, Baron, torturing myself to attain to the fervor of an initiate, and I confess, in all simplicity of soul, that these *roman-feuilletons* worded in pathos and in double or triple gobbledygook ('Esther happy,' 'Where the wrong paths lead,' 'The price old men pay for love')[24] have always had the effect on me of Rocambole[25] mysteries elevated by some inexplicable favor to the precarious status of masterpiece...." "You say that because you know nothing of life," said the Baron, doubly irritated, for he sensed that Brichot would understand neither his artistic nor his other reasons. "I quite understand," replied Brichot, "that, to talk like Master François Rabelais, you mean I am *moult sorbonagre, sorbonicole et sorboniforme.*[26]

Yet, equally as much as my fellows, I like a book to give an impression of life and sincerity, I am not one of those clerks—" "The *quart d'heure de Rabelais*,"[27] broke in Dr. Cottard, with an expression no longer of uncertainty but of witty self-assurance. "—who take a vow of literature following the rule of l'Abbaye-aux-Bois in the obedience of M. le Vicomte de Chateaubriand, grand master of humbug, according to the strict rule of the humanists. M. le Vicomte de Chateaubriand—" "*Chateaubriand aux pommes?*"[28] broke in Dr. Cottard. "He is the patron saint of the brotherhood," Brichot continued, without picking up on the doctor's joke, who, in return, alarmed by the university man's words, looked anxiously at M. de Charlus. Brichot had seemed lacking in tact to Cottard, whose pun had brought a delicate smile to the lips of the Princesse Sherbatoff. "With the professor, the mordant irony of the complete skeptic never loses its rights," she said, out of friendliness and to show that the doctor's "witticism" had not gone unnoticed by her. "The wise man is of necessity a skeptic," replied the doctor. "What do I know? '*Gnothi seauton*,' said Socrates. That's very true, excess in anything is a fault. But I'm flabbergasted when I reflect that that was enough for the name of Socrates to have endured until our own day. What is there in that philosophy? Little enough, when all's said and done. When you reflect that Charcot and others have done work a thousand times more remarkable and which at least rests on something, on the suppression of the pupillary reflex as a syndrome of general paralysis, and that they're almost forgotten! When all's said and done, Socrates isn't so extraordinary. They're people who had nothing to do, who spent their whole day walking about chopping logic. It's like Jesus Christ: '*Love one another*,' how very pretty." "My friend . . . ," pleaded Mme Cottard. "Naturally, my wife is protesting, women are all neurotics." "But, *mon petit docteur*, I'm not a neurotic," murmured Mme Cottard. "What, she's not a neurotic? When her son's ill, she presents phenomena of insomnia. Still, I acknowledge that Socrates and the others, they're necessary for a superior culture, to get a gift for exposition. I always quote the *gnothi seauton* to my pupils at the first lecture. Old Bouchard, who found that out, congratulated me." "I'm not one of the supporters of form for form's sake, any more than in poetry I'd hoard millionaire rhymes,"[29] resumed Brichot. "All the same, the *Comédie humaine*—not so very human—is too much the opposite of those works in which the art outweighs the subject matter, as that faithful old steed Ovid has it.[30] And it's permissible to prefer a path halfway up the slope, which leads to the vicarage of Meudon or the hermitage of Ferney, equidistant from the Vallée-aux-Loups, where René majestically fulfilled the functions of an unyielding pontificate, and from Les Jardies, where Honoré de Balzac, harassed by the bailiff's men, never stopped cacographying, for the sake of a Polish woman, as a zealous apostle of double Dutch."[31] "Chateaubriand is much more alive than you say, and Balzac is a great writer nonetheless," replied M. de Charlus, still too imbued with the tastes of Swann not to be irritated by Brichot, "and Balzac was familiar with those passions even that everyone ignores or studies only in order to castigate them. Not to refer again to the immortal *Illusions perdues*, *Sarrasine*, *La Fille aux yeux d'or*, *Une Passion dans le désert*, even the somewhat enigmatic *Fausse Maîtresse* will bear out what I'm saying. When I spoke of this 'outside-nature' side of Balzac with Swann, he used to say, 'You're of the same opinion as Taine.'[32] I didn't have the honor of meeting Taine," added M. de Charlus (with that irritating habit among society people of the pointless "Monsieur," as if they believed that, by qualifying a great writer as "Monsieur," they were bestowing an honor on him, or perhaps keeping their distance, and letting it be seen that they did not know him), "I didn't know M. Taine, but I took it as a great honor to be of the same opinion as him." Despite these ridiculous society habits, M. de Charlus was in fact highly intelligent, and it is probable that if some ancient marriage had established links between his family and that of Balzac, he would have felt (no less than Balzac, for that matter) a self-satisfaction of which he would not, however, have been able to stop himself boasting, as though of a mark of admirable condescension.

On occasion, at the station that came after Saint-Martin-du-Chêne, some young men would get into the train. M. de Charlus could not help looking at them, but since he cut short and disguised the attention he was paying to them, it came to look as though it were concealing a secret, more particular even than the real one; you would have said that he knew them, and had let this show in spite of himself after accepting the sacrifice, before turning back to us, as those children do who, following a quarrel between parents, have been forbidden to greet certain classmates, but who, when they meet them, cannot forbear to raise their heads before falling back under the ferrule of their tutor.

At the word coming from the Greek with which M. de Charlus, in speaking of Balzac, had followed the allusion to the "Tristesse d'Olympio" in *Splendeurs et misères,* Ski, Brichot, and Cottard had looked at one another with a smile that was less ironic perhaps than imbued with the satisfaction that dinner guests might feel who had succeeded in getting Dreyfus to talk about his own Affair, or the Empress about her reign. They were counting indeed on pressing him a little further on the subject, but already we were at Doncières, where Morel joined us. In front of him, M. de Charlus kept careful watch on the conversation, and when Ski wanted to bring him back to the love of Carlos Herrera for Lucien de Rubempré, the Baron assumed the annoyed, mysterious, and finally (seeing they were not listening to him) severe and judicial expression of a father hearing improprieties being spoken in front of his daughter. Ski having shown persistence in pursuing the matter, M. de Charlus, his eyes bulging and raising his voice, said meaningfully, indicating Albertine, who could not, however, hear us, being busy talking to Mme Cottard and the Princesse Sherbatoff, and in the ambiguous tone of someone wishing to teach a lesson to people of no breeding: "I think it might be time to talk about things that might interest this young lady." But I saw clearly that for him the young lady was not Albertine but Morel; he later confirmed the accuracy of my interpretation by the expressions he used when asking that we should not have any more such conversations in front of Morel. "You know," he said to me, referring to the violinist, "he's not at all what you might think, he's a very decent boy who's always stayed very sensible, very responsible." And you felt from these words that M. de Charlus looked on sexual inversion as a danger equally as threatening for young men as prostitution is for women, and that, if he used the epithet "responsible" in connection with Morel, it was in the sense that it acquires when applied to a young working girl. Then, to change the conversation, Brichot asked me whether I was counting on staying much longer in Incarville. For all that I had pointed out to him more than once that I was living not in Incarville but in Balbec, he always fell back into his error, because it was under the name of Incarville or of Balbec-Incarville that he designated this part of the littoral. There are people who talk in this way about the same things as ourselves but calling them by a slightly different name. A certain lady of the Faubourg Saint-Germain always asked me, when she wanted to talk about the Duchesse de Guermantes, whether I had seen Zénaïde lately, or Oriane-Zénaïde, which meant that at the outset I did not understand. There had probably been a time when, a relation of Mme de Guermantes's being called Oriane, she, for her part, had been called, to avoid confusion, Oriane-Zénaïde. Perhaps, too, there had originally been a station only in Incarville, and you went on from there to Balbec by carriage. "What were you talking about, then?" said Albertine, surprised by the solemn, paterfamilias tone that M. de Charlus had just usurped. "About Balzac," the Baron hastened to reply, "and this evening you're wearing the exact outfit of the Princesse de Cadignan,[33] not the first one, the one at the dinner, but the second." This coincidence derived from the fact that, in choosing Albertine's outfits, I drew my inspiration from the taste she had acquired thanks to Elstir, who greatly valued a sobriety that might have been called British had it not been accompanied by a greater comfort, a French softness. The dresses he preferred most often offered to the eye a harmonious combination of gray shades, like that of Diane de Cadignan. M. de Charlus was almost alone in knowing how to appreciate Albertine's outfits at their true worth; his eye would at once pick out what constituted their rarity, their price; he would never have named one fabric in mistake for another, and he recognized the maker. Only he preferred—for women—rather more dash and color than Elstir could tolerate. And so, on that particular evening, she threw me a glance, half smiling, half anxious, lowering her little pink kitten's nose. Indeed, overlapping with her gray crêpe-de-chine skirt, her gray cheviot jacket made you suppose that Albertine was all in gray. But, signaling to me to help her, because her bouffant sleeves needed smoothing down or pulling up for her to get into or out of her jacket, she took the latter off, and since her sleeves were of a very soft tartan, pink, pale blue, greeny, dove-colored, it was if a rainbow had formed in a gray sky. And she had been wondering whether M. de Charlus was going to like it. "Ah!" exclaimed the latter, in ecstasies. "Look there, a sunbeam, a prism of color. All my compliments to you." "But Monsieur alone has earned any," replied Albertine kindly, indicating me, for she liked to show what had come to her from me. "It's only the women who don't know how to dress that are afraid of color," M. de Charlus went on. "One can be brilliant without vulgarity and soft without being drab. Anyway, you don't have the same reasons as Mme de Cadignan to want to appear detached from life, because that was the idea she wanted to instill in d'Arthez with that gray outfit." Albertine, interested in this wordless language of dresses, questioned M. de Charlus about the Princesse de Cadignan. "Oh, it's an exquisite short novel," said the Baron dreamily. "I know the little garden where Diane de Cadignan walked with Mme d'Espard. It's the garden of one of my cousins." "All these things about his cousin's garden," muttered Brichot to Cottard, "may, just like his genealogy, be something that the excellent Baron values. But what interest can it have for us, who don't have the privilege of walking in it, don't know the lady, and have no claim to a title?" For Brichot did not suspect that one might be interested in a dress or a garden as in a work of art, and that it was as if in Balzac that M. de Charlus could again see Mme de Cadignan's little garden paths. The Baron continued: "But you know her," he said to me, referring to the cousin in question, and in order to flatter me by addressing himself to me as if to someone who, exiled among the little clan, was, for M. de Charlus, if not of his world, then at least went into his world. "At all events, you must have met her at Mme de Villeparisis's." "The Marquise de Villeparisis that the château of Baucreux belongs to?" asked Brichot, looking captivated. "Yes, you know her?" M. de Charlus asked curtly. "Not at all," replied Brichot, "but our colleague Norpois spends part of his vacation every year at Baucreux. I've had occasion to write to him there." I told Morel, thinking to interest him, that M. de Norpois was a friend of my father's. But not a single movement of his face attested to his having heard, so poor an opinion did he have of my parents, as having not come near to being what my great-uncle had been, whose manservant his father was, and who, moreover, unlike the rest of the family, rather liked "cutting a dash" and had left his servants dazzled by the memory of him. "It seems that Mme de Villeparisis is a superior woman; but I've never been admitted to judge of that for myself, any more than my colleagues, for that matter. For Norpois, who is, as it happens, the soul of courtesy and amiability at the Institute, has never introduced any of us to the Marquise. The only one I know who's been received by her is our friend Thureau-Dangin, who had an old family connection, and also Gaston Boissier,[34] whom she wanted to meet following a study she found especially interesting. He dined there once and came back under the spell. Mme Boissier hasn't been asked, though." At these names, Morel gave a feeling smile. "Ah, Thureau-Dangin!" he said to me, with an expression as interested as that which he had displayed on hearing speak of the Marquis de Norpois and of my father had remained indifferent. "Thureau-Dangin and your uncle were inseparable. When a lady wanted a center seat for a reception at the Academy, your uncle used to say, 'I'll write to Thureau-Dangin.' And of course the seat was sent straight away, for you can well understand that M. Thureau-Dangin wouldn't have risked refusing your uncle anything, who'd have got his own back on him. It amuses me, too, to hear the name Boissier, for it was there your great-uncle did all his shopping for the ladies at the New Year.[35] I know because I know the person who was responsible for doing it." He had done more than know him, it was his own father. Certain of these affectionate allusions by Morel to my uncle's memory touched on the fact that we were not counting on remaining forever in the Guermantes *hôtel,* where we had only come to lodge on account of my grandmother. There was talk now and again of a possible move. But in order to understand the advice that Charles Morel was giving me in this regard, you need to know that in the old days my great-uncle had lived at 40 *bis* Boulevard Malesherbes.[36] The consequence of which was that, in the family, since we used to go frequently to my uncle Adolphe's until the fateful day when I had caused a rift between him and my parents by retailing the story of the lady in pink, instead of saying "at your uncle's" we would say "at 40 *bis.*" Some of Mamma's cousins would say to her, in the most natural way, "Ah, we can't have you on Sunday, you're dining at 40 *bis.*" If I was going to visit a relative, I was advised to go first of all to "40 *bis,*" so that my uncle would not be offended that we had not begun with him. He was the owner of the house and proved, truth to tell, very difficult when it came to choosing his tenants, who were all friends, or became so. Colonel le Baron de Vatry came every day to smoke a cigar with him in order to get his repairs done more easily. The porte cochère was always closed. If my uncle caught sight of any washing or a carpet at a window, he would enter in a fury and have it taken back in more quickly than a policeman would today. He nonetheless rented out part of the house, keeping for himself only two floors and the stables. In spite of which, knowing how to please him by praising the excellent state of upkeep of the house, we extolled the comfort of the "little *hôtel*," as if my uncle had been its sole occupant, and he let it pass, without offering any formal denial, as he should have done. The "little *hôtel*" was certainly comfortable (my uncle having introduced all the new inventions of the day). But there was nothing extraordinary about it. My uncle alone, while talking with false modesty about "my little hovel," was convinced, or had at all events instilled into his manservant, his manservant's wife, the coachman, and the cook, the idea that nowhere in Paris did there exist anything comparable, where comfort, luxury, and attraction were concerned, to the little *hôtel*. Charles Morel had grown up in this belief. In it he had remained. And so, even on the days when he was not talking to me, if on the train I mentioned to someone the possibility of our moving, he would at once smile at me and wink knowingly, saying: "Ah, what you need is something in the style of 40 *bis*! You'd be really comfortable there! It can be said your uncle knew what he was doing. I'm quite sure there's nothing that comes up to 40 *bis* in the whole of Paris."

From the melancholy expression that M. de Charlus had assumed when talking about the Princesse de Cadignan, I had a clear sense that that novel had not set him thinking only about the small garden of a cousin who meant little to him. He fell into a profound reverie and, as if talking to himself: *"Les Secrets de la Princesse de Cadignan!"* he exclaimed, "What a masterpiece! So very profound, so very painful, and Diane's bad reputation, which she's so afraid of the man she loves finding out about! How eternally true, and more general than it may appear! There's so much to it!" M. de Charlus uttered these words with a sadness that you felt he found not without its charm, however. Certainly, M. de Charlus, not knowing the precise extent to which his habits were or were not known, had been fearful for some time past that, once he had returned to Paris and he was seen with Morel, the latter's family might step in and his happiness be thus put in jeopardy.

This eventuality had probably appeared to him hitherto only as something profoundly disagreeable and painful. But the Baron was very much the artist. And now that he had, in these past few moments, merged his own situation with that described by Balzac, he had in some sense taken refuge in the novel, and in the misfortune that perhaps threatened him, or which did not at all events fail to alarm him, he had the consolation of discovering in his own anxiety what Swann, and Saint-Loup also, would have called something "very Balzacian." This identification with the Princesse de Cadignan had been made easy for M. de Charlus by virtue of the mental transposition that had become habitual with him and of which he had already given various examples. This was enough, indeed, for the mere replacement of the woman, as the beloved object, by a young man, at once to set in train around the latter that whole process of social complications which develops around a normal liaison. When, for whatever reason, they introduce a change once and for all into the calendar, or into timetables, if the year is made to start a few weeks later, or midnight to strike a quarter of an hour earlier, since the days will nevertheless contain twenty-four hours and the months thirty days, everything that depends on the measurement of time will remain identical. Everything can have been changed without leading to any disturbance, since the ratio between the figures is still the same. So, too, with the lives that adopt Central European Time or the Eastern calendar. It even seems that the pride we take in keeping an actress may have played a part in this particular liaison. When, from the very first day, M. de Charlus had made inquiries into Morel's origins, he had certainly learned that he was of humble extraction, but a demimondaine with whom we are in love is no less glamorous in our eyes for being a daughter of poor people. On the other hand, the well-known musicians to whom he had written—not even out of self-interest, like the friends who, when introducing Swann to Odette, had portrayed her as more difficult and more sought-after than she was—but out of the simple triteness of men in the public eye overpraising a beginner, had replied to the Baron, "Ah, a great talent, considerable position, given how young he is, of course, much appreciated by the cognoscenti, will make his way." And out of that obsession which people who know nothing of inversion have, to talk about masculine beauty: "And, then,

he looks pretty when he's playing; he does better than anyone at a concert; he has pretty hair and distinguished attitudes, his expression is ravishing, he's the very picture of a violinist." And so M. de Charlus,
overexcited in any case by Morel, who did not fail to let him know of
how many propositions he was the object, was flattered to take him
back with him, and to create for him a garret to which he often returned. For he wanted the rest of the time free, as was necessitated by
his career, with which M. de Charlus was anxious, however much
money he might have to give him, that Morel should continue, either
in the very Guermantes-like belief that a man has to do something, that
we are only as good as our talents, and that noble birth or money is
merely the zero that multiplies a value, or because he was afraid that, if
he was unoccupied and never out of his sight, the violinist might become bored. He did not want in any case to deprive himself of the pleasure he got, at certain major concerts, from telling himself, "The man
they're applauding at this moment will be at home with me tonight."
Fashionable people, when they are in love and whatever the form of
that love, stake their vanity on what may destroy the advantages in
which their vanity would previously have found satisfaction.

Morel, sensing that I bore him no malice, genuinely attached to
M. de Charlus, and moreover, perfectly indifferent physically to both
of us, ended by displaying in my own case the same feelings of warm
sympathy as a cocotte who knows that you do not desire her and that in
you her lover has a genuine friend who will not try to make trouble between them. Not only did he talk to me exactly as Rachel, Saint-Loup's
mistress, had once done, but even, judging by what M. de Charlus repeated to me, said the same things about me in my absence as Rachel
had said about me to Robert. Indeed, M. de Charlus said to me, "He's
very fond of you," like Robert's "She's very fond of you." And, like the
nephew for the sake of his mistress, it was for Morel's sake that the uncle frequently invited me to go and dine with them. There were moreover no fewer storms between them than between Robert and Rachel. It
is true that Charlie (Morel) once out of the way, M. de Charlus never
tired of singing his praises, repeating, what he found flattering, that the
violinist was so good to him. It was noticeable nonetheless that frequently, even in front of all the faithful, Charlie wore an irritated ex-

pression instead of appearing always happy and submissive, as the Baron would have wished. This irritation even got later on to the point where, in consequence of the weakness that led M. de Charlus to forgive Morel any unseemliness in his attitude, the violinist did not try to conceal it, or even affected it. I have seen M. de Charlus, on entering a railway compartment where Charlie was sitting with some of his soldier friends, greeted by a shrug of the shoulders from the musician, accompanied by a wink to his comrades. Or else he would make out he was asleep, like someone overcome by boredom at this new arrival. Or he would start to cough, and the others would laugh, jokingly adopt the mincing speech of men of M. de Charlus's kind, and draw Charlie into a corner, who finally returned, as though having been forced, next to M. de Charlus, whose heart had been pierced by all these arrows. It is inconceivable that he should have borne with them; and these everchanging forms of suffering posed once again for M. de Charlus the problem of happiness, forced him not only to demand more, but to long for something other, the previous arrangement finding itself vitiated by an awful memory. Yet, however painful these scenes were afterward to become, it has to be acknowledged that, in the early stages, the genius of the French man of the people traced for Morel, caused him to be clothed in, charming forms of simplicity, of apparent candor, of an independent pride even that seemed inspired by disinterestedness. This was false, but the advantage of such an attitude lay all the more with Morel, inasmuch as, while the one who loves is forever obliged to return to the charge, to raise the bidding, it is, on the contrary, easy for the one who does not love to follow a straight line, at once inflexible and graceful. It existed by virtue of a racial privilege in the very open face of the same Morel whose heart was so tightly closed, a face embellished by that neo-Hellenic grace which flowers in the basilicas of Champagne. For all his simulated pride, often, on catching sight of M. de Charlus at a moment when he was not expecting it, he was embarrassed for the little clan's sake, blushed, and looked down, to the great delight of the Baron, who read a whole novel into it. It was a sign merely of irritation and of shame. There were times when he gave vent to the first; for, however calm and strenuously proper Morel's attitude might normally be, it did not go without being frequently belied. At times even, at some remark made to him by the Baron, there would burst from Morel, in a harsh voice, an insolent riposte by which everyone was shocked. M. de Charlus would lower his head with a sad expression, without making any answer, and, with that ability which idolatrous fathers have of believing that their children's coldness or harshness has gone unnoticed, continued just the same to sing the violinist's praises. M. de Charlus was not always so submissive, but his rebellions generally failed to achieve their end, mainly because, having lived among society people, in calculating the reactions he might evoke, he made allowance for obsequiousness, if not inborn then acquired through upbringing. But with Morel he came up instead against some plebeian whim of momentary indifference. Alas for M. de Charlus, he had not understood that, as far as Morel was concerned, everything else took second place to matters where the Conservatoire and the Conservatoire's good reputation (though this, which was to become more serious, was not as yet an issue) were at stake. Thus does the bourgeoisie, for example, find it easy to change their names out of vanity, great noblemen for advantage. For the young violinist, on the contrary, the name Morel was indissolubly linked to his first prize for violin, hence any modification was out of the question. M. de Charlus would have liked Morel to have everything from him, including his name. Having remarked that Morel's first name was Charles, which resembled Charlus, and that the property where they used to meet was called Les Charmes, he sought to persuade Morel that, a pretty name agreeable to pronounce being one half of an artistic reputation, the virtuoso should not hesitate to take the name of "Charmel," a discreet allusion to the scene of their rendezvous. Morel gave a shrug. As a clinching argument, M. de Charlus had the unfortunate idea of adding that he had a manservant of that name. All this did was to arouse the young man to a furious indignation. "There was a time when my forebears were proud of the title of *valet de chambre*, of *maître d'hôtel* to the King." "There was another time," answered Morel haughtily, "when my forebears cut the throats of yours." M. de Charlus would have been greatly surprised had he been able to imagine that, failing "Charmel," and resigned to adopting Morel and bestowing on him one of the Guermantes family titles that he had at his disposal, but which circumstances, as we shall see, did not permit him to offer the violinist, the latter might refuse, thinking of the artistic reputation attaching to the name Morel and to the comments that would have been made "in class." So far above the Faubourg Saint-Germain did he set the rue Bergère! M. de Charlus had of necessity to content himself for the present with having symbolic rings made for Morel bearing the ancient inscription, PLUS ULTRA CAROL's.[37] Certainly, faced by an adversary of a kind of which he had no experience, M. de Charlus ought to have changed his tactics. But who is capable of that? Moreover, if M. de Charlus had moments of awkwardness, so, equally, did Morel. Far more than the actual circumstance that brought about the rupture, what was, at least temporarily (but this temporary turned out to be final), to prove his undoing with M. de Charlus was that there was in him not just the servility that made him grovel before any harshness and answer gentleness with insolence. Along with this servile nature there went a neurasthenia, made more complicated by his faulty upbringing, which, being aroused in circumstances where he was in the wrong or was becoming a responsibility, meant that, at the very moment when he would have needed all his kindness, all his gentleness, all his cheerfulness to disarm the Baron, he became gloomy and quarrelsome, attempting to start arguments where he knew people did not agree with him, and maintaining his own hostile point of view with a weakness of reasoning and a peremptory violence that even enhanced that weakness. For, soon running out of arguments, he would invent some nonetheless, in which he laid bare the full extent of his ignorance and stupidity. These scarcely showed through when he was being friendly and seeking only to please. Conversely, you saw nothing else during his fits of moroseness, when, from having been inoffensive, they became hateful. M. de Charlus would then feel overcome and invest all his hopes in a better tomorrow, whereas Morel, forgetting that the Baron was keeping him in luxury, would give an ironic smile of pitying condescension and say: "I've never accepted anything from anybody. That way, I've no one I have to say a single thank-you to."

Meanwhile, and as if he were dealing with a man of the world, M. de Charlus continued to exercise his rages, whether genuine or feigned, but by now without effect. They were not always so, however. Thus, one day (which belongs in fact after this early period), when the Baron was returning with Charlie and myself from a lunch at the Verdurins', and expecting to spend the late afternoon and evening with the violinist in Doncières, the latter's taking leave of him the moment we left the train, with, "No, I've got things to do," caused so keen a disappointment in M. de Charlus that, although he may have tried to put a brave face on it, I saw tears melting the makeup on his eyelashes, as he stood bewildered before the train. Such was his grief that, since she and I were planning on ending the day in Doncières, I whispered to Albertine that I would certainly not like for us to leave M. de Charlus on his own, because he seemed, I had no idea why, unhappy. The dear child agreed with all her heart. I then asked M. de Charlus if he would not like me to accompany him for a little way. He, too, agreed, but refused to put my cousin to any trouble on that account. I derived a certain comfort (and no doubt for the last time, since I was resolved to break with her) from ordering her gently, as though she had been my wife, "You go home in your direction, I'll see you again this evening," and from hearing her, as a wife would have done, giving me permission to do as I wished, and agreeing that if M. de Charlus, of whom she was very fond, had need of me I should make myself available. We went, the Baron and I, he swaying his fat body, his Jesuit's eyes lowered, and I following, as far as a café, where they brought us some beer. I sensed that, in his anxiety, M. de Charlus had some plan in view. He suddenly demanded paper and ink and began writing with a strange rapidity. As he covered sheet after sheet, his eyes were flashing with some furious daydream. Once he had written eight pages, he said: "Can I ask a great favor of you? Forgive my sealing this note. But I must. You are to take a cab, a motorcar if you can, to get there quicker. You'll certainly find Morel still in his room, where he's gone to change. Poor boy, he tried to play the bully just as he was leaving us, but you may be sure that his heart is heavier than my own. You are to give him this note and, if he asks where you saw me, you will tell him that you stopped off in Doncières—which is in any case the truth—in order to see Robert—which is not, perhaps—but that you met me with someone you don't know, that I seemed to be in a furious temper, that you thought you caught something about sending seconds—I am fighting tomorrow, indeed. Above all, don't tell him that I'm asking for him, don't try to bring him back, but if he wants to come with you, don't stop him from doing so. Off you go, my boy, it's for his own good, you may be averting a great drama. While you're gone, I shall write to my seconds. I have kept you from going off with your cousin. I hope she won't hold it against me; I believe so, even. For hers is a noble soul, and I know she's one of those women who know how not to overlook the greatness of the occasion. You must thank her on my behalf. I am personally indebted to her, and it pleases me that it should be so." I felt much pity for M. de Charlus; it seemed to me that Charlie might have prevented this duel, of which he was perhaps the cause, and I was revolted, were this the case, that he should have gone off so unfeelingly instead of assisting his patron. My indignation grew when, on arriving at the house where Morel was lodging, I recognized the violinist's voice, who, in the need he felt to broadcast his high spirits, was singing lustily, "On Saturday evenings, after the weekly grind!"[38] If only poor M. de Charlus could have heard him, he who wanted you to believe, and himself believed no doubt, that Morel at this moment was heavy at heart! Charlie started jigging with delight when he saw me. "Hello, *mon vieux*. Forgive me calling you that, one picks up vile habits from this ghastly life in the army. What a stroke of good luck, seeing you! I've got my evening to myself. Do, please, let's spend it together. We can stay here if you like that, we can take a boat out if you'd rather, we can have some music, I don't have any preference." I told him that I was obliged to dine in Balbec; he was most anxious for me to invite him, but I refused. "But if you're in such a hurry, why did you come?" "I've brought you a note from M. de Charlus." At that name, all his high spirits evaporated; his face contracted. "What, he has to come pestering me even here! Then I'm a slave! Do me a kindness, *mon vieux*. I'm not opening the letter. You can tell him you couldn't find me." "Wouldn't you do better to open it? I imagine it's something serious." "No, a hundred times over; you don't know that old crook's lies, his infernal stratagems. It's a device to get me to go and see him. Well, I'm not going; I want a peaceful evening." "But isn't there a duel tomorrow?" I asked Morel, who I had supposed was in the know. "A duel?" he said, looking stupefied. "I've not heard a word about that. And anyway, I don't give a damn, that disgusting old man can happily go and get himself massacred if he wants. But hold on, you intrigue me; I'm going to take a look at his letter all the same. You can tell him you left it on the off chance, in case I came home." As Morel was talking, I was gazing in amazement at the splendid books that M. de Charlus had given him and which were cluttering the room. The violinist having refused those that bore "I belong to the Baron" and the like, a device that he found insulting to himself, as signifying possession, the Baron, with that sentimental ingenuity in which an unhappy love takes pleasure, had varied it with others, originating with his forebears but ordered from the binder's according to the circumstances of a melancholy affection. Sometimes these were brief and confident, such as *"Spes mea"* or *"Exspectata non eludet";*[39] sometimes merely resigned, such as *"J'attendrai";*[40] some were gallant, *"Mesmes plaisirs du mestre,"*[41] or recommending chastity, like that borrowed from the Simiane, semy of towers azure and fleurs-de-lis, and twisted as to its meaning, *"Sustentant lilia turres";*[42] others, finally, despairing and fixing a rendezvous in heaven with him who had wanted nothing to do with him on earth, *"Manet ultima caelo",*[43] and, finding the bunch of grapes he had been unable to reach too green, and pretending not to have been seeking what he had not obtained, in one of them M. de Charlus had said, *"Non mortale quod opto."*[44] But I did not have time to look at them all.

If, in dashing this letter down on paper, M. de Charlus seemed to have fallen prey to the demon of inspiration that was causing his pen to fly, the moment Morel had broken the seal, *"Atavis et armis,"*[45] charged with a leopard accompanied by two roses gules, he began to read with a feverishness as great as that which M. de Charlus had shown when writing, and his eyes traveled no less quickly across these hastily scrawled pages than had the Baron's pen. "Oh my God," he exclaimed, "that's all it needed. But where can I find him? God knows where he is now." I hinted that, by hurrying, he would still find him perhaps at a brasserie, where he had asked for beer in order to recompose himself. "I don't know whether I'll be coming back," he said to his housekeeper, and added *in petto:* "It'll depend on how things turn out." A few minutes later, we arrived at the café. I observed M. de Charlus's expression at the moment he caught sight of me. Finding that I had not returned alone, I had the feeling that breath, that life itself, had been restored to him. Being in a mood that evening not to be able to do without Morel, he had invented that it had been reported to him that two of the regimental officers had slandered him in connection with the violinist, and that he was going to send his seconds to them. Morel had glimpsed the scandal, his life in the regiment made impossible, and had come running. In which he was not altogether wrong. For, to make his falsehood more plausible, M. de Charlus had already written to two friends (one was Cottard) to ask them to be his seconds. And had the violinist not come, it is certain that, out of control as he was, M. de Charlus (to turn his unhappiness into rage) would have sent them at random to some officer or another, whom he would have found solace in fighting. In the meantime, M. de Charlus, reminding himself that he was of purer stock than the House of France, told himself that it was very good of him to be thus fretting and fuming for the son of a *maître d'hôtel* with whose master he would not have deigned to associate. On the other hand, if he now took pleasure in consorting with hardly anyone except debauchees, the latter's ingrained habit of not answering letters, and of failing to keep an assignation, without warning and without apologizing afterward, produced so many emotions in him, since a love affair was often involved, and the rest of the time caused him so much irritation, inconvenience, and rage, that there were times when he felt nostalgia for the multiplicity of letters about nothing at all and the scrupulous exactitude of ambassadors and princes, who, though, sadly, they might have no attraction for him, yet afforded him a sort of respite. Accustomed to Morel's ways, and knowing how little hold he had over him and how incapable he was of insinuating himself into a life in which vulgar companionships, consecrated by habit, took up too much space and time for an hour to be set aside for the evicted, proud, and vainly imploring nobleman, M. de Charlus was so convinced that the musician would not come, was so afraid of having caused a permanent rift between them by overstepping the mark, that it was all he could do to stifle a cry when he saw him. But, feeling himself victorious, he insisted on dictating the peace terms, and on extracting such advantages as he could. "What have you come here for?" he said. "And you?" he added, looking at me. "I specifically told you not to bring me him back." "He didn't want to bring me," said Morel, rolling toward M. de Charlus, in his artless coquettishness, conventionally sad and languorously old-fashioned glances, with an expression he no doubt thought irresistible, of wanting to kiss the Baron and longing to burst into tears. "It's I who came in spite of him. I've come in the name of our friendship, to implore you on both knees not to commit this folly." M. de Charlus was delirious with joy. The reaction was almost too much for his nerves; in spite of this, he retained control of them. "The friendship which you invoke somewhat inopportunely," he replied curtly, "ought, on the contrary, to make you approve of me when I do not think I should allow the impertinences of a fool to go unchecked. In any case, if I wanted to obey the entreaties of an affection that I have known better inspired, it would no longer be in my power to do so, my letters to my seconds have gone and I don't doubt their accepting. You have always behaved toward me like a young imbecile, and, instead of priding yourself, as you had a right to do, on the predilection I had shown you, instead of letting that rabble of noncommissioned officers and domestic servants among whom military law obliges you to live see what a source of incomparable pride a friendship such as mine was for you, you sought to apologize, to make a stupid virtue almost out of being insufficiently grateful. I know that in this," he added, so as not to let it be seen how deeply humiliated he had been by certain scenes, "you are guilty only of allowing yourself to be led on by the jealousy of others. But how, at your age, can you be such a child—and a rather badly brought-up child—as not to have guessed right away that your election by me and all the advantages that would result from it for you were going to stir up jealousy, that all your comrades, while they were egging you on to quarrel with me, would be working to take your place? I did not see fit to warn you of the letters I have received in that connection from all those whom you trust the most. I despise the overtures of these flunkies just as I do their ineffectual mockery. The one person who concerns me is you, because I am very fond of you, but affection has its limits, as you should have suspected." However harsh the word "flunky" might sound in the ears of Morel, whose father had been one, indeed precisely because his father had been one, the explanation of every social misadventure by "jealousy," a simplistic and absurd explanation, yet hard-wearing, and which, among a certain class, always "takes," just as unfailingly as do old tricks of the trade with audiences in the theater, or the threat of the clerical menace in political assemblies,[46] found almost as ready an acceptance with him as with Françoise or Mme de Guermantes's servants, for whom it was the one source of humanity's misfortunes. He did not doubt that his comrades had been trying to nab his place and was all the more unhappy about this calamitous, albeit imaginary duel. "Oh, I despair!" exclaimed Charlie. "I shan't survive it. But aren't they to see you before they go and find this officer?" "I don't know, I think so, yes. I sent to tell one of them I'd be remaining here this evening and I shall give him my instructions." "I hope between now and him coming to make you hear reason; just allow me to remain here with you," Morel asked him fondly. This was all that M. de Charlus had wanted. He did not give in right away. "You'd be wrong to apply here the proverbial 'Spare the rod and spoil the child,' for it's you who are the child, and I intend to use the rod, even after our quarrel, on those who tried despicably to do you harm. Until now, to their prying insinuations, daring to ask me how a man like myself could consort with a gigolo of your sort, risen from nowhere, my one response was the motto of my La Rochefoucauld cousins, *'C'est mon plaisir.'*[47] I have even stressed to you more than once that this pleasure was susceptible of becoming my greatest pleasure, without your arbitrary elevation resulting in my own abasement." And, in an almost insane impulse of pride, he exclaimed, raising his arms, *"Tantus ab uno splendor!"*[48] To condescend is not to descend," he added, more calmly, after this delirium of pride and joy. "I hope at least that my two adversaries, despite the inequality of rank, are of a blood that I can cause to flow without shame. I have made discreet inquiries in that regard which have reassured me. If you retained any gratitude to me, you ought on the contrary to be proud to see that, because of you, I am recovering the bellicose temperament of my forebears, saying, like them, in the event of a fatal outcome, now that I have realized what a young rogue you are, *'Mort m'est vie.'* "[49] And M. de Charlus spoke with sincerity, not only out of love for Morel, but because a taste for combat that he innocently believed he had got from his forefathers put him in such good heart at the thought of fighting that he would now have felt regret at giving up this duel, originally contrived only in order to get Morel to come. He had never had an affair of honor without at once seeing himself as valorous and identifying himself with the celebrated Connétable de Guermantes, whereas for anyone else this same act of taking the field would have seemed of the utmost insignificance. "I think it'll be very beautiful," he said to us with sincerity, intoning each word. "To see Sarah Bernhardt in *L'Aiglon,* what is that? Excrement. Mounet-Sully in *Oedipus*?[50] Excrement. It acquires at most a certain pallor of transfiguration when it takes place in the Arena in Nîmes. But what is it compared with that unprecedented thing, of seeing the actual descendant of the Connétable do battle?" At the mere thought of which, M. de Charlus, unable to contain his delight, began to perform *contre-de-quartes* reminiscent of Molière,[51] leading us to move our beer glasses closer for safety, and to fear that the first clash of blades might wound the adversaries, the doctor, and the seconds. "What a tempting spectacle it would be for a painter! You who know M. Elstir," he said to me, "you should bring him along." I replied that he was not on the coast. M. de Charlus hinted that he might be sent a telegram. "Oh, I say that for his sake," he added, faced by my silence. "It's always interesting for a master—in my opinion, he is one—to capture such an example of ethnic reviviscence. There's perhaps only one a century."

But if M. de Charlus was enchanted by the prospect of a fight that he had at first thought purely fictitious, Morel was reflecting in terror on the rumors that, thanks to the stir that the duel would make, might be hawked all the way from the regimental band to the temple on the rue Bergère. Already seeing his "class" knowing everything, he became more and more insistent with M. de Charlus, who continued to gesticulate before the heady prospect of fighting. He implored the Baron to allow him not to leave him until the next day but one, the supposed day of the duel, so as to keep him in sight and try to make him hear the voice of reason. So affectionate a proposal overcame M. de Charlus's last hesitations. He said that he would try to find a way out, that he would defer a final decision until the next day but one. In this way, by not settling the matter all at once, M. de Charlus would be able to keep Charlie for two days at least and use them to obtain from him undertakings for the future in exchange for his giving up the duel, an exercise that in itself, he said, enchanted him, and which he would not forgo without regret. And in this, moreover, he was being sincere, for he had always found pleasure in taking the field when it was a matter of crossing steel or exchanging shots with an adversary. Cottard finally arrived although having been much delayed, for, overjoyed to be acting as a second but even more excited, he had been obliged to stop at every café and farmhouse along the way, asking whether they would be kind enough to direct him to "number 100" or "the smallest room." The moment he was there, the Baron led him off into a room apart, for he thought it more in keeping with the rules that Charlie and I should not be present at their interview, and he excelled in the temporary appointment of some nondescript room as a throne room or debating chamber. Once alone with Cottard, he thanked him warmly but declared that it was likely that the remark retailed had not in actual fact been made, and that in these circumstances the doctor might be so good as to warn the other second that, barring possible complications, the incident was considered closed. The danger receding, Cottard was disappointed. He even wanted momentarily to display anger, but remembered that one of his mentors, who had enjoyed the most successful medical career of his day, having failed to get into the Académie the first time by only two votes, had put a brave face on things and gone to shake the hand of his successful rival. And so the doctor dispensed with an expression of pique that would no longer have changed anything and, after muttering, he the most fearful of men, that there are some things that one cannot let pass, he added that it was better this way, that this solution delighted him. M. de Charlus, anxious to evince his gratitude to the doctor, in the same way as M. le Duc his brother might have arranged the collar of my father's overcoat, or a duchess above all have put an arm around the waist of some woman of the people, brought his chair up close to that of the doctor, in spite of the distaste with which the latter filled him. And not only without any physical pleasure, but overcoming a physical revulsion, as a Guermantes, not as an invert, in order to take leave of the doctor, he held his hand and stroked it for a moment, with the kindness of a master fondling the muzzle of his horse and giving it a lump of sugar. Cottard, however, who had never allowed the Baron to see that he had heard even the vaguest dark rumors circulating as to his habits, but nevertheless saw him, in his heart of hearts,

as forming part of the class of the "abnormal" (with his usual termino-
logical impropriety, and in the most serious tone, he even used to say of
one of M. Verdurin's manservants, "Isn't he the Baron's mistress?"),
persons of whom he had scant experience, imagined that this stroking
of his hand was the immediate prelude to a rape, for the accomplish-
ment of which, the duel having served merely as a pretext, he had been
drawn into an ambush and led by the Baron into this lonely hall, where
he was about to be taken by force. Not daring to leave his chair, to
which fear kept him rooted, he rolled his eyes in alarm, as though he
had fallen into the hands of a savage who he was not altogether certain
might not feed off human flesh. Finally, M. de Charlus letting go his
hand, and wishing to be affable to the bitter end: "You'll take a little
something with us, as they say, what in the old days was called a *mazagran* or a *gloria*,[52] drinks you now meet with, except as archaeological cu-
riosities, only in the plays of Labiche and the cafés of Doncières. A
*gloria* would be quite appropriate to the setting, would it not? And to
the occasion, what d'you say?" "I am president of the Anti-Alcohol
League," replied Cottard. "It would only need some provincial quack to
come past, for them to say I don't practice what I preach. *Os homini sublime dedit caelumque tueri*,"[53] he added, although there was no connection, but because his stock of Latin quotations was somewhat meager, if
adequate for impressing his students. M. de Charlus gave a shrug and
brought Cottard back to us, having demanded from him a confidential-
ity that mattered all the more to him inasmuch as, the motive for the
abortive duel being purely imaginary, it had to be prevented from
reaching the ears of the officer thus arbitrarily accused. As we were all
four of us drinking, Mme Cottard, who had been waiting for her husband outside, in front of the door, and whom M. de Charlus had certainly seen but had not troubled to bring in, entered and bid the Baron
good day, who held out his hand to her as if to a chambermaid, without
moving from his chair, partly as a king receiving homage, partly as a
snob who does not want a less-than-fashionable woman to sit down at
his table, partly as an egotist who takes pleasure in being alone with his
friends and does not wish to be intruded on. Mme Cottard remained
standing therefore, talking to M. de Charlus and her husband. But per-

haps because politeness, the "done thing," is not the exclusive privilege of the Guermantes, but may suddenly illuminate and guide the most uncertain brains, or because, having frequently been unfaithful to his wife, there were moments when Cottard, by a sort of requital, felt the need to protect her against whoever was being disrespectful to her, the doctor suddenly gave a frown, something that I had never seen him do, and, without consulting M. de Charlus, magisterially: "Come, Léontine, don't stay standing up, sit down." "But am I not disturbing you?" Mme Cottard asked M. de Charlus timidly, who, taken aback by the doctor's tone, had made no answer. And, not allowing him a second opportunity, Cottard went on authoritatively: "I told you to sit down."

A moment or two later, we broke up, and then M. de Charlus said to Morel, "I conclude from this whole business, which has ended better than you deserved, that you do not know how to conduct yourself, and that at the end of your military service I shall take you back myself to your father, as did the Archangel Raphael, sent by God to the young Tobias."[54] And the Baron began to smile with an air of grandeur, and a delight that Morel, who found scant pleasure in the prospect of being thus taken home, did not seem to share. In the headiness of likening himself to the Archangel, and Morel to the son of Tobit, M. de Charlus had lost sight of the object of his remark, which had been to test the ground to learn whether, as he wanted, Morel would consent to go with him to Paris. Intoxicated by his love, or by his vanity, the Baron did not see, or pretended not to see, the face that the violinist pulled, for, having left the latter on his own in the café, he said to me with an arrogant smile: "Did you notice, when I compared him to the son of Tobit, how delirious with joy he was? That's because, highly intelligent as he is, he realized at once that the Father with whom he was going henceforth to live was not his father according to the flesh, who must be some frightful mustachioed manservant, but his spiritual father, that is to say Myself. How glorious for him! How proudly he drew back his head! What joy he felt at having realized! I'm sure he'll repeat every day, 'O God, who didst give the blessed Archangel Raphael to be a *guide* to Thy servant Tobias on a long journey, grant to us, Thy servants, that we may be always protected by him and armed with his succor.' I had no need even," added the Baron, strongly persuaded that he would one day sit before the throne of God, "to tell him that I was the heavenly messenger, he realized that for himself and was speechless with happiness!" And M. de Charlus (who, on the contrary, had not been deprived of the power of speech by happiness), unconcerned by the few passersby who looked around thinking they had a lunatic on their hands, exclaimed all alone and at the top of his voice, raising his hands, "Alleluia!"

This reconciliation put an end to M. de Charlus's torments only for a time; often Morel, having left on maneuvers, too far away for M. de Charlus to be able to go visit him or send me to talk to him, would write the Baron fond and despairing letters, in which he assured him that he would have to put an end to his life because some frightful affair meant that he needed twenty-five thousand francs. He did not say what the frightful affair was, and had he done so, it would no doubt have been a fabrication. As for the money itself, M. de Charlus would willingly have sent it had he not felt that this would have provided Charlie with the means of dispensing with him and also of enjoying the favors of someone else. Thus he refused, and his telegrams had the curt, sharp-edged tone of his voice. Once he was certain of their effect, he wished that Morel might have fallen out with him for good, for, convinced that it was the opposite that would materialize, he was made aware of all the disadvantages that would be reborn from this inevitable liaison. But if no reply came from Morel, he could no longer sleep, he no longer knew a moment's peace of mind, so many in number, indeed, are the things that we experience without knowing them, and the profound inner realities that remain hidden from us. He then entertained all manner of suppositions as to the enormity that had led to Morel's having need of twenty-five thousand francs; he made it take every form and attached many proper names to it, one after the other. I believe that at such moments M. de Charlus (and although by that time his snobbery was on the decline, and had already been caught up, if not overtaken, by the growing curiosity the Baron felt toward the common people) must have recalled with a certain nostalgia the graceful, variegated whirl of social gatherings at which the most charming men and women sought him out only for the disinterested pleasure that he afforded them, and where no one would have dreamed of "taking him for a ride," or of inventing some "frightful affair" for which one is ready to put an end to one's days unless one is in immediate receipt of twenty-five thousand francs. I believe that, and perhaps because he had all the same remained more a man of Combray than had I, and had grafted a feudal pride onto German arrogance, he must then have discovered that you do not become the fancy man of a domestic servant with impunity, that the common people are not quite the same thing as society, and "did not have confidence" in the people as I myself always have.

The little train's next stop, Maineville, reminds me indeed of an incident relating to Morel and M. de Charlus. Before speaking of it, I ought to say that the stop in Maineville (when you were conducting a fashionable new arrival to Balbec, someone who, so as not to be in the way, preferred not to stay at La Raspelière) was the occasion of scenes less painful than the one that I shall recount in a moment. The new arrival, having his hand luggage in the train, generally found the Grand-Hôtel a little too far away, but since, before Balbec, there were only small beach resorts with uncomfortable villas, he had, out of a taste for luxury and well-being, resigned himself to the long journey when, just as the train came to a stop in Maineville, he saw, suddenly looming up, the Palace, which he could not have suspected was a house of prostitution. "Don't let's go any further," he would invariably say to Mme Cottard, a woman known for being of a practical bent and for her sound advice. "That's exactly what I need. What's the point of going all the way to Balbec, where it certainly won't be any better? Simply from the look of it, I adjudge it'll have every comfort; I could perfectly well bring Mme Verdurin there, for, in return for her civility, I count on giving a few small gatherings in her honor. She won't have so far to travel as if I stay in Balbec. This strikes me as exactly right for her, and for your wife, my dear professor. They must have private rooms; we'll bring the ladies here. Between ourselves, I don't know why, instead of leasing La Raspelière, Mme Verdurin didn't come and live here. It's a lot healthier than old houses like La Raspelière, which is bound to be damp, without being clean, for that matter; they don't have hot water, one can't wash as one would like to. Maineville strikes me as far pleasanter. Mme Verdurin could have played her role of patronne there to perfection. Everyone to his own taste anyway, I shall establish myself here; Mme

Cottard, will you not alight with me? Wasting no time, for it won't be long before the train leaves again. You must pilot me into the establishment, which will be yours and which you must have often frequented. It's a setting simply made for you." We had the utmost difficulty in silencing the luckless newcomer and above all in preventing him from alighting, for, with the obstinacy that often emanates from a gaffe, he would insist, would pick up his suitcases and refuse to hear another word until he had been assured that neither Mme Verdurin nor Mme Cottard would come and visit him there. "At all events, I shall elect domicile there. Mme Verdurin will only have to write to me there."

The recollection concerning Morel relates to an incident of a more particular order. There were others, but I shall content myself here, as the "slow coach" comes to a halt and the porter shouts out Doncières, Grattevast,[55] Maineville, etc., with noting what the small beach resort or garrison evokes for me. I have already spoken of Maineville (*media villa*) and of the importance it had acquired on account of the sumptuous house of prostitution that had recently been constructed there, not without exciting futile protests from the mothers. But before saying how Maineville comes to be linked in my memory to Morel and M. de Charlus, I must note the disproportion (which I shall have to go into more thoroughly later) between the importance that Morel attached to keeping certain hours free and the insignificance of the occupations to which he claimed to devote them, this same disproportion being found again amid the explanations of another kind that he gave to M. de Charlus. He, who played at being disinterested with the Baron (and could do so without risk, given his patron's generosity) when he wanted to have the evening to himself, in order to give a lesson and so on, did not fail to add to his excuse these words, spoken with an avaricious smile: "Besides, it may earn me forty francs. That's not nothing. Allow me to go there, because you can see it's in my interest. I mean, I don't have a private income like you, I've a position to make, it's time to be earning a few sous." In wanting to give his lesson, Morel was not being altogether insincere. For one thing, to say that money has no color is untrue. A new means of earning it can make coins grown dull with use shine like new. Had he really gone out for the sake of a lesson, it is possible that two louis handed him on leaving by a pupil would

have affected him differently from two louis fallen from the hand of
M. de Charlus. And then the wealthiest of men would journey miles for
the sake of two louis, which become leagues when you are the son of a
manservant. But M. de Charlus often had his doubts as to the reality of
the violin lesson, made all the stronger by the fact that the musician
often invoked pretexts of another kind, of an entirely disinterested order materially speaking, and in any case absurd. Morel could thus not
help presenting a picture of his life, but intentionally, as well as unintentionally, of such murkiness that certain bits of it alone let themselves
be clearly seen. For a whole month, he placed himself at M. de Charlus's disposal on condition that he had his evenings free, for he wanted
to keep up with a course of lectures on algebra. Come and see M. de
Charlus afterward? Ah, that was impossible, the lectures sometimes
went on very late. "Past two in the morning, even?" asked the Baron.
"Sometimes." "But you can learn algebra just as easily from a book."
"Even more easily, because I don't understand much at the lectures."
"Well, then? Anyway, algebra's not going to be of any use to you." "I
love it. It drives away my neurasthenia." "It can't be algebra that makes
him ask for leave at nights," M. de Charlus said to himself. "Can he be
attached to the police?" At all events, Morel, whatever objections might
be raised, reserved certain late hours, whether on account of the algebra
or of the violin. On one occasion, it was neither one nor the other but
the Prince de Guermantes, who, having come to spend a few days on
the coast to pay a visit to the Duchess of Luxembourg, encountered the
musician, without knowing who he was and without being known to
him, and offered him fifty francs to spend the night together at the
house of prostitution in Maineville; a twofold pleasure, where Morel
was concerned, of the profit he would make out of M. de Guermantes
and the voluptuousness of being surrounded by women whose dark-
skinned breasts were displayed quite openly. Somehow or other, M. de
Charlus had an idea of what had transpired and where, but not of
the seducer. Frantic with jealousy, and to know who this latter was, he
telegraphed to Jupien, who arrived two days later, and when, at the beginning of the following week, Morel announced that he would again
be absent, the Baron asked Jupien if he would undertake to bribe the
madam of the establishment and arrange that Jupien and he be hidden

in order to witness the scene. "Understood. Leave it to me, my little charmer," Jupien replied to the Baron. It is hard to credit the extent to which his anxiety had disturbed, and by the same token had even momentarily enriched, M. de Charlus's mind. Love causes these veritable geological upheavals in our thoughts. In those of M. de Charlus, which, a few days before, had resembled a plain so smooth that, away into the distance, he would not have been able to spot an idea lying on the surface, there had abruptly arisen, hard as stone, a mountain massif, but of mountains so sculpted it was as if some statuary, instead of carrying the marble away, had carved it where it lay, and where there writhed, in giant, titanic groups, Fury, Jealousy, Curiosity, Envy, Hatred, Suffering, Pride, Terror, and Love.

The evening on which Morel was to be absent had meanwhile arrived. Jupien's mission had been successful. He and the Baron were to go there around eleven o'clock at night, and they would be hidden. Three streets before reaching this magnificent house of prostitution (to which they came from all the fashionable places round about), M. de Charlus was walking on tiptoe, disguising his voice, and begging Jupien to lower his voice, in case Morel should hear them from inside. But, the moment he made his stealthy entrance into the hallway, M. de Charlus, who had little experience of places of this sort, found himself, to his terror and amazement, in a place noisier than the Bourse or the Hôtel des Ventes.[56] It was in vain that he recommended the soubrettes who were crowding round him to talk more quietly; their voices were being drowned, in any case, by the noise of lots being cried and knocked down, made by an old *sous-maîtresse*[57] with a very dark wig and a face creased with the gravity of a lawyer or a Spanish priest, who, with a noise like thunder, was forever coming out, as she allowed doors to be alternately opened and closed again, like someone controlling the traffic, with: "Put Monsieur in number 28, in the Spanish room." "No more to go in." "Open the door again, these gentlemen are asking for Mlle Noémie. She's waiting for them in the Persian saloon." M. de Charlus was as terrified as a provincial having to cross the boulevards; and, to choose a comparison infinitely less sacrilegious than the subject portrayed on the capitals in the porch of the old church in Couliville, the voices of the young maids tirelessly repeated, in a lower register, the *sous-maîtresse*'s orders, like the catechisms you can hear schoolchildren chanting in the sonority of a country church. Alarmed though he was, M. de Charlus, who, in the street, had been fearful of being overheard, having persuaded himself that Morel was at the window, was perhaps less frightened even so amid the bellowing on these immense staircases, where you realized that from the bedrooms nothing could be seen. Finally, his calvary at an end, he found Mlle Noémie, who was to hide him together with Jupien, but who began by shutting him in a very sumptuous Persian saloon from where he could see nothing. She told him that Morel had asked for a drink of orangeade and that as soon as he had been served it the two travelers would be taken into a viewing room. Meanwhile, since she was being asked for, she promised them, as in a folk tale, that, to help them pass the time, she would send them in "an intelligent little lady." For she herself was being sent for. The intelligent little lady wore a Persian wrap, which she wanted to take off. M. de Charlus asked her to do nothing of the sort, and she had champagne brought up that cost forty francs a bottle. In point of fact, during this time Morel was with the Prince de Guermantes; he had, for form's sake, made a pretense of mistaking the room, and had gone into one in which there were two women, who had made haste to leave the two gentlemen to themselves. M. de Charlus knew nothing of all this, but was cursing and trying to open doors, and he asked for Mlle Noémie again, who, having overheard the intelligent little lady giving M. de Charlus details concerning Morel that did not accord with those that she herself had given Jupien, sent her packing and quickly sent in, as a replacement for the intelligent little lady, "a nice little lady," who did not show them anything, either, but told them what a responsible establishment it was and likewise asked for champagne. The Baron, fuming, got Mlle Noémie back once more, who told them, "Yes, it's a bit long-winded, the ladies are adopting poses, he doesn't look as though he wants to do anything." At last, faced with the Baron's promises, and his threats, Mlle Noémie went off looking annoyed, assuring them they would not have to wait more than another five minutes. These five minutes lasted for an hour, after which Noémie led a M. de Charlus mad with rage and a despondent Jupien stealthily toward a door that was ajar, telling them: "You'll have a very good view. On the other hand, it's not very interesting at present, he's with three ladies, he's telling them about his life in the army." Finally, the Baron was able to see through the gap in the doorway, as well as in the mirrors. But a mortal terror forced him to lean against the wall. It was indeed Morel that he had before him, but, as though the pagan mysteries and enchantments still existed, it was the shade of Morel rather, Morel embalmed, not even Morel resuscitated like Lazarus, an apparition of Morel, a spectral Morel, Morel revenant, or conjured up in this room (where the walls and divans everywhere repeated emblems of sorcery), who was a few meters away from him, in profile. Morel was, as after death, drained of color; between the women, with whom it seemed he should have been disporting himself joyously, livid, he remained frozen in an artificial immobility; in order to drink the goblet of champagne that stood in front of him, his lifeless arm tried slowly to reach out and fell back. You got the impression of that equivocation where a religion speaks of immortality but means by it something that does not exclude nothingness. The women were plying him with questions: "You see," said Mlle Noémie in a low voice to the Baron, "they're talking to him about his life in the army, amusing, isn't it?" And she laughed. "Are you satisfied? He's peaceful, isn't he?" she added, as she might have said of a dying man. The women plied him with questions, but Morel, inanimate, did not have the strength to answer them. The miracle of even one murmured word did not occur. M. de Charlus knew only a moment's hesitation before grasping the truth, that, whether it was Jupien's gaucheness when going to make the arrangements, or the potentiality of secrets to expand once confided, which means that they are never kept, or the indiscreet natures of the women, or fear of the police, Morel had been warned that two gentlemen had paid a lot of money in order to watch him, and they had brought out the Prince de Guermantes metamorphosed into three women, and so positioned poor Morel, quaking and paralyzed by stupefaction, that, if M. de Charlus could see him only with difficulty, he, terror-stricken, incapable of speech, not daring to pick up his glass for fear of dropping it, had a clear view of the Baron.

Nor did the story end any more happily for the Prince de Guermantes. When he had been made to leave so that M. de Charlus might not see him, furious at this setback but unsuspecting of who was behind it, he had pleaded with Morel, though still unwilling to let him know who he was, to fix a rendezvous for the following night in a small villa that he had rented, and which, despite the short time he would be staying there, he had, in accordance with the same obsessive habit as we have earlier remarked in Mme de Villeparisis, decorated with a number of family mementos, so as to feel more at home. The next day, therefore, Morel, looking behind him the whole time, fearful of being followed and spied on by M. de Charlus, had finally, not having observed any suspicious passersby, entered the villa. A valet showed him into the drawing room, saying that he would go and inform Monsieur (his master had warned him not to utter the word "Prince" for fear of arousing suspicion). But once Morel found himself alone and wanted to look in the mirror, to see whether his lock of hair might have been disarranged, it was like a hallucination. On the mantelpiece, the photographs, recognizable to the violinist, he having seen them at M. de Charlus's, of the Princesse de Guermantes, the Duchess of Luxembourg, and Mme de Villeparisis, petrified him at first with fright. At the same moment, he caught sight of that of M. de Charlus, which stood a little farther back. The Baron seemed to have immobilized Morel with a strange, fixed stare. Wild with terror, Morel, recovering from his initial stupefaction, and not doubting that this was an ambush into which M. de Charlus had led him as a test of his fidelity, tumbled down the villa's few steps four at a time, and began running as fast as his legs could carry him along the road, so that, when the Prince de Guermantes (after believing that he had made this passing acquaintance serve his period of probation, and not without wondering whether it was altogether wise and whether the individual in question might not be dangerous) entered the drawing room, he found no one there any longer. In vain did he explore with his valet and, for fear of burglars, revolver in hand, the whole house, which was not large, every corner of the little garden and the basement, the companion whose presence he had thought certain had vanished. He came across him several times in the course of the following week. But each time it was Morel, the dangerous individual, who ran off, as if the Prince had been more dangerous still. Immovable in his suspicions, Morel never dispelled them, and even in Paris the sight of the Prince de Guermantes was enough to cause him to turn tail. Whereby M. de Charlus was protected against an infidelity that made him despair, and avenged, without ever having imagined it, or above all in what way.

But already the memories of what had been retailed to me on this matter are being replaced by others, for the TSN, resuming its snail-like progress, is continuing to set down and pick up passengers at the next stations.

At Grattevast, where his sister lived, with whom he had gone to spend the afternoon, there sometimes got in M. Pierre de Verjus, Comte de Crécy (who was known simply as the Comte de Crécy), a poor but extremely distinguished member of the gentry whom I had met through the Cambremers, with whom, however, he was by no means intimate. As he was reduced to an exceedingly modest, almost impoverished way of life, I felt that a cigar and a "glass of something" were things so agreeable to him that I acquired the habit, on the days when I was unable to meet Albertine, of inviting him to Balbec. Very discerning, expressing himself beautifully, his hair quite white, with charming blue eyes, he talked above all, in an artificial way, very tactfully, about the comforts of the seigneurial life, which he had evidently known, as well as about genealogies. When I asked him what was engraved on his ring, he told me, smiling modestly, "It's a sprig of verjuice." And he added, with the pleasure of a wine-taster, "Our arms are a branch of verjuice—symbolic, since my name is Verjus—stalked and foliated vert." But I imagine he would have felt disappointment if in Balbec I had offered him only verjuice to drink. He liked the most expensive wines, from deprivation no doubt, and a profound knowledge of what he had been deprived of, from taste, perhaps also from a propensity for exaggeration. Thus, when I invited him to dinner in Balbec, he would order the meal with a knowledgeable refinement but ate rather too much, and above all drank, making them serve the wines that need it at room temperature, and chill those that demand to be put on ice. Before dinner and after, he would indicate the date or the number he wanted for a port or a *fine*, as he might have done for the generally unknown raising of a marquisate, with which he was also familiar.

As I was for Aimé a favorite guest, he was overjoyed that I should be giving these extra dinners and would shout to the waiters, "Quick, get table 25 ready"; he did not even say "get" but "get me," as though it had been for him. And since the language of *maîtres d'hôtel* is not altogether the same as that of *chefs de rang, demi-chefs, commis,* and so on, just as I was asking for the bill he would say to the waiter who had been serving us, with a repeated, soothing gesture with the back of his hand, as though he were trying to quiet a horse preparing to take the bit between its teeth: "Don't rush things"—over the bill. "Gently, very gently does it." Then, as the waiter went off, armed with this *aide-mémoire,* Aimé, fearing that his injunctions might not be strictly adhered to, called him back: "Wait, I'm going to reckon it up myself." And as I was telling him that it was no matter: "I hold it as a principle that, in the common parlance, one mustn't fleece a guest." As for the manager, seeing my guest's simple clothes, always the same and somewhat threadbare (yet no one would have been more adept at the art of dressing ostentatiously, like one of Balzac's dandies, had he had the means), he contented himself, on my account, with inspecting from a distance to see that everything was in order, and by a glance getting a wedge set beneath one of the legs of the table, which was not level. It was not that he would have been unable, although he had concealed his origins as a dishwasher, to lend a hand like anyone else. It required some exceptional circumstance, however, for him one day to carve the guinea fowls himself. I had gone out, but I learned that he had done so with a sacerdotal majesty, surrounded, at a respectful distance from the sideboard, by a ring of waiters less intent on learning thereby than on letting themselves be seen, and who appeared vacuously admiring. Seen, however, by the manager (plunging with a slow gesture into the flanks of his victims, and no more removing from them eyes imbued with his high office than if an augury were to be read there), they were not. The sacrificer did not even remark my own absence. When he learned of it, he was desolate. "What, you didn't see me carve the guinea fowls myself?" I replied that, having not been able thus far to see Rome, Venice, Siena, the Prado, the Dresden museum, India, or Sarah in *Phèdre,* I knew all about resignation, and that I would add his carving of the guinea fowls to my list. The comparison with the dramatic art (Sarah in *Phèdre*) was the only one he appeared to understand, for he knew through me that, on days of gala performances, the elder Coquelin[58] had accepted begin-ners' roles, even that of a character who has only one line or no lines at all. "It's no matter, I'm distressed for your sake. When shall I carve again? It would require an event, it would require a war." (It required, in fact, the Armistice.) From that day forward, the calendar was changed, and was reckoned thus: "It was the day after the day when I carved the guinea fowls myself." "It was a week to the day after the manager carved the guinea fowls himself." This prosectomy thus provided, like the birth of Christ or the Hegira, the starting point for a calendar different from the others, but which did not achieve their extension or match their duration.

The sadness of M. de Crécy's life derived, equally as much as from his no longer keeping horses or a succulent table, from rubbing shoul-ders only with people capable of believing that Cambremer and Guer-mantes were all one. When he found that I knew that Legrandin, who now styled himself Legrand de Méséglise, had no sort of title to it, and being inflamed moreover by the wine he was drinking, he experienced a sort of transport of delight. His sister used to say to me with a knowing look, "My brother's never so happy as when he can talk with you." He had felt himself to exist indeed since discovering someone who knew how second-rate the Cambremers were, and how grand the Guer-mantes, someone for whom the social world existed. Just so, following a conflagration of all the libraries on the globe, and the rise of a wholly ignorant race, might an old Latinist regain his footing and his trust in life on hearing someone quote him a line from Horace. And so, if he never left the compartment without saying to me, "When's our next lit-tle get-together to be?," it was as much from the gourmandise of a scholar as the avidity of a parasite, and because he saw these Balbec agapes as an opportunity to talk, at the same time, about subjects close to his heart that he could not talk about with anyone else, and analo-gous in this to the dinners at which the Société des Bibliophiles gathers, on certain fixed dates, at the especially succulent board of the Cercle de l'Union.[59] Very unassuming where his own family was concerned, it was not through M. de Crécy that I learned that it was very grand and a genuine offshoot in France of the English family that bears the title of Crécy. When I learned that he was a true Crécy, I told him that a niece of Mme de Guermantes had married an American by the name of Charles Crécy and said that I supposed there was no connection with himself. "None," he said. "Any more than–though my family's not so very illustrious in any case–the many Americans calling themselves Montgomery, Berry, Chandos, or Capel have any connection with the families of Pembroke, Buckingham, or Essex, or with the Duc de Berry."[60] I thought several times of telling him, to amuse him, that I had known Mme Swann, who, as a cocotte, had gone in the old days under the name of Odette de Crécy; but although the Duc d'Alençon may not have taken offense had anyone spoken of Émilienne d'Alençon,[61] I did not feel sufficiently well in with M. de Crécy to carry the joke as far as that. "He comes from a very great family," M. de Montsurvent said to me one day. "His patronymic is Saylor." And he added that on his old *castel* above Incarville, grown all but uninhabitable in fact and which, although born very wealthy, he was today too penniless to repair, there could still be read his family's ancient motto. I thought this motto very fine, whether it be applied to the impatience of a predatory race perched in that aerie from which they must once have taken flight, or, today, to the contemplation of its decline, and the anticipation of impending death in that savage and imposing retreat. It is in this double sense indeed that the motto makes play with the name of Saylor: *"Ne sçais l'heure."*[62]

At Hermonville, M. de Chevregny sometimes got in, whose name, Brichot told us, signified, like that of Monseigneur de Cabrières, "a place where goats gather." He was related to the Cambremers, on which account, and out of a false appreciation of what was fashionable, the latter frequently invited him to Féterne, but only when they had no guests to dazzle. Living all year round at Beausoleil, M. de Chevregny had remained more provincial than they were. Thus, when he went to spend a few weeks in Paris, there was not a single day to be wasted, on account of "all there was to see"; to the point where, at times, a little dazed by the number of spectacles too rapidly digested, when he was asked whether he had seen a certain play it happened that he was no longer quite sure. But this vagueness was rare, for he had that detailed knowledge of things Parisian peculiar to the people who rarely go there. He recommended to me the "new things" to go and see ("It's worth the effort"), regarding them, on the other hand, purely from the point of view of the pleasant evening they enabled you to spend, and ignoring the aesthetic point of view to the extent of not even suspecting that they might in fact constitute a "new thing" in the history of art. Thus, speaking of everything on the same plane, he would say: "We went once to the Opéra-Comique, but the show isn't up to much. It's called *Pelléas et Mélisande*. It's insignificant. Périer[63] is always good, but you'd do better to see him in something else. On the other hand, at the Gymnase, they're doing *La Châtelaine*.[64] We went back twice; don't fail to go, it's worth seeing; and then the acting is a joy; you've got Frévalles, Marie Magnier, Baron *fils*."[65] He even quoted the names of actors to me that I had never heard spoken, and without preceding them by "Monsieur," "Madame," or "Mademoiselle," as the Duc de Guermantes would have done, who referred in the same ceremoniously contemptuous tone to the "songs of Mlle Yvette Guilbert"[66] and "the experiments of M. Charcot." That was not M. de Chevregny's way; he said "Cornaglia" and "Dehelly"[67] as he might have said "Voltaire" and "Montesquieu." For, with him, with regard to actors as to everything to do with Paris, the aristocrat's desire to display his contempt came second to the provincial man's desire to show familiarity.

Straight after the first dinner party that I had been to at La Raspelière, with what was still referred to at Féterne as "the young couple" although M. and Mme Cambremer were no longer, far from it, in the first flush of youth, the old Marquise had written me one of those letters whose style you could have picked out from among thousands. It said, "Bring your delightful–charming–agreeable cousin. It will be an enchantment, a pleasure," always failing so infallibly to achieve the progression anticipated by whoever received the letter that I ended by altering my opinion as to the nature of these diminuendos, believing them now to be deliberate, and finding in them the same depravation of taste–transposed into the social order–that drove Sainte-Beuve to break all the alliances between words and to alter any expression that was in the least usual. Two methods, taught no doubt by different teachers, were contrasted in this epistolary style, the second of them leading Mme de Cambremer to redeem the banality of her multiple adjectives by employing them on a descending scale and avoiding ending on a common chord. On the other hand, I tended to see in these inverse gradations, no longer refinement, as when they were the work of the dowager Marquise, but awkwardness, every time they were employed by her son the Marquis or by her cousins. For throughout the family, to quite a remote degree and in admiring imitation of Aunt Zélia, the three-adjective rule was held in high esteem, as was a certain enthusiastic way of catching your breath when speaking. An imitation that had passed into the blood, what was more; when in the family, a girl, from childhood on, broke off from speaking to swallow her saliva, they would say, "She takes after Aunt Zélia," and felt that later on her lips would quite soon tend to be shadowed by a faint mustache and promised themselves they would cultivate the aptitude that she must show for music. It was not long before the Cambremers' relations with Mme Verdurin were less ideal than with myself, for various reasons. They wanted to invite her. The "young" Marquise said to me contemptuously, "I don't see why we shouldn't invite the woman; you can see anyone at all in the country, it doesn't lead to anything." But, somewhat impressed deep down, they never ceased consulting me as to the manner in which they should realize their desire to be polite. As they had invited us, Albertine and me, to dinner, with some friends of Saint-Loup's, fashionable people from the region, the owners of the château in Gourville, who represented rather more than the cream of Norman society, to which Mme Verdurin, without appearing to touch it, was partial, I advised the Cambremers to invite the Patronne at the same time. But the châtelains of Féterne, from fear (so timid were they) of upsetting their noble friends, or (so naïve were they) of boring M. and Mme Verdurin with people who were not intellectuals, or again (so impregnated were they by a spirit of routine that experience had not fertilized) of mixing kinds and "putting their foot in it," declared that they would not go together, that they would not "hit it off," and that it would be better to keep Mme Verdurin (who would be invited with all her little group) in reserve for another dinner party. For the next one—the fashionable one, with Saint-Loup's friends—they invited only Morel from the little nucleus, so that M. de Charlus might be informed indirectly of the brilliant people whom they entertained, and also so that the musician might be a source of entertainment for the guests, for he would be asked to bring his violin. To him they added Cottard, because M. de Cambremer declared that he was a live wire and "an asset" at a dinner party; besides, it might prove convenient to be on good terms with a doctor should they ever have someone who was ill. But he was asked on his own, so as "not to start anything with the wife." Mme Verdurin was outraged when she learned that two members of the little group had been invited without her to an "informal dinner" at Féterne. She dictated to the doctor, whose first instinct had been to accept, a haughty reply, in which he said, "*We* are dining that evening at Mme Verdurin's," a plural intended as a lesson to the Cambremers and to show them he was not separable from Mme Cottard. As for Morel, Mme Verdurin had no need to trace out an impolite course of action for him, he adopted one spontaneously, and for the following reason. If, in regard to M. de Charlus, and where his pleasures were concerned, he enjoyed an independence that saddened the Baron, we have seen that the latter's influence made itself felt more in other spheres, that he had, for example, broadened the virtuoso's musical knowledge and purified his style. But, at this point in our story at least, it was still only an influence. There was one terrain, on the other hand, where what M. de Charlus said was believed and acted on blindly by Morel. Blindly and crazily, for not only were M. de Charlus's teachings false, but, even had they been valid for a great nobleman, as applied to the letter by Morel they became ludicrous. The terrain on which Morel had become so credulous and so easily led by his mentor was that of society. The violinist, who, before he met M. de Charlus had had no notion of society, had taken literally the arrogant and summary sketch map of it drawn for him by the Baron. "There are a certain number of preponderant families," M. de Charlus had told him, "the Guermantes above all, who can count fourteen alliances with the House of France, which is flattering mainly in fact for the House of France, moreover, for it was to Aldonce de Guermantes and not to Louis the Fat, his younger half-brother, that the throne of France should have passed.[68] Under Louis XIV, we wore black at the death of Monsieur, as having the same grandmother as the King. Far beneath the Guermantes, one can nevertheless cite the La Tremoïlles, descendants of the Kings of Naples and the Comtes de

Poitiers;[69] the d'Uzès,[70] far from ancient as a family but the most ancient peers; the Luynes,[71] altogether recent, but with the distinction of great alliances; the Choiseuls, the Harcourts, the La Rochefoucaulds.[72] Add the Noailles, despite the Comte de Toulouse, the Montesquious, the Castellanes,[73] and, barring some oversight, that's all. As for all those nobodies who call themselves the Marquis de Cambremerde or de Vatefairefiche,[74] there's no difference between them and the meanest private in your regiment. Whether you go and piss at the Comtesse Shit's, or shit at the Comtesse Piss's, it's the same thing, you'll have risked your reputation and used a brown-stained rag as toilet paper. Which is unhygienic." Morel had piously taken in this perhaps somewhat cursory history lesson; he judged things as if he were himself a Guermantes and hoped for an opportunity of finding himself with the false La Tour d'Auvergnes so that he could let them see, by a contemptuous shake of the hand, that he hardly took them seriously. As for the Cambremers, he could show them here and now that they were "no better than the meanest private in his regiment." He did not reply to their invitation, and on the evening of the dinner begged off at the very last moment by telegram, as overjoyed as if he had just behaved like a prince of the blood. It must be added, however, that one cannot imagine just how, in a more general way, unbearable, niggling, and even, he who was so discerning, stupid M. de Charlus could be, on all those occasions when the defects of his character came into play. It can be said indeed that these are like an intermittent sickness of the mind. Who has not observed this fact with women, or even with men, endowed with a remarkable intelligence, but afflicted by nervousness? When they are happy, at peace, content with their surroundings, they cause us to admire their precious gifts; it is literally the truth that speaks through their mouths. A migraine, some small puncturing of their *amour-propre* is enough to change everything. The luminous intelligence, abrupt, convulsive, shrunken, now reflects only a self that is irritated, suspicious, coquettish, doing all it can to be unattractive. The anger of the Cambremers ran high; and in the meantime, other incidents led to a certain tension in their relations with the little clan. As we were returning, the Cottards, Charlus, Brichot, Morel, and I, from a dinner at La

Raspelière, and the Cambremers, who had been going to have lunch with some friends in Arembouville, had made part of the outward journey with us: "You who are so fond of Balzac and able to recognize him in contemporary society," I had said to M. de Charlus, "you must think that the Cambremers have escaped from the *Scènes de la vie de province.*"[75] But M. de Charlus, absolutely as if he had been their friend and as if I had offended him by my remark, abruptly cut me short: "You're saying that because the wife is superior to the husband," he said curtly. "Oh, I didn't mean that she was the 'Muse du Département,' or Mme de Bargeton,[76] although . . ." M. de Charlus interrupted me once more: "Say, rather, Mme de Mortsauf."[77] The train stopped, and Brichot got out. "No good our signaling to you, you're terrible." "What d'you mean?" "Oh, come, haven't you noticed that Brichot is madly in love with Mme de Cambremer?" I could see by the attitude of the Cottards and of Charlie that there was not a shred of doubt about this among the little nucleus. I thought it showed ill-will on their part. "Come, you didn't notice how agitated he was when you were talking about her," M. de Charlus went on, who liked to show that he had experience of women and spoke naturally of the sentiment they inspire, as if it were one that he himself was in the habit of feeling. But a certain tone of equivocal fatherliness with all the young men—despite his exclusive love for Morel—gave the lie by his tone to the ladies'-man views he was expressing: "Oh, these children," he said, in a high-pitched, affected, measured voice, "you have to teach them everything, they're innocent as a newborn babe, they can't recognize when a man's in love with a woman. I knew what's what better than that at your age," he added, for he liked using these expressions from the world of the Paris apaches, perhaps from taste, perhaps so as not to appear, by avoiding them, to be admitting that he associated with those whose current vocabulary they were. A few days later, I had indeed to yield to the evidence and recognize that Brichot was smitten with the Marquise. Unfortunately, he accepted several lunch invitations from her. Mme Verdurin adjudged that it was time to put her oar in. Apart from the usefulness she could see in an intervention where the politics of the little nucleus was concerned, she took an increasingly keen enjoyment in these sorts of explanation and the dramas they gave rise to, an enjoyment born of idleness as much among the bourgeoisie as in the world of the aristocracy. It was a day of high emotion at La Raspelière when Mme Verdurin was seen to disappear for a whole hour with Brichot, whom she was known to have told that Mme de Cambremer made fun of him, that he was the laughingstock of her drawing room, that he was about to dishonor his old age and jeopardize his position in academic life. She even went so far as to refer in touching terms to the washerwoman he had lived with in Paris and to their little girl. She carried the day, Brichot stopped going to Féterne, but his unhappiness was such that for two days it was thought he was going to lose his sight altogether, and his malady had in any case taken a leap forward from which there was no going back. Meanwhile, the Cambremers, whose anger against Morel was great, invited M. de Charlus one time, and very deliberately, without him. Not receiving any reply from the Baron, they feared they had made a gaffe, and, deciding that resentment was a poor counselor, wrote rather belatedly to Morel, an obsequiousness that made M. de Charlus smile by revealing the extent of his influence. "You will answer for the two of us, that I accept," the Baron told Morel. The day of the dinner having arrived, they were waiting in the large drawing room at Féterne. The Cambremers were in point of fact giving the dinner for the flower of fashion that were M. and Mme Féré. But so afraid were they of displeasing M. de Charlus that, although she had met the Férés through M. de Chevregny, Mme de Cambremer became frantic when, on the day of the dinner, she found the latter arriving to pay a call on them at Féterne. They invented all manner of excuses to send him back to Beausoleil as quickly as possible, not quickly enough, however, to stop him from running into the Férés in the courtyard, who were as shocked to see him being expelled as he was ashamed. But, whatever the cost, the Cambremers wanted to spare M. de Charlus the sight of M. de Chevregny, judging the latter to be provincial on the strength of nuances that are overlooked *en famille* and of which account is taken only in the presence of outsiders, the very people who would alone fail to notice them. But we do not like to show off to them relations who have remained what we have tried hard to cease from being. As for M. and Mme Féré, they were in the highest degree people out of what is called "the top drawer." In the eyes of those who described them thus, no doubt the Guermantes, the Rohans, and many others were also people out of the top drawer, but their name excused you from saying so. Since not everyone knew of the high birth of M. Féré's mother, or of Mme Féré's mother, and the extraordinarily closed circle in which she and her husband moved, when they had just been introduced, in order to explain, it was always added that they were people "of the very best kind." Had their obscure name dictated a sort of haughty reserve in them? The fact was that the Férés did not visit people whom the La Tremoïlles would have frequented. It had taken her position as queen of the seaside, which the old Marquise de Cambremer held in the Manche, for the Férés to come to one of her matinées each year. They had been invited to dinner, and great store was set on the effect that M. de Charlus would have on them. It was given out discreetly that he would be among the guests. By chance, Mme Féré did not know him. Mme de Cambremer experienced a keen satisfaction at this, and the smile of the chemist who is about to bring into contact for the first time two especially important bodies strayed across her face. The door opened, and Mme de Cambremer almost felt sick when she saw Morel enter alone. Like a private secretary charged with making his minister's apologies, or like a morganatic spouse expressing the Prince's regrets that he is feeling unwell (as Mme de Clinchamp used to do in respect of the Duc d'Aumale[78]), Morel said, in the airiest of tones: "The Baron won't be able to come. He's slightly indisposed, at least I think that's the reason; I haven't come across him this week," he added, these last words causing Mme de Cambremer quite to despair, she having told M. and Mme Féré that Morel saw M. de Charlus at all hours of the day. The Cambremers pretended that the Baron's absence merely added to the pleasures of the occasion and, without letting themselves be overheard by Morel, said to their guests: "We can make do without him, can we not? It'll be all the pleasanter." But they were furious, suspecting a conspiracy mounted by Mme Verdurin, and, tit for tat, when the latter invited them once again to La Raspelière, M. de Cambremer, unable to resist the pleasure of revisiting his house and of finding himself once again among the little group, went, but alone, saying that the Marquise was most upset, but that her doctor had ordered her to keep to her room. By this half-presence, the Cambremers thought both to teach M. de

Charlus a lesson and to show the Verdurins that only a limited polite-
ness was due to them, just as in the old days princesses of the blood
used to escort duchesses out, but only as far as halfway across the sec-
ond chamber. After a few weeks, the breach was more or less complete.
M. de Cambremer justified it to me thus: "I must tell you that with
M. de Charlus it was difficult. He's an out-and-out Dreyfusard. . . ."
"Not so!" "Oh yes, he is. . . . At all events, his cousin the Prince de
Guermantes is, they've met with a fair bit of hostility on that account.
I've relations who are very touchy about that. I can't mix with such people, I'd fall out with the whole of my family." "Since the Prince de
Guermantes is a Dreyfusard, it'll be all the better," said Mme de Cambremer, "because Saint-Loup, who, they say, is to marry his niece, is
one, too. It could even be the reason for the marriage." "Come, my
dear, don't say that Saint-Loup, of whom we're so fond, is a Dreyfusard. You shouldn't broadcast these allegations lightly," said M. de
Cambremer. "What might they not think of him in the army!" "He was
one, but he isn't any longer," I said to M. de Cambremer. "As for his
marrying Mlle de Guermantes-Brassac, is that true?" "It's all people talk
about, but you're in a good position to know." "But I say again, he told
me himself he was a Dreyfusard," said Mme de Cambremer. "He's got
every excuse anyway, the Guermantes are half German." "In the case of
the rue-de-Varenne Guermantes, you can say one hundred percent,"
said Cancan. "But Saint-Loup's a different kettle of fish; he may well
have any number of German relations, but his father claimed his title
above all as a great French nobleman; he served again in 1871 and was
killed in the finest manner during the war. I may well fuss too much
about that sort of thing, but one mustn't exaggerate either in one direction or the other. *In medio . . . virtus,*[79] oh, I don't remember! It's something Dr. Cottard says. He's never at a loss for the right words. You
ought to have a *Petit Larousse* here." To avoid having to pronounce on
the Latin quotation, and to get off the subject of Saint-Loup, on which
her husband seemed to find her lacking in tact, Mme de Cambremer
fell back on the Patronne, whose quarrel with them was even more
in need of an explanation. "We were happy to lease La Raspelière to
Mme Verdurin," said the Marquise. "Only she has appeared to think
that, along with the house, and everything she's found a way of laying

claim to, the use of the meadow, the old hangings, all things that certainly weren't in the lease, she'd have in addition the right to become friends with us. Those are two quite distinct things. Our mistake is simply not to have done things through a factor or an agency. At Féterne that's of no account, but I can see now the expression on my aunt de Ch'nouville's face if she saw old Mother Verdurin turning up on my at-home day, with her hair all over the place. In the case of M. de Charlus, of course, he knows some highly respectable people, but he also knows some who were far from it." I asked who. Pressed by questions, Mme de Cambremer finally said: "They claim it's he who was keeping a M. Moreau, Morille, Morue,[80] I no longer know. No connection, of course, with Morel, the violinist," she added, blushing. "When I sensed that Mme Verdurin imagined that, because she was our tenant in the Manche, she'd have the right to call on me in Paris, I realized we had to cut our moorings."

Despite this breach with the Patronne, the Cambremers were on good enough terms with the faithful, and gladly got into our compartment when they were on the line. When we were on the point of arriving in Douville, Albertine, pulling her mirror out one last time, sometimes found it helpful to change her gloves or remove her hat for a moment, and with the tortoiseshell comb I had given her and which she wore in her hair, would smooth down her ringlets, fluff them up, and, if necessary, put up her chignon above the undulations that descended in regular valleys as far as her nape. Once in the carriages that were waiting for us, we no longer had any idea at all where we were; the roads were not lit; we could tell by the louder sound the wheels made that we were passing through a village, we thought we had arrived, we found ourselves in open country again, we could hear church bells in the distance, we forgot we were in dinner jackets, and we had almost dozed off when, at the end of this long margin of darkness that, because of the distance we had traveled and the incidents characteristic of any journey by train, seemed to have borne us on to an advanced hour of the night and almost halfway back to Paris, all of a sudden, after we felt the carriage glide on a finer sand, revealing that we had just entered the park, there burst forth, reintroducing us into the life of society, the brilliant lights of the drawing room, then of the dining room, where we were suddenly made to recoil by hearing it strike eight, an hour we thought long since past, whereas the numerous courses and fine wines were about to follow one another, around men in tails and women semi-décolletées, in a dinner rutilant with light, like a true *dîner en ville,* which was surrounded only, and had its character thereby altered, by the strange, somber double sash woven by the nocturnal, pastoral, and marine hours, deflected by this worldly use from their original solemnity, of the double journey. This latter obliged us indeed to abandon the radiant, quickly forgotten splendor of the brightly lit drawing room for the carriages, where I contrived to be with Albertine so that my loved one might not be with other people without me, and frequently for another reason also, which was that we could the two of us do lots of things in a dark carriage, where the jolts of the descent would anyway excuse us, in the event of a sudden shaft of light entering, for our having clutched hold of each other. When M. de Cambremer had not as yet fallen out with the Verdurins, he used to ask me: "You don't think, with this fog, that you'll have one of your breathless attacks? My sister had terrible ones this morning. Ah, you did, too," he would say, with satisfaction. "I shall tell her so tonight. I know that when I get back she'll be inquiring right away how long it is since you had them." He talked to me about mine in fact only in order to get on to those of his sister, and made me describe the particulars of the first the better to mark the differences there were between the two. In spite of these, as his sister's attacks seemed to him to carry authority, he could not believe that what "worked" with hers was not advisable for my own, and he was annoyed that I should not have tried them, for there is one thing even more difficult than sticking to a regimen, and that is not imposing it on others. "Anyway, what am I saying, me, a layman, when you're here in front of the Areopagus, the very fountainhead. What does Professor Cottard think?"

I saw his wife again another time, it so happens, because she had said that my "cousin" had a funny style, and I wanted to know what she meant by this. She denied having said it, but finally owned that she had been talking about someone whom she thought she had met with my cousin. She did not know her name but said finally that, if she was not mistaken, it was the wife of a banker, of the name of Lina, Linette,

Lisette, Lia, or something of the sort. I fancied that "wife of a banker" was inserted only in order to remove any marks of identity. I wanted to ask Albertine whether it was true. But I preferred appearing to be the one who knew rather than the one asking questions. Albertine would in any case either not have given me any answer or else a "no" in which the "n" would have been too hesitant and the "o" too resonant. Albertine never recounted facts that might harm her, but others that could only be explained by the earlier ones, the truth being a current that flows from what we are told and which we pick up, invisible though it is, rather than the actual thing we have been told. Thus, when I assured her that a woman whom she had met in Vichy was disreputable, she swore that the woman in question was certainly not what I imagined and had never tried to make her do anything bad. But another day she added, when I was speaking of my curiosity regarding that sort of person, that the lady in Vichy had a friend like that whom Albertine did not meet, but to whom the lady had "*promised* to introduce her." For her to have made such a promise must mean that Albertine had wanted it, or that the lady had, by so offering, known how to please her. But if I had raised this objection with Albertine, I would have seemed to have had my revelations from her alone, I would at once have put a stop to them, I would have learned nothing further, I would have ceased to make myself feared. Moreover, we were in Balbec, and the Vichy lady and her friend lived in Menton; the remoteness, the impossibility of any danger, would have soon put an end to my suspicions.

Often, when M. de Cambremer hailed me from the station, I had, with Albertine, just been taking advantage of the darkness, and with all the more difficulty inasmuch as the latter had fought somewhat, fearing it was not sufficiently total. "You know, I'm sure that Cottard saw us; anyway, even without seeing, he certainly heard you choking back your voice, just when they were talking about your other sort of choking," Albertine said to me on arrival at the station in Douville, where we caught the little train for the return journey. But this return journey, like the outward one, if, by giving me a certain impression of poetry, it reawoke in me the longing to travel, to lead a new life, and thereby made me wish to abandon any plan of marrying Albertine, and even to break off our relationship once and for all, it also, by the very fact of this relationship's contradictory nature, made the break easier. For, on the return journey, as on the outward one, at each station there either got in with us or greeted us from the platform people of our acquaintance; the furtive pleasures of the imagination were dominated by the—continual—pleasures of sociability, which are so calming, so soporific. Already, before the stations themselves, their names (which had so set me to dreaming ever since the day I first heard them, on that first evening when I had been traveling with my grandmother) had been humanized, had lost their strangeness since the evening when Brichot, at Albertine's request, had explained their etymologies to us more fully. I had found the *-fleur* charming that ended certain names, such as Fiquefleur, Honfleur, Flers, Barfleur, Harfleur, and so on, and the *-boeuf* to be found at the end of Bricqueboeuf amusing. But the *fleur* vanished along with the *boeuf* when Brichot (and he had told me this that first day, in the train) taught us that *fleur* means "harbor" (like *fiord*) and that *boeuf*, *budh* in Norman, signifies "hut." As he cited various examples, what had seemed to me particular became general: Bricqueboeuf went to join Elbeuf, and even in a name at first sight as individual as the place itself, such as the name of Pennedepie, in which oddities impossible of elucidation by reason seemed to have become amalgamated since time immemorial into a vocable as hard, strong-tasting, and unpleasant as a certain Normandy cheese, I was distressed to discover the Gallic *pen*, which signifies "mountain" and is found in Penmarch as well as in the Apennines. As, each time the train stopped, I felt that we should have friendly hands to shake, if not visits to receive, I said to Albertine: "Hurry up and ask Brichot the names you want to know about. You mentioned Marcouville-l'Orgueilleuse." "Yes, I just love that *orgueil*, it's a proud village," said Albertine. "You'd think it prouder still," replied Brichot, "if, instead of its French form, or even the Low Latin, such as you find it in the Bishop of Bayeux's cartulary, *Marcovilla superba*, you were to take the more ancient form, closer to the Norman, *Marculphivilla superba*, the village, or domain, of Merculph. In almost all these names that end in *-ville*, you can still see, erect above this coast, the ghost of the rude Norman invaders. At Hermonville, you had, standing in the carriage doorway, only our excellent doctor, who obviously has nothing of the Norse chieftain about him. But by closing your eyes, you might have seen the celebrated Herimund (*Herimundivilla*). Although, I don't know why, people go by these roads, between Loigny and Balbec-Plage, rather than the very picturesque ones that go from Loigny to old Balbec, Mme Verdurin has perhaps taken you out in that direction by carriage. In which case you'll have seen Incarville or the village of Wiscar, and Tourville, before you get to Mme Verdurin's, is the village of Turold. Moreover, there weren't only the Normans. It seems that Germans may have got this far (Aumenancourt, *Alemanicurtis*); don't tell this to the young officer I see there; he'd be capable of refusing to go to his cousins' any more. There were Saxons, too, witness the fountain of Sissonne"—one of Mme Verdurin's favorite destinations for her excursions, and rightly so—"just as, in England, Middlesex and Wessex. Something inexplicable, it seems that the Goths, *gueux*, as they used to say, got this far, and even Moors, for 'Mortagne' comes from *Mauretania*. The trace of them has remained in 'Gourville' (*Gothorumvilla*). The odd vestige of the Latins survives, too, moreover, 'Lagny' (*Latiniacum*)." "I shall ask for an explanation of Thorpehomme," said M. de Charlus. "I can understand *homme*," he added, as the sculptor and Cottard exchanged meaningful glances. "But *Thorp*?" "*Homme* does not at all signify what you are naturally led to believe, Baron," replied Brichot, glancing mischievously at Cottard and the sculptor. "*Homme* has nothing to do in this case with the sex to which I am not indebted for my mother. *Homme* is *Holm*, which signifies 'small island,' and so on. As for *thorp*, or 'village,' you find it again in dozens of words with which I've already bored our young friend. So in Thorpehomme there isn't the name of a Norman chieftain, but words of the Norman tongue. You can see how this whole region was Germanized." "I think he's exaggerating," said M. de Charlus. "Yesterday I went to Orgeville . . ." "This time I give you back the man I took away in Thorpehomme, Baron. Let it be said without pedantry, a charter of Robert I gives us, for Orgeville, the domain of Otger. All these names are those of ancient lords. Octeville-la-Venelle is for l'Avenel. The Avenels were a family well known in the Middle Ages. Bourguenolles, which Mme Verdurin took us to the other day, used to be written 'Bourg de Môles,' because the village belonged in the eleventh century to Baudoin de Môles, as did La Chaise–Baudoin; but here we are in Doncières." "Good Lord, all the lieutenants that are going to try and get in!" said M. de Charlus in mock terror. "I'm thinking of you, it doesn't trouble me, as I'm getting out." "You hear, Doctor?" said Brichot. "The Baron's afraid of having officers clambering over his person. Yet they're quite in character, by being here in strength, for Doncières is none other than Saint-Cyr,[81] *Dominus Cyriacus*. There are lots of names of towns in which *sanctus* and *sancta* have been replaced by *dominus* and *domina*. Moreover, this peaceful army town sometimes gives a false impression of being Saint-Cyr, Versailles, or even Fontainebleau."

During these homeward journeys (as on the outward one), I used to tell Albertine to dress well, for I knew that at Amnancourt, Doncières, Epreville, and Saint-Vast, we would be receiving brief visits. I did not find these at all disagreeable, as it happens, whether it was, at Hermonville (the domain of Herimund), that of M. de Chevregny, taking advantage of having come to fetch guests to ask me to go and have lunch the following day at Montsurvent, or, at Doncières, the abrupt invasion of one of Saint-Loup's charming friends, sent by him (if he was not free) to pass on an invitation from Captain de Borodino, from the officers' mess at the Coq Hardi, or from the NCOs at the Faisan Doré. Saint-Loup often came in person, and all the time he was there, without its being apparent to anyone, I held Albertine captive with my eyes, pointlessly vigilant as it happens. On one occasion, however, I interrupted my watch. The stop being prolonged, Bloch, having greeted us, ran off almost immediately to rejoin his father, who had just inherited from his uncle and, having leased a château called La Commanderie, thought it very much the grand seigneur to travel about only in a post chaise, with postilions in livery. Bloch asked me to go with him as far as the carriage. "But make haste, for these quadrupeds are impatient; come, man beloved of the gods, you will bring pleasure to my father." But I could not bear to leave Albertine in the train with Saint-Loup; they might, while my back was turned, talk together, get into another carriage, smile at each other, touch each other; my adhesive gaze could not be removed from Albertine for as long as Saint-Loup was there. But I could see very well that Bloch, who had asked me as a favor to go and greet his father, found it first of all unfriendly that I should refuse when nothing was stopping me, the porters having warned us that the train would be remaining for another quarter of an hour at least in the station, and that almost all the passengers, without whom it would not leave, had alighted; and, for another thing, he did not doubt that it was definitely because—my conduct on this occasion was a decisive response—I was a snob. For he was not unaware of the names of the people I was with. Indeed, M. de Charlus had said to me, some time before and not remembering or caring that this had been done in the old days, in order to get close to him, "But introduce me to your friend then, what you're doing shows a lack of respect for me," and he had talked with Bloch, with whom he seemed exceedingly taken, to the point where he had gratified him with an "I shall hope to meet you again." "It's irrevocable then, you refuse to walk those hundred meters to say hello to my father, to whom it'd give so much pleasure?" Bloch said. I was unhappy at seeming to be failing in comradeship, and even more so at the reason Bloch imagined I had for failing in it, and at sensing that he supposed I was not the same with my bourgeois friends when people of "birth" were present. From that day forward, he ceased to show me the same affection and, what I found more hurtful, no longer had the same high regard for my character. But in order to undeceive him as to the motive that had led me to remain in the train, I would have needed to tell him something—namely, that I was jealous of Albertine—that would have been even more painful than allowing him to believe that I was stupidly worldly. Thus it is that, in theory, we find we ought always to explain ourselves frankly, to avoid misunderstandings. But very often life combines these in such a way that, in order to dispel them, in the rare circumstances when that might prove possible, we would have to reveal either—which was not the case here—something that would offend our friend even more than the imaginary wrong he imputes to us, or a secret the divulging of which—this was what had just happened in my own case—strikes us as even worse than the misunderstanding. Moreover, even without explaining to Bloch, since I was unable to, the reason I had for not accompanying him, had I begged him not to be offended I would merely have doubled the offense by showing that I had been aware of it. There was nothing to be done but to submit to this *fatum* which had decreed that the presence of Albertine should prevent me from escorting him and that he should believe that, on the contrary, it was the presence of brilliant people, who, had they been a hundred times more so, would have simply had the effect of making me concern myself exclusively with Bloch and reserve all my courtesies for him. It is thus enough that, accidentally, absurdly, an incident (in this case, the coming together of Albertine and Saint-Loup) should interpose itself between two destinies whose lines had been converging, for these to be made to deviate, to grow farther and farther apart and never approach each other again. And more beautiful friendships than mine with Bloch have found themselves destroyed, without the involuntary author of the quarrel having ever been able to explain to the one quarreled with what would surely have healed his *amour-propre* and retrieved his fugitive sympathy.

Friendships more beautiful than Bloch's would not be saying very much, on the other hand. He had all the defects that displeased me the most. My fondness for Albertine, it so happened, made them quite unbearable. Thus, at that simple moment when I was talking with him while keeping an eye on Robert, Bloch told me he had lunched at Mme Bontemps's and that everyone had talked about me in the most laudatory terms until "the declension of Helios." "Good," I thought, "since Mme Bontemps thinks Bloch is a genius, the enthusiastic vote of approval he will have given me will do more than what all the others may have said; it'll get back to Albertine. She can't fail to find out someday soon, and it surprises me that her aunt hasn't already repeated it to her, that I'm a 'superior' man." "Yes," added Bloch, "everyone heaped praises on you. I alone preserved a silence as profound as if I had absorbed, in place of the, in fact somewhat mediocre, meal that we were served, the poppies beloved of the blessed brother of Thanatos and Lethe, the divine Hypnos, who envelops the body and the tongue in his sweet bonds. It's not that I admire you any less than the band of ravening dogs with whom I had been invited. But I admire you because I understand you, and they admire you without understanding you. The truth is, I admire you too much to speak of you in that way in public; it would have seemed to me a profanation to praise aloud what I carry in the deepest recesses of my heart. It was in vain that they questioned me about you; a sacred Pudor, the daughter of Kronion, made me remain mute." I was not so tasteless as to appear disgruntled, but this particular

Pudor seemed to me akin—much more than to Kronion—to the reticence that prevents a critic who admires you from talking about you because the secret temple where you sit enthroned would be invaded by the mob of ignorant readers and journalists; to the reticence of the statesman who does not give you a decoration so that you should not be lost to view amid people of less worth than yourself; to the reticence of the Academician who does not give you his vote so as to spare you the shame of being the colleague of X, who is without talent; to the reticence, finally, more respectable yet more criminal, of the sons who beg you not to write about their late father, who was full of fine qualities, in order to ensure silence and repose, to prevent people's maintaining him in life and creating a halo around the poor dead man, who would rather have his name issuing from men's mouths than the wreaths borne, however piously, to his grave.

If Bloch, while distressing me by not being able to understand the reason that had prevented me from going to salute his father, had exasperated me by confessing that he had depreciated me at Mme Bontemps's (I now understood why Albertine had never alluded to that lunch and remained silent when I spoke to her of Bloch's affection for me), the young Israelite had had an effect on M. de Charlus that was anything but irritation. Certainly Bloch now believed, not only that I could not for one second keep away from people of fashion, but that, jealous of the overtures they might have made to him (like M. de Charlus), I was trying to put a spoke in his wheel and prevent him from becoming friendly with them; but for his part, the Baron regretted not having seen more of my schoolmate. As was his habit, he was careful not to show it. He began by putting to me, without appearing to, a few questions about Bloch, but in so offhand a tone, and with an interest that appeared so put on, that you would not have supposed that he was attending to the answers. With an air of detachment, in a singsong voice expressive of more than indifference, of distraction, and as if out of simple politeness toward myself: "He looks intelligent, he said he was writing, has he any talent?" I told M. de Charlus it had been very good of him to say he hoped to meet him again. The Baron gave not the slightest indication that he might have heard my words, and as I repeated them four times without getting any reply, I finally suspected I might have been the victim of an acoustic mirage when I thought I heard what M. de Charlus had said. "Is he staying in Balbec?" crooned the Baron, with so uninquiring an expression it is unfortunate that the French language has no sign other than the question mark with which to end these sentences that appear so unlike questions. It is true that such a sign would be of scant use save to M. de Charlus. "No, they're renting near here, La Commanderie." Having learned what he wanted, M. de Charlus pretended to despise Bloch. "How ghastly!" he exclaimed, restoring to his voice all its clarion vigor. "All the localities or properties called 'La Commanderie' were built or owned by the Knights of the Order of Malta (of whom I am one), just as the places known as 'Le Temple' or 'La Cavalerie' were by the Templars. Were I staying at La Commanderie, nothing could be more natural. But a Jew! Not, however, that it surprises me; it comes from a curious liking for sacrilege, peculiar to that race. As soon as a Jew has enough money to buy a château, he always chooses one called Le Prieuré, L'Abbaye, Le Monastère, La Maison-Dieu. I had dealings with a Jewish functionary, can you guess where he resided? In Pont-l'Évêque.[82] Having fallen out of favor, he got himself sent to Brittany, to Pont-l'Abbé. When, in Holy Week, they put on those indecent spectacles known as Passion plays, half the auditorium is filled with Jews, exulting at the thought that they are going to put Christ on the cross for a second time, at least in effigy. At the Lamoureux concerts, I had for my neighbor one day a rich Jewish banker. They were giving Berlioz's *L'Enfance du Christ;* he was appalled. But he soon recovered the beatific expression that is usual with him on hearing 'L'Enchantement du Vendredi Saint.'[83] Your friend is staying at La Commanderie, the wretch! What sadism! You must show me how to get there," he added, resuming his indifferent air, "so that I can go one day and see how our ancient domains are withstanding such a profanation. It's unfortunate, for he's polite, he seems clever. All he needs now is to live in Paris on the rue du Temple!" With these words, M. de Charlus seemed simply to be looking for a fresh example by which to support his theory; but in reality he was posing a question whose intention was twofold, the principal one being to learn Bloch's address. "Indeed," Brichot pointed out, "the rue du Temple used to be called the rue de la Chevalerie-du-Temple. Apropos of which, will you permit me an observation, Baron?" said the university man. "What? What is it?" said M. de Charlus curtly, the remark having prevented him from obtaining his information. "No, nothing," replied Brichot, abashed. "It was apropos of the etymology of 'Balbec' that I was asked for. The rue du Temple was once called the rue Barre-du-Bec, because the Abbey of Bec, in Normandy, had its bar of justice there in Paris." M. de Charlus made no reply and pretended not to have heard, which was one of the forms his insolence took. "Where does your friend live in Paris? Since three-quarters of the streets take their name from a church or an abbey, there's a good chance of the sacrilege's continuing. You can't stop Jews from living on the Boulevard de la Madeleine, in the Faubourg Saint-Honoré, or the Place Saint-Augustin. As long as they don't carry perfidy to the point of electing domicile in the Place du Parvis–Notre-Dame, the Quai de l'Archevêché, the rue Chanoinesse, or the rue de l'Ave Maria, allowance must be made for their difficulties." We were unable to satisfy M. de Charlus, Bloch's current address not being known to us. But I knew that his father's offices were on the rue des Blancs-Manteaux.[84] "Oh, the very height of perversity," exclaimed M. de Charlus, seeming to derive a profound satisfaction from his own cry of ironic indignation. "Rue des Blancs-Manteaux," he repeated, laying weight on each syllable and laughing. "What sacrilege! To think that these Blancs-Manteaux polluted by M. Bloch were those of the mendicant friars, known as serfs of the Holy Virgin, that Saint Louis established there.[85] And the street has always belonged to the religious orders. The profanation is all the more diabolical in that, no distance from the rue des Blancs-Manteaux, there's a street whose name escapes me but which is entirely given over to the Jews; there are Hebrew characters on the shops, factories making unleavened bread, Jewish butchers, it's quite simply the Judengasse of Paris. M. de Rochegude calls that street the Paris ghetto.[86] That's where M. Bloch should have been living. Of course," he went on, in a somewhat emphatic, lordly tone, and, to make his aesthetic pronouncements, lending to the face that he had drawn back, by a reaction addressed to him in spite of himself by his heredity, the look of one of Louis XIII's old musketeers, "I concern myself with all that only from the point of view of art. Politics are not my thing, and I can't condemn en bloc, even if Blochs there are, a nation that numbers Spinoza among its illustrious sons. And I admire Rembrandt too much not to know what beauty may be had from the frequentation of the synagogue.[87] But, then, a ghetto is all the better the more homogeneous and the more complete it is. You may be sure, in any case, so closely bound up are the practical instinct and cupidity with sadism among that race, that the proximity of the Hebraic street I am speaking of, and the convenience of having Israelite butchers close at hand, led your friend to choose the rue des Blancs-Manteaux. How curious it is! It was there, as it happens, that there lived a strange Jew who boiled the Host,[88] after which I believe they boiled him, which is stranger still, since that seems to signify that the body of a Jew can be of equal value to the body of God. Perhaps something could be arranged with your friend so that he takes us to see the church of the Blancs-Manteaux. To think that it was there they laid the body of Louis d'Orléans after his assassination by Jean the Fearless, who, alas, did not deliver us from the Orléans.[89] Personally, I get along very well as it happens with my cousin the Duc de Chartres, but in the end they're a race of usurpers, who had Louis XVI assassinated, and Charles X and Henri V despoiled.[90] They've much to live up to, moreover, having for ancestors Monsieur, so called no doubt because he was the most astonishing old woman, and the Regent and all the rest. What a family!" This speech, anti-Jewish or pro-Hebrew—according to whether you fastened on the surface of the words or the intentions they concealed—had been comically watered down for me by a remark whispered to me by Morel that would have made M. de Charlus despair. Morel, who had not failed to observe the impression Bloch had been making, thanked me surreptitiously for having "dispatched" him, adding cynically: "He'd have liked to stay, all that's jealousy, he'd like to take my place. Typical of a Yid!" "We could have profited from this prolonged stoppage to ask for a few ritual explanations from your friend. Couldn't you catch up with him?" M. de Charlus asked me, with the anxiety of doubt. "No, it's impossible, he went off in a carriage and angry with me, moreover." "Thank you, thank you," breathed Morel. "The reason's absurd, you can always overtake a carriage, there's nothing to stop you taking a motorcar," replied M. de Charlus, as a man accustomed to having everything submit to him. But, observing my silence: "What is this more or less imaginary carriage?" he said, insolently, and with a last flicker of hope. "It's an open post chaise which must already have got to La Commanderie." Faced by an impossibility, M. de Charlus resigned himself and affected to joke. "I can understand that they should have been put off by the superfluous brougham. It would have been a new broom." Finally, we were advised that the train was departing, and Saint-Loup left us. But that was the one day when, by getting into our compartment, he unwittingly caused me to suffer, from the thought I entertained for an instant of leaving him with Albertine in order to go with Bloch. On the other occasions, his presence did not torment me. For, of her own accord, Albertine, to spare me any anxiety, took up a position, on some pretext or other, such that she would have been unable, even involuntarily, to brush against Robert, almost too far away even to have to offer him her hand; looking the other way, she would begin, as soon as he was there, to talk, ostensibly and almost with affection, with one or another of the other travelers, keeping up this game until Saint-Loup had gone. In this way, the visits he made to us in Doncières, causing me neither pain nor even embarrassment, did not form an exception to the others, all of which were agreeable for bringing me in some sense the homage and the invitation of this land. Already, from the end of the summer, on our journey from Balbec to Douville, when I spotted the station of Saint-Pierre-des-Ifs in the distance where, for a moment, in the evenings, the crest of the cliffs sparkled pink like the snow on a mountain in the setting sun, it no longer put me in mind (I do not say of the sadness even that the sight of its sudden strange looming had produced in me on that first evening, by giving me so strong a desire to catch the train back to Paris instead of going on to Balbec) of the spectacle that you could see from there in the mornings, so Elstir had told me, in the hour before the sun came up, when all the colors of the rainbow are refracted on the rocks, and where he had so many times woken up the young boy who, one year, had served him as a model, to paint him, stark naked, against the sand. The name of Saint-Pierre-des-Ifs merely announced to me that there was about to appear a strange, witty, bedizened fifty-year-old, with whom I would be able to discuss Chateaubriand and Balzac. And now, in the mists of evening, behind the Incarville cliffs that had so set me to dreaming in the old days, what

I could see, as if its ancient sandstone had grown transparent, was the beautiful house of an uncle of M. de Cambremer's, where I knew they would always be glad to take me in if I did not want to dine at La Raspelière or return to Balbec. Thus it was not simply the place-names of the region that had lost their original mystery, but the places themselves. The names, already half voided of a mystery that etymology had replaced by reason, had descended one step further still. On our return journeys to Hermonville, Saint-Vast, Arembouville, just as the train was stopping, we would catch sight of shadows that we did not at first recognize, and which Brichot, who could not see a thing, might perhaps have mistaken in the darkness for the phantoms of Herimund, Wiscar, and Herimbald. But they approached the carriage. It was merely M. de Cambremer, his breach with the Verdurins now complete, seeing guests off, and who, on behalf of his wife and his mother, came to ask me whether I would not like him to "kidnap" me, to keep me for a few days at Féterne, where there would be, in succession, an excellent lady musician who would sing me the whole of Gluck, and a chess-player of repute with whom I would have excellent games, which would not get in the way of the fishing or yachting parties in the bay, or even the Verdurin dinners, for which the Marquis gave his word of honor that he would "lend" me, having me driven there and fetched again so as to make it easier as well as safer. "But I can't imagine it's good for you to go that high up. I know my sister wouldn't be able to stand it. She'd come back in such a state! She's not as it happens all that good at present. . . . Really, you've had that bad an attack! Tomorrow you won't be able to stand up!" And he doubled up, not out of unkindness, but for the same reason that he could not not laugh when he saw a lame man go sprawling in the street, or talked with a deaf person. "And before that? What, you hadn't had one for a fortnight? D'you know, that's very fine! You really ought to come and install yourself at Féterne, you could discuss your attacks with my sister." At Incarville, it was the Marquis de Montpeyroux who, not having been able to go to Féterne, for he had been away hunting, had come "to the train" in boots and a hat decorated with a pheasant feather, to shake the hand of some relations and of myself at the same time, announcing, for the day of the week that would not inconvenience me, the visit of his son, whom he thanked me for entertaining and would be very happy if I got him to do some reading; or else M. de Crécy, come there, so he said, smoking his pipe, to settle his digestion, who accepted one or even several cigars, and said to me: "Well, you haven't told me what day our next get-together à la Lucullus is to be? We've nothing to say to each other? Permit me to remind you that we left unfinished the question of the two families of Montgommerys. We have to settle that. I'm counting on you." Others had come simply to buy their newspapers. Many also exchanged a few words with us, whom I have always suspected of finding themselves on the platform, at the station nearest to their small château, only because they had nothing better to do except meet for a moment with people of their acquaintance. These stops the little train made were, all in all, as much a setting for social life as any other. It seemed aware itself of the role that had devolved on it, and had developed a certain human friendliness: patient and docile in character, it waited for as long as was required for the stragglers, and even once it had left would stop to pick up those who signaled to it; they would then run after it, puffing, in which they resembled the train itself, with the difference that they caught up with it going at full speed, whereas it had resorted to a sensible dilatoriness. Thus Hermonville, Arembouville, Incarville no longer even evoked for me the savage magnificence of the Norman Conquest, not content with having entirely divested themselves of the unaccountable sadness in which, once upon a time, I had seen them bathed in the evening damp. Doncières! Even after I had come to know it and had woken up from my dream, how long there had remained in that name for me agreeably icy streets, lighted shop-windows and succulent poultry! Doncières! Now it was nothing more than the station at which Morel got in; Egleville (*Aquilaevilla*) that where the Princesse Sherbatoff was generally waiting for us; Maineville, the station where Albertine would alight on fine evenings, when, not feeling too tired, she was anxious to spend a moment or two longer with me, having scarcely any farther to walk, up a steep path, than if she had alighted at Parville (*Paterni villa*). Not only did I no longer experience the anxious fear of isolation that had gripped me that first evening, but I no longer had to fear that it might reawaken, or that I might feel homesick or find myself alone in this land productive not only of chestnut trees and tamarisks but of friendships, which, all along the journey, formed a long chain, broken, like that of the blue-colored hills, hidden now and again in the anfractuosity of the rocks or behind the lime trees of the avenue, but at each relay delegating an amiable gentleman who came, with a cordial shake of the hand, to interrupt my journey, to prevent my becoming conscious of its length, if need be to offer to continue it with me. Another one would be at the next station, so that the little tram's whistle made us abandon one friend only so as to enable us to meet again with others. Between the more scattered châteaux and the train that skirted them almost at a fast walking pace, the distance was so short that, at the moment when, on the platform, in front of the waiting room, their owners hailed us, we might almost have thought that they were doing so from their own doorsteps or from their bedroom windows, as if the little departmental railway line were nothing more than a provincial street, and the isolated manor house an urban *hôtel;* and even at the rare stations where I did not hear anyone's "good evening," the silence had a calming and nutritious fullness, because I knew it to be formed of the sleep of friends who had retired early in the nearby manor, where my arrival would have been greeted with delight had I had to awaken them in order to ask for some favor of hospitality. Except that habit takes up so much of our time that, at the end of a few months, we no longer have a free moment in a town where, when we arrived, the day offered us the free disposal of its twelve hours; had by any chance one of these become vacant, I would no longer have thought of using it in order to visit some church or other for the sake of which I had once come to Balbec, or even to compare a beauty spot painted by Elstir with the sketch of it I had seen in his house, but to go and have one more game of chess with M. Féré. Indeed, such was the degrading influence, and also the charm, of the country around Balbec, that it had become truly familiar ground for me; if their territorial distribution, their being sown along the full extent of the coast in diverse crops, necessarily lent to the visits I made to these various friends the form of a journey, they also now confined the attractions of that journey to the social ones, of a succession of visits. The same place-names, so disturbing for me in the old days that merely leafing through the chapter for the *département* of the Manche in the *Annuaire des châteaux* produced as much emotion in me as the railway timetable, had become so familiar that I might have consulted that same timetable, on the page for Balbec–Douville via Doncières, with the same contented peace of mind as a dictionary of addresses. In this too social valley, to the sides of which I sensed there clung, whether visible or not, a numerous company of friends, the poetic cry of evening was no longer that of the owl or the frog but the "How goes it?" of M. de Criquetot, or the "Kaire" of Brichot. The atmosphere no longer aroused anxieties and, laden with purely human effluvia, was breathable without difficulty, too soothing even. The benefit that I derived from it, at least, was no longer to see things except from the practical point of view. Marriage with Albertine struck me as foolishness.

## CHAPTER 4

*Sudden reversion to Albertine—*
*Desolation at break of day—*
*I leave at once for Paris with Albertine.*

I WAS ONLY awaiting an opportunity for the final rupture. And one evening, as Mamma was leaving the next day for Combray, where she was going to attend a sister of her mother's in her last illness, leaving me behind so that I might benefit, as Grandmother would have wanted, from the sea air, I announced to her that I had decided irrevocably not to marry Albertine and would shortly stop seeing her. I was pleased to have been able, by these words, to give my mother satisfaction on the eve of her departure. She made no secret of the fact that it was indeed for her a very keen satisfaction. I needed also to have things out with Albertine. As I was returning with her from La Raspelière, the faithful having alighted, some at Saint-Mars-le-Vêtu, others at Saint-Pierre-des-Ifs, still others at Doncières, feeling especially happy and detached from her, I had made up my mind, now that there were only the two of us in the compartment, finally to broach the conversation. The truth, in any case, was that that one of the Balbec girls whom I loved, although she was then away, along with her friends, but would be returning (I enjoyed being with all of them, for each of them had for me, as on the first day, something of the essence of the others, was as if from a race apart), was Andrée. Since she would be arriving back in Balbec in a few days' time, she would certainly come and see me right away, and then, in order to remain free and not to marry her if I did not want to, so as to be able to go to Venice, but yet to have her all to my-self in the meantime, the means I would adopt would be not to appear to be going to her but, as soon as she arrived, when we were talking to-gether, I would say: "What a pity I didn't see you a few weeks earlier! I'd have loved you; now my heart is taken. But that doesn't matter, we'll see each other often, for I'm unhappy in my other love and you will help to console me." I smiled inwardly on imagining this conversation, for in this way I would be giving Andrée the illusion that I did not really love her; thus she would not grow tired of me, and I would take joyful and consoling advantage of her affection. But all this only made it the more necessary, finally, to talk seriously to Albertine, so as not to act unscrupulously, and since I was resolved to devote myself to her friend, she, Albertine, needed certainly to know that I did not love her. She needed to be told right away, since Andrée might arrive any day. But as we were nearing Parville, I felt that we would not have time that evening and that it would be better to put off until the following day what had now been irrevocably decided on. I contented myself there-fore with talking to her about the dinner we had been to at the Ver-durins'. As she was putting her coat back on, the train having just left Incarville, the last station before Parville, she said, "Tomorrow, then, re-Verdurin, you won't forget that it's you who are coming to fetch me." I could not help answering, somewhat curtly: "Yes, unless I 'default,' be-cause I'm beginning to find this life really stupid. At all events, if we go there, so that my time at La Raspelière shouldn't be time totally wasted, I shall have to think of asking Mme Verdurin something that could in-terest me greatly, be a subject for study, and give me pleasure, because I'm really getting very little this year in Balbec." "That's not being very nice, but I won't hold it against you, because I can tell you're nervous. What is this pleasure?" "That Mme Verdurin should get them to play me things by a musician whose works she knows very well. I, too, know one of them, but it seems there are others, and I'd need to find out if it's been published, if it differs from the early ones." "What musician?" "If I tell you that his name's Vinteuil, my sweet one, are you any the wiser?" We may have turned over in our minds every possible idea with-out the truth's ever entering, and it is from outside, when we least ex-pect it, that it delivers its fearsome sting and wounds us forever. "You can't know how much you amuse me," replied Albertine, standing up, for the train was about to stop. "Not only does it mean much more to me than you think, but even without Mme Verdurin I can get you all the information you want. You remember my speaking to you about a girlfriend, older than me, who was like both a mother and sister to me, whom I spent my best years with in Trieste, and who, moreover, I'm due to meet in Cherbourg in a few weeks' time, from where we'll be traveling together (it's a little weird, but you know how I love the sea), well, this friend (oh, not at all the type of woman you might suppose!), and isn't this extraordinary, is in actual fact the best friend of this Vinteuil's daughter, and I know Vinteuil's daughter almost as well. I only ever call them my two big sisters. I'm not unhappy to show you that your little Albertine can be useful to you in these musical matters, where you say, rightly as it happens, that I don't understand a thing." At these words, uttered as we were entering the station in Parville, so far from Combray and from Montjouvain, so long after Vinteuil's death, a picture came to life in my heart, a picture held in reserve during so many years that, even had I been able to guess, when long ago storing it away, that it had the power to do harm, I would have supposed that in the course of time it had lost it entirely; preserved alive deep inside me—like Orestes, whose death the gods had prevented so that on the day appointed he might return to his homeland to punish the murder of Agamemnon—as my torment, as my punishment perhaps, who knows, for having allowed my grandmother to die; suddenly rising up out of the depths of that darkness where it had seemed to lie forever entombed and striking like an Avenger, in order to inaugurate for me a new life, terrible and deserved, perhaps also to explode before my eyes the fateful consequences to which wicked actions give rise indefinitely, not only for those who have committed them but for those who were no more than, who thought they were merely, onlookers at a curious and diverting spectacle, like me, alas, on that far-off day's end in Montjouvain, hidden behind a bush, where (as when I had listened complaisantly to the account of Swann's amours) I had perilously allowed to broaden out within me the fateful path of Knowledge, destined to become so sorrowful. And at that same moment of my greatest sorrow, I had a feeling, proud almost, almost joyful, that of a man caused to leap so far upward by the shock that he has received that he has attained a point to which no effort could have raised him. Albertine the friend of Mlle Vinteuil and of her friend, a practicing and professional sapphist, this, compared with what I had imagined at my most suspicious, was what, in comparison with the little acoustic device at the 1889 Exhibition, which you hardly hoped might reach from one end of the house to the other, the telephone now is, soaring over streets, towns, fields, and seas, linking regions. This was a terrible *terra incognita* on which I had just set foot, a new phase of unsuspected suffering that was opening. And yet the deluge of reality that submerges us, enormous though it may be compared with our timid and negligible suppositions, had been anticipated by them. It was no doubt something like what I had just learned, something like the friendship between Albertine and Mlle Vinteuil, something that my mind would have been incapable of inventing, but which I had obscurely apprehended when I was so concerned at seeing Albertine next to Andrée. It is often only for want of the creative spirit that we do not go far enough in suffering. And the most terrible reality brings us, at the same time as suffering, the joy of a beautiful discovery, for all that it does is to lend a new and explicit form to what we had long been turning over in our minds without suspecting it. The train had stopped in Parville, and as we were the only passengers to be found on it, it was in a voice made limp by his sense of the futility of the task, by the same habit that yet made him fulfill it and inspired him at once with indolence and punctiliousness, and even more out of the longing for sleep, that the porter shouted, "Parville!" Albertine, standing facing me and seeing that she had reached her destination, took a few steps from the back of the carriage where we were and opened the door. But the movement that she thus performed in order to alight tore unbearably at my heart as if, contrary to the position that Albertine's body, independently of my own, seemed to be occupying a short step away, this separation in space, which a truthful draftsman would have been obliged to represent between us, was only an appearance, and as if whoever might have wanted, in accordance with the true reality, to redraw things would have now had to place Albertine, not at some little distance from me, but inside me. Her moving away caused me such pain that, catching up with her, I pulled her despairingly by the arm. "Would it be physically impossible," I asked her, "for you to come and spend the night in Balbec?" "Physically, no. But I can't keep awake." "You'd be doing me an immense favor . . ." "All right, then, though I don't understand; why didn't you say sooner? Anyway, I'll stay." My mother was asleep when, after getting them to give Albertine a room on another floor, I returned to my own room. I sat down near the window, stifling my sobs so that my mother, who was separated from me only by a thin partition, might not hear me. I had not even thought to close the shutters, for at one moment, raising my eyes, I saw facing me in the sky that same faint glow of a dull red that was to be seen in the restaurant at Rivebelle in a study Elstir had made of a sunset. I recalled the exaltation that, when I had caught sight of it from the train on the day of my arrival in Balbec, this same image of a dusk that was the prelude not to the night but to a new day had given me. But no day now would ever again be new for me, would ever again awaken the longing for an unknown happiness; it would merely prolong my sufferings, until I would no longer have the strength to withstand them. The truth of what Cottard had said to me in the casino in Parville[1] was no longer in any doubt. What I had dreaded, had long vaguely suspected of Albertine, what my instinct had isolated from her whole being, but what my arguments, guided by my desire, had slowly led me to deny, was true! Behind Albertine I no longer saw the blue mountains of the sea, but the room in Montjouvain where she was falling into the arms of Mlle Vinteuil, with that laugh in which she made you hear, as it were, the unknown sound of her sexual pleasure. For, pretty as Albertine was, how could Mlle Vinteuil, with her proclivities, not have asked her to satisfy them? And the proof that Albertine had not been shocked by this but had consented was that they had not quarreled, that their intimacy had not ceased to grow. And that graceful movement of Albertine's, resting her chin on Rosemonde's shoulder, gazing at her with a smile, and planting a kiss on her neck, that movement which had reminded me of Mlle Vinteuil, and in the interpretation of which I had yet hesitated to admit that the same line traced by a gesture had necessarily to result from the same penchant, who knows whether Albertine had not simply learned it from Mlle Vinteuil? The colorless sky was slowly catching fire. I, who until now had never woken up without smiling at the humblest things, at the bowl of *café au lait,* the sound of the rain, the thunder of the wind, I felt that the day that would be breaking in a moment, and all the days that came after, would never again bring me the hope of an unknown happiness, but a prolonging of my martyrdom. I still held to life; I knew that I could now expect from it only what was cruel. I ran to the lift, despite the unseemly hour, to ring for the "lift" who filled the duties of night watchman, and I asked him to go to Albertine's room, to tell her I had something important to convey to her, if she was able to receive me. "Mademoiselle would rather she come to you," was the reply. "She'll be here in a moment." And soon, indeed, Albertine came in, in a dressing gown. "Albertine," I said very softly, and warning her not to raise her voice, so as not to wake my mother, from whom we were separated only by the same partition, the thinness of which, inopportune today and obliging us to whisper, had once resembled, when my grandmother's intentions had been so clearly depicted on it, a sort of musical diaphaneity, "I'm ashamed to have disturbed you. Here. So that you'll understand, I must tell you something you don't know. When I came here, I left a woman whom I was due to marry, who was ready to give up everything for my sake. She was due to leave on a journey this morning, and for the past week, every day, I've been wondering whether I'd have the courage not to telegraph her that I was returning. I had the courage, but I was so wretched that I thought I'd kill myself. That's why I asked you last night if you couldn't come and sleep in Balbec. If I was going to die, I'd have liked to say goodbye to you." And I gave free rein to the tears that my fiction had made natural. "My poor lamb, had I known, I'd have spent the night with you," exclaimed Albertine, into whose head the idea that I would perhaps marry this woman, and that her own opportunity of making a "good marriage" had vanished, never even entered, so sincerely moved was she by an unhappiness whose source I could keep from her, but not its reality and its strength. "Anyway," she said, "yesterday, during the whole journey from La Raspelière, I could certainly tell you were on edge and unhappy, I was afraid of something." In actual fact, my unhappiness had begun only at Parville, and my edginess, very different but which Albertine happily had confused with it, came from the tedium of living a few more days with her. She went on, "I won't leave you again, I'm going to stay here all the time." She was in fact offering me—and she alone could offer it—the one remedy against the poison that was burning me, homogeneous with it, moreover; the one sweet, the other cruel, both alike had derived from Albertine. At that moment, Albertine—my sickness—relenting from causing me to suffer, left me—she, Albertine, the remedy—as susceptible as a convalescent. But I reflected that she would soon be leaving Balbec for Cherbourg and thence for Trieste. Her habits of old were going to be revived. What I wanted above all else was to prevent Albertine from catching the boat, to try and take her to Paris. Admittedly, from Paris she could, if she wanted, more easily than from Balbec, go to Trieste, but in Paris we would see; perhaps I would be able to ask Mme de Guermantes to influence Mlle Vinteuil's friend indirectly, so that she would not remain in Trieste, to get her to accept a position elsewhere, perhaps with the Prince de ——, whom I had met at Mme de Villeparisis's and even at Mme de Guermantes's. And he, even if Albertine wanted to go there in order to meet her friend, might, forewarned by Mme de Guermantes, prevent them from coming together. True, I might have told myself that in Paris, if Albertine had these proclivities, she would find a great many other people with whom to gratify them. But each impulse of jealousy is particular and bears the stamp of the individual—on this occasion, Mlle Vinteuil's friend—who has excited it. It was Mlle Vinteuil's friend who remained my chief preoccupation. The mysterious passion with which I had once thought about Austria because it was the country from which Albertine had come (her uncle had been a counselor in the embassy there), so that I was able to study its geographical singularity, the race that inhabited it, its monuments, its landscapes, as if in an atlas, in a collection of views, in Albertine's smile and her mannerisms, I experienced that passion again, but, its signs now inverted, in the domain of horror. Yes, it was from there that Albertine had come. It was there that, in every house, she would be sure to find again either Mlle Vinteuil's friend or else others. Childhood habits would revive, they would be gathering in three months' time for Christmas, then the First of January, dates that were already sad for me in themselves, because of the unconscious memory of the unhappiness I had experienced when, in the old days, they had separated me, all through the New Year holiday, from Gilberte. After the long dinners, after the *réveillons*,[2] when everyone would be joyful and animated, Albertine would be adopting, with her friends from there, the same attitudes that I had seen her take up with Andrée, and whereas Albertine's friendship with her was innocent, who knows, perhaps the ones that had brought Mlle Vinteuil, pursued by her friend, close before me at Montjouvain. To Mlle Vinteuil, while her friend was tickling her before pouncing on her, I now lent the inflamed features of Albertine, of Albertine whom I could hear, as she ran off, then gave herself up, letting out that strange, deep laugh. What, compared with the pain I was experiencing, was the jealousy I had been able to feel on the day when Saint-Loup had met Albertine with me in Doncières, and when she had led him on? Or that which I had felt when thinking back to the unknown initiator to whom I may have owed the first kisses she had given me in Paris, on the day when I was awaiting Mlle de Stermaria's letter? That other jealousy, provoked by Saint-Loup or by some other young man, was nothing. I might in that case have had to fear at most a rival over whom I could have tried to prevail. But this time the rival was not of my own kind, their weapons were different, I could not give battle on the same terrain, or afford Albertine the same pleasures, or even conceive of them accurately. At many moments in our lives, we would barter the whole of the future against a power in itself insignificant. In the old days, I would have renounced all life's advantages to get to know Mme Blatin, because she was a friend of Mme Swann's. Today, in order that Albertine should not go to Trieste, I would have endured all manner of suffering and, were that insufficient, would have inflicted it on her, would have isolated her, locked her away, would have taken away the little money she had so that penury might prevent her physically from making the journey. As, in the old days, when I had wanted to go to Balbec, what drove me to leave was the longing for a Persian church, or for a storm at dawn, what now rent my heart, when I thought that Albertine would perhaps be going to Trieste, was that she would spend Christmas night there with Mlle Vinteuil's friend; for the imagination, when it changes its nature and is transformed into sensibility, does not thereby have at its dis-

posal a greater number of simultaneous images. Had I been told that
she was not at that moment in Cherbourg, or in Trieste, that she could
not meet Albertine, how I would have wept, for joy and in relief! How
my life and its future would have changed! Yet I knew very well that this
localization of my jealousy was arbitrary, that if Albertine had these
tastes she could gratify them with others. Perhaps even these same girls,
if they could have met her elsewhere, would not have tortured my heart
so. It was from Trieste, from that unknown world where I felt that
Albertine had found enjoyment, where her memories were, her friendships, her childhood loves, that there was exhaled this hostile, inexplicable atmosphere, like that which used to rise up into my room of
old in Combray from the dining room, where I could hear, laughing
and talking with strangers, amid the sound of forks, Mamma, who
would not be coming up to say good night; like that which, for Swann,
had filled the houses where Odette had gone to a soirée in search of
unimaginable delights. It was no longer as of some delectable land
where the people are pensive, the sunsets golden, the carillons sad that I
now thought of Trieste, but as an accursed city that I would have liked
instantly to have burned down and erased from the real world. That
town had become lodged in my heart like a permanent arrowhead.
To let Albertine leave soon for Cherbourg and Trieste filled me with
horror—or even to remain in Balbec. For, now that the revelation of my
loved one's intimacy with Mlle Vinteuil had made me all but certain, I
imagined that at every moment when Albertine was not with me (and
there were whole days when, on account of her aunt, I could not see
her) she was at the mercy of Bloch's cousins, and perhaps of others. The
thought that this very evening she might be meeting Bloch's cousins
drove me mad. And so, after she had told me that she would not leave
me for the next few days, I replied: "But the fact is I'd like to leave for
Paris. Won't you leave with me? And wouldn't you like to come and
live with us for a bit in Paris?" I had at all costs to prevent her from being on her own, at least for a few days, to keep her beside me so as to be
sure that she could not meet Mlle Vinteuil's friend. It would in reality
mean her staying alone with me, for my mother, taking advantage of a
tour of inspection that my father would be making, had prescribed it as
her duty to obey my grandmother's wish, who had wanted her to go for

a few days to Combray to be with one of Grandmother's sisters. Mamma did not like her aunt, because she had not been for Grandmother, so affectionate toward her, the sister that she should have been. Thus, once grown up, do children remember with resentment those who have treated them badly. But Mamma having become like my grandmother, herself incapable of resentment, her mother's life was for her like a pure and innocent childhood she would draw on for those memories whose sweetness or bitterness governed her actions toward this person or that. My aunt might have supplied Mamma with certain invaluable details, but now it would be hard for her to obtain them; her aunt had fallen seriously ill (it was said with cancer), and she reproached herself for not having gone sooner, so as to keep my father company, and saw this simply as one more reason to do as her mother would have done; and just as she went on the anniversary of my grandmother's father's death, who had been such a bad father, to take to his grave the flowers that my grandmother had been in the habit of taking, so, to the side of the grave that was about to open, my mother wanted to bring the consoling conversations that my aunt had not come to offer my grandmother. While she was in Combray, my mother would be taken up with certain building work that my grandmother had always wanted, but only if it was carried out under her daughter's supervision. Thus it had not yet been begun, Mamma not wanting, by leaving Paris before my father, to make him feel too much the weight of a loss in which he shared, but which could not afflict him as much as it did her. "Oh, it wouldn't be possible at this moment," replied Albertine. "Anyway, why do you need to go back to Paris so soon, when the lady in question has gone?" "Because I shall be calmer in a place where I knew her, rather than in Balbec, which she has never seen, and which I've come to abominate." Did Albertine later come to realize that this other woman did not exist, and that if on that particular night I had truly wanted to die, it was because she had thoughtlessly revealed to me that she was friendly with the friend of Mlle Vinteuil? It is possible. There are times when it strikes me as probable. At all events, on the morning in question, she believed in the woman's existence. "But you should marry this lady, *mon petit*," she said. "You'd be happy, and she would surely be happy also." I answered that the thought that I might make this woman happy had indeed all but decided me; recently, when I had come into a large inheritance that would enable me to give my wife every pleasure and luxury, I had been on the verge of accepting the sacrifice of her whom I loved. Intoxicated by the gratitude inspired in me by Albertine's kindness, so soon after the atrocious suffering she had caused me, just as we would gladly promise the café waiter a fortune who is pouring us a sixth glass of brandy, I told her that my wife would have a motorcar and a yacht; that, from this point of view, since Albertine was so fond of motoring and of yachting, it was unfortunate that it was not she whom I loved; that I would have been the perfect husband for her, but that we would see, we would perhaps find it agreeable to see each other. In spite of everything, just as, in a state of drunkenness, we refrain from accosting passersby for fear of blows, I refrained from the imprudence I would have committed in the days of Gilberte, of telling her that it was she, Albertine, that I loved. "You see, I all but married her. But I didn't dare do it, however; I wouldn't have wanted to make a young woman live with someone so sickly and so tiresome." "But you're crazy, everyone would like to live with you, look how everyone seeks you out. You're all they ever talk about at Mme Verdurin's, and in the wider world, too, so I'm told. So she wasn't being nice to you, this lady, was she, by causing you to doubt yourself? I can tell what she is, she's spiteful and I hate her, oh, if it'd been me . . . !" "No, no, she's very kind, too kind. As for the Verdurins and all the rest, I don't give a fig. Apart from the woman that I love and whom I've anyway given up, I care only for my little Albertine, she's the only one, by seeing a lot of me—in the early days at least," I added, so as not to alarm her and to be able to ask a lot of her during these days—"who can console me a little." I made only a vague allusion to the possibility of marriage, while saying that it was unrealizable because our characters would not be in harmony. In spite of myself, still pursued in my jealousy by the memory of Saint-Loup's relations with "Rachel when of the Lord" and of those of Swann with Odette, I was too given to believing that the moment I was in love I could not be loved, and that self-interest alone could attach a woman to me. It was no doubt foolish to judge Albertine in terms of Odette and Rachel. But it was not her, it was me; it was the sentiments I might inspire that my jealousy caused me to underestimate. And of this—perhaps erroneous—judgment were no doubt born many of the misfortunes that would befall us. "You refuse my invitation for Paris, then?" "My aunt wouldn't want me to leave at present. Anyway, even if I can later on, wouldn't it look funny, my coming to stay with you like that? In Paris they'd know very well I'm not your cousin." "Well, we'll say we're more or less engaged. What does it matter, since you know it isn't true?" Albertine's neck, the whole of which was protruding from her nightgown, was powerful, golden, coarse-grained. I kissed it as innocently as if I had been kissing my mother, to still a childish unhappiness that I thought I would never be able to tear out from my heart. Albertine left me to go and get dressed. Her devotion was already weakening, in any case; a little earlier, she had said she would not leave me for a second. (And I felt indeed that her resolution would not last, because I was afraid that if we stayed in Balbec she might, that same evening, if it were not for me, meet Bloch's cousins.) Yet now she had just told me she wanted to go over to Maineville and would come back and see me during the afternoon. She had not been home the previous evening; there might be letters for her; moreover, her aunt might be worried. I had replied, "If that's the only reason, we can send the 'lift' to tell your aunt you're here and fetch your letters." And, wanting to show she was kind, though annoyed at being subjugated, she had wrinkled her brow and then, suddenly, very kindly, said, "That's right," and had sent the "lift." Albertine had left me only for a moment before the "lift" came and tapped on the door. I had not expected him, while I was talking with Albertine, to have had the time to go to Maineville and then return. He came to tell me that Albertine had written a note to her aunt and that she could, if I wanted, come to Paris that same day. She had, on the other hand, been wrong to give him the message orally, for already, despite the earliness of the hour, the manager had heard, and came, distraught, to ask me if I was unhappy about something, if I really was leaving, if I could not wait at least for a few days, the wind today being somewhat fearful (to be feared). I refused to explain that I wanted at all costs for Albertine no longer to be in Balbec at the hour when Bloch's cousins took their walk, especially with Andrée, who alone might have been able to shield her, not being there, and that Balbec was like those places in which an invalid, who can no longer breathe there, has decided, even though he may die along the way, not to spend another night. For the rest, I was going to have to battle against entreaties of the same kind, in the hotel first of all, where Marie Gineste and Céleste Albaret were red-eyed. (Marie, moreover, gave vent to the urgent sobbing of a mountain torrent; the more lethargic Céleste urged her to calm down; but Marie having murmured the only lines of poetry that she knew, *"Ici-bas tous les lilas meurent,"* Céleste could not contain herself, and a sheet of tears spilled across her lilac-colored face; I imagine, on the other hand, that they had forgotten me by that same evening.) Then, on the little branch-line train, despite all my precautions against being seen, I encountered M. de Cambremer, who at the sight of my trunks, turned pale, for he had been counting on me for two days hence; he exasperated me by trying to persuade me that my breathless attacks depended on the change in the weather, and that October would be ideal for them, and he asked me whether, at all events, I could not "put off my departure for a week," an expression whose stupidity enraged me only perhaps because what he was proposing made me feel sick. And while he was speaking to me in the carriage, I was afraid at each station of seeing there, more terrible than Herimbald or Guiscard, M. de Crécy, begging for an invitation, or more dreadful still, Mme Verdurin, insisting on inviting me. But that would happen only in a few hours' time. I had not yet reached that point. I had to confront only the despairing lamentations of the manager. I showed him the door, because I was afraid that, though he was whispering, he would wake Mamma. I remained alone in the room, that same room with the too high ceiling where I had been so unhappy on my first arrival, where I had had such tender thoughts of Mlle de Stermaria, had watched out for Albertine and her friends to go past like migrating birds that had paused on the beach, where I had possessed her with such indifference when I had sent the "lift" to fetch her, where I had experienced my grandmother's goodness, then learned that she was dead; these shutters, at the foot of which the morning light was falling, I had opened them that first time to see the first foothills of the sea (the shutters that Albertine had made me close so that we should not be seen kissing). I became more clearly aware of my own transformations by contrasting them with the self-identity of things. Yet we become accustomed to these as we do to people, and when, suddenly, we recall the different meaning that they carried, and then, once they had lost all meaning, the events, very different from those of today, for which they had been the setting, the diversity of the actions performed beneath the same ceiling, between the same glass-fronted bookcases, the change in our hearts and in our lives which that diversity implies seems further enhanced by the immutable permanence of the décor, reinforced by the unity of place.

I two or three times had the idea, momentarily, that the world in which this room and these bookcases were, and in which Albertine counted for so little, was perhaps an intellectual world, which was the sole reality, and my unhappiness something like that which we get from reading a novel, and which a madman alone could make into a lasting and permanent unhappiness, extending into his life; that it would take only a slight effort of will perhaps to attain to that real world, to return into it by passing beyond my grief, as though bursting through a paper hoop, and no more to care about what Albertine had done than we care about the actions of the imaginary heroine of a novel after we have finished reading it. Moreover, the mistresses whom I have loved the most have never coincided with my love for them. This love was true, since I subordinated everything else to seeing them, to keeping them for myself alone, since I would sob if, one evening, I had had to wait for them. But they had the peculiar quality of arousing that love, of carrying it to a paroxysm, rather than of being the image of it. When I saw them, when I listened to them, I found nothing in them that might resemble my love or be able to explain it. Yet my one joy was to see them, my one anxiety to wait for them. It was as if a virtue having no connection with them had been adjoined to them incidentally by nature, and that this virtue, this electricity-like power, had the effect on me of exciting my love, that is to say of directing all my actions and causing all my sufferings. But from this, the beauty, or the intelligence, or the goodness of these women was wholly distinct. As though by an electric current that moves you, I have been shaken by my love affairs, I have lived them, I have felt them; never have I succeeded in seeing them or thinking them. I incline even to think that in these affairs (I leave aside the physical pleasure, which is of course their habitual accompaniment but is not enough to constitute them), beneath the outward appearance of the woman, it is to these invisible forces by which she is incidentally accompanied that we address ourselves, as if to obscure divinities. It is they whose goodwill is necessary to us, contact with which we seek without finding any positive pleasure in it. During our assignations, the woman puts us in touch with these goddesses, and hardly anything more. We have, as offerings, promised jewels and voyages, and uttered forms of words that signify that we adore her, and contrary forms of words that signify our indifference. We have expended all our influence on obtaining a fresh assignation, but one to be accorded without annoyance. But is it for the woman herself, were she not completed by these occult forces, that we would go to so much trouble, when, once she has gone, we would be unable to say how she was dressed, and we realize that we have not even looked at her?

What a deceitful sense sight is! A human body, even when loved, as was that of Albertine, seems, from a few meters, a few centimeters away, distant from us. And the soul that belongs to it likewise. Except that, should something come violently to alter the position of that soul in relation to us, to show us that it loves other human beings and not ourselves, then, by the beating of our dislocated hearts, we feel that the cherished creature was not a few feet away but inside us. Inside us, in more or less superficial regions. But the words "That friend is Mlle Vinteuil" had been the "Open sesame" that I would have been incapable of finding for myself, which had caused Albertine to penetrate deep into my lacerated heart. And I might have searched for a hundred years without knowing how the door might be reopened that had closed on her.

I had ceased hearing these words momentarily while Albertine was with me a little earlier. In kissing her as I had used to kiss my mother in Combray to calm my anguish, I almost believed in Albertine's innocence, or at least did not think in any coherent way of the discovery I had made of her vice. But now that I was alone, the words rang out once more like those noises inside the ear that we hear as soon as someone has stopped talking to us. Her vice was now no longer in any doubt. The light of the sun, which was about to come up, by modifying the objects around me made me once again, as if shifting my position for a moment in relation to it, aware, even more cruelly, of my pain. Never had I seen so beautiful and so sorrowful a morning. Reflecting on all the indifferent landscapes that were about to be illuminated, and which, just yesterday, would have filled me only with the desire to visit them, I could not contain a sob when, in a mechanically executed gesture of oblation, seeming to symbolize for me the bloody sacrifice that I was about to have to make of all joy, each morning, until the end of my life, a renewal, solemnly celebrated at each dawning of my daily unhappiness and of the blood from my wound, the golden egg of the sun, as if propelled by the break in equilibrium produced at the moment of coagulation by a change of density, barbed with flames as in paintings, burst in one bound through the curtain behind which I had sensed it quivering for the past few moments, ready to enter onto the stage and to spring upward, and whose mysterious, congealed purple it erased beneath floods of light. I could hear myself crying. But at that moment, against all expectation, the door opened, and, my heart pounding, I seemed to see my grandmother before me, as in one of those apparitions that I had already had, but only in my sleep. Was all this only a dream, then? Alas, I was wide awake. "You think I look like your poor grandmother," said Mamma—for it was she—gently, as if to calm my fright, admitting, however, to the resemblance, with a lovely smile of modest pride in which coquettishness had never had any part. Her disordered hair, in which the gray strands had not been hidden but were wound about her anxious eyes and her aging cheeks, my grandmother's dressing gown even that she was wearing, all had prevented me for a second from recognizing her and made me unsure whether I was asleep or whether my grandmother had been resurrected. For a long time now, my mother had resembled my grandmother far more than the young and laughing mamma that my childhood had known. But I had never given it another thought. Thus it is, when we have been sitting for a long time reading, distracted, we have not noticed that time has been passing, and we suddenly find, round about us, the sun, drawn inevitably to pass through the same phases, unmistakably recalling the sun at the same hour the day before, and awakening around it the same harmonies, the same correspondences preparatory to the sunset. It was with a smile that my mother drew my attention to my mistake, for it was a comfort to her to bear so close a resemblance to her mother. "I came," she said, "because when I was asleep I thought I could hear someone crying. It woke me up. But how is it you're not in bed? And your eyes are full of tears. What's the matter?" I took her head in my arms: "Mamma, there, I'm afraid you'll think me very changeable. But, first of all, yesterday I didn't talk to you very nicely about Albertine; what I said was unfair." "But why should that matter?" my mother said, and, catching sight of the rising sun, she gave a sad smile, thinking of her mother, and, so that I should not lose the benefit of a spectacle that my grandmother regretted that I never watched, she pointed to the window. But behind the beach of Balbec, the sea, and the sunrise, to which Mamma was pointing, I could see, in a fit of despair that did not escape her, the room in Montjouvain where Albertine, pink, curled up in a ball like a big cat, with her mischievous nose, had taken the place of Mlle Vinteuil's friend and was saying, to peals of her voluptuous laughter: "Oh well, if we're seen, that'll only make it better. Me, I wouldn't dare spit on that old ape?" This was the scene I could see behind that spread out in the window, which was nothing more than a mournful veil, superimposed on the other like a reflection. It seemed indeed almost unreal, like a painted view. Facing us, where the Parville cliffs jutted out, the leafy tableau of the little wood where we had played hunt-the-ring sloped all the way down to the sea, beneath the still-golden sheen of the water, as at that hour when often, at the day's end, when I had gone to have a siesta there with Albertine, we had got to our feet on seeing the sun go down. In the disorder of the night mists that still hung in blue and pink shreds over waters littered with the pearly debris of the dawn, boats were passing, smiling at the oblique light that had turned their sails and the tips of their bowsprits yellow, as when they return home in the evening: an imaginary scene, shivering and deserted, a pure evocation of the sunset, which did not rest, like the dusk, on the succession of hours of the day that I was in the habit of seeing precede it, slender, interpolated, more insubstantial even than the horrible image of Montjouvain that it had not succeeded in canceling out, in covering, in concealing—a vain and poetic image of the memory and of the dream. "But come," said my mother, "you didn't speak any ill of her, you told me she bored you a little, that you were happy at having given up the idea of marrying her. That's no reason to cry like that. Remember that your mamma is leaving today and is going to be desolate at leaving her darling in this state. All the more, my poor child, because I hardly have time to console you. For, though my things may be ready, one doesn't have all that much time on a day of departure." "It's not that." And then, calculating the future, carefully weighing my determination, realizing that an affection such as that of Albertine for the friend of Mlle Vinteuil and over so long a period, cannot have been innocent, that Albertine had been initiated, and, as all her gestures had demonstrated to me, had been born, moreover, with a predisposition to vice of which my anxiety had all too often had a presentiment, to which she can never have ceased to yield (to which she was perhaps yielding at this very minute, taking advantage of a moment when I was not present), I told my mother, knowing the pain I was causing her, which she did not show, and which betrayed itself in her only by that look of serious concern she wore when she compared the gravity of making me unhappy or of doing me harm, the look she had worn in Combray for the first time when she had resigned herself to spending the night beside me, that look which at this moment bore an extraordinary resemblance to that of my grandmother when she allowed me to drink cognac, I said to my mother: "I know the pain I'm going to cause you. First of all, instead of remaining here, as you wanted, I'm going to leave at the same time as you. But that's by no means all. I don't feel well here, I prefer to go home. But listen, don't be too upset. It's this. I was mistaken, I misled you in good faith yesterday, I've been thinking it over all night. I absolutely must, and let that be decided here and now, because I now realize clearly, because I shan't change again, and I couldn't live without it, I absolutely must marry Albertine."

# Notes

1. **"Gomorrah . . . Sodom":** the two "cities of the plain" destroyed by God because of the depravity of their inhabitants, representing here the spiritual homes of female and male homosexuality respectively. See Genesis 18, 19.

2. **transparent mica . . . foothills:** the "mica" and "foothills" in this description are metaphorical; Proust has described this same prospect earlier (in *The Guermantes Way*) in terms of the Swiss Alps.

3. **the Jockey Club . . . the Bois:** the Jockey Club was the smartest and most exclusive of Parisian male institutions; the Bois is the Bois de Boulogne, then a very fashionable park.

4. **the scene in Montjouvain:** a reference to the scene in *Swann's Way* when the Narrator witnesses the profanation of the composer Vinteuil's photograph by his lesbian daughter during a lesbian encounter.

5. **far-from-convincing example in the *Golden Legend*:** according to the thirteenth-century *Golden Legend*, the Roman Emperor Nero had sex with one of his freedmen, whom he was then anxious to see give birth; after being given a philter, the freedman did so, to a frog.

6. **"the question of the tram-driver":** this episode in Charlus's love life did not find its way into the final text of the novel.

7. **"the Caliph . . . simple merchant":** a reference to the Caliph of Baghdad in the *Arabian Nights*.

8. **"young person . . . good health":** *personne* is a feminine noun, as is the French word for "highness," *altesse*.

9. **"Orléans Cathedral . . . ophthalmia":** the cathedral of Orléans, surprisingly, is a modern building, begun in the seventeenth century and finished in 1829.

10. **"Diane de Poitiers's house":** a Renaissance house in Orléans that was destroyed in June 1940.

**11. "I have three popes in my family"**: possibly an allusion to three Renaissance popes from the Medici family in Florence from whom Charlus is supposedly descended: Leo X, Clement VII, and Leo XI.

**12. Athena**: the goddess who protects Ulysses in both the *Iliad* and the *Odyssey*. In Book XIII of the *Odyssey*, she finally reveals herself to him, having earlier appeared in the guise of an adolescent.

**13. Mene, Tekel, Upharsin**: the prophetic words written on the wall by the fingers of a man's hand during King Belshazzar's fatal feast in Babylon. They were interpreted by the prophet Daniel to mean that Belshazzar's reign, and indeed his life, were over (see Daniel 5).

**14. the poet ... lay his head**: the "poet" is Oscar Wilde, whose homosexuality led to his imprisonment on vice charges in 1895.

**15. "The two sexes will die each on its own side"**: *"Les deux sexes mourront chacun de son côté,"* a line from Alfred de Vigny's poem "La Colère de Samson," or "The Wrath of Samson," Samson having become disillusioned with women following his betrayal by Delilah.

**16. sons of the Indre**: i.e., natives of the *département* of the Indre, in central France.

**17. Union des Gauches ... Fédération Socialiste**: the Union des Gauches was formed from a merger between two radical groups in 1885; there seems never to have been a Fédération Socialiste as such, though a Fédération des Gauches was formed in 1899 to support the government in its attempt to liquidate the Dreyfus Affair.

**18. Schola Cantorum**: a music school founded in Paris in 1894.

**19. the Iénas ... Potin's**: the Iénas' title dates back to the First Empire, and commemorates one of Napoleon's victories (at Jena, in Prussia); to the old, pre-1789 aristocracy of the novel, such Napoleonic creations are vulgar and parvenu. Felix Potin, now the name of a minimarket chain, was then a grocery on the Boulevard Malesherbes where Proust's housekeeper did her food shopping.

**20. Saint-Simonism**: the collectivist school of left-wing political thought inaugurated by Claude-Henri de Rouvroy, Comte de Saint-Simon (1760–1825); at one time in the nineteenth century it functioned as a sort of secular religion.

**21. Galatea**: a sea nymph loved by the giant Polyphemus, who crushed the shepherd she loved, Acis, underneath a rock.

**22. beneath the satellite of Saturn perhaps**: Saturn was the planet thought traditionally by astrologers to preside over "unnatural" love; the satellite invoked by Proust is perhaps Titan.

**23. Rob Roy and not Diana Vernon:** Diana Vernon is the heroine of Scott's novel *Rob Roy*, of which Rob Roy himself is the very masculine hero.

**24. Griselda:** a legendary wife, found in Petrarch, Boccaccio, and Chaucer, as a symbol of patience and conjugal fidelity.

**25. Michelet:** Jules Michelet (1798–1874), the great French historian, wrote about jellyfish in *La Mer* (*The Sea*), which he co-authored with his wife.

**26. "here below every soul" . . . "fragrance":** quotation from a poem by Victor Hugo.

**27. the Montagues and the Capulets:** the warring families in Shakespeare's *Romeo and Juliet.*

**28. *Primula veris:*** these prolonged botanical analogies are based on what Proust had learned from Maeterlinck's *L'Intelligence des fleurs* (1907) and Amédée Coutance's introduction to a translation of some of Darwin's botanical writings.

**29. initial hermaphroditism . . . conserve the trace:** the concept of an "initial hermaphroditism," preceding the division of the human race into two sexes, is to be found in Darwin and in the Greek myth, recounted in Plato's *Symposium,* that explains the phenomenon of love between the sexes by supposing that each is in search of a lost transsexual unity.

**30. For the two angels . . . pillars of salt:** see Genesis 18 and 19; the angel with the flaming sword appears in the story of the expulsion of Adam and Eve from the Garden of Eden, not at the destruction of Sodom, a city from which Lot alone survived, according to Genesis.

**31. "So that if a man . . . numbered":** Genesis 13:16. The verse applies to the descendants of Abraham.

**32. Petrograd:** the name of Saint Petersburg between 1914 and 1924, when it was renamed Leningrad.


PART II: CHAPTER I

**1. Courvoisier-like:** this "cousin," the Prince de Guermantes, is the grandson, on his mother's side, of a Courvoisier, a family described in *The Guermantes Way* as the "opposite camp" to the Guermantes, with whose family values and characteristics Proust compares the Courvoisiers at length, to the latter's disadvantage.

**2. M. Detaille:** Édouard Detaille (1848–1912) specialized in painting military scenes and was a strong anti-Dreyfusard.

**3. *The Dream:*** an allegorical painting showing modern French soldiers on maneuvers, sleeping, as victorious French soldiers of the past pass overhead. The painting won a medal at the 1888 Salon; we can be sure that Proust despised it.

4. **Huxley ... literary world:** T. H. Huxley (1825–95), the great nineteenth-century popularizer of Darwinism; the "nephew" is the novelist and essayist Aldous Huxley (1894–1963), who had reviewed an earlier volume of Proust's novel in November 1919, but was the grandson, not the nephew, of the other Huxley.

5. **"And to do them honor ...":** François de Malherbe (1555–1628) was a poet whose spare, rigorous methods strongly influenced seventeenth-century French classicism. The allusion is to a poem in which the Innocents massacred by Herod arrive in heaven. In French, *"Et pour leur faire honneur les Anges se lever."*

6. **as a famous sonnet has it:** the sonnet, hardly "famous," is by Alexis-Félix Arvers (1806–50), and the relevant lines go: "My soul has its secret, my life has its mystery; / An everlasting love conceived in an instant: / The malady is hopeless, and so I have had to keep silent, / And she who caused it has known nothing of it."

7. **incidents during his youth ... M. de Charlus:** These "incidents" were described by Proust in the manuscript of the novel, but not included in the published text.

8. **the Quai d'Orsay:** where the French Foreign Ministry is situated in Paris.

9. *La Presse:* a daily newspaper founded in 1836, which survived, with one or two gaps in publication, until 1935.

10. **a Jacobin:** i.e., a political radical.

11. *Phèdre:* the tragedy by Racine (1639–99).

12. **A former German chancellor ... Italian woman:** Bernhard von Bülow (1849–1929), German chancellor under Kaiser Wilhelm II, married Maria Beccadelli in 1886.

13. **eminent French diplomat ... illustrious in the East:** Maurice Paléologue (1859–1944), whose family name was also that of the dynasty who provided the Emperors of Byzantium between 1261 and its conquest by the Turks in 1453.

14. **Princesse Palatine ... court of Louis XIV:** Charlotte-Élisabeth de Bavière (1652–1722) was the second wife of Philippe, Duc d'Orléans, the brother of Louis XIV. She was of masculine appearance, and her much-republished letters are full of scandalous details concerning homosexuality among the nobility at Versailles.

15. **entertainment that unfolds in** *Tannhäuser* **... famous March:** the scene

occurs in the second act of Wagner's opera, when the singers arrive to take part in the tournament and sing of love.

**16. Whistler:** James McNeill Whistler (1834–1903), a painter born in the United States but living mainly in France and in England, who specialized in works of muted, subtle harmonies of color.

**17. Hubert Robert's celebrated fountain:** Hubert Robert (1733–1808), better known as a landscape painter and engraver, designed some of the fountains at Versailles.

**18. Grand Duke Vladimir:** Vladimir (1847–1909), the second son of Tsar Alexander II; he spent long periods in Paris with his wife, Maria Pavlovna, who appears in the final volume of the novel.

**19. the Queen of Italy's:** the wife of Victor Emmanuel III, who became King of Italy in 1900.

**20. *agrégé:*** someone having passed the *agrégation,* a competitive examination—in this case, in history—and thus qualified to teach in higher education.

**21. Mme Standish ... the Duchesse de Doudeauville:** Proust met Mrs. Henry Standish (1847–1933, née Hélène de Prusse des Cars) for the first time in 1912; the Doudeauvilles were a branch of the La Rochefoucauld family, hence highly aristocratic.

**22. "Mama ... him":** Amanien d'Osmond, cousin of the Duc de Guermantes, was terminally ill at the end of *The Guermantes Way;* his nickname was "Mama."

**23. the Duchesse de Montmorency:** the Montmorencys were one of the oldest and most illustrious of Ancien Régime families; the son of the last of them, Alix, was given the title of Duc de Montmorency by Napoleon III under the Second Empire.

**24. École des Sciences Politiques:** a private institution, founded in 1871, to teach law, economics, and history, which quickly came to specialize in training future senior civil servants. It was nationalized in 1945, when it became the Institut des Études Politiques.

**25. in Racine's tragedies ... "Yids":** neither of the two tragedies referred to, *Athalie* and *Esther,* has any homosexual theme; the "race" Racine is concerned with in both plays is that of the Jews. All the quotations that follow are from *Esther,* as modified by Proust.

**26. throne room of Suze:** in 1912, the Comtesse Blanche de Clermont-Tonnerre gave a famous "Persian" party, the décor of which reproduced that of the walls of the recently discovered ancient palace of Suze, in Tunisia.

**27. "Great Heaven! . . .":** *Ciel! Quel nombreux essaim d'innocentes beautés / S'offre à mes yeux en foule et sort de tous côtés! / Quelle aimable pudeur sur leur visage est peinte!*

**28. "Meanwhile his love . . .":** *Cependant son amour pour notre nation / A peuplé ce palais de filles de Sion, / Jeunes et tendres fleurs par le sort agitées, / Sous un ciel étranger comme moi transplantées. / Dans un lieu séparé de profanes témoins / Il met à les former son étude et ses soins.*

**29. "To this day . . .":** *Le roi jusqu'à ce jour ignore qui je suis, / Et ce secret toujours tient ma langue enchaînée.*

**30. "D'Annunzio":** Gabriele D'Annunzio (1863–1938), an Italian writer with a spectacular reputation as a womanizer.

**31. "Isvolsky":** Alexander Pavlovich Isvolsky (1856–1919), Russian ambassador in Paris from 1910 until the Revolution of 1917.

**32. "three of Ibsen's plays":** Ibsen died in 1906, and his appearance contemporary with Isvolsky is implausible—whence, perhaps, the doubts the Duc de Guermantes is about to display.

**33.** *Le Gaulois: Le Gaulois,* founded in 1868, was famous before 1914 for its social coverage, which took readers away from *Le Figaro*—the paper it was eventually merged with in 1928.

**34. the Grand Prix:** the Grand Prix de Paris was a leading flat race run at Longchamp.

**35. Mme Alphonse de Rothschild . . . Baron Hirsch:** Alphonse de Rothschild (1827–1905) was head of the family bank in Paris and a prominent businessman; the Duchesse de La Trémoïlle was the wife of Charles, Duc de La Trémoïlle (1838–1911), a gentleman-scholar; the Princesse de Sagan was the wife of Charles-Guillaume Boson de Talleyrand-Périgord (1832–1910), an arbiter of fashion in the *fin de siècle;* the Baron Maurice de Hirsch de Gereuth (1831–96) was a Jewish businessman and philanthropist.

**36. the Duc de Berry:** Charles-Ferdinand, Duc de Berry (1778–1820), second son of King Charles X, was stabbed to death by a workman. His dying wish to his wife was that she should bring up as her own the two illegitimate daughters he had had in England by a Mrs. Brown; this she did.

**37. "where Monaldeschi was murdered":** the favorite of Queen Christina of Sweden, who had him murdered at Fontainebleau in 1657.

**38. Duchesses d'Uzès:** either the widowed Anne de Rochechouart-Mortemart (1847–1933), novelist, poet, sculptress, yachtswoman, and feminist; or else Thérèse de Luynes, whose husband became Duc d'Uzès in 1893.

**39. the Academicians . . . count on their vote:** candidates for election to the various academies, the Académie Française above all, are expected to gather support in this way.

**40. Mme de Durfort:** the Durfort family appears in the *Memoirs* of Saint-Simon, one of Proust's principal sources of aristocratic names; various members of it were still prominent in Parisian society in his own day.

**41. "Mélanie Pourtalès's":** the Comtesse Edmond de Pourtalès, née Mélanie de Bussière (c. 1832–1914), had been a lady-in-waiting to the Empress Eugénie, the wife of Napoleon III.

**42. "the Holy Synod and the Oratorian temple":** the Holy Synod was an ecclesiastical body of the Russian Orthodox church, founded in 1721 and suppressed in 1917; the monastery of the Oratory, on the rue de Rivoli in Paris, was handed over to the Protestants by Napoleon in 1811.

**43. "the aforenamed Charleval":** in fact, of the aforenamed Chanlivault.

**44. "Labiche":** Eugéne Labiche (1815–88), a writer of comedies and vaudeville sketches, noted for his portrayal of very down-to-earth members of the bourgeoisie.

**45. the Prince de Chimay:** Joseph de Riquet, Prince de Chimay et de Caraman (1836–92), was at one time the Belgian foreign minister.

**46. *concours général:*** an annual nationwide academic competition between the best pupils in French *lycées* and colleges.

**47. "Chartres":** the Duc de Chartres (1840–1910), grandson of King Louis-Philippe and younger brother of the Comte de Paris.

**48. the burgomaster Six:** whose portrait, along with that of his wife, is in the Six Collection in Amsterdam.

**49. " 'Ab uno disce omnes' ":** a line from Virgil's *Aeneid,* meaning, "By the one we can know the others."

**50. " 'the Princesse de Parme's' ":** the duchy of Parma became part of the kingdom of Italy in 1860. Proust knew the illegitimate daughter of the last reigning Prince of Parma, who, as Mme d'Hervey de Saint-Denis, will make her appearance in the novel shortly.

**51. "I'm astonished . . . Duc de Bouillon":** rival claims to the ancient family name of La Tour d'Auvergne had become something of a cause célèbre during the nineteenth and early twentieth centuries; the Duc de Guermantes naturally takes the purist view that the claims were false, though the claims of the Duc de Bouillon appear not to have been too sound, either.

**52. the Vicomte d'Arlincourt and Loïsa Puget:** Charles-Victor Prévôt,

Vicomte d'Arlincourt (1789–1856), was a writer whose historical novels were disguised attacks on the regime of King Louis-Philippe; Loïsa Puget (1810–89) was a poetess and musician who sang her own songs at social functions. The "days" Proust is referring to are thus those of the July Monarchy, after 1830.

**53. "Montfort-l'Amaury":** a village to the west of Paris, near Rambouillet, whose church has some renowned sixteenth-century stained glass.

**54. " 'Campo Santo' ":** the Campo Santo in Pisa has celebrated frescos showing such funereal scenes as *The Triumph of Death* and *The Last Judgment.*

**55. an Aumale-Lorraine:** a family dating back to the early fifteenth century and related by marriage to the junior or Orléans branch of the Bourbons.

**56. *"la barbe":*** literally, "the beard," an expression meaning "what a drag."

**57. *more geometrico:*** in the geometrical mode.

**58. *suave mari magno* and *memento quia pulvis: "suave, mari magno"* ("how sweet when, on the open sea") are the first words of a passage by the Roman poet Lucretius where he reflects on the comfort of watching from the shore as the lives of others are imperiled by a storm out at sea; *memento quia pulvis* ("remember thou art dust") are words drawn from Genesis 3:19 and God's promise to Adam: "for dust thou art, and unto dust shalt thou return."

**59. an inquisitive Valois:** the Valois were the reigning dynasty in France from 1328 to 1589.

**60. married to a Bourbon princess:** this is the only mention of Charlus's late wife's having been a Bourbon—that is, a member of the family of the Kings of France between 1589 and 1848.

**61. one louis:** a gold coin worth twenty francs.

**62. Jacquet:** Gustave Jacquet (1846–1909), a painter of genre scenes and of society portraits.

**63. *Uncle and Nephew: Der Neffe als Onkels* (*The Nephew Mistaken for the Uncle*), a play by the German dramatist Schiller (1759–1805).

**64. "Giorgione-like":** Giorgione (c. 1477–1511) was a painter credited with instituting the great tradition of Venetian painting.

**65. Scapin ... with a stick:** Scapin was the traditional figure of the insolent valet in Italian comedy, imported into France by Molière in his comedy *Les Fourberies de Scapin* (*The Impostures of Scapin*).

**66. "Right down to the household dog ...":** a quotation, slightly modified, from Molière.

**67. "Victurnien, like in the *Cabinet des antiques":*** Victurnien d'Esgrignon is the beautiful young hero of Balzac's novel of this title, published in 1838.

68. **"Loubet"**: Émile Loubet (1838–1929) was president of the Republic from 1899 to 1906, and thus during the time when the Dreyfus case was reopened. He was in favor of a review and reprieved Dreyfus after he had been found guilty for a second time.

69. **"a Polignac and a Montesquiou"**: probably Prince Edmond de Polignac (1834–1901), who married Winnaretta Singer, daughter of the sewing-machine magnate, and whose religious and other music Proust much admired; and Robert, Comte de Montesquiou-Fezensac (1855–1921), a celebrated poetaster, aesthete, socialite, homosexual, and snob, whom Proust knew well, and who is often taken to have been his prime model for the character of the Baron de Charlus.

70. **"Would you believe ... whether I had the colic"**: the writer Jean Cocteau claims in his *Journal* that Charlus's "diatribe" is one actually delivered by Robert de Montesquiou.

71. **"the Restoration"**: the Restoration was the period immediately following the fall of Napoleon and the First Empire.

72. **" 'vertes' "**: *vert* here in the sense not of green but of "spicy."

73. **" 'Ah! Green . . .' "**: the line (slightly mis-)quoted comes from a volume of parodies of Symbolist poetry entitled *Déliquescences: Poèmes décadents d'André Floupette* (1885), written by Gabriel Vicaire and Henri Beauclair. In French, the quote reads, *"Ah! Verte, combien verte était mon âme ce jour-là. . . ."*

74. **"like Mazarin with his books"**: Jules Mazarin (1602–61), one of the great statesmen of seventeenth-century France, founded the Bibliothèque Mazarine in Paris in 1642, a public library that became part of the Bibliothèque Nationale in 1930.

75. **Athena Hippia ... outruns horsemen**: Athena Hippia was so called because she was supposed to have taught men how to control horses.

76. **" 'the Grand Duke of Hesse' "**: the Landgraves of Hesse became grand dukes under Napoleon I. At the time of the Dreyfus Affair, the Grand Duke was Ernest Ludwig (b. 1868).

77. **" 'the Swedish Crown Prince' "**: Gustav (1858–1950), the elder son of King Oscar II and Sophie of Nassau.

78. **" 'Empress Eugénie was a Dreyfusist' "**: Eugénie (1826–1920), the widow of Napoleon III, was indeed a Dreyfusard.

79. **Bourg l'Abbé, Bois-le-Roi, and the like**: in the Middle Ages, the titles of local dignitaries, such as Abbé, or Abbot, could become part of a place-name.

80. **a peer of France**: between the Restoration in 1814 and the "Revolution" of

1848, the Pairs (or Peers) de France formed the upper house of the French Parliament. From 1815 to 1830, the peerage was hereditary, but later new members were appointed by the King from among the bourgeoisie.

**81. "Nattier's *Duchesse de Châteauroux*"**: Jean-Marc Nattier (1685–1766) was court painter to King Louis XV, and the Duchesse de Châteauroux in question (1714–44) was for two years the King's mistress.

**82. " 'the Henry document' "**: Major Hubert-Joseph Henry (1846–98) forged or tampered with a number of documents in order to incriminate Dreyfus retrospectively, at a time when his superior, Colonel Picquart, was building a case against Esterhazy, the real culprit. One forgery in particular, a note purporting to have been written by the Italian military attaché in Paris, was known ever after as the "faux Henry" and is clearly the document referred to by Proust. Henry later committed suicide in prison.

**83. " '*Le Siècle* and *L'Aurore*' "**: *Le Siècle,* a Paris daily that began publishing in 1836, supported the case for a review of Dreyfus's conviction; *L'Aurore* was a daily founded (in 1897) in the Dreyfusard interest. Zola's celebrated pro-Dreyfus article, "J'accuse," appeared in *L'Aurore*.

**84. "Mme de Ligne, Mme de Tarente, Mme de Chevreuse, and the Duchesse d'Arenberg"**: the Princesses de Ligne, de Tarente, and d'Arenberg can all be found in the 1908 social directory, *Tout-Paris;* a Mme de Chevreuse appears in the *Memoirs* of Saint-Simon.

**85. "Picquart"**: Colonel Georges Picquart (1854–1914), having been instrumental in exposing the conspiracy against Dreyfus, was himself eventually arrested and dismissed from the service. When he was, even as a civilian, threatened with a military court-martial, there were widespread protests, and a petition in Picquart's favor was signed by many prominent professors, artists, writers, etc. Picquart was later reinstated in the army, became a general, and was a reforming minister of war from 1906 to 1909.

**86. the decoration he had won . . . in '70**: at the time of the disastrous war with Prussia, when the militia, the Garde Nationale, was called into action.

**87. chevalier of the Légion d'Honneur**: the lowest of the five grades of the Légion d'Honneur, an order instituted by Napoleon I in 1802.

**88. "Dreyfus rehabilitated"**: Dreyfus was rehabilitated in 1906.

**89. the very different story . . . intimidated**: sadly, Proust did not include this episode in the finished text.

**90. " 'Why is Pascal . . .' "**: a schoolmasterish play on words: *troublant/troublé* = troubling/troubled, *trou* = "hole," *blé* = wheat, *blanc* = white.

**91. "Hervey de Saint-Denis"**: the Marquis Hervey de Saint-Denis (1823–92) became professor of Chinese at the Collège de France in 1874. Proust knew his widow.

**92. Monseigneur Dupanloup:** Dupanloup (1802–78), a liberal Catholic who took a particular interest in education and was one of the prime movers of the Loi Falloux of 1850, which freed education in France from church control.

**93. the Castellanes:** Count Boni de Castellane was one of Proust's closest friends.

**94. the Prince de Sagan:** Boni de Castellane's uncle, who died in 1910.

**95. "some cartoon or other . . .":** a cartoon answering to this description appeared in a French paper in 1923, and may well have been reproducing an earlier version of the same theme.

**96. *Annuaire des châteaux:*** it appeared for the first time in 1887–88, as an extension of *Tout-Paris,* the annual guide to Parisian society, of which Proust makes copious use.

**97. "they're exaggerating":** a response supposedly based on one actually made by Aimery de La Rochefoucauld when told of the (for him) untimely death of his cousin, the brother of Robert de Montesquiou.

**98. Bailleau-le-Pin:** a village near Illiers—i.e., Proust's Combray.

**99. Edison's discovery:** the telephone was of course the invention, not of Edison, but of Alexander Graham Bell (1847–1922).

**100. the brandished scarf . . . *Tristan:*** the waving of the scarf is a prearranged signal given by Isolde to Tristan in Act II of Wagner's opera; the shepherd's pipe in Act III tells the dying Tristan that Isolde's ship has sailed.

**101. "Jojotte":** a nickname given to a portrait painter, Georges Clarin (1843–1919), who signed the first petition in favor of Dreyfus, following the publication of Zola's "J'accuse."

**102. Cours-la-Reine:** an avenue that runs along the Seine between the Place de la Concorde and the Grand-Palais.

**103. *Rape of Europa:*** a copy of this 1747 painting by Boucher, now in the Louvre, served as a cartoon for tapestries.

**104. Consulate . . . Directory:** the Consulate lasted from 1799 to 1804, with Napoleon the *de facto* ruler of France as First Consul (out of three); the Directory had lasted from 1795 to the *coup d'état* of November 1799, when Napoleon seized power. The two regimes fostered distinct cultural styles.

**105. Ballets Russes . . . Princess Yourbeletieff:** Diaghilev's Ballets Russes created a sensation in Paris from their first appearance there in 1909. Léon Bakst (1866–1924) was the foremost designer of their sets and costumes; Vaslav Nijinsky (1890–1950) was the most celebrated of the Russian male dancers;

Alexandre Benois (1870–1960) was a painter who also designed stage sets; Igor Stravinsky (1882–1971) wrote some of his best-known music for Diaghilev, notably *The Firebird* and *The Rite of Spring;* the Princess Yourbeletieff is an invention.

**106. a Communard salon:** the Paris Commune of 1871 was a radical insurrection that turned to violence and was bloodily suppressed by government troops; it had few if any supporters among "society people."

**107. Patrie Française:** the Ligue de la Patrie Française was founded in 1898 to bring together those opposed to Dreyfus, and as an answer to the Dreyfusard Ligue des Droits de l'Homme.

**108. the Marquis du Lau . . . the Duc d'Estrées:** the Marquis Armand du Lau d'Allemans was a prominent member of the Jockey Club, and an associate of Comte Louis de Turenne. Prince Giovanni Borghese (1855–1918) married, in 1902, Alice de Riquet, Comtesse de Caraman-Chimay. Charles, Vicomte de La Rochefoucauld, Duc d'Estrées (1863–1907), was the eldest son of Duc Sosthène de La Rochefoucauld–Doudeauville, who is about to be mentioned.

**109. M. Doumer and M. Deschanel:** Paul Doumer (1857–1932), a radical politician who became president of the Republic in 1931, only to be assassinated a year later; Paul Deschanel (1855–1922) became president in 1920 but had to resign that same year because of ill health.

**110. the Charettes, the Doudeauvilles, etc.:** François-Athanase de Charette de La Contrie (1763–96) led the counterrevolutionary Royalist uprising in the Vendée in 1793; his family remained strongly Royalist throughout the nineteenth century. Sosthène de Doudeauville (1825–1908), descended from another ultra-Royalist family, was a right-wing deputy for many years and ambassador in London 1873–74.

**111. Committee of Public Safety:** the Comité de Salut Public was the most ferocious of the ruling institutions created by the French Revolution, lasting from 1793 to 1795 and being dominated first by Danton and then by Robespierre.

**112. Picquart, Clemenceau, Zola, Reinach, and Labori:** Georges Picquart is described in note 85 above; Georges Clemenceau (1841–1929), a left-wing journalist and politician, was prime minister from 1906 to 1909 and again in the final months of the Great War, but failed subsequently to be elected president; Émile Zola (1840–1902), by then the country's leading writer, was the most prominent of all Dreyfus supporters during the Affair; Joseph Reinach (1856–1921), a left-wing politician, eventually wrote a seven-volume history of the Affair; Fernand Labori (1860–1917), a left-wing lawyer, appeared for the defense in the Dreyfus trial.

113. **Colonne concerts:** Judas Colonna, alias Édouard Colonne (1838–1910), a conductor who founded the Concert National in Paris in 1871 and later the Association des Concerts Colonne.

114. *Revue des deux mondes:* a review started in 1828 and devoted to both cultural and political topics. Its heyday was the late nineteenth and early twentieth centuries.

115. **Falconet:** Étienne Falconet (1716–91), sculptor and ceramic artist, a protégé of Louis XV's mistress, Mme de Pompadour.

116. **The Intermittences of the Heart:** the title that Proust envisaged at one time giving to his novel as a whole.

117. *bâtonnier:* the president of the lawyers pleading in a particular court.

118. **First President:** a judicial appointment, roughly equivalent to "senior judge."

119. *Écho de Paris:* a daily founded in 1884, literary and artistic to begin with, later conservative and Catholic.

120. **M. Caillaux's:** Joseph Caillaux (1863–1944), a radical politician who served as prime minister from 1911 to 1912. He had to negotiate with Germany after the so-called Agadir Affair, in which a German warship provoked a crisis by entering the harbor there. Caillaux was forced to resign as a minister in 1914, after his wife assassinated Gaston Calmette, the editor of *Le Figaro*, which paper had been leading a campaign against him.

121. **"under the thimble ... thumb":** the manager says *"sous la coupole"* instead of *"sous la coupe,"* which improves the joke, since *"sous la coupole"* is the phrase used to describe the meeting place of the Académie Française: to be received *sous la coupole* means to be elected to the Academy.

122. **"M. Paillard":** the name of a well-known Paris restaurant, patronized by some of Proust's friends.

123. **Lethe:** the river of forgetfulness or oblivion in Greek mythology.

124. **"stags, stags, Francis Jammes, fork":** Francis Jammes (1868–1938) wrote poetry of a naïve and sentimental kind, often on the theme of innocence recovered. The stag in this dream sequence appears to derive from a story by Gustave Flaubert, "The Legend of Saint Julien the Hospitaler," in which a stag predicts to Julien that he will kill both his father and his mother; the reference may be connected with the guilt felt by Proust at the death of his mother. The fork comes from an earlier draft of the novel, in which the sound of a fork

striking a plate acts as a trigger for the Narrator's involuntary memories (in the same way as the better-known madeleine). In the published text (in *Finding Time Again*), the fork has become a spoon.

**125. Aias:** the Greek form of Ajax, who, in his madness in the *Iliad,* massacred shepherds and sheep after mistaking them for fellow Greeks.

**126. "Jonathan":** i.e., John the Baptist.

**127. Duc d'Orléans** . . . **Duc de Guermantes:** only two of the four separate houses of Orléans ever succeeded to the throne, the second such occasion coming in 1830, with King Louis-Philippe; the title of Prince de Tarente belonged indeed to the house of La Trémoïlle.

**128. Mme de Sévigné:** Marie de Sévigné (1626–96), thought by many to be the greatest of all French letter-writers, and admired particularly by Proust for the quick, spirited impressionism of her style.

**129. Mme de Beausergent:** Proust's own invention.

**130. *en-tout-cas:*** an umbrella that can also be used as a sunshade.

**131. "witty Marquise"** . . . **"good old La Fontaine":** these were descriptions used by the great nineteenth-century critic Charles-Augustin Sainte-Beuve (1804–69), whose work Proust detested and regarded as philistine.

**132. *cuiller* . . . *cueiller:*** the difference phonetically being, roughly, between *kwee-air* and *ker-i-yea.*

**133. Fénelon:** Bertrand de Salignac-Fénelon (1878–1914) was killed in the opening months of the 1914–18 war. He was descended from a brother of François de Salignac de La Mothe–Fénelon (1651–1715), writer, theologian, and Archbishop–also known as the "Swan"–of Cambrai, whose *Aventures de Télémaque* were interpreted as a veiled attack on Louis XIV.

**134. Duguay-Trouin:** René Duguay-Trouin, Sieur du Guay (1673–1736), a sailor whose statue stands in his native Saint-Malo.

**135. Mme de Montespan:** Marie-Madeleine Gabrielle de Rochechouart (1645–1704), Abbess of Fontevrault, the sister of Françoise-Athénaïs de Rochechouart (1641–1707), Marquise de Montespan and mistress of King Louis XIV, who had eight children by her in eight years.

**136. Panathenaea:** a festival held in Athens in honor of the goddess Athena; its procession was depicted on a frieze on the Parthenon, fragments of which are now in the British Museum and the Louvre.

**137. *"un peuple florissant":*** "a flourishing race," a quotation from *Esther.* The following quotations all come from *Athalie* and are in some cases slightly modified (or else inaccurately quoted).

138. **"What, then, is your occupation?"**: *"Quel est donc votre emploi?"*
139. **"But this whole people ..."**: *"Mais tout ce peuple enfermé dans ce lieu, / À quoi s'occupe-t-il?"*
140. **" 'I see the stately order ...' "**: *" 'Je vois l'ordre pompeux de ces cérémonies.' "*
141. **"raised far from the world"**: *"loin du monde élevés."*
142. **"young and faithful troupe"**: *"troupe jeune et fidèle."*

PART II: CHAPTER 2

1. ***Decauville:*** Paul Decauville (1846–1922), industrialist and politician, who invented a narrow-gauge railway that could be demounted and transported.
2. **Rosemonde:** a slip of the pen for Albertine.
3. ***"ascenseur"* ... *"accenseur":*** the difference in sound is between "assenseur" and "acksenseur." *Ascenseur* means "elevator" or "lift."
4. **the recidivism ... single negative:** Proust's lift boy omits the normal *ne* in front of the verb used negatively. Bélise is a character in *Les Femmes savantes,* in which Molière makes fun of grammatical pedantry.
5. **"Sappho":** legend has the poetess Sappho throwing herself into the sea off Lesbos as a result of her unrequited love for a boatman.
6. **Le Sidaner:** Henri le Sidaner (1862–1939), a minor Impressionist, best known for his cityscapes of Bruges and Venice.
7. **"M. Degas assures us ... Chantilly":** Degas had much to do with the revival of Poussin's reputation during the 1890s.
8. **" 'Their giant's wings ...' ":** a line from a celebrated sonnet in which Baudelaire describes the ungainliness of an albatross when it is on the ground, using the bird as a symbol for the Poet. In French, *"Leurs ailes de géant les empêchent de marcher."*
9. **the Congrégations ... Yellow Peril, etc.:** the Congrégations were religious bodies that ran many schools (and some hospitals) in France; after 1900, they fell foul of secularist politicians and were finally dissolved in 1904. The "wars in the East" refers to the war of 1904–5 between Russia and Japan, the Japanese victory in which led to fears in Europe that the "yellow" races might prove too strong for the white.
10. ***Tetralogy:*** the four operas of Wagner's *Ring* cycle.
11. **Massenet:** Jules Massenet (1842–1912), a composer best known for his operas, notably *Manon* and *Don Quichotte.*
12. ***Latude or 35 years of Captivity:*** a historical melodrama by Guilbert de

Pixérécourt and Anicet Bourgeois, first performed in 1834, based on the story of Jean-Henri Latude (1725–1805), who sent Louis XV's mistress, Mme de Pompadour, an explosive device and then denounced his own plot in hopes of getting a reward. His reward was to spend the next thirty-five years in prison.

**13. "the air that gives life":** the chorus in *Fidelio* sings to this effect at the end of Act III.

**14. *particule:*** i.e., the *de* in front of "Chenouville."

**15. Caro's lectures:** Elme Marie Caro (1826–87) was a philosophy professor at the Sorbonne.

**16. the Lamoureux concerts:** regular Sunday concerts started in 1881 by Charles Lamoureux (1834–99), a violinist, conductor, and keen Wagnerian.

**17. *"talentueuse":*** a rare usage meaning "talented."

**18. twenty-eight days:** the annual service required of an army conscript once in the reserve.

**19. Galland's . . . and Mardrus's *Arabian Nights:*** the Galland translation appeared in twelve volumes early in the eighteenth century; the Mardrus appeared between 1899 and 1904, and restored the risqué elements that Galland had censored.

**20. Thierry:** Augustin Thierry (1795–1856), a medieval historian of Romantic views, who wrote notably about the Merovingians and the Norman Conquest of England. Part of his search for local color involved using the Germanic forms of Merovingian names long since Gallicized by other writers.

**21. Leconte de Lisle:** Charles-Marie Leconte de Lisle (1818–94), the most prominent of the post-Romantic Parnassian school of poets, who took much of his subject matter from antiquity.

**22. Lamartine:** Alphonse de Lamartine (1790–1869), the most lyrical and thus least Parnassian of Romantic poets.

**23. Viviane . . . Puss in Boots:** Viviane is a good fairy in Chrétien de Troyes's twelfth-century romance of *Lancelot,* who turns the hero into a perfect knight. Puss in Boots is a character in one of Perrault's fairy tales.

**24. vague as fragrances:** this and the classical references that follow come from Leconte de Lisle's French translation of the *Orphic Hymns.*

**25. choruses:** all the quotations that follow come from *Athalie.*

**26. "Great heaven . . .":** *"Mon Dieu, qu'une vertu naissante / Parmi tant de périls marche à pas incertains! / Qu'une âme qui te cherche et veut être innocente / Trouve d'obstacle à ses desseins!"*

27. **"Put not your trust ..."**: *"Sur la richesse et l'or ne mets point ton appui."*

28. **"And whether from fear ..."**: *"Et soit frayeur encor ou pour le caresser, / De ses bras innocents il se sentit presser."*

29. **"From flowers to flowers ..."**: *"De fleurs en fleurs, de plaisirs en plaisirs / Promenons nos désirs. / De nos ans passagers le nombre est incertain. / Hâtons-nous aujourd'hui de jouir de la vie! / L'honneur et les emplois / Sont le prix d'une aveugle et douce obéissance, / Pour la triste innocence / Qui viendrait élever la voix."*

30. **a ballet dancer ... Degas:** Degas drew and painted many scenes of ballet dancers.

31. **La Juive:** an opera, with music by Fromental Halévy (1799–1862), first performed in 1835.

32. **"O God ..."**: *"O Dieu de nos pères, / Parmi nous descends, / Cache nos mystères / À l'oeil des méchants!"*

33. **"He's a ministerial messenger"**: the best-known aria from *Les Brigands,* an opera with music by Jacques Offenbach (1819–80). In French, *"C'est un courrier de cabinet."*

34. **Mlle Marie Gineste and Mme Céleste Albaret:** Céleste Albaret (née Gineste, 1891–1984), the wife of a Paris taxi-driver used by Proust, became his housekeeper in 1914, and worked for him until his death in 1922. Her memories of the writer were published in 1973 as *Monsieur Proust.* Marie Gineste was her unmarried sister; they came originally from Auvergne.

35. **Saint-Léger Léger:** Alexis Saint-Léger Léger (1887–1975), a diplomat, born in the West Indies, who wrote poetry under the name of Saint-John Perse. His *Éloges* appeared in 1911.

36. **"Here below ..."**: the first line of a poem by Sully Prudhomme (1839–1907), who received the first Nobel Prize for Literature, in 1901. Proust had mixed views about Sully Prudhomme's merits. In French, *"Ici-bas tous les lilas meurent."*

37. **Amphitryon:** in Greek mythology, the betrothed of Alcmene. He was cuckolded in his absence by Zeus, who took on the features of Amphitryon in order to seduce her and thus became the father of Hercules.

38. **the Maxims:** the *Maxims,* first published in 1665, were the work of François, Duc de La Rochefoucauld (1613–80), whose links with the Guermantes family have already been established.

39. **"But you, indolent traveler ..."**: a couplet from a poem by Alfred de Vigny. In French, *"Mais toi, ne veux-tu pas, voyageuse indolente, / Rêver sur mon épaule en y posant ton front?"*

**40. pecus:** the Latin word for "cattle."

**41. Emmaus:** the place outside Jerusalem where two disciples met the risen Christ.

**42. where German-style notions . . . humanism:** higher education was considerably reorganized in France between 1885 and 1896, and new university disciplines were created, often on the German model.

**43. the Princesse de Caprarola:** a made-up title; Caprarola is a small town near Viterbo, Italy, where Proust had once thought of renting a palazzo.

**44. "Villemain":** Abel-François Villemain (1790–1870), critic, Sorbonne professor, and politician, who became permanent secretary of the Académie Française.

**45. "M. le Prince de Talleyrand":** Charles-Maurice de Talleyrand-Périgord (1754–1838), statesman, diplomat, and supreme political opportunist and survivor. The phrase Talleyrand actually used was *plaisir de vivre,* not *douceur de vivre,* referring to the agreeableness of life (for him) in France during the 1780s.

**46. "M. le Cardinal de Retz . . . Marcillac":** Paul de Gondi (1613–79), later Cardinal de Retz, was powerful in both the church and the state; he wrote some famous memoirs. "Struggle-for-lifer," a phrase used in English by Proust, derives from the vulgar Darwinism of the late nineteenth century. The Duc de La Rochefoucauld who wrote the *Maxims* was Prince de Marcillac before succeeding his father in the title; the *boulangistes* were the supporters of Général Boulanger (1837–91), a rabid nationalist, suspected at one time of being a potential dictator.

**47. William:** the German Emperor Wilhelm II.

**48. the Abbaye-aux-Bois:** where the celebrated hostess Mme de Récamier had her salon in Paris, at which, during the 1820s, the great Romantic writers, Chateaubriand among them, read their works in public.

**49. Mme de Châtelet:** Émilie, Marquise du Châtelet (1706–49), who had a long liaison with Voltaire.

**50. the Roman Empress:** possibly Agrippina, wife of Claudius I and mother of Nero, famous for her domineering ways.

**51. like Christ or the Kaiser:** a reference to Christ's injunction in Matthew 10:37; and to Kaiser Wilhelm II's declarations of 1891 that "The will of the King is the supreme law" and that soldiers should obey "without a murmur" if ordered to fire on their own families.

**52. "You alone appeared . . .":** *"Toi seule me parus ce qu'on cherche toujours."*

**53. Potain and Charcot:** Pierre-Carl-Édouard Potain (1825–1901), a prominent Paris medical man, with several literary patients (see the Goncourts' *Journal*);

Jean-Martin Charcot (1825–93), greatest of nineteenth-century neurologists in France, who considerably influenced the young Freud when he was a medical student in Paris.

**54. just as in Marivaux ... she ever had one:** the comedies of Pierre de Marivaux (1688–1763) contain numerous aristocrats, but no baronnes.

**55. Viollet-le-Duc:** Eugène-Emmanuel Viollet-le-Duc (1814–79) was a champion of Gothic architecture, and responsible for the (sometimes brutal) restoration of many medieval buildings.

**56. "Charles-Maurice, abbé of Périgord":** i.e., Talleyrand, at one time both an unbeliever and a Catholic bishop.

**57. Were d'Indy and Debussy ... over the Affair:** Vincent d'Indy (1851–1931), the composer, was outspokenly anti-Dreyfus, and also anti-Semitic. The position of Claude Debussy (1862–1918) was more nuanced; ironically, the fiercely partisan disagreements as to the merits or otherwise of his opera, *Pelléas et Mélisande,* caused it later to be likened to the Dreyfus Affair.

**58. "Meilhac":** Henri Meilhac (1831–97) wrote plays and comic operas, the best-known of which is *La Belle Hélène.* Brichot is referring to Pascal's famous *pensée:* "If Cleopatra's nose had been shorter, the whole face of the earth would have been changed."

**59. *"gâcher. Jachères . . . gâtines":*** *gâcher* is a verb meaning "to waste"; *jachère* and *gâtine* are terms for different kinds of fallow or sterile land.

**60. "Saint-Merd":** a name echoing *merde,* or "shit," hence Brichot's *honni soit qui mal y pense.*

**61. "Poquelin":** Jean-Baptiste Poquelin was the real name of Molière, whose absurd doctor Argan, in *Le Malade imaginaire,* is the model for Proust's pastiche of medical jargon.

**62. "Uncle, I mean Sarcey":** Francisque Sarcey (1827–99) was the leading drama critic of the day, nicknamed "Uncle" for his good sense and middlebrow tastes.

**63. "Saint Barnum":** Phineas Taylor Barnum (1810–91), the archetypal American showman and publicist.

**64. "Planté, Paderewski, Risler even":** Francis Planté (1839–1934), French pianist; Ignacy Jan Paderewski (1860–1941), a virtuoso pianist who twice became prime minister of his native Poland; Édouard Risler (1873–1929), a French pianist best known for his playing of Liszt and Beethoven.

**65. *"Qualis artifex pereo!":*** "What an artist perishes in me!," supposedly the Emperor Nero's last words. German classicists had been unable to agree on the worth or authenticity of the Latin poetry attributed to him.

**66. "the Mass in D":** Beethoven's *Missa Solemnis*.

**67.** *"garde-française":* an infantry regiment of the King's household, disbanded in 1789.

**68. "O Cottard . . . as Theocritus has it":** the vocative construction was freely used in Leconte de Lisle's translations of Theocritus.

**69.** *"demoiselles de Caen . . .* **Pampille":** *demoiselles de Caen* are small Normandy lobsters; Pampille was the pen name of Mme Léon Daudet, who wrote fashion and cooking columns in the extreme right-wing paper *L'Action française*, run by her husband.

**70. Ronsard . . . unknown there:** Pierre de Ronsard (1524–85), one of the greatest of French Renaissance poets. He hinted that his family had once been great noblemen in Southeastern Europe, but there is no evidence that they were.

**71.** *buen retiro:* a Spanish phrase literally meaning "good retreat."

**72. An important publisher . . . paper knife:** possibly a description of Eugène Fasquelle, a Paris publisher known to Proust.

**73. "M. de Persigny":** Jean-Gilbert-Victor Fialin, Duc de Persigny (1808–72), a right-wing politician who became minister of the interior and ambassador to London under the Second Empire.

**74. Dumas** *fils:* Alexandre Dumas (1824–95), son of the novelist of the same name, himself a novelist and dramatist, best known as the author of the decidedly middlebrow *La Dame aux camélias*.

**75. Cancan:** the word can refer to either an item of unkind gossip, or the quack of a duck.

**76. a fable of La Fontaine's and another by Florian:** Jean de La Fontaine (1621–95), the greatest of French fabulists; Jean-Pierre Claris de Florian (1755–94), Voltaire's great-nephew and, as a writer of fables, much influenced by Rousseau.

**77. Julien de Monchâteau . . . "Pico della Mirandola":** François (not Julien) de Monchâteau was celebrated in France as a child prodigy (as was Pico della Mirandola in Renaissance Florence).

**78. Place Saint-Sulpice:** where, in Paris, the cheapest and most tasteless religious objects can be bought.

**79. "Barbedienne bronzes":** Ferdinand Barbedienne (1810–92) specialized in casting bronze reproductions of classical statuary, popular among the nineteenth-century bourgeoisie.

**80. Harpagon:** the paranoid miser in Molière's comedy *L'Avare*.

**81. "Chantepie . . . Does it deserve its name?":** *une pie* is "a magpie," *chan-*

*ter* means "to sing," so that the name should refer to a place where magpies sing.

82. **Lachelier:** Jules Lachelier (1832–1918) wrote influentially about the problem of induction, and is opposed here to John Stuart Mill, a philosopher known in France in Proust's day as an extreme empiricist.

83. **Millet's peasants:** Jean-François Millet (1814–75), celebrated for painting scenes of peasant life, notably the much reproduced *L'Angélus*.

84. **"Chantereine . . . the queen in question is":** because *reine* is French for "queen."

85. **"Pont-à-Couleuvre . . . nasty serpents":** Pont-à-Couleuvre would literally mean "Snake Bridge."

86. **the second fable:** in none of La Fontaine's or Florian's fables does a frog find itself before the Areopagus, or supreme court of Athens.

87. **" 'She has good qualities . . .' ":** the quotation from Mme de Sévigné, modified by Proust, refers to her daughter-in-law.

88. **"conscript fathers":** the name by which senators were referred to in ancient Rome, here applied to members of the French Senate, like Charles-Louis de Saulces de Freycinet (1828–1923) and Justin de Selves (1848–1934).

89. **"*sylva*":** the Latin word for a wood.

90. **"Tour d'Argent . . . Hôtel Meurice":** the Tour d'Argent, on the Left Bank, was, and remains, one of the great restaurants of Paris; the Hôtel Meurice, on the rue de Rivoli, was one of the city's best in Proust's day.

91. **"M. Boutroux":** Émile Boutroux (1845–1921) taught philosophy at the Sorbonne, and at one time had Henri Bergson for a pupil.

92. **"the Forty":** the Forty are the "Immortals," or the forty members of the Académie Française. Not all the names that Brichot cites are those of actual Academicians.

93. **"Porel . . . Odéonia":** Porel was the pseudonym of Désiré-Paul Parfouru (1842–1917), an actor and theater director, who ran the Odéon on the Left Bank, from 1884 to 1892, hence the reference to "Odéonia"; his son, Jacques Porel, was a friend of Proust's.

94. **"Saint-Martin-du-Chêne and Saint-Pierre-des-Ifs":** *un chêne* is "an oak tree," *un if* is "a yew."

95. **a verb . . . "*-arder*":** a possible verb would be *pétarder*, meaning to "blow one's top."

96. **"*La Chercheuse*":** *La Chercheuse d'esprit*, a comic opera with words by Charles-Simon Favart (1710–92), which was put on in Paris in 1888 and again in 1900.

97. "*Anna Karenina* or *Resurrection* . . . architrave": both novels were indeed adapted for the stage and performed in Paris, one of them at the Odéon, between 1899 and 1905.

98. "It's a stock role . . . see *Le Capitaine Fracasse*": La Zerbine is indeed a stock role in the French comic repertoire, for a soubrette; but there is no such role in *La Chercheuse d'esprit*. There is one, however, in *Le Capitaine Fracasse,* a novel involving a troupe of actors by Théophile Gautier, which was one of Proust's favorite books.

99. "Brillat-Savarin . . . *pommes frites*": Anthelme Brillat-Savarin (1755–1826), the most celebrated of French gastronomes, and author of *The Physiology of Taste* (1825).

100. an *à-peu-près:* literally, an "approximation."

101. "Believing that the Édit de Nantes was an Englishwoman": as pronounced in French, the words could be taken to refer to an imaginary Englishwoman of title, Lady de Nantes.

102. *agrégé:* the *agrégation* is the competitive examination by which students are recruited into the higher echelons of the teaching profession.

103. "Helleu": Paul Helleu (1859–1927), painter and engraver, whose style was very eighteenth-century.

104. "Watteau *à vapeur*": this is Saniette's *à-peu-près*—"Watteau *à vapeur*" is a pun on *bateau à vapeur,* or "steamboat."

105. "*Croyez à mon amitié vraie.*" "*Croyez à ma sympathie vraie*": Formulas roughly equivalent to "Yours truly" or "Faithfully yours."

106. "this Hohenzollern . . . King of Hanover": with the abdication of Kaiser Wilhelm II in 1918, the Hohenzollern dynasty of German emperors came to an end. The short-lived kingdom of Hanover was annexed by Prussia in 1866, and its last King was indeed dispossessed, but by Kaiser Wilhelm I, not his son. Prussia annexed Alsace-Lorraine from France following its victory in the 1870 war.

107. "M. Tschudi": Hugo von Tschudi (1851–1911), director of the National Gallery in Berlin and, unlike the Emperor, a supporter of Impressionism; he was forced eventually to resign.

108. the Eulenburg Affair: Philipp, Prinz von Eulenburg and Hertfeld (1847–1921), a confidant of the German Emperor and ambassador in Vienna 1894–1902, was in 1906 charged with homosexuality. In the chronology of the novel, the affair is misplaced, since Charlus is alluding to it some five or six years before it occurred.

**109. "as mediatized princes we are *Durchlaucht*":** the "mediatized" families are those appearing in the second section, or *Durchlaucht,* of the *Almanach de Gotha,* the first section being reserved for the genealogies of Europe's royal houses. The *Durchlaucht* families were recognized as being equal in birth to the royal families, and intermediate in rank between them and the merely princely families of the *Almanach*'s third section.

**110. "the *émigrés*":** those aristocrats and others who emigrated during the revolutionary and Napoleonic years.

**111. "Monsieur":** this title was given to the eldest brother of the King. The pretensions of the Croy family are noted in Proust's major historical source, the *Memoirs* of the Duc de Saint-Simon.

**112. " '*Passavant*' ":** from the verb *passer* (to pass) and *avant* (before), the utterance means roughly "forward."

**113. "the Prince of Hanover, later King of England":** a reference to the Elector of Hanover, who became King George I of England in 1714.

**114. *"Maecenas atavis edite regibus!":*** "Maecenas, descended from royal ancestors!"—a quotation from Horace, *Odes,* bk. I.

**115. Fauré's sonata for piano and violin:** Sonata No. 1 for Violin and Piano, Opus 13, by Fauré, first performed in 1875, and antedating by ten years the Franck sonata that Proust used as one of his models for the Vinteuil sonata, which occupies such an important place in his novel.

**116. *Fêtes:*** the second of Debussy's three orchestral nocturnes, a complex piece hardly suitable for a violin transposition.

**117. *Robert le Diable:*** Meyerbeer's Romantic opera of 1831, thus rather primitive musically compared with Debussy.

**118. Scarlatti:** Domenico Scarlatti (1685–1757), known for his harpsichord music.

**119. "Je-Men-Fou":** i.e., *Je m'en fous,* or "I couldn't care less."

**120. "Asnières or Bois-Colombes":** both are suburbs of the city.

**121. *soutenances de thèses:*** doctoral theses are "defended" before a jury by their authors in France, in front of an audience.

**122. "Rosicrucian":** a reference not to the seventeenth-century German illuminati, but to a *fin-de-siècle* aesthetic movement in France, comparable to the "deliquescent" movement in poetry referred to earlier.

**123. "the Great Condé":** Louis II, Prince de Condé (1621–86), a successful army commander and a leader of the so-called Fronde des Princes, or revolt against the regime of Cardinal Mazarin during Louis XIV's minority. He later re-entered the King's service.

**124. "the Abbaye du Mont":** the celebrated Benedictine Abbey of Mont-Saint-Michel.

**125. "Galli-Marié":** Célestine Galli-Marié (1840–1905), a singer whose heyday was in the 1860s and 1870s.

**126. "Ingalli-Marié":** a reference to another singer, Speranza Engally, who made her debut in 1878.

**127. Bouchard or Charcot:** Charles Bouchard (1837–1915), doctor and biologist; for Charcot, see note 53 to this chapter.

**128. "Bouffe de Saint-Blaise or Courtois-Suffit":** two doctors listed as practicing in the fashionable quarters of Paris before 1914.

**129. "345 port":** an unknown brand of port.

**130. "the nickname of Arrachepel":** from the verb *arracher,* meaning "to pull up," and *pel,* an old French word for "stake" or "picket," the historical Arrachepels were a noble family whose seat was near Illiers (the Combray of the novel).

**131. "La Fontaine":** one of whose fables is entitled "The Camel and the Floating Sticks."

**132. Molière's word:** the word is "cuckold."

**133. *"fraisette":*** a strawberry drink.

**134. a Christian . . . Grace to himself:** in the seventeenth century, the Abbey of Port-Royal became the center of Jansenism, whose adherents believed in the Augustinian doctrine that Grace was a free gift from God, not necessarily related to the virtue of those receiving it.

**135. "David":** the king of spades.

**136. the doctors of Salerno . . . the crossing:** a reference to a medieval legend whereby, Virgil having created a miraculous spa near Naples, the jealous doctors of Salerno set out to destroy it.

PART II: CHAPTER 3

**1. "like a dulcimer":** the reference is to a couplet from Baudelaire's *Fleurs du mal:* "Your memory, like uncertain fables, / Wearies the reader like a dulcimer."

**2. "Prosper, dear hope . . .":** a line from Racine's *Esther,* wrongly attributed here to *Athalie.* In French, *"Prospérez, cher espoir d'une nation sainte."*

**3. "Come, come, my daughters":** *"Venez, venez, mes filles."*

**4. "they must be summoned":** *"il faut les appeler."*

**5. the old nurse Euryclea:** in the *Odyssey*, when Ulysses returns to Ithaca in disguise, and Euryclea recognizes him by a scar on his foot.

**6. faulty restorations at Notre-Dame:** a reference to the restorations carried out by Viollet-le-Duc and others between 1844 and 1864.

**7. those objects . . . mantelpiece:** a reference to Edgar Allan Poe's story "The Purloined Letter," which was translated into French by Baudelaire, and in which a much-sought incriminating letter lies unconcealed.

**8. "diplomats":** biscuits soaked in rum or kirsch.

**9. La Sanseverina:** the spirited and sophisticated heroine of Stendhal's novel *La Chartreuse de Parme*.

**10. "the Baronne de Rothschild or the Maréchale Niel":** the former is a rose named in 1868 after the wife of Baron Alphonse de Rothschild; the latter should in fact be the "Maréchal Niel," named in 1864 after Adolphe Niel (1802–69).

**11. "Jupien's daughter":** in fact, his niece.

**12. "Stamati":** Camille Stamati (1811–70), a pianist and composer, and the teacher, among others, of Saint-Saëns.

**13. "the Comtesse d'Escarbagnas . . . 'bon Chrétien'":** *La Comtesse d'Escarbagnas* is a one-act comedy by Molière, in which the heroine is sent some *bon Chrétien* pears as a love offering by her suitor, M. Thibaudier. The other pear names that follow came from Élisabeth (not Émilie, as Proust writes) de Clermont-Tonnerre's *Almanach des bonnes choses de France* (1920).

**14. Godard:** Benjamin Godard (1849–95), a writer of successful operas; Proust found his music facile.

**15. "Work . . . to Chateaubriand":** "Work, work, my dear friend, achieve renown." Chateaubriand cites these words as having been written to him in 1798 by the Marquis Louis de Fontanes (1757–1821), a mediocre writer with whom he had become friendly during his exile in England.

**16. Napoleon's love letters:** a collection of Napoleon's letters to Josephine was published in 1913 under the title *Tendresses impériales*, or *Imperial Tendernesses*.

**17. rue Bergère:** the address of the Paris Conservatoire until 1913.

**18. "tapette":** a (feminine) noun that can be applied both to someone who talks too much and to a homosexual.

**19. "In proeliis non semper" . . . "Non sine labore":** meaning, respectively, "Not always in combat" and "Nothing is gained without effort" (the motto of the Cardinal de Retz).

20. *"Parmi les hommes"*: meaning "among men." Henry Roujon (1853–1914) was a writer and critic; the book's actual title was *Au milieu des hommes,* and it was a collection of his critical essays.

21. **Fournier-Sarlovèze**: the name of a former *préfet* who founded a connoisseurs' club known as the Société Artistique des Amateurs.

22. **"It's so fine ... pederasty"**: the satanic Carlos Herrera, alias Vautrin, had "befriended," first Eugène de Rastignac (in *Le Père Goriot*) and then Lucien de Rubempré, who is with him when they find themselves passing Rastignac; "Tristesse d'Olympio" is one of Victor Hugo's best-known and most beautiful poems, in which he revisits the scenes where he first fell in love with his mistress, Juliette Drouet.

23. **"man of taste"**: this was Oscar Wilde, who in his essay "The Decay of Lying" wrote, "One of the greatest tragedies of my life is the death of Lucien de Rubempré."

24. **" 'Esther happy ...' "**: these are the titles of three of the four parts into which *Splendeurs et misères des courtisanes* is divided.

25. **"Rocambole"**: the hero of some thirty adventure novels written by Pierre-Alexis Ponson du Terrail (1829–71); the adjective *rocambolesque* subsequently entered the language, to mean "far-fetched" as applied to a story or event.

26. *"moult sorbonagre, sorbonicole et sorboniforme"*: a scathing Rabelaisian way of referring to a pedantic doctor from the Sorbonne; translatable perhaps as "Sorbonnified, Sorbonniculous, and Sorbonniform."

27. *"The quart d'heure de Rabelais"*: a stock phrase meaning "the hour of reckoning."

28. *"Chateaubriand aux pommes"*: i.e., a Chateaubriand steak, served with apple.

29. **"millionaire rhymes"**: i.e., very rich rhymes.

30. **"as ... Ovid has it"**: Ovid wrote *Materiam superabat opus* (*Metamorphoses* II, 5), or "The work surpassed the matter."

31. **"Meudon ... double Dutch"**: Meudon, now part of Paris, was the parish of which Rabelais was the *curé;* Ferney was the Genevan home of Voltaire; the Vallée-aux-Loups, near Sceaux, was where Chateaubriand lived for several years; Les Jardies was the name of Balzac's house in Villa d'Avray; the "Polish woman" was Mme Hanska, whom Balzac married in 1850, shortly before his death.

32. **" 'You're of the same opinion as Taine' "**: Taine complained, in a well-

known essay on Balzac, that the *Comédie humaine* contained too much that was morbid or unnatural.

33. **"the Princesse de Cadignan"**: the *Comédie humaine* includes a volume entitled *Les Secrets de la Princesse de Cadignan.*

34. **"Thureau-Dangin . . . Boissier"**: Paul Thureau-Dangin (1837–1913) was a right-wing Catholic historian; Gaston Boissier (1823–1908) was a Latinist and a professor of rhetoric at the Collège de France.

35. **"Boissier . . . New Year"**: Boissier was the name of a smart confectioner on the Boulevard des Capucines.

36. **40 *bis* Boulevard Malesherbes**: Proust himself had lived with his parents at 9 Boulevard Malesherbes, until 1900; his maternal grandparents lived at 40 *bis* rue du Faubourg-Poissonnière.

37. **PLUS ULTRA CAROL'S**: the device of the Habsburg Emperor Charles V: *Plus ultra Carol' Quint.*

38. **"On Saturday evenings . . ."**: the opening words of a popular song of 1902 called "Viens, Poupoule" ("Come, Poppet").

39. ***"Spes mea"* or *"Exspectata non eludet"*:** respectively, "My hope" and "He will not disappoint hopes."

40. ***"J'attendrai"*:** "I shall wait."

41. ***"Mesmes plaisirs du mestre"*:** "The same pleasures as the master."

42. ***"Sustentant lilia turres"*:** "The towers support the lilies."

43. ***"Manet ultima caelo"*:** "The end belongs to heaven."

44. ***"Non mortale quod opto"*:** "I have the ambition of an immortal."

45. ***"Atavis et armis"*:** "By ancestors and by arms."

46. **the clerical menace in political assemblies**: in France, church and state had not become separate in 1905, and political parties of the center and the left saw clerical influence as a permanent threat of reaction.

47. **" 'C'est mon plaisir' "**: "It is my pleasure."

48. ***"Tantus ab uno splendor"*:** "Such brilliance coming from one person."

49. **" 'Mort m'est vie' "**: "Death is life to me."

50. **Sarah Bernhardt . . . *Oedipus*:** Sarah Bernhardt created the title role in Edmond Rostand's very successful *L'Aiglon* in 1900; Jean-Sully Mounet (1841–1916), stage name Mounet-Sully, had played the role of Oedipus early in the century, but in the Roman arena at Orange, not Nîmes.

51. ***contre-de-quartes* reminiscent of Molière**: a reference to the fencing lesson in *Le Bourgeois Gentilhomme;* a *contre-de-quarte* is a circular parrying movement of the sword.

52. **"a *mazagran* or a *gloria*":** a *mazagran* was coffee laced with rum, a *gloria* a mixture of sweet coffee and rum or eau-de-vie.

53. **"*Os homini . . . tueri*":** "He has given man a face turned toward the sky," a line from Ovid's *Metamorphoses*.

54. **"as did the Archangel Raphael . . . Tobias":** the story is in the book of Tobit, in the Apocrypha.

55. **Grattevast:** this was previously on a different branch line.

56. **Hôtel des Ventes:** i.e., an auction room.

57. ***sous-maîtresse:*** a brothel-keeper's assistant.

58. **the elder Coquelin:** Constant Coquelin, known as Coquelin *aîné*, a well-known actor (1841–1909).

59. **Société des Bibliophiles . . . Cercle de l'Union:** the Société des Bibliophiles Français was founded in 1820 and comprised mainly aristocrats; the Cercle de l'Union was founded in 1828 and was the most exclusive of the Paris clubs during the Second Empire.

60. **"the many Americans . . . Duc de Berry":** the Montgomery and Pembroke families were associated, as were the Buckinghams and the Chandoses. A Capel became Count of Essex in 1661, and Proust knew a Berthe Capel in Paris. The Duc de Berry (1844–1910) was a member of the Orléans family.

61. **Émilienne d'Alençon:** Émilienne Andrée was a celebrated cocotte around 1900, who dabbled in music and poetry and appeared with her performing rabbits at the Folies-Bergère.

62. **"*Ne sçais l'heure*":** literally, "Know not the hour," words pronounced in French like the name Saylor.

63. **"Périer":** Jean-Alexis Périer (1869–1954) created the role of Pelléas in Debussy's opera in 1902.

64. **"the Gymnase . . . *La Châtelaine*":** the Théâtre du Gymnase specialized in comedy; *La Châtelaine* was a comedy by Alfred Capus (1858–1922), a dramatist and journalist who was elected to the Académie Française in 1914.

65. **"Frévalles, Marie Magnier, Baron *fils*":** Frévalles might be Simone Frévalles, a member of the company at the Théâtre de la Porte-Saint-Martin, or Eugène-Félix-Constant Langlois, known as Fréville (1826–90), an actor who wrote several comedies; Marie Magnier (1848–1913) made her debut in 1867 and played in many Paris theaters; Louis Baron (1870–1939), known as Baron *fils* to distinguish him from his father, also an actor, was a well-known comic actor at the turn of the century.

66. **"Guilbert":** Yvette Guilbert (1867–1944) began her celebrated career as a chanteuse around 1885.

67. **"Cornaglia" and "Dehelly":** Ernest Cornaglia (1834–1912), an actor who joined the company at the Théâtre de l'Odéon in 1880; Émile Dehelly (1871–1969) made his debut at the Comédie-Française in 1890.

68. **"Aldonce de Guermantes . . . should have passed":** Aldonce de Guermantes is an invention. Louis VI, known as le Gros (1081–1137), had an illegitimate younger half-brother, called Philippe de Mantes, and had himself crowned in a hurry in 1108 in order to ensure his own succession.

69. **"the La Tremoïlles . . . the Comtes de Poitiers":** the La Tremoïlles became heirs to the Kings of Naples in 1605; their descent from the Comtes de Poitiers is uncertain.

70. **"the d'Uzès":** Uzès did not become a duchy until 1572.

71. **"the Luynes":** the first Duc de Luynes was created in 1619.

72. **"the Choiseuls, the Harcourts, the La Rochefoucaulds":** these three families all traced their origins back to the tenth century.

73. **"the Noailles . . . the Montesquious, the Castellanes":** families tracing their origins back to the eleventh century.

74. **"Marquis de Cambremerde or de Vatefairefiche":** *va-te-faire-fiche* is a phrase meaning "scram!" The turning of "Cambremer" into "Cambremerde" looks ahead to the "Comtesse Shit."

75. *"Scènes de la vie de province":* one of the major sections into which Balzac's *Comédie humaine* is divided.

76. **" 'Muse du Département,' or Mme de Bargeton":** *La Muse du département* (*The Muse of the Department*) forms part of the *Scènes de la vie de province;* its heroine, Mme de la Baudraye, writes literary essays and has an adulterous love affair. Mme de Bargeton is a character in *Illusions perdues,* a provincial wife who becomes the lover of the young hero, Lucien de Rubempré.

77. **"Mme de Mortsauf":** the heroine of *Le Lys dans la vallée,* who overcomes her passion for the young Félix de Vandenesse and dies a saintly death.

78. **Mme de Clinchamp . . . Duc d'Aumale:** Berthe de Clinchamp, the companion of the Duchesse d'Aumale, came eventually to run the Duc's household, and in 1899 published a memoir of him: *Le Duc d'Aumale, prince, soldat.*

79. *"In medio . . . virtus":* *in medio stat virtus,* or "virtue lies in the middle."

80. **"M. Moreau, Morille, Morue":** *moreau* can mean a horse's nosebag; a *morille* is a morel, a kind of mushroom; and *morue* means a codfish.

81. **"Saint-Cyr":** the military academy where French Army officers are trained.

82. **"Pont-l'Évêque":** *évêque* being French for "bishop."

83. *"L'Enfance . . . 'Vendredi Saint' ":* *L'Enfance du Christ* is an oratorio written by Berlioz between 1850 and 1854; "L'Enchantement du Vendredi Saint," or the

"Good Friday Music," forms part of Act III of Wagner's opera *Parsifal,* but is sometimes performed separately, notably at Easter.

**84. Blancs-Manteaux:** literally, White Mantles, or White Friars, a Carmelite order.

**85. "that Saint Louis established there":** in 1258; Louis IX, or Saint Louis, King of France 1226–70.

**86. "M. de Rochegude ... ghetto":** Proust's source here was F. de Rochegude's twenty-volume work *Promenades dans toutes les rues de Paris* (1910). The street whose name Charlus cannot remember was the rue des Rosiers; and "du Rozier" will become the name adopted later in the book by Bloch in order to hide his Jewishness.

**87. "and I admire Rembrandt ... synagogue":** Rembrandt was not Jewish but lived in the Jewish quarter of Amsterdam and painted Jewish subjects.

**88. "a strange Jew who boiled the Host":** a legend concerning a thirteenth-century Jew convicted of burning a consecrated Host, which was itself miraculously preserved.

**89. "laid the body ... Orléans":** according to Rochegude, this Duc d'Orléans was murdered on coming out from supper with Isabeau de Bavière, his sister-in-law and mistress. The Duc de Chartres (1840–1910) was the grandson of Louis-Philippe, Duc d'Orléans (also known as Philippe-Égalité), and not obviously related to the Baron de Charlus.

**90. "a race of usurpers ... despoiled":** as a legitimist, Charlus condemns the Orléans family for having conspired against the Bourbons; Charles X was the last Bourbon King, and was replaced in 1830 by Louis-Philippe, son of the Duc d'Orléans referred to above. "Henri V" was the son of Charles X, recognized as the rightful King of France only by fanatical legitimists.


PART II: CHAPTER 4

**1. the casino in Parville:** the casino was previously in Incarville.

**2. *réveillons:*** midnight celebrations at Christmas and New Year's.

# Synopsis

posterity of the ashamed Sodomists (32). I have missed the fertilization of the orchid by the bee (33).

Swann eyes Mme de Surgis's corsage (106). How the Prince de Guermantes came to be convinced of Dreyfus's innocence (106). History of the name "Surgis-le-Duc" (107). The adventures of Mme de Surgis: ups and downs of her social situation (107). M. de Charlus's flattery of her (107). Swann's allusions to M. de Charlus's love life (109). Return to the Prince's conversion to Dreyfusism (109). I refuse a select supper party after the soirée, remembering my rendezvous with Albertine (110). Comparison between the different orders of pleasure (110). Swann's fatigue (111). For her part, the Princesse de Guermantes had also become convinced of Dreyfus's innocence (112). Swann's sympathy for those who share his opinion about Dreyfus (112). He finds them all intelligent (113). Limits of Swann's Dreyfusism (113). His invitation to visit Gilberte leaves me indifferent (114). The Princesse de Guermantes's secret passion for M. de Charlus (115).

Departure and return: the Duc and Duchesse accompany me back (117). M. de Guermantes says goodbye to his brother: tender feelings and a gaffe (117). Tableau of the staircase when leaving the *hôtel* (119). Last appearance of the Prince de Sagan (120). Belated arrival of Mme d'Orvillers (121). The Duchesse's friendliness toward Mme de Gallardon (121). Return with the Guermantes in their coupé (123). My two desires: Mlle d'Orgeville and the Baronne Putbus's lady's maid (123). Mme de Guermantes refuses to introduce me to the Baronne Putbus (124). The Guermantes prepare to go to the fancy-dress ball despite the death of their cousin d'Osmond (124).

Visit from Albertine after the soirée: Albertine has not arrived (126). Françoise and her daughter, installed in the kitchen (126). Their language (126). Observations on linguistic geography (128). I await Albertine's arrival (129). The irritation caused by waiting turns to anxiety (130). Telephone call from Albertine (131). I try to make her come without asking her to (132). This terrible need for someone: comparison between my feelings toward Albertine and toward my mother (133). The mysteries of Albertine (133). How Françoise announces Albertine (134). Françoise's antipathy for Albertine (135). The latter's visit (137). Kisses, the gift of the slipcase (137). I then write to Gilberte, without the emotion of the old days (138). The Duc de Guermantes's conversion to Dreyfusism: the three charming ladies (139).

Visits before the second stay in Balbec: I visit other fairies in their dwellings (141). Observations concerning the history of salons (141). Odette's salon, crystallized around Bergotte, becomes one of the leaders (142). One reason is Odette's anti-Dreyfusism (143). Another, her discretion (144). My pleasures in the salons, in particular that of Mme de Montmorency (149).

The intermittences of the heart (150). Second stay in Balbec (150). The welcome from the manager of the Grand-Hôtel (150). His malapropisms (150). Reason for the second stay: the hope of meeting Mme de Putbus's lady's maid at the Verdurins' (151). Saint-Loup has put in a word for me with the Cambremers (152). Hope of also meeting beautiful unknowns (153). Comparison with my first arrival in Balbec (154). More of the manager's malapropisms (154). A convulsion of my entire being: my grandmother's presence given back to me as I am taking my boots off (154). Doctrine of the intermittences of the heart (155). I understand for the first time that I have lost her forever (156). My remorse for the unhappiness I caused her, especially on the occasion of the photograph taken by Saint-Loup (157). Pain of mourning (158). A dream (159). Awakening and heartrending recollections (161).

Albertine is at a neighboring resort, but I no longer wish to see her, or anyone (161). Recalling the pleasure of my arrival, before the upset (162). Mme de Cambremer has stopped by (163). Her fame in the vicinity (164). Refusal of an invitation to her house (166). My unhappiness is less profound, however, than my mother's (166). My mother has become like my grandmother (168). Encounter with Mme Poussin (169). The new *chasseur* at the hotel entrance (171). Comparison between the staff of the hotel and the choruses in Racine (172). The memories of my grandmother cause me to suffer (173). Revelations from Françoise concerning the circumstances of the photograph taken by Saint-Loup (174). Revelations from the manager: my grandmother's fainting fits (176). New dream about her (177). I become used to the painful memory (177). I finally decide to receive Albertine, whom I wish to see again (177). Dazzled by the apple blossom (178).

## PART II: CHAPTER 2

Resumption of intimacy with Albertine and first suspicions. My unhappiness decreases, Albertine begins to instill a desire for happiness in me again (179). Description of the rural sea (181). Return of unhappiness in the little train that I take to go and fetch Albertine (183). I abandon joining her (183). A death notice sent by the Cambremers (184). I send Françoise to fetch Albertine (185). Albertine's first visit to Balbec (185). Françoise warns me against Albertine (185). The Princesse de Parme at the Grand-Hôtel (186). Albertine's girlfriends (187). I send the lift boy to fetch her when I need her (188). The ways and language of the lift boy (189). One evening, the lift boy returns without her, announcing that she will come later on (191). How my cruel mistrust will arise with respect to Albertine (192). They dance breast against breast, as Cottard remarks while Albertine is dancing with Andrée (193). Rivalry between Cottard and his confrère du Boulbon (193). Return to the evening when Albertine did not come, despite the lift boy's announcement (195). Waiting and anxiety (195). Painful curiosity about Albertine's life (196). How she sacrifices her visit to a lady in Infreville when I propose going with her (197). In the Balbec casino: Bloch's sister and cousin, whom she watches in the mirror (199).

Fits of anger against Albertine, followed by truces (200). I construct Albertine's character based on the memory of that of Odette (201)

Visit from Mme de Cambremer, while I am on the esplanade with Albertine and her friends (201). The old Mme de Cambremer's gear (202). The lawyer, an admirer of Le Sidaner, who is accompanying her (203). The two politenesses of the young Mme de Cambremer (203). With her, I talk like Legrandin (204). The outlook from La Raspelière (205). The Combray *curé*'s etymologies (206). The young Mme de Cambremer's aesthetic biases and snobberies (207). Her hostility against her mother-in-law (208). Evolution of artistic doctrines (210). Return to the fashion for Poussin and Chopin, to the delight of the old Marquise (213). How the young Mme de Cambremer pronounces certain names (214). She has lost all memory of having been born a Legrandin (216). The affability of the Cambremers' friend, the admirer of Le Sidaner (217). Invitation from the Cambremers (217). Their departure, humiliation of the First President (219).

Albertine comes up into my room with me (220). Lift boy's air of dejection and concern (221). Its cause: the absence of the usual tip (222). Remarks concerning a revolution (222). The hotel staff and money (222). Calculated protestations of coldness toward Albertine and love for Andrée (223). The binary rhythm of love (224). Having told Albertine of the indifference she inspires in me, I can experience affection and pity for her (226). Albertine gives me the hour that she should have spent without me (227). She denies having had a relationship with Andrée (228). Reconciliation and caresses (229). I ought to have left her at that moment of happiness (230). Easier in my mind, I live more in the company of my mother (230). Reading the *Arabian Nights* (231). Excursions with Albertine (232). Brief lusts after other girls (232). Desires and disappointments (233). Jealousy over Albertine and renewed suspicions as the season reaches its peak (235). She and Andrée calculate their remarks with a view to removing my suspicions (236).

Scandal provoked in the hotel by Bloch's sister and an actress (237). It is suppressed, thanks to the protection of M. Nissim Bernard (237). The reason for his loyalty to the Grand-Hôtel: he is keeping a young *commis* waiter (237). The *chasseurs* and the young Israelites in *Esther* and *Athalie* (238). Friendship with two young guests' maids, Marie Gineste and Céleste Albaret (240). Their language (241). Giggles of Bloch's sister and her friend as Albertine goes past (245). Fresh reasons for suspecting Albertine's habits (245). An unknown woman with radiant eyes (245). Albertine's suspicious rudeness to a woman friend of her aunt's (248). Suspension of my jealousy of the women Albertine may have loved (248).

M. Nissim Bernard and the tomato brothers (249). I am invited to the Verdurins' (249). Albertine and I go to pay a call on Saint-Loup in Doncières, by the little train (250). Invitation to the Verdurins' receptions at La Raspelière (251). In our compartment, a large, vulgar, and pretentious lady (252). Albertine's attitude toward Saint-Loup excites my jealousy (253). Argument after Saint-Loup's departure (254).

Appearance of M. de Charlus, much aged, on the platform at the Doncières station, waiting for the Paris train (254). I chat with him (255). M. de Charlus's first meeting with Morel (255). The Baron asks me to go and talk to the bandsman, and I recognize Morel (255). M. de Charlus joins us; he had never met Morel (255). M. de Charlus does not board the train for Paris (257). Our changing perspectives on people (258). Return with Albertine in her rubber raincoat (259).

Soirée at La Raspelière with the Verdurins: I go to La Raspelière by the little train, to Mme Verdurin's Wednesday (259). The little train's "habitués": Cottard, Ski, Brichot (261). Portrait of Brichot (261). The Verdurin salon's evolution toward society: the "temple of music" (262). Saniette (265). Ski (266). The Princesse Sherbatoff, ideally faithful (269). Cottard and the Wednesdays (273). The unknown girl of Saint-Pierre-des-Ifs (276). Morel has defaulted two days before (277). Mme Verdurin has invited the Cambremers, whose tenant she is (277). How she has prepared the faithful for this invitation (278). Remarks of the faithful concerning the Cambremers (279). Brichot's first comments on the local place-names and their etymologies (280). The Princesse Sherbatoff is the large, vulgar woman from the other day (285). Morel has been found again and will come this evening with a friend of his father's (286). News of the death of Dechambre, formerly Mme Verdurin's favorite pianist (286). Arrival at Douville-Féterne, continuation by carriage for La Raspelière (287). Mme Verdurin and the death of the faithful (289). Intoxicating beauty of the countryside; emotion (289). Arrival at La Raspelière, M. Verdurin's welcome (291). Dechambre renounced in favor of Morel (294), awaited along with a purported friend of his family: the Baron de Charlus (294). The Baron's habits are better known among the Verdurin clan than in the Faubourg Saint-Germain (294). Common errors concerning people's true situation (296). A Paris publisher (296). The Verdurins' indifference toward the beauties of nature (296). Their insight into the locality nonetheless (297).

Entrance of Morel and M. de Charlus (298). Evidence of the latter's feminine nature (299). The profaned mothers (300). Morel asks me to lie to the Verdurins about his origins (301). His rudeness once he has obtained satisfaction (302). First rough outline of his character (302). Arrival of the Cambremers (303). Bizarre behavior of Cottard (304). The Marquis de Cambremer's coarse features (304); his wife is haughty and morose (306). Introductions (307). M. de Cambremer's fables (307). Mme de Cambremer distorts names (308). Mme Verdurin and protocol (308). Mme Verdurin's taste is better than that of Mme de Cambremer (309). The Cambremers' garden (309). Brief misunderstanding of M. de Charlus, who mistakes Cottard for an invert (310). Harshness of inverts toward those they attract (311). The name Chantepie (313). Association between culture and snobbery in Mme de Cambremer (315). Fresh etymologies from Brichot (316). Why M. de Cambremer is interested in my breathless attacks (317). My mother's hesitant opinion of a marriage with Albertine recalled (318). Mme de Cambremer's remarks concerning Saint-Loup's marriage (319), and M. de Charlus (320). Still more etymologies from Brichot (320). Interlude of the Norwegian philosopher (321). M. Verdurin torments Saniette (324). More etymologies (328). Conversation about Elstir (329). Mme Verdurin prefers Ski (330). His marriage, his stupidity (330).

M. Verdurin's explanation to M. de Charlus about their lapse in protocol (332). M. de Charlus's laughter, his insolence (332). Elstir's roses (333). M. de Charlus emphasizes a gesture of politeness hinted at by M. de Cambremer (334). My enthusiasm for a piece of green luster (334). The Cambremers' severity over the taste of the Verdurins (334). I read the old Mme de Cambremer's letter, brought by her son: the rule of the three adjectives (335). M. de Charlus's claim to the title of Highness (336). Irony concealed by the apparent friendliness of the Verdurins toward Brichot (337). The clan spirit (338). Suffering produced in Brichot by the Verdurins' barbs (341). Mme Verdurin defends herself against being unkind to Saniette (341). Historical anecdotes with which M. de Charlus illustrates his pretensions (341). Artistic qualities that M. de Charlus's nature adds to the Guermantes race (343). Mme de Cambremer's musical snobbery, and the mischievousness of Morel, who plays Meyerbeer instead of Debussy (344). Brichot's comments (345). M. de Charlus's devotion to the Archangel Michael (346). Cottard and Morel play *écarté* (347). Cottard's puns (347). Professor Cottard's identity revealed to M. de Cambremer (349). Mme Cottard's sleepiness (349). Sleeping medications (350). Mme Verdurin's eulogy of Cottard (352). The Arrachepel coat of arms (352). The card game (353). Conversation with Mme Cottard (354).

M. de Charlus reveals his nature by expressing his preference for the strawberry drink (356). His first skirmish with Mme Verdurin, his insolence (356). Mme Verdurin does not understand that M. de Charlus might be the brother of the Duc de Guermantes (358). She dissuades me from going to the Cambremers' (358). She invites me to the next "Wednesday" along with my cousin and my friends (359). She runs Swann down in my presence (360). Comparison of the wit of Swann, Brichot, and the Guermantes (360). Mme Verdurin even proposes that I become a houseguest together with my cousin (362). She proposes to put in a word for Saint-Loup where necessary (362). New fury of M. Verdurin against Saniette (362). Cottard's witticisms as he wins at cards (363), and farewells (364). Outside (364). Rivalry between Cottard and his colleague du Boulbon (365). By carriage as far as Douville-Féterne (366). M. de Cambremer's tip (366). In the train (366). Mme de Cambremer's goodbye (366). The pleasure M. de Cambremer takes in his wife's passing fancies (368).

PART II: CHAPTER 3

Reflections on sleep. On my return from the soirée, gossip with the cross-eyed *chasseur* who has replaced the lift boy (369). His sister's habits (369). My sleep when I return from La Raspelière (370). The team of sleep (371). Time in sleep and time when awake (372). The effect of hypnotics on the memory: disagreement with Bergson (373). Sleep and memory (373). Waking up after deep sleep (374).

M. de Charlus dines at the Grand-Hôtel with a footman (376). The Baron compares the *chasseurs* with the choruses in Racine (376). The footman offers to put him in touch with the Prince de Guermantes (377). The domestic staff recognize the footman for what he is (377). Conversation with Aimé about M. de Charlus (379). Aimé is ignorant of the Baron's identity, is surprised when he learns it (379). Strange and passionate letter that the Baron had written to Aimé (380).

Excursions with Albertine: Albertine starts painting again (382). Heat (383). The forest of Chantepie (383). After a toque and veil for Albertine, I order an automobile (384). Aimé's pride (384). The car reduces distances and even modifies art (385). Visit to the Verdurins' (386). M. Verdurin knows the locality (387). Beauty of the "views" at La Raspelière (388). The countryside renews the charms of social life (388). Mme Verdurin had needed to have company (390). She tries to make us stay to tea, or to return with us (391). I refuse her proposals, not without being rude (392). Effect of the automobile on space and time (393). Comparison with the railway (393). Others of the chauffeur's customers: M. de Charlus and Morel (394). One of their meals in a restaurant along the coast (395). The Baron's sadistic pleasure at Morel's plans for deflowering a young girl (396). M. de Charlus's musical advice to Morel (398). The pears (398). Morel responds to M. de Charlus's kindnesses with increasing harshness (399). When Albertine is painting, I go off alone, but my mind is wholly taken up with her (399). Why sacrifice everything to phantoms? (400). Nature appears to be advising me to get down to work (401).

The small Normandy churches (401). Albertine's opinion on their restoration (402). The life of couples in love (403). Drinking Calvados or cider in the car (403). My jealousy over Albertine is not cured: the waiter in the Rivebelle hotel (404). Temporary calm of solitary excursions (405). Vow to leave Albertine (405). My mother's remonstrations have a contrary effect on this vow (406). Evening rendezvous with Albertine (407), and anxiety each morning over how she is to spend her day (408). I see less of my other connections: Saint-Loup, whom I dread Albertine's meeting (409), and Saniette (410). The latter's lack of boldness (411), and his indiscretion (411). Aimé's curiosity regarding the chauffeur's tip (412). The lift boy's message, calling the chauffeur a "gentleman" (413). The verbal lesson I get from this (414). Friendships with workingmen, and my mother's objections (414). The chauffeur leaves Balbec before the off season (415). I no longer get any pleasure with Albertine (416). Moving encounter with an airplane in the course of a solitary excursion (416).

Morel's machinations to get the Verdurins' coachman dismissed and at once replaced by his friend the chauffeur (417). Change for the better in Morel's attitude toward me (419). The contradictions in his predominantly ugly character (420). His absolute respect for the Conservatoire (420).

M. de Charlus and the Verdurins: as summer comes to an end, charm of the preparations for evenings at La Raspelière (421). The First President's remonstrations against idleness (423). Nighttime journey to La Raspelière with Albertine (423). The vanity case from Cartier's (424). M. de Charlus, the Verdurins' new habitué (424). The faithful are embarrassed at first to travel with him (424). The devices on his books (426). His piety (427). The faithful finally join him (427), and take pleasure in his conversation (427), in which he does not hesitate to broach certain subjects before the arrival of Morel (429). M. de Charlus's illusions concerning the secrecy of his love life (429). Mme Verdurin's allusions during his absence (430). He becomes temporarily the most faithful of the faithful (431). The Princesse Sherbatoff's animosity toward me, following an encounter with Mme de Villeparisis in the train (432).

A great musician furthers M. de Charlus's relationship with Morel (434). Psychological value of the "gossip" (435). M. de Charlus's blindness toward the Verdurins' true feelings toward him (436). Argument between M. de Charlus and Brichot about Balzac and Chateaubriand (437). Cottard's interruptions (438). Praise of Balzac's "outside-nature" side by M. de Charlus (439). He eyes the young men (439). M. de Charlus's discretion on his favorite topic in the presence of Morel (440). Albertine's outfits, inspired by the taste of Elstir, are appreciated by M. de Charlus and compared to the outfits of the Princesse de Cadignan (441). Morel's admiring consideration for my great-uncle and his townhouse at "40 *bis*" (443). M. de Charlus's melancholy in identifying himself with the Princesse de Cadignan (444). Morel's behavior toward M. de Charlus reminds me of that of Rachel toward Saint-Loup (446). Morel's affectation of unkindness with M. de Charlus, along with his apparent disinterestedness (447). M. de Charlus's clumsiness trying to get him to change his name to Charmel (448). Morel's servile nature, neurasthenia, and faulty upbringing (449).

The fictitious duel. M. de Charlus's sorrow one day when Morel refuses to remain with him after a lunch at the Verdurins' (449). He invents a duel in order to avenge Morel's honor (450). He hopes to get him brought back by me, and sends me to Morel with a letter (451). Devices in the books given to Morel by M. de Charlus (452). Morel is worried about his reputation and follows me (453). A triumphant M. de Charlus dictates the peace terms (453). Morel does not doubt that others covet his position with M. de Charlus (454). M. de Charlus is enthusiastic at the thought of a duel (455), but Morel succeeds in making him give it up (456). Cottard, an alarmed second, then disappointed (457). M. de Charlus sees himself as the Archangel Raphael with the young Tobias (459). Morel's demands for money from M. de Charlus (460). The little train's stopping-places. Memories tied to them. Maineville: the Palace that is a house of prostitution (461). Mishap that befell Morel there (463). His algebra lectures in the middle of the night (463). The Prince de Guermantes arranged a rendezvous with him in the Maineville Palace of which M. de Charlus got wind (463). M. de Charlus and Jupien sneak into the house (465). They are shown Morel, forewarned but terrified, with women (466). Second disappointment for the Prince de Guermantes: Morel catches sight of a photograph of M. de Charlus in his house, and takes flight (467).

Grattevast: the Comte de Crécy (468). The dinners I offer him (468). Episode of the guinea fowls carved by the manager (469). I do not dare tell M. de Crécy that Mme Swann had been known under the name of Odette de Crécy (471). Hermonville: M. de Chevregny, a man from the provinces very taken with Paris (471). Mme de Cambremer's three-adjective rule once again (472). Mme Verdurin's complaints against the Cambremers: they invited only Cottard and Morel to a smart dinner party (473). Effect of M. de Charlus's noble pretensions on Morel (474), and the latter's coarseness with the Cambremers (475). Mme Verdurin makes Brichot, who is secretly in love with Mme de Cambremer, stop going to Féterne (477). The Cambremers cannot have M. de Charlus to the dinner party they are giving for M. and Mme Féré (477). Morel's fresh insolence toward them (478). The Cambremers suspect a cabal of the Verdurins (479). Reasons for the falling-out given by the Cambremers: Charlus's Dreyfusism (479), and the Verdurins' familiarity (479).

Apparent length of the journey to La Raspelière (480). Caresses in the carriage (481). Mme de Cambremer's allusions to Albertine's "funny style" (481). The pleasures of the imagination and of sociability, in the course of journeys to La Raspelière, make me want to break up with Albertine and lead a new life (482). Brichot's final etymologies (483). Brief visits, at the stops on the return journey, while I keep my eye on Albertine (485). At Doncières: Saint-Loup (485). One day, when there is a long stop and Bloch asks me to get out and greet his father, I refuse, so as not to leave Albertine with Saint-Loup (486). Erroneous interpretation of my behavior by Bloch, who takes me to be a snob (486). Fatality of such misunderstandings that destroy friendships (486). Bloch's silence regarding me, on the occasion of a lunch party at Mme Bontemps's (487). M. de Charlus's interest in Bloch (488). M. de Charlus's anti-Semitic tirade (489). Morel's gratitude toward me for not catching up with Bloch (491).

Habit and socializing have emptied all the place-names along the little train's trajectory, and the places themselves, of their mystery and poetry (493). Charm and damaging influence of a knowledge of the locality (495). Marriage with Albertine seems like foolishness (496).

PART II: CHAPTER 4

Intermittences of the heart II: I prepare to break up with Albertine (497), I wish to set myself free for the arrival of Andrée (498). But on the return from La Raspelière, in the little train, shortly before leaving me, Albertine reveals to me that she knows Mlle Vinteuil and her friend intimately and is soon to join them (499). Cruel reminiscence of the scene at Montjouvain (499).

I ask Albertine not to leave me this evening (501). Solitary desolation in my room until daybreak (501), and certainty about Albertine's Gomorran habits (501). I summon her (502), and invent a reason for my unhappiness: I have just renounced a marriage (502). My jealousy becomes fixed on Mlle Vinteuil's friend (503); I want to stop Albertine from joining her (503). Plan to get her to come to Paris, to my parents' apartment, while they are away (505). Albertine's objections, then her abrupt decision to leave with me that same day (508). Effects of this abrupt departure: visit from the manager, anticipated objections of M. de Cambremer (508). The truth of love is within us and not outside (510). The beloved creature, too, is within us (511). Description of the sunrise (512). My mother, alerted by my tears, comes into my room (512); she has become altogether like my grandmother (512). Horrible picture of Albertine with Mlle Vinteuil at Montjouvain (513). "I absolutely must marry Albertine" (514).

# Marcel Proust's *In Search of Lost Time*
## Available in Penguin Classics Deluxe Editions

The first completely new translation of Marcel Proust's masterwork since the 1920s, these superb editions offer us a more rich, comic, and lucid Proust than American readers have previously been able to enjoy.

### Christopher Prendergast, General Editor

*Swann's Way*
**Translated by Lydia Davis**
*Swann's Way* is one of the preeminent novels of childhood—a sensitive boy's impressions of his family and neighbors, all brought dazzlingly back to life years later by the famous taste of a madeleine. The first volume of the book that established Proust as one of the finest voices of the modern age—satirical, skeptical, confiding, and endlessly varied in his response to the human condition—*Swann's Way* also stands on its own as a perfect rendering of a life in art, of the past re-created through memory.

*ISBN 0-14-243796-4*

*In the Shadow of Young Girls in Flower*
**Translated by James Grieve**
*In the Shadow of Young Girls in Flower*, the second volume of *In Search of Lost Time*, is a spectacular dissection of male and female adolescence, charged with the narrator's memories of Paris and the Normandy seaside. Here Proust introduces some of his greatest comic inventions, from the magnificently dull M. de Norpois to the enchanting Robert de Saint-Loup, as well as the two figures who will later dominate the narrator's life—the Baron de Charlus and the mysterious Albertine. As a meditation on different forms of love, *In the Shadow of Young Girls in Flower* has no equal.

*ISBN 0-14-303907-5*

*The Guermantes Way*
**Translated by Mark Treharne**
After the relative intimacy of the first two volumes of *In Search of Lost Time*, *The Guermantes Way* opens up a vast, dazzling landscape of fashionable Parisian life in the late nineteenth century, as the narrator enters the brilliant, shallow world of the literary and aristocratic salons. Both a salute to and a devastating satire of a time, place, and culture, *The Guermantes Way* is a part of the great tradition of novels that follow the initiation of a young man into the ways of the world.

*ISBN 0-14-303922-9*

# FOR THE BEST IN PAPERBACKS, LOOK FOR THE

In every corner of the world, on every subject under the sun, Penguin represents quality and variety—the very best in publishing today.

For complete information about books available from Penguin—including Penguin Classics, Penguin Compass, and Puffins—and how to order them, write to us at the appropriate address below. Please note that for copyright reasons the selection of books varies from country to country.

**In the United States:** Please write to *Penguin Group (USA), P.O. Box 12289 Dept. B, Newark, New Jersey 07101-5289* or call 1-800-788-6262.

**In the United Kingdom:** Please write to *Dept. EP, Penguin Books Ltd, Bath Road, Harmondsworth, West Drayton, Middlesex UB7 0DA.*

**In Canada:** Please write to *Penguin Books Canada Ltd, 90 Eglinton Avenue East, Suite 700, Toronto, Ontario M4P 2Y3.*

**In Australia:** Please write to *Penguin Books Australia Ltd, P.O. Box 257, Ringwood, Victoria 3134.*

**In New Zealand:** Please write to *Penguin Books (NZ) Ltd, Private Bag 102902, North Shore Mail Centre, Auckland 10.*

**In India:** Please write to *Penguin Books India Pvt Ltd, 11 Panchsheel Shopping Centre, Panchsheel Park, New Delhi 110 017.*

**In the Netherlands:** Please write to *Penguin Books Netherlands bv, Postbus 3507, NL-1001 AH Amsterdam.*

**In Germany:** Please write to *Penguin Books Deutschland GmbH, Metzlerstrasse 26, 60594 Frankfurt am Main.*

**In Spain:** Please write to *Penguin Books S. A., Bravo Murillo 19, 1° B, 28015 Madrid.*

**In Italy:** Please write to *Penguin Italia s.r.l., Via Benedetto Croce 2, 20094 Corsico, Milano.*

**In France:** Please write to *Penguin France, Le Carré Wilson, 62 rue Benjamin Baillaud, 31500 Toulouse.*

**In Japan:** Please write to *Penguin Books Japan Ltd, Kaneko Building, 2-3-25 Koraku, Bunkyo-Ku, Tokyo 112.*

**In South Africa:** Please write to *Penguin Books South Africa (Pty) Ltd, Private Bag X14, Parkview, 2122 Johannesburg.*